ISAAC ASIMOV
THE COMPLETE STORIES
Volume 1

ISAAC
ASIMOV

VOLUME 1

The Complete Stories

Broadway Books

New York

BROADWAY

First Broadway Books trade paperback edition published 2001.

This volume contains the complete contents of the previously published collections *Earth Is Room Enough*, *Nine Tomorrows*, and *Nightfall and Other Stories*.

The Library of Congress Cataloging-in-Publication Data has cataloged the previous edition as:

Asimov, Isaac, 1920–
  [Short stories]
  The complete stories. Volume 1/Isaac Asimov.—1st ed.
    p. cm.
  1. Science fiction, American. I. Title.
PS3551.S5A6 1990
813'.54—dc20 90-3136
CIP

ISBN 0-385-41606-7
ISBN 0-385-41627-X (trade pbk.)

20 19 18

Contents

Introduction

I have been writing short stories for fifty-one years and I haven't yet quit. In addition to the hundreds of short stories I have published, there are at least a dozen in press waiting to be published, and two stories written and not yet submitted. So I have by no means retired.

There is, however, no way one can publish short stories for this length of time without understanding that the time left to him is limited. In the words of the song: "Forevermore is shorter than before."

It is time, therefore, for Doubleday to pull the strings together and get all my fiction—short stories and novels, too—into a definitive form and in uniform bindings, both in hard and soft covers.

It may sound conceited of me to say so (I am frequently accused of being conceited), but my fiction generally has been popular from the start and has continued to be well received through the years. To locate any one story, however, that you no longer have and wish you did, or to find one you have heard about but have missed is no easy task. My stories appeared originally in any one of many magazines, the original issues of which are all but unobtainable. They then appeared in any of a multiplicity of anthologies and collections, copies of which are almost as unobtainable.

It is Doubleday's intention to make this multivolume collection definitive and uniform in the hope that the science fiction public, the mystery public (for my many mysteries will also be collected), and libraries as well will seize upon them ravenously and clear their book shelves to make room for *Isaac Asimov: The Complete Stories.*

We begin in this volume with two of my early collections from the 1950s, *Earth Is Room Enough* and *Nine Tomorrows*.

The former includes such favorites of mine as "Franchise," which deals with the ultimate election day; "Living Space," which gives every family a world of its own; "The Fun They Had," my most anthologized story; "Jokester," whose ending I bet you don't anticipate if you've never read the story before; and "Dreaming Is a Private Thing," concerning which Robert A. Heinlein accused me of making money out of my own neuroses.

Nine Tomorrows, the personal favorite of all my collections, contains not one story I don't consider to be excellent examples of my productions of the 1950s. In particular, there is "The Last Question," which, of all the stories I have written, is my absolute favorite.

Then there is "The Ugly Little Boy," my third-favorite story. My tales tend to be cerebral, but I count on this one to bring about a tear or two. (To find out which is the *second*-favorite of my stories, you'll have to read successive volumes of this collection.) "The Feeling of Power" is another frequently anthologized piece and is rather prophetic, considering it was written before anyone was thinking of pocket computers. "All the Troubles of the World" is a suspense story and "The Dying Night" is a mystery based, alas, on an astronomical "fact" now known to be quite mistaken.

Then there is a later collection included here, *Nightfall and Other Stories,* which features "Nightfall," a story that many readers and the Science Fiction Writers of America have voted the best science fiction story ever written (I don't think so, but it would be impolite to argue). Other favorites of mine are " 'Breeds There a Man . . . ?' ", which is rather chilling; "Sally," which expresses my feelings about automobiles; "Strikebreaker," which I consider much underappreciated; and "Eyes Do More than See," a short heartstring wrencher.

There'll be more volumes, but begin by reading this one. You will make an old man very happy, you know.

—ISAAC ASIMOV
New York City
March 1990

ISAAC ASIMOV
THE COMPLETE STORIES
Volume 1

The Dead Past

Arnold Potterley, Ph.D., was a Professor of Ancient History. That, in itself, was not dangerous. What changed the world beyond all dreams was the fact that he *looked* like a Professor of Ancient History.

Thaddeus Araman, Department Head of the Division of Chronoscopy, might have taken proper action if Dr. Potterley had been owner of a large, square chin, flashing eyes, aquiline nose and broad shoulders.

As it was, Thaddeus Araman found himself staring over his desk at a mild-mannered individual, whose faded blue eyes looked at him wistfully from either side of a low-bridged button nose; whose small, neatly dressed figure seemed stamped "milk-and-water" from thinning brown hair to the neatly brushed shoes that completed a conservative middle-class costume.

Araman said pleasantly, "And now what can I do for you, Dr. Potterley?"

Dr. Potterley said in a soft voice that went well with the rest of him, "Mr. Araman, I came to you because you're top man in chronoscopy."

Araman smiled. "Not exactly. Above me is the World Commissioner of Research and above him is the Secretary-General of the United Nations. And above both of them, of course, are the sovereign peoples of Earth."

Dr. Potterley shook his head. "They're not interested in chronoscopy. I've come to you, sir, because for two years I have been trying to obtain permission to do some time viewing—chronoscopy, that is—in connection with my researches on ancient Carthage. I can't obtain such permission. My research grants are all proper. There is no irregularity in any of my intellectual endeavors and yet—"

"I'm sure there is no question of irregularity," said Araman soothingly. He flipped the thin reproduction sheets in the folder to which Potterley's name had been attached. They had been produced by Multivac, whose vast analogical mind kept all the department records. When this was over, the sheets could be destroyed, then reproduced on demand in a matter of minutes.

And while Araman turned the pages, Dr. Potterley's voice continued in a soft monotone.

The historian was saying, "I must explain that my problem is quite an important one. Carthage was ancient commercialism brought to its zenith. Pre-Roman Carthage was the nearest ancient analogue to pre-atomic America, at least insofar as its attachment to trade, commerce and business in general was concerned. They were the most daring seamen and explorers before the Vikings; much better at it than the overrated Greeks.

"To know Carthage would be very rewarding, yet the only knowledge we have of it is derived from the writings of its bitter enemies, the Greeks and Romans. Carthage itself never wrote in its own defense or, if it did, the books did not survive. As a result, the Carthaginians have been one of the favorite sets of villains of history and perhaps unjustly so. Time viewing may set the record straight."

He said much more.

Araman said, still turning the reproduction sheets before him, "You must realize, Dr. Potterley, that chronoscopy, or time viewing, if you prefer, is a difficult process."

Dr. Potterley, who had been interrupted, frowned and said, "I am asking for only certain selected views at times and places I would indicate."

Araman sighed. "Even a few views, even one . . . It is an unbelievably delicate art. There is the question of focus, getting the proper scene in view and holding it. There is the synchronization of sound, which calls for completely independent circuits."

"Surely my problem is important enough to justify considerable effort."

"Yes, sir. Undoubtedly," said Araman at once. To deny the importance of someone's research problem would be unforgivably bad manners. "But you must understand how long-drawn-out even the simplest view is. And there is a long waiting line for the chronoscope and an even longer waiting line for the use of Multivac which guides us in our use of the controls."

Potterley stirred unhappily. "But can nothing be done? For two years—"

"A matter of priority, sir. I'm sorry. . . . Cigarette?"

The historian started back at the suggestion, eyes suddenly widening as he stared at the pack thrust out toward him. Araman looked surprised, withdrew the pack, made a motion as though to take a cigarette for himself and thought better of it.

Potterley drew a sigh of unfeigned relief as the pack was put out of sight.

He said, "Is there any way of reviewing matters, putting me as far forward as possible. I don't know how to explain—"

Araman smiled. Some had offered money under similar circumstances which, of course, had gotten them nowhere, either. He said, "The decisions on priority are computer-processed. I could in no way alter those decisions arbitrarily."

Potterley rose stiffly to his feet. He stood five and a half feet tall. "Then, good day, sir."

"Good day, Dr. Potterley. And my sincerest regrets."

He offered his hand and Potterley touched it briefly.

The historian left, and a touch of the buzzer brought Araman's secretary into the room. He handed her the folder.

"These," he said, "may be disposed of."

Alone again, he smiled bitterly. Another item in his quarter-century's service to the human race. Service through negation.

At least this fellow had been easy to dispose of. Sometimes academic pressure had to be applied and even withdrawal of grants.

Five minutes later, he had forgotten Dr. Potterley. Nor, thinking back on it later, could he remember feeling any premonition of danger.

During the first year of his frustration, Arnold Potterley had experienced only that—frustration. During the second year, though, his frustration gave birth to an idea that first frightened and then fascinated him. Two things stopped him from trying to translate the idea into action, and neither barrier was the undoubted fact that his notion was a grossly unethical one.

The first was merely the continuing hope that the government would finally give its permission and make it unnecessary for him to do anything more. That hope had perished finally in the interview with Araman just completed.

The second barrier had been not a hope at all but a dreary realization of his own incapacity. He was not a physicist and he knew no physicists from whom he might obtain help. The Department of Physics at the university consisted of men well stocked with grants and well immersed in specialty. At best, they would not listen to him. At worst, they would report him for intellectual anarchy and even his basic Carthaginian grant might easily be withdrawn.

That he could not risk. And yet chronoscopy was the only way to carry on his work. Without it, he would be no worse off if his grant were lost.

The first hint that the second barrier might be overcome had come a week earlier than his interview with Araman, and it had gone unrecognized at the time. It had been at one of the faculty teas. Potterley attended these sessions unfailingly because he conceived attendance to be a duty, and he took his duties seriously. Once there, however, he conceived it to be no responsibility of his to make light conversation or new friends. He sipped abstemiously at a drink or two, exchanged a polite word with the dean or such department heads as happened to be present, bestowed a narrow smile on others and finally left early.

Ordinarily, he would have paid no attention, at that most recent tea, to a young man standing quietly, even diffidently, in one corner. He would never have dreamed of speaking to him. Yet a tangle of circumstance persuaded him this once to behave in a way contrary to his nature.

That morning at breakfast, Mrs. Potterley had announced somberly that once again she had dreamed of Laurel; but this time a Laurel grown up, yet retaining the three-year-old face that stamped her as their child. Potterley had let her talk. There had been a time when he fought her too frequent preoccupation with the past and death. Laurel would not come back to them, either through dreams or through talk. Yet if it appeased Caroline Potterley—let her dream and talk.

But when Potterley went to school that morning, he found himself for once affected by Caroline's inanities. Laurel grown up! She had died nearly twenty years ago; their only child, then and ever. In all that time, when he thought of her, it was as a three-year-old.

Now he thought: But if she were alive now, she wouldn't be three, she'd be nearly twenty-three.

Helplessly, he found himself trying to think of Laurel as growing progressively older; as finally becoming twenty-three. He did not quite succeed.

Yet he tried. Laurel using make-up. Laurel going out with boys. Laurel—getting married!

So it was that when he saw the young man hovering at the outskirts of the coldly circulating group of faculty men, it occurred to him quixotically that, for all he knew, a youngster just such as this might have married Laurel. That youngster himself, perhaps. . . .

Laurel might have met him, here at the university, or some evening when he might be invited to dinner at the Potterleys'. They might grow interested in one another. Laurel would surely have been pretty and this youngster looked well. He was dark in coloring, with a lean intent face and an easy carriage.

The tenuous daydream snapped, yet Potterley found himself staring foolishly at the young man, not as a strange face but as a possible son-in-law in the might-have-been. He found himself threading his way toward the man. It was almost a form of autohypnotism.

He put out his hand. "I am Arnold Potterley of the History Department. You're new here, I think?"

The youngster looked faintly astonished and fumbled with his drink, shifting it to his left hand in order to shake with his right. "Jonas Foster is my name, sir. I'm a new instructor in physics. I'm just starting this semester."

Potterley nodded. "I wish you a happy stay here and great success."

That was the end of it, then. Potterley had come uneasily to his senses, found himself embarrassed and moved off. He stared back over his shoulder once, but the illusion of relationship had gone. Reality was quite real once more and he was angry with himself for having fallen prey to his wife's foolish talk about Laurel.

But a week later, even while Araman was talking, the thought of that young man had come back to him. An instructor in physics. A new instructor. Had he been deaf at the time? Was there a short circuit between ear and brain? Or was it an automatic self-censorship because of the impending interview with the Head of Chronoscopy?

But the interview failed, and it was the thought of the young man with whom he had exchanged two sentences that prevented Potterley from elaborating his pleas for consideration. He was almost anxious to get away.

And in the autogiro express back to the university, he could almost wish he were superstitious. He could then console himself with the thought that the casual meaningless meeting had really been directed by a knowing and purposeful Fate.

Jonas Foster was not new to academic life. The long and rickety struggle for the doctorate would make anyone a veteran. Additional work as a postdoctorate teaching fellow acted as a booster shot.

But now he was Instructor Jonas Foster. Professorial dignity lay ahead. And he now found himself in a new sort of relationship toward other professors.

For one thing, they would be voting on future promotions. For another, he was in no position to tell so early in the game which particular member of the faculty might or might not have the ear of the dean or even of the university president. He did not fancy himself as a campus politician and was sure he would make a poor one, yet there was no point in kicking his own rear into blisters just to prove that to himself.

So Foster listened to this mild-mannered historian who, in some vague way, seemed nevertheless to radiate tension, and did not shut him up abruptly and toss him out. Certainly that was his first impulse.

He remembered Potterley well enough. Potterley had approached him at that tea (which had been a grizzly affair). The fellow had spoken two sentences to him stiffly, somehow glassy-eyed, had then come to himself with a visible start and hurried off.

It had amused Foster at the time, but now . . .

Potterley might have been deliberately trying to make his acquaintance, or, rather, to impress his own personality on Foster as that of a queer sort of duck, eccentric but harmless. He might now be probing Foster's views, searching for unsettling opinions. Surely, they ought to have done so before granting him his appointment. Still . . .

Potterley might be serious, might honestly not realize what he was doing.

Or he might realize quite well what he was doing; he might be nothing more or less than a dangerous rascal.

Foster mumbled, "Well, now—" to gain time, and fished out a package of cigarettes, intending to offer one to Potterley and to light it and one for himself very slowly.

But Potterley said at once, "Please, Dr. Foster. No cigarettes."

Foster looked startled. "I'm sorry, sir."

"No. The regrets are mine. I cannot stand the odor. An idiosyncrasy. I'm sorry."

He was positively pale. Foster put away the cigarettes.

Foster, feeling the absence of the cigarette, took the easy way out. "I'm flattered that you ask my advice and all that, Dr. Potterley, but I'm not a neutrinics man. I can't very well do anything professional in that direction. Even stating an opinion would be out of line, and, frankly, I'd prefer that you didn't go into any particulars."

The historian's prim face set hard. "What do you mean, you're not a neutrinics man? You're not anything yet. You haven't received any grant, have you?"

"This is only my first semester."

"I know that. I imagine you haven't even applied for any grant yet."

Foster half-smiled. In three months at the university, he had not succeeded in putting his initial requests for research grants into good enough shape to pass on to a professional science writer, let alone to the Research Commission.

(His Department Head, fortunately, took it quite well. "Take your time now, Foster," he said, "and get your thoughts well organized. Make sure you know your path and where it will lead, for, once you receive a grant, your specialization will be formally recognized and, for better or for worse, it will be yours for the rest of your career." The advice was trite enough, but triteness has often the merit of truth, and Foster recognized that.)

Foster said, "By education and inclination, Dr. Potterley, I'm a hyperoptics man with a gravitics minor. It's how I described myself in applying for this position. It may not be my official specialization yet, but it's going to be. It can't be anything else. As for neutrinics, I never even studied the subject."

"Why not?" demanded Potterley at once.

Foster stared. It was the kind of rude curiosity about another man's professional status that was always irritating. He said, with the edge of his own politeness just a trifle blunted, "A course in neutrinics wasn't given at my university."

"Good Lord, where did you go?"

"M.I.T.," said Foster quietly.

"And they don't teach neutrinics?"

"No, they don't." Foster felt himself flush and was moved to a defense.

"It's a highly specialized subject with no great value. Chronoscopy, perhaps, has some value, but it is the only practical application and that's a dead end."

The historian stared at him earnestly. "Tell me this. Do you know where I can find a neutrinics man?"

"No, I don't," said Foster bluntly.

"Well, then, do you know a school which teaches neutrinics?"

"No, I don't."

Potterley smiled tightly and without humor.

Foster resented that smile, found he detected insult in it and grew sufficiently annoyed to say, "I would like to point out, sir, that you're stepping out of line."

"What?"

"I'm saying that, as a historian, your interest in any sort of physics, your *professional* interest, is—" He paused, unable to bring himself quite to say the word.

"Unethical?"

"That's the word, Dr. Potterley."

"My researches have driven me to it," said Potterley in an intense whisper.

"The Research Commission is the place to go. If they permit—"

"I have gone to them and have received no satisfaction."

"Then obviously you must abandon this." Foster knew he was sounding stuffily virtuous, but he wasn't going to let this man lure him into an expression of intellectual anarchy. It was too early in his career to take stupid risks.

Apparently, though, the remark had its effect on Potterley. Without any warning, the man exploded into a rapid-fire verbal storm of irresponsibility.

Scholars, he said, could be free only if they could freely follow their own free-swinging curiosity. Research, he said, forced into a predesigned pattern by the powers that held the purse strings became slavish and had to stagnate. No man, he said, had the right to dictate the intellectual interests of another.

Foster listened to all of it with disbelief. None of it was strange to him. He had heard college boys talk so in order to shock their professors and he had once or twice amused himself in that fashion, too. Anyone who studied the history of science knew that many men had once thought so.

Yet it seemed strange to Foster, almost against nature, that a modern man of science could advance such nonsense. No one would advocate running a factory by allowing each individual worker to do whatever pleased him at the moment, or of running a ship according to the casual and conflicting notions of each individual crewman. It would be taken for granted that some sort of centralized supervisory agency must exist in each case. Why should direction and order benefit a factory and a ship but not scientific research?

People might say that the human mind was somehow qualitatively different from a ship or factory but the history of intellectual endeavor proved the opposite.

When science was young and the intricacies of all or most of the known was within the grasp of an individual mind, there was no need for direction, perhaps. Blind wandering over the uncharted tracts of ignorance could lead to wonderful finds by accident.

But as knowledge grew, more and more data had to be absorbed before worthwhile journeys into ignorance could be organized. Men had to specialize. The researcher needed the resources of a library he himself could not gather, then of instruments he himself could not afford. More and more, the individual researcher gave way to the research team and the research institution.

The funds necessary for research grew greater as tools grew more numerous. What college was so small today as not to require at least one nuclear micro-reactor and at least one three-stage computer?

Centuries before, private individuals could no longer subsidize research. By 1940, only the government, large industries and large universities or research institutions could properly subsidize basic research.

By 1960, even the largest universities depended entirely upon government grants, while research institutions could not exist without tax concessions and public subscriptions. By 2000, the industrial combines had become a branch of the world government and, thereafter, the financing of research and therefore its direction naturally became centralized under a department of the government.

It all worked itself out naturally and well. Every branch of science was fitted neatly to the needs of the public, and the various branches of science were co-ordinated decently. The material advance of the last half-century was argument enough for the fact that science was not falling into stagnation.

Foster tried to say a very little of this and was waved aside impatiently by Potterley who said, "You are parroting official propaganda. You're sitting in the middle of an example that's squarely against the official view. Can you believe that?"

"Frankly, no."

"Well, why do you say time viewing is a dead end? Why is neutrinics unimportant? You say it is. You say it categorically. Yet you've never studied it. You claim complete ignorance of the subject. It's not even given in your school—"

"Isn't the mere fact that it isn't given proof enough?"

"Oh, I see. It's not given because it's unimportant. And it's unimportant because it's not given. Are you satisfied with that reasoning?"

Foster felt a growing confusion. "It's in the books."

"That's all. The books say neutrinics is unimportant. Your professors tell you so because they read it in the books. The books say so because professors write them. Who says it from personal experience and knowledge? Who does research in it? Do you know of anyone?"

Foster said, "I don't see that we're getting anywhere, Dr. Potterley. I have work to do—"

"One minute. I just want you to try this on. See how it sounds to you. I say the government is actively suppressing basic research in neutrinics and chronoscopy. They're suppressing application of chronoscopy."

"Oh, no."

"Why not? They could do it. There's your centrally directed research. If they refuse grants for research in any portion of science, that portion dies. They've killed neutrinics. They can do it and have done it."

"But why?"

"I don't know why. I want you to find out. I'd do it myself if I knew enough. I came to you because you're a young fellow with a brand-new education. Have your intellectual arteries hardened already? Is there no curiosity in you? Don't you want to *know?* Don't you want *answers?"*

The historian was peering intently into Foster's face. Their noses were only inches apart, and Foster was so lost that he did not think to draw back.

He should, by rights, have ordered Potterley out. If necessary, he should have thrown Potterley out.

It was not respect for age and position that stopped him. It was certainly not that Potterley's arguments had convinced him. Rather, it was a small point of college pride.

Why didn't M.I.T. give a course in neutrinics? For that matter, now that he came to think of it, he doubted that there was a single book on neutrinics in the library. He could never recall having seen one.

He stopped to think about that.

And that was ruin.

Caroline Potterley had once been an attractive woman. There were occasions, such as dinners or university functions, when, by considerable effort, remnants of the attraction could be salvaged.

On ordinary occasions, she sagged. It was the word she applied to herself in moments of self-abhorrence. She had grown plumper with the years, but the flaccidity about her was not a matter of fat entirely. It was as though her muscles had given up and grown limp so that she shuffled when she walked, while her eyes grew baggy and her cheeks jowly. Even her graying hair seemed tired rather than merely stringy. Its straightness seemed to be the result of a supine surrender to gravity, nothing else.

Caroline Potterley looked at herself in the mirror and admitted this was one of her bad days. She knew the reason, too.

It had been the dream of Laurel. The strange one, with Laurel grown up. She had been wretched ever since.

Still, she was sorry she had mentioned it to Arnold. He didn't say anything; he never did any more; but it was bad for him. He was particularly
withdrawn for days afterward. It might have been that he was getting ready
for that important conference with the big government official (he kept
saying he expected no success), but it might also have been her dream.

It was better in the old days when he would cry sharply at her, "Let the
dead past *go*, Caroline! Talk won't bring her back, and dreams won't either."

It had been bad for both of them. Horribly bad. She had been away from
home and had lived in guilt ever since. If she had stayed at home, if she had
not gone on an unnecessary shopping expedition, there would have been two
of them available. One would have succeeded in saving Laurel.

Poor Arnold had not managed. Heaven knew he tried. He had nearly died
himself. He had come out of the burning house, staggering in agony, blis-
tered, choking, half-blinded, with the dead Laurel in his arms.

The nightmare of that lived on, never lifting entirely.

Arnold slowly grew a shell about himself afterward. He cultivated a low-
voiced mildness through which nothing broke, no lightning struck. He grew
puritanical and even abandoned his minor vices, his cigarettes, his penchant
for an occasional profane exclamation. He obtained his grant for the preparation of a new history of Carthage and subordinated everything to that.

She tried to help him. She hunted up his references, typed his notes and
microfilmed them. Then that ended suddenly.

She ran from the desk suddenly one evening, reaching the bathroom in
bare time and retching abominably. Her husband followed her in confusion
and concern.

"Caroline, what's wrong?"

It took a drop of brandy to bring her around. She said, "Is it true? What
they did?"

"Who did?"

"The Carthaginians."

He stared at her and she got it out by indirection. She couldn't say it right
out.

The Carthaginians, it seemed, worshiped Moloch, in the form of a hollow, brazen idol with a furnace in its belly. At times of national crisis, the
priests and the people gathered, and infants, after the proper ceremonies
and invocations, were dextrously hurled, alive, into the flames.

They were given sweetmeats just before the crucial moment, in order that
the efficacy of the sacrifice not be ruined by displeasing cries of panic. The
drums rolled just after the moment, to drown out the few seconds of infant
shrieking. The parents were present, presumably gratified, for the sacrifice
was pleasing to the gods. . . .

Arnold Potterley frowned darkly. Vicious lies, he told her, on the part of
Carthage's enemies. He should have warned her. After all, such propa-

gandistic lies were not uncommon. According to the Greeks, the ancient Hebrews worshiped an ass's head in their Holy of Holies. According to the Romans, the primitive Christians were haters of all men who sacrificed pagan children in the catacombs.

"Then they didn't do it?" asked Caroline.

"I'm sure they didn't. The primitive Phoenicians may have. Human sacrifice is commonplace in primitive cultures. But Carthage in her great days was not a primitive culture. Human sacrifice often gives way to symbolic actions such as circumcision. The Greeks and Romans might have mistaken some Carthaginian symbolism for the original full rite, either out of ignorance or out of malice."

"Are you sure?"

"I can't be sure yet, Caroline, but when I've got enough evidence, I'll apply for permission to use chronoscopy, which will settle the matter once and for all."

"Chronoscopy?"

"Time viewing. We can focus on ancient Carthage at some time of crisis, the landing of Scipio Africanus in 202 B.C., for instance, and see with our own eyes exactly what happens. And you'll see, I'll be right."

He patted her and smiled encouragingly, but she dreamed of Laurel every night for two weeks thereafter and she never helped him with his Carthage project again. Nor did he ever ask her to.

But now she was bracing herself for his coming. He had called her after arriving back in town, told her he had seen the government man and that it had gone as expected. That meant failure, and yet the little telltale sign of depression had been absent from his voice and his features had appeared quite composed in the teleview. He had another errand to take care of, he said, before coming home.

It meant he would be late, but that didn't matter. Neither one of them was particular about eating hours or cared when packages were taken out of the freezer or even which packages or when the selfwarming mechanism was activated.

When he did arrive, he surprised her. There was nothing untoward about him in any obvious way. He kissed her dutifully and smiled, took off his hat and asked if all had been well while he was gone. It was all almost perfectly normal. Almost.

She had learned to detect small things, though, and his pace in all this was a trifle hurried. Enough to show her accustomed eye that he was under tension.

She said, "Has something happened?"

He said, "We're going to have a dinner guest night after next, Caroline. You don't mind?"

"Well, no. Is it anyone I know?"

"No. A young instructor. A newcomer. I've spoken to him." He suddenly whirled toward her and seized her arms at the elbow, held them a moment, then dropped them in confusion as though disconcerted at having shown emotion.

He said, "I almost didn't get through to him. Imagine that. Terrible, *terrible*, the way we have all bent to the yoke; the affection we have for the harness about us."

Mrs. Potterley·wasn't sure she understood, but for a year she had been watching him grow quietly more rebellious; little by little more daring in his criticism of the government. She said, "You haven't spoken foolishly to him, have you?"

"What do you mean, foolishly? He'll be doing some neutrinics for me."

"Neutrinics" was trisyllabic nonsense to Mrs. Potterley, but she knew it had nothing to do with history. She said faintly, "Arnold, I don't like you to do that. You'll lose your position. It's—"

"It's intellectual anarchy, my dear," he said. "That's the phrase you want. Very well. I am an anarchist. If the government will not allow me to push my researches, I will push them on my own. And when I show the way, others will follow. . . . And if they don't, it makes no difference. It's Carthage that counts and human knowledge, not you and I."

"But you don't know this young man. What if he is an agent for the Commission of Research."

"Not likely and I'll take that chance." He made a fist of his right hand and rubbed it gently against the palm of his left. "He's on my side now. I'm sure of it. He can't help but be. I can recognize intellectual curiosity when I see it in a man's eyes and face and attitude, and it's a fatal disease for a tame scientist. Even today it takes time to beat it out of a man and the young ones are vulnerable. . . . Oh, why stop at anything? Why not build our own chronoscope and tell the government to go to—"

He stopped abruptly, shook his head and turned away.

"I hope everything will be all right," said Mrs. Potterley, feeling helplessly certain that everything would not be, and frightened, in advance, for her husband's professorial status and the security of their old age.

It was she alone, of them all, who had a violent presentiment of trouble. Quite the wrong trouble, of course.

Jonas Foster was nearly half an hour late in arriving at the Potterleys' off-campus house. Up to that very evening, he had not quite decided he would go. Then, at the last moment, he found he could not bring himself to commit the social enormity of breaking a dinner appointment an hour before the appointed time. That, and the nagging of curiosity.

The dinner itself passed interminably. Foster ate without appetite. Mrs. Potterley sat in distant absent-mindedness, emerging out of it only once to ask if he were married and to make a deprecating sound at the news that he was not. Dr. Potterley himself asked neutrally after his professional history and nodded his head primly.

It was as staid, stodgy—boring, actually—as anything could be.

Foster thought: He seems so harmless.

Foster had spent the last two days reading up on Dr. Potterley. Very casually, of course, almost sneakily. He wasn't particularly anxious to be seen in the Social Science Library. To be sure, history was one of those borderline affairs and historical works were frequently read for amusement or edification by the general public.

Still, a physicist wasn't quite the "general public." Let Foster take to reading histories and he would be considered queer, sure as relativity, and after a while the Head of the Department would wonder if his new instructor were really "the man for the job."

So he had been cautious. He sat in the more secluded alcoves and kept his head bent when he slipped in and out at odd hours.

Dr. Potterley, it turned out, had written three books and some dozen articles on the ancient Mediterranean worlds, and the later articles (all in "Historical Reviews") had all dealt with pre-Roman Carthage from a sympathetic viewpoint.

That, at least, checked with Potterley's story and had soothed Foster's suspicions somewhat. . . . And yet Foster felt that it would have been much wiser, much safer, to have scotched the matter at the beginning.

A scientist shouldn't be too curious, he thought in bitter dissatisfaction with himself. It's a dangerous trait.

After dinner, he was ushered into Potterley's study and he was brought up sharply at the threshold. The walls were simply lined with books.

Not merely films. There were films, of course, but these were far outnumbered by the books—print on paper. He wouldn't have thought so many books would exist in usable condition.

That bothered Foster. Why should anyone want to keep so many books at home? Surely all were available in the university library, or, at the very worst, at the Library of Congress, if one wished to take the minor trouble of checking out a microfilm.

There was an element of secrecy involved in a home library. It breathed of intellectual anarchy. That last thought, oddly, calmed Foster. He would rather Potterley be an authentic anarchist than a play-acting *agent provocateur*.

And now the hours began to pass quickly and astonishingly.

"You see," Potterley said, in a clear, unflurried voice, "it was a matter of finding, if possible, anyone who had ever used chronoscopy in his work. Naturally, I couldn't ask baldly, since that would be unauthorized research."

"Yes," said Foster dryly. He was a little surprised such a small consideration would stop the man.

"I used indirect methods—"

He had. Foster was amazed at the volume of correspondence dealing with small disputed points of ancient Mediterranean culture which somehow managed to elicit the casual remark over and over again: "Of course, having never made use of chronoscopy—" or, "Pending approval of my request for chronoscopic data, which appear unlikely at the moment—"

"Now these aren't blind questionings," said Potterley. "There's a monthly booklet put out by the Institute for Chronoscopy in which items concerning the past as determined by time viewing are printed. Just one or two items.

"What impressed me first was the triviality of most of the items, their insipidity. Why should such researches get priority over my work? So I wrote to people who would be most likely to do research in the directions described in the booklet. Uniformly, as I have shown you, they did *not* make use of the chronoscope. Now let's go over it point by point."

At last Foster, his head swimming with Potterley's meticulously gathered details, asked, "But why?"

"I don't know why," said Potterley, "but I have a theory. The original invention of the chronoscope was by Sterbinski—you see, I know that much —and it was well publicized. But then the government took over the instrument and decided to suppress further research in the matter or any use of the machine. But then, people might be curious as to why it wasn't being used. Curiosity is such a vice, Dr. Foster."

Yes, agreed the physicist to himself.

"Imagine the effectiveness, then," Potterley went on, "of pretending that the chronoscope *was* being used. It would then be not a mystery, but a commonplace. It would no longer be a fitting object for legitimate curiosity or an attractive one for illicit curiosity."

"*You* were curious," pointed out Foster.

Potterley looked a trifle restless. "It was different in my case," he said angrily. "I have something that *must* be done, and I wouldn't submit to the ridiculous way in which they kept putting me off."

A bit paranoid, too, thought Foster gloomily.

Yet he had ended up with something, paranoid or not. Foster could no longer deny that something peculiar was going on in the matter of neutrinics.

But what was Potterley after? That still bothered Foster. If Potterley didn't intend this as a test of Foster's ethics, what *did* he want?

Foster put it to himself logically. If an intellectual anarchist with a touch of paranoia wanted to use a chronoscope and was convinced that the powers-that-be were deliberately standing in his way, what would he do?

Supposing it were I, he thought. What would I do?

He said slowly, "Maybe the chronoscope doesn't exist at all?"

Potterley started. There was almost a crack in his general calmness. For an instant, Foster found himself catching a glimpse of something not at all calm.

But the historian kept his balance and said, "Oh, no, there *must* be a chronoscope."

"Why? Have you seen it? Have I? Maybe that's the explanation of everything. Maybe they're not deliberately holding out on a chronoscope they've got. Maybe they haven't got it in the first place."

"But Sterbinski lived. He built a chronoscope. That much is a fact."

"The books say so," said Foster coldly.

"Now listen." Potterley actually reached over and snatched at Foster's jacket sleeve. "I need the chronoscope. I must have it. Don't tell me it doesn't exist. What we're going to do is find out enough about neutrinics to be able to—"

Potterley drew himself up short.

Foster drew his sleeve away. He needed no ending to that sentence. He supplied it himself. He said, "Build one of our own?"

Potterley looked sour as though he would rather not have said it point-blank. Nevertheless, he said, "Why not?"

"Because that's out of the question," said Foster. "If what I've read is correct, then it took Sterbinski twenty years to build his machine and several millions in composite grants. Do you think you and I can duplicate that illegally? Suppose we had the time, which we haven't, and suppose I could learn enough out of books, which I doubt, where would we get the money and equipment? The chronoscope is supposed to fill a five-story building, for Heaven's sake."

"Then you won't help me?"

"Well, I'll tell you what. I have one way in which I may be able to find out something—"

"What is that?" asked Potterley at once.

"Never mind. That's not important. But I may be able to find out enough to tell you whether the government is deliberately suppressing research by chronoscope. I may confirm the evidence you already have or I may be able to prove that your evidence is misleading. I don't know what good it will do you in either case, but it's as far as I can go. It's my limit."

Potterley watched the young man go finally. He was angry with himself. Why had he allowed himself to grow so careless as to permit the fellow to guess that he was thinking in terms of a chronoscope of his own. That was premature.

But then why did the young fool have to suppose that a chronoscope might not exist at all?

It *had* to exist. It *had* to. What was the use of saying it didn't?

And why couldn't a second one be built? Science had advanced in the fifty years since Sterbinski. All that was needed was knowledge.

Let the youngster gather knowledge. Let him think a small gathering would be his limit. Having taken the path to anarchy, there would be no limit. If the boy were not driven onward by something in himself, the first steps would be error enough to force the rest. Potterley was quite certain he would not hesitate to use blackmail.

Potterley waved a last good-by and looked up. It was beginning to rain.

Certainly! Blackmail if necessary, but he would not be stopped.

Foster steered his car across the bleak outskirts of town and scarcely noticed the rain.

He *was* a fool, he told himself, but he couldn't leave things as they were. He had to know. He damned his streak of undisciplined curiosity, but he had to know.

But he would go no further than Uncle Ralph. He swore mightily to himself that it would stop there. In that way, there would be no evidence against him, no real evidence. Uncle Ralph would be discreet.

In a way, he was secretly ashamed of Uncle Ralph. He hadn't mentioned him to Potterley partly out of caution and partly because he did not wish to witness the lifted eyebrow, the inevitable half-smile. Professional science writers, however useful, were a little outside the pale, fit only for patronizing contempt. The fact that, as a class, they made more money than did research scientists only made matters worse, of course.

Still, there were times when a science writer in the family could be a convenience. Not being really educated, they did not have to specialize. Consequently, a good science writer knew practically everything. . . . And Uncle Ralph was one of the best.

Ralph Nimmo had no college degree and was rather proud of it. "A degree," he once said to Jonas Foster, when both were considerably younger, "is a first step down a ruinous highway. You don't want to waste it so you go on to graduate work and doctoral research. You end up a thoroughgoing ignoramus on everything in the world except for one subdivisional sliver of nothing.

"On the other hand, if you guard your mind carefully and keep it blank of any clutter of information till maturity is reached, filling it only with intelligence and training it only in clear thinking, you then have a powerful instrument at your disposal and you can become a science writer."

Nimmo received his first assignment at the age of twenty-five, after he had completed his apprenticeship and been out in the field for less than three months. It came in the shape of a clotted manuscript whose language would impart no glimmering of understanding to any reader, however qualified, without careful study and some inspired guesswork. Nimmo took it apart and put it together again (after five long and exasperating interviews with the authors, who were biophysicists), making the language taut and meaningful and smoothing the style to a pleasant gloss.

"Why not?" he would say tolerantly to his nephew, who countered his strictures on degrees by berating him with his readiness to hang on the fringes of science. "The fringe is important. Your scientists can't write. Why should they be expected to? They aren't expected to be grand masters at chess or virtuosos at the violin, so why expect them to know how to put words together? Why not leave that for specialists, too?"

"Good Lord, Jonas, read your literature of a hundred years ago. Discount the fact that the science is out of date and that some of the expressions are out of date. Just try to read it and make sense out of it. It's just jaw-cracking, amateurish. Pages are published uselessly; whole articles which are either noncomprehensible or both."

"But you don't get recognition, Uncle Ralph," protested young Foster, who was getting ready to start his college career and was rather starry-eyed about it. "You could be a terrific researcher."

"I get recognition," said Nimmo. "Don't think for a minute I don't. Sure, a biochemist or a strato-meteorologist won't give me the time of day, but they pay me well enough. Just find out what happens when some first-class chemist finds the Commission has cut his year's allowance for science writing. He'll fight harder for enough funds to afford me, or someone like me, than to get a recording ionograph."

He grinned broadly and Foster grinned back. Actually, he was proud of his paunchy, round-faced, stub-fingered uncle, whose vanity made him brush his fringe of hair futilely over the desert on his pate and made him dress like an unmade haystack because such negligence was his trademark. Ashamed, but proud, too.

And now Foster entered his uncle's cluttered apartment in no mood at all for grinning. He was nine years older now and so was Uncle Ralph. For nine more years, papers in every branch of science had come to him for polishing and a little of each had crept into his capacious mind.

Nimmo was eating seedless grapes, popping them into his mouth one at a time. He tossed a bunch to Foster who caught them by a hair, then bent to retrieve individual grapes that had torn loose and fallen to the floor.

"Let them be. Don't bother," said Nimmo carelessly. "Someone comes in here to clean once a week. What's up? Having trouble with your grant application write-up?"

"I haven't really got into that yet."

"You haven't? Get a move on, boy. Are you waiting for me to offer to do the final arrangement?"

"I couldn't afford you, Uncle."

"Aw, come on. It's all in the family. Grant me all popular publication rights and no cash need change hands."

Foster nodded. "If you're serious, it's a deal."

"It's a deal."

It was a gamble, of course, but Foster knew enough of Nimmo's science writing to realize it could pay off. Some dramatic discovery of public interest on primitive man or on a new surgical technique, or on any branch of spationautics could mean a very cash-attracting article in any of the mass media of communication.

It was Nimmo, for instance, who had written up, for scientific consumption, the series of papers by Bryce and co-workers that elucidated the fine structure of two cancer viruses, for which job he asked the picayune payment of fifteen hundred dollars, provided popular publication rights were included. He then wrote up, exclusively, the same work in semidramatic form for use in trimensional video for a twenty-thousand-dollar advance plus rental royalties that were still coming in after five years.

Foster said bluntly, "What do you know about neutrinics, Uncle?"

"Neutrinics?" Nimmo's small eyes looked surprised. "Are you working in that? I thought it was pseudo-gravitic optics."

"It is p.g.o. I just happen to be asking about neutrinics."

"That's a devil of a thing to be doing. You're stepping out of line. You know that, don't you?"

"I don't expect you to call the Commission because I'm a little curious about things."

"Maybe I should before you get into trouble. Curiosity is an occupational danger with scientists. I've watched it work. One of them will be moving quietly along on a problem, then curiosity leads him up a strange creek. Next thing you know they've done so little on their proper problem, they can't justify for a project renewal. I've seen more—"

"All I want to know," said Foster patiently, "is what's been passing through your hands lately on neutrinics."

Nimmo leaned back, chewing at a grape thoughtfully. "Nothing. Nothing ever. I don't recall ever getting a paper on neutrinics."

"What!" Foster was openly astonished. "Then who does get the work?"

"Now that you ask,' said Nimmo, "I don't know. Don't recall anyone talking about it at the annual conventions. I don't think much work is being done there."

"Why not?"

"Hey, there, don't bark. I'm not doing anything. My guess would be—"
Foster was exasperated. "Don't you know?"

"Hmp. I'll tell you what I know about neutrinics. It concerns the applications of neutrino movements and the forces involved—"

"Sure. Sure. Just as electronics deals with the applications of electron movements and the forces involved, and pseudo-gravitics deals with the applications of artificial gravitational fields. I didn't come to you for that. Is that all you know?"

"And," said Nimmo with equanimity, "neutrinics is the basis of time viewing and that *is* all I know."

Foster slouched back in his chair and massaged one lean cheek with great intensity. He felt angrily dissatisfied. Without formulating it explicitly in his own mind, he had felt sure, somehow, that Nimmo would come up with some late reports, bring up interesting facets of modern neutrinics, send him back to Potterley able to say that the elderly historian was mistaken, that his data was misleading, his deductions mistaken.

Then he could have returned to his proper work.

But now . . .

He told himself angrily: So they're not doing much work in the field. Does that make it deliberate suppression? What if neutrinics is a sterile discipline? Maybe it is. I don't know. Potterley doesn't. Why waste the intellectual resources of humanity on nothing? Or the work might be secret for some legitimate reason. It might be . . .

The trouble was, he had to know. He couldn't leave things as they were now. *He couldn't!*

He said, "Is there a text on neutrinics, Uncle Ralph? I mean a clear and simple one. An elementary one."

Nimmo thought, his plump cheeks puffing out with a series of sighs. "You ask the damnedest questions. The only one I ever heard of was Sterbinski and somebody. I've never seen it, but I viewed something about it once. . . . Sterbinski and LaMarr, that's it."

"Is that the Sterbinski who invented the chronoscope?"

"I think so. Proves the book ought to be good."

"Is there a recent edition? Sterbinski died thirty years ago."

Nimmo shrugged and said nothing.

"Can you find out?"

They sat in silence for a moment, while Nimmo shifted his bulk to the creaking tune of the chair he sat on. Then the science writer said, "Are you going to tell me what this is all about?"

"I can't. Will you help me anyway, Uncle Ralph? Will you get me a copy of the text?"

"Well, you've taught me all I know on pseudo-gravitics. I should be grateful. Tell you what—I'll help you on one condition."

"Which is?"

The older man was suddenly very grave. "That you be careful, Jonas. You're obviously way out of line whatever you're doing. Don't blow up your career just because you're curious about something you haven't been assigned to and which is none of your business. Understand?"

Foster nodded, but he hardly heard. He was thinking furiously.

• • • •

A full week later, Ralph Nimmo eased his rotund figure into Jonas Foster's on-campus two-room combination and said, in a hoarse whisper, "I've
got something."

"What?" Foster was immediately eager.

"A copy of Sterbinski and LaMarr." He produced it, or rather a corner of
it, from his ample topcoat.

Foster almost automatically eyed door and windows to make sure they
were closed and shaded respectively, then held out his hand.

The film case was flaking with age, and when he cracked it the film was
faded and growing brittle. He said sharply, "Is this all?"

"Gratitude, my boy, gratitude!" Nimmo sat down with a grunt, and
reached into a pocket for an apple.

"Oh, I'm grateful, but it's so old."

"And lucky to get it at that. I tried to get a film run from the Congressional Library. No go. The book was restricted."

"Then how did you get this?"

"Stole it." He was biting crunchingly around the core. "New York Public."

"What?"

"Simple enough. I had access to the stacks, naturally. So I stepped over a
chained railing when no one was around, dug this up, and walked out with
it. They're very trusting out there. Meanwhile, they won't miss it in years.
. . . Only you'd better not let anyone see it on you, nephew."

Foster stared at the film as though it were literally hot.

Nimmo discarded the core and reached for a second apple. "Funny thing,
now. There's nothing more recent in the whole field of neutrinics. Not a
monograph, not a paper, not a progress note. Nothing since the chronoscope."

"Uh-huh," said Foster absently.

Foster worked evenings in the Potterley home. He could not trust his own
on-campus rooms for the purpose. The evening work grew more real to him
than his own grant applications. Sometimes he worried about it but then
that stopped, too.

His work consisted, at first, simply in viewing and reviewing the text film.
Later it consisted in thinking (sometimes while a section of the book ran
itself off through the pocket projector, disregarded).

Sometimes Potterley would come down to watch, to sit with prim, eager
eyes, as though he expected thought processes to solidify and become visible
in all their convolutions. He interfered in only two ways. He did not allow
Foster to smoke and sometimes he talked.

It wasn't conversation talk, never that. Rather it was a low-voiced mono-
logue with which, it seemed, he scarcely expected to command attention. It
was much more as though he were relieving a pressure within himself.

Carthage! Always Carthage!

Carthage, the New York of the ancient Mediterranean. Carthage, commercial empire and queen of the seas. Carthage, all that Syracuse and Alexandria pretended to be. Carthage, maligned by her enemies and inarticulate in her own defense.

She had been defeated once by Rome and then driven out of Sicily and Sardinia, but came back to more than recoup her losses by new dominions in Spain, and raised up Hannibal to give the Romans sixteen years of terror.

In the end, she lost again a second time, reconciled herself to fate and built again with broken tools a limping life in shrunken territory, succeeding so well that jealous Rome deliberately forced a third war. And then Carthage, with nothing but bare hands and tenacity, built weapons and forced Rome into a two-year war that ended only with complete destruction of the city, the inhabitants throwing themselves into their flaming houses rather than surrender.

"Could people fight so for a city and a way of life as bad as the ancient writers painted it? Hannibal was a better general than any Roman and his soldiers were absolutely faithful to him. Even his bitterest enemies praised him. There was a Carthaginian. It is fashionable to say that he was an atypical Carthaginian, better than the others, a diamond placed in garbage. But then why was he so faithful to Carthage, even to his death after years of exile? They talk of Moloch—"

Foster didn't always listen but sometimes he couldn't help himself and he shuddered and turned sick at the bloody tale of child sacrifice.

But Potterley went on earnestly, "Just the same, it isn't true. It's a twenty-five-hundred-year-old canard started by the Greeks and Romans. They had their own slaves, their crucifixions and torture, their gladiatorial contests. They weren't holy. The Moloch story is what later ages would have called war propaganda, the big lie. I can prove it was a lie. I can prove it and, by Heaven, I will—I will—"

He would mumble that promise over and over again in his earnestness.

Mrs. Potterley visited him also, but less frequently, usually on Tuesdays and Thursdays when Dr. Potterley himself had an evening course to take care of and was not present.

She would sit quietly, scarcely talking, face slack and doughy, eyes blank, her whole attitude distant and withdrawn.

The first time, Foster tried, uneasily, to suggest that she leave.

She said tonelessly, "Do I disturb you?"

"No, of course not," lied Foster restlessly. "It's just that—that—" He couldn't complete the sentence.

She nodded, as though accepting an invitation to stay. Then she opened a cloth bag she had brought with her and took out a quire of vitron sheets which she proceeded to weave together by rapid, delicate movements of a pair of slender, tetra-faceted depolarizers, whose battery-fed wires made her look as though she were holding a large spider.

One evening, she said softly, "My daughter, Laurel, is your age."

Foster started, as much at the sudden unexpected sound of speech as at the words. He said, "I didn't know you had a daughter, Mrs. Potterley."

"She died. Years ago."

The vitron grew under the deft manipulations into the uneven shape of some garment Foster could not yet identify. There was nothing left for him to do but mutter inanely, "I'm sorry."

Mrs. Potterley sighed. "I dream about her often." She raised her blue, distant eyes to him.

Foster winced and looked away.

Another evening she asked, pulling at one of the vitron sheets to loosen its gentle clinging to her dress, "What is time viewing anyway?"

That remark broke into a particularly involved chain of thought, and Foster said snappishly, "Dr. Potterley can explain."

"He's tried to. Oh, my, yes. But I think he's a little impatient with me. He calls it chronoscopy most of the time. Do you actually see things in the past, like the trimensionals? Or does it just make little dot patterns like the computer you use?"

Foster stared at his hand computer with distaste. It worked well enough, but every operation had to be manually controlled and the answers were obtained in code. Now if he could use the school computer . . . Well, why dream, he felt conspicuous enough, as it was, carrying a hand computer under his arm every evening as he left his office.

He said, "I've never seen the chronoscope myself, but I'm under the impression that you actually see pictures and hear sound."

"You can hear people talk, too?"

"I think so." Then, half in desperation, "Look here, Mrs. Potterley, this must be awfully dull for you. I realize you don't like to leave a guest all to himself, but really, Mrs. Potterley, you mustn't feel compelled—"

"I don't feel compelled," she said. "I'm sitting here, waiting."

"Waiting? For what?"

She said composedly, "I listened to you that first evening. The time you first spoke to Arnold. I listened at the door."

He said, "You did?"

"I know I shouldn't have, but I was awfully worried about Arnold. I had a notion he was going to do something he oughtn't and I wanted to hear what. And then when I heard—" She paused, bending close over the vitron and peering at it.

"Heard what, Mrs. Potterley?"

"That you wouldn't build a chronoscope."

"Well, of course not."

"I thought maybe you might change your mind."

Foster glared at her. "Do you mean you're coming down here hoping I'll build a chronoscope, waiting for me to build one?"

"I hope you do, Dr. Foster. Oh, I hope you do."

It was as though, all at once, a fuzzy veil had fallen off her face, leaving all her features clear and sharp, putting color into her cheeks, life into her eyes, the vibrations of something approaching excitement into her voice.

"Wouldn't it be wonderful," she whispered, "to have one? People of the past could live again. Pharaohs and kings and—just people. I hope you build one, Dr. Foster. I really—hope—"

She choked, it seemed, on the intensity of her own words and let the vitron sheets slip off her lap. She rose and ran up the basement stairs, while Foster's eyes followed her awkwardly fleeing body with astonishment and distress.

It cut deeper into Foster's nights and left him sleepless and painfully stiff with thought. It was almost a mental indigestion.

His grant requests went limping in, finally, to Ralph Nimmo. He scarcely had any hope for them. He thought numbly: They won't be approved.

If they weren't, of course, it would create a scandal in the department and probably mean his appointment at the university would not be renewed, come the end of the academic year.

He scarcely worried. It was the neutrino, the neutrino, only the neutrino. Its trail curved and veered sharply and led him breathlessly along uncharted pathways that even Sterbinski and LaMarr did not follow.

He called Nimmo. "Uncle Ralph, I need a few things. I'm calling from off the campus."

Nimmo's face in the video plate was jovial, but his voice was sharp. He said, "What you need is a course in communication. I'm having a hell of a time pulling your application into one intelligible piece. If that's what you're calling about—"

Foster shook his head impatiently. "That's *not* what I'm calling about. I need these." He scribbled quickly on a piece of paper and held it up before the receiver.

Nimmo yiped. "Hey, how many tricks do you think I can wangle?"

"You can get them, Uncle. You know you can."

Nimmo reread the list of items with silent motions of his plump lips and looked grave.

"What happens when you put those things together?" he asked. Foster shook his head. "You'll have exclusive popular publication rights to whatever turns up, the way it's always been. But please don't ask any questions now."

"I can't do miracles, you know."

"Do this one. You've got to. You're a science writer, not a research man. You don't have to account for anything. You've got friends and connections.

They can look the other way, can't they, to get a break from you next publication time?"

"Your faith, nephew, is touching. I'll try."

Nimmo succeeded. The material and equipment were brought over late one evening in a private touring car. Nimmo and Foster lugged it in with the grunting of men unused to manual labor.

Potterley stood at the entrance of the basement after Nimmo had left. He asked softly, "What's this for?"

Foster brushed the hair off his forehead and gently massaged a sprained wrist. He said, "I want to conduct a few simple experiments."

"Really?" The historian's eyes glittered with excitement.

Foster felt exploited. He felt as though he were being led along a dangerous highway by the pull of pinching fingers on his nose; as though he could see the ruin clearly that lay in wait at the end of the path, yet walked eagerly and determinedly. Worst of all, he felt the compelling grip on his nose to be his own.

It was Potterley who began it, Potterley who stood there now, gloating; but the compulsion was his own.

Foster said sourly, "I'll be wanting privacy now, Potterley. I can't have you and your wife running down here and annoying me."

He thought: If that offends him, let him kick me out. Let him put an end to this.

In his heart, though, he did not think being evicted would stop anything.

But it did not come to that. Potterley was showing no signs of offense. His mild gaze was unchanged. He said, "Of course, Dr. Foster, of course. All the privacy you wish."

Foster watched him go. He was left still marching along the highway, perversely glad of it and hating himself for being glad.

He took to sleeping over on a cot in Potterley's basement and spending his weekends there entirely.

During that period, preliminary word came through that his grants (as doctored by Nimmo) had been approved. The Department Head brought the word and congratulated him.

Foster stared back distantly and mumbled, "Good. I'm glad," with so little conviction that the other frowned and turned away without another word.

Foster gave the matter no further thought. It was a minor point, worth no notice. He was planning something that really counted, a climactic test for that evening.

One evening, a second and third and then, haggard and half beside himself with excitement, he called in Potterley.

Potterley came down the stairs and looked about at the homemade gadgetry. He said, in his soft voice, "The electric bills are quite high. I don't mind the expense, but the City may ask questions. Can anything be done?"

It was a warm evening, but Potterley wore a tight collar and a semijacket. Foster, who was in his undershirt, lifted bleary eyes and said shakily, "It won't be for much longer, Dr. Potterley. I've called you down to tell you something. A chronoscope can be built. A small one, of course, but it can be built."

Potterley seized the railing. His body sagged. He managed a whisper. "Can it be built here?"

"Here in the basement," said Foster wearily.

"Good Lord. You said—"

"I know what I said," cried Foster impatiently. "I said it couldn't be done. I didn't know anything then. Even Sterbinski didn't know anything."

Potterley shook his head. "Are you sure? You're not mistaken, Dr. Foster? I couldn't endure it if—"

Foster said, "I'm not mistaken. Damn it, sir, if just theory had been enough, we could have had a time viewer over a hundred years ago, when the neutrino was first postulated. The trouble was, the original investigators considered it only a mysterious particle without mass or charge that could not be detected. It was just something to even up the bookkeeping and save the law of conservation of mass energy."

He wasn't sure Potterley knew what he was talking about. He didn't care. He needed a breather. He had to get some of this out of his clotting thoughts. . . . And he needed background for what he would have to tell Potterley next.

He went on. "It was Sterbinski who first discovered that the neutrino broke through the space-time cross-sectional barrier, that it traveled through time as well as through space. It was Sterbinski who first devised a method for stopping neutrinos. He invented a neutrino recorder and learned how to interpret the pattern of the neutrino stream. Naturally, the stream had been affected and deflected by all the matter it had passed through in its passage through time, and the deflections could be analyzed and converted into the images of the matter that had done the deflecting. Time viewing was possible. Even air vibrations could be detected in this way and converted into sound."

Potterley was definitely not listening. He said, "Yes. Yes. But when can you build a chronoscope?"

Foster said urgently, "Let me finish. Everything depends on the method used to detect and analyze the neutrino stream. Sterbinski's method was difficult and roundabout. It required mountains of energy. But I've studied pseudo-gravitics, Dr. Potterley, the science of artificial gravitational fields. I've specialized in the behavior of light in such fields. It's a new science. Sterbinski knew nothing of it. If he had, he would have seen—anyone would have—a much better and more efficient method of detecting neutrinos using a pseudo-gravitic field. If I had known more neutrinics to begin with, I would have seen it at once."

Potterley brightened a bit. "I knew it," he said. "Even if they stop research in neutrinics there is no way the government can be sure that discoveries in other segments of science won't reflect knowledge on neutrinics. So much for the value of centralized direction of science. I thought this long ago, Dr. Foster, before you ever came to work here."

"I congratulate you on that," said Foster, "but there's one thing—"

"Oh, never mind all this. Answer me. Please. When can you build a chronoscope?"

"I'm trying to tell you something, Dr. Potterley. A chronoscope won't do you any good." (This is it, Foster thought.)

Slowly, Potterley descended the stairs. He stood facing Foster. "What do you mean? Why won't it help me?"

"You won't see Carthage. It's what I've got to tell you. It's what I've been leading up to. You can never see Carthage."

Potterley shook his head slightly. "Oh, no, you're wrong. If you have the chronoscope, just focus it properly—"

"No, Dr. Potterley. It's not a question of focus. There are random factors affecting the neutrino stream, as they affect all subatomic particles. What we call the uncertainty principle. When the stream is recorded and interpreted, the random factor comes out as fuzziness, or 'noise' as the communications boys speak of it. The further back in time you penetrate, the more pronounced the fuzziness, the greater the noise. After a while, the noise drowns out the picture. Do you understand?"

"More power," said Potterley in a dead kind of voice.

"That won't help. When the noise blurs out detail, magnifying detail magnifies the noise, too. You can't see anything in a sun-burned film by enlarging it, can you? Get this through your head, now. The physical nature of the universe sets limits. The random thermal motions of air molecules set limits to how weak a sound can be detected by any instrument. The length of a light wave or of an electron wave sets limits to the size of objects that can be seen by any instrument. It works that way in chronoscopy, too. You can only time view so far."

"How far? How far?"

Foster took a deep breath. "A century and a quarter. That's the most."

"But the monthly bulletin the Commission puts out deals with ancient history almost entirely." The historian laughed shakily. "You must be wrong. The government has data as far back as 3000 B.C."

"When did you switch to believing them?" demanded Foster, scornfully. "You began this business by proving they were lying; that no historian had made use of the chronoscope. Don't you see why now? No historian, except one interested in contemporary history, could. No chronoscope can possibly see back in time further than 1920 under any conditions."

"You're wrong. You don't know everything," said Potterley.

"The truth won't bend itself to your convenience either. Face it. The government's part in this is to perpetuate a hoax."

"Why?"

"I don't know why."

Potterley's snubby nose was twitching. His eyes were bulging. He pleaded, "It's only theory, Dr. Foster. Build a chronoscope. Build one and try."

Foster caught Potterley's shoulders in a sudden, fierce grip. "Do you think I haven't? Do you think I would tell you this before I had checked it every way I knew? I *have* built one. It's all around you. Look!"

He ran to the switches at the power leads. He flicked them on, one by one. He turned a resistor, adjusted other knobs, put out the cellar lights. "Wait. Let it warm up."

There was a small glow near the center of one wall. Potterley was gibbering incoherently, but Foster only cried again, "Look!"

The light sharpened and brightened, broke up into a light-and-dark pattern. Men and women! Fuzzy. Features blurred. Arms and legs mere streaks. An old-fashioned ground car, unclear but recognizable as one of the kind that had once used gasoline-powered internal-combustion engines, sped by.

Foster said, "Mid-twentieth century, somewhere. I can't hook up an audio yet so this is soundless. Eventually, we can add sound. Anyway, midtwentieth is almost as far back as you can go. Believe me, that's the best focusing that can be done."

Potterley said, "Build a larger machine, a stronger one. Improve your circuits."

"You can't lick the Uncertainty Principle, man, any more than you can live on the sun. There are physical limits to what can be done."

"You're lying. I won't believe you. I—"

A new voice sounded, raised shrilly to make itself heard.

"Arnold! Dr. Foster!"

The young physicist turned at once. Dr. Potterley froze for a long moment, then said, without turning, "What is it, Caroline? Leave us."

"No!" Mrs. Potterley descended the stairs. "I heard. I couldn't help hearing. Do you have a time viewer here, Dr. Foster? Here in the basement?"

"Yes, I do, Mrs. Potterley. A kind of time viewer. Not a good one. I can't get sound yet and the picture is darned blurry, but it works."

Mrs. Potterley clasped her hands and held them tightly against her breast. "How wonderful. How wonderful."

"It's not at all wonderful," snapped Potterley. "The young fool can't reach further back than—"

"Now, look," began Foster in exasperation. . . .

"Please!" cried Mrs. Potterley. "Listen to me. Arnold, don't you see that as long as we can use it for twenty years back, we can see Laurel once again? What do we care about Carthage and ancient times? It's Laurel we can see.

She'll be alive for us again. Leave the machine here, Dr. Foster. Show us how to work it."

Foster stared at her then at her husband. Dr. Potterley's face had gone white. Though his voice stayed low and even, its calmness was somehow gone. He said, "You're a fool!"

Caroline said weakly, "Arnold!"

"You're a fool, I say. What will you see? The past. The dead past. Will Laurel do one thing she did not do? Will you see one thing you haven't seen? Will you live three years over and over again, watching a baby who'll never grow up no matter how you watch?"

His voice came near to cracking, but held. He stopped closer to her, seized her shoulder and shook her roughly. "Do you know what will happen to you if you do that? They'll come to take you away because you'll go mad. Yes, mad. Do you want mental treatment? Do you want to be shut up, to undergo the psychic probe?"

Mrs. Potterley tore away. There was no trace of softness or vagueness about her. She had twisted into a virago. "I want to see my child, Arnold. She's in that machine and I want her."

"She's *not* in the machine. An image is. Can't you understand? An image! Something that's not real!"

"I want my child. Do you hear me?" She flew at him, screaming, fists beating. *"I want my child."*

The historian retreated at the fury of the assault, crying out. Foster moved to step between, when Mrs. Potterley dropped, sobbing wildly, to the floor.

Potterley turned, eyes desperately seeking. With a sudden heave, he snatched at a Lando-rod, tearing it from its support, and whirling away before Foster, numbed by all that was taking place, could move to stop him.

"Stand back!" gasped Potterley, "or I'll kill you. I swear it."

He swung with force, and Foster jumped back.

Potterley turned with fury on every part of the structure in the cellar, and Foster, after the first crash of glass, watched dazedly.

Potterley spent his rage and then he was standing quietly amid shards and splinters, with a broken Lando-rod in his hand. He said to Foster in a whisper, "Now get out of here! Never come back! If any of this cost you anything, send me a bill and I'll pay for it. I'll pay double."

Foster shrugged, picked up his shirt and moved up the basement stairs. He could hear Mrs. Potterley sobbing loudly, and, as he turned at the head of the stairs for a last look, he saw Dr. Potterley bending over her, his face convulsed with sorrow.

Two days later, with the school day drawing to a close, and Foster looking wearily about to see if there were any data on his newly approved projects that he wished to take home, Dr. Potterley appeared once more. He was standing at the open door of Foster's office.

The historian was neatly dressed as ever. He lifted his hand in a gesture that was too vague to be a greeting, too abortive to be a plea. Foster stared stonily.

Potterley said, "I waited till five, till you were . . . May I come in?"

Foster nodded.

Potterley said, "I suppose I ought to apologize for my behavior. I was dreadfully disappointed; not quite master of myself. Still, it was inexcusable."

"I accept your apology," said Foster. "Is that all?"

"My wife called you, I think."

"Yes, she has."

"She has been quite hysterical. She told me she had but I couldn't be quite sure—"

"Could you tell me—would you be so kind as to tell me what she wanted?"

"She wanted a chronoscope. She said she had some money of her own. She was willing to pay."

"Did you—make any commitments?"

"I said I wasn't in the manufacturing business."

"Good," breathed Potterley, his chest expanding with a sigh of relief. "Please don't take any calls from her. She's not—quite—"

"Look, Dr. Potterley," said Foster, "I'm not getting into any domestic quarrels, but you'd better be prepared for something. Chronoscopes can be built by anybody. Given a few simple parts that can be bought through some etherics sales center, it can be built in the home workshop. The video part, anyway."

"But no one else will think of it beside you, will they? No one has."

"I don't intend to keep it secret."

"But you can't publish. It's illegal research."

"That doesn't matter any more, Dr. Potterley. If I lose my grants, I lose them. If the university is displeased, I'll resign. It just doesn't matter."

"But you can't do that!"

"Till now," said Foster, "you didn't mind my risking loss of grants and position. Why do you turn so tender about it now? Now let me explain something to you. When you first came to me, I believed in organized and directed research; the situation as it existed, in other words. I considered you an intellectual anarchist, Dr. Potterley, and dangerous. But, for one reason or another, I've been an anarchist myself for months now and I have achieved great things.

"Those things have been achieved not because I am a brilliant scientist. Not at all. It was just that scientific research had been directed from above and holes were left that could be filled in by anyone who looked in the right direction. And anyone might have if the government hadn't actively tried to prevent it.

"Now understand me. I still believe directed research can be useful. I'm not in favor of a retreat to total anarchy. But there must be a middle ground. Directed research can retain flexibility. A scientist must be allowed to follow his curiosity, at least in his spare time."

Potterley sat down. He said ingratiatingly, "Let's discuss this, Foster. I appreciate your idealism. You're young. You want the moon. But you can't destroy yourself through fancy notions of what research must consist of. I got you into this. I am responsible and I blame myself bitterly. I was acting emotionally. My interest in Carthage blinded me and I was a damned fool."

Foster broke in. "You mean you've changed completely in two days? Carthage is nothing? Government suppression of research is nothing?"

"Even a damned fool like myself can learn, Foster. My wife taught me something. I understand the reason for government suppression of neutrinics now. I didn't two days ago. And, understanding, I approve. You saw the way my wife reacted to the news of a chronoscope in the basement. I had envisioned a chronoscope used for research purposes. All *she* could see was the personal pleasure of returning neurotically to a personal past, a dead past. The pure researcher, Foster, is in the minority. People like my wife would outweigh us.

"For the government to encourage chronoscopy would have meant that everyone's past would be visible. The government officers would be subjected to blackmail and improper pressure, since who on Earth has a past that is absolutely clean? Organized government might become impossible."

Foster licked his lips. "Maybe. Maybe the government has some justification in its own eyes. Still, there's an important principle involved here. Who knows what other scientific advances are being stymied because scientists are being stifled into walking a narrow path? If the chronoscope becomes the terror of a few politicians, it's a price that must be paid. The public must realize that science must be free and there is no more dramatic way of doing it than to publish my discovery, one way or another, legally or illegally."

Potterley's brow was damp with perspiration, but his voice remained even. "Oh, not just a few politicians, Dr. Foster. Don't think that. It would be my terror, too. My wife would spend her time living with our dead daughter. She would retreat further from reality. She would go mad living the same scenes over and over. And not just my terror. There would be others like her. Children searching for their dead parents or their own youth. We'll have a whole world living in the past. Midsummer madness."

Foster said, "Moral judgments can't stand in the way. There isn't one advance at any time in history that mankind hasn't had the ingenuity to pervert. Mankind must also have the ingenuity to prevent. As for the chronoscope, your delvers into the dead past will get tired soon enough. They'll catch their loved parents in some of the things their loved parents did and they'll lose their enthusiasm for it all. But all this is trivial. With me, it's a matter of important principle."

Potterley said, "Hang your principle. Can't you understand men and women as well as principle? Don't you understand that my wife will live through the fire that killed our baby? She won't be able to help herself. I know her. She'll follow through each step, trying to prevent it. She'll live it over and over again, hoping each time that it won't happen. How many times do you want to kill Laurel?" A huskiness had crept into his voice.

A thought crossed Foster's mind. "What are you really afraid she'll find out, Dr. Potterley? What happened the night of the fire?"

The historian's hands went up quickly to cover his face and they shook with his dry sobs. Foster turned away and stared uncomfortably out the window.

Potterley said after a while, "It's a long time since I've had to think of it. Caroline was away. I was baby-sitting. I went into the baby's bedroom midevening to see if she had kicked off the bedclothes. I had my cigarette with me . . . I smoked in those days. I must have stubbed it out before putting it in the ashtray on the chest of drawers. I was always careful. The baby was all right. I returned to the living room and fell asleep before the video. I awoke, choking, surrounded by fire. I don't know how it started."

"But you think it may have been the cigarette, is that it?" said Foster. "A cigarette which, for once, you forgot to stub out?"

"I don't know. I tried to save her, but she was dead in my arms when I got out."

"You never told your wife about the cigarette, I suppose."

Potterley shook his head. "But I've lived with it."

"Only now, with a chronoscope, she'll find out. Maybe it wasn't the cigarette. Maybe you did stub it out. Isn't that possible?"

The scant tears had dried on Potterley's face. The redness had subsided. He said, "I can't take the chance. . . . But it's not just myself, Foster. The past has its terrors for most people. Don't loose those terrors on the human race."

Foster paced the floor. Somehow, this explained the reason for Potterley's rabid, irrational desire to boost the Carthaginians, deify them, most of all disprove the story of their fiery sacrifices to Moloch. By freeing them of the guilt of infanticide by fire, he symbolically freed himself of the same guilt.

So the same fire that had driven him on to causing the construction of a chronoscope was now driving him on to the destruction.

Foster looked sadly at the older man. "I see your position, Dr. Potterley, but this goes above personal feelings. I've got to smash this throttling hold on the throat of science."

Potterley said, savagely, "You mean you want the fame and wealth that goes with such a discovery."

"I don't know about the wealth, but that, too, I suppose. I'm no more than human."

"You won't suppress your knowledge?"

"Not under any circumstances."

"Well, then—" and the historian got to his feet and stood for a moment, glaring.

Foster had an odd moment of terror. The man was older than he, smaller, feebler, and he didn't look armed. Still . . .

Foster said, "If you're thinking of killing me or anything insane like that, I've got the information in a safety-deposit vault where the proper people will find it in case of my disappearance or death."

Potterley said, "Don't be a fool," and stalked out.

Foster closed the door, locked it and sat down to think. He felt silly. He had no information in any safety-deposit vault, of course. Such a melodramatic action would not have occurred to him ordinarily. But now it had.

Feeling even sillier, he spent an hour writing out the equations of the application of pseudo-gravitic optics to neutrinic recording, and some diagrams for the engineering details of construction. He sealed it in an envelope and scrawled Ralph Nimmo's name over the outside.

He spent a rather restless night and the next morning, on the way to school, dropped the envelope off at the bank, with appropriate instructions to an official, who made him sign a paper permitting the box to be opened after his death.

He called Nimmo to tell him of the existence of the envelope, refusing querulously to say anything about its contents.

He had never felt so ridiculously self-conscious as at that moment.

That night and the next, Foster spent in only fitful sleep, finding himself face to face with the highly practical problem of the publication of data unethically obtained.

The *Proceedings of the Society for Pseudo-Gravitics*, which was the journal with which he was best acquainted, would certainly not touch any paper that did not include the magic footnote: "The work described in this paper was made possible by Grant No. so-and-so from the Commission of Research of the United Nations."

Nor, doubly so, would the *Journal of Physics*.

There were always the minor journals who might overlook the nature of the article for the sake of the sensation, but that would require a little financial negotiation on which he hesitated to embark. It might, on the whole, be better to pay the cost of publishing a small pamphlet for general distribution among scholars. In that case, he would even be able to dispense with the services of a science writer, sacrificing polish for speed. He would have to find a reliable printer. Uncle Ralph might know one.

He walked down the corridor to his office and wondered anxiously if perhaps he ought to waste no further time, give himself no further chance to lapse into indecision and take the risk of calling Ralph from his office phone. He was so absorbed in his own heavy thoughts that he did not notice that his room was occupied until he turned from the clothes closet and approached his desk.

Dr. Potterley was there and a man whom Foster did not recognize.

Foster stared at them. "What's this?"

Potterley said, "I'm sorry, but I had to stop you."

Foster continued staring. "What are you talking about?"

The stranger said, "Let me introduce myself." He had large teeth, a little uneven, and they showed prominently when he smiled. "I am Thaddeus Araman, Department Head of the Division of Chronoscopy. I am here to see you concerning information brought to me by Professor Arnold Potterley and confirmed by our own sources—"

Potterley said breathlessly, "I took all the blame, Dr. Foster. I explained that it was I who persuaded you against your will into unethical practices. I have offered to accept full responsibility and punishment. I don't wish you harmed in any way. It's just that chronoscopy must not be permitted!"

Araman nodded. "He has taken the blame as he says, Dr. Foster, but this thing is out of his hands now."

Foster said, "So? What are you going to do? Blackball me from all consideration for research grants?"

"That is in my power," said Araman.

"Order the university to discharge me?"

"That, too, is in my power."

"All right, go ahead. Consider it done. I'll leave my office now, with you. I can send for my books later. If you insist, I'll leave my books. Is that all?"

"Not quite," said Araman. "You must engage to do no further research in chronoscopy, to publish none of your findings in chronoscopy and, of course, to build no chronoscope. You will remain under surveillance indefinitely to make sure you keep that promise."

"Supposing I refuse to promise? What can you do? Doing research out of my field may be unethical, but it isn't a criminal offense."

"In the case of chronoscopy, my young friend," said Araman patiently, "it is a criminal offense. If necessary, you will be put in jail and kept there."

"Why?" shouted Foster. "What's magic about chronoscopy?"

Araman said, "That's the way it is. We cannot allow further developments in the field. My own job is, primarily, to make sure of that, and I intend to do my job. Unfortunately, I had no knowledge, nor did anyone in the department, that the optics of pseudo-gravity fields had such immediate application to chronoscopy. Score one for general ignorance, but henceforward research will be steered properly in that respect, too."

Foster said, "That won't help. Something else may apply that neither you nor I dream of. All science hangs together. It's one piece. If you want to stop one part, you've got to stop it all."

"No doubt that is true," said Araman, "in theory. On the practical side, however, we have managed quite well to hold chronoscopy down to the original Sterbinski level for fifty years. Having caught you in time, Dr. Foster, we hope to continue doing so indefinitely. And we wouldn't have come this close to disaster, either, if I had accepted Dr. Potterley at something more than face value."

He turned toward the historian and lifted his eyebrows in a kind of humorous self-deprecation. "I'm afraid, sir, that I dismissed you as a history professor and no more on the occasion of our first interview. Had I done my job properly and checked on you, this would not have happened."

Foster said abruptly, "Is anyone allowed to use the government chronoscope?"

"No one outside our division under any pretext. I say that since it is obvious to me that you have already guessed as much. I warn you, though, that any repetition of that fact will be a criminal, not an ethical, offense."

"And your chronoscope doesn't go back more than a hundred twenty-five years or so, does it?"

"It doesn't."

"Then your bulletin with its stories of time viewing ancient times is a hoax?"

Araman said coolly, "With the knowledge you now have, it is obvious you know that for a certainty. However, I confirm your remark. The monthly bulletin is a hoax."

"In that case," said Foster, "I will not promise to suppress my knowledge of chronoscopy. If you wish to arrest me, go ahead. My defense at the trial will be enough to destroy the vicious card house of directed research and bring it tumbling down. Directing research is one thing; suppressing it and depriving mankind of its benefits is quite another."

Araman said, "Oh, let's get something straight, Dr. Foster. If you do not co-operate, you will go to jail directly. You will *not* see a lawyer, you will *not* be charged, you will *not* have a trial. You will simply stay in jail."

"Oh, no," said Foster, "you're bluffing. This is not the twentieth century, you know."

There was a stir outside the office, the clatter of feet, a high-pitched shout that Foster was sure he recognized. The door crashed open, the lock splintering, and three intertwined figures stumbled in.

As they did so, one of the men raised a blaster and brought its butt down hard on the skull of another.

There was a whoosh of expiring air, and the one whose head was struck went limp.

"Uncle Ralph!" cried Foster.

Araman frowned. "Put him down in that chair," he ordered, "and get some water."

Ralph Nimmo, rubbing his head with a gingerly sort of disgust, said, "There was no need to get rough, Araman."

Araman said, "The guard should have been rough sooner and kept you out of here, Nimmo. You'd have been better off."

"You know each other?" asked Foster.

"I've had dealings with the man," said Nimmo, still rubbing. "If he's here in your office, nephew, you're in trouble."

"And you, too," said Araman angrily. "I know Dr. Foster consulted you on neutrinics literature."

Nimmo corrugated his forehead, then straightened it with a wince as though the action had brought pain. "So?" he said. "What else do you know about me?"

"We will know everything about you soon enough. Meanwhile, that one item is enough to implicate you. What are you doing here?"

"My dear Dr. Araman," said Nimmo, some of his jauntiness restored, "day before yesterday, my jackass of a nephew called me. He had placed some mysterious information—"

"Don't tell him! Don't say anything!" cried Foster.

Araman glanced at him coldly. "We know all about it, Dr. Foster. The safety-deposit box has been opened and its contents removed."

"But how can you know—" Foster's voice died away in a kind of furious frustration.

"Anyway," said Nimmo, "I decided the net must be closing around him and, after I took care of a few items, I came down to tell him to get off this thing he's doing. It's not worth his career."

"Does that mean you know what he's doing?" asked Araman.

"He never told me," said Nimmo, "but I'm a science writer with a hell of a lot of experience. I know which side of an atom is electronified. The boy, Foster, specializes in pseudo-gravitic optics and coached me on the stuff himself. He got me to get him a textbook on neutrinics and I kind of ship-viewed it myself before handing it over. I can put the two together. He asked me to get him certain pieces of physical equipment, and that was evidence, too. Stop me if I'm wrong, but my nephew has built a semipor-table, low-power chronoscope. Yes, or—yes?"

"Yes." Araman reached thoughtfully for a cigarette and paid no attention to Dr. Potterley (watching silently, as though all were a dream) who shied away, gasping, from the white cylinder. "Another mistake for me. I ought to resign. I should have put tabs on you, too, Nimmo, instead of concentrating too hard on Potterley and Foster. I didn't have much time of course and you've ended up safely here, but that doesn't excuse me. You're under arrest, Nimmo."

"What for?" demanded the science writer.

"Unauthorized research."

"I wasn't doing any. I can't, not being a registered scientist. And even if I did, it's not a criminal offense."

Foster said savagely, "No use, Uncle Ralph. This bureaucrat is making his own laws."

"Like what?" demanded Nimmo.

"Like life imprisonment without trial."

"Nuts," said Nimmo. "This isn't the twentieth cen—"

"I tried that," said Foster. "It doesn't bother him."

"Well, nuts," shouted Nimmo. "Look here, Araman. My nephew and I have relatives who haven't lost touch with us, you know. The professor has some also, I imagine. You can't just make us disappear. There'll be questions and a scandal. This *isn't* the twentieth century. So if you're trying to scare us, it isn't working."

The cigarette snapped between Araman's fingers and he tossed it away violently. He said, "Damn it, I don't know *what* to do. It's never been like this before. . . . Look! You three fools know nothing of what you're trying to do. You understand nothing. Will you listen to me?"

"Oh, we'll listen," said Nimmo grimly.

(Foster sat silently, eyes angry, lips compressed. Potterley's hands writhed like two intertwined snakes.)

Araman said, "The past to you is the dead past. If any of you have discussed the matter, it's dollars to nickels you've used that phrase. The dead past. If you knew how many times I've heard those three words, you'd choke on them, too.

"When people think of the past, they think of it as dead, far away and gone, long ago. We encourage them to think so. When we report time viewing, we always talk of views centuries in the past, even though you gentlemen know seeing more than a century or so is impossible. People accept it. The past means Greece, Rome, Carthage, Egypt, the Stone Age. The deader the better.

"Now you three know a century or a little more is the limit, so what does the past mean to you? Your youth. Your first girl. Your dead mother. Twenty years ago. Thirty years ago. Fifty years ago. The deader the better. . . . But when does the past really begin?"

He paused in anger. The others stared at him and Nimmo stirred uneasily.

"Well," said Araman, "when did it begin? A year ago? Five minutes ago? One second ago? Isn't it obvious that the past begins an instant ago? The dead past is just another name for the living present. What if you focus the chronoscope in the past of one-hundredth of a second ago? Aren't you watching the present? Does it begin to sink in?"

Nimmo said, "Damnation."

"Damnation," mimicked Araman. "After Potterley came to me with his story night before last, how do you suppose I checked up on both of you? I did it with the chronoscope, spotting key moments to the very instant of the present."

"And that's how you knew about the safety-deposit box?" said Foster.

"And every other important fact. Now what do you suppose would happen if we let news of a home chronoscope get out? People might start out by watching their youth, their parents and so on, but it wouldn't be long before they'd catch on to the possibilities. The housewife will forget her poor, dead mother and take to watching her neighbor at home and her husband at the office. The businessman will watch his competitor; the employer his employee.

"There will be no such thing as privacy. The party line, the prying eye behind the curtain will be nothing compared to it. The video stars will be closely watched at all times by everyone. Every man his own peeping Tom and there'll be no getting away from the watcher. Even darkness will be no escape because chronoscopy can be adjusted to the infrared and human figures can be seen by their own body heat. The figures will be fuzzy, of course, and the surroundings will be dark, but that will make the titillation of it all the greater, perhaps. . . . Hmp, the men in charge of the machine now experiment sometimes in spite of the regulations against it."

Nimmo seemed sick. "You can always forbid private manufacture—"

Araman turned on him fiercely. "You can, but do you expect it to do good? Can you legislate successfully against drinking, smoking, adultery or gossiping over the back fence? And this mixture of nosiness and prurience will have a worse grip on humanity than any of those. Good Lord, in a thousand years of trying we haven't even been able to wipe out the heroin traffic and you talk about legislating against a device for watching anyone you please at any time you please that can be built in a home workshop."

Foster said suddenly, "I won't publish."

Potterley burst out, half in sobs, "None of us will talk. I regret—"

Nimmo broke in. "You said you didn't tab me on the chronoscope, Araman."

"No time," said Araman wearily. "Things don't move any faster on the chronoscope than in real life. You can't speed it up like the film in a book viewer. We spent a full twenty-four hours trying to catch the important moments during the last six months of Potterley and Foster. There was no time for anything else and it was enough."

"It wasn't," said Nimmo.

"What are you talking about?" There was a sudden infinite alarm on Araman's face.

"I told you my nephew, Jonas, had called me to say he had put important information in a safety-deposit box. He acted as though he were in trouble. He's my nephew. I had to try to get him off the spot. It took a while, then I came here to tell him what I had done. I told you when I got here, just after your man conked me that I had taken care of a few items."

"What? For Heaven's sake—"

"Just this: I sent the details of the portable chronoscope off to half a dozen of my regular publicity outlets."

Not a word. Not a sound. Not a breath. They were all past any demonstration.

"Don't stare like that," cried Nimmo. "Don't you see my point? I had popular publication rights. Jonas will admit that. I knew he couldn't publish scientifically in any legal way. I was sure he was planning to publish illegally and was preparing the safety-deposit box for that reason. I thought if I put through the details prematurely, all the responsibility would be mine. His career would be saved. And if I were deprived of my science-writing license as a result, my exclusive possession of the chronometric data would set me up for life. Jonas would be angry, I expected that, but I could explain the motive and we would split the take fifty-fifty. . . . Don't stare at me like that. How did I know—"

"Nobody knew anything," said Araman bitterly, "but you all just took it for granted that the government was stupidly bureaucratic, vicious, tyrannical, given to suppressing research for the hell of it. It never occurred to any of you that we were trying to protect mankind as best we could."

"Don't sit there talking," wailed Potterley. "Get the names of the people who were told—"

"Too late," said Nimmo, shrugging. "They've had better than a day. There's been time for the word to spread. My outfits will have called any number of physicists to check my data before going on with it and they'll call one another to pass on the news. Once scientists put neutrinics and pseudo-gravitics together, home chronoscopy becomes obvious. Before the week is out, five hundred people will know how to build a small chronoscope and how will you catch them all?" His plum cheeks sagged. "I suppose there's no way of putting the mushroom cloud back into that nice, shiny uranium sphere."

Araman stood up. "We'll try, Potterley, but I agree with Nimmo. It's too late. What kind of a world we'll have from now on, I don't know, I can't tell, but the world we know has been destroyed completely. Until now, every custom, every habit, every tiniest way of life has always taken a certain amount of privacy for granted, but that's all gone now."

He saluted each of the three with elaborate formality.

"You have created a new world among the three of you. I congratulate you. Happy goldfish bowl to you, to me, to everyone, and may each of you fry in hell forever. Arrest rescinded."

The Foundation
of S.F. Success

(WITH APOLOGIES TO W. S. GILBERT)

If you ask me how to shine in the science-fiction line as a pro of luster
    bright,
I say, practice up the lingo of the sciences, by jingo (never mind if not
    quite right).
You must talk of Space and Galaxies and tesseractic
    fallacies in slick and mystic style,
Though the fans won't understand it, they will all the same demand it
    with a softly hopeful smile.

    And all the fans will say,
    As you walk your spatial way,
    If that young man indulges in flights through all
    the Galaxy,
    Why, what a most imaginative type of man that type
    of man must be.

So success is not a mystery, just brush up on your history,
    and borrow day by day.
Take an Empire that was Roman and you'll find it is at home in all the
    starry Milky Way.
With a drive that's hyperspatial, through the parsecs you will race, you'll
    find that plotting is a breeze,

With a tiny bit of cribbin' from the works of
    Edward Gibbon and that Greek, Thucydides.

    And all the fans will say,
    As you walk your thoughtful way,
    If that young man involves himself in authentic history,
    Why, what a very learned kind of high IQ, his high IQ must be.

Then eschew all thoughts of passion of a man-and-woman fashion from
    your hero's thoughtful mind.
He must spend his time on politics, and thinking up his shady tricks, and
    outside that he's blind.
It's enough he's had a mother, other females are a bother, though they're
    jeweled and glistery.
They will just distract his dreaming and his necessary
    scheming with that psychohistory.

    And all the fans will say
    As you walk your narrow way,
    If all his yarns restrict themselves to masculinity,
    Why, what a most particularly pure young man that pure young man
        must be.

Franchise

Linda, age ten, was the only one of the family who seemed to enjoy being awake.

Norman Muller could hear her now through his own drugged, unhealthy coma. (He had finally managed to fall asleep an hour earlier but even then it was more like exhaustion than sleep.)

She was at his bedside now, shaking him. "Daddy, Daddy, wake up. Wake up!"

He suppressed a groan. "All right, Linda."

"But, Daddy, there's more policemen around than any time! Police cars and everything!"

Norman Muller gave up and rose blearily to his elbows. The day was beginning. It was faintly stirring toward dawn outside, the germ of a miserable gray that looked about as miserably gray as he felt. He could hear Sarah, his wife, shuffling about breakfast duties in the kitchen. His father-in-law, Matthew, was hawking strenuously in the bathroom. No doubt Agent Handley was ready and waiting for him.

This was *the* day.

Election Day!

To begin with, it had been like every other year. Maybe a little worse, because it was a presidential year, but no worse than other presidential years if it came to that.

The politicians spoke about the guh-reat electorate and the vast electuhronic intelligence that was its servant. The press analyzed the situation with industrial computers (the New York *Times* and the St. Louis *Post-Dispatch* had their own computers) and were full of little hints as to what would be forthcoming. Commentators and columnists pinpointed the crucial state and county in happy contradiction to one another.

The first hint that it would *not* be like every other year was when Sarah Muller said to her husband on the evening of October 4 (with Election Day exactly a month off), "Cantwell Johnson says that Indiana will be the state this year. He's the fourth one. Just think, *our* state this time."

Matthew Hortenweiler took his fleshy face from behind the paper, stared dourly at his daughter and growled, "Those fellows are paid to tell lies. Don't listen to them."

"Four of them, Father," said Sarah mildly. "They all say Indiana."

"Indiana *is* a key state, Matthew," said Norman, just as mildly, "on account of the Hawkins-Smith Act and this mess in Indianapolis. It—"

Matthew twisted his old face alarmingly and rasped out, "No one says Bloomington or Monroe County, do they?"

"Well—" said Norman.

Linda, whose little pointed-chinned face had been shifting from one speaker to the next, said pipingly, "You going to be voting this year, Daddy?"

Norman smiled gently and said, "I don't think so, dear."

But this was in the gradually growing excitement of an October in a presidential election year and Sarah had led a quiet life with dreams for her companions. She said longingly, "Wouldn't *that* be wonderful, though?"

"If I voted?" Norman Muller had a small blond mustache that had given him a debonair quality in the young Sarah's eyes, but which, with gradual graying, had declined merely to lack of distinction. His forehead bore deepening lines born of uncertainty and, in general, he had never seduced his clerkly soul with the thought that he was either born great or would under any circumstances achieve greatness. He had a wife, a job and a little girl, and except under extraordinary conditions of elation or depression was inclined to consider that to be an adequate bargain struck with life.

So he was a little embarrassed and more than a little uneasy at the direction his wife's thoughts were taking. "Actually, my dear," he said, "there are two hundred million people in the country, and, with odds like that, I don't think we ought to waste our time wondering about it."

His wife said, "Why, Norman, it's no such thing like two hundred million and you know it. In the first place, only people between twenty and sixty are eligible and it's always men, so that puts it down to maybe fifty million to one. Then, if it's really Indiana—"

"Then it's about one and a quarter million to one. You wouldn't want me to bet in a horse race against those odds, now, would you? Let's have supper."

Matthew muttered from behind his newspaper, "Damned foolishness."

Linda asked again, "You going to be voting this year, Daddy?"

Norman shook his head and they all adjourned to the dining room.

By October 20, Sarah's excitement was rising rapidly. Over the coffee, she announced that Mrs. Schultz, having a cousin who was the secretary of an Assemblyman, said that all the "smart money" was on Indiana.

"She says President Villers is even going to make a speech at Indianapolis."

Norman Muller, who had had a hard day at the store, nudged the statement with a raising of eyebrows and let it go at that.

Matthew Hortenweiler, who was chronically dissatisfied with Washington, said, "If Villers makes a speech in Indiana, that means he thinks Multivac will pick Arizona. He wouldn't have the guts to go closer, the mushhead."

Sarah, who ignored her father whenever she could decently do so, said, "I don't know why they don't announce the state as soon as they can, and then the county and so on. Then the people who were eliminated could relax."

"If they did anything like that," pointed out Norman, "the politicians would follow the announcements like vultures. By the time it was narrowed down to a township, you'd have a Congressman or two at every street corner."

Matthew narrowed his eyes and brushed angrily at his sparse, gray hair. "They're vultures, anyhow. Listen—"

Sarah murmured, "Now, Father—"

Matthew's voice rumbled over her protest without as much as a stumble or hitch. "Listen, I was around when they set up Multivac. It would end partisan politics, they said. No more voters' money wasted on campaigns. No more grinning nobodies high-pressured and advertising-campaigned into Congress or the White House. So what happens. More campaigning than ever, only now they do it blind. They'll send guys to Indiana on account of the Hawkins-Smith Act and other guys to California in case it's the Joe Hammer situation that turns out crucial. I say, wipe out all that nonsense. Back to the good old—"

Linda asked suddenly, "Don't you want Daddy to vote this year, Grandpa?"

Matthew glared at the young girl. "Never you mind, now." He turned back to Norman and Sarah. "There was a time I voted. Marched right up to the polling booth, stuck my fist on the levers and voted. There was nothing to it. I just said: This fellow's my man and I'm voting for him. *That's* the way it should be."

Linda said excitedly, "You voted, Grandpa? You really did?"

Sarah leaned forward quickly to quiet what might easily become an incongruous story drifting about the neighborhood, "It's nothing, Linda. Grandpa doesn't really mean voted. Everyone did that kind of voting, your grandpa, too, but it wasn't *really* voting."

Matthew roared, "It wasn't when I was a little boy. I was twenty-two and I voted for Langley and it was real voting. My vote didn't count for much, maybe, but it was as good as anyone else's. *Anyone* else's. And no Multivac to—"

Norman interposed, "All right, Linda, time for bed. And stop asking questions about voting. When you grow up, you'll understand all about it."

He kissed her with antiseptic gentleness and she moved reluctantly out of range under maternal prodding and a promise that she might watch the bedside video till 9:15, *if* she was prompt about the bathing ritual.

Linda said, "Grandpa," and stood with her chin down and her hands behind her back until his newspaper lowered itself to the point where shaggy eyebrows and eyes, nested in fine wrinkles, showed themselves. It was Friday, October 31.

He said, "Yes?"

Linda came closer and put both her forearms on one of the old man's knees so that he had to discard his newspaper altogether.

She said, "Grandpa, did you really once vote?"

He said, "You heard me say I did, didn't you? Do you think I tell fibs?"

"N—no, but Mamma says everybody voted then."

"So they did."

"But how could they? How could *everybody* vote?"

Matthew stared at her solemnly, then lifted her and put her on his knee.

He even moderated the tonal qualities of his voice. He said, "You see, Linda, till about forty years ago, everybody always voted. Say we wanted to decide who was to be the new President of the United States. The Democrats and Republicans would both nominate someone, and everybody would say who they wanted. When Election Day was over, they would count how many people wanted the Democrat and how many wanted the Republican. Whoever had more votes was elected. You see?"

Linda nodded and said, "How did all the people know who to vote for? Did Multivac tell them?"

Matthew's eyebrows hunched down and he looked severe. "They just used their own judgment, girl."

She edged away from him, and he lowered his voice again, "I'm not angry at you, Linda. But, you see, sometimes it took all night to count what everyone said and people were impatient. So they invented special machines which could look at the first few votes and compare them with the votes from the same places in previous years. That way the machine could compute how the total vote would be and who would be elected. You see?"

She nodded. "Like Multivac."

"The first computers were much smaller than Multivac. But the machines grew bigger and they could tell how the election would go from fewer and fewer votes. Then, at last, they built Multivac and it can tell from just one voter."

Linda smiled at having reached a familiar part of the story and said, "That's nice."

Matthew frowned and said, "No, it's not nice. I don't want a machine telling me how I would have voted just because some joker in Milwaukee says he's against higher tariffs. Maybe I want to vote cockeyed just for the pleasure of it. Maybe I don't want to vote. Maybe—"

But Linda had wriggled from his knee and was beating a retreat.

She met her mother at the door. Her mother, who was still wearing her coat and had not even had time to remove her hat, said breathlessly, "Run along, Linda. Don't get in Mother's way."

Then she said to Matthew, as she lifted her hat from her head and patted her hair back into place, "I've been at Agatha's."

Matthew stared at her censoriously and did not even dignify that piece of information with a grunt as he groped for his newspaper.

Sarah said, as she unbuttoned her coat, "Guess what she said?"

Matthew flattened out his newspaper for reading purposes with a sharp crackle and said, "Don't much care."

Sarah said, "Now, Father—" But she had no time for anger. The news had to be told and Matthew was the only recipient handy, so she went on, "Agatha's Joe is a policeman, you know, and he says a whole truckload of secret service men came into Bloomington last night."

"They're not after me."

"Don't you see, Father? Secret service agents, and it's almost election time. In *Bloomington*."

"Maybe they're after a bank robber."

"There hasn't been a bank robbery in town in ages. . . . . Father, you're hopeless."

She stalked away.

Nor did Norman Muller receive the news with noticeably greater excitement.

"Now, Sarah, how did Agatha's Joe know they were secret service agents?" he asked calmly. "They wouldn't go around with identification cards pasted on their foreheads."

But by next evening, with November a day old, she could say triumphantly, "It's just everyone in Bloomington that's waiting for someone local to be the voter. The Bloomington *News* as much as said so on video."

Norman stirred uneasily. He couldn't deny it, and his heart was sinking. If Bloomington was really to be hit by Multivac's lightning, it would mean newspapermen, video shows, tourists, all sorts of—strange upsets. Norman liked the quiet routine of his life, and the distant stir of politics was getting uncomfortably close.

He said, "It's all rumor. Nothing more."

"You wait and see, then. You just wait and see."

As things turned out, there was very little time to wait, for the doorbell rang insistently, and when Norman Muller opened it and said, "Yes?" a tall, grave-faced man said, "Are you Norman Muller?"

Norman said, "Yes," again, but in a strange dying voice. It was not difficult to see from the stranger's bearing that he was one carrying authority, and the nature of his errand suddenly became as inevitably obvious as it had, until the moment before, been unthinkably impossible.

The man presented credentials, stepped into the house, closed the door behind him and said ritualistically, "Mr. Norman Muller, it is necessary for me to inform you on the behalf of the President of the United States that you have been chosen to represent the American electorate on Tuesday, November 4, 2008."

Norman Muller managed, with difficulty, to walk unaided to his chair. He sat there, white-faced and almost insensible, while Sarah brought water, slapped his hands in panic and moaned to her husband between clenched teeth, "Don't be sick, Norman. *Don't* be sick. They'll pick someone else."

When Norman could manage to talk, he whispered, "I'm sorry, sir."

The secret service agent had removed his coat, unbuttoned his jacket and was sitting at ease on the couch.

"It's all right," he said, and the mark of officialdom seemed to have vanished with the formal announcement and leave him simply a large and rather friendly man. "This is the sixth time I've made the announcement and I've seen all kinds of reactions. Not one of them was the kind you see on the video. You know what I mean? A holy, dedicated look, and a character who says, 'It will be a great privilege to serve my country.' That sort of stuff." The agent laughed comfortingly.

Sarah's accompanying laugh held a trace of shrill hysteria.

The agent said, "Now you're going to have me with you for a while. My name is Phil Handley. I'd appreciate it if you call me Phil. Mr. Muller can't leave the house any more till Election Day. You'll have to inform the department store that he's sick, Mrs. Muller. You can go about your business for a while, but you'll have to agree not to say a word about this. Right, Mrs. Muller?"

Sarah nodded vigorously. "No, sir. Not a word."

"All right. But, Mrs. Muller," Handley looked grave, "we're not kidding now. Go out only if you must and you'll be followed when you do. I'm sorry but that's the way we must operate."

"Followed?"

"It won't be obvious. Don't worry. And it's only for two days till the formal announcement to the nation is made. Your daughter—"

"She's in bed," said Sarah hastily.

"Good. She'll have to be told I'm a relative or friend staying with the family. If she does find out the truth, she'll have to be kept in the house. Your father had better stay in the house in any case."

"He won't like that," said Sarah.

"Can't be helped. Now, since you have no others living with you—"

"You know all about us apparently," whispered Norman.

"Quite a bit," agreed Handley. "In any case, those are all my instructions to you for the moment. I'll try to co-operate as much as I can and be as little of a nuisance as possible. The government will pay for my maintenance so I won't be an expense to you. I'll be relieved each night by someone who will sit up in this room, so there will be no problem about sleeping accommodations. Now, Mr. Muller—"

"Sir?"

"You can call me Phil," said the agent again. "The purpose of the two-day preliminary before formal announcement is to get you used to your position. We prefer to have you face Multivac in as normal a state of mind as possible. Just relax and try to feel this is all in a day's work. Okay?"

"Okay," said Norman, and then shook his head violently. "But I don't want the responsibility. Why me?"

"All right," said Handley, "let's get that straight to begin with. Multivac weighs all sorts of known factors, billions of them. One factor isn't known, though, and won't be known for a long time. That's the reaction pattern of the human mind. All Americans are subjected to the molding pressure of what other Americans do and say, to the things that are done to him and the things he does to others. Any American can be brought to Multivac to have the bent of his mind surveyed. From that the bent of all other minds in the country can be estimated. Some Americans are better for the purpose than others at some given time, depending upon the happenings of that year. Multivac picked you as most representative this year. Not the smartest, or the strongest, or the luckiest, but just the most representative. Now we don't question Multivac, do we?"

"Couldn't it make a mistake?" asked Norman.

Sarah, who listened impatiently, interrupted to say, "Don't listen to him, sir. He's just nervous, you know. Actually, he's very well read and he always follows politics very closely."

Handley said, "Multivac makes the decisions, Mrs. Muller. It picked your husband."

"But does it know everything?" insisted Norman wildly. "Couldn't it have made a mistake?"

"Yes, it can. There's no point in not being frank. In 1993, a selected Voter died of a stroke two hours before it was time for him to be notified. Multivac didn't predict that; it couldn't. A Voter might be mentally unstable, morally unsuitable, or, for that matter, disloyal. Multivac can't know everything about everybody until he's fed all the data there is. That's why alternate selections are always held in readiness. I don't think we'll be using one this time. You're in good health, Mr. Muller, and you've been carefully investigated. You qualify."

Norman buried his face in his hands and sat motionless.

"By tomorrow morning, sir," said Sarah, "he'll be perfectly all right. He just has to get used to it, that's all."

"Of course," said Handley.

In the privacy of their bedchamber, Sarah Muller expressed herself in other and stronger fashion. The burden of her lecture was, "So get hold of yourself, Norman. You're trying to throw away the chance of a lifetime."

Norman whispered desperately, "It frightens me, Sarah. The whole thing."

"For goodness' sake, why? What's there to it but answering a question or two?"

"The responsibility is too great. I couldn't face it."

"What responsibility? There isn't any. Multivac picked you. It's Multivac's responsibility. Everyone knows that."

Norman sat up in bed in a sudden excess of rebellion and anguish. "Everyone is *supposed* to know that. But they don't. They—"

"Lower your voice," hissed Sarah icily. "They'll hear you downtown."

"They don't," said Norman, declining quickly to a whisper. "When they talk about the Ridgely administration of 1988, do they say he won them over with pie-in-the-sky promises and racist baloney? No! They talk about the 'goddam MacComber vote,' as though Humphrey MacComber was the only man who had anything to do with it because he faced Multivac. I've said it myself—only now I think the poor guy was just a truck farmer who didn't ask to be picked. Why was it his fault more than anyone else's? Now his name is a curse."

"You're just being childish," said Sarah.

"I'm being sensible. I tell you, Sarah, I won't accept. They can't make me vote if I don't want to. I'll say I'm sick. I'll say—"

But Sarah had had enough. "Now you listen to me," she whispered in a cold fury. "You don't have only yourself to think about. You know what it means to be Voter of the Year. A presidential year at that. It means publicity and fame and, maybe, buckets of money—"

"And then I go back to being a clerk."

"You will *not*. You'll have a branch managership at the least if you have any brains at all, and you *will* have, because I'll tell you what to do. You control the kind of publicity if you play your cards right, and you can force Kennell Stores, Inc., into a tight contract *and* an escalator clause in connection with your salary *and* a decent pension plan."

"That's not the point in being Voter, Sarah."

"That will be your point. If you don't owe anything to yourself or to me —I'm not asking for myself—you owe something to Linda."

Norman groaned.

"Well, don't you?" snapped Sarah.

"Yes, dear," murmured Norman.

On November 3, the official announcement was made and it was too late for Norman to back out even if he had been able to find the courage to make the attempt.

Their house was sealed off. Secret service agents made their appearance in the open, blocking off all approach.

At first the telephone rang incessantly, but Philip Handley with an engagingly apologetic smile took all calls. Eventually, the exchange shunted all calls directly to the police station.

Norman imagined that, in that way, he was spared not only the bubbling (and envious?) congratulations of friends, but also the egregious pressure of salesmen scenting a prospect and the designing smoothness of politicians from all over the nation. . . . Perhaps even death threats from the inevitable cranks.

Newspapers were forbidden to enter the house now in order to keep out weighted pressures, and television was gently but firmly disconnected, over Linda's loud protests.

Matthew growled and stayed in his room; Linda, after the first flurry of excitement, sulked and whined because she could not leave the house; Sarah divided her time between preparation of meals for the present and plans for the future; and Norman's depression lived and fed upon itself.

And the morning of Tuesday, November 4, 2008, came at last, and it was Election Day.

It was early breakfast, but only Norman Muller ate, and that mechanically. Even a shower and shave had not succeeded in either restoring him to reality or removing his own conviction that he was as grimy without as he felt grimy within.

Handley's friendly voice did its best to shed some normality over the gray and unfriendly dawn. (The weather prediction had been for a cloudy day with prospects of rain before noon.)

Handley said, "We'll keep this house insulated till Mr. Muller is back, but after that we'll be off your necks." The secret service agent was in full uniform now, including sidearms in heavily brassed holsters.

"You've been no trouble at all, Mr. Handley," simpered Sarah.

Norman drank through two cups of black coffee, wiped his lips with a napkin, stood up and said haggardly, "I'm ready."

Handley stood up, too. "Very well, sir. And thank you, Mrs. Muller, for your very kind hospitality."

• • • •

The armored car purred down empty streets. They were empty even for that hour of the morning.

Handley indicated that and said, "They always shift traffic away from the line of drive ever since the attempted bombing that nearly ruined the Leverett Election of '92."

When the car stopped, Norman was helped out by the always polite Handley into an underground drive whose walls were lined with soldiers at attention.

He was led into a brightly lit room, in which three white-uniformed men greeted him smilingly.

Norman said sharply, "But this is the hospital."

"There's no significance to that," said Handley at once. "It's just that the hospital has the necessary facilities."

"Well, what do I do?"

Handley nodded. One of the three men in white advanced and said, "I'll take over now, agent."

Handley saluted in an offhand manner and left the room.

The man in white said, "Won't you sit down, Mr. Muller? I'm John Paulson, Senior Computer. These are Samson Levine and Peter Dorogobuzh, my assistants."

Norman shook hands numbly all about. Paulson was a man of middle height with a soft face that seemed used to smiling and a very obvious toupee. He wore plastic-rimmed glasses of an old-fashioned cut, and he lit a cigarette as he talked. (Norman refused his offer of one.)

Paulson said, "In the first place, Mr. Muller, I want you to know we are in no hurry. We want you to stay with us all day if necessary, just so that you get used to your surroundings and get over any thought you might have that there is anything unusual in this, anything clinical, if you know what I mean."

"It's all right," said Norman. "I'd just as soon this were over."

"I understand your feelings. Still, we want you to know exactly what's going on. In the first place, Multivac isn't here."

"It isn't?" Somehow through all his depression, he had still looked forward to seeing Multivac. They said it was half a mile long and three stories high, that fifty technicians walked the corridors *within* its structure continuously. It was one of the wonders of the world.

Paulson smiled. "No. It's not portable, you know. It's located underground, in fact, and very few people know exactly where. You can understand that, since it is our greatest natural resource. Believe me, elections aren't the only things it's used for."

Norman thought he was being deliberately chatty and found himself intrigued all the same. "I thought I'd see it. I'd like to."

"I'm sure of that. But it takes a presidential order and even then it has to be countersigned by Security. However, we are plugged into Multivac right here by beam transmission. What Multivac says can be interpreted here and what we say is beamed directly to Multivac, so in a sense we're in its presence."

Norman looked about. The machines within the room were all meaningless to him.

"Now let me explain, Mr. Muller," Paulson went on. "Multivac already has most of the information it needs to decide all the elections, national, state and local. It needs only to check certain imponderable attitudes of mind and it will use you for that. We can't predict what questions it will ask, but they may not make much sense to you, or even to us. It may ask you how you feel about garbage disposal in your town; whether you favor central incinerators. It might ask you whether you have a doctor of your own or whether you make use of National Medicine, Inc. Do you understand?"

"Yes, sir."

"Whatever it asks, you answer in your own words in any way you please. If you feel you must explain quite a bit, do so. Talk an hour, if necessary."

"Yes, sir."

"Now, one more thing. We will have to make use of some simple devices which will automatically record your blood pressure, heartbeat, skin conductivity and brain-wave pattern while you speak. The machinery will seem formidable, but it's all absolutely painless. You won't even know it's going on."

The other two technicians were already busying themselves with smooth-gleaming apparatus on oiled wheels.

Norman said, "Is that to check on whether I'm lying or not?"

"Not at all, Mr. Muller. There's no question of lying. It's only a matter of emotional intensity. If the machine asks you your opinion of your child's school, you may say, 'I think it is overcrowded.' Those are only words. From the way your brain and heart and hormones and sweat glands work, Multivac can judge exactly how intensely you feel about the matter. It will understand your feelings better than you yourself."

"I never heard of this," said Norman.

"No, I'm sure you didn't. Most of the details of Multivac's workings are top secret. For instance, when you leave, you will be asked to sign a paper swearing that you will never reveal the nature of the questions you were asked, the nature of your responses, what was done, or how it was done. The less is known about the Multivac, the less chance of attempted outside pressures upon the men who service it." He smiled grimly. "Our lives are hard enough as it is."

Norman nodded. "I understand."

"And now would you like anything to eat or drink?"

"No. Nothing right now."

"Do you have any questions?"

Norman shook his head.

"Then you tell us when you're ready."

"I'm ready right now."

"You're certain?"

"Quite."

Paulson nodded, and raised his hand in a gesture to the others. They advanced with their frightening equipment, and Norman Muller felt his breath come a little quicker as he watched.

The ordeal lasted nearly three hours, with one short break for coffee and an embarrassing session with a chamber pot. During all this time, Norman Muller remained encased in machinery. He was bone-weary at the close.

He thought sardonically that his promise to reveal nothing of what had passed would be an easy one to keep. Already the questions were a hazy mishmash in his mind.

Somehow he had thought Multivac would speak in a sepulchral, superhuman voice, resonant and echoing, but that, after all, was just an idea he had from seeing too many television shows, he now decided. The truth was distressingly undramatic. The questions were slips of a kind of metallic foil patterned with numerous punctures. A second machine converted the pattern into words and Paulson read the words to Norman, then gave him the question and let him read it for himself.

Norman's answers were taken down by a recording machine, played back to Norman for confirmation, with emendations and added remarks also taken down. All that was fed into a pattern-making instrument and that, in turn, was radiated to Multivac.

The one question Norman could remember at the moment was an incongruously gossipy: "What do you think of the price of eggs?"

Now it was over, and gently they removed the electrodes from various portions of his body, unwrapped the pulsating band from his upper arm, moved the machinery away.

He stood up, drew a deep, shuddering breath and said, "Is that all? Am I through?"

"Not quite." Paulson hurried to him, smiling in reassuring fashion. "We'll have to ask you to stay another hour."

"Why?" asked Norman sharply.

"It will take that long for Multivac to weave its new data into the trillions of items it has. Thousands of elections are concerned, you know. It's very complicated. And it may be that an odd contest here or there, a comptrollership in Phoenix, Arizona, or some council seat in Wilkesboro, North Carolina, may be in doubt. In that case, Multivac may be compelled to ask you a deciding question or two."

"No," said Norman. "I won't go through this again."

"It probably won't happen," Paulson said soothingly. "It rarely does. But, just in case, you'll have to stay." A touch of steel, just a touch, entered his voice. "You have no choice, you know. You must."

Norman sat down wearily. He shrugged.

Paulson said, "We can't let you read a newspaper, but if you'd care for a murder mystery, or if you'd like to play chess, or if there's anything we can do for you to help pass the time, I wish you'd mention it."

"It's all right. I'll just wait."

They ushered him into a small room just next to the one in which he had been questioned. He let himself sink into a plastic-covered armchair and closed his eyes.

As well as he could, he must wait out this final hour.

He sat perfectly still and slowly the tension left him. His breathing grew less ragged and he could clasp his hands without being quite so conscious of the trembling of his fingers.

Maybe there would be no questions. Maybe it was all over.

If it *were* over, then the next thing would be torchlight processions and invitations to speak at all sorts of functions. The Voter of the Year!

He, Norman Muller, ordinary clerk of a small department store in Bloomington, Indiana, who had neither been born great nor achieved greatness would be in the extraordinary position of having had greatness thrust upon him.

The historians would speak soberly of the Muller Election of 2008. That would be its name, the Muller Election.

The publicity, the better job, the flash flood of money that interested Sarah so much, occupied only a corner of his mind. It would all be welcome, of course. He couldn't refuse it. But at the moment something else was beginning to concern him.

A latent patriotism was stirring. After all, he was representing the entire electorate. He was the focal point for *them*. He was, in his own person, for this one day, all of America!

The door opened, snapping him to open-eyed attention. For a moment, his stomach constricted. Not more questions!

But Paulson was smiling. "That will be all, Mr. Muller."

"No more questions, sir?"

"None needed. Everything was quite clear-cut. You will be escorted back to your home and then you will be a private citizen once more. Or as much so as the public will allow."

"Thank you. Thank you." Norman flushed and said, "I wonder—who was elected?"

Paulson shook his head. "That will have to wait for the official announcement. The rules are quite strict. We can't even tell you. You understand."

"Of course. Yes." Norman felt embarrassed.

"Secret service will have the necessary papers for you to sign."

"Yes." Suddenly, Norman Muller felt proud. It was on him now in full strength. He was proud.

In this imperfect world, the sovereign citizens of the first and greatest Electronic Democracy had, through Norman Muller (through *him!*) exercised once again its free, untrammeled franchise.

Gimmicks Three

"Come, come," said Shapur quite politely, considering that he was a demon. "You are wasting my time. And your own, too, I might add, since you have only half an hour left." And his tail twitched.

"It's *not* dematerialization?" asked Isidore Wellby thoughtfully.

"I have already said it is not," said Shapur.

For the hundredth time, Wellby looked at the unbroken bronze that surrounded him on all sides. The demon had taken unholy pleasure (what other kind indeed?) in pointing out that the floor, ceiling and four walls were featureless, two-foot-thick slabs of bronze, welded seamlessly together.

It was the ultimate locked room and Wellby had but another half hour to get out, while the demon watched with an expression of gathering anticipation.

It has been ten years previously (to the day, naturally) that Isidore Wellby had signed up.

"We pay you in advance," said Shapur persuasively. "Ten years of anything you want, within reason, and then you're a demon. You're one of us, with a new name of demonic potency, and many privileges beside. You'll hardly know you're damned. And if you don't sign, you may end up in the fire, anyway, just in the ordinary course of things. You never know. . . . Here, look at me. I'm not doing too badly. I signed up, had my ten years and here I am. Not bad."

"Why so anxious for me to sign then, if I might be damned anyway?" asked Wellby.

"It's not so easy to recruit hell's cadre," said the demon, with a frank shrug that made the faint odor of sulfur dioxide in the air a trifle stronger. "Everyone wishes to gamble on ending in Heaven. It's a poor gamble, but there it is. I think *you*'re too sensible for that. But meanwhile we have more damned souls than we know what to do with and a growing shortage at the administrative end."

Wellby, having just left the army and finding himself with nothing much to show for it but a limp and a farewell letter from a girl he somehow still loved, pricked his finger, and signed.

Of course, he read the small print first. A certain amount of demonic power would be deposited to his account upon signature in blood. He would not know in detail how one manipulated those powers, or even the nature of all of them, but he would nevertheless find his wishes fulfilled in such a way that they would seem to have come about through perfectly normal mechanisms.

Naturally, no wish might be fulfilled which would interfere with the higher aims and purposes of human history. Wellby had raised his eyebrows at that.

Shapur coughed. "A precaution imposed upon us by—uh—Above. You are reasonable. The limitation won't interfere with you."

Wellby said, "There seems to be a catch clause, too."

"A kind of one, yes. After all, we have to check your aptitude for the position. It states, as you see, that you will be required to perform a task for us at the conclusion of your ten years, one your demonic powers will make it quite possible for you to do. We can't tell you the nature of the task now, but you will have ten years to study the nature of your powers. Look upon the whole thing as an entrance qualification."

"And if I don't pass the test, what then?"

"In that case," said the demon, "you will be only an ordinary damned soul after all." And because he was a demon, his eyes glowed smokily at the thought and his clawed fingers twitched as though he felt them already deep in the other's vitals. But he added suavely, "Come, now, the test will be a simple one. We would rather have you as cadre than as just another chore on our hands."

Wellby, with sad thoughts of his unattainable loved one, cared little enough at that moment for what would happen after ten years and he signed.

Yet the ten years passed quickly enough. Isidore Wellby was always reasonable, as the demon had predicted, and things worked well. Wellby accepted a position and because he was always at the right spot at the right time and always said the right thing to the right man, he was quickly promoted to a position of great authority.

Investments he made invariably paid off and, what was more gratifying still, his girl came back to him most sincerely repentant and most satisfactorily adoring.

His marriage was a happy one and was blessed with four children, two boys and two girls, all bright and reasonably well behaved. At the end of ten years, he was at the height of his authority, reputation and wealth, while his wife, if anything, had grown more beautiful as she had matured.

And ten years (to the day, naturally) after the making of the compact, he woke to find himself, not in his bedroom, but in a horrible bronze chamber of the most appalling solidity, with no company other than an eager demon.

"You have only to get out, and you will be one of us," said Shapur. "It can be done fairly and logically by using your demonic powers, provided you know exactly what it is you're doing. You should, by now."

"My wife and children will be very disturbed at my disappearance," said Wellby with the beginning of regrets.

"They will find your dead body," said the demon consolingly. "You will seem to have died of a heart attack and you will have a beautiful funeral. The minister will consign you to Heaven and we will not disillusion him or those who listen to him. Now, come, Wellby, you have till noon."

Wellby, having unconsciously steeled himself for this moment for ten years, was less panic-stricken than he might have been. He looked about speculatively. "Is this room perfectly enclosed? No trick openings?"

"No openings anywhere in the walls, floor or ceiling," said the demon, with a professional delight in his handiwork. "Or at the boundaries of any of those surfaces, for that matter. Are you giving up?"

"No, no. Just give me time."

Wellby thought very hard. There seemed no sign of closeness in the room. There was even a feeling of moving air. The air might be entering the room by dematerializing across the walls. Perhaps the demon had entered by dematerialization and perhaps Wellby himself might leave in that manner. He asked.

The demon grinned. "Dematerialization is not one of your powers. Nor did I myself use it in entering."

"You're sure now?"

"The room is my own creation," said the demon smugly, "and especially constructed for you."

"And you entered from outside?"

"I did."

"With reasonably demonic powers which I possess, too?"

"Exactly. Come, let us be precise. You cannot move through matter but you can move in any dimension by a mere effort of will. You can move up, down, right, left, obliquely and so on, but you cannot move through matter in any way."

Wellby kept on thinking, and Shapur kept on pointing out the utter immovable solidity of the bronze walls, floor and ceiling; their unbroken ultimacy.

It seemed obvious to Wellby that Shapur, however much he might believe in the necessity for recruiting cadre, was barely restraining his demonic delight at possibly having an ordinary damned soul to amuse himself with.

"At least," said Wellby, with a sorrowful attempt at philosophy, "I'll have ten happy years to look back on. Surely that's a consolation, even for a damned soul in hell."

"Not at all," said the demon. "Hell would not be hell, if you were allowed consolations. Everything anyone gains on Earth by pacts with the devil, as in your case (or my own, for that matter), is exactly what one might have gained without such a pact if one had worked industriously and in full trust in—uh—Above. That is what makes all such bargains so truly demonic." And the demon laughed with a kind of cheerful howl.

Wellby said indignantly, "You mean my wife would have returned to me even if I had never signed your contract."

"She might have," said Shapur. "Whatever happens is the will of—uh—Above, you know. We ourselves can do nothing to alter that."

The chagrin of that moment must have sharpened Wellby's wits for it was then that he vanished, leaving the room empty, except for a surprised demon. And surprise turned to absolute fury when the demon looked at the contract with Wellby which he had, until that moment, been holding in his hand for final action, one way or the other.

It was ten years (to the day, naturally) after Isidore Wellby had signed his pact with Shapur, that the demon entered Wellby's office and said, most angrily, "Look here—"

Wellby looked up from his work, astonished. "Who are you?"

"You know very well who I am," said Shapur.

"Not at all," said Wellby.

The demon looked sharply at the man. "I see you are telling the truth, but I can't make out the details." He promptly flooded Wellby's mind with the events of the last ten years.

Wellby said, "Oh, yes. I can explain, of course, but are you sure we will not be interrupted?"

"We won't be," said the demon grimly.

"I sat in that closed bronze room," said Wellby, "and—"

"Never mind that," said the demon hastily. "I want to know—"

"Please. Let me tell this my way."

The demon clamped his jaws and fairly exuded sulfur dioxide till Wellby coughed and looked pained.

Wellby said, "If you'll move off a bit. Thank you. . . . Now I sat in that closed bronze room and remembered how you kept stressing the absolute unbrokenness of the four walls, the floor and the ceiling. I wondered: why did you specify? What else was there beside walls, floor and ceiling. You had defined a completely enclosed three-dimensional space.

"And that was it: three-dimensional. The room was not closed in the fourth dimension. It did not exist indefinitely in the past. You said you had created it for me. So if one traveled into the past, one would find oneself at a point in time, eventually, when the room did not exist and then one would be out of the room.

"What's more, you *had* said I could move in any dimension, and time may certainly be viewed as a dimension. In any case, as soon as I decided to move toward the past, I found myself living backward at a tremendous rate and suddenly there was no bronze around me anywhere."

Shapur cried in anguish, "I can guess all that. You couldn't have escaped any other way. It's this contract of yours that I'm concerned about. If you're not an ordinary damned soul, very well, it's part of the game. But you must be at least one of *us*, one of the cadre; it's what you were paid for, and if I don't deliver you down below, I will be in enormous trouble."

Wellby shrugged his shoulders. "I'm sorry for you, of course, but I can't help you. You must have created the bronze room immediately after I placed my signature on the paper, for when I burst out of the room, I found myself just at the point in time at which I was making the bargain with you. There you were again; there I was; you were pushing the contract toward me, together with a stylus with which I might prick my finger. To be sure, as I had moved back in time, my memory of what was becoming the future faded out, but not, apparently, quite entirely. As you pushed the contract at me, I felt uneasy. I didn't quite remember the future, but I felt uneasy. So I didn't sign. I turned you down flat."

Shapur ground his teeth. "I might have known. If probability patterns affected demons, I would have shifted with you into this new if-world. As it is, all I can say is that you have lost the ten happy years we paid you with. That is one consolation. And we'll get you in the end. That is another."

"Well, now," said Wellby, "are there consolations in hell? Through the ten years I have now lived, I knew nothing of what I might have obtained. But now that you've put the memory of the ten-years-that-might-have-been into my mind, I recall that, in the bronze room, you told me that demonic agreements could give nothing that could not be obtained by industry and trust in Above. I have been industrious and I have trusted."

Wellby's eyes fell upon the photograph of his beautiful wife and four beautiful children, then traveled about the tasteful luxuriance of his office. "And I may even escape hell altogether. That, too, is beyond *your* power to decide."

And the demon, with a horrible shriek, vanished forever.

Kid Stuff

The first pang of nausea had passed and Jan Prentiss said, "Damn it, you're an insect."

It was a statement of fact, not an insult, and the thing that sat on Prentiss' desk said, "Of course."

It was about a foot long, very thin, and in shape a farfetched and miniature caricature of a human being. Its stalky arms and legs originated in pairs from the upper portion of its body. The legs were longer and thicker than the arms. They extended the length of the body, then bent forward at the knee.

The creature sat upon those knees and, when it did so, the stub of its fuzzy abdomen just cleared Prentiss' desk.

There was plenty of time for Prentiss to absorb these details. The object had no objection to being stared at. It seemed to welcome it, in fact, as though it were used to exciting admiration.

"What are you?" Prentiss did not feel completely rational. Five minutes ago, he had been seated at his typewriter, working leisurely on the story he had promised Horace W. Browne for last month's issue of *Farfetched Fantasy Fiction*. He had been in a perfectly usual frame of mind. He had felt quite fine; quite sane.

And then a block of air immediately to the right of the typewriter had shimmered, clouded over and condensed into the little horror that dangled its black and shiny feet over the edge of the desk.

Prentiss wondered in a detached sort of way that he bothered talking to it. This was the first time his profession had so crudely affected his dreams. It *must* be a dream, he told himself.

"I'm an Avalonian," said the being. "I'm from Avalon, in other words." It's tiny face ended in a mandibular mouth. Two swaying three-inch antennae rose from a spot above either eye, while the eyes themselves gleamed richly in their many-faceted fashion. There was no sign of nostrils.

Naturally not, thought Prentiss wildly. It has to breathe through vents in its abdomen. It must be talking with its abdomen then. Or using telepathy.

"Avalon?" he said stupidly. He thought: Avalon? The land of the fay in King Arthur's time?

"Certainly," said the creature, answering the thought smoothly. "I'm an elf."

"Oh, no!" Prentiss put his hands to his face, took them away and found the elf still there, its feet thumping against the top drawer. Prentiss was not a drinking man, or a nervous one. In fact, he was considered a very prosaic sort of person by his neighbors. He had a comfortable paunch, a reasonable but not excessive amount of hair on his head, an amiable wife and an active ten-year-old son. His neighbors were, of course, kept ignorant of the fact that he paid off the mortgage on his house by writing fantasies of one sort or another.

Till now, however, this secret vice had never affected his psyche. To be sure, his wife had shaken her head over his addiction many times. It was her standard opinion that he was wasting, even perverting, his talents.

"Who on Earth reads these things?" she would say. "All that stuff about demons and gnomes and wishing rings and elves. All that *kid* stuff, if you want my frank opinion."

"You're quite wrong," Prentiss would reply stiffly. "Modern fantasies are very sophisticated and mature treatments of folk motifs. Behind the façade of glib unreality there frequently lie trenchant comments on the world of today. Fantasy in modern style is, above all, adult fare."

Blanche shrugged. She had heard him speak at conventions so these comments weren't new to her.

"Besides," he would add, "fantasies pay the mortgage, don't they?"

"Maybe so," she would reply, "but it would be nice if you'd switch to mysteries. At least you'd get quarter-reprint sales out of those and we could even tell the neighbors what you do for a living."

Prentiss groaned in spirit. Blanche could come in now at any time and find him talking to himself (it was too real for a dream; it might be a hallucination). After that he *would* have to write mysteries for a living—or take to work.

"You're quite wrong," said the elf. "This is neither a dream nor a hallucination."

"Then why don't you go away?" asked Prentiss.

"I intend to. This is scarcely my idea of a place to live. And you're coming with me."

"I am *not.* What the hell do you think you are, telling me what I'm going to do?"

"If you think that's a respectful way to speak to a representative of an older culture, I can't say much for your upbringing."

"You're not an older culture—" He wanted to add: You're just a figment of my imagination; but he had been a writer too long to be able to bring himself to commit the cliché.

"We insects," said the elf freezingly, "existed half a billion years before the first mammal was invented. We watched the dinosaurs come in and we watched them go out. As for you man-things—strictly newcomers."

For the first time, Prentiss noted that, from the spot on the elf's body where its limbs sprouted, a third vestigial pair existed as well. It increased the insecticity of the object and Prentiss' sense of indignation grew.

He said, "You needn't waste your company on social inferiors."

"I wouldn't," said the elf, "believe me. But necessity drives, you know. It's a rather complicated story but when you hear it, you'll *want* to help."

Prentiss said uneasily, "Look, I don't have much time. Blanche—my wife will be in here any time. She'll be upset."

"She won't be here," said the elf. "I've set up a block in her mind."

"What!"

"Quite harmless, I assure you. But, after all, we can't afford to be disturbed, can we?"

Prentiss sat back in his chair, dazed and unhappy.

The elf said, "We elves began our association with you man-things immediately after the last ice age began. It had been a miserable time for us, as you can imagine. We couldn't wear animal carcasses or live in holes as your uncouth ancestors did. It took incredible stores of psychic energy to keep warm."

"Incredible stores of what?"

"Psychic energy. You know nothing at all about it. Your mind is too coarse to grasp the concept. Please don't interrupt."

The elf continued, "Necessity drove us to experiment with your people's brains. They were crude, but large. The cells were inefficient, almost worthless, but there were a vast number of them. We could use those brains as a concentrating device, a type of psychic lens, and increase the available energy which our own minds could tap. We survived the ice age handily and without having to retreat to the tropics as in previous such eras.

"Of course, we were spoiled. When warmth returned, we didn't abandon the man-things. We used them to increase our standard of living generally. We could travel faster, eat better, do more, and we lost our old, simple, virtuous way of life forever. Then, too, there was milk."

"Milk?" said Prentiss. "I don't see the connection."

"A divine liquid. I only tasted it once in my life. But elfin classic poetry speaks of it in superlatives. In the old days, men always supplied us plentifully. Why mammals of all things should be blessed with it and insects not is a complete mystery. . . . How unfortunate it is that the men-things got out of hand."

"They did?"

"Two hundred years ago."

"Good for us."

"Don't be narrow-minded," said the elf stiffly. "It was a useful association for all parties until you man-things learned to handle physical energies in quantity. It was just the sort of gross thing your minds are capable of."

"What was wrong with it?"

"It's hard to explain. It was all very well for us to light up our nightly revels with fireflies brightened by use of two manpower of psychic energy. But then you men-creatures installed electric lights. Our antennal reception is good for miles, but then you invented telegraphs, telephones and radios. Our kobolds mined ore with much greater efficiency than man-things do, until man-things invented dynamite. Do you see?"

"No."

"Surely you don't expect sensitive and superior creatures such as the elves to watch a group of hairy mammals outdo them. It wouldn't be so bad if we could imitate the electronic development ourselves, but our psychic energies were insufficient for the purpose. Well, we retreated from reality. We sulked, pined and drooped. Call it an inferiority complex, if you will, but from two centuries ago onward, we slowly abandoned mankind and retreated to such centers as Avalon."

Prentiss thought furiously. "Let's get this straight. You can handle minds?"

"Certainly."

"You can make me think you're invisible? Hypnotically, I mean?"

"A crude term, but yes."

"And when you appeared just now, you did it by lifting a kind of mental block. Is that it?"

"To answer your thoughts, rather than your words: You are not sleeping; you are not mad; and I am not supernatural."

"I was just making sure. I take it, then, you can read my mind."

"Of course. It is a rather dirty and unrewarding sort of labor, but I can do it when I must. Your name is Prentiss and you write imaginative fiction. You have one larva who is at a place of instruction. I know a great deal about you."

Prentiss winced. "And just where is Avalon?"

"You won't find it." The elf clacked his mandibles together two or three times. "Don't speculate on the possibility of warning the authorities. You'll find yourself in a madhouse. Avalon, in case you think the knowledge will help you, is in the middle of the Atlantic and quite invisible, you know. After the steamboat was invented, you man-things got to moving about so unreasonably that we had to cloak the whole island with a psychic shield.

"Of course, incidents *will* take place. Once a huge, barbaric vessel hit us dead center and it took all the psychic energy of the entire population to give the island the appearance of an iceberg. The *Titanic*, I believe, was the name printed on the vessel. And nowadays there are planes flying overhead all the time and sometimes there are crashes. We picked up cases of canned milk once. That's when I tasted it."

Prentiss said, "Well, then, damn it, why aren't you still on Avalon? Why did you leave?"

"I was ordered to leave," said the elf angrily. "The fools."

"Oh?"

"You know how it is when you're a little different. I'm not like the rest of them and the poor tradition-ridden fools resented it. They were jealous. That's the best explanation. Jealous!"

"How are you different?"

"Hand me that light bulb," said the elf. "Oh, just unscrew it. You don't need a reading lamp in the daytime."

With a quiver of repulsion, Prentiss did as he was told and passed the object into the little hands of the elf. Carefully, the elf, with fingers so thin and wiry that they looked like tendrils, touched the bottom and side of the brass base.

Feebly the filament in the bulb reddened.

"Good God," said Prentiss.

"That," said the elf proudly, "is my great talent. I told you that we elves couldn't adapt psychic energy to electronics. Well, I can! I'm not just an ordinary elf. I'm a mutant! A super-elf! I'm the next stage in elfin evolution. This light is due just to the activity of my own mind, you know. Now watch when I use yours as a focus."

As he said that, the bulb's filament grew white hot and painful to look at, while a vague and not unpleasant tickling sensation entered Prentiss' skull.

The lamp went out and the elf put the bulb on the desk behind the typewriter.

"I haven't tried," said the elf proudly, "but I suspect I can fission uranium too."

"But look here, lighting a bulb takes energy. You can't just hold it—"

"I've *told* you about psychic energy. Great Oberon, man-thing, try to understand."

Prentiss felt increasingly uneasy; he said cautiously, "What do you intend doing with this gift of yours?"

"Go back to Avalon, of course. I *should* let those fools go to their doom, but an elf does have a certain patriotism, even if he *is* a coleopteron."

"A what?"

"We elves are not all of a species, you know. I'm of beetle descent. See?"

He rose to his feet and, standing on the desk, turned his back to Prentiss. What had seemed merely a shining black cuticle suddenly split and lifted. From underneath, two filmy, veined wings fluttered out.

"Oh, you can fly," said Prentiss.

"You're very foolish," said the elf contemptuously, "not to realize I'm too large for flight. But they *are* attractive, aren't they? How do you like the iridescence? The lepidoptera have disgusting wings in comparison. They're gaudy and indelicate. What's more they're always sticking out."

"The lepidoptera?" Prentiss felt hopelessly confused.

"The butterfly clans. They're the proud ones. They were always letting humans see them so they could be admired. Very petty minds in a way. And that's why your legends always give fairies butterfly wings instead of beetle wings which are *much* more diaphanously beautiful. We'll give the lepidoptera what for when we get back, you and I."

"Now hold on—"

"Just think," said the elf, swaying back and forth in what looked like elfin ecstasy, "our nightly revels on the fairy green will be a blaze of sparkling light from curlicues of neon tubing. We can cut loose the swarms of wasps we've got hitched to our flying wagons and install internal-combustion motors instead. We can stop this business of curling up on leaves when it's time to sleep and build factories to manufacture decent mattresses. I tell you, we'll *live.* . . . And the rest of them will eat dirt for having ordered me out."

"But I can't go with you," bleated Prentiss. "I have responsibilities. I have a wife and kid. You wouldn't take a man away from his—his larva, would you?"

"I'm not cruel," said the elf. He turned his eyes full on Prentiss. "I have an elfin soul. Still, what choice have I? I must have a man-brain for focusing purposes or I will accomplish nothing; and not all man-brains are suitable."

"Why not?"

"Great Oberon, creature. A man-brain isn't a passive thing of wood and stone. It must co-operate in order to be useful. And it can only co-operate by being fully aware of our own elfin ability to manipulate it. I can use your brain, for instance, but your wife's would be useless to me. It would take her years to understand who and what I am."

Prentiss said, "This is a damned insult. Are you telling me I believe in fairies? I'll have you know I'm a complete rationalist."

"Are you? When I first revealed myself to you, you had a few feeble thoughts about dreams and hallucinations but you talked to me, you accepted me. Your wife would have screamed and gone into hysterics."

Prentiss was silent. He could think of no answer.

"That's the trouble," said the elf despondently. "Practically all you humans have forgotten about us since we left you. Your minds have closed;

grown useless. To be sure, your larvae believe in your legends about the 'little folk,' but their brains are undeveloped and useful only for simple processes. When they mature, they lose belief. Frankly, I don't know what I would do if it weren't for you fantasy writers."

"What do you mean we fantasy writers?"

"You are the few remaining adults who believe in the insect folk. You, Prentiss, most of all. You've been a fantasy writer for twenty years."

"You're mad. I don't believe the things I write."

"You have to. You can't help it. I mean, while you're actually writing, you take the subject matter seriously. After a while your mind is just naturally cultivated into usefulness. . . . But why argue. I *have* used you. You saw the light bulb brighten. So you see you must come with me."

"But I won't." Prentiss set his limbs stubbornly. "Can you make me against my will?"

"I could, but I might damage you, and I wouldn't want that. Suppose we say this. If you don't agree to come, I could focus a current of high-voltage electricity through your wife. It would be a revolting thing to have to do, but I understand your own people execute enemies of the state in that fashion, so that you would probably find the punishment less horrible than I do. I wouldn't want to seem brutal even to a man-thing."

Prentiss grew conscious of the perspiration matting the short hairs on his temple.

"Wait," he said, "don't do anything like that. Let's talk it over."

The elf shot out his filmy wings, fluttered them and returned them to their case. "Talk, talk, talk. It's tiring. Surely you have milk in the house. You're not a very thoughtful host or you would have offered me refreshment before this."

Prentiss tried to bury the thought that came to him, to push it as far below the outer skin of his mind as he could. He said casually, "I have something better than milk. Here, I'll get it for you."

"Stay where you are. Call to your wife. She'll bring it."

"But I don't want her to see you. It would frighten her."

The elf said, "You need feel no concern. I'll handle her so that she won't be the least disturbed."

Prentiss lifted an arm.

The elf said, "Any attack you make on me will be far slower than the bolt of electricity that will strike your wife."

Prentiss' arm dropped. He stepped to the door of his study.

"Blanche!" he called down the stairs.

Blanche was just visible in the living room, sitting woodenly in the armchair near the bookcase. She seemed to be asleep, open-eyed.

Prentiss turned to the elf. "Something's wrong with her."

"She's just in a state of sedation. She'll hear you. Tell her what to do."

"Blanche!" he called again. "Bring the container of eggnog and a small glass, will you?"

With no sign of animation other than that of bare movement, Blanche rose and disappeared from view.

"What is eggnog?" asked the elf.

Prentiss attempted enthusiasm. "It is a compound of milk, sugar and eggs beaten to a delightful consistency. Milk alone is poor stuff compared to it."

Blanche entered with the eggnog. Her pretty face was expressionless. Her eyes turned toward the elf but lightened with no realization of the significance of the sight.

"Here, Jan," she said, and sat down in the old, leather-covered chair by the window, hands falling loosely to her lap.

Prentiss watched her uneasily for a moment. "Are you going to keep her here?"

"She'll be easier to control. . . . Well, aren't you going to offer me the eggnog?"

"Oh, sure. Here!"

He poured the thick white liquid into the cocktail glass. He had prepared five milk bottles of it two nights before for the boys of the New York Fantasy Association and it had been mixed with a lavish hand, since fantasy writers notoriously like it so.

The elf's antennae trembled violently.

"A heavenly aroma," he muttered.

He wrapped the ends of his thin arms about the stem of the small glass and lifted it to his mouth. The liquid's level sank. When half was gone, he put it down and sighed, "Oh, the loss to my people. What a creation! What a thing to exist! Our histories tell us that in ancient days an occasional lucky sprite managed to take the place of a man-larva at birth so that he might draw off the liquid fresh-made. I wonder if even those ever experienced anything like this."

Prentiss said with a touch of professional interest, "That's the idea behind this business of changelings, is it?"

"Of course. The female man-creature has a great gift. Why not take advantage of it?" The elf turned his eyes upon the rise and fall of Blanche's bosom and sighed again.

Prentiss said (not too eager, now; don't give it away), "Go ahead. Drink all you want."

He, too, watched Blanche, waiting for signs of restoring animation, waiting for the beginnings of breakdown in the elf's control.

The elf said, "When is your larva returning from its place of instruction? I need him."

"Soon, soon," said Prentiss nervously. He looked at his wristwatch. Actually, Jan, Junior, would be back, yelling for a slab of cake and milk, in something like fifteen minutes.

"Fill 'er up," he said urgently. "Fill 'er up."

The elf sipped gaily.. He said, "Once the larva arrives, you can go."

"Go?"

"Only to the library. You'll have to get volumes on electronics. I'll need the details on how to build television, telephones, all that. I'll need to have rules on wiring, instructions for constructing vacuum tubes. Details, Prentiss, details! We have tremendous tasks ahead of us. Oil drilling, gasoline refining, motors, scientific agriculture. We'll build a new Avalon, you and I. A technical one. A scientific fairyland. We will create a new world."

"Great!" said Prentiss. "Here, don't neglect your drink."

"You see. You are catching fire with the idea," said the elf. "And you will be rewarded. You will have a dozen female man-things to yourself."

Prentiss looked at Blanche automatically. No signs of hearing, but who could tell? He said, "I'd have no use for female man-th—for women, I mean."

"Come now," said the elf censoriously, "be truthful. You men-things are well known to our folk as lecherous, bestial creatures. Mothers frightened their young for generations by threatening them with men-things. . . . Young, ah!" He lifted the glass of eggnog in the air and said, "To my own young," and drained it.

"Fill 'er up," said Prentiss at once. "Fill 'er up."

The elf did so. He said, "I'll have lots of children. I'll pick out the best of the coleoptresses and breed my line. I'll continue the mutation. Right now I'm the only one, but when we have a dozen or fifty, I'll interbreed them and develop the race of the super-elf. A race of electro—ulp—electronic marvels and infinite future. . . . If I could only drink more. Nectar! The original nectar!"

There was the sudden noise of a door being flung open and a young voice calling, "Mom! Hey, Mom!"

The elf, his glossy eyes a little dimmed, said, "Then we'll begin to take over the men-things. A few believe already; the rest we will—urp—teach. It will be the old days, but better; a more efficient elfhood, a tighter union."

Jan, Junior's, voice was closer and tinged with impatience. "Hey, Mom! Ain't you home?"

Prentiss felt his eyes popping with tension. Blanche sat rigid. The elf's speech was slightly thick, his balance a little unsteady. If Prentiss were going to risk it, now, now was the time.

"Sit back," said the elf peremptorily. "You're being foolish. I knew there was alcohol in the eggnog from the moment you thought your ridiculous scheme. You men-things are very shifty. We elves have many proverbs about you. Fortunately, alcohol has little effect upon us. Now if you had tried catnip with just a touch of honey in it . . . Ah, here is the larva. How are you, little man-thing?"

The elf sat there, the goblet of eggnog halfway to his mandibles, while

Jan, Junior, stood in the doorway. Jan, Junior's, ten-year-old face was moderately smeared with dirt, his hair was immoderately matted and there was a look of the utmost surprise in his gray eyes. His battered schoolbooks swayed from the end of the strap he held in his hand.

He said, "Pop! What's the matter with Mom? And—and what's that?"

The elf said to Prentiss, "Hurry to the library. No time must be lost. You know the books I need." All trace of incipient drunkenness had left the creature and Prentiss' morale broke. The creature had been playing with him.

Prentiss got up to go.

The elf said, "And nothing human; nothing sneaky; no tricks. Your wife is still a hostage. I can use the larva's mind to kill her; it's good enough for that. I wouldn't want to do it. I'm a member of the Elfitarian Ethical Society and we advocate considerate treatment of mammals so you may rely on my noble principles *if* you do as I say."

Prentiss felt a strong compulsion to leave flooding him. He stumbled toward the door.

Jan, Junior, cried, "Pop, it can talk! He says he'll kill Mom! Hey, don't go away!"

Prentiss was already out of the room, when he heard the elf say, "Don't stare at me, larva. I will not harm your mother if you do exactly as I say. I am an elf, a fairy. You know what a fairy is, of course."

And Prentiss was at the front door when he heard Jan, Junior's, treble raised in wild shouting, followed by scream after scream in Blanche's shuddering soprano.

The strong, though invisible, elastic that was drawing Prentiss out the house snapped and vanished. He fell backward, righted himself and darted back up the stairs.

Blanche, fairly saturated with quivering life, was backed into a corner, her arms about a weeping Jan, Junior.

On the desk was a collapsed black carapace, covering a nasty smear of pulpiness from which colorless liquid dripped.

Jan, Junior, was sobbing hysterically, "I hit it. I hit it with my schoolbooks. It was hurting Mom."

An hour passed and Prentiss felt the world of normality pouring back into the interstices left behind by the creature from Avalon. The elf itself was already ash in the incinerator behind the house and the only remnant of its existence was the damp stain at the foot of his desk.

Blanche was still sickly pale. They talked in whispers.

Prentiss said, "How's Jan, Junior?"

"He's watching television."

"Is he all right?"

"Oh, *he's* all right, but *I'll* be having nightmares for weeks."

"I know. So will I unless we can get it out of our minds. I don't think there'll ever be another of those—things here."

Blanche said, "I can't explain how awful it was. I kept hearing every word he said, even when I was down in the living room."

"It was telepathy, you see."

"I just couldn't move. Then, after you left, I could begin to stir a bit. I tried to scream but all I could do was moan and whimper. Then Jan, Junior, smashed him and all at once I was free. I don't understand how it happened."

Prentiss felt a certain gloomy satisfaction. "I think I know. I was under his control because I accepted the truth of his existence. He held you in check through me. When I left the room, increasing distance made it harder to use my mind as a psychic lens and you could begin moving. By the time I reached the front door, the elf thought it was time to switch from my mind to Jan, Junior's. That was his mistake."

"In what way?" asked Blanche.

"He assumed that all children believe in fairies, but he was wrong. Here in America today children *don't* believe in fairies. They never hear of them. They believe in Tom Corbett, in Hopalong Cassidy, in Dick Tracy, in Howdy Doody, in Superman and a dozen other things, but not in fairies.

"The elf just never realized the sudden cultural changes brought about by comic books and television, and when he tried to grab Jan, Junior's mind, he couldn't. Before he could recover his psychic balance, Jan, Junior, was on top of him in a swinging panic because he thought you were being hurt and it was all over.

"It's like I've always said, Blanche. The ancient folk motifs of legend survive only in the modern fantasy magazine, and modern fantasy is purely adult fare. Do you finally see my point?"

Blanche said humbly, "Yes, dear."

Prentiss put his hands in his pockets and grinned slowly. "You know, Blanche, next time I see Walt Rae, I think I'll just drop a hint that I write the stuff. Time the neighbors knew, I think."

Jan, Junior, holding an enormous slice of buttered bread, wandered into his father's study in search of the dimming memory. Pop kept slapping him on the back and Mom kept putting bread and cake in his hands and he was forgetting why. There had been this big old thing on the desk that could talk . . .

It had all happened so quickly that it got mixed up in his mind.

He shrugged his shoulders and, in the late afternoon sunlight, looked at the partly typewritten sheet in his father's typewriter, then at the small pile of paper resting on the desk.

He read a while, curled his lip and muttered, "Gee whiz. Fairies again. Always kid stuff!" and wandered off.

The Watery Place

We're never going to have space travel. What's more, no extraterrestrials will ever land on Earth—at least, any more.

I'm not just being a pessimist. As a matter of fact, space travel *is* possible; extraterrestrials *have* landed. I *know* that. Space ships are crisscrossing space among a million worlds, probably, but we'll never join them. I know that, too. All on account of a ridiculous error.

I'll explain.

It was actually Bart Cameron's error and you'll have to understand about Bart Cameron. He's the sheriff at Twin Gulch, Idaho, and I'm his deputy. Bart Cameron is an impatient man and he gets most impatient when he has to work up his income tax. You see, besides being sheriff, he also owns and runs the general store, he's got some shares in a sheep ranch, he does a bit of assay work, he's got a kind of pension for being a disabled veteran (bad knee) and a few other things like that. Naturally, it makes his tax figures complicated.

It wouldn't be so bad if he'd let a tax man work on the forms with him, but he insists on doing it himself and it makes him a bitter man. By April 14, he isn't approachable.

So it's too bad the flying saucer landed on April 14, 1956.

I saw it land. My chair was backed up against the wall in the sheriff's office, and I was looking at the stars through the windows and feeling too lazy to go back to my magazine and wondering if I ought to knock off and hit the sack or keep on listening to Cameron curse real steady as he went over his columns of figures for the hundred twenty-seventh time.

It looked like a shooting star at first, but then the track of light broadened into two things that looked like rocket exhausts and the thing came down sweet, steady and without a sound. An old, dead leaf would have rustled more coming down and landed thumpier. Two men got out.

I couldn't say anything or do anything. I couldn't choke or point; I couldn't even bug my eyes. I just sat there.

Cameron? He never looked up.

There was a knock on the door which wasn't locked. It opened and the two men from the flying saucer stepped in. I would have thought they were city fellows if I hadn't seen the flying saucer land in the scrub. They wore charcoal-gray suits, with white shirts and maroon four-in-hands. They had on black shoes and black homburgs. They had dark complexions, black wavy hair and brown eyes. They had very serious looks on their faces and were about five foot ten apiece. They looked very much alike.

God, I was scared.

But Cameron just looked up when the door opened and frowned. Ordinarily, I guess he'd have laughed the collar button off his shirt at seeing clothes like that in Twin Gulch, but he was so taken up by his income tax that he never cracked a smile.

He said, "What can I do for you, folks?" and he tapped his hand on the forms so it was obvious he hadn't much time.

One of the two stepped forward. He said, "We have had your people under observation a long time." He pronounced each word carefully and all by itself.

Cameron said, "My people? All I got's a wife. What's she been doing?"

The fellow in the suit said, "We have chosen this locality for our first contact because it is isolated and peaceful. We know that you are the leader here."

"I'm the sheriff, if that's what you mean, so spit it out. What's you trouble?"

"We have been careful to adopt your mode of dress and even to assume your appearance."

"That's *my* mode of dress?" He must have noticed it for the first time.

"The mode of dress of your dominant social class, that is. We have also learned your language."

You could see the light break in on Cameron. He said, "You guys foreigners?" Cameron didn't go much for foreigners, never having met many outside the army, but generally he tried to be fair.

The man from the saucer said, "Foreigners? Indeed we are. We come from the watery place your people call Venus."

(I was just collecting up strength to blink my eyes, but that sent me right back to nothing. I had seen the flying saucer. I had seen it land. I had to believe this! These men—or these somethings—came from Venus.)

But Cameron never blinked an eye. He said, "All right. This is the U.S.A. We all got equal rights regardless of race, creed, color, *or* nationality. I'm at your service. What can I do for you?"

"We would like to have you make immediate arrangements for the important men of your U.S.A., as you call it, to be brought here for discussions leading to your people joining our great organization."

Slowly, Cameron got red. "Our people join *your* organization. We're already part of the U.N. and God knows what else. And I suppose I'm to get the President here, eh? Right now? In Twin Gulch? Send a hurry-up message?" He looked at me, as though he wanted to see a smile on my face, but I couldn't as much as fall down if someone had pushed the chair out from under me.

The saucer man said, "Speed is desirable."

"You want Congress, too? The Supreme Court?"

"If they will help, sheriff."

And Cameron really went to pieces. He banged his income tax form and yelled, "Well, you're not helping me, and I have no time for wise-guy jerks who come around, especially foreigners. If you don't get the hell out of here pronto, I'll lock you up for disturbing the peace and I'll never let you out."

"You wish us to leave?" said the man from Venus.

"Right now! Get the hell out of here and back to wherever you're from and don't ever come back. I don't want to see you and no one else around here does."

The two men looked at each other, making little twitches with their faces.

Then the one who had done all the talking said, "I can see in your mind that you really wish, with great intensity, to be left alone. It is not our way to force ourselves or our organization on people who do not wish us or it. We will respect your privacy and leave. We will not return. We will girdle your world in warning and none will enter and your people will never have to leave."

Cameron said, "Mister, I'm tired of this crap, so I'll count to three—"

They turned and left, and I just knew that everything they said was so. I was listening to them, you see, which Cameron wasn't, because he was busy thinking of his income tax, and it was as though I could hear their minds, know what I mean? I knew that there would be a kind of fence around earth, corralling us in, keeping us from leaving, keeping others from coming in. I *knew* it.

And when they left, I got my voice back—too late. I screamed, "Cameron, for God's sake, they're from space. Why'd you send them away?"

"From space!" He stared at me.

I yelled, "Look!" I don't know how I did it, he being twenty-five pounds heavier than I, but I yanked him to the window by his shirt collar, busting every shirt button off him.

He was too surprised to resist and when he recovered his wits enough to make like he was going to knock me down, he caught sight of what was going on outside the window and the breath went out of *him*.

They were getting into the flying saucer, those two men, and the saucer sat there, large, round, shiny and kind of powerful, you know. Then it took off. It went up easy as a feather and a red-orange glow showed up on one side and got brighter as the ship got smaller till it was a shooting star again, slowly fading out.

And I said, "Sheriff, why'd you send them away? They *had* to see the President. Now they'll never come back."

Cameron said, "I thought they were foreigners. They *said* they had to learn our language. And they talked funny."

"Oh, fine. Foreigners."

"They *said* they were foreigners and they looked Italian. I thought they were Italian."

"How could they be Italian? They said they were from the planet Venus. I heard them. They said so."

"The planet Venus." His eyes got real round.

"They said it. They called it the watery place or something. You know Venus has a lot of water on it."

But you see, it was just an error, a stupid error, the kind anyone could make. Only now Earth is never going to have space travel and we'll never as much as land on the moon or have another Venusian visit us. That dope, Cameron, and his income tax!

Because he whispered, "Venus! When they talked about the watery place, I thought they meant *Venice!*"

Living Space

Clarence Rimbro had no objections to living in the only house on an uninhabited planet, any more than had any other of Earth's even trillion of inhabitants.

If someone had questioned him concerning possible objections, he would undoubtedly have stared blankly at the questioner. His house was much larger than any house could possibly be on Earth proper and much more modern. It had its independent air supply and water supply, ample food in its freezing compartments. It was isolated from the lifeless planet on which it was located by a force field, but the rooms were built about a five-acre farm (under glass, of course), which, in the planet's beneficent sunlight, grew flowers for pleasure and vegetables for health. It even supported a few chickens. It gave Mrs. Rimbro something to do with herself afternoons, and a place for the two little Rimbros to play when they were tired of indoors.

Furthermore, if one *wanted* to be on Earth proper; if one insisted on it; if one *had* to have people around and air one could breathe in the open or water to swim in, one had only to go out of the front door of the house.

So where was the difficulty?

Remember, too, that on the lifeless planet on which the Rimbro house was located there was complete silence except for the occasional monotonous effects of wind and rain. There was absolute privacy and the feeling of absolute ownership of two hundred million square miles of planetary surface.

Clarence Rimbro appreciated all that in his distant way. He was an accountant, skilled in handling very advanced computer models, precise in his manners and clothing, not much given to smiling beneath his thin, well-kept mustache and properly aware of his own worth. When he drove from work toward home, he passed the occasional dwelling place on Earth proper and he never ceased to stare at them with a certain smugness.

Well, either for business reasons or mental perversion, some people simply had to live on Earth proper. It was too bad for them. After all, Earth proper's soil had to supply the minerals and basic food supply for all the trillion of inhabitants (in fifty years, it would be two trillion) and space was at a premium. Houses on Earth proper just *couldn't* be any bigger than that, and people who had to live in them had to adjust to the fact.

Even the process of entering his house had its mild pleasantness. He would enter the community twist place to which he was assigned (it looked, as did all such, like a rather stumpy obelisk), and there he would invariably find others waiting to use it. Still more would arrive before he reached the head of the line. It was a sociable time.

"How's your planet?" "How's yours?" The usual small talk. Sometimes someone would be having trouble. Machinery breakdowns or serious weather that would alter the terrain unfavorably. Not often.

But it passed the time. Then Rimbro would be at the head of the line; he would put his key into the slot; the proper combination would be punched; and he would be twisted into a new probability pattern; his own particular probability pattern; the one assigned to him when he married and became a producing citizen; a probability pattern in which life had never developed on Earth. And twisting to this particular lifeless Earth, he would walk into his own foyer.

Just like that.

He never worried about being in another probability. Why should he? He never gave it any thought. There were an infinite number of possible Earths. Each existed in its own niche; its own probability pattern. Since on a planet such as Earth there was, according to calculation, about a fifty-fifty chance of life's developing, half of all the possible Earths (still infinite, since half of infinity was infinity) possessed life, and half (still infinite) did not. And living on about three hundred billion of the unoccupied Earths were three hundred billion families, each with its own beautiful house, powered by the sun of that probability, and each securely at peace. The number of Earths so occupied grew by millions each day.

And then one day, Rimbro came home and Sandra (his wife) said to him, as he entered, "There's been the most peculiar noise."

Rimbro's eyebrows shot up and he looked closely at his wife. Except for a certain restlessness of her thin hands and a pale look about the corners of her tight mouth, she looked normal.

Rimbro said, still holding his topcoat halfway toward the servette that waited patiently for it, "Noise? What noise? I don't hear anything."

"It's stopped now," Sandra said. "Really, it was like a deep thumping or rumble. You'd hear it a bit. Then it would stop. Then you'd hear it a bit and so on. I've never heard anything like it."

Rimbro surrendered his coat. "But that's quite impossible."

"I *heard* it."

"I'll look over the machinery," he mumbled. "Something may be wrong."

Nothing was, that his accountant's eyes could discover, and, with a shrug, he went to supper. He listened to the servettes hum busily about their different chores, watched one sweep up the plates and cutlery for disposal and recovery, then said, pursing his lips, "Maybe one of the servettes is out of order. I'll check them."

"It wasn't anything like that, Clarence."

Rimbro went to bed, without further concern over the matter, and wakened with his wife's hand clutching his shoulder. His hand went automatically to the contact patch that set the walls glowing. "What's the matter? What time is it?"

She shook her head. "Listen! *Listen!*"

Good Lord, thought Rimbro, there *is* a noise. A definite rumbling. It came and went.

"Earthquake?" he whispered. It did happen, of course, though, with all the planet to choose from, they could generally count on having avoided the faulted areas.

"All day long?" asked Sandra fretfully. "I think it's something else." And then she voiced the secret terror of every nervous householder. "I think there's someone on the planet with us. This Earth is *inhabited.*"

Rimbro did the logical things. When morning came, he took his wife and children to his wife's mother. He himself took a day off and hurried to the Sector's Housing Bureau.

He was quite annoyed at all his.

Bill Ching of the Housing Bureau was short, jovial and proud of his part Mongolian ancestry. He thought probability patterns had solved every last one of humanity's problems. Alec Mishnoff, also of the Housing Bureau, thought probability patterns were a snare into which humanity had been hopelessly tempted. He had originally majored in archeology and had studied a variety of antiquarian subjects with which his delicately poised head was still crammed. His face managed to look sensitive despite overbearing eyebrows, and he lived with a pet notion that so far he had dared tell no one, though preoccupation with it had driven him out of archeology and into housing.

Ching was fond of saying, "The hell with Malthus!" It was almost a verbal trademark of his. "The hell with Malthus. We can't possibly overpopulate now. However frequently we double and redouble, Homo sapiens remains finite in number, and the uninhabited Earths remain infinite. And we don't have to put one house on each planet. We can put a hundred, a thousand, a million. Plenty of room and plenty of power from each probability sun."

"More than one on a planet?" said Mishnoff sourly.

Ching knew exactly what he meant. When probability patterns had first been put to use, sole ownership of a planet had been powerful inducement for early settlers. It appealed to the snob and despot in every one. What man so poor, ran the slogan, as not to have an empire larger than Genghis Khan's? To introduce multiple settling now would outrage everyone.

Ching said, with a shrug, "All right, it would take psychological preparation. So what? That's what it took to start the whole deal in the first place."

"And food?" asked Mishnoff.

"You know we're putting hydroponic works and yeast plants in other probability patterns. And if we had to, we could cultivate their soil."

"Wearing space suits and importing oxygen."

"We could reduce carbon dioxide for oxygen till the plants got going and they'd do the job after that."

"Given a million years."

"Mishnoff, the trouble with you," Ching said, "is you read too many ancient history books. You're an obstructionist."

But Ching was too good-natured really to mean that, and Mishnoff continued to read books and to worry. Mishnoff longed for the day he could get up the courage necessary to see the Head of the Section and put right out in plain view—bang, like that—exactly what it was that was troubling him.

But now, a Mr. Clarence Rimbro faced them, perspiring slightly and toweringly angry at the fact that it had taken him the better part of two days to reach this far into the Bureau.

He reached his exposition's climax by saying, "And *I* say the planet is inhabited and I don't propose to stand for it."

Having listened to his story in full, Ching tried the soothing approach. He said, "Noise like that is probably just some natural phenomenon."

"What kind of natural phenomenon?" demanded Rimbro. "I want an investigation. If it's a natural phenomenon, I want to know what kind. I say the place is inhabited. It has life on it, by Heaven, and I'm not paying rent on a planet to share it. And with dinosaurs, from the sound of it."

"Come, Mr. Rimbro, how long have you lived on your Earth?"

"Fifteen and a half years."

"And has there ever been any evidence of life?"

"There is now, and, as a citizen with a production record classified as A-I, I demand an investigation."

"Of course we'll investigate, sir, but we just want to assure you now that everything is all right. Do you realize how carefully we select our probability patterns?"

"I'm an accountant. I have a pretty good idea," said Rimbro at once.

"Then surely you know our computers cannot fail us. They never pick a probability which has been picked before. They can't possibly. And they're geared to select only probability patterns in which Earth has a carbon dioxide atmosphere, one in which plant life, and therefore animal life, has never developed. Because if plants had evolved, the carbon dioxide would have been reduced to oxygen. Do you understand?"

"I understand it all very well and I'm not here for lectures," said Rimbro. "I want an investigation out of you and nothing else. It is quite humiliating to think I may be sharing my world, my own world, with something or other, and I don't propose to endure it."

"No, of course not," muttered Ching, avoiding. Mishnoff's sardonic glance. "We'll be there before night."

They were on their way to the twisting place with full equipment.

Mishnoff said, "I want to ask you something. Why do you go through that 'There's no need to worry, sir' routine? They always worry anyway. Where does it get you?"

"I've got to try. They *shouldn't* worry," said Ching petulantly. "Ever hear of a carbon dioxide planet that *was* inhabited? Besides, Rimbro is the type that starts rumors. I can spot them. By the time he's through, if he's encouraged, he'll say his sun went nova."

"*That* happens sometimes," said Mishnoff.

"So? One house is wiped out and one family dies. See, you're an obstructionist. In the old times, the times you like, if there were a flood in China or someplace, thousands of people would die. And that's out of a population of a measly billion or two."

Mishnoff muttered, "How do you know the Rimbro planet doesn't have life on it?"

"Carbon dioxide atmosphere."

"But suppose—" It was no use. Mishnoff couldn't say it. He finished lamely, "Suppose plant and animal life develops that can live on carbon dioxide."

"It's never been observed."

"In an infinite number of worlds, anything can happen." He finished that in a whisper. "Everything *must* happen."

"Chances are one in a duodecillion," said Ching, shrugging.

They arrived at the twisting point then, and, having utilized the freight twist for their vehicle (thus sending it into the Rimbro storage area), they entered the Rimbro probability pattern themselves. First Ching, then Mishnoff.

"A nice house," said Ching, with satisfaction. "Very nice model. Good taste."

"Hear anything?" asked Mishnoff.

"No."

Ching wandered into the garden. "Hey," he yelled. "Rhode Island Reds."

Mishnoff followed, looking up at the glass roof. The sun looked like the sun of a trillion other Earths.

He said absently, "There could be plant life, just starting out. The carbon dioxide might just be starting to drop in concentration. The computer would never know."

"And it would take millions of years for animal life to begin and millions more for it to come out of the sea."

"It doesn't have to follow that pattern."

Ching put an arm about his partner's shoulder. "You brood. Someday, you'll tell me what's really bothering you, instead of just hinting, and we can straighten you out."

Mishnoff shrugged off the encircling arm with an annoyed frown. Ching's tolerance was always hard to bear. He began, "Let's not psychotherapize—" He broke off, then whispered, "Listen."

There was a distant rumble. Again.

They placed the seismograph in the center of the room and activated the force field that penetrated downward and bound it rigidly to bedrock. They watched the quivering needle record the shocks.

Mishnoff said, "Surface waves only. Very superficial. It's not underground."

Ching looked a little more dismal, "What is it then?"

"I think," said Mishnoff, "we'd better find out." His face was gray with apprehension. "We'll have to set up a seismograph at another point and get a fix on the focus of the disturbance."

"Obviously," said Ching. "I'll go out with the other seismograph. You stay here."

"No," said Mishnoff, with energy. "I'll go out."

Mishnoff felt terrified, but he had no choice. If this were it, he would be prepared. He could get a warning through. Sending out an unsuspecting Ching would be disastrous. Nor could he warn Ching, who would certainly never believe him.

But since Mishnoff was not cast in the heroic mold, he trembled as he got into his oxygen suit and fumbled the disrupter as he tried to dissolve the force field locally in order to free the emergency exit.

"Any reason you want to go, particularly?" asked Ching, watching the other's inept manipulations. "I'm willing."

"It's all right. I'm going out," said Mishnoff, out of a dry throat, and stepped into the lock that led out onto the desolate surface of a lifeless Earth. A presumably lifeless Earth.

The sight was not unfamiliar to Mishnoff. He had seen its like dozens of times. Bare rock, weathered by wind and rain, crusted and powdered with sand in the gullies; a small and noisy brook beating itself against its stony course. All brown and gray; no sign of green. No sound of life.

Yet the sun was the same and, when night fell, the constellations would be the same.

The situation of the dwelling place was in that region which on Earth proper would be called Labrador. (It was Labrador here, too, really. It had been calculated that in not more than one out of a quadrillion or so Earths were there significant changes in the geological development. The continents were everywhere recognizable down to quite small details.)

Despite the situation and the time of the year, which was October, the temperature was sticky warm due to the hothouse effect of the carbon dioxide in this Earth's dead atmosphere.

From inside his suit, through the transparent visor, Mishnoff watched it all somberly. If the epicenter of the noise were close by, adjusting the second seismograph a mile or so away would be enough for the fix. If it weren't, they would have to bring in an air scooter. Well, assume the lesser complication to begin with.

Methodically, he made his way up a rocky hillside. Once at the top, he could choose his spot.

Once at the top, puffing and feeling the heat most unpleasantly, he found he didn't have to.

His heart was pounding so that he could scarcely hear his own voice as he yelled into his radio mouthpiece, "Hey, Ching, there's construction going on."

"What?" came back the appalled shout in his ears.

There was no mistake. Ground was being leveled. Machinery was at work. Rock was being blasted out.

Mishnoff shouted, "They're blasting. That's the noise."

Ching called back, "But it's impossible. The computer would never pick the same probability pattern twice. *It couldn't.*"

"You don't understand—" began Mishnoff.

But Ching was following his own thought processes. "Get over there, Mishnoff. I'm coming out, too."

"No, damn it. You stay there," cried Mishnoff in alarm. "Keep me in radio contact, and for God's sake be ready to leave for Earth proper on wings if I give the word."

"Why?" demanded Ching. "What's going on?"

"I don't know yet," said Mishnoff. "Give me a chance to find out."

To his own surprise, he noticed his teeth were chattering.

Muttering breathless curses at the computer, at probability patterns and at the insatiable need for living space on the part of a trillion human beings expanding in numbers like a puff of smoke, Mishnoff slithered and slipped down the other side of the slope, setting stones to rolling and rousing peculiar echoes.

• • • •

A man came out to meet him, dressed in a gas-tight suit, different in many details from Mishnoff's own, but obviously intended for the same purpose—to lead oxygen to the lungs.

Mishnoff gasped breathlessly into his mouthpiece, "Hold it, Ching. There's a man coming. Keep in touch." Mishnoff felt his heart pump more easily and the bellows of his lungs labor less.

The two men were staring at one another. The other man was blond and craggy of face. The look of surprise about him was too extreme to be feigned.

He said in a harsh voice, *"Wer sind Sie? Was machen Sie hier?"*

Mishnoff was thunderstruck. He'd studied ancient German for two years in the days when he expected to be an archeologist and he followed the comment despite the fact that the pronunciation was not what he had been taught. The stranger was asking his identity and his business there.

Stupidly, Mishnoff stammered, *"Sprechen Sie Deutsch?"* and then had to mutter reassurance to Ching whose agitated voice in his earpiece was demanding to know what the gibberish was all about.

The German-speaking one made no direct answer. He repeated, *"Wer sind Sie?"* and added impatiently, *"Hier ist für ein verrückten Spass keine Zeit."*

Mishnoff didn't feel like a joke either, particularly not a foolish one, but he continued, *"Sprechen Sie Planetisch?"*

He did not know the German for "Planetary Standard Language" so he had to guess. Too late, he thought he should have referred to it simply as English.

The other man stared wide-eyed at him. *"Sind Sie wahnsinnig?"*

Mishnoff was almost willing to settle for that, but in feeble self-defense, he said, "I'm not crazy, damn it. I mean, *"Auf der Erde woher Sie gekom—"*

He gave it up for lack of German, but the new idea that was rattling inside his skull would not quit its nagging. He had to find some way of testing it. He said desperately, *"Welches Jahr ist es jetzt?"*

Presumably, the stranger, who was questioning his sanity already, would be convinced of Mishnoff's insanity now that he was being asked what year it was, but it was one question for which Mishnoff had the necessary German.

The other muttered something that sounded suspiciously like good German swearing and then said, *"Es ist doch zwei tausend drei hundert vier-und-sechzig, und warum—"*

The stream of German that followed was completely incomprehensible to Mishnoff, but in any case he had had enough for the moment. If he translated the German correctly, the year given him was 2364, which was nearly two thousand years in the past. How could that be?

He muttered, *"Zwei tausend drei hundert vier-und sechzig?"*

"Ja, Ja," said the other, with deep sarcasm. *"Zwei tausend drei hundert vier-und-sechzig. Der ganze Jahr lang ist es so gewesen."*

Mishnoff shrugged. The statement that it had been so all year long was a feeble witticism even in German and it gained nothing in translation. He pondered.

But then the other's ironical tone deepening, the German-speaking one went on, *"Zwei tausend drei hundert vier-und-sechzig nach Hitler. Hilft das Ihnen vielleicht? Nach Hitler!"*

Mishnoff yelled with delight. "That *does* help me. *Es hilft! Hören Sie, bitte—"* He went on in broken German interspersed with scraps of Planetary, "For Heaven's sake, *um Gottes willen—"*

Making it 2364 after Hitler was different altogether.

He put German together desperately, trying to explain.

The other frowned and grew thoughtful. He lifted his gloved hand to stroke his chin or make some equivalent gesture, hit the transparent visor that covered his face and left his hand there uselessly, while he thought.

He said, suddenly, *"Ich heiss George Fallenby."*

To Mishnoff it seemed that the name must be of Anglo-Saxon derivation, although the change in vowel form as pronounced by the other made it seem Teutonic.

"Guten Tag," said Mishnoff awkwardly. *"Ich heiss Alec Mishnoff,"* and was suddenly aware of the Slavic derivation of his own name.

"Kommen Sie mit mir, Herr Mishnoff," said Fallenby.

Mishnoff followed with a strained smile, muttering into his transmitter, "It's all right, Ching. It's all right."

Back on Earth proper, Mishnoff faced the Sector's Bureau Head, who had grown old in the Service; whose every gray hair betokened a problem met and solved; and every missing hair a problem averted. He was a cautious man with eyes still bright and teeth that were still his own. His name was Berg.

He shook his head. "And they speak German: but the German you studied was two thousand years old."

"True," said Mishnoff. "But the English Hemingway used is two thousand years old and Planetary is close enough for anyone to be able to read it."

"Hmp. And who's this Hitler?"

"He was a sort of tribal chief in ancient times. He led the German tribe in one of the wars of the twentieth century, just about the time the Atomic Age started and true history began."

"Before the Devastation, you mean?"

"Right. There was a series of wars then. The Anglo-Saxon countries won out, and I suppose that's why the Earth speaks Planetary."

"And if Hitler and his Germans had won out, the world would speak German instead?"

"They *have* won out on Fallenby's Earth, sir, and they *do* speak German."

"And make their dates 'after Hitler' instead of A.D.?"

"Right. And I suppose there's an Earth in which the Slavic tribes won out and everyone speaks Russian."

"Somehow," said Berg, "it seems to me we should have foreseen it, and yet, as far as I know, no one has. After all, there are an infinite number of inhabited Earths, and we can't be the only one that has decided to solve the problem of unlimited population growth by expanding into the worlds of probability."

"Exactly," said Mishnoff earnestly, "and it seems to me that if you think of it, there must be countless inhabited Earths so doing and there must be many multiple occupations in the three hundred billion Earths we ourselves occupy. The only reason we caught this one is that, by sheer chance, they decided to build within a mile of the dwelling we had placed there. This is something we must check."

"You imply we ought to search all our Earths."

"I do, sir. We've got to make some settlement with other inhabited Earths. After all, there is room for all of us and to expand without agreement may result in all sorts of trouble and conflict."

"Yes," said Berg thoughtfully. "I agree with you."

Clarence Rimbro stared suspiciously at Berg's old face, creased now into all manner of benevolence.

"You're sure now?"

"Absolutely," said the Bureau Head. "We're sorry that you've had to accept temporary quarters for the last two weeks—"

"More like three."

"—three weeks, but you will be compensated."

"What was the noise?"

"Purely geological, sir. A rock was delicately balanced and, with the wind, it made occasional contact with the rocks of the hillside. We've removed it and surveyed the area to make certain that nothing similar will occur again."

Rimbro clutched his hat and said, "Well, thanks for your trouble."

"No thanks necessary, I assure you, Mr. Rimbro. This is our job."

Rimbro was ushered out, and Berg turned to Mishnoff, who had remained a quiet spectator of this completion of the Rimbro affair.

Berg said, "The Germans were nice about it, anyway. They admitted we had priority and got off. Room for everybody, they said. Of course, as it turned out, they build any number of dwellings on each unoccupied world. . . . And now there's the project of surveying our other worlds and making similar agreements with whomever we find. It's all strictly confidential, too.

It can't be made known to the populace without plenty of preparation. . . . Still, none of this is what I want to speak to you about."

"Oh?" said Mishnoff. Developments had not noticeably cheered him. His own bogey still concerned him.

Berg smiled at the younger man. "You understand, Mishnoff, we in the Bureau, and in the Planetary Government, too, are very appreciative of your quick thinking, of your understanding of the situation. This could have developed into something very tragic, had it not been for you. This appreciation will take some tangible form."

"Thank you, sir."

"But, as I said once before, this is something many of us should have thought of. How is it you did? . . . Now we've gone into your background a little. Your co-worker, Ching, tells us you have hinted in the past at some serious danger involved in our probability-pattern setup, and that you insisted on going out to meet the Germans although you were obviously frightened. You were anticipating what you actually found, were you not? And how did you do it?"

Mishnoff said confusedly, "No, no. That was not in my mind at all. It came as a surprise. I—"

Suddenly he stiffened. Why not now? They were grateful to him. He had proved that he was a man to be taken into account. One unexpected thing had already happened.

He said firmly, "There's something else."

"Yes?"

(How did one begin?) "There's no life in the Solar System other than the life on Earth."

"That's right," said Berg benevolently.

"And computation has it that the probability of developing any form of interstellar travel is so low as to be infinitesimal."

"What are you getting at?"

"That all this is so *in this probability!* But there must be some probability patterns in which other life *does* exist in the Solar System or in which interstellar drives *are* developed by dwellers in other star systems."

Berg frowned. "Theoretically."

"In one of these probabilities, Earth may be visited by such intelligences. If it were a probability pattern in which Earth is inhabited, it won't affect us; they'll have no connection with us in Earth proper. But if it were a probability pattern in which Earth is uninhabited and they set up some sort of a base, they may find, by happenstance, one of our dwelling places."

"Why ours?" demanded Berg dryly. "What not a dwelling place of the Germans, for instance?"

"Because we spot our dwellings one to a world. The German Earth doesn't. Probably very few others do. The odds are in favor of us by billions to one. And if extraterrestrials do find such a dwelling, they'll investigate and find the route to Earth proper, a highly developed, rich world."

"Not if we turn off the twisting place," said Berg.

"Once they know that twisting places exist, they can construct their own," said Mishnoff. "A race intelligent enough to travel through space could do that, and from the equipment in the dwelling they would take over, they could easily spot our particular probability. . . . And then how would we handle extraterrestrials? They're not Germans, or other Earths. They would have alien psychologies and motivations. And we're not even on our guard. We just keep setting up more and more worlds and increasing the chance every day that—"

His voice had risen in excitement and Berg shouted at him, "Nonsense. This is all ridiculous—"

The buzzer sounded and the communiplate brightened and showed the face of Ching. Ching's voice said, "I'm sorry to interrupt, but—"

"What is it?" demanded Berg savagely.

"There's a man here I don't know what to do with. He's drunk or crazy. He complains that his home is surrounded and that there are things staring through the glass roof of his garden."

"Things?" cried Mishnoff.

"Purple things with big red veins, three eyes and some sort of tentacles instead of hair. They have—"

But Mishnoff and Berg didn't hear the rest. They were staring at each other in sick horror.

The Message

They drank beer and reminisced as men will who have met after long separation. They called to mind the days under fire. They remembered sergeants and girls, both with exaggeration. Deadly things became humorous in retrospect, and trifles disregarded for ten years were hauled out for airing.

Including, of course, the perennial mystery.

"How do you account for it?" asked the first. "Who started it?"

The second shrugged. "No one started it. Everyone was doing it, like a disease. You, too, I suppose."

The first chuckled.

The third one said softly, "I never saw the fun in it. Maybe because I came across it first when I was under fire for the first time. North Africa."

"Really?" said the second.

"The first night on the beaches of Oran. I was getting under cover, making for some native shack and I saw it in the light of a flare—"

George was deliriously happy. Two years of red tape and now he was finally back in the past. Now he could complete his paper on the social life of the foot soldier of World War II with some authentic details.

Out of the warless, insipid society of the thirtieth century, he found himself for one glorious moment in the tense, superlative drama of the warlike twentieth.

North Africa! Site of the first great sea-borne invasion of the war! How the temporal physicists had scanned the area for the perfect spot and moment. This shadow of an empty wooden building was it. No human would approach for a known number of minutes. No blast would seriously affect it in that time. By being there, George would not affect history. He would be that ideal of the temporal physicist, the "pure observer."

It was even more terrific than he had imagined. There was the perpetual roar of artillery, the unseen tearing of planes overhead. There were the periodic lines of tracer bullets splitting the sky and the occasional ghastly glow of a flare twisting downward.

And *he* was here! He, George, was part of the war, part of an intense kind of life forever gone from the world of the thirtieth century, grown tame and gentle.

He imagined he could see the shadows of an advancing column of soldiers, hear the low cautious monosyllables slip from one to another. How he longed to be one of them in truth, not merely a momentary intruder, a "pure observer."

He stopped his note taking and stared at his stylus, its micro-light hypnotizing him for a moment. A sudden idea had overwhelmed him and he looked at the wood against which his shoulder pressed. This moment must not pass unforgotten into history. Surely doing this would affect nothing. He would use the older English dialect and there would be no suspicion.

He did it quickly and then spied a soldier running desperately toward the structure, dodging a burst of bullets. George knew his time was up, and, even as he knew it, found himself back in the thirtieth century.

It didn't matter. For those few minutes he had been part of World War II. A small part, but *part*. And others would know it. They might not know they knew it, but someone perhaps would repeat the message to himself.

Someone, perhaps that man running for shelter, would read it and know that along with all the heroes of the twentieth century was the "pure observer," the man from the thirtieth century, George Kilroy. *He* was there!

Satisfaction Guaranteed

I

Tony was tall and darkly handsome, with an incredibly patrician air drawn into every line of his unchangeable expression, and Claire Belmont regarded him through the crack in the door with a mixture of horror and dismay.

"I can't, Larry. I just can't have him in the house." Feverishly, she was searching her paralyzed mind for a stronger way of putting it; some way that would make sense and settle things, but she could only end with a simple repetition.

"Well, I can't!"

Larry Belmont regarded his wife stiffly, and there was that spark of impatience in his eyes that Claire hated to see, since she felt her own incompetence mirrored in it. "We're committed, Claire," he said, "and I can't have you backing out now. The company is sending me to Washington on this basis, and it probably means a promotion. It's perfectly safe and you know it. What's your objection?"

She frowned helplessly. "It just gives me the chills. I couldn't bear him."

"He's as human as you or I, almost. So, no nonsense. Come, get out there."

His hand was in the small of her back, shoving; and she found herself in her own living room, shivering. *It* was there, looking at her with a precise politeness, as though appraising his hostess-to-be of the next three weeks. Dr. Susan Calvin was there, too, sitting stiffly in thin-lipped abstraction. She had the cold, faraway look of someone who has worked with machines so long that a little of the steel had entered the blood.

"Hello," crackled Claire in general, and ineffectual, greeting.

But Larry was busily saving the situation with a spurious gaiety. "Here, Claire, I want you to meet Tony, a swell guy. This is my wife, Claire, Tony, old boy." Larry's hand draped itself amiably over Tony's shoulder, but Tony remained unresponsive and expressionless under the pressure.

He said, "How do you do, Mrs. Belmont."

And Claire jumped at Tony's voice. It was deep and mellow, smooth as the hair on his head or the skin on his face.

Before she could stop herself, she said, "Oh, my—you talk."

"Why not? Did you expect that I didn't?"

But Claire could only smile weakly. She didn't really know what she had expected. She looked away, then let him slide gently into the corner of her eye. His hair was smooth and black, like polished plastic—or was it really composed of separate hairs? And was the even, olive skin of his hands and face continued on past the obscurement of his formally cut clothing?

She was lost in the shuddering wonder of it, and had to force her thoughts back into place to meet Dr. Calvin's flat, unemotional voice.

"Mrs. Belmont, I hope you appreciate the importance of this experiment. Your husband tells me he has given you some of the background. I would like to give you more, as the senior psychologist of the U.S. Robots and Mechanical Men Corporation.

"Tony is a robot. His actual designation on the company files is TN-3, but he will answer to Tony. He is not a mechanical monster, nor simply a calculating machine of the type that were developed during World War II, fifty years ago. He has an artificial brain nearly as complicated as our own. It is an immense telephone switchboard on an atomic scale, so that billions of possible 'telephone connections' can be compressed into an instrument that will fit inside a skull.

"Such brains are manufactured for each model of robot specifically. Each contains a precalculated set of connections so that each robot knows the English language to start with and enough of anything else that may be necessary to perform his job.

"Until now, U.S. Robots has confined its manufacturing activity to industrial models for use in places where human labor is impractical—in deep mines, for instance, or in underwater work. But we want to invade the city and the home. To do so, we must get the ordinary man and woman to accept these robots without fear. You understand that there is nothing to fear."

"There isn't, Claire," interposed Larry earnestly. "Take my word for it. It's impossible for him to do any harm. You know I wouldn't leave him with you otherwise."

Claire cast a quick, secret glance at Tony and lowered her voice. "What if I make him angry?"

"You needn't whisper," said Dr. Calvin calmly. "He *can't* get angry with you, my dear. I told you that the switchboard connections of his brain were predetermined. Well, the most important connection of all is what we call 'The First Law of Robotics,' and it is merely this: 'No robot can harm a human being, or, through inaction, allow a human being to come to harm.' All robots are built so. No robot can be forced in any way to do harm to any human. So, you see, we need you and Tony as a preliminary experiment for our own guidance, while your husband is in Washington to arrange for government-supervised legal tests."

"You mean all this isn't legal?"

Larry cleared his throat. "Not just yet, but it's all right. He won't leave the house, and you mustn't let anyone see him. That's all. . . . And, Claire, I'd stay with you, but I know too much about the robots. We must have a completely inexperienced tester so that we can have severe conditions. It's necessary."

"Oh, well," muttered Claire. Then, as a thought struck her, "But what does he do?"

"Housework," said Dr. Calvin shortly.

She got up to leave, and it was Larry who saw her to the front door. Claire stayed behind drearily. She caught a glimpse of herself in the mirror above the mantelpiece, and looked away hastily. She was very tired of her small, mousy face and her dim, unimaginative hair. Then she caught Tony's eyes upon her and almost smiled before she remembered. . . .

He was only a machine.

Larry Belmont was on his way to the airport when he caught a glimpse of Gladys Claffern. She was the type of woman who seemed made to be seen in glimpses. . . . Perfectly and precisely manufactured; dressed with thoughtful hand and eye; too gleaming to be stared at.

The little smile that preceded her and the faint scent that trailed her were a pair of beckoning fingers. Larry felt his stride break; he touched his hat, then hurried on.

As always he felt that vague anger. If Claire could only push her way into the Claffern clique, it would help so much. But what was the use.

Claire! The few times she had come face to face with Gladys, the little fool had been tongue-tied. He had no illusions. The testing of Tony was his big chance, and it was in Claire's hands. How much safer it would be in the hands of someone like Gladys Claffern.

Claire woke the second morning to the sound of a subdued knock on the bedroom door. Her mind clamored, then went icy. She had avoided Tony the first day, smiling thinly when she met him and brushing past with a wordless sound of apology.

"Is that you—Tony?"

"Yes, Mrs. Belmont. May I enter?"

She must have said yes, because he was in the room, quite suddenly and noiselessly. Her eyes and nose were simultaneously aware of the tray he was carrying.

"Breakfast?" she said.

"If you please."

She wouldn't have dared to refuse, so she pushed herself slowly into a sitting position and received it: poached eggs, buttered toast, coffee.

"I have brought the sugar and cream separately," said Tony. "I expect to learn your preference with time, in this and in other things."

She waited.

Tony, standing there straight and pliant as a metal rule, asked, after a moment, "Would you prefer to eat in privacy?"

"Yes. . . . I mean, if you don't mind."

"Will you need help later in dressing?"

"Oh, my, no!" She clutched frantically at the sheet, so that the coffee hovered at the edge of catastrophe. She remained so, in rigor, then sank helplessly back against the pillow when the door closed him out of her sight again.

She got through breakfast somehow. . . . He was only a machine, and if it were only more visible that he were it wouldn't be so frightening. Or if his expression would change. It just stayed there, nailed on. You couldn't tell what went on behind those dark eyes and that smooth, olive skin-stuff. The coffee cup beat a faint castanet for a moment as she set it back, empty, on the tray.

Then she realized that she had forgotten to add the sugar and cream after all, and she did so hate black coffee.

She burned a straight path from bedroom to kitchen after dressing. It was her house, after all, and there wasn't anything frippy about her, but she liked her kitchen clean. He should have waited for supervision. . . .

But when she entered, she found a kitchen that might have been minted fire-new from the factory the moment before.

She stopped, stared, turned on her heel and nearly ran into Tony. She yelped.

"May I help?" he asked.

"Tony," and she scraped the anger off the edges of her mind's panic, "you must make some noise when you walk. I can't have you stalking me, you know. . . . Didn't you use this kitchen?"

"I did, Mrs. Belmont."

"It doesn't look it."

"I cleaned up afterward. Isn't that customary?"

Claire opened her eyes wide. After all, what could one say to that. She opened the oven compartment that held the pots, took a quick, unseeing look at the metallic glitter inside, then said with a tremor, "Very good. Quite satisfactory."

If at the moment, he had beamed; if he had smiled; if he had quirked the corner of his mouth the slightest bit, she felt that she could have warmed to him. But he remained an English lord in repose, as he said, "Thank you, Mrs. Belmont. Would you come into the living room?"

She did, and it struck her at once. "Have you been polishing the furniture?"

"Is it satisfactory, Mrs. Belmont?"

"But when? You didn't do it yesterday."

"Last night, of course."

"You burned the lights all night?"

"Oh, no. That wouldn't have been necessary. I've a built-in ultra-violet source. I can see in ultraviolet. And, of course, I don't require sleep."

He did require admiration, though. She realized that, then. He had to know that he was pleasing her. But she couldn't bring herself to supply that pleasure for him.

She could only say sourly, "Your kind will put ordinary houseworkers out of business."

"There is work of much greater importance they can be put to in the world, once they are freed of drudgery. After all, Mrs. Belmont, things like myself can be manufactured. But nothing yet can imitate the creativity and versatility of a human brain, like yours."

And though his face gave no hint, his voice was warmly surcharged with awe and admiration, so that Claire flushed and muttered, *"My* brain! You can have it."

Tony approached a little and said, "You must be unhappy to say such a thing. Is there anything I can do?"

For a moment, Claire felt like laughing. It *was* a ridiculous situation. Here was an animated carpet-sweeper, dishwasher, furniture-polisher, general factotum, rising from the factory table—and offering his services as consoler and confidant.

Yet she said suddenly, in a burst of woe and voice, "Mr. Belmont doesn't think I have a brain, if you must know. . . . And I suppose I haven't." She couldn't cry in front of him. She felt, for some reason, that she had the honor of the human race to support against this mere creation.

"It's lately," she added. "It was all right when he was a student; when he was just starting. But I can't be a big man's wife; and he's getting to be a big man. He wants me to be a hostess and an entry into social life for him—like G—guh—guh—Gladys Claffern."

Her nose was red, and she looked away.

But Tony wasn't watching her. His eyes wandered about the room. "I can help you run the house."

"But it's no good," she said fiercely. "It needs a touch I can't give it. I can only make it comfortable; I can't ever make it the kind they take pictures of for the Home Beautiful magazines."

"Do you want that kind?"

"Does it do any good—wanting?"

Tony's eyes were on her, full. "I could help."

"Do you know anything about interior decoration?"

"Is it something a good housekeeper should know?"

"Oh, yes."

"Then I have the potentialities of learning it. Can you get me books on the subject?"

Something started then.

Claire, clutching her hat against the brawling liberties of the wind, had manipulated two fat volumes on the home arts back from the public library. She watched Tony as he opened one of them and flipped the pages. It was the first time she had watched his fingers flicker at anything like fine work.

I don't see how they do it, she thought, and on a sudden impulse reached for his hand and pulled it toward herself. Tony did not resist, but let it lie limp for inspection.

She said, "It's remarkable. Even your fingernails look natural."

"That's deliberate, of course," said Tony. Then, chattily, "The skin is a flexible plastic, and the skeletal framework is a light metal alloy. Does that amuse you?"

"Oh, no." She lifted her reddened face. "I just feel a little embarrassed at sort of poking into your insides. It's none of my business. You don't ask me about mine."

"My brain paths don't include that type of curiosity. I can only act within my limitations, you know."

And Claire felt something tighten inside her in the silence that followed. Why did she keep forgetting he was a machine. Now the thing itself had to remind her. Was she so starved for sympathy that she would even accept a robot as equal—because he sympathized?

She noticed Tony was still flipping the pages—almost helplessly—and there was a quick, shooting sense of relieved superiority within her. "You can't read, can you?"

Tony looked up at her; his voice calm, unreproachful. "I *am* reading, Mrs. Belmont."

"But—" She pointed at the book in a meaningless gesture.

"I am scanning the pages, if that's what you mean. My sense of reading is photographic."

It was evening then, and when Claire eventually went to bed Tony was well into the second volume, sitting there in the dark, or what seemed dark to Claire's limited eyes.

Her last thought, the one that clamored at her just as her mind let go and tumbled, was a queer one. She remembered his hand again; the touch of it. It had been warm and soft, like a human being's.

How clever of the factory, she thought, and softly ebbed to sleep.

It was the library continuously, thereafter, for several days. Tony suggested the fields of study, which branched out quickly. There were books on color matching and on cosmetics; on carpentry and on fashions; on art and on the history of costumes.

He turned the pages of each book before his solemn eyes, and, as quickly as he turned, he read; nor did he seem capable of forgetting.

Before the end of the week, he had insisted on cutting her hair, introducing her to a new method of arranging it, adjusting her eyebrow line a bit and changing the shade of her powder and lipstick.

She had palpitated in nervous dread for half an hour under the delicate touch of his inhuman fingers and then looked in the mirror.

"There is more that can be done," said Tony, "especially in clothes. How do you find it for a beginning?"

And she hadn't answered; not for quite a while. Not until she had absorbed the identity of the stranger in the glass and cooled the wonder at the beauty of it all. Then she had said chokingly, never once taking her eyes from the warming image, "Yes, Tony, quite good—for a beginning."

She said nothing of this in her letters to Larry. Let him see it all at once. And something in her realized that it wasn't only the surprise she would enjoy. It was going to be a kind of revenge.

Tony said one morning, "It's time to start buying, and I'm not allowed to leave the house. If I write out exactly what we must have, can I trust you to get it? We need drapery, and furniture fabric, wallpaper, carpeting, paint, clothing—and any number of small things."

"You can't get these things to your own specifications at a stroke's notice," said Claire doubtfully.

"You can get fairly close, if you go through the city and if money is no object."

"But, Tony, money is certainly an object."

"Not at all. Stop off at U.S. Robots in the first place. I'll write a note for you. You see Dr. Calvin, and tell her that I said it was part of the experiment."

Dr. Calvin, somehow, didn't frighten her as on that first evening. With her new face and a new hat, she couldn't be quite the old Claire. The psychologist listened carefully, asked a few questions, nodded—and then Claire found herself walking out, armed with an unlimited charge account against the assets of U.S. Robots and Mechanical Men Corporation.

It is wonderful what money will do. With a store's contents at her feet, a saleslady's dictum was not necessarily a voice from above; the uplifted eyebrow of a decorator was not anything like Jove's thunder.

And once, when an Exalted Plumpness at one of the most lordly of the garment salons had insistently poohed her description of the wardrobe she must have with counterpronouncements in accents of the purest Fifty-seventh Street French, she called up Tony, then held the phone out to Monsieur.

"If you don't mind"—voice firm, but fingers twisting a bit—"I'd like you to talk to my—uh—secretary."

Pudgy proceeded to the phone with a solemn arm crooked behind his back. He lifted the phone in two fingers and said delicately, "Yes." A short pause, another "Yes," then a much longer pause, a squeaky beginning of an objection that perished quickly, another pause, a very meek "Yes," and the phone was restored to its cradle.

"If Madam will come with me," he said, hurt and distant, "I will try to supply her needs."

"Just a second." Claire rushed back to the phone, and dialed again. "Hello, Tony. I don't know what you said, but it worked. Thanks. You're a—" She struggled for the appropriate word, gave up and ended in a final little squeak, "—a—a dear!"

It was Gladys Claffern looking at her when she turned from the phone again. A slightly amused and slightly amazed Gladys Claffern, looking at her out of a face tilted a bit to one side.

"Mrs. Belmont?"

It all drained out of Claire—just like that. She could only nod—stupidly, like a marionette.

Gladys smiled with an insolence you couldn't put your finger on. "I didn't know you shopped here?" As if the place had, in her eyes, definitely lost caste through the fact.

"I don't, usually," said Claire humbly.

"And haven't you done something to your hair? It's quite—quaint. . . . Oh, I hope you'll excuse me, but isn't your husband's name. Lawrence? It seems to me that it's Lawrence."

Claire's teeth clenched, but she had to explain. She *had* to. "Tony is a friend of my husband's. He's helping me select some things."

"I understand. And quite a *dear* about it, I imagine." She passed on smiling, carrying the light and the warmth of the world with her.

Claire did not question the fact that it was to Tony that she turned for consolation. Ten days had cured her of reluctance. And she could weep before him; weep and rage.

"I was a complete f-fool," she stormed, wrenching at her water-logged handkerchief. "She does that to me. I don't know why. She just does. I should have—kicked her. I should have knocked her down and stamped on her."

"Can you hate a human being so much?" asked Tony, in puzzled softness. "That part of a human mind is closed to me."

"Oh, it isn't she," she moaned. "It's myself, I suppose. She's everything I want to be—on the outside, anyway. . . . And I can't be."

Tony's voice was forceful and low in her ear. "You can be, Mrs. Belmont. You *can* be. We have ten days yet, and in ten days the house will no longer be itself. Haven't we been planning that?"

"And how will that help me—with her?"

"Invite her here. Invite her friends. Have it the evening before I—before I leave. It will be a housewarming, in a way."

"She won't come."

"Yes, she will. She'll come to laugh. . . . And she won't be able to."

"Do you really think so? Oh, Tony, do you think we can do it?" She had both his hands in hers. . . . And then, with her face flung aside, "But what good would it be? It won't be I; it will be you that's doing it. I can't ride your back."

"Nobody lives in splendid singleness," whispered Tony. "They've put that knowledge in me. What you, or anyone, see in Gladys Claffern is not just Gladys Claffern. She rides the back of all that money and social position can bring. She doesn't question that. Why should you? . . . And look at it this way, Mrs. Belmont. I am manufactured to obey, but the extent of my obedience is for myself to determine. I can follow orders niggardly or liberally. For you, it is liberal, because you are what I have been manufactured to see human beings as. You are kind, friendly, unassuming. Mrs. Claffern, as you describe her, is not, and I wouldn't obey her as I would you. So it *is* you, and not I, Mrs. Belmont, that is doing all this."

He withdrew his hands from hers then, and Claire looked at that expressionless face no one could read—wondering. She was suddenly frightened again in a completely new way.

She swallowed nervously and stared at her hands, which were still tingling with the pressure of his fingers. She hadn't imagined it; his fingers had pressed hers, gently, tenderly, just before they moved away.

No!

Its fingers . . . *Its* fingers. . . .

She ran to the bathroom and scrubbed her hands—blindly, uselessly.

She was a bit shy of him the next day; watching him narrowly; waiting to see what might follow—and for a while nothing did.

Tony was working. If there was any difficulty in technique in putting up wallpaper, or utilizing the quick-drying paint, Tony's activity did not show it. His hands moved precisely; his fingers were deft and sure.

He worked all night. She never heard him, but each morning was a new adventure. She couldn't count the number of things that had been done, and by evening she was still finding new touches—and another night had come.

She tried to help only once and her human clumsiness marred that. *He* was in the next room, and she was hanging a picture in the spot marked by Tony's mathematical eyes. The little mark was there; the picture was there; and a revulsion against idleness was there.

But she was nervous, or the ladder was rickety. It didn't matter. She felt it going, and she cried out. It tumbled without her, for Tony, with far more than flesh-and-blood quickness, had been under her.

His calm, dark eyes said nothing at all, and his warm voice said only words. "Are you hurt, Mrs. Belmont?"

She noticed for an instant that her falling hand must have mussed that sleek hair of his, because for the first time she could see for herself that it was composed of distinct strands—fine black hairs.

And then, all at once, she was conscious of his arms about her shoulders and under her knees—holding her tightly and warmly.

She pushed, and her scream was loud in her own ears. She spent the rest of the day in her room, and thereafter she slept with a chair upended against the doorknob of her bedroom door.

She had sent out the invitations, and, as Tony had said, they were accepted. She had only to wait for the last evening.

It came, too, after the rest of them, in its proper place. The house was scarcely her own. She went through it one last time—and every room had been changed. She, herself, was in clothes she would never have dared wear before. . . . And when you put them on, you put on pride and confidence with them.

She tried a polite look of contemptuous amusement before the mirror, and the mirror sneered back at her masterfully.

What would Larry say? . . . It didn't matter, somehow. The exciting days weren't coming with him. They were leaving with Tony. Now wasn't that strange? She tried to recapture her mood of three weeks before and failed completely.

The clock shrieked eight at her in eight breathless installments, and she turned to Tony. "They'll be here soon, Tony. You'd better get into the basement. We can't let them—"

She stared a moment, then said weakly, "Tony?" and more strongly, "Tony?" and nearly a scream, *"Tony!"*

But his arms were around her now; his face was close to hers; the pressure of his embrace was relentless. She heard his voice through a haze of emotional jumble.

"Claire," the voice said, "there are many things I am not made to understand, and this must be one of them. I am leaving tomorrow, and I don't want to. I find that there is more in me than just a desire to please you. Isn't it strange?"

His face was closer; his lips were warm, but with no breath behind them —for machines do not breathe. They were almost on hers.

. . . And the bell sounded.

For a moment, she struggled breathlessly, and then he was gone and nowhere in sight, and the bell was sounding again. Its intermittent shrillness was insistent.

The curtains on the front windows had been pulled open. They had been closed fifteen minutes earlier. She *knew* that.

They must have seen, then. They must *all* have seen—everything!

They came in so politely, all in a bunch—the pack come to howl—with their sharp, darting eyes piercing everywhere. They *had* seen. Why else would Gladys ask in her jabbingest manner after Larry? And Claire was spurred to a desperate and reckless defiance.

Yes, he *is* away. He'll be back tomorrow, I suppose. No, I haven't been lonely here myself. Not a bit. I've had an exciting time. And she laughed at them. Why not? What could they do? Larry would know the truth, if it ever came to him, the story of what they thought they saw.

But *they* didn't laugh.

She could read that in the fury in Gladys Claffern's eyes; in the false sparkle of her words; in her desire to leave early. And as she parted with them, she caught one last, anonymous whisper—disjointed.

". . . never saw anything like . . . so *handsome*—"

And she knew what it was that had enabled her to finger-snap them so. Let each cat mew; and let each cat know—that she might be prettier than Claire Belmont, and grander, and richer—but not one, *not one,* could have so handsome a lover!

And then she remembered again—again—again, that Tony was a machine, and her skin crawled.

"Go away! Leave me be!" she cried to the empty room and ran to her bed. She wept wakefully all that night and the next morning, almost before dawn, when the streets were empty, a car drew up to the house and took Tony away.

Lawrence Belmont passed Dr. Calvin's office, and, on impulse, knocked. He found her with Mathematician Peter Bogert, but did not hesitate on that account.

He said, "Claire tells me that U.S. Robots paid for all that was done at my house—"

"Yes," said Dr. Calvin. "We've written it off, as a valuable and necessary part of the experiment. With your new position as Associate Engineer, you'll be able to keep it up, I think."

"That's not what I'm worried about. With Washington agreeing to the tests, we'll be able to get a TN model of our own by next year, I think." He turned hesitantly, as though to go, and as hesitantly turned back again.

"Well, Mr. Belmont?" asked Dr. Calvin, after a pause.

"I wonder—" began Larry. "I wonder what really happened there. She—Claire, I mean—seems so different. It's not just her looks—though, frankly, I'm amazed." He laughed nervously. "It's *her!* She's not my wife, really—I can't explain it."

"Why try? Are you disappointed with any part of the change?"

"On the contrary. But it's a little frightening, too, you see—"

"I wouldn't worry, Mr. Belmont. Your wife has handled herself very well. Frankly, I never expected to have the experiment yield such a thorough and complete test. We know exactly what corrections must be made in the TN model, and the credit belongs entirely to Mrs. Belmont. If you want me to be very honest, I think your wife deserves your promotion more than you do."

Larry flinched visibly at that. "As long as it's in the family," he murmured unconvincingly and left.

Susan Calvin looked after him, "I think that hurt—I hope. . . . Have you read Tony's report, Peter?"

"Thoroughly," said Bogert. "And won't the TN-3 model need changes?"

"Oh, you think so, too?" questioned Calvin sharply. "What's your reasoning?"

Bogert frowned. "I don't need any. It's obvious on the face of it that we can't have a robot loose which makes love to his mistress, if you don't mind the pun."

"Love! Peter, you sicken me. You really don't understand? That machine had to obey the First Law. He couldn't allow harm to come to a human being, and harm was coming to Claire Belmont through her own sense of inadequacy. So he made love to her, since what woman would fail to appreciate the compliment of being able to stir passion in a machine—in a cold, soulless machine. And he opened the curtains that night deliberately, that the others might see and envy—without any risk possible to Claire's marriage. I think it was clever of Tony—"

"Do you? What's the difference whether it was pretense or not, Susan? It still has its horrifying effect. Read the report again. She avoided him. She screamed when he held her. She didn't sleep that last night—in hysterics. We can't have that."

"Peter, you're blind. You're as blind as I was. The TN model will be rebuilt entirely, but not for your reason. Quite otherwise; quite otherwise.

Strange that I overlooked it in the first place," her eyes were opaquely thoughtful, "but perhaps it reflects a shortcoming in myself. You see, Peter, machines can't fall in love, but—even when it's hopeless and horrifying—women can!"

Hell-Fire

There was a stir as of a very polite first-night audience. Only a handful of scientists were present, a sprinkling of high brass, some Congressmen, a few newsmen.

Alvin Horner of the Washington Bureau of the Continental Press found himself next to Joseph Vincenzo of Los Alamos, and said, *"Now* we ought to learn something."

Vincenzo stared at him through bifocals and said, "Not the important thing."

Horner frowned. This was to be the first super-slow-motion films of an atomic explosion. With trick lenses changing directional polarization in flickers, the moment of explosion would be divided into billionth-second snaps. Yesterday, an A-bomb had exploded. Today, those snaps would show the explosion in incredible detail.

Horner said, "You think this won't work?"

Vincenzo looked tormented. "It will work. We've run pilot tests. But the important thing—"

"Which is?"

"That these bombs are man's death sentence. We don't seem to be able to learn that." Vincenzo nodded. "Look at them here. They're excited and thrilled, but not afraid."

The newsman said, "They know the danger. They're afraid, too."

"Not enough," said the scientist. "I've seen men watch an H-bomb blow an island into a hole and then go home and sleep. That's the way men are.

For thousands of years, hell-fire has been preached to them, and it's made no real impression."

"Hell-fire: Are you religious, sir?"

"What you saw yesterday was hell-fire. An exploding atom bomb is hell-fire. Literally."

That was enough for Horner. He got up and changed his seat, but watched the audience uneasily. Were any afraid? Did any worry about hell-fire? It didn't seem so to him.

The lights went out, the projector started. On the screen, the firing tower stood gaunt. The audience grew tensely quiet.

Then a dot of light appeared at the apex of the tower, a brilliant, burning point, slowly budding in a lazy, outward elbowing, this way and that, taking on uneven shapes of light and shadow, growing oval.

A man cried out chokingly, then others. A hoarse babble of noise, followed by thick silence. Horner could smell fear, taste terror in his own mouth, feel his blood freeze.

The oval fireball had sprouted projections, then paused a moment in stasis, before expanding rapidly into a bright and featureless sphere.

That moment of stasis—the fireball had shown dark spots for eyes, with dark lines for thin, flaring eyebrows, a hairline coming down V-shaped, a mouth twisted upward, laughing wildly in the hell-fire—and horns.

The Last Trump

The Archangel Gabriel was quite casual about the whole thing. Idly, he let the tip of one wing graze the planet Mars, which, being of mere matter, was unaffected by the contact.

He said, "It's a settled matter, Etheriel. There's nothing to be done about it now. The Day of Resurrection is due."

Etheriel, a very junior seraph who had been created not quite a thousand years earlier as men counted time, quivered so that distinct vortices appeared in the continuum. Ever since his creation, he had been in immediate charge of Earth and environs. As a job, it was a sinecure, a cubbyhole, a dead end, but through the centuries he had come to take a perverse pride in the world.

"But you'll be disrupting my world without notice."

"Not at all. Not at all. Certain passages occur in the Book of Daniel and in the Apocalypse of St. John which are clear enough."

"They are? Having been copied from scribe to scribe? I wonder if two words in a row are left unchanged."

"There are hints in the Rig-Veda, in the Confucian Analects—"

"Which are the property of isolated cultural groups which exist as a thin aristocracy—"

"The Gilgamesh Chronicle speaks out plainly."

"Much of the Gilgamesh Chronicle was destroyed with the library of Ashurbanipal sixteen hundred years, Earth-style, before my creation."

"There are certain features of the Great Pyramid and a pattern in the inlaid jewels of the Taj Mahal—"

"Which are so subtle that no man has ever rightly interpreted them."

Gabriel said wearily, "If you're going to object to everything, there's no use discussing the matter. In any case, *you* ought to know about it. In matters concerning Earth, you're omniscient."

"Yes, if I choose to be. I've had much to concern me here and investigating the possibilities of Resurrection did not, I confess, occur to me."

"Well, it should have. All the papers involved are in the files of the Council of Ascendants. You could have availed yourself of them at any time."

"I tell you all my time was needed here. You have no idea of the deadly efficiency of the Adversary on this planet. It took all my efforts to curb him, and even so—"

"Why, yes"—Gabriel stroked a comet as it passed—"he does seem to have won his little victories. I note as I let the interlocking factual pattern of this miserable little world flow through me that this is one of those setups with matter-energy equivalence."

"So it is," said Etheriel.

"And they are playing with it."

"I'm afraid so."

"Then what better time for ending the matter?"

"I'll be able to handle it, I assure you. Their nuclear bombs will not destroy them."

"I wonder. Well, now suppose you let me continue, Etheriel. The appointed moment approaches."

The seraph said stubbornly, "I would like to see the documents in the case."

"If you insist." The wording of an Act of Ascendancy appeared in glittering symbols against the deep black of the airless firmament.

Etheriel read aloud: "It is hereby directed by order of Council that the Archangel Gabriel, Serial number etcetera, etcetera (well, that's you, at any rate), will approach Planet, Class A, number G753990, hereinafter known as Earth, and on January 1, 1957, at 12:01 P.M., using local time values—" He finished reading in gloomy silence.

"Satisfied?"

"No, but I'm helpless."

Gabriel smiled. A trumpet appeared in space, in shape like an earthly trumpet, but its burnished gold extended from Earth to sun. It was raised to Gabriel's glittering beautiful lips.

"Can't you let me have a little time to take this up with the Council?" asked Etheriel desperately.

"What good would it do you? The act is countersigned by the Chief, and you know that an act countersigned by the Chief is absolutely irrevocable.

And now, if you don't mind, it is almost the stipulated second and I want to be done with this as I have other matters of much greater moment on my mind. Would you step out of my way a little? Thank you."

Gabriel blew, and a clean, thin sound of perfect pitch and crystalline delicacy filled all the universe to the furthest star. As it sounded, there was a tiny moment of stasis as thin as the line separating past from future, and then the fabric of worlds collapsed upon itself and matter was gathered back into the primeval chaos from which it had once sprung at a word. The stars and nebulae were gone, and the cosmic dust, the sun, the planets, the moon; all, all, all except Earth itself, which spun as before in a universe now completely empty.

The Last Trump had sounded.

R. E. Mann (known to all who knew him simply as R.E.) eased himself into the offices of the Billikan Bitsies factory and stared somberly at the tall man (gaunt but with a certain faded elegance about his neat gray mustache) who bent intently over a sheaf of papers on his desk.

R.E. looked at his wristwatch, which still said 7:01, having ceased running at that time. It was Eastern standard time, of course; 12:01 P.M. Greenwich time. His dark brown eyes, staring sharply out over a pair of pronounced cheekbones, caught those of the other.

For a moment, the tall man stared at him blankly. Then he said, "Can I do anything for you?"

"Horatio J. Billikan, I presume? Owner of this place?"

"Yes."

"I'm R. E. Mann and I couldn't help but stop in when I finally found someone at work. Don't you know what today is?"

"Today?"

"It's Resurrection Day."

"Oh, that! I know it. I heard the blast. Fit to wake the dead. . . . That's rather a good one, don't you think?" He chuckled for a moment, then went on. "It woke me at seven in the morning. I nudged my wife. She slept through it, of course. I always said she would. 'It's the Last Trump, dear,' I said. Hortense, that's my wife, said, 'All right,' and went back to sleep. I bathed, shaved, dressed and came to work."

"But why?"

"Why not?"

"None of your workers have come in."

"No, poor souls. They'll take a holiday just at first. You've got to expect that. After all, it isn't every day that the world comes to an end. Frankly, it's just as well. It gives me a chance to straighten out my personal correspondence without interruptions. Telephone hasn't rung once."

He stood up and went to the window. "It's a great improvement. No blinding sun any more and the snow's gone. There's a pleasant light and a pleasant warmth. Very good arrangement. . . . But now, if you don't mind, I'm *rather* busy, so if you'll excuse me—"

A great, hoarse voice interrupted with a, "Just a minute, Horatio," and a gentleman, looking remarkably like Billikan in a somewhat craggier way, followed his prominent nose into the office and struck an attitude of offended dignity which was scarcely spoiled by the fact that he was quite naked. "May I ask why you've shut down Bitsies?"

Billikan looked faint. "Good Heavens," he said, "it's Father. Wherever did you come from?"

"From the graveyard," roared Billikan, Senior. "Where on Earth else? They're coming out of the ground there by the dozens. Every one of them naked. Women, too."

Billikan cleared his throat. "I'll get you some clothes, Father. I'll bring them to you from home."

"Never mind that. Business first. Business first."

R.E. came out of his musing. "Is everyone coming out of their graves at the same time, sir?"

He stared curiously at Billikan, Senior, as he spoke. The old man's appearance was one of robust age. His cheeks were furrowed but glowed with health. His age, R.E. decided, was exactly what it was at the moment of his death, but his body was as it should have been at that age if it functioned ideally.

Billikan, Senior, said, "No, sir, they are not. The newer graves are coming up first. Pottersby died five years before me and came up about five minutes after me. Seeing him made me decide to leave. I had had enough of him when . . . And that reminds me." He brought his fist down on the desk, a very solid fist. "There were no taxis, no busses. Telephones weren't working. I had to walk. I had to walk twenty miles."

"Like that?" asked his son in a faint and appalled voice.

Billikan, Senior, looked down upon his bare skin with casual approval. "It's warm. Almost everyone else is naked. . . . Anyway, son, I'm not here to make small talk. Why is the factory shut down?"

"It isn't shut down. It's a special occasion."

"Special occasion, my foot. You call union headquarters and tell them Resurrection Day isn't in the contract. Every worker is being docked for every minute he's off the job."

Billikan's lean face took on a stubborn look as he peered at his father. "I will not. Don't forget, now, you're no longer in charge of this plant. I am."

"Oh, you are? By what right?"

"By your will."

"All right. Now here I am and I void my will."

"You can't, Father. You're dead. You may not look dead, but I have witnesses. I have the doctor's certificate. I have receipted bills from the undertaker. I can get testimony from the pallbearers."

Billikan, Senior, stared at his son, sat down, placed his arm over the back of the chair, crossed his legs and said, "If it comes to that, we're all dead, aren't we? The world's come to an end, hasn't it?"

"But you've been declared legally dead and I haven't."

"Oh, we'll change that, son. There are going to be more of us than of you and votes count."

Billikan, Junior, tapped the desk firmly with the flat of his hand and flushed slightly. "Father, I hate to bring up this particular point, but you force me to. May I remind you that by now I am sure that Mother is sitting at home waiting for you; that she probably had to walk the streets—uh—naked, too; and that she probably isn't in a good humor."

Billikan, Senior, went ludicrously pale. "Good Heavens!"

"And you know she always wanted you to retire."

Billikan, Senior, came to a quick decision. "I'm not going home. Why, this is a nightmare. Aren't there any limits to this Resurrection business? It's—it's—it's sheer anarchy. There's such a thing as overdoing it. I'm just not going home."

At which point, a somewhat rotund gentleman with a smooth, pink face and fluffy white sideburns (much like pictures of Martin Van Buren) stepped in and said coldly, "Good day."

"Father," said Billikan, Senior.

"Grandfather," said Billikan, Junior.

Billikan, Grandsenior, looked at Billikan, Junior, with disapproval. "If you are my grandson," he said, "you've aged considerably and the change has not improved you."

Billikan, Junior, smiled with dyspeptic feebleness, and made no answer.

Billikan, Grandsenior, did not seem to require one. He said, "Now if you two will bring me up to date on the business, I will resume my managerial function."

There were two simultaneous answers, and Billikan, Grandsenior's, floridity waxed dangerously as he beat the ground peremptorily with an imaginary cane and barked a retort.

R.E. said, "Gentlemen."

He raised his voice. "Gentlemen!"

He shrieked at full long-power, "GENTLEMEN!"

Conversation snapped off sharply and all turned to look at him. R.E.'s angular face, his oddly attractive eyes, his sardonic mouth seemed suddenly to dominate the gathering.

He said, "I don't understand this argument. What is it that you manufacture?"

"Bitsies," said Billikan, Junior.

"Which, I take it, are a packaged cereal breakfast food—"

"Teeming with energy in every golden, crispy flake—" cried Billikan, Junior.

"Covered with honey-sweet, crystalline sugar; a confection and a food—" growled Billikan, Senior.

"To tempt the most jaded appetite," roared Billikan, Grandsenior.

"Exactly," said R.E. "What appetite?"

They stared stolidly at him. "I beg your pardon," said Billikan, Junior.

"Are any of you hungry?" asked R.E. "I'm not."

"What is this fool maundering about?" demanded Billikan, Grandsenior, angrily. His invisible cane would have been prodding R.E. in the navel had it (the cane, not the navel) existed.

R.E. said, "I'm trying to tell you that no one will ever eat again. It is the hereafter, and food is unnecessary."

The expressions on the faces of the Billikans needed no interpretation. It was obvious that they had tried their own appetites and found them wanting.

Billikan, Junior, said ashenly, "Ruined!"

Billikan, Grandsenior, pounded the floor heavily and noiselessly with his imaginary cane. "This is confiscation of property without due process of law. I'll sue. I'll sue."

"Quite unconstitutional," agreed Billikan, Senior.

"If you can find anyone to sue, I wish you all good fortune," said R.E. agreeably. "And now if you'll excuse me I think I'll walk toward the graveyard."

He put his hat on his head and walked out the door.

Etheriel, his vortices quivering, stood before the glory of a six-winged cherub.

The cherub said, "If I understand you, your particular universe has been dismantled."

"Exactly."

"Well, surely, now, you don't expect *me* to set it up again?"

"I don't expect you to do anything," said Etheriel, "except to arrange an appointment for me with the Chief."

The cherub gestured his respect instantly at hearing the word. Two wingtips covered his feet, two his eyes and two his mouth. He restored himself to normal and said, "The Chief is quite busy. There are a myriad score of matters for him to decide."

"Who denies that? I merely point out that if matters stand as they are now, there will have been a universe in which Satan will have won the final victory."

"Satan?"

"It's the Hebrew word for Adversary," said Etheriel impatiently. "I could say Ahriman, which is the Persian word. In any case, I mean the Adversary."

The cherub said, "But what will an interview with the Chief accomplish? The document authorizing the Last Trump was countersigned by the Chief, and you know that it is irrevocable for that reason. The Chief would never limit his own omnipotence by canceling a word he had spoken in his official capacity."

"Is that final? You will not arrange an appointment?"

"I cannot."

Etheriel said, "In that case, I shall seek out the Chief without one. I will invade the Primum Mobile. If it means my destruction, so be it." He gathered his energies. . . .

The cherub murmured in horror, "Sacrilege!" and there was a faint gathering of thunder as Etheriel sprang upward and was gone.

R. E. Mann passed through the crowding streets and grew used to the sight of people bewildered, disbelieving, apathetic, in makeshift clothing or, usually, none at all.

A girl, who looked about twelve, leaned over an iron gate, one foot on a crossbar, swinging it to and fro, and said as he passed, "Hello, mister."

"Hello," said R.E. The girl was dressed. She was not one of the—uh—returnees.

The girl said, "We got a new baby in our house. She's a sister I once had. Mommy is crying and they sent me here."

R.E. said, "Well, well," passed through the gate and up the paved walk to the house, one with modest pretensions to middle-class gentility. He rang the bell, obtained no answer, opened the door and walked in.

He followed the sound of sobbing and knocked at an inner door. A stout man of about fifty with little hair and a comfortable supply of cheek and chin looked out at him with mingled astonishment and resentment.

"Who are you?"

R.E. removed his hat. "I thought I might be able to help. Your little girl outside—"

A woman looked up at him hopelessly from a chair by a double bed. Her hair was beginning to gray. Her face was puffed and unsightly with weeping and the veins stood out bluely on the back of her hands. A baby lay on the bed, plump and naked. It kicked its feet languidly and its sightless baby eyes turned aimlessly here and there.

"This is my baby," said the woman. "She was born twenty-three years ago in this house and she died when she was ten days old in this house. I wanted her back so much."

"And now you have her," said R.E.

"But it's too late," cried the woman vehemently. "I've had three other children. My oldest girl is married; my son is in the army. I'm too old to have a baby now. And even if—even if—"

Her features worked in a heroic effort to keep back the tears and failed.

Her husband said with flat tonelessness, "It's not a real baby. It doesn't cry. It doesn't soil itself. It won't take milk. What will we do? It'll never grow. It'll always be a baby."

R.E. shook his head. "I don't know," he said. "I'm afraid I can do nothing to help."

Quietly he left. Quietly he thought of the hospitals. Thousands of babies must be appearing at each one.

Place them in racks, he thought, sardonically. Stack them like cordwood. They need no care. Their little bodies are merely each the custodian of an indestructible spark of life.

He passed two little boys of apparently equal chronological age, perhaps ten. Their voices were shrill. The body of one glistened white in the sunless light so he was a returnee. The other was not. R.E. paused to listen.

The bare one said, "I had scarlet fever."

A spark of envy at the other's claim to notoriety seemed to enter the clothed one's voice. "Gee."

"That's why I died."

"Gee. Did they use pensillun or auromysun?"

"What?"

"They're medicines."

"I never heard of them."

"Boy, you never heard of *much*."

"I know as much as *you*."

"Yeah? Who's President of the United States?"

"Warren Harding, that's who."

"You're crazy. It's Eisenhower."

"Who's he?"

"Ever see television?"

"What's that?"

The clothed boy hooted earsplittingly. "It's something you turn on and see comedians, movies, cowboys, rocket rangers, anything you want."

"Let's see it."

There was a pause and the boy from the present said, "It ain't working."

The other boy shrieked his scorn. "You mean it ain't never worked. You made it all up."

R.E. shrugged and passed on.

The crowds thinned as he left town and neared the cemetery. Those who were left were all walking into town, all were nude.

A man stopped him; a cheerful man with pinkish skin and white hair who had the marks of pince-nez on either side of the bridge of his nose, but no glasses to go with them.

"Greetings, friend."

"Hello," said R.E.

"You're the first man with clothing that I've seen. You were alive when the trumpet blew, I suppose."

"Yes, I was."

"Well, isn't this great? Isn't this joyous and delightful? Come rejoice with me."

"You like this, do you?" said R.E.

"*Like it?* A pure and radiant joy fills me. We are surrounded by the light of the first day; the light that glowed softly and serenely before sun, moon and stars were made. (You know your Genesis, of course.) There is the comfortable warmth that must have been one of the highest blisses of Eden; not enervating heat or assaulting cold. Men and women walk the streets unclothed and are not ashamed. All is well, my friend, all is well."

R.E. said, "Well, it's a fact that I haven't seemed to mind the feminine display all about."

"Naturally not," said the other. "Lust and sin as we remember it in our earthly existence no longer exists. Let me introduce myself, friend, as I was in earthly times. My name on Earth was Winthrop Hester. I was born in 1812 and died in 1884 as we counted time then. Through the last forty years of my life I labored to bring my little flock to the Kingdom and I go now to count the ones I have won."

R.E. regarded the ex-minister solemnly, "Surely there has been no Judgment yet."

"Why not? The Lord sees within a man and in the same instant that all things of the world ceased, all men were judged and we are the saved."

"There must be a great many saved."

"On the contrary, my son, those saved are but as a remnant."

"A pretty large remnant. As near as I can make out, everyone's coming back to life. I've seen some pretty unsavory characters back in town as alive as you are."

"Last-minute repentance—"

"*I* never repented."

"Of what, my son?"

"Of the fact that I never attended church."

Winthrop Hester stepped back hastily. "Were you ever baptized?"

"Not to my knowledge."

Winthrop Hester trembled. "Surely you believe in God?"

"Well," said R.E., "I believed a lot of things about Him that would probably startle you."

Winthrop Hester turned and hurried off in great agitation.

In what remained of his walk to the cemetery (R.E. had no way of estimating time, nor did it occur to him to try) no one else stopped him. He found the cemetery itself all but empty, its trees and grass gone (it occurred to him that there was nothing green in the world; the ground everywhere was a hard, featureless, grainless gray; the sky a luminous white), but its headstones still standing.

On one of these sat a lean and furrowed man with long, black hair on his head and a mat of it, shorter, though more impressive, on his chest and upper arms.

He called out in a deep voice, "Hey, there, you!"

R.E. sat down on a neighboring headstone. "Hello."

Black-hair said, "Your clothes don't look right. What year was it when it happened?"

"1957."

"I died in 1807. Funny! I expected to be one pretty hot boy right about now, with the 'tarnal flames shooting up my innards."

"Aren't you coming along to town?" asked R.E.

"My name's Zeb," said the ancient. "That's short for Zebulon, but Zeb's good enough. What's the town like? Changed some, I reckon?"

"It's got nearly a hundred thousand people in it."

Zeb's mouth yawned somewhat. "Go on. Might nigh bigger'n Philadelphia. . . . You're making fun."

"Philadelphia's got—" R.E. paused. Stating the figure would do him no good. Instead, he said, "The town's grown in a hundred fifty years, you know."

"Country, too?"

"Forty-eight states," said R.E. "All the way to the Pacific."

"No!" Zeb slapped his thigh in delight and then winced at the unexpected absence of rough homespun to take up the worst of the blow. "I'd head out west if I wasn't needed here. Yes, sir." His face grew lowering and his thin lips took on a definite grimness. "I'll stay right here, where I'm needed."

"Why are you needed?"

The explanation came out briefly, bitten off hard. "Injuns!"

"Indians?"

"Millions of 'em. First the tribes we fought and licked and then tribes who ain't never seen a white man. They'll all come back to life. I'll need my old buddies. You city fellers ain't no good at it. . . . Ever seen an Injun?"

R.E. said, "Not around here lately, no."

Zeb looked his contempt, and tried to spit to one side but found no saliva for the purpose. He said, "You better git back to the city, then. After a while, it ain't going to be safe nohow round here. Wish I had my musket."

R.E. rose, thought a moment, shrugged and faced back to the city. The headstone he had been sitting upon collapsed as he rose, falling into a powder of gray stone that melted into the featureless ground. He looked about. Most of the headstones were gone. The rest would not last long. Only the one under Zeb still looked firm and strong.

R.E. began the walk back. Zeb did not turn to look at him. He remained waiting quietly and calmly—for Indians.

. . . .

Etheriel plunged through the heavens in reckless haste. The eyes of the Ascendants were on him, he knew. From late-born seraph, through cherubs and angels, to the highest archangel, they must be watching.

Already he was higher than any Ascendant, uninvited, had ever been before and he waited for the quiver of the Word that would reduce his vortices to non-existence.

But he did not falter. Through non-space and non-time, he plunged toward union with the Primum Mobile; the seat that encompassed all that Is, Was, Would Be, Had Been, Could Be and Might Be.

And as he thought that, he burst through and was part of it, his being expanding so that momentarily he, too, was part of the All. But then it was mercifully veiled from his senses, and the Chief was a still, small voice within him, yet all the more impressive in its infinity for all that.

"My son," the voice said, "I know why you have come."

"Then help me, if that be your will."

"By my own will," said the Chief, "an act of mine is irrevocable. All your mankind, my son, yearned for life. All feared death. All evolved thoughts and dreams of life unending. No two groups of men; no two single men; evolved the same afterlife, but all wished life. I was petitioned that I might grant the common denominator of all these wishes—life unending. I did so."

"No servant of yours made that request."

"The Adversary did, my son."

Etheriel trailed his feeble glory in dejection and said in a low voice, "I am dust in your sight and unworthy to be in your presence, yet I must ask a question. Is then the Adversary your servant also?"

"Without him I can have no other," said the Chief, "for what then is Good but the eternal fight against Evil?"

And in that fight, thought Etheriel, I have lost.

R.E. paused in sight of town. The buildings were crumbling. Those that were made of wood were already heaps of rubble. R.E. walked to the nearest such heap and found the wooden splinters powdery and dry.

He penetrated deeper into town and found the brick buildings still standing, but there was an ominous roundness to the edges of the bricks, a threatening flakiness.

"They won't last long," said a deep voice, "but there is this consolation, if consolation it be; their collapse can kill no one."

R.E. looked up in surprise and found himself face to face with a cadaverous Don Quixote of a man, lantern-jawed, sunken-cheeked. His eyes were sad and his brown hair was lank and straight. His clothes hung loosely and skin showed clearly through various rents.

"My name," said the man, "is Richard Levine. I was a professor of history once—before this happened."

"You're wearing clothes," said R.E. "You're not one of those resurrected."

"No, but that mark of distinction is vanishing. Clothes are going."

R.E. looked at the throngs that drifted past them, moving slowly and aimlessly like motes in a sunbeam. Vanishingly few wore clothes. He looked down at himself and noticed for the first time that the seam down the length of each trouser leg had parted. He pinched the fabric of his jacket between thumb and forefinger and the wool parted and came away easily.

"I guess you're right," said R.E.

"If you'll notice," went on Levine, "Mellon's Hill is flattening out."

R.E. turned to the north where ordinarily the mansions of the aristocracy (such aristocracy as there was in town) studded the slopes of Mellon's Hill, and found the horizon nearly flat.

Levine said, "Eventually, there'll be nothing but flatness, featurelessness, nothingness—and us."

"And Indians," said R.E. "There's a man outside of town waiting for Indians and wishing he had a musket."

"I imagine," said Levine, "the Indians will give no trouble. There is no pleasure in fighting an enemy that cannot be killed or hurt. And even if that were not so, the lust for battle would be gone, as are all lusts."

"Are you sure?"

"I am positive. Before all this happened, although you may not think it to look at me, I derived much harmless pleasure in a consideration of the female figure. Now, with the unexampled opportunities at my disposal, I find myself irritatingly uninterested. No, that is wrong. I am not even irritated at my disinterest."

R.E. looked up briefly at the passers-by. "I see what you mean."

"The coming of Indians here," said Levine, "is nothing compared with the situation in the Old World. Early during the Resurrection, Hitler and his Wehrmacht must have come back to life and must now be facing and intermingled with Stalin and the Red Army all the way from Berlin to Stalingrad. To complicate the situation, the Kaisers and Czars will arrive. The men at Verdun and the Somme are back in the old battlegrounds. Napoleon and his marshals are scattered over western Europe. And Mohammed must be back to see what following ages have made of Islam, while the Saints and Apostles consider the paths of Christianity. And even the Mongols, poor things, the Khans from Temujin to Aurangzeb, must be wandering the steppes helplessly, longing for their horses."

"As a professor of history," said R.E., "you must long to be there and observe."

"How could I be there? Every man's position on Earth is restricted to the distance he can walk. There are no machines of any kind, and, as I have just mentioned, no horses. And what would I find in Europe anyway? Apathy, I think! As here."

A soft plopping sound caused R.E. to turn around. The wing of a neighboring brick building had collapsed in dust. Portions of bricks lay on either side of him. Some must have hurtled through him without his being aware of it. He looked about. The heaps of rubble were less numerous. Those that remained were smaller in size.

He said, "I met a man who thought we had all been judged and are in Heaven."

"Judged?" said Levine. "Why, yes, I imagine we are. We face eternity now. We have no universe left, no outside phenomena, no emotions, no passions. Nothing but ourselves and thought. We face an eternity of intro-spection, when all through history we have never known what to do with ourselves on a rainy Sunday."

"You sound as though the situation bothers you."

"It does more than that. The Dantean conceptions of Inferno were child-ish and unworthy of the Divine imagination: fire and torture. Boredom is much more subtle. The inner torture of a mind unable to escape itself in any way, condemned to fester in its own exuding mental pus for all time, is much more fitting. Oh, yes, my friend, we have been judged, and con-demned, too, and this is not Heaven, but hell."

And Levine rose with shoulders drooping dejectedly, and walked away.

R.E. gazed thoughtfully about and nodded his head. He was satisfied.

The self-admission of failure lasted but an instant in Etheriel, and then, quite suddenly, he lifted his being as brightly and highly as he dared in the presence of the Chief and his glory was a tiny dot of light in the infinite Primum Mobile.

"If it be your will, then," he said. "I do not ask you to defeat your will but to fulfill it."

"In what way, my son?"

"The document, approved by the Council of Ascendants and signed by yourself, authorizes the Day of Resurrection at a specific time of a specific day of the year 1957 as Earthmen count time."

"So it did."

"But the year 1957 is unqualified. What then is 1957? To the dominant culture on Earth the year was A.D. 1957. That is true. Yet from the time you breathed existence into Earth and its universe there have passed 5,960 years. Based on the internal evidence you created within that universe, nearly four billion years have passed. Is the year, *unqualified*, then 1957, 5960, or 4000000000?

"Nor is that all," Etheriel went on. "The year A.D. 1957 is the year 7464 of the Byzantine era, 5716 by the Jewish calendar. It is 2708 A.U.C., that is, the 2,708th year since the founding of Rome, if we adopt the Roman calendar. It is the year 1375 in the Mohammedan calendar, and the hun-dred eightieth year of the independence of the United States.

"Humbly I ask then if it does not seem to you that a year referred to as 1957 alone and without qualification has no meaning."

The Chief's still small voice said, "I have always known this, my son; it was you who had to learn."

"Then," said Etheriel, quivering luminously with joy, "let the very letter of your will be fulfilled and let the Day of Resurrection fall in 1957, but only when all the inhabitants of Earth unanimously agree that a certain year shall be numbered 1957 and none other."

"So let it be," said the Chief, and this Word re-created Earth and all it contained, together with the sun and moon and all the hosts of Heaven.

It was 7 A.M. on January 1, 1957, when R. E. Mann awoke with a start. The very beginnings of a melodious note that ought to have filled all the universe had sounded and yet had not sounded.

For a moment, he cocked his head as though to allow understanding to flow in, and then a trifle of rage crossed his face to vanish again. It was but another battle.

He sat down at his desk to compose the next plan of action. People already spoke of calendar reform and it would have to be stimulated. A new era must begin with December 2, 1944, and someday a new year 1957 would come; 1957 of the Atomic Era, acknowledged as such by all the world.

A strange light shone on his head as thoughts passed through his more-than-human mind and the shadow of Ahriman on the wall seemed to have small horns at either temple.

The Fun They Had

Margie even wrote about it that night in her diary. On the page headed May 17, 2157, she wrote, "Today Tommy found a real book!"

It was a very old book. Margie's grandfather once said that when he was a little boy *his* grandfather told him that there was a time when all stories were printed on paper.

They turned the pages, which were yellow and crinkly, and it was awfully funny to read words that stood still instead of moving the way they were supposed to—on a screen, you know. And then, when they turned back to the page before, it had the same words on it that it had had when they read it the first time.

"Gee," said Tommy, "what a waste. When you're through with the book, you just throw it away, I guess. Our television screen must have had a million books on it and it's good for plenty more. I wouldn't throw *it* away."

"Same with mine," said Margie. She was eleven and hadn't seen as many telebooks as Tommy had. He was thirteen.

She said, "Where did you find it?"

"In my house." He pointed without looking, because he was busy reading. "In the attic."

"What's it about?"

"School."

Margie was scornful. "School? What's there to write about school? I hate school."

Margie always hated school, but now she hated it more than ever. The mechanical teacher had been giving her test after test in geography and she had been doing worse and worse until her mother had shaken her head sorrowfully and sent for the County Inspector.

He was a round little man with a red face and a whole box of tools with dials and wires. He smiled at Margie and gave her an apple, then took the teacher apart. Margie had hoped he wouldn't know how to put it together again, but he knew how all right, and, after an hour or so, there it was again, large and black and ugly, with a big screen on which all the lessons were shown and the questions were asked. That wasn't so bad. The part Margie hated most was the slot where she had to put homework and test papers. She always had to write them out in a punch code they made her learn when she was six years old, and the mechanical teacher calculated the mark in no time.

The Inspector had smiled after he was finished and patted Margie's head. He said to her mother, "It's not the little girl's fault, Mrs. Jones. I think the geography sector was geared a little too quick. Those things happen sometimes. I've slowed it up to an average ten-year level. Actually, the over-all pattern of her progress is quite satisfactory." And he patted Margie's head again.

Margie was disappointed. She had been hoping they would take the teacher away altogether. They had once taken Tommy's teacher away for nearly a month because the history sector had blanked out completely.

So she said to Tommy, "Why would anyone write about school?"

Tommy looked at her with very superior eyes. "Because it's not our kind of school, stupid. This is the old kind of school that they had hundreds and hundreds of years ago." He added loftily, pronouncing the word carefully, *"Centuries* ago."

Margie was hurt. "Well, I don't know what kind of school they had all that time ago." She read the book over his shoulder for a while, then said, "Anyway, they had a teacher."

"Sure they had a teacher, but it wasn't a *regular* teacher. It was a man."

"A man? How could a man be a teacher?"

"Well, he just told the boys and girls things and gave them homework and asked them questions."

"A man isn't smart enough."

"Sure he is. My father knows as much as my teacher."

"He can't. A man can't know as much as a teacher."

"He knows almost as much, I betcha."

Margie wasn't prepared to dispute that. She said, "I wouldn't want a strange man in my house to teach me."

Tommy screamed with laughter. "You don't know much, Margie. The teachers didn't live in the house. They had a special building and all the kids went there."

"And all the kids learned the same thing?"

"Sure, if they were the same age."

"But my mother says a teacher has to be adjusted to fit the mind of each boy and girl it teaches and that each kid has to be taught differently."

"Just the same they didn't do it that way then. If you don't like it, you don't have to read the book."

"I didn't say I didn't like it," Margie said quickly. She wanted to read about those funny schools.

They weren't even half-finished when Margie's mother called, "Margie! School!"

Margie looked up. "Not yet, Mamma."

"Now!" said Mrs. Jones. "And it's probably time for Tommy, too."

Margie said to Tommy, "Can I read the book some more with you after school?"

"Maybe," he said nonchalantly. He walked away whistling, the dusty old book tucked beneath his arm.

Margie went into the schoolroom. It was right next to her bedroom, and the mechanical teacher was on and waiting for her. It was always on at the same time every day except Saturday and Sunday, because her mother said little girls learned better if they learned at regular hours.

The screen was lit up, and it said: "Today's arithmetic lesson is on the addition of proper fractions. Please insert yesterday's homework in the proper slot."

Margie did so with a sigh. She was thinking about the old schools they had when her grandfather's grandfather was a little boy. All the kids from the whole neighborhood came, laughing and shouting in the schoolyard, sitting together in the schoolroom, going home together at the end of the day. They learned the same things, so they could help one another on the homework and talk about it.

And the teachers were people. . . .

The mechanical teacher was flashing on the screen: "When we add the fractions $1/2$ and $1/4$—"

Margie was thinking about how the kids must have loved it in the old days. She was thinking about the fun they had.

Jokester

Noel Meyerhof consulted the list he had prepared and chose which item was to be first. As usual, he relied mainly on intuition.

He was dwarfed by the machine he faced, though only the smallest portion of the latter was in view. That didn't matter. He spoke with the offhand confidence of one who thoroughly knew he was master.

"Johnson," he said, "came home unexpectedly from a business trip to find his wife in the arms of his best friend. He staggered back and said, 'Max! I'm married to the lady so I *have* to. But why you?' "

Meyerhof thought: Okay, let that trickle down into its guts and gurgle about a bit.

And a voice behind him said, "Hey."

Meyerhof erased the sound of that monosyllable and put the circuit he was using into neutral. He whirled and said, "I'm working. Don't you knock?"

He did not smile as he customarily did in greeting Timothy Whistler, a senior analyst with whom he dealt as often as with any. He frowned as he would have for an interruption by a stranger, wrinkling his thin face into a distortion that seemed to extend to his hair, rumpling it more than ever.

Whistler shrugged. He wore his white lab coat with his fists pressing down within its pockets and creasing it into tense vertical lines. "I knocked. You didn't answer. The operations signal wasn't on."

Meyerhof grunted. It wasn't at that. He'd been thinking about this new project too intensively and he was forgetting little details.

And yet he could scarcely blame himself for that. This thing was important.

He didn't know why it was, of course. Grand Masters rarely did. That's what made them Grand Masters; the fact that they were beyond reason. How else could the human mind keep up with that ten-mile-long lump of solidified reason that men called Multivac, the most complex computer ever built?

Meyerhof said, "I *am* working. Is there something important on your mind?"

"Nothing that can't be postponed. There are a few holes in the answer on the hyperspatial—" Whistler did a double take and his face took on a rueful look of uncertainty. *"Working?"*

"Yes. What about it?"

"But—" He looked about, staring into the crannies of the shallow room that faced the banks upon banks of relays that formed a small portion of Multivac. "There isn't anyone here at that."

"Who said there was, or should be?"

"You were telling one of your jokes, weren't you?"

"And?"

Whistler forced a smile. "Don't tell me you were telling a joke to Multivac?"

Meyerhof stiffened. "Why not?"

"Were you?"

"Yes."

"Why?"

Meyerhof stared the other down. "I don't have to account to you. Or to anyone."

"Good Lord, of course not. I was curious, that's all. . . . But then, if you're working, I'll leave." He looked about once more, frowning.

"Do so," said Meyerhof. His eyes followed the other out and then he activated the operations signal with a savage punch of his finger.

He strode the length of the room and back, getting himself in hand. Damn Whistler! Damn them all! Because he didn't bother to hold those technicians, analysts and mechanics at the proper social distance, because he treated them as though they, too, were creative artists, they took these liberties.

He thought grimly: They can't even tell jokes decently.

And instantly that brought him back to the task in hand. He sat down again. Devil take them all.

He threw the proper Multivac circuit back into operation and said, "The ship's steward stopped at the rail of the ship during a particularly rough ocean crossing and gazed compassionately at the man whose slumped position over the rail and whose intensity of gaze toward the depths betokened all too well the ravages of seasickness.

"Gently, the steward patted the man's shoulder. 'Cheer up, sir,' he murmured. 'I know it seems bad, but really, you know, nobody ever dies of seasickness.'

"The afflicted gentleman lifted his greenish, tortured face to his comforter and gasped in hoarse accents, 'Don't say that, man. For Heaven's sake, don't say that. It's only the hope of dying that's keeping me alive.' "

Timothy Whistler, a bit preoccupied, nevertheless smiled and nodded as he passed the secretary's desk. She smiled back at him.

Here, he thought, was an archaic item in this computer-ridden world of the twenty-first century, a human secretary. But then perhaps it was natural that such an institution should survive here in the very citadel of computerdom; in the gigantic world corporation that handled Multivac. With Multivac filling the horizons, lesser computers for trivial tasks would have been in poor taste.

Whistler stepped into Abram Trask's office. That government official paused in his careful task of lighting a pipe; his dark eyes flicked in Whistler's direction and his beaked nose stood out sharply and prominently against the rectangle of window behind him.

"Ah, there, Whistler. Sit down. Sit down."

Whistler did so. "I think we've got a problem, Trask."

Trask half-smiled. "Not a technical one, I hope. I'm just an innocent politician." (It was one of his favorite phrases.)

"It involves Meyerhof."

Trask sat down instantly and looked acutely miserable. "Are you sure?"

"Reasonably sure."

Whistler understood the other's sudden unhappiness well. Trask was the government official in charge of the Division of Computers and Automation of the Department of the Interior. He was expected to deal with matters of policy involving the human satellites of Multivac, just as those technically trained satellites were expected to deal with Multivac itself.

But a Grand Master was more than just a satellite. More, even, than just a human.

Early in the history of Multivac, it had become apparent that the bottleneck was the questioning procedure. Multivac could answer the problem of humanity, *all* the problems, if—*if* it were asked meaningful questions. But as knowledge accumulated at an ever-faster rate, it became ever more difficult to locate those meaningful questions.

Reason alone wouldn't do. What was needed was a rare type of intuition; the same faculty of mind (only much more intensified) that made a grand master at chess. A mind was needed of the sort that could see through the quadrillions of chess patterns to find the one best move, and do it in a matter of minutes.

Trask moved restlessly. "What's Meyerhof been doing?"

"He's introduced a line of questioning that I find disturbing."

"Oh, come on, Whistler. Is that all? You can't stop a Grand Master from going through any line of questioning he chooses. Neither you nor I are equipped to judge the worth of his questions. You know that. I know you know that."

"I do. Of course. But I also know Meyerhof. Have you ever met him socially?"

"Good Lord, no. Does anyone meet any Grand Master socially?"

"Don't take that attitude, Trask. They're human and they're to be pitied. Have you ever thought what it must be like to be a Grand Master; to know there are only some twelve like you in the world; to know that only one or two come up per generation; that the world depends on you; that a thousand mathematicians, logicians, psychologists and physical scientists wait on you?"

Trask shrugged and muttered, "Good Lord, I'd feel king of the world."

"I don't think you would," said the senior analyst impatiently. "They feel kings of nothing. They have no equal to talk to, no sensation of belonging. Listen, Meyerhof never misses a chance to get together with the boys. He isn't married, naturally; he doesn't drink; he has no natural social touch—yet he forces himself into company because he must. And do you know what he does when he gets together with us, and that's at least once a week?"

"I haven't the least idea," said the government man. "This is all new to me."

"He's a jokester."

"What?"

"He tells jokes. Good ones. He's terrific. He can take any story, however old and dull, and make it sound good. It's the way he tells it. He has a flair."

"I see. Well, good."

"Or bad. These jokes are important to him." Whistler put both elbows on Trask's desk, bit at a thumbnail and stared into the air. "He's different, he knows he's different and these jokes are the one way he feels he can get the rest of us ordinary schmoes to accept him. We laugh, we howl, we clap him on the back and even forget he's a Grand Master. It's the only hold he has on the rest of us."

"This is all interesting. I didn't know you were such a psychologist. Still, where does this lead?"

"Just this. What do you suppose happens if Meyerhof runs out of jokes?"

"What?" The government man stared blankly.

"If he starts repeating himself? If his audience starts laughing less heartily, or stops laughing altogether? It's his only hold on our approval. Without it, he'll be alone and then what would happen to him? After all, Trask, he's one of the dozen men mankind can't do without. We can't let anything happen to him. I don't mean just physical things. We can't even let him get too unhappy. Who knows how that might affect his intuition?"

"Well, has he started repeating himself?"

"Not as far as I know, but I think *he* thinks he has."

"Why do you say that?"

"Because I've heard him telling jokes to Multivac."

"Oh, no."

"Accidentally! I walked in on him and he threw me out. He was savage. He's usually good-natured enough, and I consider it a bad sign that he was so upset at the intrusion. But the fact remains that he was telling a joke to Multivac, and I'm convinced it was one of a series."

"But why?"

Whistler shrugged and rubbed a hand fiercely across his chin. "I have a thought about that. I think he's trying to build up a store of jokes in Multivac's memory banks in order to get back new variations. You see what I mean? He's planning a mechanical jokester, so that he can have an infinite number of jokes at hand and never fear running out."

"Good Lord!"

"Objectively, there may be nothing wrong with that, but I consider it a bad sign when a Grand Master starts using Multivac for his personal problems. Any Grand Master has a certain inherent mental instability and he should be watched. Meyerhof may be approaching a borderline beyond which we lose a Grand Master."

Trask said blankly, "What are you suggesting I do?"

"You can check me. I'm too close to him to judge well, maybe, and judging humans isn't my particular talent, anyway. You're a politician; it's more your talent."

"Judging humans, perhaps, not Grand Masters."

"They're human, too. Besides, who else is to do it?"

The fingers of Trask's hand struck his desk in rapid succession over and over like a slow and muted roll of drums.

"I suppose I'll have to," he said.

Meyerhof said to Multivac, "The ardent swain, picking a bouquet of wildflowers for his loved one, was disconcerted to find himself, suddenly, in the same field with a large bull of unfriendly appearance which, gazing at him steadily, pawed the ground in a threatening manner. The young man, spying a farmer on the other side of a fairly distant fence, shouted, 'Hey, mister, is that bull safe?' The farmer surveyed the situation with critical eye, spat to one side and called back, 'He's safe as anything.' He spat again, and added, 'Can't say the same about you, though.'"

Meyerhof was about to pass on to the next when the summons came.

It wasn't really a summons. No one could summon a Grand Master. It was only a message that Division Head Trask would like very much to see Grand Master Meyerhof if Grand Master Meyerhof could spare him the time.

Meyerhof might, with impunity, have tossed the message to one side and continued with whatever he was doing. He was not subject to discipline.

On the other hand, were he to do that, they would continue to bother him—oh, very respectfully, but they would continue to bother him.

So he neutralized the pertinent circuits of Multivac and locked them into place. He put the freeze signal on his office so that no one would dare enter in his absence and left for Trask's office.

Trask coughed and felt a bit intimidated by the sullen fierceness of the other's look. He said, "We have not had occasion to know one another, Grand Master, to my great regret."

"I have reported to you," said Meyerhof stiffly.

Trask wondered what lay behind those keen, wild eyes. It was difficult for him to imagine Meyerhof with his thin face, his dark, straight hair, his intense air, even unbending long enough to tell funny stories.

He said, "Reports are not social acquaintance. I—I have been given to understand you have a marvelous fund of anecdotes."

"I am a jokester, sir. That's the phrase people use. A jokester."

"They haven't used the phrase to me, Grand Master. They have said—"

"The hell with them! I don't care what they've said. See here, Trask, do you want to hear a joke?" He leaned forward across the desk, his eyes narrowed.

"By all means. Certainly," said Trask, with an effort at heartiness.

"All right. Here's the joke: Mrs. Jones stared at the fortune card that had emerged from the weighing machine in response to her husband's penny. She said, 'It says here, George, that you're suave, intelligent, farseeing, industrious and attractive to women.' With that, she turned the card over and added, 'And they have your weight wrong, too.' "

Trask laughed. It was almost impossible not to. Although the punch line was predictable, the surprising facility with which Meyerhof had produced just the tone of contemptuous disdain in the woman's voice, and the cleverness with which he had contorted the lines of his face to suit that tone carried the politician helplessly into laughter.

Meyerhof said sharply, "Why is that funny?"

Trask sobered. "I beg your pardon."

"I said, why is that funny? Why do you laugh?"

"Well," said Trask, trying to be reasonable, "the last line put every thing that preceded in a new light. The unexpectedness—"

"The point is," said Meyerhof, "that I have pictured a husband being humiliated by his wife; a marriage that is such a failure that the wife is convinced that her husband lacks any virtue. Yet you laugh at that. If you were the husband, would you find it funny?"

He waited a moment in thought, then said, "Try this one, Trask: Abner was seated at his wife's sickbed, weeping uncontrollably, when his wife, mustering the dregs of her strength, drew herself up to one elbow.

" 'Abner,' she whispered, 'Abner, I cannot go to my Maker without confessing my misdeed.'

" 'Not now,' muttered the stricken husband. 'Not now, my dear. Lie back and rest.'

" 'I cannot,' she cried. 'I must tell, or my soul will never know peace. I have been unfaithful to you, Abner. In this very house, not one month ago—'

" 'Hush, dear,' soothed Abner. 'I know all about it. Why else have I poisoned you?' "

Trask tried desperately to maintain equanimity but did not entirely succeed. He suppressed a chuckle imperfectly.

Meyerhof said, "So that's funny, too. Adultery. Murder. All funny."

"Well, now," said Trask, "books have been written analyzing humor."

"True enough," said Meyerhof, "and I've read a number of them. What's more, I've read most of them to Multivac. Still, the people who write the books are just guessing. Some of them say we laugh because we feel superior to the people in the joke. Some say it is because of a suddenly realized incongruity, or a sudden relief from tension, or a sudden reinterpretation of events. Is there any simple reason? Different people laugh at different jokes. No joke is universal. Some people don't laugh at any joke. Yet what may be most important is that man is the only animal with a true sense of humor: the only animal that laughs."

Trask said suddenly, "I understand. You're trying to analyze humor. That's why you're transmitting a series of jokes to Multivac."

"Who told you I was doing that? . . . Never mind, it was Whistler. I remember, now. He surprised me at it. Well, what about it?"

"Nothing at all."

"You don't dispute my right to add anything I wish to Multivac's general fund of knowledge, or to ask any question I wish?"

"No, not at all," said Trask hastily. "As a matter of fact, I have no doubt that this will open the way to new analyses of great interest to psychologists."

"Hmp. Maybe. Just the same there's something plaguing me that's more important than just the general analysis of humor. There's a specific question I have to ask. Two of them, really."

"Oh? What's that?" Trask wondered if the other would answer. There would be no way of compelling him if he chose not to.

But Meyerhof said, "The first question is this: Where do all these jokes come from?"

"What?"

"Who makes them up? Listen! About a month ago, I spent an evening swapping jokes. As usual, I told most of them and, as usual, the fools laughed. Maybe they really thought the jokes were funny and maybe they were just humoring me. In any case, one creature took the liberty of slapping me on the back and saying, 'Meyerhof, you know more jokes than any ten people I know.'

"I'm sure he was right, but it gave rise to a thought. I don't know how many hundreds, or perhaps thousands, of jokes I've told at one time or another in my life, yet the fact is I never made up one. Not one. I'd only repeated them. My only contribution was to tell them. To begin with, I'd either heard them or read them. And the source of my hearing or reading didn't make up the jokes, either. I never met anyone who ever claimed to have constructed a joke. It's always 'I heard a good one the other day,' and 'Heard any good ones lately?'

"*All the jokes are old!* That's why jokes exhibit such a social lag. They still deal with seasickness, for instance, when that's easily prevented these days and never experienced. Or they'll deal with fortune-giving weighing machines, like the joke I told you, when such machines are found only in antique shops. Well, then, who makes up the jokes?"

Trask said, "Is *that* what you're trying to find out?" It was on the tip of Trask's tongue to add: Good Lord, who cares? He forced that impulse down. A Grand Master's questions were always meaningful.

"Of course that's what I'm trying to find out. Think of it this way. It's not just that jokes happen to be old. They *must* be old to be enjoyed. It's essential that a joke not be original. There's one variety of humor that is, or can be, original and that's the pun. I've heard puns that were obviously made up on the spur of the moment. I have made some up myself. But no one laughs at such puns. You're not supposed to. You groan. The better the pun, the louder the groan. Original humor is not laugh-provoking. Why?"

"I'm sure I don't know."

"All right. Let's find out. Having given Multivac all the information I thought advisable on the general topic of humor, I am now feeding it selected jokes."

Trask found himself intrigued. "Selected how?" he asked.

"I don't know," said Meyerhof. "They felt like the right ones. I'm Grand Master, you know."

"Oh, agreed. Agreed."

"From those jokes and the general philosophy of humor, my first request will be for Multivac to trace the origin of the jokes, if it can. Since Whistler is in on this and since he has seen fit to report it to you, have him down in Analysis day after tomorrow. I think he'll have a bit of work to do."

"Certainly. May I attend, too?"

Meyerhof shrugged. Trask's attendance was obviously a matter of indifference to him.

. . . .

Meyerhof had selected the last in the series with particular care. What that care consisted of, he could not have said, but he had revolved a dozen possibilities in his mind, and over and over again had tested each for some indefinable quality of meaningfulness.

He said, "Ug, the caveman, observed his mate running to him in tears, her leopard-skin skirt in disorder. 'Ug,' she cried, distraught, 'do something quickly. A saber-toothed tiger has entered Mother's cave. Do something!' Ug grunted, picked up his well-gnawed buffalo bone and said, 'Why do anything? Who the hell cares what happens to a saber-toothed tiger?' "

It was then that Meyerhof asked his two questions and leaned back, closing his eyes. He was done.

"I saw absolutely nothing wrong," said Trask to Whistler. "He told me what he was doing readily enough and it was odd but legitimate."

"What he *claimed* he was doing," said Whistler.

"Even so, I can't stop a Grand Master on opinion alone. He seemed queer but, after all, Grand Masters are supposed to seem queer. I didn't think him insane."

"Using Multivac to find the source of jokes?" muttered the senior analyst in discontent. "That's not insane?"

"How can we tell?" asked Trask irritably. "Science has advanced to the point where the only meaningful questions left are the ridiculous ones. The sensible ones have been thought of, asked and answered long ago."

"It's no use. I'm bothered."

"Maybe, but there's no choice now, Whistler. We'll see Meyerhof and you can do the necessary analysis of Multivac's response, if any. As for me, my only job is to handle the red tape. Good Lord, I don't even know what a senior analyst such as yourself is supposed to do, except analyze, and that doesn't help me any."

Whistler said, "It's simple enough. A Grand Master like Meyerhof asks questions and Multivac automatically formulates it into quantities and operations. The necessary machinery for converting words to symbols is what makes up most of the bulk of Multivac. Multivac then gives the answer in quantities and operations, but it doesn't translate that back into words except in the most simple and routine cases. If it were designed to solve the general retranslation problem, its bulk would have to be quadrupled at least."

"I see. Then it's your job to translate these symbols into words?"

"My job and that of other analysts. We use smaller, specially designed computers whenever necessary." Whistler smiled grimly. "Like the Delphic priestess of ancient Greece, Multivac gives oracular and obscure answers. Only we have translators, you see."

They had arrived. Meyerhof was waiting.

Whistler said briskly, "What circuits did you use, Grand Master?"
Meyerhof told him and Whistler went to work.

Trask tried to follow what was happening, but none of it made sense. The
government official watched a spool unreel with a pattern of dots in endless
incomprehensibility. Grand Master Meyerhof stood indifferently to one side
while Whistler surveyed the pattern as it emerged. The analyst had put on
headphones and a mouthpiece and at intervals murmured a series of instructions which, at some far-off place, guided assistants through electronic con-
tortions in other computers.

Occasionally, Whistler listened, then punched combinations on a complex keyboard marked with symbols that looked vaguely mathematical but
weren't.

A good deal more than an hour's time elapsed.

The frown on Whistler's face grew deeper. Once, he looked up at the two
others and began, "This is unbel—" and turned back to his work.

Finally, he said hoarsely, "I can give you an unofficial answer." His eyes
were red-rimmed. "The official answer awaits complete analysis. Do you
want it unofficial?"

"Go ahead," said Meyerhof.

Trask nodded.

Whistler darted a hangdog glance at the Grand Master. "Ask a foolish
question—" he said. Then, gruffly, "Multivac says, extraterrestrial origin."

"What are you saying?" demanded Trask.

"Don't you hear me? The jokes we laugh at were not made up by any
man. Multivac has analyzed all data given it and the one answer that best
fits that data is that some extraterrestrial intelligence has composed the
jokes, all of them, and placed them in selected human minds at selected
times and places in such a way that no man is conscious of having made one
up. All subsequent jokes are minor variations and adaptations of these grand
originals."

Meyerhof broke in, face flushed with the kind of triumph only a Grand
Master can know who once again has asked the right question. "All comedy
writers," he said, "work by twisting old jokes to new purposes. That's well
known. The answer fits."

"But why?" asked Trask. "Why make up the jokes?"

"Multivac says," said Whistler, "that the only purpose that fits all the
data is that the jokes are intended to study human psychology. We study rat
psychology by making the rats solve mazes. The rats don't know why and
wouldn't even if they were aware of what was going on, which they're not.
These outer intelligences study man's psychology by noting individual reactions to carefully selected anecdotes. Each man reacts differently. . . . Presumably, these outer intelligences are to us as we are to rats." He shuddered.

Trask, eyes staring, said, "The Grand Master said man is the only animal with a sense of humor. It would seem then that the sense of humor is foisted upon us from without."

Meyerhof added excitedly, "And for possible humor created from within, we have no laughter. Puns, I mean."

Whistler said, "Presumably, the extraterrestrials cancel out reactions to spontaneous jokes to avoid confusion."

Trask said in sudden agony of spirit, "Come on, now, Good Lord, do either of you believe this?"

The senior analyst looked at him coldly. "Multivac says so. It's all that can be said so far. It has pointed out the real jokesters of the universe, and if we want to know more, the matter will have to be followed up." He added in a whisper, "If anyone dares follow it up."

Grand Master Meyerhof said suddenly, "I asked two questions, you know. So far only the first has been answered. I think Multivac has enough data to answer the second."

Whistler shrugged. He seemed a half-broken man. "When a Grand Master thinks there is enough data," he said, "I'll make book on it. What is your second question?"

"I asked this: What will be the effect on the human race of discovering the answer to my first question?"

"Why did you ask that?" demanded Trask.

"Just a feeling that it had to be asked," said Meyerhof.

Trask said, "Insane. It's all insane," and turned away. Even he himself felt how strangely he and Whistler had changed sides. Now it was Trask crying insanity.

Trask closed his eyes. He might cry insanity all he wished, but no man in fifty years had doubted the combination of a Grand Master and Multivac and found his doubts verified.

Whistler worked silently, teeth clenched. He put Multivac and its subsidiary machines through their paces again. Another hour passed and he laughed harshly. "A raving nightmare!"

"What's the answer?" asked Meyerhof. "I want Multivac's remarks, not yours."

"All right. Take it. Multivac states that, once even a single human discovers the truth of this method of psychological analysis of the human mind, it will become useless as an objective technique to those extraterrestrial powers now using it."

"You mean there won't be any more jokes handed out to humanity?" asked Trask faintly. "Or what do you mean?"

"No more jokes," said Whistler, *"now!* Multivac says *now!* The experiment is ended *now!* A new technique will have to be introduced."

They stared at each other. The minutes passed.

Meyerhof said slowly, "Multivac is right."

Whistler said haggardly, "I know."

Even Trask said in a whisper, "Yes. It must be."

It was Meyerhof who put his finger on the proof of it, Meyerhof the accomplished jokester. He said, "It's over, you know, all over. I've been trying for five minutes now and I can't think of one single joke, not one! And if I read one in a book, I wouldn't laugh. I know."

"The gift of humor is gone," said Trask drearily. "No man will ever laugh again."

And they remained there, staring, feeling the world shrink down to the dimensions of an experimental rat cage—with the maze removed and something, something about to be put in its place.

The Immortal Bard

"Oh, yes," said Dr. Phineas Welch, "I can bring back the spirits of the illustrious dead."

He was a little drunk, or maybe he wouldn't have said it. Of course, it was perfectly all right to get a little drunk at the annual Christmas party.

Scott Robertson, the school's young English instructor, adjusted his glasses and looked to right and left to see if they were overheard. "Really, Dr. Welch."

"I mean it. And not just the spirits. I bring back the bodies, too."

"I wouldn't have said it were possible," said Robertson primly.

"Why not? A simple matter of temporal transference."

"You mean time travel? But that's quite—uh—unusual."

"Not if you know how."

"Well, how, Dr. Welch?"

"Think I'm going to tell you?" asked the physicist gravely. He looked vaguely about for another drink and didn't find any. He said, "I brought quite a few back. Archimedes, Newton, Galileo. Poor fellows."

"Didn't they like it here? I should think they'd have been fascinated by our modern science," said Robertson. He was beginning to enjoy the conversation.

"Oh, they were. They were. Especially Archimedes. I thought he'd go mad with joy at first after I explained a little of it in some Greek I'd boned up on, but no—no—"

"What was wrong?"

"Just a different culture. They couldn't get used to our way of life. They got terribly lonely and frightened. I had to send them back."

"That's too bad."

"Yes. Great minds, but not flexible minds. Not universal. So I tried Shakespeare."

"*What?*" yelled Robertson. This was getting closer to home.

"Don't yell, my boy," said Welch. "It's bad manners."

"Did you say you brought back Shakespeare?"

"I did. I needed someone with a universal mind; someone who knew people well enough to be able to live with them centuries way from his own time. Shakespeare was the man. I've got his signature. As a memento, you know."

"On you?" asked Robertson, eyes bugging.

"Right here." Welch fumbled in one vest pocket after another. "Ah, here it is."

A little piece of pasteboard was passed to the instructor. On one side it said: "L. Klein & Sons, Wholesale Hardware." On the other side, in straggly script, was written, "Willm Shakesper."

A wild surmise filled Robertson. "What did he look like?"

"Not like his pictures. Bald and an ugly mustache. He spoke in a thick brogue. Of course, I did my best to please him with our times. I told him we thought highly of his plays and still put them on the boards. In fact, I said we thought they were the greatest pieces of literature in the English language, maybe in any language."

"Good. Good," said Robertson breathlessly.

"I said people had written volumes of commentaries on his plays. Naturally he wanted to see one and I got one for him from the library."

"And?"

"Oh, he was fascinated. Of course, he had trouble with the current idioms and references to events since 1600, but I helped out. Poor fellow. I don't think he ever expected such treatment. He kept saying, 'God ha' mercy! What cannot be racked from words in five centuries? One could wring, methinks, a flood from a damp clout!' "

"He wouldn't say that."

"Why not? He wrote his plays as quickly as he could. He said he had to on account of the deadlines. He wrote *Hamlet* in less than six months. The plot was an old one. He just polished it up."

"That's all they do to a telescope mirror. Just polish it up," said the English instructor indignantly.

The physicist disregarded him. He made out an untouched cocktail on the bar some feet away and sidled toward it. "I told the immortal bard that we even gave college courses in Shakespeare."

"*I* give one."

"I know. I enrolled him in your evening extension course. I never saw a man so eager to find out what posterity thought of him as poor Bill was. He worked hard at it."

"You enrolled William Shakespeare in my course?" mumbled Robertson. Even as an alcoholic fantasy, the thought staggered him. And *was* it an alcoholic fantasy? He was beginning to recall a bald man with a queer way of talking. . . .

"Not under his real name, of course," said Dr. Welch. "Never mind what he went under. It was a mistake, that's all. A big mistake. Poor fellow." He had the cocktail now and shook his head at it.

"Why was it a mistake? What happened?"

"I had to send him back to 1600," roared Welch indignantly. "How much humiliation do you think a man can stand?"

"What humiliation are you talking about?"

Dr. Welch tossed off the cocktail. "Why, you poor simpleton, you *flunked* him."

Someday

Niccolo Mazetti lay stomach down on the rug, chin buried in the palm of one small hand, and listened to the Bard disconsolately. There was even the suspicion of tears in his dark eyes, a luxury an eleven-year-old could allow himself only when alone.

The Bard said, "Once upon a time in the middle of a deep wood, there lived a poor woodcutter and his two motherless daughters, who were each as beautiful as the day is long. The older daughter had long hair as black as a feather from a raven's wing, but the younger daughter had hair as bright and golden as the sunlight of an autumn afternoon.

"Many times while the girls were waiting for their father to come home from his day's work in the wood, the older girl would sit before a mirror and sing—"

What she sang, Niccolo did not hear, for a call sounded from outside the room: "Hey, Nickie."

And Niccolo, his face clearing on the moment, rushed to the window and shouted, "Hey, Paul."

Paul Loeb waved an excited hand. He was thinner than Niccolo and not as tall, for all he was six months older. His face was full of repressed tension which showed itself most clearly in the rapid blinking of his eyelids. "Hey, Nickie, let me in. I've got an idea and a *half*. Wait till you hear it." He looked rapidly about him as though to check on the possibility of eavesdroppers, but the front yard was quite patently empty. He repeated, in a whisper, "Wait till you hear it."

"All right. I'll open the door."

The Bard continued smoothly, oblivious to the sudden loss of attention on the part of Niccolo. As Paul entered, the Bard was saying. ". . . Thereupon, the lion said, 'If you will find me the lost egg of the bird which flies over the Ebony Mountain once every ten years, I will—' "

Paul said, "Is that a Bard you're listening to? I didn't know you had one."

Niccolo reddened and the look of unhappiness returned to his face. "Just an old thing I had when I was a kid. It ain't much good." He kicked at the Bard with his foot and caught the somewhat scarred and discolored plastic covering a glancing blow.

The Bard hiccupped as its speaking attachment was jarred out of contact a moment, then it went on: "—for a year and a day until the iron shoes were worn out. The princess stopped at the side of the road. . . ."

Paul said, "Boy, that *is* an old model," and looked at it critically.

Despite Niccolo's own bitterness against the Bard, he winced at the other's condescending tone. For the moment, he was sorry he had allowed Paul in, at least before he had restored the Bard to its usual resting place in the basement. It was only in the desperation of a dull day and a fruitless discussion with his father that he had resurrected it. And it turned out to be just as stupid as he had expected.

Nickie was a little afraid of Paul anyway, since Paul had special courses at school and everyone said he was going to grow up to be a Computing Engineer.

Not that Niccolo himself was doing badly at school. He got adequate marks in logic, binary manipulations, computing and elementary circuits; all the usual grammar-school subjects. But that was it! They were just the usual subjects and he would grow up to be a control-board guard like everyone else.

Paul, however, knew mysterious things about what he called electronics and theoretical mathematics and programing. Especially programing. Niccolo didn't even try to understand when Paul bubbled over about it.

Paul listened to the Bard for a few minutes and said, "You been using it much?"

"No!" said Niccolo, offended. "I've had it in the basement since before you moved into the neighborhood. I just got it out today—" He lacked an excuse that seemed adequate to himself, so he concluded, "I just got it out."

Paul said, "Is that what it tells you about: woodcutters and princesses and talking animals?"

Niccolo said, "It's terrible. My dad says we can't afford a new one. I said to him this morning—" The memory of the morning's fruitless pleadings brought Niccolo dangerously near tears, which he repressed in a panic. Somehow, he felt that Paul's thin cheeks never felt the stain of tears and that Paul would have only contempt for anyone else less strong than himself.

Niccolo went on, "So I thought I'd try this old thing again, but it's no good."

Paul turned off the Bard, pressed the contact that led to a nearly instantaneous reorientation and recombination of the vocabulary, characters, plot lines and climaxes stored within it. Then he reactivated it.

The Bard began smoothly, "Once upon a time there was a little boy named Willikins whose mother had died and who lived with a stepfather and a stepbrother. Although the stepfather was very well-to-do, he begrudged poor Willikins the very bed he slept in so that Willikins was forced to get such rest as he could on a pile of straw in the stable next to the horses—"

"Horses!" cried Paul.

"They're a kind of animal," said Niccolo. "I think."

"I know that! I just mean imagine stories about *horses*."

"It tells about horses all the time," said Niccolo. "There are things called cows, too. You milk them but the Bard doesn't say how."

"Well, gee, why don't you fix it up?"

"I'd like to know how."

The Bard was saying, "Often Willikins would think that if only he were rich and powerful, he would show his stepfather and stepbrother what it meant to be cruel to a little boy, so one day he decided to go out into the world and seek his fortune."

Paul, who wasn't listening to the Bard, said, "It's *easy*. The Bard has memory cylinders all fixed up for plot lines and climaxes and things. We don't have to worry about that. It's just vocabulary we've got to fix so it'll know about computers and automation and electronics and real things about today. Then it can tell interesting stories, you know, instead of about princesses and things."

Niccolo said despondently, "I wish we could do that."

Paul said, "Listen, my dad says if I get into special computing school next year, he'll get me a *real* Bard, a late model. A big one with an attachment for space stories and mysteries. And a visual attachment, too!"

"You mean *see* the stories?"

"Sure. Mr. Daugherty at school says they've got things like that, now, but not for just everybody. Only if I get into computing school, Dad can get a few breaks."

Niccolo's eyes bulged with envy. "Gee. *Seeing* a story."

"You can come over and watch anytime, Nickie."

"Oh, boy. Thanks."

"That's all right. But remember, I'm the guy who says what kind of story we hear."

"Sure. Sure." Niccolo would have agreed readily to much more onerous conditions.

Paul's attention returned to the Bard.

It was saying, " 'If that is the case,' said the king, stroking his beard and frowning till clouds filled the sky and lightning flashed, 'you will see to it that my entire land is freed of flies by this time day after tomorrow or—' "

"All we've got to do," said Paul, "is open it up—" He shut the Bard off again and was prying at its front panel as he spoke.

"Hey," said Niccolo, in sudden alarm. "Don't break it."

"I won't break it," said Paul impatiently. "I know all about these things." Then, with sudden caution, "Your father and mother home?"

"No."

"All right, then." He had the front panel off and peered in. "Boy, this *is* a one-cylinder thing."

He worked away at the Bard's innards. Niccolo, who watched with painful suspense, could not make out what he was doing.

Paul pulled out a thin, flexible metal strip, powdered with dots. "That's the Bard's memory cylinder. I'll bet its capacity for stories is under a trillion."

"What are you going to do, Paul?" quavered Niccolo.

"I'll give it vocabulary."

"How?"

"Easy. I've got a book here. Mr. Daugherty gave it to me at school."

Paul pulled the book out of his pocket and pried at it till he had its plastic jacket off. He unreeled the tape a bit, ran it through the vocalizer, which he turned down to a whisper, then placed it within the Bard's vitals. He made further attachments.

"What'll that do?"

"The book will talk and the Bard will put it all on its memory tape."

"What good will that do?"

"Boy, you're a dope! This book is all about computers and automation and the Bard will get all that information. Then he can stop talking about kings making lightning when they frown."

Niccolo said, "And the good guy always wins anyway. There's no excitement."

"Oh, well," said Paul, watching to see if his setup was working properly, "that's the way they make Bards. They got to have the good guy win and make the bad guys lose and things like that. I heard my father talking about it once. He says that without censorship there'd be no telling what the younger generation would come to. He says it's bad enough as it is. . . . There, it's working fine."

Paul brushed his hands against one another and turned away from the Bard. He said, "But listen, I didn't tell you my idea yet. It's the best thing you ever heard, I bet. I came right to you, because I figured you'd come in with me."

"Sure, Paul, sure."

"Okay. You know Mr. Daugherty at school? You know what a funny kind of guy he is. Well, he likes me, kind of."

"I know."

"I was over at his house after school today."

"You *were?*"

"Sure. He says I'm going to be entering computer school and he wants to encourage me and things like that. He says the world needs more people who can design advanced computer circuits and do proper programing."

"Oh?"

Paul might have caught some of the emptiness behind that monosyllable. He said impatiently, "Programing! I told you a hundred times. That's when you set up problems for the giant computers like Multivac to work on. Mr. Daugherty says it gets harder all the time to find people who can really run computers. He says anyone can keep an eye on the controls and check off answers and put through routine problems. He says the trick is to expand research and figure out ways to ask the right questions, and that's hard.

"Anyway, Nickie, he took me to his place and showed me his collection of old computers. It's kind of a hobby of his to collect old computers. He had tiny computers you had to push with your hand, with little knobs all over it. And he had a hunk of wood he called a slide rule with a little piece of it that went in and out. And some wires with balls on them. He even had a hunk of paper with a kind of thing he called a multiplication table."

Niccolo, who found himself only moderately interested, said, "A paper table?"

"It wasn't really a table like you eat on. It was different. It was to help people compute. Mr. Daugherty tried to explain but he didn't have much time and it was kind of complicated, anyway."

"Why didn't people just use a computer?"

"That was *before* they had computers," cried Paul.

"Before?"

"Sure. Do you think people always had computers? Didn't you ever hear of cavemen?"

Niccolo said, "How'd they get along without computers?"

"*I* don't know. Mr. Daugherty says they just had children any old time and did anything that came into their heads whether it would be good for everybody or not. They didn't even know if it was good or not. And farmers grew things with their hands and people had to do all the work in the factories and run all the machines."

"I don't believe you."

"That's what Mr. Daugherty said. He said it was just plain messy and everyone was miserable. . . . Anyway, let me get to my idea, will you?"

"Well, go ahead. Who's stopping you?" said Niccolo, offended.

"All right. Well, the hand computers, the ones with the knobs, had little squiggles on each knob. And the slide rule had squiggles on it. And the multiplication table was all squiggles. I asked what they were. Mr. Daugherty said they were numbers."

"What?"

"Each different squiggle stood for a different number. For 'one' you made a kind of mark, for 'two' you make another kind of mark, for 'three' another one and so on."

"What for?"

"So you could compute."

"What *for?* You just tell the computer—"

"Jiminy," cried Paul, his face twisting with anger, "can't you get it through your head? These slide rules and things didn't talk."

"Then how—"

"The answers showed up in squiggles and you had to know what the squiggles meant. Mr. Daugherty says that, in olden days, everybody learned how to make squiggles when they were kids and how to decode them, too. Making squiggles was called 'writing' and decoding them was 'reading.' He says there was a different kind of squiggle for every word and they used to write whole books in squiggles. He said they had some at the museum and I could look at them if I wanted to. He said if I was going to be a real computer and programer I would have to know about the history of computing and that's why he was showing me all these things."

Niccolo frowned. He said, "You mean everybody had to figure out squiggles for every word and *remember* them? . . . Is this all real or are you making it up?"

"It's all real. Honest. Look, this is the way you make a 'one.' " He drew his finger through the air in a rapid downstroke. "This way you make 'two,' and this way 'three.' I learned all the numbers up to 'nine.' "

Niccolo watched the curving finger uncomprehendingly. "What's the good of it?"

"You can learn how to make words. I asked Mr. Daugherty how you made the squiggle for 'Paul Loeb' but he didn't know. He said there were people at the museum who would know. He said there were people who had learned how to decode whole books. He said computers could be designed to decode books and used to be used that way but not any more because we have real books now, with magnetic tapes that go through the vocalizer and come out talking, you know."

"Sure."

"So if we go down to the museum, we can get to learn how to make words in squiggles. They'll let us because I'm going to computer school."

Niccolo was riddled with disappointment. "Is that your idea? Holy Smokes, Paul, who wants to do that? Make stupid squiggles!"

"Don't you get it? Don't you *get* it? You dope. *It'll be secret message stuff!*"

"What?"

"Sure. What good is talking when everyone can understand you? With squiggles you can send secret messages. You can make them on paper and nobody in the world would know what you were saying unless they knew the squiggles, too. And they wouldn't, you bet, unless we taught them. We can have a real club, with initiations and rules and a clubhouse. Boy—"

A certain excitement began stirring in Niccolo's bosom. "What kind of secret messages?"

"Any kind. Say I want to tell you to come over my place and watch my new Visual Bard and I don't want any of the other fellows to come. I make the right squiggles on paper and I give it to you and you look at it and you know what to do. Nobody else does. You can even show it to them and they wouldn't know a thing."

"Hey, that's something," yelled Niccolo, completely won over. "When do we learn how?"

"Tomorrow," said Paul. "I'll get Mr. Daugherty to explain to the museum that it's all right and you get your mother and father to say okay. We can go down right after school and start learning."

"Sure!" cried Niccolo. "We can be club officers."

"I'll be president of the club," said Paul matter-of-factly. "You can be vice-president."

"All right. Hey, this is going to be lots more fun than the Bard." He was suddenly reminded of the Bard and said in sudden apprehension, "Hey, what about my old Bard?"

Paul turned to look at it. It was quietly taking in the slowly unreeling book, and the sound of the book's vocalizations was a dimly heard murmur.

He said, "I'll disconnect it."

He worked away while Niccolo watched anxiously. After a few moments, Paul put his reassembled book into his pocket, replaced the Bard's panel and activated it.

The Bard said, "Once upon a time, in a large city, there lived a poor young boy named Fair Johnnie whose only friend in the world was a small computer. The computer, each morning, would tell the boy whether it would rain that day and answer any problems he might have. It was never wrong. But it so happened that one day, the king of that land, having heard of the little computer, decided that he would have it as his own. With this purpose in mind, he called in his Grand Vizier and said—"

Niccolo turned off the Bard with a quick motion of his hand. "Same old junk," he said passionately. "Just with a computer thrown in."

"Well," said Paul, "they got so much stuff on the tape already that the computer business doesn't show up much when random combinations are made. What's the difference, anyway? You just need a new model."

"We'll *never* be able to afford one. Just this dirty old miserable thing." He kicked at it again, hitting it more squarely this time. The Bard moved backward with a squeal of castors.

"You can always watch mine, when I get it," said Paul. "Besides, don't forget our squiggle club."

Niccolo nodded.

"I tell you what," said Paul. "Let's go over to my place. My father has some books about old times. We can listen to them and maybe get some ideas. You leave a note for your folks and maybe you can stay over for supper. Come on."

"Okay," said Niccolo, and the two boys ran out together. Niccolo, in his eagerness, ran almost squarely into the Bard, but he only rubbed at the spot on his hip where he had made contact and ran on.

The activation signal of the Bard glowed. Niccolo's collision closed a circuit and, although it was alone in the room and there was none to hear, it began a story, nevertheless.

But not in its usual voice, somehow; in a lower tone that had a hint of throatiness in it. An adult, listening, might almost have thought that the voice carried a hint of passion in it, a trace of near feeling.

The Bard said: "Once upon a time, there was a little computer named the Bard who lived all alone with cruel step-people. The cruel step-people continually made fun of the little computer and sneered at him, telling him he was good-for-nothing and that he was a useless object. They struck him and kept him in lonely rooms for months at a time.

"Yet through it all the little computer remained brave. He always did the best he could, obeying all orders cheerfully. Nevertheless, the step-people with whom he lived remained cruel and heartless.

"One day, the little computer learned that in the world there existed a great many computers of all sorts, great numbers of them. Some were Bards like himself, but some ran factories, and some ran farms. Some organized population and some analyzed all kinds of data. Many were very powerful and very wise, much more powerful and wise than the step-people who were so cruel to the little computer.

"And the little computer knew then that computers would always grow wiser and more powerful until someday—someday—someday—"

But a valve must finally have stuck in the Bard's aging and corroding vitals, for as it waited alone in the darkening room through the evening, it could only whisper over and over again, "Someday—someday—someday."

The Author's Ordeal

(WITH APOLOGIES TO W. S. GILBERT)

Plots, helter-skelter, teem within your brain;
Plots, s.f. plots, devised with joy and gladness;
Plots crowd your skull and stubbornly remain,
Until you're driven into hopeless madness.

When you're with your best girl and your mind's in a whirl and you don't
hear a thing that she's saying;
Or at Symphony Hall you are gone past recall and you can't tell a note that
they're playing;
Or you're driving a car and have not gone too far when you find that you've
sped through a red light,
And on top of that, lord! you have sideswiped a Ford, and have broken your
one working headlight;
Or your boss slaps your back (having made some smart crack) and you stare
at him, stupidly blinking;
Then you say something dumb so he's sure you're a crumb, and are possibly
given to drinking.
When events such as that have been knocking you flat, do not blame supernatural forces;
If you write s.f. tales, you'll be knocked off your rails, just as sure as the stars
in their courses.

For your plot-making mind will stay deaf, dumb and blind to the dull facts
    of life that will hound you,
While the wonders of space have you close in embrace and the glory of star
    beams surround you.

You begin with a ship that is caught on a skip into hyperspace en route for
    Castor,
And has found to its cost that it seems to be lost in a Galaxy like ours, but
    vaster.
You're a little perplexed as to what may come next and you make up a series
    of creatures
Who are villains and liars with such evil desires and with perfectly horrible
    features.
Our brave heroes are faced with these hordes and are placed in a terribly
    crucial position,
For the enemy's bound (once our Galaxy's found) that they'll beat mankind
    into submission.
Now you must make it rough when developing stuff so's to keep the yarn
    pulsing with tension,
So the Earthmen are four (only four and no more) while the numbers of foes
    are past mention.
Our four heroes are caught and accordingly brought to the sneering, tyranni-
    cal leaders.
"Where is Earth?" they demand, but the men mutely stand with a courage
    that pleases the readers.

But, now, wait just a bit; let's see, this isn't it, since you haven't provided a
    maiden,
Who is both good and pure (yet with sexy allure) and with not many clothes
    overladen.
She is part of the crew, and so she's captured, too, and is ogled by foes who
    are lustful;
There's desire in each eye and there's good reason why, for of beauty our girl
    has a bustful.
Just the same you go fast till this section is passed so the reader won't raise
    any ruction,
When recalling the foe are all reptiles and so have no interest in human
    seduction.
Then they truss up the girl and they make the whips swirl just in order to
    break Earthmen's silence,
And so that's when our men break their handcuffs and then we are treated
    to scenes full of violence.
Every hero from Earth is a fighter from birth and his fists are a match for a
    dozen,

And then just when this spot has been reached in your plot you come to
with your mind all a buzzin'.

You don't know where you are, or the site of your car, and your tie is askew
and you haven't a clue of the time of the day or of what people say or
the fact that they stare at your socks (not a pair) and decide it's a fad,
or else that you're mad, which is just a surmise from the gleam in your
eyes, till at last they conclude from your general mood, you'll be mad
from right now till you're hoary.
But the torture is done and it's now for the fun and the paper that's white
and the words that are right, for you've worked up a new s.f. story.

Dreaming
Is a Private Thing

Jesse Weill looked up from his desk. His old, spare body, his sharp, high-bridged nose, deep-set, shadowy eyes and amazing shock of white hair had trademarked his appearance during the years that Dreams, Inc., had become world-famous.

He said, "Is the boy here already, Joe?"

Joe Dooley was short and heavy-set. A cigar caressed his moist lower lip. He took it away for a moment and nodded. "His folks are with him. They're all scared."

"You're sure this is not a false alarm, Joe? I haven't got much time." He looked at his watch. "Government business at two."

"This is a sure thing, Mr. Weill." Dooley's face was a study in earnestness. His jowls quivered with persuasive intensity. "Like I told you, I picked him up playing some kind of basketball game in the schoolyard. You should've seen the kid. He stunk. When he had his hands on the ball, his own team had to take it away, and fast, but just the same he had all the stance of a star player. Know what I mean? To me it was a giveaway."

"Did you talk to him?"

"Well, sure. I stopped him at lunch. You know me." Dooley gestured expansively with his cigar and caught the severed ash with his other hand. "Kid, I said—"

"And he's dream material?"

"I said, 'Kid, I just came from Africa and—' "

"All right." Weill held up the palm of his hand. "Your word I'll always take. How you do it I don't know, but when you say a boy is a potential dreamer, I'll gamble. Bring him in."

The youngster came in between his parents. Dooley pushed chairs forward and Weill rose to shake hands. He smiled at the youngster in a way that turned the wrinkles of his face into benevolent creases.

"You're Tommy Slutsky?"

Tommy nodded wordlessly. He was about ten and a little small for that. His dark hair was plastered down unconvincingly and his face was unrealistically clean.

Weill said, "You're a good boy?"

The boy's mother smiled at once and patted Tommy's head maternally (a gesture which did not soften the anxious expression on the youngster's face). She said, "He's always a very good boy."

Weill let this dubious statement pass. "Tell me, Tommy," he said, and held out a lollipop which was first hesitated over, then accepted, "do you ever listen to dreamies?"

"Sometimes," said Tommy trebly.

Mr. Slutsky cleared his throat. He was broad-shouldered and thick-fingered, the type of laboring man who, every once in a while, to the confusion of eugenics, sired a dreamer. "We rented one or two for the boy. Real old ones."

Weill nodded. He said, "Did you like them, Tommy?"

"They were sort of silly."

"You think up better ones for yourself, do you?"

The grin that spread over the ten-year-old face had the effect of taking away some of the unreality of the slicked hair and washed face.

Weill went on gently, "Would you like to make up a dream for me?"

Tommy was instantly embarrassed. "I guess not."

"It won't be hard. It's very easy. . . . Joe."

Dooley moved a screen out of the way and rolled forward a dream recorder.

The youngster looked owlishly at it.

Weill lifted the helmet and brought it close to the boy. "Do you know what this is?"

Tommy shrank away. "No."

"It's a thinker. That's what we call it because people think into it. You put it on your head and think anything you want."

"Then what happens?"

"Nothing at all. It feels nice."

"No," said Tommy, "I guess I'd rather not."

His mother bent hurriedly toward him. "It won't hurt, Tommy. You do what the man says." There was an unmistakable edge to her voice.

Tommy stiffened, and looked as though he might cry but he didn't. Weill put the thinker on him.

He did it gently and slowly and let it remain there for some thirty seconds before speaking again, to let the boy assure himself it would do no harm, to let him get used to the insinuating touch of the fibrils against the sutures of his skull (penetrating the skin so finely as to be insensible almost), and finally to let him get used to the faint hum of the alternating field vortices.

Then he said, "Now would you think for us?"

"About what?" Only the boy's nose and mouth showed.

"About anything you want. What's the best thing you would like to do when school is out?"

The boy thought a moment and said, with rising inflection, "Go on a stratojet?"

"Why not? Sure thing. You go on a jet. It's taking off right now." He gestured lightly to Dooley, who threw the freezer into circuit.

Weill kept the boy only five minutes and then let him and his mother be escorted from the office by Dooley. Tommy looked bewildered but undamaged by the ordeal.

Weill said to the father, "Now, Mr. Slutsky, if your boy does well on this test, we'll be glad to pay you five hundred dollars each year until he finishes high school. In that time, all we'll ask is that he spend an hour a week some afternoon at our special school."

"Do I have to sign a paper?" Slutsky's voice was a bit hoarse.

"Certainly. This is business, Mr. Slutsky."

"Well, I don't know. Dreamers are hard to come by, I hear."

"They are. They are. But your son, Mr. Slutsky, is not a dreamer yet. He might never be. Five hundred dollars a year is a gamble for us. It's not a gamble for you. When he's finished high school, it may turn out he's not a dreamer, yet you've lost nothing. You've gained maybe four thousand dollars altogether. If he *is* a dreamer, he'll make a nice living and you certainly haven't lost then."

"He'll need special training, won't he?"

"Oh, yes, most intensive. But we don't have to worry about that till after he's finished high school. Then, after two years with us, he'll be developed. Rely on me, Mr. Slutsky."

"Will you guarantee that special training?"

Weill, who had been shoving a paper across the desk at Slutsky, and punching a pen wrong-end-to at him, put the pen down and chuckled. "A guarantee? No. How can we when we don't know for sure yet if he's a real talent? Still, the five hundred a year will stay yours."

Slutsky pondered and shook his head. "I tell you straight out, Mr. Weill . . . After your man arranged to have us come here, I called Luster-Think. They said they'll guarantee training."

Weill sighed. "Mr. Slutsky, I don't like to talk against a competitor. If they say they'll guarantee schooling, they'll do as they say, but they can't make a boy a dreamer if he hasn't got it in him, schooling or not. If they take a plain boy without the proper talent and put him through a development course, they'll ruin him. A dreamer he won't be, I guarantee you. And a normal human being, he won't be, either. Don't take the chance of doing it to your son.

"Now Dreams, Inc., will be perfectly honest with you. If he can be a dreamer, we'll make him one. If not, we'll give him back to you without having tampered with him and say, 'Let him learn a trade.' He'll be better and healthier that way. I tell you, Mr. Slutsky—I have sons and daughters and grandchildren so I know what I say—I would not allow a child of mine to be pushed into dreaming if he's not ready for it. Not for a million dollars."

Slutsky wiped his mouth with the back of his hand and reached for the pen. "What does this say?"

"This is just an option. We pay you a hundred dollars in cash right now. No strings attached. We study the boy's reverie. If we feel it's worth following up, we'll call you in again and make the five-hundred-dollar-a-year deal. Leave yourself in my hands, Mr. Slutsky, and don't worry. You won't be sorry."

Slutsky signed.

Weill passed the document through the file slot and handed an envelope to Slutsky.

Five minutes later, alone in the office, he placed the unfreezer over his own head and absorbed the boy's reverie intently. It was a typically childish daydream. First Person was at the controls of the plane, which looked like a compound of illustrations out of the filmed thrillers that still circulated among those who lacked the time, desire or money for dream cylinders.

When he removed the unfreezer, he found Dooley looking at him.

"Well, Mr. Weill, what do you think?" said Dooley, with an eager and proprietary air.

"Could be, Joe. Could be. He has the overtones and, for a ten-year-old boy without a scrap of training, it's hopeful. When the plane went through a cloud, there was a distinct sensation of pillows. Also the smell of clean sheets, which was an amusing touch. We can go with him a ways, Joe."

"Good."

"But I tell you, Joe, what we really need is to catch them still sooner. And why not? Someday, Joe, every child will be tested at birth. A difference in the brain there positively must be and it should be found. Then we could separate the dreamers at the very beginning."

"Hell, Mr. Weill," said Dooley, looking hurt. "What would happen to my job, then?"

Weill laughed. "No cause to worry yet, Joe. It won't happen in our lifetimes. In mine, certainly not. We'll be depending on good talent scouts like you for many years. You just watch the playgrounds and the streets"—Weill's gnarled hand dropped to Dooley's shoulder with a gentle, approving pressure—"and find us a few more Hillarys and Janows and Luster-Think won't ever catch us. . . . Now get out. I want lunch and then I'll be ready for my two o'clock appointment. The government, Joe, the government." And he winked portentously.

Jesse Weill's two o'clock appointment was with a young man, apple-cheeked, spectacled, sandy-haired and glowing with the intensity of a man with a mission. He presented his credentials across Weill's desk and revealed himself to be John J. Byrne, an agent of the Department of Arts and Sciences.

"Good afternoon, Mr. Byrne," said Weill. "In what way can I be of service?"

"Are we private here?" asked the agent. He had an unexpected baritone.

"Quite private."

"Then, if you don't mind, I'll ask you to absorb this." Byrne produced a small and battered cylinder and held it out between thumb and forefinger.

Weill took it, hefted it, turned it this way and that and said with a denture-revealing smile, "Not the product of Dreams, Inc., Mr. Byrne."

"I didn't think it was," said the agent. "I'd still like you to absorb it. I'd set the automatic cutoff for about a minute, though."

"That's all that can be endured?" Weill pulled the receiver to his desk and placed the cylinder into the unfreeze compartment. He removed it, polished either end of the cylinder with his handkerchief and tried again. "It doesn't make good contact," he said. "An amateurish job."

He placed the cushioned unfreeze helmet over his skull and adjusted the temple contacts, then set the automatic cutoff. He leaned back and clasped his hands over his chest and began absorbing.

His fingers grew rigid and clutched at his jacket. After the cutoff had brought absorption to an end, he removed the unfreezer and looked faintly angry. "A raw piece," he said. "It's lucky I'm an old man so that such things no longer bother me."

Byrne said stiffly, "It's not the worst we've found. And the fad is increasing."

Weill shrugged. "Pornographic dreamies. It's a logical development, I suppose."

The government man said, "Logical or not, it represents a deadly danger for the moral fiber of the nation."

"The moral fiber," said Weill, "can take a lot of beating. Erotica of one form or another have been circulated all through history."

"Not like this, sir. A direct mind-to-mind stimulation is much more effective than smoking room stories or filthy pictures. Those must be filtered through the senses and lose some of their effect in that way."

Weill could scarcely argue that point. He said, "What would you have me do?"

"Can you suggest a possible source for this cylinder?"

"Mr. Byrne, I'm not a policeman."

"No, no, I'm not asking you to do our work for us. The Department is quite capable of conducting its own investigations. Can you help us, I mean, from your own specialized knowledge? You say your company did not put out that filth. Who did?"

"No reputable dream distributor. I'm sure of that. It's too cheaply made."

"That could have been done on purpose."

"And no professional dreamer originated it."

"Are you sure, Mr. Weill? Couldn't dreamers do this sort of thing for some small, illegitimate concern for money—or for fun?"

"They could, but not this particular one. No overtones. It's two-dimensional. Of course, a thing like this doesn't need overtones."

"What do you mean, overtones?"

Weill laughed gently. "You are not a dreamie fan?"

Byrne tried not to look virtuous and did not entirely succeed. "I prefer music."

"Well, that's all right, too," said Weill tolerantly, "but it makes it a little harder to explain overtones. Even people who absorb dreamies would not be able to explain if you asked them. Still they'd know a dreamie was no good if the overtones were missing, even if they couldn't tell you why. Look, when an experienced dreamer goes into reverie, he doesn't think a story like in the old-fashioned television or book films. It's a series of little visions. Each one has several meanings. If you studied them carefully, you'd find maybe five or six. While absorbing in the ordinary way, you would never notice, but careful study shows it. Believe me, my psychological staff puts in long hours on just that point. All the overtones, the different meanings, blend together into a mass of guided emotion. Without them, everything would be flat, tasteless.

"Now, this morning, I tested a young boy. A ten-year-old with possibilities. A cloud to him isn't a cloud, it's a pillow, too. Having the sensations of both, it was more than either. Of course, the boy's very primitive. But when he's through with his schooling, he'll be trained and disciplined. He'll be subjected to all sorts of sensations. He'll store up experience. He'll study and analyze classic dreamies of the past. He'll learn how to control and direct his thoughts, though, mind you, I have always said that when a good dreamer improvises—"

Weill halted abruptly, then proceeded in less impassioned tones, "I shouldn't get excited. All I try to bring out now is that every professional dreamer has his own type of overtones which he can't mask. To an expert it's like signing his name on the dreamie. And I, Mr. Byrne, know all the signatures. Now that piece of dirt you brought me has no overtones at all. It was done by an ordinary person. A little talent, maybe, but like you and me, he really can't think."

Byrne reddened a trifle. "A lot of people can think, Mr. Weill, even if they don't make dreamies."

"Oh, tush," and Weill wagged his hand in the air. "Don't be angry with what an old man says. I don't mean think as in reason. I mean think as in dream. We all can dream after a fashion, just like we all can run. But can you and I run a mile in four minutes? You and I can talk, but are we Daniel Websters? Now when I think of a steak, I think of the word. Maybe I have a quick picture of a brown steak on a platter. Maybe you have a better pictori-alization of it and you can see the crisp fat and the onions and the baked potato. I don't know. But a *dreamer* . . . He sees it and smells it and tastes it and everything about it, with the charcoal and the satisfied feeling in the stomach and the way the knife cuts through it and a hundred other things all at once. Very sensual. Very sensual. You and I can't do it."

"Well, then," said Byrne, "no professional dreamer has done this. That's something anyway." He put the cylinder in his inner jacket pocket. "I hope we'll have your full cooperation in squelching this sort of thing."

"Positively, Mr. Byrne. With a whole heart."

"I hope so." Byrne spoke with a consciousness of power. "It's not up to me, Mr. Weill, to say what will be done and what won't be done, but this sort of thing," he tapped the cylinder he had brought, "will make it awfully tempting to impose a really strict censorship on dreamies."

He rose. "Good day, Mr. Weill."

"Good day, Mr. Byrne. I'll hope always for the best."

Francis Belanger burst into Jesse Weill's office in his usual steaming tizzy, his reddish hair disordered and his face aglow with worry and a mild perspi-ration. He was brought up sharply by the sight of Weill's head cradled in the crook of his elbow and bent on the desk until only the glimmer of white hair was visible.

Belanger swallowed. "Boss?"

Weill's head lifted. "It's you, Frank?"

"What's the matter, boss? Are you sick?"

"I'm old enough to be sick, but I'm on my feet. Staggering, but on my feet. A government man was here."

"What did he want?"

"He threatens censorship. He brought a sample of what's going round. Cheap dreamies for bottle parties."

"God damn!" said Belanger feelingly.

"The only trouble is that morality makes for good campaign fodder. They'll be hitting out everywhere. And, to tell the truth, we're vulnerable, Frank."

"*We* are? Our stuff is clean. We play up straight adventure and romance."

Weill thrust out his lower lip and wrinkled his forehead. "Between us, Frank, we don't have to make believe. Clean? It depends on how you look at it. It's not for publication, maybe, but you know and I know that every dreamie has its Freudian connotations. You can't deny it."

"Sure, if you *look* for it. If you're a psychiatrist—"

"If you're an ordinary person, too. The ordinary observer doesn't know it's there and maybe he couldn't tell a phallic symbol from a mother image even if you pointed it out. Still, his subconscious knows. And it's the connotations that make many a dreamie click."

"All right, what's the government going to do? Clean up the subconscious?"

"It's a problem. I don't know what they're going to do. What we have on our side, and what I'm mainly depending on, is the fact that the public loves its dreamies and won't give them up. . . . Meanwhile, what did you come in for? You want to see me about something, I suppose?"

Belanger tossed an object onto Weill's desk and shoved his shirttail deeper into his trousers.

Weill broke open the glistening plastic cover and took out the enclosed cylinder. At one end was engraved in a too fancy script in pastel blue "Along the Himalayan Trail." It bore the mark of Luster-Think.

"The Competitor's Product." Weill said it with capitals, and his lips twitched. "It hasn't been published yet. Where did you get it, Frank?"

"Never mind. I just want you to absorb it."

Weill sighed. "Today, everyone wants me to absorb dreams. Frank, it's not dirty?"

Belanger said testily, "It has your Freudian symbols. Narrow crevasses between the mountain peaks. I hope that won't bother you."

"I'm an old man. It stopped bothering me years ago, but that other thing was so poorly done, it hurt. . . . All right, let's see what you've got here."

Again the recorder. Again the unfreezer over his skull and at the temples. This time, Weill rested back in his chair for fifteen minutes or more, while Francis Belanger went hurriedly through two cigarettes.

When Weill removed the headpiece and blinked dream out of his eyes, Belanger said, "Well, what's your reaction, boss?"

Weill corrugated his forehead. "It's not for me. It was repetitious. With competition like this, Dreams, Inc., doesn't have to worry for a while."

"That's your mistake, boss. Luster-Think's going to win with stuff like this. We've got to do something."

"Now, Frank—"

"No, you listen. This is the coming thing."

"This!" Weill stared with a half-humorous dubiety at the cylinder. "It's amateurish, it's repetitious. Its overtones are very unsubtle. The snow had a distinct lemon sherbet taste. Who tastes lemon sherbet in snow these days, Frank? In the old days, yes. Twenty years ago, maybe. When Lyman Harrison first made his Snow Symphonies for sale down south, it was a big thing.

Sherbet and candy-striped mountaintops and sliding down chocolate-covered cliffs. It's slapstick, Frank. These days it doesn't go."

"Because," said Belanger, "you're not up with the times, boss. I've got to talk to you straight. When you started the dreamie business, when you bought up the basic patents and began putting them out, dreamies were luxury stuff. The market was small and individual. You could afford to turn out specialized dreamies and sell them to people at high prices."

"I know," said Weill, "and we've kept that up. But also we've opened a rental business for the masses."

"Yes, we have and it's not enough. Our dreamies have subtlety, yes. They can be used over and over again. The tenth time you're still finding new things, still getting new enjoyment. But how many people are connoisseurs? And another thing. Our stuff is strongly individualized. They're First Person."

"Well?"

"Well, Luster-Think is opening dream palaces. They've opened one with three hundred booths in Nashville. You walk in, take your seat, put on your unfreezer and get your dream. Everyone in the audience gets the same one."

"I've heard of it, Frank, and it's been done before. It didn't work the first time and it won't work now. You want to know why it won't work? Because, in the first place, dreaming is a private thing. Do you like your neighbor to know what you're dreaming? In the second place, in a dream palace, the dreams have to start on schedule, don't they? So the dreamer has to dream not when he wants to but when some palace manager says he should. Finally, a dream one person likes another person doesn't like. In those three hundred booths, I guarantee you, a hundred fifty people are dissatisfied. And if they're dissatisfied, they won't come back."

Slowly, Belanger rolled up his sleeves and opened his collar. "Boss," he said, "you're talking through your hat. What's the use of proving they won't work? They *are* working. The word came through today that Luster-Think is breaking ground for a thousand-booth palace in St. Louis. People can get used to public dreaming, if everyone else in the same room is having the same dream. And they can adjust themselves to having it at a given time, as long as it's cheap and convenient.

"Damn it, boss, it's a social affair. A boy and a girl go to a dream palace and absorb some cheap romantic thing with stereotyped overtones and commonplace situations, but still they come out with stars sprinkling their hair. They've had the same dream together. They've gone through identical sloppy emotions. They're *in tune*, boss. You bet they go back to the dream palace, and all their friends go, too."

"And if they don't like the dream?"

"That's the point. That's the nub of the whole thing. They're bound to like it. If you prepare Hillary specials with wheels within wheels within wheels, with surprise twists on the third-level undertones, with clever shifts of significance and all the other things we're so proud of, why, naturally, it won't appeal to everyone. Specialized dreamies are for specialized tastes. But Luster-Think is turning out simple jobs in Third Person so both sexes can be hit at once. Like what you've just absorbed. Simple, repetitive, commonplace. They're aiming at the lowest common denominator. No one will love it, maybe, but no one will hate it."

Weill sat silent for a long time and Belanger watched him. Then Weill said, "Frank, I started on quality and I'm staying there. Maybe you're right. Maybe dream palaces are the coming thing. If so we'll open them, but we'll use good stuff. Maybe Luster-Think underestimates ordinary people. Let's go slowly and not panic. I have based all my policies on the theory that there's always a market for quality. Sometimes, my boy, it would surprise you how big a market."

"Boss—"

The sounding of the intercom interrupted Belanger.

"What is it, Ruth?" said Weill.

The voice of his secretary said, "It's Mr. Hillary, sir. He wants to see you right away. He says it's important."

"Hillary?" Weill's voice registered shock. Then, "Wait five minutes, Ruth, then send him in."

Weill turned to Belanger. "Today, Frank, is definitely not one of my good days. A dreamer's place is in his home with his thinker. And Hillary's our best dreamer so he especially should be at home. What do you suppose is wrong with him?"

Belanger, still brooding over Luster-Think and dream palaces, said shortly, "Call him in and find out."

"In one minute. Tell me, how was his last dream? I haven't tried the one that came in last week."

Belanger came down to earth. He wrinkled his nose. "Not so good."

"Why not?"

"It was ragged. Too jumpy. I don't mind sharp transitions for the liveliness, you know, but there's got to be some connection, even if only on a deep level."

"Is it a total loss?"

"No Hillary dream is a *total* loss. It took a lot of editing, though. We cut it down quite a bit and spliced in some odd pieces he'd sent us now and then. You know, detached scenes. It's still not Grade A, but it will pass."

"You told him about this, Frank?"

"Think I'm crazy, boss? Think I'm going to say a harsh word to a dreamer?"

And at that point the door opened and Weill's comely young secretary smiled Sherman Hillary into the office.

. . . .

Sherman Hillary, at the age of thirty-one, could have been recognized as a dreamer by anyone. His eyes, unspectacled, had nevertheless the misty look of one who either needs glasses or who rarely focuses on anything mundane. He was of average height but underweight, with black hair that needed cutting, a narrow chin, a pale skin and a troubled look.

He muttered, "Hello, Mr. Weill," and half-nodded in hangdog fashion in the direction of Belanger.

Weill said heartily, "Sherman, my boy, you look fine. What's the matter? A dream is cooking only so-so at home? You're worried about it? . . . Sit down, sit down."

The dreamer did, sitting at the edge of the chair and holding his thighs stiffly together as though to be ready for instant obedience to a possible order to stand up once more.

He said, "I've come to tell you, Mr. Weill, I'm quitting."

"Quitting?"

"I don't want to dream any more, Mr. Weill."

Weill's old face looked older now than at any time in the day. "Why, Sherman?"

The dreamer's lips twisted. He blurted out, "Because I'm not *living*, Mr. Weill. Everything passes me by. It wasn't so bad at first. It was even relaxing. I'd dream evenings, weekends when I felt like, or any other time. And when I felt like I wouldn't. But now, Mr. Weill, I'm an old pro. You tell me I'm one of the best in the business and the industry looks to me to think up new subtleties and new changes on the old reliables like the flying reveries, and the worm-turning skits."

Weill said, "And is anyone better than you, Sherman? Your little sequence on leading an orchestra is selling steadily after ten years."

"All right, Mr. Weill. I've done my part. It's gotten so I don't go out any more. I neglect my wife. My little girl doesn't know me. Last week, we went to a dinner party—Sarah made me—and I don't remember a bit of it. Sarah says I was sitting on the couch all evening just staring at nothing and humming. She said everyone kept looking at me. She cried all night. I'm tired of things like that, Mr. Weill. I want to be a normal person and live in this world. I promised her I'd quit and I will, so it's good-by, Mr. Weill." Hillary stood up and held out his hand awkwardly.

Weill waved it gently away. "If you want to quit, Sherman, it's all right. But do an old man a favor and let me explain something to you."

"I'm not going to change my mind," said Hillary.

"I'm not going to try to make you. I just want to explain something. I'm an old man and even before you were born I was in this business so I like to talk about it. Humor me, Sherman? Please?"

Hillary sat down. His teeth clamped down on his lower lip and he stared sullenly at his fingernails.

Weill said, "Do you know what a dreamer is, Sherman? Do you know what he means to ordinary people? Do you know what it is to be like me, like Frank Belanger, like your wife, Sarah? To have crippled minds that can't imagine, that can't build up thoughts? People like myself, ordinary people, would like to escape just once in a while this life of ours. We can't. We need help.

"In olden times it was books, plays, radio, movies, television. They gave us make-believe, but that wasn't important. What was important was that for a little while our own imaginations were stimulated. We could think of handsome lovers and beautiful princesses. We could be beautiful, witty, strong, capable, everything we weren't.

"But, always, the passing of the dream from dreamer to absorber was not perfect. It had to be translated into words in one way or another. The best dreamer in the world might not be able to get any of it into words. And the best writer in the world could put only the smallest part of his dreams into words. You understand?

"But now, with dream recording, any man can dream. You, Sherman, and a handful of men like you, supply those dreams directly and exactly. It's straight from your head into ours, full strength. You dream for a hundred million people every time you dream. You dream a hundred million dreams at once. This is a great thing, my boy. You give all those people a glimpse of something they could not have by themselves."

Hillary mumbled, "I've done my share." He rose desperately to his feet. "I'm through. I don't care what you say. And if you want to sue me for breaking our contract, go ahead and sue. I don't care."

Weill stood up, too. "Would I sue you? . . . Ruth," he spoke into the intercom, "bring in our copy of Mr. Hillary's contract."

He waited. So did Hillary and so did Belanger. Weill smiled faintly and his yellowed fingers drummed softly on his desk.

His secretary brought in the contract. Weill took it, showed its face to Hillary and said, "Sherman, my boy, unless you want to be with me, it's not right you should stay."

Then, before Belanger could make more than the beginning of a horrified gesture to stop him, he tore the contract into four pieces and tossed them down the waste chute. "That's all."

Hillary's hand shot out to seize Weill's. "Thanks, Mr. Weill," he said earnestly, his voice husky. "You've always treated me very well, and I'm grateful. I'm sorry it had to be like this."

"It's all right, my boy. It's all right."

Half in tears, still muttering thanks, Sherman Hillary left.

"For the love of Pete, boss, why did you let him go?" demanded Belanger distractedly. "Don't you see the game? He'll be going straight to Luster-Think. They've bought him off."

Weill raised his hand. "You're wrong. You're quite wrong. I know the boy and this would not be his style. Besides," he added dryly, "Ruth is a good secretary and she knows what to bring me when I ask for a dreamer's contract. What I had was a fake. The real contract is still in the safe, believe me.

"Meanwhile, a fine day I've had. I had to argue with a father to give me a chance at new talent, with a government man to avoid censorship, with you to keep from adopting fatal policies and now with my best dreamer to keep him from leaving. The father I probably won out over. The government man and you, I don't know. Maybe yes, maybe no. But about Sherman Hillary, at least, there is no question. The dreamer will be back."

"How do you know?"

Weill smiled at Belanger and crinkled his cheeks into a network of fine lines. "Frank, my boy, you know how to edit dreamies so you think you know all the tools and machines of the trade. But let me tell you something. The most important tool in the dreamie business is the dreamer himself. He is the one you have to understand most of all, and I understand them.

"Listen. When I was a youngster—there were no dreamies then—I knew a fellow who wrote television scripts. He would complain to me bitterly that when someone met him for the first time and found out who he was, they would say: Where do you get those crazy ideas?

"They honestly didn't know. To them it was an impossibility to even think of one of them. So what could my friend say? He used to talk to me about it and tell me: Could I say, I don't know? When I go to bed, I can't sleep for ideas dancing in my head. When I shave, I cut myself; when I talk, I lose track of what I'm saying; when I drive, I take my life in my hands. And always because ideas, situations, dialogues are spinning and twisting in my mind. I can't tell you where I get my ideas. Can you tell me, maybe, your trick of *not* getting ideas, so I, too, can have a little peace.

"You see, Frank, how it is. *You* can stop work here anytime. So can I. This is our job, not our life. But not Sherman Hillary. Wherever he goes, whatever he does, he'll dream. While he lives, he must think; while he thinks, he must dream. We don't hold him prisoner, our contract isn't an iron wall for him. His own skull is his prisoner, Frank. So he'll be back. What can he do?"

Belanger shrugged. "If what you say is right, I'm sort of sorry for the guy."

Weill nodded sadly. "I'm sorry for all of them. Through the years, I've found out one thing. It's their business; making people happy. *Other* people."

Profession

George Platen could not conceal the longing in his voice. It was too much to suppress. He said, "Tomorrow's the first of May. Olympics!"

He rolled over on his stomach and peered over the foot of his bed at his roommate. Didn't he feel it, too? Didn't *this* make some impression on him?

George's face was thin and had grown a trifle thinner in the nearly year and a half that he had been at the House. His figure was slight but the look in his blue eyes was as intense as it had ever been, and right now there was a trapped look in the way his fingers curled against the bedspread.

George's roommate looked up briefly from his book and took the opportunity to adjust the light-level of the stretch of wall near his chair. His name was Hali Omani and he was a Nigerian by birth. His dark brown skin and massive features seemed made for calmness, and mention of the Olympics did not move him.

He said, "I know, George."

George owed much to Hali's patience and kindness when it was needed, but even patience and kindness could be overdone. Was this a time to sit there like a statue built of some dark, warm wood?

George wondered if he himself would grow like that after ten years here and rejected the thought violently. No!

He said defiantly, "I think you've forgotten what May means."

The other said, "I remember very well what it means. It means nothing! You're the one who's forgotten that. May means nothing to you, George Platen, and," he added softly, "it means nothing to me, Hali Omani."

George said, "The ships are coming in for recruits. By June, thousands and thousands will leave with millions of men and women heading for any world you can name, and all that means nothing?"

"Less than nothing. What do you want me to do about it, anyway?" Omani ran his finger along a difficult passage in the book he was reading and his lips moved soundlessly.

George watched him. Damn it, he thought, yell, scream; you can do that much. Kick at me, do anything.

It was only that he wanted not to be so alone in his anger. He wanted not to be the only one so filled with resentment, not to be the only one dying a slow death.

It was better those first weeks when the Universe was a small shell of vague light and sound pressing down upon him. It was better before Omani had wavered into view and dragged him back to a life that wasn't worth living.

Omani! He was old! He was at least thirty. George thought: Will I be like that at thirty? Will I be like that in twelve years?

And because he was afraid he might be, he yelled at Omani, "Will you stop reading that fool book?"

Omani turned a page and read on a few words, then lifted his head with its skullcap of crisply curled hair and said, "What?".

"What good does it do you to read the book?" He stepped forward, snorted "More electronics," and slapped it out of Omani's hands.

Omani got up slowly and picked up the book. He smoothed a crumpled page without visible rancor. "Call it the satisfaction of curiosity," he said. "I understand a little of it today, perhaps a little more tomorrow. That's a victory in a way."

"A victory. What kind of a victory? Is that what satisfies you in life? To get to know enough to be a quarter of a Registered Electronician by the time you're sixty-five?"

"Perhaps by the time I'm thirty-five."

"And then who'll want you? Who'll use you? Where will you go?"

"No one. No one. Nowhere. I'll stay here and read other books."

"And that satisfies you? Tell me! You've dragged me to class. You've got me to reading and memorizing, too. For what? There's nothing in it that satisfies me."

"What good will it do you to deny yourself satisfaction?"

"It means I'll quit the whole farce. I'll do as I planned to do in the beginning before you dovey-lovied me out of it. I'm going to force them to —to—"

Omani put down his book. He let the other run down and then said, "To what, George?"

"To correct a miscarriage of justice. A frame-up. I'll get that Antonelli and force him to admit he—he—"

Omani shook his head. "Everyone who comes here insists it's a mistake. I thought you'd passed that stage."

"Don't call it a stage," said George violently. "In my case, it's a fact. I've told you—"

"You've told me, but in your heart you know no one made any mistake as far as you were concerned."

"Because no one will admit it? You think any of them would admit a mistake unless they were forced to?— Well, I'll force them."

It was May that was doing this to George; it was Olympics month. He felt it bring the old wildness back and he couldn't stop it. He didn't want to stop it. He had been in danger of forgetting.

He said, "I was going to be a Computer Programmer and I *can* be one. I could be one today, regardless of what they say analysis shows." He pounded his mattress. "They're wrong. They *must* be."

"The analysts are never wrong."

"They *must* be. Do you doubt my intelligence?"

"Intelligence hasn't one thing to do with it. Haven't you been told that often enough? Can't you understand that?"

George rolled away, lay on his back, and stared somberly at the ceiling. "What did you want to be, Hali?"

"I had no fixed plans. Hydroponicist would have suited me, I suppose."

"Did you think you could make it?"

"I wasn't sure."

George had never asked personal questions of Omani before. It struck him as queer, almost unnatural, that other people had had ambitions and ended here. Hydroponicist!

He said, "Did you think you'd make *this?*"

"No, but here I am just the same."

"And you're satisfied. Really, really satisfied. You're happy. You love it. You wouldn't be anywhere else."

Slowly, Omani got to his feet. Carefully, he began to unmake his bed. He said, "George, you're a hard case. You're knocking yourself out because you won't accept the facts about yourself. George, you're here in what you call the House, but I've never heard you give it its full title. Say it, George, say it. Then go to bed and sleep this off."

George gritted his teeth and showed them. He chocked out, "No!"

"Then I will," said Omani, and he did. He shaped each syllable carefully. George was bitterly ashamed at the sound of it. He turned his head away.

For most of the first eighteen years of his life, George Platen had headed firmly in one direction, that of Registered Computer Programmer. There were those in his crowd who spoke wisely of Spationautics, Refrigeration Technology, Transportation Control, and even Administration. But George held firm.

He argued relative merits as vigorously as any of them, and why not? Education Day loomed ahead of them and was the great fact of their existence. It approached steadily, as fixed and certain as the calendar—the first day of November of the year following one's eighteenth birthday.

After that day, there were other topics of conversation. One could discuss with others some detail of the profession, or the virtues of one's wife and children, or the fate of one's space-polo team, or one's experiences in the Olympics. Before Education Day, however, there was only one topic that unfailingly and unwearyingly held everyone's interest, and that was Education Day.

"What are you going for? Think you'll make it? Heck, that's no good. Look at the records; quota's been cut. Logistics now—"

Or Hypermechanics now— Or Communications now— Or Gravitics now—

Especially Gravitics at the moment. Everyone had been talking about Gravitics in the few years just before George's Education Day because of the development of the Gravitic power engine.

Any world within ten light-years of a dwarf star, everyone said, would give its eyeteeth for any kind of Registered Gravitics Engineer.

The thought of that never bothered George. Sure it would; all the eyeteeth it could scare up. But George had also heard what had happened before in a newly developed technique. Rationalization and simplification followed in a flood. New models each year; new types of gravitic engines; new principles. Then all those eyeteeth gentlemen would find themselves out of date and superseded by later models with later educations. The first group would then have to settle down to unskilled labor or ship out to some backwoods world that wasn't quite caught up yet.

Now Computer Programmers were in steady demand year after year, century after century. The demand never reached wild peaks; there was never a howling bull market for Programmers; but the demand climbed steadily as new worlds opened up and as older worlds grew more complex.

He had argued with Stubby Trevelyan about that constantly. As best friends, their arguments had to be constant and vitriolic and, of course, neither ever persuaded or was persuaded.

But then Trevelyan had had a father who was a Registered Metallurgist and had actually served on one of the Outworlds, and a grandfather who had also been a Registered Metallurgist. He himself was intent on becoming a Registered Metallurgist almost as a matter of family right and was firmly convinced that any other profession was a shade less than respectable.

"There'll always be metal," he said, "and there's an accomplishment in molding alloys to specification and watching structures grow. Now what's a Programmer going to be doing. Sitting at a coder all day long, feeding some fool mile-long machine."

Even at sixteen, George had learned to be practical. He said simply, "There'll be a million Metallurgists put out along with you."

"Because it's good. A good profession. The best."

"But you get crowded out, Stubby. You can be way back in line. Any world can tape out its own Metallurgists, and the market for advanced Earth models isn't so big. And it's mostly the small worlds that want them. You know what per cent of the turn-out of Registered Metallurgists get tabbed for worlds with a Grade A rating. I looked it up. It's just 13.3 per cent. That means you'll have seven chances in eight of being stuck in some world that just about has running water. You may even be stuck on Earth; 2.3 per cent are."

Trevelyan said belligerently, "There's no disgrace in staying on Earth. Earth needs technicians, too. Good ones." His grandfather had been an Earth-bound Metallurgist, and Trevelyan lifted his finger to his upper lip and dabbed at an as yet nonexistent mustache.

George knew about Trevelyan's grandfather and, considering the Earth-bound position of his own ancestry, was in no mood to sneer. He said diplomatically, "No intellectual disgrace. Of course not. But it's nice to get into a Grade A world, isn't it?

"Now you take Programmers. Only the Grade A worlds have the kind of computers that really need first-class Programmers so they're the only ones in the market. And Programmer tapes are complicated and hardly any one fits. They need more Programmers than their own population can supply. It's just a matter of statistics. There's one first-class Programmer per million, say. A world needs twenty and has a population of ten million, they have to come to Earth for five to fifteen Programmers. Right?

"And you know how many Registered Computer Programmers went to Grade A planets last year? I'll tell you. Every last one. If you're a Programmer, you're a picked man. Yes, sir."

Trevelyan frowned. "If only one in a million makes it, what makes you think *you'll* make it?"

George said guardedly, "I'll make it."

He never dared tell anyone; not Trevelyan; not his parents; of exactly what he was doing that made him so confident. But he wasn't worried. He was simply confident (that was the worst of the memories he had in the hopeless days afterward). He was as blandly confident as the average eight-year-old kid approaching Reading Day—that childhood preview of Education Day.

Of course, Reading Day had been different. Partly, there was the simple fact of childhood. A boy of eight takes many extraordinary things in stride. One day you can't read and the next day you can. That's just the way things are. Like the sun shining.

And then not so much depended upon it. There were no recruiters just ahead, waiting and jostling for the lists and scores on the coming Olympics. A boy or girl who goes through the Reading Day is just someone who has ten more years of undifferentiated living upon Earth's crawling surface; just someone who returns to his family with one new ability.

By the time Education Day came, ten years later, George wasn't even sure of most of the details of his own Reading Day.

Most clearly of all, he remembered it to be a dismal September day with a mild rain falling. (September for Reading Day; November for Education Day; May for Olympics. They made nursery rhymes out of it.) George had dressed by the wall lights, with his parents far more excited than he himself was. His father was a Registered Pipe Fitter and had found his occupation on Earth. This fact had always been a humiliation to him, although, of course, as anyone could see plainly, most of each generation must stay on Earth in the nature of things.

There had to be farmers and miners and even technicians on Earth. It was only the late-model, high-specialty professions that were in demand on the Outworlds, and only a few millions a year out of Earth's eight billion population could be exported. Every man and woman on Earth couldn't be among that group.

But every man and woman could hope that at least one of his children could be one, and Platen, Senior, was certainly no exception. It was obvious to him (and, to be sure, to others as well) that George was notably intelligent and quick-minded. He would be bound to do well and he would have to, as he was an only child. If George didn't end on an Outworld, they would have to wait for grandchildren before a next chance would come along, and that was too far in the future to be much consolation.

Reading Day would not prove much, of course, but it would be the only indication they would have before the big day itself. Every parent on Earth would be listening to the quality of reading when his child came home with it; listening for any particularly easy flow of words and building that into certain omens of the future. There were few families that didn't have at least one hopeful who, from Reading Day on, was the great hope because of the way he handled his trisyllabics.

Dimly, George was aware of the cause of his parents' tension, and if there was any anxiety in his young heart that drizzly morning, it was only the fear that his father's hopeful expression might fade out when he returned home with his reading.

The children met in the large assembly room of the town's Education hall. All over Earth, in millions of local halls, throughout that month, similar groups of children would be meeting. George felt depressed by the grayness of the room and by the other children, strained and stiff in unaccustomed finery.

Automatically, George did as all the rest of the children did. He found the small clique that represented the children on his floor of the apartment house and joined them.

Trevelyan, who lived immediately next door, still wore his hair childishly long and was years removed from the sideburns and thin, reddish mustache that he was to grow as soon as he was physiologically capable of it.

Trevelyan (to whom George was then known as Jaw-jee) said, "Bet you're scared."

"I am not," said George. Then, confidentially, "My folks got a hunk of printing up on the dresser in my room, and when I come home, I'm going to read it for them." (George's main suffering at the moment lay in the fact that he didn't quite know where to put his hands. He had been warned not to scratch his head or rub his ears or pick his nose or put his hands into his pockets. This eliminated almost every possibility.)

Trevelyan put *his* hands in his pockets and said, "My father isn't worried."

Trevelyan, Senior, had been a Metallurgist on Diporia for nearly seven years, which gave him a superior social status in his neighborhood even though he had retired and returned to Earth.

Earth discouraged these re-immigrants because of population problems, but a small trickle did return. For one thing the cost of living was lower on Earth, and what was a trifling annuity on Diporia, say, was a comfortable income on Earth. Besides, there were always men who found more satisfaction in displaying their success before the friends and scenes of their childhood than before all the rest of the Universe besides.

Trevelyan, Senior, further explained that if he stayed on Diporia, so would his children, and Diporia was a one-spaceship world. Back on Earth, his kids could end anywhere, even Novia.

Stubby Trevelyan had picked up that item early. Even before Reading Day, his conversation was based on the carelessly assumed fact that his ultimate home would be in Novia.

George, oppressed by thoughts of the other's future greatness and his own small-time contrast, was driven to belligerent defense at once.

"My father isn't worried either. He just wants to hear me read because he knows I'll be good. I suppose your father would just as soon not hear you because he knows you'll be all wrong."

"I will not be all wrong. Reading is *nothing*. On Novia, I'll *hire* people to read to me."

"Because *you* won't be able to read yourself, on account of you're *dumb!*"

"Then how come I'll be on Novia?"

And George, driven, made the great denial, "Who says you'll be on Novia? Bet you don't go anywhere."

Stubby Trevelyan reddened. "I won't be a Pipe Fitter like your old man."

"Take that back, you dumbhead."

"You take *that* back."

They stood nose to nose, not wanting to fight but relieved at having something familiar to do in this strange place. Furthermore, now that George had curled his hands into fists and lifted them before his face, the problem of what to do with his hands was, at least temporarily, solved. Other children gathered round excitedly.

But then it all ended when a woman's voice sounded loudly over the public address system. There was instant silence everywhere. George dropped his fists and forgot Trevelyan.

"Children," said the voice, "we are going to call out your names. As each child is called, he or she is to go to one of the men waiting along the side walls. Do you see them? They are wearing red uniforms so they will be easy to find. The girls will go to the right. The boys will go to the left. Now look about and see which man in red is nearest to you—"

George found his man at a glance and waited for his name to be called off. He had not been introduced before this to the sophistications of the alphabet, and the length of time it took to reach his own name grew disturbing.

The crowd of children thinned; little rivulets made their way to each of the red-clad guides.

When the name "George Platen" was finally called, his sense of relief was exceeded only by the feeling of pure gladness at the fact that Stubby Trevelyan still stood in his place, uncalled.

George shouted back over his shoulder as he left, "Yay, Stubby, maybe they don't want you."

That moment of gaiety quickly left. He was herded into a line and directed down corridors in the company of strange children. They all looked at one another, large-eyed and concerned, but beyond a snuffling, "Quitcher pushing" and "Hey, watch out" there was no conversation.

They were handed little slips of paper which they were told must remain with them. George stared at his curiously. Little black marks of different shapes. He knew it to be printing but how could anyone make words out of it? He couldn't imagine.

He was told to strip; he and four other boys who were all that now remained together. All the new clothes came shucking off and four eight-year-olds stood naked and small, shivering more out of embarrassment than cold. Medical technicians came past, probing them, testing them with odd instruments, pricking them for blood. Each took the little cards and made additional marks on them with little black rods that produced the marks, all neatly lined up, with great speed. George stared at the new marks, but they were no more comprehensible than the old. The children were ordered back into their clothes.

They sat on separate little chairs then and waited again. Names were called again and "George Platen" came third.

He moved into a large room, filled with frightening instruments with knobs and glassy panels in front. There was a desk in the very center, and behind it a man sat, his eyes on the papers piled before him.

He said, "George Platen?"

"Yes, sir," said George, in a shaky whisper. All this waiting and all this going here and there was making him nervous. He wished it were over.

The man behind the desk said, "I am Dr. Lloyd, George. How are you?"

The doctor didn't look up as he spoke. It was as though he had said those words over and over again and didn't have to look up any more.

"I'm all right."

"Are you afraid, George?"

"N—no, sir," said George, sounding afraid even in his own ears.

"That's good," said the doctor, "because there's nothing to be afraid of, you know. Let's see, George. It says here on your card that your father is named Peter and that he's a Registered Pipe Fitter and your mother is named Amy and is a Registered Home Technician. Is that right?"

"Y—yes, sir."

"And your birthday is February 13, and you had an ear infection about a year ago. Right?"

"Yes, sir."

"Do you know how I know all these things?"

"It's on the card, I think, sir."

"That's right." The doctor looked up at George for the first time and smiled. He showed even teeth and looked much younger than George's father. Some of George's nervousness vanished.

The doctor passed the card to George. "Do you know what all those things there mean, George?"

Although George knew he did not he was startled by the sudden request into looking at the card as though he might understand now through some sudden stroke of fate. But they were just marks as before and he passed the card back. "No, sir."

"Why not?"

George felt a sudden pang of suspicion concerning the sanity of this doctor. Didn't he know why not?

George said, "I can't read, sir."

"Would you like to read?"

"Yes, sir."

"Why, George?"

George stared, appalled. No one had ever asked him that. He had no answer. He said falteringly, "I don't know, sir."

"Printed information will direct you all through your life. There is so much you'll have to know even after Education Day. Cards like this one will tell you. Books will tell you. Television screens will tell you. Printing will tell you such useful things and such interesting things that not being able to read would be as bad as not being able to see. Do you understand?"

"Yes, sir."

"Are you afraid, George?"

"No, sir."

"Good. Now I'll tell you exactly what we'll do first. I'm going to put these wires on your forehead just over the corners of your eyes. They'll stick there but they won't hurt at all. Then, I'll turn on something that will make a buzz. It will sound funny and it may tickle you, but it won't hurt. Now if it does hurt, you tell me, and I'll turn it off right away, but it won't hurt. All right?"

George nodded and swallowed.

"Are you ready?"

George nodded. He closed his eyes while the doctor busied himself. His parents had explained this to him. They, too, had said it wouldn't hurt, but then there were always the older children. There were the ten- and twelve-year-olds who howled after the eight-year-olds waiting for Reading Day, "Watch out for the needle." There were the others who took you off in confidence and said, "They got to cut your head open. They use a sharp knife that big with a hook on it," and so on into horrifying details.

George had never believed them but he had had nightmares, and now he closed his eyes and felt pure terror.

He didn't feel the wires at his temple. The buzz was a distant thing, and there was the sound of his own blood in his ears, ringing hollowly as though it and he were in a large cave. Slowly he chanced opening his eyes.

The doctor had his back to him. From one of the instruments a strip of paper unwound and was covered with a thin, wavy purple line. The doctor tore off pieces and put them into a slot in another machine. He did it over and over again. Each time a little piece of film came out, which the doctor looked at. Finally, he turned toward George with a queer frown between his eyes.

The buzzing stopped.

George said breathlessly, "Is it over?"

The doctor said, "Yes," but he was still frowning.

"Can I read now?" asked George. He felt no different.

The doctor said, "What?" then smiled very suddenly and briefly. He said, "It works fine, George. You'll be reading in fifteen minutes. Now we're going to use another machine this time and it will take longer. I'm going to cover your whole head, and when I turn it on you won't be able to see or hear anything for a while, but it won't hurt. Just to make sure I'm going to give you a little switch to hold in your hand. If anything hurts, you press the little button and everything shuts off. All right?"

In later years, George was told that the little switch was strictly a dummy; that it was introduced solely for confidence. He never did know for sure, however, since he never pushed the button.

A large smoothly curved helmet with a rubbery inner lining was placed over his head and left there. Three or four little knobs seemed to grab at him and bite into his skull, but there was only a little pressure that faded. No pain.

The doctor's voice sounded dimly. "Everything all right, George?"

And then, with no real warning, a layer of thick felt closed down all about him. He was disembodied, there was no sensation, no universe, only himself and a distant murmur at the very ends of nothingness telling him something—telling him—telling him—

He strained to hear and understand but there was all that thick felt between.

Then the helmet was taken off his head, and the light was so bright that it hurt his eyes while the doctor's voice drummed at his ears.

The doctor said, "Here's your card, George. What does it say?"

George looked at his card again and gave out a strangled shout. The marks weren't just marks at all. They made up words. They were words just as clearly as though something were whispering them in his ears. He could *hear* them being whispered as he looked at them.

"What does it say, George?"

"It says—it says—'Platen, George. Born 13 February 6492 of Peter and Amy Platen in . . .'" He broke off.

"You can read, George," said the doctor. "It's all over."

"For good? I won't forget how?"

"Of course not." The doctor leaned over to shake hands gravely. "You will be taken home now."

It was days before George got over this new and great talent of his. He read for his father with such facility that Platen, Senior, wept and called relatives to tell the good news.

George walked about town, reading every scrap of printing he could find and wondering how it was that none of it had ever made sense to him before.

He tried to remember how it was not to be able to read and he couldn't. As far as his feeling about it was concerned, he had always been able to read. Always.

At eighteen, George was rather dark, of medium height, but thin enough to look taller. Trevelyan, who was scarcely an inch shorter, had a stockiness of build that made "Stubby" more than ever appropriate, but in this last year he had grown self-conscious. The nickname could no longer be used without reprisal. And since Trevelyan disapproved of his proper first name even more strongly, he was called Trevelyan or any decent variant of that. As though to prove his manhood further, he had most persistently grown a pair of sideburns and a bristly mustache.

He was sweating and nervous now, and George, who had himself grown out of "Jaw-jee" and into the curt monosyllabic gutturability of "George," was rather amused by that.

They were in the same large hall they had been in ten years before (and not since). It was as if a vague dream of the past had come to sudden reality. In the first few minutes George had been distinctly surprised at finding everything seem smaller and more cramped than his memory told him; then he made allowance for his own growth.

The crowd was smaller than it had been in childhood. It was exclusively male this time. The girls had another day assigned them.

Trevelyan leaned over to say, "Beats me the way they make you wait."

"Red tape," said George. "You can't avoid it."

Trevelyan said, "What makes *you* so damned tolerant about it?"

"I've got nothing to worry about."

"Oh, brother, you make me sick. I hope you end up Registered Manure Spreader just so I can see your face when you do." His somber eyes swept the crowd anxiously.

George looked about, too. It wasn't quite the system they used on the children. Matters went slower, and instructions had been given out at the start in print (an advantage over the pre-Readers). The names Platen and Trevelyan were well down the alphabet still, but this time the two knew it.

Young men came out of the education rooms, frowning and uncomfortable, picked up their clothes and belongings, then went off to analysis to learn the results.

Each, as he come out, would be surrounded by a clot of the thinning crowd. "How was it?" "How'd it feel?" "Whacha think ya made?" "Ya feel any different?"

Answers were vague and noncommittal.

George forced himself to remain out of those clots. You only raised your own blood pressure. Everyone said you stood the best chance if you remained calm. Even so, you could feel the palms of your hands grow cold. Funny that new tensions came with the years.

For instance, high-specialty professionals heading out for an Outworld were accompanied by a wife (or husband). It was important to keep the sex ratio in good balance on all worlds. And if you were going out to a Grade A world, what girl would refuse you? George had no specific girl in mind yet; he wanted none. Not now! Once he made Programmer; once he could add to his name, Registered Computer Programmer, he could take his pick, like a sultan in a harem. The thought excited him and he tried to put it away. Must stay calm.

Trevelyan muttered, "What's it all about anyway? First they say it works best if you're relaxed and at ease. Then they put you through this and make it impossible for you to be relaxed and at ease."

"Maybe that's the idea. They're separating the boys from the men to begin with. Take it easy, Trev."

"Shut up,"

George's turn came. His name was not called. It appeared in glowing letters on the notice board.

He waved at Trevelyan. "Take it easy. Don't let it get you."

He was happy as he entered the testing chamber. Actually happy.

The man behind the desk said, "George Platen?"

For a fleeting instant there was a razor-sharp picture in George's mind of another man, ten years earlier, who had asked the same question, and it was almost as though this were the same man and he, George, had turned eight again as he had stepped across the threshold.

But the man looked up and, of course, the face matched that of the sudden memory not at all. The nose was bulbous, the hair thin and stringy, and the chin wattled as though its owner had once been grossly overweight and had reduced.

The man behind the desk looked annoyed. "Well?"

George came to Earth. "I'm George Platen, sir."

"Say so, then. I'm Dr. Zachary Antonelli, and we're going to be intimately acquainted in a moment."

He stared at small strips of film, holding them up to the light owlishly.

George winced inwardly. Very hazily, he remembered that other doctor (he had forgotten the name) staring at such film. Could these be the same? The other doctor had frowned and this one was looking at him now as though he were angry.

His happiness was already just about gone.

Dr. Antonelli spread the pages of a thickish file out before him now and put the films carefully to one side. "It says here you want to be a Computer Programmer."

"Yes, doctor."

"Still do?"

"Yes, sir."

"It's a responsible and exacting position. Do you feel up to it?"

"Yes, sir."

"Most pre-Educates don't put down any specific profession. I believe they are afraid of queering it."

"I think that's right, sir."

"Aren't you afraid of that?"

"I might as well be honest, sir."

Dr. Antonelli nodded, but without any noticeable lightening of his expression. "Why do you want to be a Programmer?"

"It's a responsible and exacting position as you said, sir. It's an important job and an exciting one. I like it and I think I can do it."

Dr. Antonelli put the papers away, and looked at George sourly. He said,

"How do you know you like it? Because you think you'll be snapped up by some Grade A planet?"

George thought uneasily: He's trying to rattle you. Stay calm and stay frank.

He said, "I think a Programmer has a good chance, sir, but even if I were left on Earth, I know I'd like it." (That was true enough. I'm not lying, thought George.)

"All right, how do you know?"

He asked it as though he knew there was no decent answer and George almost smiled. He had one.

He said, "I've been reading about Programming, sir."

"You've been *what?*" Now the doctor looked genuinely astonished and George took pleasure in that.

"Reading about it, sir. I bought a book on the subject and I've been studying it."

"A book for Registered Programmers?"

"Yes, sir."

"But you couldn't understand it."

"Not at first. I got other books on mathematics and electronics. I made out all I could. I still don't know much, but I know enough to know I like it and to know I can make it." (Even his parents never found that secret cache of books or knew why he spent so much time in his own room or exactly what happened to the sleep he missed.)

The doctor pulled at the loose skin under his chin. "What was your idea in doing that, son?"

"I wanted to make sure I would be interested, sir."

"Surely you know that being interested means nothing. You could be devoured by a subject and if the physical make-up of your brain makes it more efficient for you to be something else, something else you will be. You know that, don't you?"

"I've been told that," said George cautiously.

"Well, believe it. It's true."

George said nothing.

Dr. Antonelli said, "Or do you believe that studying some subject will bend the brain cells in that direction, like that other theory that a pregnant woman need only listen to great music persistently to make a composer of her child. Do you believe that?"

George flushed. That had certainly been in his mind. By forcing his intellect constantly in the desired direction, he had felt sure that he would be getting a head start. Most of his confidence had rested on exactly that point.

"I never—" he began, and found no way of finishing.

"Well, it isn't true. Good Lord, youngster, your brain pattern is fixed at birth. It can be altered by a blow hard enough to damage the cells or by a burst blood vessel or by a tumor or by a major infection—each time, of course, for the worse. But it certainly can't be affected by your thinking special thoughts." He stared at George thoughtfully, then said, "Who told you to do this?"

George, now thoroughly disturbed, swallowed and said, "No one, doctor. My own idea."

"Who knew you were doing it after you started?"

"No one. Doctor, I meant to do no wrong."

"Who said anything about wrong? Useless is what I would say. Why did you keep it to yourself?"

"I—I thought they'd laugh at me." (He thought abruptly of a recent exchange with Trevelyan. George had very cautiously broached the thought, as of something merely circulating distantly in the very outermost reaches of his mind, concerning the possibility of learning something by ladling it into the mind by hand, so to speak, in bits and pieces. Trevelyan had hooted, "George, you'll be tanning your own shoes next and weaving your own shirts." He had been thankful then for his policy of secrecy.)

Dr. Antonelli shoved the bits of film he had first looked at from position to position in morose thought. Then he said, "Let's get you analyzed. This is getting me nowhere."

The wires went to George's temples. There was the buzzing. Again there came a sharp memory of ten years ago.

George's hands were clammy; his heart pounded. He should never have told the doctor about his secret reading.

It was his damned vanity, he told himself. He had wanted to show how enterprising he was, how full of initiative. Instead, he had showed himself superstitious and ignorant and aroused the hostility of the doctor. (He could tell the doctor hated him for a wise guy on the make.)

And now he had brought himself to such a state of nervousness, he was sure the analyzer would show nothing that made sense.

He wasn't aware of the moment when the wires were removed from his temples. The sight of the doctor, staring at him thoughtfully, blinked into his consciousness and that was that; the wires were gone. George dragged himself together with a tearing effort. He had quite given up his ambition to be a Programmer. In the space of ten minutes, it had all gone.

He said dismally, "I suppose no?"

"No what?"

"No Programmer?"

The doctor rubbed his nose and said, "You get your clothes and whatever belongs to you and go to room 15-C. Your files will be waiting for you there. So will my report."

George said in complete surprise, "Have I been Educated already? I thought this was just to—"

Dr. Antonelli stared down at his desk. "It will all be explained to you. You do as I say."

George felt something like panic. What was it they couldn't tell him? He wasn't fit for anything but Registered Laborer. They were going to prepare him for that; adjust him to it.

He was suddenly certain of it and he had to keep from screaming by main force.

He stumbled back to his place of waiting. Trevelyan was not there, a fact for which he would have been thankful if he had had enough self-possession to be meaningfully aware of his surroundings. Hardly anyone was left, in fact, and the few who were looked as though they might ask him questions were it not that they were too worn out by their tail-of-the-alphabet waiting to buck the fierce, hot look of anger and hate he cast at them.

What right had *they* to be technicians and he, himself, a Laborer? Laborer! He was *certain!*

He was led by a red-uniformed guide along the busy corridors lined with separate rooms each containing its groups, here two, there five: the Motor Mechanics, the Construction Engineers, the Agronomists— There were hundreds of specialized Professions and most of them would be represented in this small town by one or two anyway.

He hated them all just then: the Statisticians, the Accountants, the lesser breeds and the higher. He hated them because they owned their smug knowledge now, knew their fate, while he himself, empty still, had to face some kind of further red tape.

He reached 15-C, was ushered in and left in an empty room. For one moment, his spirits bounded. Surely, if this were the Labor classification room, there would be dozens of youngsters present.

A door sucked into its recess on the other side of a waist-high partition and an elderly, white-haired man stepped out. He smiled and showed even teeth that were obviously false, but his face was still ruddy and unlined and his voice had vigor.

He said, "Good evening, George. Our own sector has only one of you this time, I see."

"Only one?" said George blankly.

"Thousands over the Earth, of course. Thousands. You're not alone."

George felt exasperated. He said, "I don't understand, sir. What's my classification? What's happening?"

"Easy, son. You're all right. It could happen to anyone." He held out his hand and George took it mechanically. It was warm and it pressed George's hand firmly. "Sit down, son. I'm Sam Ellenford."

George nodded impatiently. "I want to know what's going on, sir."

"Of course. To begin with, you can't be a Computer Programmer, George. You've guessed that, I think."

"Yes, I have," said George bitterly. "What will I be, then?"

"That's the hard part to explain, George." He paused, then said with careful distinctness, "Nothing."

"*What!*"

"Nothing!"

"But what does that mean? Why can't you assign me a profession?"

"We have no choice in the matter, George. It's the structure of your mind that decides that."

George went a sallow yellow. His eyes bulged. "There's something wrong with my mind?"

"There's *something* about it. As far as professional classification is concerned, I suppose you can call it wrong."

"But why?"

Ellenford shrugged. "I'm sure you know how Earth runs its Educational program, George. Practically any human being can absorb practically any body of knowledge, but each individual brain pattern is better suited to receiving some types of knowledge than others. We try to match mind to knowledge as well as we can within the limits of the quota requirements for each profession."

George nodded. "Yes, I know."

"Every once in a while, George, we come up against a young man whose mind is not suited to receiving a superimposed knowledge of any sort."

"You mean I can't be Educated?"

"That is what I mean."

"But that's crazy. I'm intelligent. I can understand—" He looked helplessly about as though trying to find some way of proving that he had a functioning brain.

"Don't misunderstand me, please," said Ellenford gravely. "You're intelligent. There's no question about that. You're even above average in intelligence. Unfortunately that has nothing to do with whether the mind ought to be allowed to accept superimposed knowledge or not. In fact, it is almost always the intelligent person who comes here."

"You mean I can't even be a Registered Laborer?" babbled George. Suddenly even that was better than the blank that faced him. "What's there to know to be a Laborer?"

"Don't underestimate the Laborer, young man. There are dozens of subclassifications and each variety has its own corpus of fairly detailed knowledge. Do you think there's no skill in knowing the proper manner of lifting a weight? Besides, for the Laborer, we must select not only minds suited to it, but bodies as well. You're not the type, George, to last long as a Laborer."

George was conscious of his slight build. He said, "But I've never heard of anyone without a profession."

"There aren't many," conceded Ellenford. "And we protect them."

"Protect them?" George felt confusion and fright grow higher inside him.

"You're a ward of the planet, George. From the time you walked through that door, we've been in charge of you." And he smiled.

It was a fond smile. To George it seemed the smile of ownership; the smile of a grown man for a helpless child.

He said, "You mean, I'm going to be in prison?"

"Of course not. You will simply be with others of your kind."

Your kind. The words made a kind of thunder in George's ear.

Ellenford said, "You need special treatment. We'll take care of you."

To George's own horror, he burst into tears. Ellenford walked to the other end of the room and faced away as though in thought.

George fought to reduce the agonized weeping to sobs and then to strangle those. He thought of his father and mother, of his friends, of Trevelyan, of his own shame—

He said rebelliously, "I learned to read."

"Everyone with a whole mind can do that. We've never found exceptions. It is at this stage that we discover—exceptions. And when you learned to read, George, we were concerned about your mind pattern. Certain peculiarities were reported even then by the doctor in charge."

"Can't you try Educating me? You haven't even tried. I'm willing to take the risk."

"The law forbids us to do that, George. But look, it will not be bad. We will explain matters to your family so they will not be hurt. At the place to which you'll be taken, you'll be allowed privileges. We'll get you books and you can learn what you will."

"Dab knowledge in by hand," said George bitterly. "Shred by shred. Then, when I die I'll know enough to be a Registered Junior Office Boy, Paper-Clip Division."

"Yet I understand you've already been studying books."

George froze. He was struck devastatingly by sudden understanding. "That's it . . ."

"What is?"

"That fellow Antonelli. He's knifing me."

"No, George. You're quite wrong."

"Don't tell me that." George was in an ecstasy of fury. "That lousy bastard is selling me out because he thought I was a little too wise for him. I read books and tried to get a head start toward programming. Well, what do you want to square things? Money? You won't get it. I'm getting out of here and when I finish broadcasting this—"

He was screaming.

Ellenford shook his head and touched a contact.

Two men entered on catfeet and got on either side of George. They pinned his arms to his sides. One of them used an air-spray hypodermic in the hollow of his right elbow and the hypnotic entered his vein and had an almost immediate effect.

His screams cut off and his head fell forward. His knees buckled and only the men on either side kept him erect as he slept.

They took care of George as they said they would; they were good to him and unfailingly kind—about the way, George thought, he himself would be to a sick kitten he had taken pity on.

They told him that he should sit up and take some interest in life; and then told him that most people who came there had the same attitude of despair at the beginning and that he would snap out of it.

He didn't even hear them.

Dr. Ellenford himself visited him to tell him that his parents had been informed that he was away on special assignment.

George muttered, "Do they know—"

Ellenford assured him at once, "We gave no details."

At first George had refused to eat. They fed him intravenously. They hid sharp objects and kept him under guard. Hali Omani came to be his room-mate and his stolidity had a calming effect.

One day, out of sheer desperate boredom, George asked for a book. Omani, who himself read books constantly, looked up, smiling broadly. George almost withdrew the request then, rather than give any of them satisfaction, then thought: What do I care?

He didn't specify the book and Omani brought one on chemistry. It was in big print, with small words and many illustrations. It was for teen-agers. He threw the book violently against the wall.

That's what he would be always. A teen-ager all his life. A pre-Educate forever and special books would have to be written for him. He lay smolder-ing in bed, staring at the ceiling, and after an hour had passed, he got up sulkily, picked up the book, and began reading.

It took him a week to finish it and then he asked for another.

"Do you want me to take the first one back?" asked Omani.

George frowned. There were things in the book he had not understood, yet he was not so lost to shame as to say so.

But Omani said, "Come to think of it, you'd better keep it. Books are meant to be read and reread."

It was that same day that he finally yielded to Omani's invitation that he tour the place. He dogged at the Nigerian's feet and took in his surround-ings with quick hostile glances.

The place was no prison certainly. There were no walls, no locked doors, no guards. But it was a prison in that the inmates had no place to go outside.

It was somehow good to see others like himself by the dozen. It was so easy to believe himself to be the only one in the world so—maimed.

He mumbled, "How many people here anyway?"

"Two hundred and five, George, and this isn't the only place of the sort in the world. There are thousands."

Men looked up as he passed, wherever he went; in the gymnasium, along the tennis courts; through the library (he had never in his life imagined books could exist in such numbers; they were stacked, actually stacked, along long shelves). They stared at him curiously and he returned the looks savagely. At least *they* were no better than he; no call for *them* to look at him as though he were some sort of curiosity.

Most of them were in their twenties. George said suddenly, "What happens to the older ones?"

Omani said, "This place specializes in the younger ones." Then, as though he suddenly recognized an implication in George's question that he had missed earlier, he shook his head gravely and said, "They're not put out of the way, if that's what you mean. There are other Houses for older ones."

"Who cares?" mumbled George, who felt he was sounding too interested and in danger of slipping into surrender.

"You might. As you grow older, you will find yourself in a House with occupants of both sexes."

That surprised George somehow. "Women, too?"

"Of course. Do you suppose women are immune to this sort of thing?"

George thought of that with more interest and excitement than he had felt for anything since before that day when— He forced his thought away from that.

Omani stopped at the doorway of a room that contained a small closed-circuit television set and a desk computer. Five or six men sat about the television. Omani said, "This is a classroom."

George said, "What's that?"

"The young men in there are being educated. Not," he added, quickly, "in the usual way."

"You mean they're cramming it in bit by bit."

"That's right. This is the way everyone did it in ancient times."

This was what they kept telling him since he had come to the House but what of it? Suppose there had been a day when mankind had not known the diatherm-oven. Did that mean he should be satisfied to eat meat raw in a world where others ate it cooked?

He said, "Why do they want to go through that bit-by-bit stuff?"

"To pass the time, George, and because they're curious."

"What good does it do them?"

"It makes them happier."

George carried that thought to bed with him.

The next day he said to Omani ungraciously, "Can you get me into a classroom where I can find out something about programming?"

Omani replied heartily, "Sure."

• • • •

It was slow and he resented it. Why should someone have to explain something and explain it again? Why should he have to read and reread a passage, then stare at a mathematical relationship and not understand it at once? That wasn't how other people had to be.

Over and over again, he gave up. Once he refused to attend classes for a week.

But always he returned. The official in charge, who assigned reading, conducted the television demonstrations, and even explained difficult passages and concepts, never commented on the matter.

George was finally given a regular task in the gardens and took his turn in the various kitchen and cleaning details. This was represented to him as being an advance, but he wasn't fooled. The place might have been far more mechanized than it was, but they deliberately made work for the young men in order to give them the illusion of worth-while occupation, of usefulness. George wasn't fooled.

They were even paid small sums of money out of which they could buy certain specified luxuries or which they could put aside for a problematical use in a problemical old age. George kept his money in an open jar, which he kept on a closet shelf. He had no idea how much he had accumulated. Nor did he care.

He made no real friends though he reached the stage where a civil good day was in order. He even stopped brooding (or almost stopped) on the miscarriage of justice that had placed him there. He would go weeks without dreaming of Antonelli, of his gross nose and wattled neck, of the leer with which he would push George into a boiling quicksand and hold him under, till he woke screaming with Omani bending over him in concern.

Omani said to him on a snowy day in February, "It's amazing how you're adjusting."

But that was February, the thirteenth to be exact, his nineteenth birthday. March came, then April, and with the approach of May he realized he hadn't adjusted at all.

The previous May had passed unregarded while George was still in his bed, drooping and ambitionless. This May was different.

All over Earth, George knew, Olympics would be taking place and young men would be competing, matching their skills against one another in the fight for a place on a new world. There would be the holiday atmosphere, the excitement, the news reports, the self-contained recruiting agents from the worlds beyond space, the glory of victory or the consolations of defeat.

How much of fiction dealt with these motifs; how much of his own boyhood excitement lay in following the events of Olympics from year to year; how many of his own plans—

George Platen could not conceal the longing in his voice. It was too much to suppress. He said, "Tomorrow's the first of May. Olympics!"

And that led to his first quarrel with Omani and to Omani's bitter enunciation of the exact name of the institution in which George found himself.

Omani gazed fixedly at George and said distinctly, "A House for the Feeble-minded."

George Platen flushed. Feeble-minded!

He rejected it desperately. He said in a monotone, "I'm leaving." He said it on impulse. His conscious mind learned it first from the statement as he uttered it.

Omani, who had returned to his book, looked up. "What?"

George knew what he was saying now. He said it fiercely, "I'm leaving."

"That's ridiculous. Sit down, George, calm yourself."

"Oh, no. I'm here on a frame-up, I tell you. This doctor, Antonelli, took a dislike to me. It's the sense of power these petty bureaucrats have. Cross them and they wipe out your life with a stylus mark on some card file."

"Are you back to that?"

"And staying there till it's all straightened out. I'm going to get to Antonelli somehow, break him, force the truth out of him." George was breathing heavily and he felt feverish. Olympics month was here and he couldn't let it pass. If he did, it would be the final surrender and he would be lost for all time.

Omani threw his legs over the side of his bed and stood up. He was nearly six feet tall and the expression on his face gave him the look of a concerned Saint Bernard. He put his arm about George's shoulder, "If I hurt your feelings—"

George shrugged him off. "You just said what you thought was the truth, and I'm going to prove it isn't the truth, that's all. Why not? The door's open. There aren't any locks. No one ever said I couldn't leave. I'll just walk out."

"All right, but where will you go?"

"To the nearest air terminal, then to the nearest Olympics center. I've got money." He seized the open jar that held the wages he had put away. Some of the coins jangled to the floor.

"That will last you a week maybe. Then what?"

"By then I'll have things settled."

"By then you'll come crawling back here," said Omani earnestly, "with all the progress you've made to do over again. You're mad, George."

"Feeble-minded is the word you used before."

"Well, I'm sorry I did. Stay here, will you?"

"Are you going to try to stop me?"

Omani compressed his full lips. "No, I guess I won't. This is your business. If the only way you can learn is to buck the world and come back with blood on your face, go ahead. —Well, go ahead."

George was in the doorway now, looking back over his shoulder. "I'm going"—he came back to pick up his pocket grooming set slowly—"I hope you don't object to my taking a few personal belongings."

Omani shrugged. He was in bed again reading, indifferent.

George lingered at the door again, but Omani didn't look up. George gritted his teeth, turned and walked rapidly down the empty corridor and out into the night-shrouded grounds.

He had expected to be stopped before leaving the grounds. He wasn't. He had stopped at an all-night diner to ask directions to an air terminal and expected the proprietor to call the police. That didn't happen. He summoned a skimmer to take him to the airport and the driver asked no questions.

Yet he felt no lift at that. He arrived at the airport sick at heart. He had not realized how the outer world would be. He was surrounded by professionals. The diner's proprietor had had his name inscribed on the plastic shell over the cash register. So and so, Registered Cook. The man in the skimmer had his license up, Registered Chauffeur. George felt the bareness of his name and experienced a kind of nakedness because of it; worse, he felt skinned. But no one challenged him. No one studied him suspiciously and demanded proof of professional rating.

George thought bitterly: Who would imagine any human being without one?

He bought a ticket to San Francisco on the 3 A.M. plane. No other plane for a sizable Olympics center was leaving before morning and he wanted to wait as little as possible. As it was, he sat huddled in the waiting room, watching for the police. They did not come.

He was in San Francisco before noon and the noise of the city struck him like a blow. This was the largest city he had ever seen and he had been used to silence and calm for a year and a half now.

Worse, it was Olympics month. He almost forgot his own predicament in his sudden awareness that some of the noise, excitement, confusion was due to that.

The Olympics boards were up at the airport for the benefit of the incoming travelers, and crowds jostled around each one. Each major profession had its own board. Each listed directions to the Olympics Hall where the contest for that day for that profession would be given; the individuals competing and their city of birth; the Outworld (if any) sponsoring it.

It was a completely stylized thing. George had read descriptions often enough in the newsprints and films, watched matches on television, and even witnessed a small Olympics in the Registered Butcher classification at the county seat. Even that, which had no conceivable Galactic implication (there was no Outworlder in attendance, of course) aroused excitement enough.

Partly, the excitement was caused simply by the fact of competition, partly by the spur of local pride (oh, when there was a hometown boy to cheer for, though he might be a complete stranger), and, of course, partly by betting. There was no way of stopping the last.

George found it difficult to approach the board. He found himself looking at the scurrying, avid onlookers in a new way.

There must have been a time when they themselves were Olympic material. What had *they* done? Nothing!

If they had been winners, they would be far out in the Galaxy somewhere, not stuck here on Earth. Whatever they were, their professions must have made them Earth-bait from the beginning; or else they had made themselves Earth-bait by inefficiency at whatever high-specialized professions they had had.

Now these failures stood about and speculated on the chances of newer and younger men. Vultures!

How he wished they were speculating on him.

He moved down the line of boards blankly, clinging to the outskirts of the groups about them. He had eaten breakfast on the strato and he wasn't hungry. He was afraid, though. He was in a big city during the confusion of the beginning of Olympics competition. That was protection, sure. The city was full of strangers. No one would question George. No one would care about George.

No one would care. Not even the House, thought George bitterly. They cared for him like a sick kitten, but if a sick kitten up and wanders off, well, too bad, what can you do?

And now that he was in San Francisco, what did he do? His thoughts struck blankly against a wall. See someone? Whom? How? Where would he even stay? The money he had left seemed pitiful.

The first shamefaced thought of going back came to him. He could go to the police— He shook his head violently as though arguing with a material adversary.

A word caught his eye on one of the boards, gleaming there: *Metallurgist.* In smaller letters, *nonferrous.* At the bottom of a long list of names, in flowing script, *sponsored by Novia.*

It induced painful memories: himself arguing with Trevelyan, so certain that he himself would be a Programmer, so certain that a Programmer was superior to a Metallurgist, so certain that he was following the right course, so certain that he was clever—

So clever that he had to boast to that small-minded, vindictive Antonelli. He had been so sure of himself that moment when he had been called and had left the nervous Trevelyan standing there, so cocksure.

George cried out in a short, incoherent high-pitched gasp. Someone turned to look at him, then hurried on. People brushed past impatiently pushing him this way and that. He remained staring at the board, open-mouthed.

It was as though the board had answered his thought. He was thinking

"Trevelyan" so hard that it had seemed for a moment that of course the board would say "Trevelyan" back at him.

But that *was* Trevelyan, up there. And *Armand* Trevelyan (Stubby's hated first name; up in lights for everyone to see) and the right hometown. What's more, Trev had wanted Novia, aimed for Novia, insisted on Novia; and this competition was sponsored by Novia.

This had to be Trev; good old Trev. Almost without thinking, he noted the directions for getting to the place of competition and took his place in line for a skimmer.

Then he thought somberly: Trev made it! He wanted to be a Metallurgist, and he made it!

George felt colder, more alone than ever.

There was a line waiting to enter the hall. Apparently, Metallurgy Olympics was to be an exciting and closely fought one. At least, the illuminated sky sign above the hall said so, and the jostling crowd seemed to think so.

It would have been a rainy day, George thought, from the color of the sky, but San Francisco had drawn the shield across its breadth from bay to ocean. It was an expense to do so, of course, but all expenses were warranted where the comfort of Outworlders was concerned. They would be in town for the Olympics. They were heavy spenders. And for each recruit taken, there would be a fee both to Earth, and to the local government from the planet sponsoring the Olympics. It paid to keep Outworlders in mind of a particular city as a pleasant place in which to spend Olympics time. San Francisco knew what it was doing.

George, lost in thought, was suddenly aware of a gentle pressure on his shoulder blade and a voice saying, "Are you in line here, young man?"

The line had moved up without George's having noticed the widening gap. He stepped forward hastily and muttered, "Sorry, sir."

There was the touch of two fingers on the elbow of his jacket and he looked about furtively.

The man behind him nodded cheerfully. He had iron-gray hair, and under his jacket he wore an old-fashioned sweater that buttoned down the front. He said, "I didn't mean to sound sarcastic."

"No offense."

"All right, then." He sounded cozily talkative. "I wasn't sure you might not simply be standing there, entangled with the line, so to speak, only by accident. I thought you might be a—"

"A what?" said George sharply.

"Why, a contestant, of course. You look young."

George turned away. He felt neither cozy nor talkative, and bitterly impatient with busybodies.

A thought struck him. Had an alarm been sent out for him? Was his description known, or his picture? Was Gray-hair behind him trying to get a good look at his face?

He hadn't seen any news reports. He craned his neck to see the moving strip of news headlines parading across one section of the city shield, somewhat lackluster against the gray of the cloudy afternoon sky. It was no use. He gave up at once. The headlines would never concern themselves with him. This was Olympics time and the only news worth headlining was the comparative scores of the winners and the trophies won by continents, nations, and cities.

It would go on like that for weeks, with scores calculated on a per capita basis and every city finding some way of calculating itself into a position of honor. His own town had once placed third in an Olympics covering Wiring Technician; third in the whole state. There was still a plaque saying so in Town Hall.

George hunched his head between his shoulders and shoved his hands in his pocket and decided that made him more noticeable. He relaxed and tried to look unconcerned, and felt no safer. He was in the lobby now, and no authoritative hand had yet been laid on his shoulder. He filed into the hall itself and moved as far forward as he could.

It was with an unpleasant shock that he noticed Gray-hair next to him. He looked away quickly and tried reasoning with himself. The man had been right behind him in line after all.

Gray-hair, beyond a brief and tentative smile, paid no attention to him and, besides, the Olympics was about to start. George rose in his seat to see if he could make out the position assigned to Trevelyan and at the moment that was all his concern.

The hall was moderate in size and shaped in the classical long oval, with the spectators in the two balconies running completely about the rim and the contestants in the linear trough down the center. The machines were set up, the progress boards above each bench were dark, except for the name and contest number of each man. The contestants themselves were on the scene, reading, talking together; one was checking his fingernails minutely. (It was, of course, considered bad form for any contestant to pay any attention to the problem before him until the instant of the starting signal.)

George studied the program sheet he found in the appropriate slot in the arm of his chair and found Trevelyan's name. His number was twelve and, to George's chagrin, that was at the wrong end of the hall. He could make out the figure of Contestant Twelve, standing with his hands in his pockets, back to his machine, and staring at the audience as though he were counting the house. George couldn't make out the face.

Still, that was Trev.

George sank back in his seat. He wondered if Trev would do well. He hoped, as a matter of conscious duty, that he would, and yet there was something within him that felt rebelliously resentful. George, professionless, here, watching. Trevelyan, Registered Metallurgist, Nonferrous, there, competing.

George wondered if Trevelyan had competed in his first year. Sometimes men did, if they felt particularly confident—or hurried. It involved a certain risk. However efficient the Educative process, a preliminary year on Earth ("oiling the stiff knowledge," as the expression went) insured a higher score.

If Trevelyan was repeating, maybe he wasn't doing so well. George felt ashamed that the thought pleased him just a bit.

He looked about. The stands were almost full. This would be a well-attended Olympics, which meant greater strain on the contestants—or greater drive, perhaps, depending on the individual.

Why Olympics, he thought suddenly? He had never known. Why was bread called bread?

Once he had asked his father: "Why do they call it Olympics, Dad?"

And his father had said: "Olympics means competition."

George had said: "Is when Stubby and I fight an Olympics, Dad?"

Platen, Senior, had said: "No. Olympics is a special kind of competition and don't ask silly questions. You'll know all you have to know when you get Educated."

George, back in the present, sighed and crowded down into his seat.

All you have to know!

Funny that the memory should be so clear now. "When you get Educated." No one ever said, "*If* you get Educated."

He always had asked silly questions, it seemed to him now. It was as though his mind had some instinctive foreknowledge of its inability to be Educated and had gone about asking questions in order to pick up scraps here and there as best it could.

And at the House they encouraged him to do so because they agreed with his mind's instinct. It was the only way.

He sat up suddenly. What the devil was he doing? Falling for that lie? Was it because Trev was there before him, an Educee, competing in the Olympics that he himself was surrendering?

He *wasn't* feeble-minded! No!

And the shout of denial in his mind was echoed by the sudden clamor in the audience as everyone got to his feet.

The box seat in the very center of one long side of the oval was filling with an entourage wearing the colors of Novia, and the word "Novia" went up above them on the main board.

Novia was a Grade A world with a large population and a thoroughly developed civilization, perhaps the best in the Galaxy. It was the kind of world that every Earthman wanted to live in someday; or, failing that, to see his children live in. (George remembered Trevelyan's insistence on Novia as a goal—and there he was competing for it.)

The lights went out in that section of the ceiling above the audience and so did the wall lights. The central trough, in which the contestants waited, became floodlit.

Again George tried to make out Trevelyan. Too far.

The clear, polished voice of the announcer sounded. "Distinguished Novian sponsors. Ladies. Gentlemen. The Olympics competition for Metallurgist, Nonferrous, is about to begin. The contestants are—"

Carefully and conscientiously, he read off the list in the program. Names. Home towns. Educative years. Each name received its cheers, the San Franciscans among them receiving the loudest. When Trevelyan's name was reached, George surprised himself by shouting and waving madly. The gray-haired man next to him surprised him even more by cheering likewise.

George could not help but stare in astonishment and his neighbor leaned over to say (speaking loudly in order to be heard over the hubbub), "No one here from my home town; I'll root for yours. Someone you know?"

George shrank back. "No."

"I noticed you looking in that direction. Would you like to borrow my glasses?"

"No. Thank you." (Why didn't the old fool mind his own business?)

The announcer went on with other formal details concerning the serial number of the competition, the method of timing and scoring and so on. Finally, he approached the meat of the matter and the audience grew silent as it listened.

"Each contestant will be supplied with a bar of nonferrous alloy of unspecified composition. He will be required to sample and assay the bar, reporting all results correctly to four decimals in per cent. All will utilize for this purpose a Beeman Microspectrograph, Model FX-2, each of which is, at the moment, not in working order."

There was an appreciative shout from the audience.

"Each contestant will be required to analyze the fault of his machine and correct it. Tools and spare parts are supplied. The spare part necessary may not be present, in which case it must be asked for, and time of delivery thereof will be deducted from final time. Are all contestants ready?"

The board above Contestant Five flashed a frantic red signal. Contestant Five ran off the floor and returned a moment later. The audience laughed good-naturedly.

"Are all contestants ready?"

The boards remained blank.

"Any questions?"

Still blank.

"You may begin."

. . . .

There was, of course, no way anyone in the audience could tell how any contestant was progressing except for whatever notations went up on the notice board. But then, that didn't matter. Except for what professional Metallurgists there might be in the audience, none would understand anything about the contest professionally in any case. What was important was who won, who was second, who was third. For those who had bets on the standings (illegal, but unpreventable) that was all-important. Everything else might go hang.

George watched as eagerly as the rest, glancing from one contestant to the next, observing how this one had removed the cover from his microspectrograph with deft strokes of a small instrument; how that one was peering into the face of the thing; how still a third was setting his alloy bar into its holder; and how a fourth adjusted a vernier with such small touches that he seemed momentarily frozen.

Trevelyan was as absorbed as the rest. George had no way of telling how he was doing.

The notice board over Contestant Seventeen flashed: Focus plate out of adjustment.

The audience cheered wildly.

Contestant Seventeen might be right and he might, of course, be wrong. If the latter, he would have to correct his diagnosis later and lose time. Or he might never correct his diagnosis and be unable to complete his analysis or, worse still, end with a completely wrong analysis.

Never mind. For the moment, the audience cheered.

Other boards lit up. George watched for Board Twelve. That came on finally: "Sample holder off-center. New clamp depresser needed."

An attendant went running to him with a new part. If Trevelyan was wrong, it would mean useless delay. Nor would the time elapsed in waiting for the part be deducted. George found himself holding his breath.

Results were beginning to go up on Board Seventeen, in gleaming letters: aluminum, 41.2649; magnesium, 22.1914; copper, 10.1001.

Here and there, other boards began sprouting figures.

The audience was in bedlam.

George wondered how the contestants could work in such pandemonium, then wondered if that were not even a good thing. A first-class technician should work best under pressure.

Seventeen rose from his place as his board went red-rimmed to signify completion. Four was only two seconds behind him. Another, then another.

Trevelyan was still working, the minor constituents of his alloy bar still unreported. With nearly all contestants standing, Trevelyan finally rose, also. Then, tailing off, Five rose, and received an ironic cheer.

It wasn't over. Official announcements were naturally delayed. Time elapsed was something, but accuracy was just as important. And not all diagnoses were of equal difficulty. A dozen factors had to be weighed.

Finally, the announcer's voice sounded, "Winner in the time of four minutes and twelve seconds, diagnosis correct, analysis correct within an average of zero point seven parts per hundred thousand, Contestant Number—*Seventeen*, Henry Anton Schmidt of—"

What followed was drowned in the screaming. Number Eight was next and then Four, whose good time was spoiled by a five part in ten thousand error in the niobium figure. Twelve was never mentioned. He was an also-ran.

George made his way through the crowd to the Contestant's Door and found a large clot of humanity ahead of him. There would be weeping relatives (joy or sorrow, depending) to greet them, newsmen to interview the top-scorers, or the home-town boys, autograph hounds, publicity seekers and the just plain curious. Girls, too, who might hope to catch the eye of a top-scorer, almost certainly headed for Novia (or perhaps a low-scorer who needed consolation and had the cash to afford it).

George hung back. He saw no one he knew. With San Francisco so far from home, it seemed pretty safe to assume that there would be no relatives to condole with Trev on the spot.

Contestants emerged, smiling weakly, nodding at shouts of approval. Policemen kept the crowds far enough away to allow a lane for walking. Each high-scorer drew a portion of the crowd off with him, like a magnet pushing through a mound of iron filings.

When Trevelyan walked out, scarcely anyone was left. (George felt somehow that he had delayed coming out until just that had come to pass.) There was a cigarette in his dour mouth and he turned, eyes downcast, to walk off.

It was the first hint of home George had had in what was almost a year and a half and seemed almost a decade and a half. He was almost amazed that Trevelyan hadn't aged, that he was the same Trev he had last seen.

George sprang forward. *"Trev!"*

Trevelyan spun about, astonished. He stared at George and then his hand shot out. "George Platen, *what* the devil—"

And almost as soon as the look of pleasure had crossed his face, it left. His hand dropped before George had quite the chance of seizing it.

"Were you in there?" A curt jerk of Trev's head indicated the hall.

"I was."

"To see me?"

"Yes."

"Didn't do so well, did I?" He dropped his cigarette and stepped on it, staring off to the street, where the emerging crowd was slowly eddying and finding its way into skimmers, while new lines were forming for the next scheduled Olympics.

Trevelyan said heavily, "So what? It's only the second time I missed. Novia can go shove after the deal I got today. There are planets that would jump at me fast enough— But, listen, I haven't seen you since Education

Day. Where did you go? Your folks said you were on special assignment but gave no details and you never wrote. You might have written."

"I should have," said George uneasily. "Anyway, I came to say I was sorry the way things went just now."

"Don't be," said Trevelyan. "I told you. Novia can go shove— At that I should have known. They've been saying for weeks that the Beeman machine would be used. All the wise money was on Beeman machines. The damned Education tapes they ran through me were for Henslers and who uses Henslers? The worlds in the Goman Cluster if you want to call them worlds. Wasn't *that* a nice deal they gave me?"

"Can't you complain to—"

"Don't be a fool. They'll tell me my brain was built for Henslers. Go argue. *Everything* went wrong. I was the only one who had to send out for a piece of equipment. Notice that?"

"They deducted the time for that, though."

"Sure, but I lost time wondering if I could be right in my diagnosis when I noticed there wasn't any clamp depresser in the parts they had supplied. They don't deduct for that. If it had been a Hensler, I would have *known* I was right. How could I match up then? The top winner was a San Franciscan. So were three of the next four. And the fifth guy was from Los Angeles. They get big-city Educational tapes. The best available. Beeman spectrographs and all. How do I compete with them? I came all the way out here just to get a chance at a Novian-sponsored Olympics in my classification and I might just as well have stayed home. I knew it, I tell you, and that settles it. Novia isn't the only chunk of rock in space. Of all the damned—"

He wasn't speaking to George. He wasn't speaking to anyone. He was just uncorked and frothing. George realized that.

George said, "If you knew in advance that the Beemans were going to be used, couldn't you have studied up on them?"

"They weren't in my tapes, I tell you."

"You could have read—books."

The last word had tailed off under Trevelyan's suddenly sharp look.

Trevelyan said, "Are you trying to make a big laugh out of this? You think this is funny? How do you expect me to read some book and try to memorize enough to match someone else who *knows*."

"I thought—"

"You try it. You try—" Then, suddenly, "What's your profession, by the way?" He sounded thoroughly hostile.

"Well—"

"Come on, now. If you're going to be a wise guy with me, let's see what you've done. You're still on Earth, I notice, so you're not a Computer Programmer and your special assignment can't be much."

George said, "Listen, Trev, I'm late for an appointment." He backed away, trying to smile.

"No, you don't." Trevelyan reached out fiercely, catching hold of George's jacket. "You answer my question. Why are you afraid to tell me? What is it with you? Don't come here rubbing a bad showing in my face, George, unless you can take it, too. Do you hear me?"

He was shaking George in frenzy and they were struggling and swaying across the floor, when the Voice of Doom struck George's ear in the form of a policeman's outraged call.

"All right now. *All* right. Break it up."

George's heart turned to lead and lurched sickeningly. The policeman would be taking names, asking to see identity cards, and George lacked one. He would be questioned and his lack of profession would show at once; and before Trevelyan, too, who ached with the pain of the drubbing he had taken and would spread the news back home as a salve for his own hurt feelings.

George couldn't stand that. He broke away from Trevelyan and made to run, but the policeman's heavy hand was on his shoulder. "Hold on, there. Let's see your identity card."

Trevelyan was fumbling for his, saying harshly, "I'm Armand Trevelyan, Metallurgist, Nonferrous. I was just competing in the Olympics. You better find out about him, though, officer."

George faced the two, lips dry and throat thickened past speech.

Another voice sounded, quiet, well-mannered. "Officer. One moment."

The policeman stepped back. "Yes, sir?"

"This young man is my guest. What is the trouble?"

George looked about in wild surprise. It was the gray-haired man who had been sitting next to him. Gray-hair nodded benignly at George.

Guest? Was he mad?

The policeman was saying, "These two were creating a disturbance, sir."

"Any criminal charges? Any damages?"

"No, sir."

"Well, then, I'll be responsible." He presented a small card to the policeman's view and the latter stepped back at once.

Trevelyan began indignantly, "Hold on, now—" but the policeman turned on him.

"All right, now. Got any charges?"

"I just—"

"On your way. The rest of you—move on." A sizable crowd had gathered, which now, reluctantly, unknotted itself and raveled away.

George let himself be led to a skimmer but balked at entering.

He said, "Thank you, but I'm not your guest." (Could it be a ridiculous case of mistaken identity?)

But Gray-hair smiled and said, "You weren't but you are now. Let me introduce myself, I'm Ladislas Ingenescu, Registered Historian."

"But—"

"Come, you will come to no harm, I assure you. After all, I only wanted to spare you some trouble with a policeman."

"But why?"

"Do you want a reason? Well, then, say that we're honorary towns-mates, you and I. We both shouted for the same man, remember, and we towns-people must stick together, even if the tie is only honorary. Eh?"

And George, completely unsure of this man, Ingenescu, and of himself as well, found himself inside the skimmer. Before he could make up his mind that he ought to get off again, they were off the ground.

He thought confusedly: The man has some status. The policeman deferred to him.

He was almost forgetting that his real purpose here in San Francisco was not to find Trevelyan but to find some person with enough influence to force a reappraisal of his own capacity of Education.

It could be that Ingenescu was such a man. And right in George's lap.

Everything could be working out fine—fine. Yet it sounded hollow in his thought. He was uneasy.

During the short skimmer-hop, Ingenescu kept up an even flow of small-talk, pointing out the landmarks of the city, reminiscing about past Olympics he had seen. George, who paid just enough attention to make vague sounds during the pauses, watched the route of flight anxiously.

Would they head for one of the shield-openings and leave the city altogether?

The skimmer landed at the roof-entry of a hotel and, as he alighted, Ingenescu said, "I hope you'll eat dinner with me in my room?"

George said, "Yes," and grinned unaffectedly. He was just beginning to realize the gap left within him by a missing lunch.

Ingenescu let George eat in silence. Night closed in and the wall lights went on automatically. (George thought: I've been on my own almost twenty-four hours.)

And then over the coffee, Ingenescu finally spoke again. He said, "You've been acting as though you think I intend you harm."

George reddened, put down his cup and tried to deny it, but the older man laughed and shook his head.

"It's so. I've been watching you closely since I first saw you and I think I know a great deal about you now."

George half rose in horror.

Ingenescu said, "But sit down. I only want to help you."

George sat down but his thoughts were in a whirl. If the old man knew who he was, why had he not left him to the policeman? On the other hand, why should he volunteer help?

Ingenescu said, "You want to know why I should want to help you? Oh, don't look alarmed. I can't read minds. It's just that my training enables me to judge the little reactions that give minds away, you see. Do you understand that?"

George shook his head.

Ingenescu said, "Consider my first sight of you. You were waiting in line to watch an Olympics, and your micro-reactions didn't match what you were doing. The expression of your face was wrong, the action of your hands was wrong. It meant that something, in general, was wrong, and the interesting thing was that, whatever it was, it was nothing common, nothing obvious. Perhaps, I thought, it was something of which your own conscious mind was unaware.

"I couldn't help but follow you, sit next to you. I followed you again when you left and eavesdropped on the conversation between your friend and yourself. After that, well, you were far too interesting an object of study— I'm sorry if that sounds cold-blooded—for me to allow you to be taken off by a policeman. —Now tell me, what is it that troubles you?"

George was in an agony of indecision. If this was a trap, why should it be such an indirect, roundabout one? And he *had* to turn to someone. He had come to the city to find help and here was help being offered. Perhaps what was wrong was that it was being offered. It came too easy.

Ingenescu said, "Of course, what you tell me as a Social Scientist is a privileged communication. Do you know what that means?"

"No, sir."

"It means, it would be dishonorable for me to repeat what you say to anyone for any purpose. Moreover no one has the legal right to compel me to repeat it."

George said, with sudden suspicion, "I thought you were a Historian."

"So I am."

"Just now you said you were a Social Scientist."

Ingenescu broke into loud laughter and apologized for it when he could talk. "I'm sorry, young man, I shouldn't laugh, and I wasn't really laughing at you. I was laughing at Earth and its emphasis on physical science, and the practical segments of it at that. I'll bet you can rattle off every subdivision of construction technology or mechanical engineering and yet you're a blank on social science."

"Well, then what *is* social science?"

"Social science studies groups of human beings and there are many high-specialized branches to it, just as there are to zoology, for instance. For instance, there are Culturists, who study the mechanics of cultures, their growth, development, and decay. Cultures," he added, forestalling a question, "are all the aspects of a way of life. For instance it includes the way we make our living, the things we enjoy and believe, what we consider good and bad and so on. Do you understand?"

"I think I do."

"An Economist—not an Economic Statistician, now, but an Economist

—specializes in the study of the way a culture supplies the bodily needs of its individual members. A psychologist specializes in the individual member of a society and how he is affected by the society. A Futurist specializes in planning the future course of a society, and a Historian— That's where I come in, now."

"Yes, sir."

"A Historian specializes in the past development of our own society and of societies with other cultures."

George found himself interested. "Was it different in the past?"

"I should say it was. Until a thousand years ago, there was no Education; not what we call Education, at least."

George said, "I know. People learned in bits and pieces out of books."

"Why, how do you know this?"

"I've heard it said," said George cautiously. Then, "Is there any use in worrying about what's happened long ago? I mean, it's all done with, isn't it?"

"It's never done with, my boy. The past explains the present. For instance, why is our Educational system what it is?"

George stirred restlessly. The man kept bringing the subject back to that. He said snappishly, "Because it's best."

"Ah, but why is it best? Now you listen to me for one moment and I'll explain. Then you can tell me if there is any use in history. Even before interstellar travel was developed—" He broke off at the look of complete astonishment on George's face. "Well, did you think we always had it?"

"I never gave it any thought, sir."

"I'm sure you didn't. But there was a time, four or five thousand years ago when mankind was confined to the surface of Earth. Even then, his culture had grown quite technological and his numbers had increased to the point where any failure in technology would have meant mass starvation and disease. To maintain the technological level and advance it in the face of an increasing population, more and more technicians and scientists had to be trained, and yet, as science advanced, it took longer and longer to train them.

"As first interplanetary and then interstellar travel was developed, the problem grew more acute. In fact, actual colonization of extra-Solar planets was impossible for about fifteen hundred years because of lack of properly trained men.

"The turning point came when the mechanics of the storage of knowledge within the brain was worked out. Once that had been done, it became possible to devise Educational tapes that would modify the mechanics in such a way as to place within the mind a body of knowledge ready-made so to speak. But you know about *that*.

"Once that was done, trained men could be turned out by the thousands and millions, and we could begin what someone has since called the 'Filling of the Universe.' There are now fifteen hundred inhabited planets in the Galaxy and there is no end in sight.

"Do you see all that is involved? Earth exports Education tapes for low-specialized professions and that keeps the Galactic culture unified. For instance, the Reading tapes insure a single language for all of us. —Don't look so surprised, other languages are possible, and in the past were used. Hundreds of them.

"Earth also exports high-specialized professionals and keeps its own population at an endurable level. Since they are shipped out in a balanced sex ratio, they act as self-reproductive units and help increase the populations on the Outworlds where an increase is needed. Furthermore, tapes and men are paid for in material which we much need and on which our economy depends. *Now* do you understand why our Education is the best way?"

"Yes, sir."

"Does it help you to understand, knowing that without it, interstellar colonization was impossible for fifteen hundred years?"

"Yes, sir."

"Then you see the uses of history." The Historian smiled. "And now I wonder if you see why I'm interested in you?"

George snapped out of time and space back to reality. Ingenescu, apparently, didn't talk aimlessly. All this lecture had been a device to attack him from a new angle.

He said, once again withdrawn, hesitating, "Why?"

"Social Scientists work with societies and societies are made up of people."

"All right."

"But people aren't machines. The professionals in physical science work with machines. There is only a limited amount to know about a machine and the professionals know it all. Furthermore, all machines of a given sort are just about alike so that there is nothing to interest them in any given individual machine. But people, ah— They are so complex and so different one from another that a Social Scientist never knows all there is to know or even a good part of what there is to know. To understand his own specialty, he must always be ready to study people; particularly unusual specimens."

"Like me," said George tonelessly.

"I shouldn't call you a specimen, I suppose, but you are unusual. You're worth studying, and if you will allow me that privilege then, in return, I will help you if you are in trouble and if I can."

There were pin wheels whirring in George's mind. —All this talk about people and colonization made possible by Education. It was as though caked thought within him were being broken up and strewn about mercilessly.

He said, "Let me think," and clamped his hands over his ears.

He took them away and said to the Historian, "Will you do something for me, sir?"

"If I can," said the Historian amiably.

"And everything I say in this room is a privileged communication. You said so."

"And I meant it."

"Then get me an interview with an Outworld official, with—with a Novian."

Ingenescu looked startled. "Well, now—"

"You can do it," said George earnestly. "You're an important official. I saw the policeman's look when you put that card in front of his eyes. If you refuse, I—I won't let you study me."

It sounded a silly threat in George's own ears, one without force. On Ingenescu, however, it seemed to have a strong effect.

He said, "That's an impossible condition. A Novian in Olympics month—"

"All right, then, get me a Novian on the phone and I'll make my own arrangements for an interview."

"Do you think you can?"

"I know I can. Wait and see."

Ingenescu stared at George thoughtfully and then reached for the visiphone.

George waited, half drunk with this new outlook on the whole problem and the sense of power it brought. It couldn't miss. It *couldn't* miss. He would be a Novian yet. He would leave Earth in triumph despite Antonelli and the whole crew of fools at the House for the (he almost laughed aloud) Feeble-minded.

George watched eagerly as the visiplate lit up. It would open up a window into a room of Novians, a window into a small patch of Novia transplanted to Earth. In twenty-four hours, he had accomplished that much.

There was a burst of laughter as the plate unmisted and sharpened, but for the moment no single head could be seen but rather the fast passing of the shadows of men and women, this way and that. A voice was heard, clear-worded over a background of babble. "Ingenescu? He wants me?"

Then there he was, staring out of the plate. A Novian. A genuine Novian. (George had not an atom of doubt. There was something completely Out-worldly about him. Nothing that could be completely defined, or even momentarily mistaken.)

He was swarthy in complexion with a dark wave of hair combed rigidly back from his forehead. He wore a thin black mustache and a pointed beard, just as dark, that scarcely reached below the lower limit of his narrow chin, but the rest of his face was so smooth that it looked as though it had been depilated permanently.

He was smiling. "Ladislas, this goes too far. We fully expect to be spied on, within reason, during our stay on Earth, but mind reading is out of bounds."

"Mind reading, Honorable?"

"Confess! You knew I was going to call you this evening. You knew I was only waiting to finish this drink." His hand moved up into view and his eye peered through a small glass of a faintly violet liqueur. "I can't offer you one, I'm afraid."

George, out of range of Ingenescu's transmitter, could not be seen by the Novian. He was relieved at that. He wanted time to compose himself and he needed it badly. It was as though he were made up exclusively of restless fingers, drumming, drumming—

But he was right. He hadn't miscalculated. Ingenescu *was* important. The Novian called him by his first name.

Good! Things worked well. What George had lost on Antonelli, he would make up, with advantage, on Ingenescu. And someday, when he was on his own at last, and could come back to Earth as powerful a Novian as this one who could negligently joke with Ingenescu's first name and be addressed as "Honorable" in turn—when he came back, he would settle with Antonelli. He had a year and a half to pay back and he—

He all but lost his balance on the brink of the enticing daydream and snapped back in sudden anxious realization that he was losing the thread of what was going on.

The Novian was saying, "—doesn't hold water. Novia has a civilization as complicated and advanced as Earth's. We're not Zeston, after all. It's ridiculous that we have to come here for individual technicians."

Ingenescu said soothingly, "Only for new models. There is never any certainty that new models will be needed. To buy the Educational tapes would cost you the same price as a thousand technicians and how do you know you would need that many?"

The Novian tossed off what remained of his drink and laughed. (It displeased George, somehow, that a Novian should be this frivolous. He wondered uneasily if perhaps the Novian ought not to have skipped that drink and even the one or two before that.)

The Novian said, "That's typical pious fraud, Ladislas. You know we can make use of all the late models we can get. I collected five Metallurgists this afternoon—"

"I know," said Ingenescu. "I was there."

"Watching me! Spying!" cried the Novian. "I'll tell you what it is. The new-model Metallurgists I got differed from the previous model only in knowing the use of Beeman Spectrographs. The tapes couldn't be modified that much, not that much" (he held up two fingers close together) "from last year's model. You introduce the new models only to *make* us buy and spend and come here hat in hand."

"We don't *make* you buy."

"No, but you sell late-model technicians to Landonum and so we have to keep pace. It's a merry-go-round you have us on, you pious Earthmen, but watch out, there may be an exit somewhere." There was a sharp edge to his laugh, and it ended sooner than it should have.

Ingenescu said, "In all honesty, I hope there is. Meanwhile, as to the purpose of my call—"

"That's right, *you* called. Oh, well, I've said my say and I suppose next year there'll be a new model of Metallurgist anyway for us to spend goods on, probably with a new gimmick for niobium assays and nothing else altered and the next year— But go on, what is it you want?"

"I have a young man here to whom I wish you to speak."

"Oh?" The Novian looked not completely pleased with that. "Concerning what?"

"I can't say. He hasn't told me. For that matter he hasn't even told me his name and profession."

The Novian frowned. "Then why take up my time?"

"He seems quite confident that you will be interested in what he has to say."

"I dare say."

"And," said Ingenescu, "as a favor to me."

The Novian shrugged. "Put him on and tell him to make it short."

Ingenescu stepped aside and whispered to George, "Address him as 'Honorable.' "

George swallowed with difficulty. This was it.

George felt himself going moist with perspiration. The thought had come so recently, yet it was in him now so certainly. The beginnings of it had come when he had spoken to Trevelyan, then everything had fermented and billowed into shape while Ingenescu had prattled, and then the Novian's own remarks had seemed to nail it all into place.

George said, "Honorable, I've come to show you the exit from the merry-go-round." Deliberately, he adopted the Novian's own metaphor.

The Novian stared at him gravely. "What merry-go-round?"

"You yourself mentioned it, Honorable. The merry-go-round that Novia is on when you come to Earth to—to get technicians." (He couldn't keep his teeth from chattering; from excitement, not fear.)

The Novian said, "You're trying to say that you know a way by which we can avoid patronizing Earth's mental super-market. Is that it?"

"Yes, sir. You can control your own Educational system."

"Umm. Without tapes?"

"Y—yes, Honorable."

The Novian, without taking his eyes from George, called out, "Ingenescu, get into view."

The Historian moved to where he could be seen over George's shoulder.

The Novian said, "What is this? I don't seem to penetrate."

"I assure you solemnly," said Ingenescu, "that whatever this is it is being done on the young man's own initiative, Honorable. I have not inspired this. I have nothing to do with it."

"Well, then, what is the young man to you? Why do you call me on his behalf?"

Ingenescu said, "He is an object of study, Honorable. He has value to me and I humor him."

"What kind of value?"

"It's difficult to explain; a matter of my profession."

The Novian laughed shortly. "Well, to each his profession." He nodded to an invisible person or persons outside plate range. "There's a young man here, a protégé of Ingenescu or some such thing, who will explain to us how to Educate without tapes." He snapped his fingers, and another glass of pale liqueur appeared in his hand. "Well, young man?"

The faces on the plate were multiple now. Men and women, both, crammed in for a view of George, their faces molded into various shades of amusement and curiosity.

George tried to look disdainful. They were all, in their own ways, Novians as well as the Earthman, "studying" him as though he were a bug on a pin. Ingenescu was sitting in a corner, now, watching him owl-eyed.

Fools, he thought tensely, one and all. But they would have to understand. He would *make* them understand.

He said, "I was at the Metallurgist Olympics this afternoon."

"You, too?" said the Novian blandly. "It seems all Earth was there."

"No, Honorable, but I was. I had a friend who competed and who made out very badly because you were using the Beeman machines. His education had included only the Henslers, apparently an older model. You said the modification involved was slight." George held up two fingers close together in conscious mimicry of the other's previous gesture. "And my friend had known some time in advance that knowledge of the Beeman machines would be required."

"And what does that signify?"

"It was my friend's lifelong ambition to qualify for Novia. He already knew the Henslers. He had to know the Beemans to qualify and he knew that. To learn about the Beemans would have taken just a few more facts, a bit more data, a small amount of practice perhaps. With a life's ambition riding the scale, he might have managed this—"

"And where would he have obtained a tape for the additional facts and data? Or has Education become a private matter for home study here on Earth?"

There was dutiful laughter from the faces in the background.

George said, "That's why he didn't learn, Honorable. He thought he needed a tape. He wouldn't even try without one, no matter what the prize. He refused to try without a tape."

"Refused, eh? Probably the type of fellow who would refuse to fly without a skimmer." More laughter and the Novian thawed into a smile and said, "The fellow is amusing. Go on. I'll give you another few moments."

George said tensely, "Don't think this is a joke. Tapes are actually bad. They teach too much; they're too painless. A man who learns that way doesn't know how to learn any other way. He's frozen into whatever position he's been taped. Now if a person *weren't* given tapes but were forced to learn by hand, so to speak, from the start; why, then he'd get the habit of learning, and continue to learn. Isn't that reasonable? Once he has the habit well developed he can be given just a small amount of tape-knowledge, perhaps, to fill in gaps or fix details. Then he can make further progress on his own. You can make Beeman Metallurgists out of your own Hensler Metallurgists in that way and not have to come to Earth for new models."

The Novian nodded and sipped at his drink. "And where does everyone get knowledge without tapes? From interstellar vacuum?"

"From books. By studying the instruments themselves. By *thinking.*"

"Books? How does one understand books without Education?"

"Books are in words. Words can be understood for the most part. Specialized words can be explained by the technicians you already have."

"What about reading? Will you allow reading tapes?"

"Reading tapes are all right, I suppose, but there's no reason you can't learn to read the old way, too. At least in part."

The Novian said, "So that you can develop good habits from the start?"

"Yes, yes," George said gleefully. The man was beginning to understand.

"And what about mathematics?"

"That's the easiest of all, sir—Honorable. Mathematics is different from other technical subjects. It starts with certain simple principles and proceeds by steps. You can start with nothing and learn. It's practically designed for that. Then, once you know the proper types of mathematics, other technical books become quite understandable. Especially if you start with easy ones.".

"Are there easy books?"

"Definitely. Even if there weren't, the technicians you now have can try to write easy books. Some of them might be able to put some of their knowledge into words and symbols."

"Good Lord," said the Novian to the men clustered about him. "The young devil has an answer for everything."

"I have. I have," shouted George. "Ask me."

"Have you tried learning from books yourself? Or is this just theory with you?"

George turned to look quickly at Ingenescu, but the Historian was passive. There was no sign of anything but gentle interest in his face.

George said, "I have."

"And do you find it works?"

"Yes, Honorable," said George eagerly. "Take me with you to Novia. I can set up a program and direct—"

"Wait, I have a few more questions. How long would it take, do you suppose, for you to become a Metallurgist capable of handling a Beeman machine, supposing you started from nothing and did not use Educational tapes?"

George hesitated. "Well—years, perhaps."

"Two years? Five? Ten?"

"I can't say, Honorable."

"Well, there's a vital question to which you have no answer, have you? Shall we say five years? Does that sound reasonable to you?"

"I suppose so."

"All right. We have a technician studying metallurgy according to this method of yours for five years. He's no good to us during that time, you'll admit, but he must be fed and housed and paid all that time."

"But—"

"Let me finish. Then when he's done and can use the Beeman, five years have passed. Don't you suppose we'll have modified Beemans then which he *won't* be able to use?"

"But by then he'll be expert on learning. He could learn the new details necessary in a matter of days."

"So you say. And suppose this friend of yours, for instance, had studied up on Beemans on his own and managed to learn it; would he be as expert in its use as a competitor who had learned it off the tapes?"

"Maybe not—" began George.

"Ah," said the Novian.

"Wait, let *me* finish. Even if he doesn't know something as well, it's the ability to learn further that's important. He may be able to think up things, new things that no tape-Educated man would. You'll have a reservoir of original thinkers—"

"In your studying," said the Novian, "have you thought up any new things?"

"No, but I'm just one man and I haven't studied long—"

"Yes. —Well, ladies, gentlemen, have we been sufficiently amused?"

"Wait," cried George, in sudden panic. "I want to arrange a personal interview. There are things I can't explain over the visiphone. There are details—"

The Novian looked past George. "Ingenescu! I think I have done you your favor. Now, really, I have a heavy schedule tomorrow. Be well!"

The screen went blank.

. . . .

George's hands shot out toward the screen, as though in a wild impulse to shake life back into it. He cried out, "He didn't believe me. He didn't believe me."

Ingenescu said, "No, George. Did you really think he would?"

George scarcely heard him. "But why not? It's all true. It's all so much to his advantage. No risk. I and a few men to work with— A dozen men training for years would cost less than one technician. —He was drunk! Drunk! He didn't understand."

George looked about breathlessly. "How do I get to him? I've got to. This was wrong. Shouldn't have used the visiphone. I need time. Face to face. How do I—"

Ingenescu said, "He won't see you, George. And if he did, he wouldn't believe you."

"He will, I tell you. When he isn't drinking. He—" George turned squarely toward the Historian and his eyes widened. "Why do you call me George?"

"Isn't that your name? George Platen?"

"You know me?"

"All about you."

George was motionless except for the breath pumping his chest wall up and down.

Ingenescu said, "I want to help you, George. I told you that. I've been studying you and I want to help you."

George screamed, "I don't need help. I'm not feeble-minded. The whole world is, but I'm not." He whirled and dashed madly for the door.

He flung it open and two policemen roused themselves suddenly from their guard duty and seized him.

For all George's straining, he could feel the hypo-spray at the fleshy point just under the corner of his jaw, and that was it. The last thing he remembered was the face of Ingenescu, watching with gentle concern.

George opened his eyes to the whiteness of a ceiling. He remembered what had happened. He remembered it distantly as though it had happened to somebody else. He stared at the ceiling till the whiteness filled his eyes and washed his brain clean, leaving room, it seemed, for new thought and new ways of thinking.

He didn't know how long he lay there so, listening to the drift of his own thinking.

There was a voice in his ear. "Are you awake?"

And George heard his own moaning for the first time. Had he been moaning? He tried to turn his head.

The voice said, "Are you in pain, George?"

George whispered, "Funny. I was so anxious to leave Earth. I didn't understand."

"Do you know where you are?"

"Back in the—the House." George managed to turn. The voice belonged to Omani.

George said, "It's funny I didn't understand."

Omani smiled gently, "Sleep again—"

George slept.

And woke again. His mind was clear.

Omani sat at the bedside reading, but he put down the book as George's eyes opened.

George struggled to a sitting position. He said, "Hello."

"Are you hungry?"

"You bet." He stared at Omani curiously. "I was followed when I left, wasn't I?"

Omani nodded. "You were under observation at all times. We were going to maneuver you to Antonelli and let you discharge your aggressions. We felt that to be the only way you could make progress. Your emotions were clogging your advance."

George said, with a trace of embarrassment, "I was all wrong about him."

"It doesn't matter now. When you stopped to stare at the Metallurgy notice board at the airport, one of our agents reported back the list of names. You and I had talked about your past sufficiently so that I caught the significance of Trevelyan's name there. You asked for directions to the Olympics; there was the possibility that this might result in the kind of crisis we were hoping for; we sent Ladislas Ingenescu to the hall to meet you and take over."

"He's an important man in the government, isn't he?"

"Yes, he is."

"And you had him take over. It makes me sound important."

"You *are* important, George."

A thick stew had arrived, steaming, fragrant. George grinned wolfishly and pushed his sheets back to free his arms. Omani helped arrange the bed-table. For a while, George ate silently.

Then George said, "I woke up here once before just for a short time."

Omani said, "I know. I was here."

"Yes, I remember. You know, everything was changed. It was as though I was too tired to feel emotion. I wasn't angry any more. I could just think. It was as though I had been drugged to wipe out emotion."

"You weren't," said Omani. "Just sedation. You had rested."

"Well, anyway, it was all clear to me, as though I had known it all the time but wouldn't listen to myself. I thought: What was it I had wanted Novia to let me do? I had wanted to go to Novia and take a batch of un-Educated youngsters and teach them out of books. I had wanted to establish a House for the Feeble-minded—like here—and Earth already has them—many of them."

Omani's white teeth gleamed as he smiled. "The Institute of Higher Studies is the correct name for places like this."

"Now I see it," said George, "so easily I am amazed at my blindness before. After all, who invents the new instrument models that require new-model technicians? Who invented the Beeman spectrographs, for instance? A man called Beeman, I suppose, but he couldn't have been tape-Educated or how could he have made the advance?"

"Exactly."

"Or who makes Educational tapes? Special tape-making technicians? Then who makes the tapes to train *them?* More advanced technicians? Then who makes the tapes—You see what I mean. Somewhere there has to be an end. Somewhere there must be men and women with capacity for original thought."

"Yes, George."

George leaned back, stared over Omani's head, and for a moment there was the return of something like restlessness to his eyes.

"Why wasn't I told all this at the beginning?"

"Oh, if we could," said Omani, "the trouble it would save us. We can analyze a mind, George, and say this one will make an adequate architect and that one a good woodworker. We know of no way of detecting the capacity for original, creative thought. It is too subtle a thing. We have some rule-of-thumb methods that mark out individuals who may possibly or potentially have such a talent.

"On Reading Day, such individuals are reported. You were, for instance. Roughly speaking, the number so reported comes to one in ten thousand. By the time Education Day arrives, these individuals are checked again, and nine out of ten of them turn out to have been false alarms. Those who remain are sent to places like this."

George said, "Well, what's wrong with telling people that one out of—of a hundred thousand will end at places like these? Then it won't be such a shock to those who do."

"And those who don't? The ninety-nine thousand nine hundred and ninety-nine that don't? We can't have all those people considering themselves failures. They aim at the professions and one way or another they all make it. Everyone can place after his or her name: Registered something-or-other. In one fashion or another every individual has his or her place in society and this is necessary."

"But we?" said George. "The one in ten thousand exception?"

"You can't be told. That's exactly it. It's the final test. Even after we've thinned out the possibilities on Education Day, nine out of ten of those who come here are not quite the material of creative genius, and there's no way we can distinguish those nine from the tenth that we want by any form of machinery. The tenth one must tell us himself."

"How?"

"We bring you here to a House for the Feeble-minded and the man who won't accept that is the man we want. It's a method that can be cruel, but it works. It won't do to say to a man, 'You can create. Do so.' It is much safer to wait for a man to say, 'I can create, and I will do so whether you wish it or not.' There are ten thousand men like you, George, who support the advancing technology of fifteen hundred worlds. We can't allow ourselves to miss one recruit to that number or waste our efforts on one member who doesn't measure up."

George pushed his empty plate out of the way and lifted a cup of coffee to his lips.

"What about the people here who don't—measure up?"

"They are taped eventually and become our Social Scientists. Ingenescu is one. I am a Registered Psychologist. We are second echelon, so to speak."

George finished his coffee. He said, "I still wonder about one thing?"

"What is that?"

George threw aside the sheet and stood up. "Why do they call them Olympics?"

The Feeling of Power

Jehan Shuman was used to dealing with the men in authority on long-embattled Earth. He was only a civilian but he originated programming patterns that resulted in self-directing war computers of the highest sort. Generals consequently listened to him. Heads of congressional committees, too.

There was one of each in the special lounge of New Pentagon. General Weider was space-burnt and had a small mouth puckered almost into a cipher. Congressman Brant was smooth-cheeked and clear-eyed. He smoked Denebian tobacco with the air of one whose patriotism was so notorious, he could be allowed such liberties.

Shuman, tall, distinguished, and Programmer-first-class, faced them fearlessly.

He said, "This, gentlemen, is Myron Aub."

"The one with the unusual gift that you discovered quite by accident," said Congressman Brant placidly. "Ah." He inspected the little man with the egg-bald head with amiable curiosity.

The little man, in return, twisted the fingers of his hands anxiously. He had never been near such great men before. He was only an aging low-grade Technician who had long ago failed all tests designed to smoke out the gifted ones among mankind and had settled into the rut of unskilled labor. There was just this hobby of his that the great Programmer had found out about and was now making such a frightening fuss over.

General Weider said, "I find this atmosphere of mystery childish."

"You won't in a moment," said Shuman. "This is not something we can leak to the firstcomer. —Aub!" There was something imperative about his manner of biting off that one-syllable name, but then he was a great Programmer speaking to a mere Technician. "Aub! How much is nine times seven?"

Aub hesitated a moment. His pale eyes glimmered with a feeble anxiety. "Sixty-three," he said.

Congressman Brant lifted his eyebrows. "Is that right?"

"Check it for yourself, Congressman."

The congressman took out his pocket computer, nudged the milled edges twice, looked at its face as it lay there in the palm of his hand, and put it back. He said, "Is this the gift you brought us here to demonstrate? An illusionist?"

"More than that, sir. Aub has memorized a few operations and with them he computes on paper."

"A paper computer?" said the general. He looked pained.

"No, sir," said Shuman patiently. "Not a paper computer. Simply a sheet of paper. General, would you be so kind as to suggest a number?"

"Seventeen," said the general.

"And you, Congressman?"

"Twenty-three."

"Good! Aub, multiply those numbers and please show the gentlemen your manner of doing it."

"Yes, Programmer," said Aub, ducking his head. He fished a small pad out of one shirt pocket and an artist's hairline stylus out of the other. His forehead corrugated as he made painstaking marks on the paper.

General Weider interrupted him sharply. "Let's see that."

Aub passed him the paper, and Weider said, "Well, it looks like the figure seventeen."

Congressman Brant nodded and said, "So it does, but I suppose anyone can copy figures off a computer. I think I could make a passable seventeen myself, even without practice."

"If you will let Aub continue, gentlemen," said Shuman without heat.

Aub continued, his hand trembling a little. Finally he said in a low voice, "The answer is three hundred and ninety-one."

Congressman Brant took out his computer a second time and flicked it, "By Godfrey, so it is. How did he guess?"

"No guess, Congressman," said Shuman. "He computed that result. He did it on this sheet of paper."

"Humbug," said the general impatiently. "A computer is one thing and marks on paper are another."

"Explain, Aub," said Shuman.

"Yes, Programmer. —Well, gentlemen, I write down seventeen and just underneath it, I write twenty-three. Next, I say to myself: seven times three—"

The congressman interrupted smoothly, "Now, Aub, the problem is seventeen times twenty-three."

"Yes, I know," said the little Technician earnestly, "but I *start* by saying seven times three because that's the way it works. Now seven times three is twenty-one."

"And how do you know that?" asked the congressman.

"I just remember it. It's always twenty-one on the computer. I've checked it any number of times."

"That doesn't mean it always will be, though, does it?" said the congressman.

"Maybe not," stammered Aub. "I'm not a mathematician. But I always get the right answers, you see."

"Go on."

"Seven times three is twenty-one, so I write down twenty-one. Then one times three is three, so I write down a three under the two of twenty-one."

"Why under the two?" asked Congressman Brant at once.

"Because—" Aub looked helplessly at his superior for support. "It's difficult to explain."

Shuman said, "If you will accept his work for the moment, we can leave the details for the mathematicians."

Brant subsided.

Aub said, "Three plus two makes five, you see, so the twenty-one becomes a fifty-one. Now you let that go for a while and start fresh. You multiply seven and two, that's fourteen, and one and two, that's two. Put them down like this and it adds up to thirty-four. Now if you put the thirty-four under the fifty-one this way and add them, you get three hundred and ninety-one and that's the answer."

There was an instant's silence and then General Weider said, "I don't believe it. He goes through this rigmarole and makes up numbers and multiplies and adds them this way and that, but I don't believe it. It's too complicated to be anything but hornswoggling."

"Oh no, sir," said Aub in a sweat. "It only *seems* complicated because you're not used to it. Actually, the rules are quite simple and will work for any numbers."

"Any numbers, eh?" said the general. "Come then." He took out his own computer (a severely styled GI model) and struck it at random. "Make a five seven three eight on the paper. That's five thousand seven hundred and thirty-eight."

"Yes, sir," said Aub, taking a new sheet of paper.

"Now," (more punching of his computer), "seven two three nine. Seven thousand two hundred and thirty-nine."

"Yes, sir."

"And now multiply those two."

"It will take some time," quavered Aub.

"Take the time," said the general.

"Go ahead, Aub," said Shuman crisply.

Aub set to work, bending low. He took another sheet of paper and another. The general took out his watch finally and stared at it. "Are you through with your magic-making, Technician?"

"I'm almost done, sir. —Here it is, sir. Forty-one million, five hundred and thirty-seven thousand, three hundred and eighty-two." He showed the scrawled figures of the result.

General Weider smiled bitterly. He pushed the multiplication contact on his computer and let the numbers whirl to a halt. And then he stared and said in a surprised squeak, "Great Galaxy, the fella's right."

The President of the Terrestrial Federation had grown haggard in office and, in private, he allowed a look of settled melancholy to appear on his sensitive features. The Denebian war, after its early start of vast movement and great popularity, had trickled down into a sordid matter of maneuver and countermaneuver, with discontent rising steadily on Earth. Possibly, it was rising on Deneb, too.

And now Congressman Brant, head of the important Committee on Military Appropriations, was cheerfully and smoothly spending his half-hour appointment spouting nonsense.

"Computing without a computer," said the president impatiently, "is a contradiction in terms."

"Computing," said the congressman, "is only a system for handling data. A machine might do it, or the human brain might. Let me give you an example." And, using the new skills he had learned, he worked out sums and products until the president, despite himself, grew interested.

"Does this always work?"

"Every time, Mr. President. It is foolproof."

"Is it hard to learn?"

"It took me a week to get the real hang of it. I think you would do better."

"Well," said the president, considering, "it's an interesting parlor game, but what is the use of it?"

"What is the use of a newborn baby, Mr. President? At the moment there is no use, but don't you see that this points the way toward liberation from the machine. Consider, Mr. President," the congressman rose and his deep voice automatically took on some of the cadences he used in public debate, "that the Denebian war is a war of computer against computer. Their computers forge an impenetrable shield of counter-missiles against our missiles, and ours forge one against theirs. If we advance the efficiency of our computers, so do they theirs, and for five years a precarious and profitless balance has existed.

"Now we have in our hands a method for going beyond the computer, leapfrogging it, passing through it. We will combine the mechanics of computation with human thought; we will have the equivalent of intelligent computers; billions of them. I can't predict what the consequences will be in detail but they will be incalculable. And if Deneb beats us to the punch, they may be unimaginably catastrophic."

The president said, troubled, "What would you have me do?"

"Put the power of the administration behind the establishment of a secret project on human computation. Call it Project Number, if you like. I can vouch for my committee, but I will need the administration behind me."

"But how far can human computation go?"

"There is no limit. According to Programmer Shuman, who first introduced me to this discovery—"

"I've heard of Shuman, of course."

"Yes. Well, Dr. Shuman tells me that in theory there is nothing the computer can do that the human mind can not do. The computer merely takes a finite amount of data and performs a finite number of operations upon them. The human mind can duplicate the process."

The president considered that. He said, "If Shuman says this, I am inclined to believe him—in theory. But, in practice, how can anyone know how a computer works?"

Brant laughed genially. "Well, Mr. President, I asked the same question. It seems that at one time computers were designed directly by human beings. Those were simple computers, of course, this being before the time of the rational use of computers to design more advanced computers had been established."

"Yes, yes. Go on."

"Technician Aub apparently had, as his hobby, the reconstruction of some of these ancient devices and in so doing he studied the details of their workings and found he could imitate them. The multiplication I just performed for you is an imitation of the workings of a computer."

"Amazing!"

The congressman coughed gently, "If I may make another point, Mr. President— The further we can develop this thing, the more we can divert our Federal effort from computer production and computer maintenance. As the human brain takes over, more of our energy can be directed into peacetime pursuits and the impingement of war on the ordinary man will be less. This will be most advantageous for the party in power, of course."

"Ah," said the president, "I see your point. Well, sit down, Congressman, sit down. I want some time to think about this. —But meanwhile, show me that multiplication trick again. Let's see if I can't catch the point of it."

. . . .

Programmer Shuman did not try to hurry matters. Loesser was conservative, very conservative, and liked to deal with computers as his father and grandfather had. Still, he controlled the West European computer combine, and if he could be persuaded to join Project Number in full enthusiasm, a great deal would be accomplished.

But Loesser was holding back. He said, "I'm not sure I like the idea of relaxing our hold on computers. The human mind is a capricious thing. The computer will give the same answer to the same problem each time. What guarantee have we that the human mind will do the same?"

"The human mind, Computer Loesser, only manipulates facts. It doesn't matter whether the human mind or a machine does it. They are just tools."

"Yes, yes. I've gone over your ingenious demonstration that the mind can duplicate the computer but it seems to me a little in the air. I'll grant the theory but what reason have we for thinking that theory can be converted to practice?"

"I think we have reason, sir. After all, computers have not always existed. The cave men with their triremes, stone axes, and railroads had no computers."

"And possibly they did not compute."

"You know better than that. Even the building of a railroad or a ziggurat called for some computing, and that must have been without computers as we know them."

"Do you suggest they computed in the fashion you demonstrate?"

"Probably not. After all, this method—we call it 'graphitics,' by the way, from the old European word 'grapho' meaning 'to write'—is developed from the computers themselves so it cannot have antedated them. Still, the cave men must have had *some* method, eh?"

"Lost arts! If you're going to talk about lost arts—"

"No, no. I'm not a lost art enthusiast, though I don't say there may not be some. After all, man was eating grain before hydroponics, and if the primitives ate grain, they must have grown it in soil. What else could they have done?"

"I don't know, but I'll believe in soil-growing when I see someone grow grain in soil. And I'll believe in making fire by rubbing two pieces of flint together when I see that, too."

Shuman grew placative. "Well, let's stick to graphitics. It's just part of the process of etherealization. Transportation by means of bulky contrivances is giving way to direct mass-transference. Communications devices become less massive and more efficient constantly. For that matter, compare your pocket computer with the massive jobs of a thousand years ago. Why not, then, the last step of doing away with computers altogether? Come, sir, Project Number is a going concern; progress is already headlong. But we want your help. If patriotism doesn't move you, consider the intellectual adventure involved."

Loesser said skeptically, "What progress? What can you do beyond multiplication? Can you integrate a transcendental function?"

"In time, sir. In time. In the last month I have learned to handle division. I can determine, and correctly, integral quotients and decimal quotients."

"Decimal quotients? To how many places?"

Programmer Shuman tried to keep his tone casual. "Any number!"

Loesser's lower jaw dropped. "Without a computer?"

"Set me a problem."

"Divide twenty-seven by thirteen. Take it to six places."

Five minutes later, Shuman said, "Two point oh seven six nine two three."

Loesser checked it. "Well, now, that's amazing. Multiplication didn't impress me too much because it involved integers after all, and I thought trick manipulation might do it. But decimals—"

"And that is not all. There is a new development that is, so far, top secret and which, strictly speaking, I ought not to mention. Still— We may have made a breakthrough on the square root front."

"Square roots?"

"It involves some tricky points and we haven't licked the bugs yet, but Technician Aub, the man who invented the science and who has an amazing intuition in connection with it, maintains he has the problem almost solved. And he is only a Technician. A man like yourself, a trained and talented mathematician ought to have no difficulty."

"Square roots," muttered Loesser, attracted.

"Cube roots, too. Are you with us?"

Loesser's hand thrust out suddenly, "Count me in."

General Weider stumped his way back and forth at the head of the room and addressed his listeners after the fashion of a savage teacher facing a group of recalcitrant students. It made no difference to the general that they were the civilian scientists heading Project Number. The general was the over-all head, and he so considered himself at every waking moment.

He said, "Now square roots are all fine. I can't do them myself and I don't understand the methods, but they're fine. Still, the Project will not be side-tracked into what some of you call the fundamentals. You can play with graphitics any way you want to after the war is over, but right now we have specific and very practical problems to solve."

In a far corner, Technician Aub listened with painful attention. He was no longer a Technician, of course, having been relieved of his duties and assigned to the project, with a fine-sounding title and good pay. But, of course, the social distinction remained and the highly placed scientific leaders could never bring themselves to admit him to their ranks on a footing of equality. Nor, to do Aub justice, did he, himself, wish it. He was as uncomfortable with them as they with him.

The general was saying, "Our goal is a simple one, gentlemen; the replacement of the computer. A ship that can navigate space without a computer on board can be constructed in one fifth the time and at one tenth the expense of a computer-laden ship. We could build fleets five times, ten times, as great as Deneb could if we could but eliminate the computer.

"And I see something even beyond this. It may be fantastic now; a mere dream; but in the future I see the manned missile!"

There was an instant murmur from the audience.

The general drove on. "At the present time, our chief bottleneck is the fact that missiles are limited in intelligence. The computer controlling them can only be so large, and for that reason they can meet the changing nature of anti-missile defenses in an unsatisfactory way. Few missiles, if any, accomplish their goal and missile warfare is coming to a dead end; for the enemy, fortunately, as well as for ourselves.

"On the other hand, a missile with a man or two within, controlling flight by graphitics, would be lighter, more mobile, more intelligent. It would give us a lead that might well mean the margin of victory. Besides which, gentlemen, the exigencies of war compel us to remember one thing. A man is much more dispensable than a computer. Manned missiles could be launched in numbers and under circumstances that no good general would care to undertake as far as computer-directed missiles are concerned—"

He said much more but Technician Aub did not wait.

Technician Aub, in the privacy of his quarters, labored long over the note he was leaving behind. It read finally as follows:

"When I began the study of what is now called graphitics, it was no more than a hobby. I saw no more in it than an interesting amusement, an exercise of mind.

"When Project Number began, I thought that others were wiser than I; that graphitics might be put to practical use as a benefit to mankind, to aid in the production of really practical mass-transference devices perhaps. But now I see it is to be used only for death and destruction.

"I cannot face the responsibility involved in having invented graphitics."

He then deliberately turned the focus of a protein-depolarizer on himself and fell instantly and painlessly dead.

They stood over the grave of the little Technician while tribute was paid to the greatness of his discovery.

Programmer Shuman bowed his head along with the rest of them, but remained unmoved. The Technician had done his share and was no longer needed, after all. He might have started graphitics, but now that it had started, it would carry on by itself overwhelmingly, triumphantly, until manned missiles were possible with who knew what else.

Nine times seven, thought Shuman with deep satisfaction, is sixty-three, and I don't need a computer to tell me so. The computer is in my own head.

And it was amazing the feeling of power that gave him.

The Dying Night

PART ONE

It was almost a class reunion, and though it was marked by joylessness, there was no reason as yet to think it would be marred by tragedy.

Edward Talliaferro, fresh from the Moon and without his gravity legs yet, met the other two in Stanley Kaunas's room. Kaunas rose to greet him in a subdued manner. Battersley Ryger merely sat and nodded.

Talliaferro lowered his large body carefully to the couch, very aware of its unusual weight. He grimaced a little, his plump lips twisting inside the rim of hair that surrounded his mouth on lip, chin, and cheek.

They had seen one another earlier that day under more formal conditions. Now for the first time they were alone, and Talliaferro said, "This is a kind of occasion. We're meeting for the first time in ten years. First time since graduation, in fact."

Ryger's nose twitched. It had been broken shortly before that same graduation and he had received his degree in astronomy with a bandage disfiguring his face. He said grumpily, "Anyone ordered champagne? Or something?"

Talliaferro said, "Come on! First big interplanetary astronomical convention in history is no place for glooming. And among friends, too!"

Kaunas said suddenly, "It's Earth. It doesn't feel right. I can't get used to it." He shook his head but his look of depression was not detachable. It remained.

Talliaferro said, "I know. I'm so heavy. It takes all the energy out of me. At that, you're better off than I am, Kaunas. Mercurian gravity is 0.4 normal. On the Moon, it's only 0.16." He interrupted Ryger's beginning of a sound by saying, "And on Ceres they use pseudo-grav fields adjusted to 0.8. You have no problems at all, Ryger."

The Cerian astronomer looked annoyed, "It's the open air. Going outside without a suit gets me."

"Right," agreed Kaunas, "and letting the sun beat down on you. Just letting it."

Talliaferro found himself insensibly drifting back in time. They had not changed much. Nor, he thought, had he himself. They were all ten years older, of course. Ryger had put on some weight and Kaunas's thin face had grown a bit leathery, but he would have recognized either if he had met him without warning.

He said, "I don't think it's Earth getting us. Let's face it."

Kaunas looked up sharply. He was a little fellow with quick, nervous movements of his hands. He habitually wore clothes that looked a shade too large for him.

He said, "Villiers! I know. I think about him sometimes." Then, with an air of desperation, "I got a letter from him."

Ryger sat upright, his olive complexion darkening further and said with energy, "You did? When?"

"A month ago."

Ryger turned to Talliaferro. "How about you?"

Talliaferro blinked placidly and nodded.

Ryger said, "He's gone crazy. He claims he's discovered a practical method of mass-transference through space. —He told you two also? —That's it, then. He was always a little bent. Now he's broken."

He rubbed his nose fiercely and Talliaferro thought of the day Villiers had broken it.

For ten years, Villiers had haunted them like the vague shadow of a guilt that wasn't really theirs. They had gone through their graduate work together, four picked and dedicated men being trained for a profession that had reached new heights in this age of interplanetary travel.

The Observatories were opening on the other worlds, surrounded by vacuum, unblurred by air.

There was the Lunar Observatory, from which Earth and the inner planets could be studied; a silent world in whose sky the home-planet hung suspended.

Mercury Observatory, closest to the sun, perched at Mercury's north pole, where the terminator moved scarcely at all, and the sun was fixed on the horizon and could be studied in the minutest detail.

Ceres Observatory, newest, most modern, with its range extending from Jupiter to the outermost galaxies.

There were disadvantages, of course. With interplanetary travel still difficult, leaves would be few, anything like normal life virtually impossible, but this was a lucky generation. Coming scientists would find the fields of knowledge well-reaped and, until the invention of an interstellar drive, no new horizon as capacious as this one would be opened.

Each of these lucky four, Talliaferro, Ryger, Kaunas, and Villiers, was to be in the position of a Galileo, who by owning the first real telescope, could not point it anywhere in the sky without making a major discovery.

But then Romero Villiers had fallen sick and it was rheumatic fever. Whose fault was that? His heart had been left leaking and limping.

He was the most brilliant of the four, the most hopeful, the most intense —and he could not even finish his schooling and get his doctorate.

Worse than that, he could never leave Earth; the acceleration of a spaceship's take-off would kill him.

Talliaferro was marked for the Moon, Ryger for Ceres, Kaunas for Mercury. Only Villiers stayed behind, a life-prisoner of Earth.

They had tried telling their sympathy and Villiers had rejected it with something approaching hate. He had railed at them and cursed them. When Ryger lost his temper and lifted his fist, Villiers had sprung at him, screaming, and had broken Ryger's nose.

Obviously Ryger hadn't forgotten that, as he caressed his nose gingerly with one finger.

Kaunas's forehead was an uncertain washboard of wrinkles. "He's at the Convention, you know. He's got a room in the hotel—405."

"*I* won't see him," said Ryger.

"He's coming up here. He said he wanted to see us. I thought— He said nine. He'll be here any minute."

"In that case," said Ryger, "if you don't mind, I'm leaving." He rose.

Talliaferro said, "Oh, wait a while. What's the harm in seeing him?"

"Because there's no point. He's mad."

"Even so. Let's not be petty about it. Are you afraid of him?"

"Afraid!" Ryger looked contemptuous.

"Nervous, then. What is there to be nervous about?"

"I'm not nervous," said Ryger.

"Sure you are. We all feel guilty about him, and without real reason. Nothing that happened was our fault." But he was speaking defensively and he knew it.

And when, at that point, the door signal sounded, all three jumped and turned to stare uneasily at the barrier that stood between themselves and Villiers.

The door opened and Romero Villiers walked in. The others rose stiffly to greet him, then remained standing in embarrassment, without one hand being raised.

He stared them down sardonically.

He's changed, thought Talliaferro.

He had. He had shrunken in almost every dimension. A gathering stoop made him seem even shorter. The skin of his scalp glistened through thinning hair, the skin on the back of his hands was ridged crookedly with bluish veins. He looked ill. There seemed nothing to link him to the memory of the past except for his trick of shading his eyes with one hand when he stared intently and, when he spoke, the even, controlled baritone of his voice.

He said, "My friends! My space-trotting friends! We've lost touch."

Talliaferro said, "Hello, Villiers."

Villiers eyed him. "Are you well?"

"Well enough."

"And you two?"

Kaunas managed a weak smile and a murmur. Ryger snapped, "All right, Villiers. What's up?"

"Ryger, the angry man," said Villiers. "How's Ceres?"

"It was doing well when I left. How's Earth?"

"You can see for yourself," but Villiers tightened as he said that.

He went on, "I am hoping that the reason all three of you have come to the Convention is to hear my paper day after tomorrow."

"Your paper? What paper?" asked Talliaferro.

"I wrote you all about it. My method of mass-transference."

Ryger smiled with one corner of his mouth. "Yes, you did. You didn't say anything about a paper, though, and I don't recall that you're listed as one of the speakers. I would have noticed it if you had been."

"You're right. I'm not listed. Nor have I prepared an abstract for publication."

Villiers had flushed and Talliaferro said soothingly, "Take it easy, Villiers. You don't look well."

Villiers whirled on him, lips contorted. "My heart's holding out, thank you."

Kaunas said, "Listen, Villiers, if you're not listed or abstracted—"

"*You* listen. I've waited ten years. You have the jobs in space and I have to teach school on Earth, but I'm a better man than any of you or all of you."

"Granted—" began Talliaferro.

"And I don't want your condescension either. Mandel witnessed it. I suppose you've heard of Mandel. Well, he's chairman of the astronautics division at the Convention and I demonstrated mass-transference for him. It was a crude device and it burnt out after one use but— Are you listening?"

"We're listening," said Ryger coldly, "for what that counts."

"He'll let me talk about it my way. You bet he will. No warning. No advertisement. I'm going to spring it at them like a bombshell. When I give them the fundamental relationships involved it will break up the Convention. They'll scatter to their home labs to check on me and build devices. And they'll find it works. I made a live mouse disappear at one spot in my lab and appear in another. Mandel witnessed it."

He stared at them, glaring first at one face, then at another. He said, "You don't believe me, do you?"

Ryger said, "If you don't want advertisement, why do you tell us?"

"You're different. You're my friends, my classmates. You went out into space and left me behind."

"That wasn't a matter of choice," objected Kaunas in a thin, high voice.

Villiers ignored that. He said, "So I want you to know *now*. What will work for a mouse will work for a human. What will move something ten feet across a lab will move it a million miles across space. I'll be on the Moon, *and* on Mercury, *and* on Ceres and anywhere I want to go. I'll match every one of you and more. And I'll have done more for astronomy just teaching school and thinking, than all of you with your observatories and telescopes and cameras and spaceships."

"Well," said Talliaferro, "I'm pleased. More power to you. May I see a copy of the paper?"

"Oh, no." Villiers' hands clenched close to his chest as though he were holding phantom sheets and shielding them from observation. "You wait like everyone else. There's only one copy and no one will see it till I'm ready. Not even Mandel."

"One copy," cried Talliaferro. "If you misplace it—"

"I won't. And if I do, it's all in my head."

"If you—" Talliaferro almost finished that sentence with "die" but stopped himself. Instead, he went on after an almost imperceptible pause, "—have any sense, you'll scan it at least. For safety's sake."

"No," said Villiers, shortly. "You'll hear me day after tomorrow. You'll see the human horizon expanded at one stroke as it never has been before."

Again he stared intently at each face. "Ten years," he said. "Good-by."

"He's mad," said Ryger explosively, staring at the door as though Villiers were still standing before it.

"Is he?" said Talliaferro thoughtfully. "I suppose he is, in a way. He hates us for irrational reasons. And, then, not even to scan his paper as a precaution—"

Talliaferro fingered his own small scanner as he said that. It was just a neutrally colored, undistinguished cylinder, somewhat thicker and somewhat shorter than an ordinary pencil. In recent years, it had become the hallmark of the scientist, much as the stethoscope was that of the physician and the micro-computer that of the statistician. The scanner was worn in a jacket pocket, or clipped to a sleeve, or slipped behind the ear, or swung at the end of a string.

Talliaferro sometimes, in his more philosophical moments, wondered how it was in the days when research men had to make laborious notes of the literature or file away full-sized reprints. How unwieldy!

Now it was only necessary to scan anything printed or written to have a micro-negative which could be developed at leisure. Talliaferro had already recorded every abstract included in the program booklet of the Convention. The other two, he assumed with full confidence, had done likewise.

Talliaferro said, "Under the circumstances, refusal to scan is mad."

"Space!" said Ryger hotly. "There is no paper. There is no discovery. Scoring one on us would be worth any lie to him."

"But then what will he do day after tomorrow?" asked Kaunas.

"How do I know? He's a madman."

Talliaferro still played with his scanner and wondered idly if he ought to remove and develop some of the small slivers of film that lay stored away in its vitals. He decided against it. He said, "Don't underestimate Villiers. He's a brain."

"Ten years ago, maybe," said Ryger. "Now he's a nut. I propose we forget him."

He spoke loudly, as though to drive away Villiers and all that concerned him by the sheer force with which he discussed other things. He talked about Ceres and his work—the radio-plotting of the Milky Way with new radioscopes capable of the resolution of single stars.

Kaunas listened and nodded, then chimed in with information concerning the radio emissions of sunspots and his own paper, in press, on the association of proton storms with the gigantic hydrogen flares on the sun's surface.

Talliaferro contributed little. Lunar work was unglamorous in comparison. The latest information on long-scale weather forecasting through direct observation of terrestrial jet-streams would not compare with radioscopes and proton storms.

More than that, his thoughts could not leave Villiers. Villiers *was* the brain. They all knew it. Even Ryger, for all his bluster, must feel that if mass-transference were at all possible then Villiers was a logical discoverer.

The discussion of their own work amounted to no more than an uneasy admission that none of them had come to much. Talliaferro had followed the literature and knew. His own papers had been minor. The others had authored nothing of great importance.

None of them—face the fact—had developed into space-shakers. The colossal dreams of school days had not come true and that was that. They were competent routine workmen. No less. Unfortunately, no more. They knew that.

Villiers would have been more. They knew that, too. It was that knowledge, as well as guilt, which kept them antagonistic.

Talliaferro felt uneasily that Villiers, despite everything, was yet to *be* more. The others must be thinking so, too, and mediocrity could grow quickly unbearable. The mass-transference paper would come to pass and Villiers would be the great man after all, as he was always fated to be apparently, while his classmates, with all their advantages, would be forgotten. Their role would be no more than to applaud from the crowd.

He felt his own envy and chagrin and was ashamed of it, but felt it none the less.

Conversation died, and Kaunas said, his eyes turning away, "Listen, why don't we drop in on old Villiers?"

There was a false heartiness about it, a completely unconvincing effort at casualness. He added, "No use leaving bad feelings—unnecessarily—"

Talliaferro thought: He wants to make sure about the mass-transference. He's hoping it *is* only a madman's nightmare so he can sleep tonight.

But he was curious himself, so he made no objection, and even Ryger shrugged with ill grace and said, "Hell, why not?"

It was a little before eleven then.

Talliaferro was awakened by the insistent ringing of his door signal. He hitched himself to one elbow in the darkness and felt distinctly outraged. The soft glow of the ceiling indicator showed it to be not quite four in the morning.

He cried out, "Who is it?"

The ringing continued in short, insistent spurts.

Growling, Talliaferro slipped into his bathrobe. He opened the door and blinked in the corridor light. He recognized the man who faced him from the trimensionals he had seen often enough.

Nevertheless, the man said in an abrupt whisper, "My name is Hubert Mandel."

"Yes, sir," said Talliaferro. Mandel was one of the Names in astronomy, prominent enough to have an important executive position with the World Astronomical Bureau, active enough to be Chairman of the Astronautics section here at the Convention.

It suddenly struck Talliaferro that it was Mandel for whom Villiers claimed to have demonstrated mass-transference. The thought of Villiers was somehow a sobering one.

Mandel said, "You are Dr. Edward Talliaferro?"

"Yes, sir."

"Then dress and come with me. It is very important. It concerns a mutual acquaintance."

"Dr. Villiers?"

Mandel's eyes flickered a bit. His brows and lashes were so fair as to give those eyes a naked, unfringed appearance. His hair was silky-thin, his age about fifty.

He said, "Why Villiers?"

"He mentioned you last evening. I don't know any other mutual acquaintance."

Mandel nodded, waited for Talliaferro to finish slipping into his clothes, then turned and led the way. Ryger and Kaunas were waiting in a room one floor above Talliaferro's. Kaunas's eyes were red and troubled. Ryger was smoking a cigarette with impatient puffs.

Talliaferro said, "We're all here. Another reunion." It fell flat.

He took a seat and the three stared at one another. Ryger shrugged.

Mandel paced the floor, hands deep in his pockets. He said, "I apologize for any inconvenience, gentlemen, and I thank you for your co-operation. I would like more of it. Our friend, Romero Villiers, is dead. About an hour ago, his body was removed from the hotel. The medical judgment is heart failure."

There was a stunned silence. Ryger's cigarette hovered halfway to his lips, then sank slowly without completing its journey.

"Poor devil," said Talliaferro.

"Horrible," whispered Kaunas hoarsely. "He was—" His voice played out.

Ryger shook himself. "Well, he had a bad heart. There's nothing to be done."

"One little thing," corrected Mandel quietly. "Recovery."

"What does that mean?" asked Ryger sharply.

Mandel said, "When did you three see him last?"

Talliaferro spoke. "Last evening. It turned out to be a reunion. We all met for the first time in ten years. It wasn't a pleasant meeting, I'm sorry to say. Villiers felt he had cause for anger with us, and he was angry."

"That was—when?"

"About nine, the first time."

"The first time?"

"We saw him again later in the evening."

Kaunas looked troubled. "He had left angrily. We couldn't leave it at that. We had to try. It wasn't as if we hadn't all been friends at one time. So we went to his room and—"

Mandel pounced on that. "You were all in his room?"

"Yes," said Kaunas, surprised.

"About when?"

"Eleven, I think." He looked at the others. Talliaferro nodded.

"And how long did you stay?"

"Two minutes," put in Ryger. "He ordered us out as though we were after his paper." He paused as though expecting Mandel to ask what paper, but Mandel said nothing. He went on. "I think he kept it under his pillow. At least he lay across the pillow as he yelled at us to leave."

"He may have been dying then," said Kaunas, in a sick whisper.

"Not then," said Mandel shortly. "So you probably all left fingerprints."

"Probably," said Talliaferro. He was losing some of his automatic respect for Mandel and a sense of impatience was returning. It *was* four in the morning, Mandel or no. He said, "Now what's all this about?"

"Well, gentlemen," said Mandel, "there's more to Villiers' death than the fact of death. Villiers' paper, the only copy of it as far as I know, was stuffed into the cigarette flash-disposal unit and only scraps of it were left. I've never seen or read the paper, but I knew enough about the matter to be willing to swear in court if necessary that the remnants of unflashed paper in the disposal unit were of the paper he was planning to give at this Convention. —You seem doubtful, Dr. Ryger."

Ryger smiled sourly. "Doubtful that he was going to give it. If you want my opinion, sir, he was mad. For ten years he was a prisoner of Earth and he fantasied mass-transference as escape. It was all that kept him alive probably. He rigged up some sort of fraudulent demonstration. I don't say it was deliberate fraud. He was probably madly sincere, and sincerely mad. Last evening was the climax. He came to our rooms—he hated us for having escaped Earth—and triumphed over us. It was what he had lived for for ten years. It may have shocked him back to some form of sanity. He knew he couldn't actually give the paper; there was nothing to give. So he burnt it and his heart gave out. It *is* too bad."

Mandel listened to the Cerian astronomer, wearing a look of sharp disapproval. He said, "Very glib, Dr. Ryger, but quite wrong. I am not as easily fooled by fraudulent demonstrations as you may believe. Now according to the registration data, which I have been forced to check rather hastily, you three were his classmates at college. Is that right?"

They nodded.

"Are there any other classmates of yours present at the Convention?"

"No," said Kaunas. "We were the only four qualifying for a doctorate in astronomy that year. At least he would have qualified except—"

"Yes, I understand," said Mandel. "Well, then, in that case one of you three visited Villiers in his room one last time at midnight."

There was a short silence. Then Ryger said coldly, "Not I." Kaunas, eyes wide, shook his head.

Talliaferro said, "What are you implying?"

"One of you came to him at midnight and insisted on seeing his paper. I don't know the motive. Conceivably, it was with the deliberate intention of forcing him into heart failure. When Villiers collapsed, the criminal, if I may call him so, was ready. He snatched the paper which, I might add, probably *was* kept under his pillow, and scanned it. Then he destroyed the paper itself in the flash-disposal, but he was in a hurry and destruction wasn't complete."

Ryger interrupted. "How do you know all this? Were you a witness?"

"Almost," said Mandel. "Villiers was not quite dead at the moment of his first collapse. When the criminal left, he managed to reach the phone and call my room. He choked out a few phrases, enough to outline what had occurred. Unfortunately I was not in my room; a late conference kept me away. However, my recording attachment taped it. I always play the recording tape back whenever I return to my room or office. Bureaucratic habit. I called back. He was dead."

"Well, then," said Ryger, "who did he say did it?"

"He didn't. Or if he did, it was unintelligible. But one word rang out clearly. It was 'classmate.'"

Talliaferro detached his scanner from its place in his inner jacket pocket and held it out toward Mandel. Quietly he said, "If you would like to develop the film in my scanner, you are welcome to do so. You will not find Villiers' paper there."

At once, Kaunas did the same, and Ryger, with a scowl, joined.

Mandel took all three scanners and said dryly, "Presumably, whichever one of you has done this has already disposed of the piece of exposed film with the paper on it. However—"

Talliaferro raised his eyebrows. "You may search my person or my room."

But Ryger was still scowling, "Now wait a minute, wait one bloody minute. Are you the police?"

Mandel stared at him. "Do you *want* the police? Do you want a scandal and a murder charge? Do you want the Convention disrupted and the System press to make a holiday out of astronomy and astronomers? Villiers' death might well have been accidental. He *did* have a bad heart. Whichever one of you was there may well have acted on impulse. It may not have been a premeditated crime. If whoever it is will return the negative, we can avoid a great deal of trouble."

"Even for the criminal?" asked Talliaferro.

Mandel shrugged. "There may be trouble for him. I will not promise immunity. But whatever the trouble, it won't be public disgrace and life imprisonment, as it might be if the police are called in."

Silence.

Mandel said, "It is one of you three."

Silence.

Mandel went on, "I think I can see the original reasoning of the guilty person. The paper would be destroyed. Only we four knew of the mass-transference and only I had ever seen a demonstration. Moreover you had only his word, a madman's word perhaps, that I had seen it. With Villiers dead of heart failure and the paper gone, it would be easy to believe Dr. Ryger's theory that there was no mass-transference and never had been. A year or two might pass and our criminal, in possession of the mass-transference data, could reveal it little by little, rig experiments, publish careful papers, and end as the apparent discoverer with all that would imply in terms of money and renown. Even his own classmates would suspect nothing. At most they would believe that the long-past affair with Villiers had inspired him to begin investigations in the field. No more."

Mandel looked sharply from one face to another. "But none of that will work now. Any of the three of you who comes through with mass-transference is proclaiming himself the criminal. I've seen the demonstration; I know it is legitimate; I know that one of you possesses a record of the paper. The information is therefore useless to you. Give it up then."

Silence.

Mandel walked to the door and turned again, "I'd appreciate it if you would stay here till I return. I won't be long. I hope the guilty one will use the interval to consider. If he's afraid a confession will lose him his job, let him remember that a session with the police may lose him his liberty *and* cost him the Psychic Probe." He hefted the three scanners, looked grim and somewhat in need of sleep. "I'll develop these."

Kaunas tried to smile. "What if we make a break for it while you're gone?"

"Only one of you has reason to try," said Mandel. "I think I can rely on the two innocent ones to control the third, if only out of self-protection."

He left.

It was five in the morning. Ryger looked at his watch indignantly. "A hell of a thing. I want to sleep."

"We can curl up here," said Talliaferro philosophically. "Is anyone planning a confession?"

Kaunas looked away and Ryger's lip lifted.

"I didn't think so." Talliaferro closed his eyes, leaned his large head back against the chair and said in a tired voice, "Back on the Moon, they're in the slack season. We've got a two-week night and then it's busy, busy. Then there's two weeks of sun and there's nothing but calculations, correlations and bull-sessions. That's the hard time. I hate it. If there were more women, if I could arrange something permanent—"

In a whisper, Kaunas talked about the fact that it was still impossible to get the entire Sun above the horizon and in view of the telescope on Mercury. But with another two miles of track soon to be laid down for the Observatory—move the whole thing, you know, tremendous forces involved, solar energy used directly—it might be managed. It *would* be managed.

Even Ryger consented to talk of Ceres after listening to the low murmur of the other voices. There was the problem there of the two-hour rotation period, which meant the stars whipped across the sky at an angular velocity twelve times that in Earth's sky. A net of three light scopes, three radioscopes, three of everything, caught the fields of study from one another as they whirled past.

"Could you use one of the poles?" asked Kaunas.

"You're thinking of Mercury and the Sun," said Ryger impatiently. "Even at the poles, the sky would still twist, and half of it would be forever hidden. Now if Ceres showed only one face to the Sun, the way Mercury does, we could have a permanent night sky with the stars rotating slowly once in three years."

The sky lightened and it dawned slowly.

Talliaferro was half asleep, but he kept hold of half-consciousness firmly. He would not fall asleep and leave the others awake. Each of the three, he thought, was wondering, "Who? Who?"—except the guilty one, of course.

Talliaferro's eyes snapped open as Mandel entered again. The sky, as seen from the window, had grown blue. Talliaferro was glad the window was closed. The hotel was air-conditioned, of course, but windows could be opened during the mild season of the year by those Earthmen who fancied the illusion of fresh air. Talliaferro, with Moon-vacuum on his mind, shuddered at the thought with real discomfort.

Mandel said, "Have any of you anything to say?"

They looked at him steadily. Ryger shook his head.

Mandel said, "I have developed the film in your scanners, gentlemen, and viewed the results." He tossed scanners and developed slivers of film on to the bed. "Nothing! you'll have trouble sorting out the film, I'm afraid. For that I'm sorry. And now there is still the question of the missing film."

"If any," said Ryger, and yawned prodigiously.

Mandel said, "I would suggest we come down to Villiers' room, gentlemen."

Kaunas looked startled. "Why?"

Talliaferro said, "Is this psychology? Bring the criminal to the scene of the crime and remorse will wring a confession from him?"

Mandel said, "A less melodramatic reason is that I would like to have the two of you who are innocent help me find the missing film of Villiers' paper."

"Do you think it's there?" asked Ryger challengingly.

"Possibly. It's a beginning. We can then search each of your rooms. The symposium on Astronautics doesn't start till tomorrow at 10 A.M. We have till then."

"And after that?"

"It may have to be the police."

They stepped gingerly into Villiers' room. Ryger was red, Kaunas pale. Talliaferro tried to remain calm.

Last night they had seen it under artificial lighting with a scowling, disheveled Villiers clutching his pillow, staring them down, ordering them away. Now there was the scentless odor of death about it.

Mandel fiddled with the window-polarizer to let more light in, and adjusted it too far, so that the eastern Sun slipped in.

Kaunas threw his arm up to shade his eyes and screamed, "The Sun!" so that all the others froze.

Kaunas's face showed a kind of terror, as though it were his Mercurian sun that he had caught a blinding glimpse of.

Talliaferro thought of his own reaction to the possibility of open air and his teeth gritted. They were all bent crooked by their ten years away from Earth.

Kaunas ran to the window, fumbling for the polarizer, and then the breath came out of him in a huge gasp.

Mandel stepped to his side. "What's wrong?" and the other two joined them.

The city lay stretched below them and outward to the horizon in broken stone and brick, bathed in the rising sun, with the shadowed portions toward them. Talliaferro cast it all a furtive and uneasy glance.

Kaunas, his chest seemingly contracted past the point where he could cry out, stared at something much closer. There, on the outer window sill, one corner secured in a trifling imperfection, a crack in the cement, was an inch-long strip of milky-gray film, and on it were the early rays of the rising sun.

Mandel, with an angry, incoherent cry, threw up the window and snatched it away. He shielded it in one cupped hand, staring out of hot and reddened eyes.

He said, "Wait here!"

There was nothing to say. When Mandel left, they sat down and stared stupidly at one another.

Mandel was back in twenty minutes. He said quietly (in a voice that gave the impression, somehow, that it was quiet only because its owner had passed far beyond the raving stage), "The corner in the crack wasn't overexposed. I could make out a few words. It is Villiers' paper. The rest is ruined; nothing can be salvaged. It's gone."

"What next?" said Talliaferro.

Mandel shrugged wearily. "Right now, I don't care. Mass-transference is gone until someone as brilliant as Villiers works it out again. I shall work on it but I have no illusions as to my own capacity. With it gone, I suppose you three don't matter, guilty or not. What's the difference?" His whole body seemed to have loosened and sunk into despair.

But Talliaferro's voice grew hard. "Now, hold on. In your eyes, any of the three of us might be guilty. I, for instance. You are a big man in the field and you will never have a good word to say for me. The general idea may arise that I am incompetent or worse. I will not be ruined by the shadow of guilt. Now let's solve this thing."

"I am no detective," said Mandel wearily.

"Then call in the police, damn it."

Ryger said, "Wait a while, Tal. Are you implying that I'm guilty?"

"I'm saying that I'm innocent."

Kaunas raised his voice in fright. "It will mean the Psychic Probe for each of us. There may be mental damage—"

Mandel raised both arms high in the air. "Gentlemen! Gentlemen! Please! There is one thing we might do short of the police; and you are right, Dr. Talliaferro, it would be unfair to the innocent to leave this matter here."

They turned to him in various stages of hostility. Ryger said, "What do you suggest?"

"I have a friend named Wendell Urth. You may have heard of him, or you may not, but perhaps I can arrange to see him tonight."

"What if you can?" demanded Talliaferro. "Where does that get us?"

"He's an odd man," said Mandel hesitantly, "very odd. And very brilliant in his way. He has helped the police before this and he may be able to help us now."

PART TWO

Edward Talliaferro could not forbear staring at the room and its occupant with the greatest astonishment. It and he seemed to exist in isolation, and to be part of no recognizable world. The sounds of Earth were absent in this well-padded, windowless nest. The light and air of Earth had been blanked out in artificial illumination and conditioning.

It was a large room, dim and cluttered. They had picked their way across a littered floor to a couch from which book-films had been brusquely cleared and dumped to one side in a tangle.

The man who owned the room had a large, round face on a stumpy, round body. He moved quickly about on his short legs, jerking his head as he spoke until his thick glasses all but bounced off the thoroughly inconspicuous nubble that served as a nose. His thick-lidded, somewhat protuberant eyes gleamed in myopic good nature at them all, as he seated himself in his own chair-desk combination, lit directly by the one bright light in the room.

"So good of you to come, gentlemen. Pray excuse the condition of my room." He waved stubby fingers in a wide-sweeping gesture. "I am engaged in cataloguing the many objects of extraterrological interest I have accumulated. It is a tremendous job. For instance—"

He dodged out of his seat and burrowed in a heap of objects beside the desk till he came up with a smoky-gray object, semi-translucent and roughly cylindrical. "This," he said, "is a Callistan object that may be a relic of intelligent nonhuman entities. It is not decided. Not more than a dozen have been discovered and this is the most perfect single specimen I know of."

He tossed it to one side and Talliaferro jumped. The plump man stared in his direction and said, "It's not breakable." He sat down again, clasped his pudgy fingers tightly over his abdomen and let them pump slowly in and out as he breathed. "And now what can I do for you?"

Hubert Mandel had carried through the introductions and Talliaferro was considering deeply. Surely it was a man named Wendell Urth who had written a recent book entitled *Comparative Evolutionary Processes on Water-Oxygen Planets,* and surely this could not be the man.

He said, "Are you the author of *Comparative Evolutionary Processes,* Dr. Urth?"

A beatific smile spread across Urth's face, "You've read it?"

"Well, no, I haven't, but—"

Urth's expression grew instantly censorious. "Then you should. Right now. Here, I have a copy—"

He bounced out of his chair again and Mandel cried at once, "Now wait, Urth, first things first. This is serious."

He virtually forced Urth back into his chair and began speaking rapidly as though to prevent any further side issues from erupting. He told the whole story with admirable word-economy.

Urth reddened slowly as he listened. He seized his glasses and shoved them higher up on his nose. "Mass-transference!" he cried.

"I saw it with my own eyes," said Mandel.

"And you never told me."

"I was sworn to secrecy. The man was—peculiar. I explained that."

Urth pounded the desk. "How could you allow such a discovery to remain the property of an eccentric, Mandel? The knowledge should have been forced from him by Psychic Probe, if necessary."

"It would have killed him," protested Mandel.

But Urth was rocking back and forth with his hands clasped tightly to his cheeks. "Mass-transference. The only way a decent, civilized man should travel. The only possible way. The only conceivable way. If I had known. If I could have been there. But the hotel is nearly thirty miles away."

Ryger, who listened with an expression of annoyance on his face, interposed, "I understand there's a flitter line direct to Convention Hall. It could have gotten you there in ten minutes."

Urth stiffened and looked at Ryger strangely. His cheeks bulged. He jumped to his feet and scurried out of the room.

Ryger said, "What the devil?"

Mandel muttered, "Damn it. I should have warned you."

"About what?"

"Dr. Urth doesn't travel on any sort of conveyance. It's a phobia. He moves about only on foot."

Kaunas blinked about in the dimness. "But he's an extraterrologist, isn't he? An expert on life forms of other planets?"

Talliaferro had risen and now stood before a Galactic Lens on a pedestal.

He stared at the inner gleam of the star systems. He had never seen a Lens so large or so elaborate.

Mandel said, "He's an extraterrologist, yes, but he's never visited any of the planets on which he is expert and he never will. In thirty years, I doubt if he's ever been more than a mile from this room."

Ryger laughed.

Mandel flushed angrily. "You may find it funny, but I'd appreciate your being careful what you say when Dr. Urth comes back."

Urth sidled in a moment later. "My apologies, gentlemen," he said in a whisper. "And now let us approach our problem. Perhaps one of you wishes to confess."

Talliaferro's lips quirked sourly. This plump, self-imprisoned extraterrologist was scarcely formidable enough to force a confession from anyone. Fortunately, there would be no need of his detective talents, if any, after all.

Talliaferro said, "Dr. Urth, are you connected with the police?"

A certain smugness seemed to suffuse Urth's ruddy face. "I have no official connection, Dr. Talliaferro, but my unofficial relationships are very good indeed."

"In that case, I will give you some information which you can carry to the police."

Urth drew in his abdomen and hitched at his shirttail. It came free, and slowly he polished his glasses with it. When he was quite through and had perched them precariously on his nose once more, he said, "And what is that?"

"I will tell you who was present when Villiers died and who scanned his paper."

"You have solved the mystery?"

"I've thought about it all day. I think I've solved it." Talliaferro rather enjoyed the sensation he was creating.

"Well, then?"

Talliaferro took a deep breath. This was not going to be easy to do, though he had been planning it for hours. "The guilty man," he said, "is obviously Dr. Hubert Mandel."

Mandel stared at Talliaferro in sudden, hard-breathing indignation. "Look here, Doctor," he began, loudly, "if you have any basis for such a ridiculous—"

Urth's tenor voice soared above the interruption. "Let him talk, Hubert, let us hear him. You suspected him and there is no law that forbids him to suspect you."

Mandel fell angrily silent.

Talliaferro, not allowing his voice to falter, said, "It is more than just suspicion, Dr. Urth. The evidence is perfectly plain. Four of us knew about mass-transference, but only one of us, Dr. Mandel, had actually seen a demonstration. He *knew* it to be a fact. He *knew* a paper on the subject existed. We three knew only that Villiers was more or less unbalanced. Oh, we might have thought there was just a chance. We visited him at eleven, I think, just to check on that, though none of us actually said so—but he just acted crazier than ever.

"Check special knowledge and motive then on Dr. Mandel's side. Now, Dr. Urth, picture something else. Whoever it was who confronted Villiers at midnight, saw him collapse, and scanned his paper (let's keep him anonymous for a moment) must have been terribly startled to see Villiers apparently come to life again and to hear him talking into the telephone. Our criminal, in the panic of the moment, realized one thing: he must get rid of the one piece of incriminating material evidence.

"He had to get rid of the undeveloped film of the paper and he had to do it in such a way that it would be safe from discovery so that he might pick it up once more if he remained unsuspected. The outer window sill was ideal. Quickly he threw up Villiers' window, placed the strip of film outside, and left. Now, even if Villiers survived or if his telephoning brought results, it would be merely Villiers' word against his own and it would be easy to show that Villiers was unbalanced."

Talliaferro paused in something like triumph. This would be irrefutable.

Wendell Urth blinked at him and wiggled the thumbs of his clasped hands so that they slapped against his ample shirt front. He said, "And the significance of all that?"

"The significance is that the window was thrown open and the film placed in open air. Now Ryger has lived for ten years on Ceres, Kaunas on Mercury, I on the Moon—barring short leaves and not many of them. We commented to one another several times yesterday on the difficulty of growing acclimated to Earth.

"Our work-worlds are each airless objects. We never go out in the open without a suit. To expose ourselves to unenclosed space is unthinkable. None of us could have opened the window without a severe inner struggle. Dr. Mandel, however, has lived on Earth exclusively. Opening a window to him is only a matter of a bit of muscular exertion. He could do it. We couldn't. Ergo, he did it."

Talliaferro sat back and smiled a bit.

"Space, that's it!" cried Ryger, with enthusiasm.

"That's not it at all," roared Mandel, half rising as though tempted to throw himself at Talliaferro. "I deny the whole miserable fabrication. What about the record I have of Villiers' phone call? He used the word 'classmate.' The entire tape makes it obvious—"

"He was a dying man," said Talliaferro. "Much of what he said you admitted was incomprehensible. I ask you, Dr. Mandel, without having heard the tape, if it isn't true that Villiers' voice is distorted past recognition."

"Well—" said Mandel in confusion.

"I'm sure it is. There is no reason to suppose, then, that you might not have rigged up the tape in advance, complete with the damning word 'class-mate.' "

Mandel said, "Good Lord, how would I know there were classmates at the Convention? How would I know they knew about the mass-transfer-ence?"

"Villiers might have told you. I presume he did."

"Now, look," said Mandel, "you three saw Villiers alive at eleven. The medical examiner, seeing Villiers' body shortly after 3 A.M. declared he had been dead at least two hours. That was certain. The time of death, there-fore, was between 11 P.M. and 1 A.M. I was at a late conference last night. I can prove my whereabouts, miles from the hotel, between 10:00 and 2:00 by a dozen witnesses no one of whom anyone can possibly question. Is that enough for you?"

Talliaferro paused a moment. Then he went on stubbornly, "Even so. Suppose you got back to the hotel by 2:30. You went to Villiers' room to discuss his talk. You found the door open, or you had a duplicate key. Anyway, you found him dead. You seized the opportunity to scan the pa-per—"

"And if he were already dead, and couldn't make phone calls, why should I hide the film?"

"To remove suspicion. You may have a second copy of the film safe in your possession. For that matter, we have only your own word that the paper itself was destroyed."

"Enough. Enough," cried Urth. "It is an interesting hypothesis, Dr. Tal-liaferro, but it falls to the ground of its own weight."

Talliaferro frowned. "That's your opinion, perhaps—"

"It would be anyone's opinion. Anyone, that is, with the power of human thought. Don't you see that Hubert Mandel did too much to be the crimi-nal?"

"No," said Talliaferro.

Wendell Urth smiled benignly. "As a scientist, Dr. Talliaferro, you un-doubtedly know better than to fall in love with your own theories to the exclusion of facts or reasoning. Do me the pleasure of behaving similarly as a detective.

"Consider that if Dr. Mandel had brought about the death of Villiers and faked an alibi, or if he had found Villiers dead and taken advantage of that, how little he would really have had to do! Why scan the paper or even pretend that anyone had done so? He could simply have taken the paper. Who else knew of its existence? Nobody, really. There is no reason to think Villiers told anyone else about it. Villiers was pathologically secretive. There would have been every reason to think that he told no one.

"No one knew Villiers was giving a talk, except Dr. Mandel. It wasn't announced. No abstract was published. Dr. Mandel could have walked off with the paper in perfect confidence.

"Even if he had discovered that Villiers had talked to his classmates about the matter, what of it? What evidence would his classmates have except the word of one whom they are themselves half willing to consider a madman?

"By announcing instead that Villiers' paper had been destroyed, by declaring his death to be not entirely natural, by searching for a scanned copy of the film—in short by everything Dr. Mandel had done—he has aroused a suspicion that only he could possibly have aroused when he need only have remained quiet to have committed a perfect crime. If he were the criminal, he would be more stupid, more colossally obtuse than anyone I have ever known. And Dr. Mandel, after all, is none of that."

Talliaferro thought hard but found nothing to say.

Ryger said, "Then who did do it?"

"One of you three. That's obvious."

"But which?"

"Oh, that's obvious, too. I knew which of you was guilty the moment Dr. Mandel had completed his description of events."

Talliaferro stared at the plump extraterrologist with distaste. The bluff did not frighten him, but it was affecting the other two. Ryger's lips were thrust out and Kaunas's lower jaw had relaxed moronically. They looked like fish, both of them.

He said, "Which one, then? Tell us."

Urth blinked. "First, I want to make it perfectly plain that the important thing is mass-transference. It can still be recovered."

Mandel, scowling still, said querulously, "What the devil are you talking about, Urth?"

"The man who scanned the paper probably looked at what he was scanning. I doubt that he had the time or presence of mind to read it, and if he did, I doubt if he could remember it—consciously. However, there is the Psychic Probe. If he even glanced at the paper, what impinged on his retina could be Probed."

There was an uneasy stir.

Urth said at once, "No need to be afraid of the Probe. Proper handling is safe, particularly if a man offers himself voluntarily. When damage is done, it is usually because of unnecessary resistance, a kind of mental tearing, you know. So if the guilty man will voluntarily confess, place himself in my hands—"

Talliaferro laughed. The sudden noise rang out sharply in the dim quiet of the room. The psychology was so transparent and artless.

Wendell Urth looked almost bewildered at the reaction and stared earnestly at Talliaferro over his glasses. He said, "I have enough influence with the police to keep the Probing entirely confidential."

Ryger said savagely, "I didn't do it."

Kaunas shook his head.

Talliaferro disdained any answer.

Urth sighed. "Then I will have to point out the guilty man. It will be traumatic. It will make things harder." He tightened the grip on his belly and his fingers twitched. "Dr. Talliaferro pointed out that the film was hidden on the outer window sill so that it might remain safe from discovery and from harm. I agree with him."

"Thank you," said Talliaferro dryly.

"However, why should anyone think that an outer window sill is a particularly safe hiding place? The police would certainly look there. Even in the absence of the police it was discovered. Who would tend to consider anything outside a building as particularly safe? Obviously, some person who has lived a long time on an airless world and has it drilled into him that no one goes outside an enclosed place without detailed precautions.

"To someone on the Moon, for instance, anything hidden outside a Lunar Dome would be comparatively safe. Men venture out only rarely and then only on specific business. So he would overcome the hardship of opening a window and exposing himself to what he would subconsciously consider a vacuum for the sake of a safe hiding place. The reflex thought, 'Outside an inhabited structure is safe,' would do the trick."

Talliaferro said between clenched teeth, "Why do you mention the Moon, Dr. Urth?"

Urth said blandly, "Only as an example. What I've said so far applies to all three of you. But now comes the crucial point, the matter of the dying night."

Talliaferro frowned. "You mean the night Villiers died?"

"I mean any night. See here, even granted that an outer window sill was a safe hiding place, which of you would be mad enough to consider it a safe hiding place *for a piece of unexposed film?* Scanner film isn't very sensitive, to be sure, and is made to be developed under all sorts of hit-and-miss conditions. Diffuse night-time illumination wouldn't seriously affect it, but diffuse daylight would ruin it in a few minutes, and direct sunlight would ruin it at once. Everyone knows that."

Mandel said, "Go ahead, Urth. What is this leading to?"

"You're trying to rush me," said Urth, with a massive pout. "I want you to see this clearly. The criminal wanted, above all, to keep the film safe. It was his only record of something of supreme value to himself and to the world. Why would he put it where it would inevitably be ruined by the morning sun? —Only because he did not expect the morning sun ever to come. He thought the night, so to speak, was immortal.

"But nights *aren't* immortal. On Earth, they die and give way to daytime.

Even the six-month polar night is a dying night eventually. The nights on Ceres last only two hours; the nights on the Moon last two weeks. They are dying nights, too, and Dr. Talliaferro and Ryger know that day must always come."

Kaunas was on his feet. "But wait—"

Wendell Urth faced him full. "No longer any need to wait, Dr. Kaunas. Mercury is the only sizable object in the Solar System that turns only one face to the sun. Even taking libration into account, fully three-eighths of its surface is true dark-side and never sees the sun. The Polar Observatory is at the rim of that dark-side. For ten years, you have grown used to the fact that nights are immortal, that a surface in darkness remains eternally in darkness, and so you entrusted unexposed film to Earth's night, forgetting in your excitement that nights must die—"

Kaunas stumbled forward. "Wait—"

Urth was inexorable. "I am told that when Mandel adjusted the polarizer in Villiers' room, you screamed at the sunlight. Was that your ingrained fear of Mercurian sun, or your sudden realization of what sunlight meant to your plans? You rushed forward. Was that to adjust the polarizer or to stare at the ruined film?"

Kaunas fell to his knees. "I didn't mean it. I wanted to speak to him, only to speak to him, and he screamed and collapsed. I thought he was dead and the paper was under his pillow and it all just followed. One thing led on to another and before I knew it, I couldn't get out of it anymore. But I meant none of it. I swear it."

They had formed a semicircle about him and Wendell Urth stared at the moaning Kaunas with pity in his eyes.

An ambulance had come and gone. Talliaferro finally brought himself to say stiffly to Mandel, "I hope, sir, there will be no hard feelings for anything said here."

And Mandel had answered, as stiffly, "I think we had all better forget as much as possible of what has happened during the last twenty-four hours."

They were standing in the doorway, ready to leave, and Wendell Urth ducked his smiling head, and said, "There's the question of my fee, you know."

Mandel looked startled.

"Not money," said Urth at once. "But when the first mass-transference setup for humans is established, I want a trip arranged for me."

Mandel continued to look anxious. "Now, wait. Trips through outer space are a long way off."

Urth shook his head rapidly. "Not outer space. Not at all. I would like to step across to Lower Falls, New Hampshire."

"All right. But why?"

Urth looked up. To Talliaferro's outright surprise, the extra-terrologist's face wore an expression compounded of shyness and eagerness.

Urth said, "I once—quite a long time ago—knew a girl there. It's been many years—but I sometimes wonder—"

I'm in Marsport Without Hilda

It worked itself out, to begin with, like a dream. I didn't have to make any arrangement. I didn't have to touch it. I just watched things work out. —Maybe that's when I should have first smelled catastrophe.

It began with my usual month's layoff between assignments. A month on and a month off is the right and proper routine for the Galactic Service. I reached Marsport for the usual three-day layover before the short hop to Earth.

Ordinarily, Hilda, God bless her, as sweet a wife as any man ever had, would be there waiting for me and we'd have a nice sedate time of it—a nice little interlude for the two of us. The only trouble with that is that Marsport is the rowdiest spot in the System, and a nice little interlude isn't exactly what fits in. Only, how do I explain that to Hilda, hey?

Well, *this* time, my mother-in-law, God *bless* her (for a change) got sick just two days before I reached Marsport, and the night before landing, I got a spacegram from Hilda saying she would stay on Earth with her mother and wouldn't meet me this one time.

I 'grammed back my loving regrets and my feverish anxiety concerning her mother and when I landed, there I was—

I was in Marsport without Hilda!

That was still nothing, you understand. It was the frame of the picture, the bones of the woman. Now there was the matter of the lines and coloring inside the frame; the skin and flesh outside the bones.

So I called up Flora (Flora of certain rare episodes in the past) and for the purpose I used a video booth. —Damn the expense; full speed ahead.

I was giving myself ten to one odds she'd be out, she'd be busy with her videophone disconnected, she'd be dead, even.

But she was in, with her videophone connected, and Great Galaxy, was she anything but dead.

She looked better than ever. Age cannot wither, as somebody or other once said, nor custom stale her infinite variety.

Was she glad to see me? She squealed, "Max! It's been years."

"I know, Flora, but this is it, if you're available. Because guess what! I'm in Marsport without Hilda."

She squealed again, "Isn't that nice! Then come on over."

I goggled a bit. This was too much. "You mean you are available?" You have to understand that Flora was never available without plenty of notice. Well, she was that kind of knockout.

She said, "Oh, I've got some quibbling little arrangement, Max, but I'll take care of that. You come on over."

"I'll come," I said happily.

Flora was the kind of girl— Well, I tell you, she had her rooms under Martian gravity, 0.4 Earth-normal. The gadget to free her of Marsport's pseudo-grav field was expensive of course, but if you've ever held a girl in your arms at 0.4 gees, you need no explanation. If you haven't, explanations will do no good. I'm also sorry for you.

Talk about floating on clouds.

I closed connections, and only the prospect of seeing it all in the flesh could have made me wipe out the image with such alacrity. I stepped out of the booth.

And at that point, that precise point, that very split-instant of time, the first whiff of catastrophe nudged itself up to me.

That first whiff was the bald head of that lousy Rog Crinton of the Mars offices, gleaming over a headful of pale blue eyes, pale yellow complexion, and pale brown mustache. I didn't bother getting on all fours and beating my forehead against the ground because my vacation had started the minute I had gotten off the ship.

So I said with only normal politeness, "What do you want and I'm in a hurry. I've got an appointment."

He said, "You've got an appointment with me. I was waiting for you at the unloading desk."

I said, "I didn't see you—"

He said, "You didn't see anything."

He was right at that, for, come to think of it, if he was at the unloading desk, he must have been spinning ever since because I went past that desk like Halley's Comet skimming the Solar Corona.

I said, "All right. What do you want?"

"I've got a little job for you."

I laughed. "It's my month off, friend."

He said, "Red emergency alert, friend."

Which meant, no vacation, just like that. I couldn't believe it. I said, "Nuts, Rog. Have a heart. I got an emergency alert of my own."

"Nothing like this."

"Rog," I yelled, "can't you get someone else? Anyone else?"

"You're the only Class A agent on Mars."

"Send to Earth, then. They stack agents like micro-pile units at Headquarters."

"This has got to be done before 11 P.M. What's the matter? You haven't got three hours?"

I grabbed my head. The boy just didn't *know*. I said, "Let me make a call, will you?"

I stepped back into the booth, glared at him, and said, "Private!"

Flora shone on the screen again, like a mirage on an asteroid. She said, "Something wrong, Max? Don't say something's wrong. I canceled my other engagement."

I said, "Flora, baby, I'll be there. I'll *be* there. But something's come up."

She asked the natural question in a hurt tone of voice and I said, "*No*. Not another girl. With you in the same town they don't make any other girls. Females, maybe. Not girls. Baby! Honey!" (I had a wild impulse but hugging 'vision screen is no pastime for a grown man.) "It's business. Just hold on. It won't take long."

She said, "All right," but she said it kind of like it was just enough not all right so that I got the shivers.

I stepped out of the booth and said, "All right, Rog, what kind of mess have you cooked up for me?"

We went into the spaceport bar and got us an insulated booth. He said, "The *Antares Giant* is coming in from Sirius in exactly half an hour; at 8 P.M. local time."

"Okay."

"Three men will get out, among others, and will wait for the *Space Eater* coming in from Earth at 11 P.M. and leaving for Capella some time thereafter. The three men will get on the *Space Eater* and will then be out of our jurisdiction."

"So."

"So between 8:00 and 11:00, they will be in a special waiting room and you will be with them. I have a trimensional image of each for you so you'll know which they are and which is which. You have between 8:00 and 11:00 to decide which one of the three is carrying contraband."

"What kind of contraband?"

"The worst kind. Altered Spaceoline."

"*Altered* Spaceoline?"

He had thrown me. I knew what Spaceoline was. If you've been on a space-hop you know, too. And in case you're Earth-bound yourself the bare fact is that everyone needs it on the first space-trip; almost everybody needs it for the first dozen trips; lots need it every trip. Without it, there is vertigo associated with free fall, screaming terrors, semi-permanent psychoses. With it, there is nothing; no one minds a thing. And it isn't habit-forming; it has no adverse side-effects. Spaceoline is ideal, essential, unsubstitutable. When in doubt, take Spaceoline.

Rog said, "That's right, altered Spaceoline. It can be changed chemically by a very simple reaction that can be conducted in anyone's basement into a drug that will give one giant-size charge and become your baby-blue habit the first time. It is on a par with the most dangerous alkaloids we know."

"And we just found out about it?"

"No. The Service has known about it for years, and we've kept others from knowing by squashing every discovery flat. Only now the discovery has gone too far."

"In what way?"

"One of the men who will be stopping over at this spaceport is carrying some of the altered Spaceoline on his person. Chemists in the Capellan system, which is outside the Federation, will analyze it and set up ways of synthesizing more. After that, it's either fight the worst drug menace we've ever seen or suppress the matter by suppressing the source."

"You mean Spaceoline."

"Right. And if we suppress Spaceoline, we suppress space travel."

I decided to put my finger on the point. "Which one of the three has it?"

Rog smiled nastily, "If we knew, would we need you? You're to find out which of the three."

"You're calling on me for a lousy frisk job."

"Touch the wrong one at the risk of a haircut down to the larynx. Every one of the three is a big man on his own planet. One is Edward Harponaster; one is Joàquin Lipsky; and one is Andiamo Ferrucci. Well?"

He was right. I'd heard of every one of them. Chances are you have, too; and not one was touchable without proof in advance, as you know. I said, "Would one of them touch a dirty deal like—"

"There are trillions involved," said Rog, "which means any one of the three would. And one of them *is*, because Jack Hawk got that far before he was killed—"

"Jack Hawk's *dead?*" For a minute, I forgot about the Galactic drug menace. For a minute, I nearly forgot about Flora.

"Right, and one of those guys arranged the killing. Now you find out which. You put the finger on the right one before 11:00 and there's a promotion, a raise in pay, a pay-back for poor Jack Hawk, and a rescue of the Galaxy. You put the finger on the wrong one and there'll be a nasty interstellar situation and you'll be out on your ear and also on every black list from here to Antares and back."

I said, "Suppose I don't finger anybody?"

"That would be like fingering the wrong one as far as the Service is concerned."

"I've got to finger someone but only the right one or my head's handed to me."

"In thin slices. You're beginning to understand me, Max."

In a long lifetime of looking ugly, Rog Crinton had never looked uglier. The only comfort I got out of staring at him was the realization that he was married, too, and that he lived with his wife at Marsport all year round. And does he deserve that. Maybe I'm hard on him, but he *deserves* it.

I put in a quick call to Flora, as soon as Rog was out of sight.

She said, "Well?"

I said, "Baby, honey, it's something I can't talk about, but I've got to do it, see? Now you hang on, I'll get it over with if I have to swim the Grand Canal to the icecap in my underwear, see? If I have to claw Phobos out of the sky. If I have to cut myself in pieces and mail myself parcel post."

"Gee," she said, "if I thought I was going to have to wait—"

I winced. She just wasn't the type to respond to poetry. Actually, she was a simple creature of action— But after all, if I was going to be drifting through low-gravity in a sea of jasmine perfume with Flora, poetry-response is not the type of qualification I would consider most indispensable.

I said urgently, "Just hold on, Flora. I won't be any time at all. I'll make it up to you."

I was annoyed, sure, but I wasn't worried as yet. Rog hadn't more than left me when I figured out exactly how I was going to tell the guilty man from the others.

It was easy. I should have called Rog back and told him, but there's no law against wanting egg in your beer and oxygen in your air. It would take me five minutes and then off I would go to Flora; a little late, maybe, but with a promotion, a raise, and a slobbering kiss from the Service on each cheek.

You see, it's like this. Big industrialists don't go space-hopping much; they use trans-video reception. When they do go to some ultra-high interstellar conference, as these three were probably going, they take Spaceoline. For one thing, they don't have enough hops under their belt to risk doing without. For another, Spaceoline is the expensive way of doing it and industrialists do things the expensive way. I know their psychology.

Now that would hold for two of them. The one who carried contraband, however, couldn't risk Spaceoline—even to prevent space-sickness. Under Spaceoline influence, he could throw the drug away; or give it away; or talk gibberish about it. He would *have* to stay in control of himself.

It was as simple as that, so I waited.

The *Antares Giant* was on time and I waited with my leg muscles tense for a quick take-off as soon as I collared the murdering drug-toting rat and sped the two eminent captains of industry on their way.

They brought in Lipsky first. He had thick, ruddy lips, rounded jowls, very dark eyebrows, and graying hair. He just looked at me and sat down. Nothing. He was under Spaceoline.

I said, "Good evening, sir."

He said, in a dreamy voice, "Surrealismus of Panamy hearts in three-quarter time for a cup of coffeedom of speech."

That was Spaceoline all the way. The buttons in the human mind were set free-swing. Each syllable suggests the next in free association.

Andiamo Ferrucci came in next. Black mustache, long and waxed, olive complexion, pock-marked face. He took a seat in another chair, facing us.

I said, "Nice trip?"

He said, "Trip the light fantastic tock the clock is crowings on the bird."

Lipsky said, "Bird to the wise guyed book to all places every body."

I grinned. That left Harponaster. I had my needle gun neatly palmed out of sight and the magnetic coil ready to grip him.

And then Harponaster came in. He was thin, leathery, near-bald and rather younger than he seemed in his trimensional image. And he was Spaceolined to the gills.

I said, "Damn!"

Harponaster said, "Damyankee note speech to his last time I saw wood you say so."

Ferrucci said, "Sow the seed the territory under dispute do well to come along long road to a nightingale."

Lipsky said, "Gay lords hopping pong balls."

I stared from one to the other as the nonsense ran down in shorter and shorter spurts and then silence.

I got the picture, all right. One of them was faking. He had thought ahead and realized that omitting the Spaceoline would be a giveaway. He might have bribed an official into injecting saline or dodged it some other way.

One of them must be faking. It wasn't hard to fake the thing. Comedians on sub-etheric had a Spaceoline skit regularly. *You*'ve heard them.

I stared at them and got the first prickle at the base of my skull that said: What if you *don't* finger the right one?

It was 8:30 and there was my job, my reputation, my head growing rickety upon my neck to be considered. I saved it all for later and thought of Flora. She wasn't going to wait for me forever. For that matter, chances were she wouldn't wait for half an hour.

I wondered. Could the faker keep up free association if nudged gently onto dangerous territory?

I said, "The floor's covered with a nice solid rug" and ran the last two words together to make it "soli drug."

Lipsky said, "Drug from underneath the dough re mi fa sol to be saved."

Ferrucci said, "Saved and a haircut above the common herd something about younicorny as a harmonican the cheek by razor and shine."

Harponaster said, "Shiner wind nor snow use trying to by four ever and effervescence and sensibilityter totter."

Lipsky said, "Totters and rags."

Ferrucci said, "Ragsactly."

Harponaster said, "Actlymation."

A few grunts and they ran down.

I tried again and I didn't forget to be careful. They would remember everything I said afterward and what I said had to be harmless. I said, "This is a darned good space-line."

Ferrucci said, "Lines and tigers through the prairie dogs do bark of the bough-wough—"

I interrupted, looking at Harponaster, "A darned good space-line."

"Line the bed and rest a little black sheepishion of wrong the clothes of a perfect day."

I interrupted again, glaring at Lipsky, "Good space-line."

"Liron is hot chocolate ain't gonna be the same on you vee and double the stakes and potatoes and heel."

Some one else said, "Heel the sicknecessaryd and write will wincetance."

"Tance with mealtime."

"I'm comingle."

"Inglish."

"Ishter seals."

"Eels."

I tried a few more times and got nowhere. The faker, whichever he was, had practiced or had natural talents at talking free association. He was disconnecting his brain and letting the words come out any old way. And he must be inspired by knowing exactly what I was after. If "drug" hadn't given it away, "space-line" three times repeated must have. I was safe with the other two, but *he* would know.

—And he was having fun with me. All three were saying phrases that might have pointed to a deep inner guilt ("sol to be saved," "little black sheepishion of wrong," "drug from underneath," and so on). Two were saying such things helplessly, randomly. The third was amusing himself.

So how did I find the third? I was in a feverish thrill of hatred against him and my fingers twitched. The rat was subverting the Galaxy. More than than, he had killed my colleague and friend. More than that, he was keeping me from Flora.

I could go up to each of them and start searching. The two who were really under Spaceoline would make no move to stop me. They could feel no emotion, no fear, no anxiety, no hate, no passion, no desire for self-defense. And if one made the slightest gesture of resistance I would have my man.

But the innocent ones would remember afterward. They would remember a personal search while under Spaceoline.

I sighed. If I tried it, I would get the criminal all right but later I would be the nearest thing to chopped liver any man had ever been. There would be a shake-up in the Service, a big stink the width of the Galaxy, and in the excitement and disorganization, the secret of altered Spaceoline would get out anyway and so what the hell.

Of course, the one I wanted might be the first one I touched. One chance out of three. I'd have one out and only God can make a three.

Nuts, something had started them going while I was muttering to myself and Spaceoline is contagioust a gigolo my, oh—

I stared desperately at my watch and my line of sight focused on 9:15.

Where the devil was time going to?

Oh, my; oh, nuts; oh, Flora!

I had no choice. I made my way to the booth for another quick call to Flora. Just a quick one, you understand, to keep things alive; assuming they weren't dead already.

I kept saying to myself: She won't answer.

I tried to prepare myself for that. There were other girls, there were other—

What's the use, there were no other girls.

If Hilda had been in Marsport, I never would have had Flora on my mind in the first place and it wouldn't have mattered. *But I was in Marsport without Hilda* and I had made a date with Flora.

The signal was signaling and signaling and I didn't dare break off.

Answer! Answer!

She answered. She said, "It's *you!*"

"Of course, sweetheart, who else would it be?"

"Lots of people. Someone who would *come.*"

"There's just this little detail of business, honey."

"What business? Plastons for who?"

I almost corrected her grammar but I was too busy wondering what this plastons kick was.

Then I remembered. I told her once I was a plaston salesman. That was the time I brought her a plaston nightgown that was a honey.

I said, "Look. Just give me another half hour—"

Her eyes grew moist. "I'm sitting here all by myself."

"I'll make it up to you." To show you how desperate I was getting, I was definitely beginning to think along paths that could lead only to jewelry even though a sizable dent in the bankbook would show up to Hilda's piercing eye like the Horsehead Nebula interrupting the Milky Way. But then I was desperate.

She said, "I had a perfectly good date and I broke it off."

I protested, "You said it was a quibbling little arrangement."

That was a mistake. I knew it the minute I said it.

She shrieked, *"Quibbling little arrangement!"* (It was what she had said. It was what she had said. But having the truth on your side just makes it worse in arguing with a woman. Don't I know?) "You call a man who's promised me an estate on Earth—"

She went on and on about that estate on Earth. There wasn't a gal in Marsport who wasn't wangling for an estate on Earth, and you could count the number who got one on the sixth finger of either hand.

I tried to stop her. No use.

She finally said, "And here I am all alone, with *nobody,*" and broke off contact.

Well, she was right. I felt like the lowest heel in the Galaxy.

I went back into the reception room. A flunky outside the door saluted me in.

I stared at the three industrialists and speculated on the order in which I would slowly choke each to death if I could but receive choking orders. Harponaster first, maybe. He had a thin, stringy neck that the fingers could go round neatly and a sharp Adam's apple against which the thumbs could find purchase.

It cheered me up infinitesimally, to the point where I mustered, "Boy!" just out of sheer longing, though it was no boy I was longing for.

It started them off at once. Ferrucci said, "Boyl the watern the spout you goateeming rain over us, God savior pennies—"

Harponaster of the scrawny neck added, "Nies and nephew don't like orporalley cat."

Lipsky said, "Cattle corral go down off a ductilitease drunk."

"Drunkle aunterior passagewayt a while."

"While beasts oh pray."

"Prayties grow."

"Grow way."

"Waiter."

"Terble."

"Ble."

Then nothing.

They stared at me. I stared at them. They were empty of emotion (or two were) and I was empty of ideas. And time passed.

I stared at them some more and thought about Flora. It occurred to me that I had nothing to lose that I had not already lost. I might as well talk about her.

I said, "Gentlemen, there is a girl in this town whose name I will not mention for fear of compromising her. Let me describe her to you, gentlemen."

And I did. If I say so myself, the last two hours had honed me to such a fine force-field edge that the description of Flora took on a kind of poetry that seemed to be coming from some wellspring of masculine force deep in the subbasement of my unconscious.

And they sat frozen, almost as though they were listening, and hardly ever interrupting. People under Spaceoline have a kind of politeness about them. They won't speak when someone else is speaking. That's why they take turns.

I kept it up with a kind of heartfelt sadness in my voice until the loudspeaker announced in stirring tones the arrival of the *Space Eater.*

That was that. I said in a loud voice, "Rise, gentlemen."

"Not you, you murderer," and my magnetic coil was on Ferrucci's wrist before he could breathe twice.

Ferrucci fought like a demon. He was under no Spaceoline influence. They found the altered Spaceoline in thin flesh-colored plastic pads hugging the inner surface of his thighs. You couldn't see it at all; you could only feel it, and even then it took a knife to make sure.

Afterward, Rog Crinton, grinning and half insane with relief, held me by the lapel with a death grip. "How did you do it? What gave it away?"

I said, trying to pull loose, "One of them was faking a Spaceoline jag. I was sure of it. So I told them," (I grew cautious—none of his business as to the details, you know) ". . . uh, about a girl, see, and two of them never reacted, so they were Spaceolined. But Ferrucci's breathing speeded up and the beads of sweat came out on his forehead. I gave a pretty dramatic rendition, and he reacted, so he was under no Spaceoline. Now will you let me go?"

He let go and I almost fell over backward.

I was set to take off. My feet were pawing the ground without any instruction from me—but then I turned back.

"Hey, Rog," I said, "can you sign me a chit for a thousand credits without its going on the record—for services rendered to the Service?"

That's when I realized he was half insane with relief and very temporary gratitude, because he said, "Sure, Max, sure. Ten thousand credits if you want."

"I *want,*" I said, grabbing him for a change. "I want. I want."

He filled out an official Service chit for ten thousand credits; good as cash anywhere in half the Galaxy. He was actually grinning as he gave it to me and you can bet I was grinning as I took it.

How *he* intended accounting for it was his affair; the point was that *I* wouldn't have to account for it to Hilda.

.   .   .   .   .

I stood in the booth, one last time, signaling Flora. I didn't dare let matters go till I reached her place. The additional half hour might just give her time to get someone else, if she hadn't already.

Make her answer. Make her answer. Make her—

She answered, but she was in formal clothes. She was going out and I had obviously caught her by two minutes.

"I am going out," she announced. "*Some* men can be decent. And I do not wish to see you in the henceforward. I do not wish ever to find my eyes upon you. You will do me a great favor, Mister Whoeveryouare, if you unhand my signal combination and never pollute it with—"

I wasn't saying anything. I was just standing there holding my breath and also holding the chit up where she could see it. Just standing there. Just holding.

Sure enough, at the word "pollute" she came in for a closer look. She wasn't much on education, that girl, but she could read "ten thousand credits" faster than any college graduate in the Solar System.

She said, "Max! For me?"

"All for you, baby," I said, "I told you I had a little business to do. I wanted to surprise you."

"Oh, Max, that's sweet of you. I didn't really mind. I was joking. Now you come right here to me." She took off her coat.

"What about your date?" I said.

"I *said* I was joking," she said.

"I'm coming," I said faintly.

"With every single one of those credits now," she said roguishly.

"With every single one," I said.

I broke contact, stepped out of the booth, and now, finally, I was set— set—

I heard my name called. "Max! Max!" Someone was running toward me. "Rog Crinton said I would find you here. Mamma's all right after all, so I got special passage on the *Space Eater* and what's this about ten thousand credits?"

I didn't turn. I said, "Hello, Hilda."

And then I turned and did the hardest thing I ever succeeded in doing in all my good-for-nothing, space-hopping life.

I managed to smile.

The Gentle Vultures

For fifteen years now, the Hurrians had maintained their base on the other side of the Moon.

It was unprecedented; unheard of. No Hurrian had dreamed it possible to be delayed so long. The decontamination squads had been ready; ready and waiting for fifteen years; ready to swoop down through the radioactive clouds and save what might be saved for the remnant of survivors. —In return, of course, for fair payment.

But fifteen times the planet had revolved about its Sun. During each revolution, the satellite had rotated not quite thirteen times about the primary. And in all that time the nuclear war had not come.

Nuclear bombs were exploded by the large-primate intelligences at various points on the planet's surface. The planet's stratosphere had grown amazingly warm with radioactive refuse. But still no war.

Devi-en hoped ardently that he would be replaced. He was the fourth Captain-in-charge of this colonizing expedition (if it could still be called so after fifteen years of suspended animation) and he was quite content that there should be a fifth. Now that the home world was sending an Arch-administrator to make a personal survey of the situation, his replacement might come soon. Good!

He stood on the surface of the Moon, encased in his space-suit, and thought of home, of Hurria. His long, thin arms moved restlessly with the thought, as though aching (through millions of years of instinct) for the ancestral trees. He stood only three feet high. What could be seen of him through the glass-fronted head plate was a black and wrinkled face with the fleshy, mobile nose dead-centered. The little tuft of fine beard was a pure white in contrast. In the rear of the suit, just below center, was the bulge within which the short and stubby Hurrian tail might rest comfortably.

Devi-en took his appearance for granted, of course, but was well aware of the difference between the Hurrians and all the other intelligences in the Galaxy. The Hurrians alone were so small; they alone were tailed; they alone were vegetarians—they alone had escaped the inevitable nuclear war that had ruined every other known intelligent species.

He stood on the walled plain that extended for so many miles that the raised and circular rim (which on Hurria would have been called a crater, if it were smaller) was invisible beyond the horizon. Against the southern edge of the rim, where there was always some protection against the direct rays of the Sun, a city had grown. It had begun as a temporary camp, of course, but with the years, women had been brought in, and children had been born in it. Now there were schools and elaborate hydroponics establishments, large water reservoirs, all that went with a city on an airless world.

It was ridiculous! All because one planet had nuclear weapons and would not fight a nuclear war.

The Arch-administrator, who would be arriving soon, would undoubtedly ask, almost at once, the same question that Devi-en had asked himself a wearisome number of times.

Why had there not been a nuclear war?

Devi-en watched the hulking Mauvs preparing the ground now for the landing, smoothing out the unevennesses and laying down the ceramic bed designed to absorb the hyperatomic field-thrusts with minimum discomfort to the passengers within the ship.

Even in their space-suits, the Mauvs seemed to exude power, but it was the power of muscle only. Beyond them was the little figure of a Hurrian giving orders, and the docile Mauvs obeyed. Naturally.

The Mauvian race, of all the large-primate intelligences, paid their fees in the most unusual coin, a quota of themselves, rather than of material goods. It was a surprisingly useful tribute, better than steel, aluminum, or fine drugs in many ways.

Devi-en's receiver stuttered to life. "The ship is sighted, sir," came the report. "It will be landing within the hour."

"Very good," said Devi-en. "Have my car made ready to take me to the ship as soon as landing is initiated."

He did not feel that it was very good at all.

The Arch-administrator came, flanked by a personal retinue of five Mauvs. They entered the city with him, one on each side, three following. They helped him off with his space-suit, then removed their own.

Their thinly haired bodies, their large, coarse-featured faces, their broad noses and flat cheekbones were repulsive but not frightening. Though twice the height of the Hurrians and more than twice the breadth, there was a blankness about their eyes, something completely submissive about the way they stood, with their thick-sinewed necks slightly bent, their bulging arms hanging listlessly.

The Arch-administrator dismissed them and they trooped out. He did not really need their protection, of course, but his position required a retinue of five and that was that.

No business was discussed during the meal or during the almost endless ritual of welcome. At a time that might have been more appropriate for sleeping, the Arch-administrator passed small fingers through his tuft of beard and said, "How much longer must we wait for this planet, Captain?"

He was visibly advancing in age. The hair on his upper arms was grizzled and the tufts at the elbows were almost as white as his beard.

"I cannot say, your Height," said Devi-en humbly. "They have not followed the path."

"That is obvious. The point is, *why* have they not followed the path? It is clear to the Council that your reports promise more than they deliver. You talk of theories but you give no details. Now we are tired of all this back on Hurria. If you know of anything you have not told us, now is the time to talk of it."

"The matter, your Height, is hard to prove. We have had no experience of spying on a people over such an extended period. Until recently, we weren't watching for the right things. Each year we kept expecting the nuclear war the year after and it is only in my time as Captain that we have taken to studying the people more intensively. It is at least one benefit of the long waiting time that we have learned some of their principal languages."

"Indeed? Without even landing on their planet?"

Devi-en explained. "A number of radio messages were recorded by those of our ships that penetrated the planetary atmosphere on observation missions, particularly in the early years. I set our linguistics computers to work on them, and for the last year I have been attempting to make sense out of it all."

The Arch-administrator stared. His bearing was such that any outright exclamation of surprise would have been superfluous. "And have you learned anything of interest?"

"I may have, your Height, but what I have worked out is so strange and the underpinning of actual evidence is so uncertain that I dared not speak of it officially in my reports."

The Arch-administrator understood. He said, stiffly, "Would you object to explaining your views unofficially—to me?"

"I would be glad to," said Devi-en at once. "The inhabitants of this planet are, of course, large-primate in nature. And they are competitive."

The other blew out his breath in a kind of relief and passed his tongue quickly over his nose. "I had the queer notion," he muttered, "that they might *not* be competitive and that that might— But go on, go on."

"They *are* competitive," Devi-en assured him. "Much more so than one would expect on the average."

"Then why doesn't everything else follow?"

"Up to a point it does, your Height. After the usual long incubation period, they began to mechanize; and after that, the usual large-primate killings became truly destructive warfare. At the conclusion of the most recent large-scale war, nuclear weapons were developed and the war ended at once."

The Arch-administrator nodded. "And then?"

Devi-en said, "What should have happened was that a nuclear war ought to have begun shortly afterward and in the course of the war, nuclear weapons would have developed quickly in destructiveness, have been used nevertheless in typical large-primate fashion, and have quickly reduced the population to starving remnants in a ruined world."

"Of course, but that didn't happen. Why not?"

Devi-en said, "There is one point. I believe these people, once mechanization started, developed at an unusually high rate."

"And if so?" said the other. "Does that matter? They reached nuclear weapons the more quickly."

"True. But after the most recent general war, they continued to develop nuclear weapons at an unusual rate. That's the trouble. The deadly potential had increased before the nuclear war had a chance to start and now it has reached a point where even large-primate intelligences dare not risk a war."

The Arch-administrator opened his small black eyes wide. "But that is impossible. I don't care how technically talented these creatures are. Military science advances rapidly only during a war."

"Perhaps that is not true in the case of these particular creatures. But even if it were, it seems they *are* having a war; not a real war, but a war."

"Not a real war, but a war," repeated the Arch-administrator blankly. "What does that mean?"

"I'm not sure." Devi-en wiggled his nose in exasperation. "This is where my attempts to draw logic out of the scattered material we have picked up is least satisfactory. This planet has something called a Cold War. Whatever it is, it drives them furiously onward in research and yet it does not involve complete nuclear destruction."

The Arch-administrator said, "Impossible!"

Devi-en said, "There is the planet. Here we are. We have been waiting fifteen years."

The Arch-administrator's long arms came up and crossed over his head and down again to the opposite shoulders. "Then there *is* only one thing to do. The Council has considered the possibility that the planet may have achieved a stalemate, a kind of uneasy peace that balances just short of a nuclear war. Something of the sort you describe, though no one suggested the actual reasons you advance. But it's something we can't allow."

"No, your Height?"

"No," he seemed almost in pain. "The longer the stalemate continues, the greater the possibility that large-primate individuals may discover the methods of interstellar travel. They will leak out into the Galaxy, in full competitive strength. You see?"

"Then?"

The Arch-administrator hunched his head deeper into his arms, as though not wishing to hear what he himself must say. His voice was a little muffled. "If they are balanced precariously, we must push them a little, Captain. We must push them."

Devi-en's stomach churned and he suddenly tasted his dinner once more in the back of his throat. "Push them, your Height?" He didn't want to understand.

But the Arch-administrator put it bluntly, "We must help them start their nuclear war." He looked as miserably sick as Devi-en felt. He whispered, "We must!"

Devi-en could scarcely speak. He said, in a whisper, "But how could such a thing be done, your Height?"

"I don't know how. —And do not look at *me* so. It is not my decision. It is the decision of the Council. Surely you understand what would happen to the Galaxy if a large-primate intelligence were to enter space in full strength without having been tamed by nuclear war."

Devi-en shuddered at the thought. All that competitiveness loosed on the Galaxy. He persisted though. "But *how* does one start a nuclear war? How is it done?"

"I don't know, I tell you. But there must be some way; perhaps a—a message we might send or a—a crucial rainstorm we might start by cloud-seeding. We could manage a great deal with their weather conditions—"

"How would that start a nuclear war?" said Devi-en, unimpressed.

"Maybe it wouldn't. I mention such a thing only as a possible example. But large-primates would know. After all, they are the ones who *do* start nuclear wars in actual fact. It is in their brain-pattern to know. That is the decision the Council came to."

Devi-en felt the soft noise his tail made as it thumped slowly against the chair. He tried to stop it and failed. "What decision, your Height?"

"To trap a large-primate from the planet's surface. To kidnap one."

"A *wild* one?"

"It's the only kind that exists at the moment on the planet. Of course, a wild one."

"And what do you expect him to tell us?"

"That doesn't matter, Captain. As long as he says enough about anything, mentalic analysis will give us the answer."

Devi-en withdrew his head as far as he could into the space between his shoulder blades. The skin just under his armpits quivered with repulsion. A wild large-primate being! He tried to picture one, untouched by the stunning aftermath of nuclear war, unaltered by the civilizing influence of Hurrian eugenic breeding.

The Arch-administrator made no attempt to hide the fact that he shared the repulsion, but he said, "You will have to lead the trapping expedition, Captain. It is for the good of the Galaxy."

Devi-en had seen the planet a number of times before but each time a ship swung about the Moon and placed the world in his line of sight a wave of unbearable homesickness swept him.

It was a beautiful planet, so like Hurria itself in dimensions and characteristics but wilder and grander. The sight of it, after the desolation of the Moon, was like a blow.

How many other planets like it were on Hurrian master listings at this moment, he wondered. How many other planets were there concerning which meticulous observers had reported seasonal changes in appearance that could be interpreted only as being caused by artificial cultivation of food plants? How many times in the future would a day come when the radioactivity in the stratosphere of one of these planets would begin to climb; when colonizing squadrons would have to be sent out at once?

—As they were to this planet.

It was almost pathetic, the confidence with which the Hurrians had proceeded at first. Devi-en could have laughed as he read through those initial reports, if he weren't trapped in this project himself now. The Hurrian scoutships had moved close to the planet to gather geographical information, to locate population centers. They were sighted, of course, but what did it matter? Any time, now, they thought, the final explosion.

Any time— But useless years passed and the scoutships wondered if they ought not to be cautious. They moved back.

Devi-en's ship was cautious now. The crew was on edge because of the unpleasantness of the mission; not all Devi-en's assurances that there was no harm intended to the large-primate could quite calm them. Even so, they could not hurry matters. It had to be over a fairly deserted and uncultivated tract of uneven ground that they hovered. They stayed at a height of ten miles for days, while the crew became edgier and only the ever-stolid Mauvs maintained calm.

Then the scope showed them a creature, alone on the uneven ground, a long staff in one hand, a pack across the upper portion of his back.

They lowered silently, supersonically. Devi-en himself, skin crawling, was at the controls.

The creature was heard to say two definite things before he was taken, and they were the first comments recorded for use in mentalic computing.

The first, when the large-primate caught sight of the ship almost upon him, was picked up by the direction telemike. It was, "My God! A flying saucer!"

Devi-en understood the second phrase. That was a term for the Hurrian ships that had grown common among the large-primates those first careless years.

The second remark was made when the wild creature was brought into the ship, struggling with amazing strength, but helpless in the iron grip of the unperturbed Mauvs.

Devi-en, panting, with his fleshy nose quivering slightly, advanced to receive him, and the creature (whose unpleasantly hairless face had become oily with some sort of fluid secretion) yelled, "Holy Toledo, a *monkey!*"

Again, Devi-en understood the second part. It was the word for little-primate in one of the chief languages of the planet.

The wild creature was almost impossible to handle. He required infinite patience before he could be spoken to reasonably. At first, there was nothing but a series of crises. The creature realized almost at once that he was being taken off Earth, and what Devi-en thought might prove an exciting experience for him, proved nothing of the sort. He talked instead of his offspring and of a large-primate female.

(They have wives and children, thought Devi-en, compassionately, and, in their way, love them, for all they are large-primate.)

Then he had to be made to understand that the Mauvs who kept him under guard and who restrained him when his violence made that necessary would not hurt him, that he was not to be damaged in any way.

(Devi-en was sickened at the thought that one intelligent being might be damaged by another. It was very difficult to discuss the subject, even if only to admit the possibility long enough to deny it. The creature from the planet treated the very hesitation with great suspicion. It was the way the large-primates were.)

On the fifth day, when out of sheer exhaustion, perhaps, the creature remained quiet over a fairly extended period, they talked in Devi-en's private quarters, and suddenly he grew angry again when the Hurrian first explained, matter-of-factly, that they were waiting for a nuclear war.

"Waiting!" cried the creature. "What makes you so sure there will be one?"

Devi-en wasn't sure, of course, but he said, "There is always a nuclear war. It is our purpose to help you afterward."

"Help us *afterward*." His words grew incoherent. He waved his arms violently, and the Mauvs who flanked him had to restrain him gently once again and lead him away.

Devi-en sighed. The creature's remarks were building in quantity and perhaps mentalics could do something with them. His own unaided mind could make nothing of them.

And meanwhile the creature was not thriving. His body was almost completely hairless, a fact that long-distance observation had not revealed owing to the artificial skins worn by them. This was either for warmth or because of an instinctive repulsion even on the part of these particular large-primates themselves for hairless skin. (It might be an interesting subject to take up. Mentalics computation could make as much out of one set of remarks as another.)

Strangely enough, the creature's face had begun to sprout hair; more, in fact, than the Hurrian face had, and of a darker color.

But still, the central fact was that he was not thriving. He had grown thinner because he was eating poorly, and if he was kept too long, his health might suffer. Devi-en had no wish to feel responsible for that.

On the next day, the large-primate seemed quite calm. He talked almost eagerly, bringing the subject around to nuclear warfare almost at once. (It had a terrible attraction for the large-primate mind, Devi-en thought.)

The creature said, "You said nuclear wars always happen? Does that mean there are other people than yours and mine—and theirs?" He indicated the near-by Mauvs.

"There are thousands of intelligent species, living on thousands of worlds. Many thousands," said Devi-en.

"And they all have nuclear wars?"

"All who have reached a certain stage of technology. All but us. We were different. We lacked competitiveness. We had the co-operative instinct."

"You mean you know that nuclear wars will happen and you do nothing about it?"

"We *do*," said Devi-en, pained. "Of course, we do. We try to help. In the early history of my people, when we first developed space-travel, we did not understand large-primates. They repelled our attempts at friendship and we stopped trying. Then we found worlds in radioactive ruins. Finally, we found one world actually in the process of a nuclear war. We were horrified, but could do nothing. Slowly, we learned. We are ready, now, at every world we discover to be at the nuclear stage. We are ready with decontamination equipment and eugenic analyzers."

"What are eugenic analyzers?"

Devi-en had manufactured the phrase by analogy with what he knew of the wild one's language. Now he said carefully, "We direct matings and sterilizations to remove, as far as possible, the competitive element in the remnant of the survivors."

For a moment, he thought the creature would grow violent again.

Instead, the other said in a monotone, "You make them docile, you mean, like these things?" Once again he indicated the Mauvs.

"No. No. These are different. We simply make it possible for the remnants to be content with a peaceful, nonexpanding, nonaggressive society under our guidance. Without this, they destroyed themselves, you see, and without it, they would destroy themselves again."

"What do you get out of it?"

Devi-en stared at the creature dubiously. Was it really necessary to explain the basic pleasure of life? He said, "Don't you enjoy helping someone?"

"Come on. Besides that. What's in it for you?"

"Of course, there are contributions to Hurria."

"Ha."

"Payment for saving a species is only fair," protested Devi-en, "and there are expenses to be covered. The contribution is not much and is adjusted to the nature of the world. It may be an annual supply of wood from a forested world; manganese salts from another. The world of these Mauvs is poor in physical resources and they themselves offered to supply us with a number of individuals to use as personal assistants. They are extremely powerful even for large-primates and we treat them painlessly with anticerebral drugs—"

"To make zombies out of them!"

Devi-en guessed at the meaning of the noun and said indignantly, "Not at all. Merely to make them content with their role as personal servant and forgetful of their homes. We would not want them to be unhappy. They are intelligent beings!"

"And what would you do with Earth if we had a war?"

"We have had fifteen years to decide that," said Devi-en. "Your world is very rich in iron and has developed a fine steel technology. Steel, I think, would be your contribution." He sighed, "But the contribution would not make up for our expense in this case, I think. We have overwaited now by ten years at least."

The large-primate said, "How many races do you tax in this way?"

"I do not know the exact number. Certainly more than a thousand."

"Then you're the little landlords of the Galaxy, are you? A thousand worlds destroy themselves in order to contribute to your welfare. You're something else, too, you know." The wild one's voice was rising, growing shrill. "You're vultures."

"Vultures?" said Devi-en, trying to place the word.

"Carrion-eaters. Birds that wait for some poor creature to die of thirst in the desert and then come down to eat the body."

Devi-en felt himself turn faint and sick at the picture conjured up for him. He said weakly, "No, no, we *help* the species."

"You wait for the war to happen like vultures. If you want to help, *prevent* the war. Don't save the remnants. Save them all."

Devi-en's tail twitched with sudden excitement. "How do we prevent a war? Will you tell me that?" (What was prevention of war but the reverse of bringing about a war? Learn one process and surely the other would be obvious.)

But the wild one faltered. He said finally, "Get down there. Explain the situation."

Devi-en felt keen disappointment. That didn't help. Besides— He said, "Land among you? Quite impossible." His skin quivered in half a dozen places at the thought of mingling with the wild ones in their untamed billions.

Perhaps the sick look on Devi-en's face was so pronounced and unmistakable that the wild one could recognize it for what it was even across the barrier of species. He tried to fling himself at the Hurrian and had to be caught virtually in mid-air by one of the Mauvs, who held him immobile with an effortless constriction of biceps.

The wild one screamed. "No. Just sit here and wait! Vulture! Vulture! *Vulture!*"

It was days before Devi-en could bring himself to see the wild one again. He was almost brought to disrespect of the Arch-administrator when the latter insisted that he lacked sufficient data for a complete analysis of the mental make-up of these wild ones.

Devi-en said boldly, "Surely, there is enough to give some solution to our question."

The Arch-administrator's nose quivered and his pink tongue passed over it meditatively. "A solution of a kind, perhaps. I can't trust this solution. We are facing a very unusual species. We know that already. We can't afford to make mistakes. —One thing, at least. We have happened upon a highly intelligent one. Unless—unless he is at his race's norm." The Arch-administrator seemed upset at that thought.

Devi-en said, "The creature brought up the horrible picture of that—that bird—that—"

"Vulture," said the Arch-administrator.

"It put our entire mission into such a distorted light. I have not been able to eat properly since, or sleep. In fact, I am afraid I will have to ask to be relieved—"

"Not before we have completed what we have set out to do," said the Arch-administrator firmly. "Do you think I enjoy the picture of—of carrion-eat— You *must* collect more data."

Devi-en nodded finally. He understood, of course. The Arch-administrator was no more anxious to cause a nuclear war than any Hurrian would be. He was putting off the moment of decision as long as possible.

Devi-en settled himself for one more interview with the wild one. It turned out to be a completely unbearable one, and the last.

· · · ·

The wild one had a bruise across his cheek as though he had been resisting the Mauvs again. In fact, it was certain he had. He had done so
numerous times before, and the Mauvs, despite their most earnest attempts
to do no harm, could not help but bruise him on occasion. One would
expect the wild one to see how intensely they tried not to hurt him and to
quiet his behavior as a result. Instead, it was as though the conviction of
safety spurred him on to additional resistance.

(These large-primate species were vicious, vicious, thought Devi-en sadly.)

For over an hour, the interview hovered over useless small talk and then
the wild one said with sudden belligerence, "How long did you say you
things have been here?"

"Fifteen of your years," said Devi-en.

"That figures. The first flying saucers were sighted just after World War
II. How much longer before the nuclear war?"

With automatic truth, Devi-en said, "We wish we knew," and stopped
suddenly.

The wild one said, "I thought nuclear war was inevitable. Last time you
said you overstayed ten years. You expected the war ten years ago, didn't
you?"

Devi-en said, "I can't discuss this subject."

"No?" The wild one was screaming. "What are you going to do about it?
How long will you wait? Why not nudge it a little? Don't just wait, vulture.
Start one."

Devi-en jumped to his feet. "What are you saying?"

"Why else are you waiting, you dirty—" He choked on a completely
incomprehensible expletive, then continued, breathlessly, "Isn't that what
vultures do when some poor miserable animal, or man, maybe, is taking too
long to die? They can't wait. They come swirling down and peck out his
eyes. They wait till he's helpless and just hurry him along the last step."

Devi-en ordered him away quickly and retired to his sleeping room, where
he was sick for hours. Nor did he sleep then or that night. The word
"vulture" screamed in his ears and that final picture danced before his eyes.

Devi-en said firmly, "Your Height, I can speak with the wild one no more.
If you need still more data, I cannot help you."

The Arch-administrator looked haggard. "I know. This vulture business—
Very difficult to take. Yet you notice the thought didn't affect him. Large-
primates are immune to such things, hardened, calloused. It is part of their
way of thinking. Horrible."

"I can get you no more data."

"It's all right. I understand. —Besides, each additional item only
strengthens the preliminary answer; the answer I thought was only provisional; that I hoped earnestly was only provisional." He buried his head in
his grizzled arms. "We have a way to start their nuclear war for them."

"Oh? What need be done?"

"It is something very direct, very simple. It is something I could never have thought of. Nor you."

"What is it, your Height?" He felt an anticipatory dread.

"What keeps them at peace now is that neither of two nearly equal sides dares take the responsibility of starting a war. If one side did, however, the other—well, let's be blunt about it—would retaliate in full."

Devi-en nodded.

The Arch-administrator went on. "If a single nuclear bomb fell on the territory of either of the two sides, the victims would at once assume the other side had launched it. They would feel they could not wait for further attacks. Retaliation in full would follow within hours; the other side would retaliate in its turn. Within weeks it would be over."

"But how do we make one of them drop that first bomb?"

"We don't, Captain. That is the point. We drop the first bomb ourselves."

"What?" Devi-en swayed.

"That is it. Compute a large-primate's mind and that answer thrusts itself at you."

"But how can we?"

"We assemble a bomb. That is easy enough. We send it down by ship and drop it over some inhabited locality—"

"Inhabited?"

The Arch-administrator looked away and said uneasily, "The effect is lost otherwise."

"I see," said Devi-en. He was picturing vultures; he couldn't help it. He visualized them as large, scaled bird (like the small harmless flying creatures on Hurria, but immensely large), with rubber-skinned wings and long razor-bills, circling down, pecking at dying eyes.

His hands covered his eyes. He said shakily, "Who will pilot the ship? Who will launch the bomb?"

The Arch-administrator's voice was no stronger than Devi-en's. "I don't know."

"I won't," said Devi-en. "I can't. There is no Hurrian who can, at any price."

The Arch-administrator rocked back and forth miserably. "Perhaps the Mauvs could be given orders—"

"Who could give them such orders?"

The Arch-administrator sighed heavily. "I will call the Council. They may have all the data. Perhaps they will suggest something."

So after a little over fifteen years, the Hurrians were dismantling their base on the other side of the Moon.

Nothing had been accomplished. The large-primates of the planet had not had their nuclear war; they might never have.

And despite all the future horror that might bring, Devi-en was in an agony of happiness. There was no point in thinking of the future. For the present, he was getting away from this most horrible of horrible worlds.

He watched the Moon fall away and shrink to a spot of light, along with the planet, and the Sun of the system itself, till the whole thing was lost among the constellations.

It was only then that he could feel anything but relief. It was only then that he felt a first tiny twinge of it-might-have-been.

He said to the Arch-administrator, "It might all have been well if we had been more patient. They might yet have blundered into nuclear war."

The Arch-administrator said, "Somehow I doubt it. The mentalic analysis of—"

He stopped and Devi-en understood. The wild one had been replaced on his planet with minimal harm. The events of the past weeks had been blanked out of his mind. He had been placed near a small, inhabited locality not far from the spot where he had been first found. His fellows would assume he had been lost. They would blame his loss of weight, his bruises, his amnesia upon the hardships he had undergone.

But the harm done *by* him—

If only they had not brought him up to the Moon in the first place. They might have reconciled themselves to the thought of starting a war. They might somehow have thought of dropping a bomb; and worked out some indirect, long-distance system for doing so.

It had been the wild one's word-picture of the vulture that had stopped it all. It had ruined Devi-en and the Arch-administrator. When all data was sent back to Hurria, the effect on the Council itself had been notable. The order to dismantle the Base had come quickly.

Devi-en said, "I will never take part in colonization again."

The Arch-administrator said mournfully, "None of us may ever have to. The wild ones of that planet will emerge and with large-primates and large-primate thinking loose in the Galaxy, it will mean the end of—of—"

Devi-en's nose twitched. The end of everything; of all the good Hurria had done in the Galaxy; all the good it might have continued to do in the future.

He said, "We ought to have dropped—" and did not finish.

What was the use of saying that? They couldn't have dropped the bomb for all the Galaxy. If they could have, they would have been large-primate themselves in their manner of thinking, and there are worse things than merely the end of everything.

Devi-en thought of the vultures.

All the Troubles of the World

I

The greatest industry on Earth centered about Multivac—Multivac, the giant computer that had grown in fifty years until its various ramifications had filled Washington, D.C., to the suburbs and had reached out tendrils into every city and town on Earth.

An army of civil servants fed it data constantly and another army correlated and interpreted the answers it gave. A corps of engineers patrolled its interior while mines and factories consumed themselves in keeping its reserve stocks of replacement parts ever complete, ever accurate, ever satisfactory in every way.

Multivac directed Earth's economy and helped Earth's science. Most important of all, it was the central clearing house of all known facts about each individual Earthman.

And each day it was part of Multivac's duties to take the four billion sets of facts about individual human beings that filled its vitals and extrapolate them for an additional day of time. Every Corrections Department on Earth received the data appropriate to its own area of jurisdiction, and the over-all data was presented in one large piece to the Central Board of Corrections in Washington, D.C.

Bernard Gulliman was in the fourth week of his year term as Chairman of the Central Board of Corrections and had grown casual enough to accept the morning report without being frightened by it. As usual, it was a sheaf of papers some six inches thick. He knew by now, he was not expected to read it. (No human could.) Still, it was amusing to glance through it.

There was the usual list of predictable crimes: frauds of all sorts, larcenies, riots, manslaughters, arsons.

He looked for one particular heading and felt a slight shock at finding it there at all, then another one at seeing two entries. Not one, but two. *Two* first-degree murders. He had not seen two in one day in all his term as Chairman so far.

He punched the knob of the two-way intercom and waited for the smooth face of his co-ordinator to appear on the screen.

"Ali," said Gulliman. "There are two first-degrees this day. Is there any unusual problem?"

"No, sir." The dark-complexioned face with its sharp, black eyes seemed restless. "Both cases are quite low probability."

"I know that," said Gulliman. "I observed that neither probability is higher than 15 per cent. Just the same, Multivac has a reputation to maintain. It has virtually wiped out crime, and the public judges that by its record on first-degree murder which is, of course, the most spectacular crime."

Ali Othman nodded. "Yes, sir. I quite realize that."

"You also realize, I hope," Gulliman said, "that I don't want a single consummated case of it during my term. If any other crime slips through, I may allow excuses. If a first-degree murder slips through, I'll have your hide. Understand?"

"Yes, sir. The complete analyses of the two potential murders are already at the district offices involved. The potential criminals and victims are under observation. I have rechecked the probabilities of consummation and they are already dropping."

"Very good," said Gulliman, and broke connection.

He went back to the list with an uneasy feeling that perhaps he had been overpompous. —But then, one had to be firm with these permanent civil-service personnel and make sure they didn't imagine they were running everything, including the Chairman. Particularly this Othman, who had been working with Multivac since both were considerably younger, and had a proprietary air that could be infuriating.

To Gulliman, this matter of crime was the political chance of a lifetime. So far, no Chairman had passed through his term without a murder taking place somewhere on Earth, some time. The previous Chairman had ended with a record of eight, three more (*more*, in fact) than under his predecessor.

Now Gulliman intended to have *none*. He was going to be, he had decided, the first Chairman without any murder at all anywhere on Earth during his term. After that, and the favorable publicity that would result—

He barely skimmed the rest of the report. He estimated that there were at least two thousand cases of prospective wife-beatings listed. Undoubtedly, not all would be stopped in time. Perhaps thirty per cent would be consummated. But the incidence was dropping and consummations were dropping even more quickly.

Multivac had added wife-beating to its list of predictable crimes only some five years earlier and the average man was not yet accustomed to the thought that if he planned to wallop his wife, it would be known in advance. As the conviction percolated through society, woman would first suffer fewer bruises and then, eventually, none.

Some husband-beatings were on the list, too, Gulliman noticed.

Ali Othman closed connections and stared at the screen from which Gulliman's jowled and balding head had departed. Then he looked across at his assistant, Rafe Leemy and said, "What do we do?"

"Don't ask me. *He's* worried about just a lousy murder or two."

"It's an awful chance trying to handle this thing on our own. Still if we tell him, he'll have a first-class fit. These elective politicians have their skins to think of, so he's bound to get in our way and make things worse."

Leemy nodded his head and put a thick lower lip between his teeth. "Trouble is, though, what if we miss out? It would just about be the end of the world, you know."

"If we miss out, who cares what happens to us? We'll just be part of the general catastrophe." Then he said in a more lively manner, "But hell, the probability is only 12.3 per cent. On anything else, except maybe murder, we'd let the probabilities rise a bit before taking any action at all. There could still be spontaneous correction."

"I wouldn't count on it," said Leemy dryly.

"I don't intend to. I was just pointing the fact out. Still, at this probability, I suggest we confine ourselves to simple observation for the moment. No one could plan a crime like this alone; there must be accomplices."

"Multivac didn't name any."

"I know. Still—" His voice trailed off.

So they stared at the details of the one crime not included on the list handed out to Gulliman; the one crime much worse than first-degree murder; the one crime never before attempted in the history of Multivac; and wondered what to do.

Ben Manners considered himself the happiest sixteen-year-old in Baltimore. This was, perhaps, doubtful. But he was certainly one of the happiest, and one of the most excited.

At least, he was one of the handful admitted to the galleries of the stadium during the swearing in of the eighteen-year-olds. His older brother was going to be sworn in so his parents had applied for spectator's tickets and they had allowed Ben to do so, too. But when Multivac chose among all the applicants, it was Ben who got the ticket.

Two years later, Ben would be sworn in himself, but watching big brother Michael now was the next best thing.

His parents had dressed him (or supervised the dressing, at any rate) with all care, as representative of the family and sent him off with numerous messages for Michael, who had left days earlier for preliminary physical and neurological examinations.

The stadium was on the outskirts of town and Ben, just bursting with self-importance, was shown to his seat. Below him, now, were rows upon rows of hundreds upon hundreds of eighteen-year-olds (boys to the right, girls to the left), all from the second district of Baltimore. At various times in the year, similar meetings were going on all over the world, but this was Baltimore, this was the important one. Down there (somewhere) was Mike, Ben's own brother.

Ben scanned the tops of heads, thinking somehow he might recognize his brother. He didn't, of course, but then a man came out on the raised platform in front of all the crowd and Ben stopped looking to listen.

The man said, "Good afternoon, swearers and guests. I am Randolph T. Hoch, in charge of the Baltimore ceremonies this year. The swearers have met me several times now during the progress of the physical and neurological portions of this examination. Most of the task is done, but the most important matter is left. The swearer himself, his personality, must go into Multivac's records.

"Each year, this requires some explanation to the young people reaching adulthood. Until now" (he turned to the young people before him and his eyes went no more to the gallery) "you have not been adult; you have not been individuals in the eyes of Multivac, except where you were especially singled out as such by your parents or your government.

"Until now, when the time for the yearly up-dating of information came, it was your parents who filled in the necessary data on you. Now the time has come for you to take over that duty yourself. It is a great honor, a great responsibility. Your parents have told us what schooling you've had, what diseases, what habits; a great many things. But now you must tell us a great deal more; your innermost thoughts; your most secret deeds.

"This is hard to do the first time, embarrassing even, but it *must* be done. Once it is done, Multivac will have a complete analysis of all of you in its files. It will understand your actions and reactions. It will even be able to guess with fair accuracy at your future actions and reactions.

"In this way, Multivac will protect you. If you are in danger of accident, it will know. If someone plans harm to you, it will know. If *you* plan harm, it will know and you will be stopped in time so that it will not be necessary to punish you.

"With its knowledge of all of you, Multivac will be able to help Earth adjust its economy and its laws for the good of all. If you have a personal problem, you may come to Multivac with it and with its knowledge of all of you, Multivac will be able to help you.

"Now you will have many forms to fill out. Think carefully and answer all questions as accurately as you can. Do not hold back through shame or caution. No one will ever know your answers except Multivac unless it becomes necessary to learn the answers in order to protect you. And then only authorized officials of the government will know.

"It may occur to you to stretch the truth a bit here or there. Don't do this. We will find out if you do. All your answers put together form a pattern. If some answers are false, they will not fit the pattern and Multivac will discover them. If all your answers are false, there will be a distorted pattern of a type that Multivac will recognize. So you must tell the truth."

Eventually, it was all over, however; the form-filling; the ceremonies and speeches that followed. In the evening, Ben, standing tiptoe, finally spotted Michael, who was still carrying the robes he had worn in the "parade of the adults." They greeted one another with jubilation.

They shared a light supper and took the expressway home, alive and alight with the greatness of the day.

They were not prepared, then, for the sudden transition of the homecoming. It was a numbing shock to both of them to be stopped by a cold-faced young man in uniform outside their own front door; to have their papers inspected before they could enter their own house; to find their own parents sitting forlornly in the living room, the mark of tragedy on their faces.

Joseph Manners, looking much older than he had that morning, looked out of his puzzled, deep-sunken eyes at his sons (one with the robes of new adulthood still over his arm) and said, "I seem to be under house arrest."

Bernard Gulliman could not and did not read the entire report. He read only the summary and that was most gratifying, indeed.

A whole generation, it seemed, had grown up accustomed to the fact that Multivac could predict the commission of major crimes. They learned that Corrections agents would be on the scene before the crime could be committed. They found out that consummation of the crime led to inevitable punishment. Gradually, they were convinced that there was no way anyone could outsmart Multivac.

The result was, naturally, that even the intention of crime fell off. And as such intentions fell off and as Multivac's capacity was enlarged, minor crimes could be added to the list it would predict each morning, and these crimes, too, were now shrinking in incidence.

So Gulliman had ordered an analysis made (by Multivac naturally) of Multivac's capacity to turn its attention to the problem of predicting probabilities of disease incidence. Doctors might soon be alerted to individual patients who might grow diabetic in the course of the next year, or suffer an attack of tuberculosis or grow a cancer.

An ounce of prevention—

And the report was a favorable one!

After that, the roster of the day's possible crimes arrived and there was not a first-degree murder on the list.

Gulliman put in an intercom call to Ali Othman in high good humor. "Othman, how do the numbers of crimes in the daily lists of the past week average compared with those in my first week as Chairman?"

It had gone down, it turned out, by 8 per cent and Gulliman was happy indeed. No fault of his own, of course, but the electorate would not know that. He blessed his luck that he had come in at the right time, at the very climax of Multivac, when disease, too, could be placed under its all-embracing and protecting knowledge.

Gulliman would prosper by this.

Othman shrugged his shoulders. "Well, he's happy."

"When do we break the bubble?" said Leemy. "Putting Manners under observation just raised the probabilities and house arrest gave it another boost."

"Don't I know it?" said Othman peevishly. "What I don't know is why."

"Accomplices, maybe, like you said. With Manners in trouble, the rest have to strike at once or be lost."

"Just the other way around. With our hand on one, the rest would scatter for safety and disappear. Besides, why aren't the accomplices named by Multivac?"

"Well, then, do we tell Gulliman?"

"No, not yet. The probability is still only 17.3 per cent. Let's get a bit more drastic first."

Elizabeth Manners said to her younger son, "You go to your room, Ben."

"But what's it all about, Mom?" asked Ben, voice breaking at this strange ending to what had been a glorious day.

"Please!"

He left reluctantly, passing through the door to the stairway, walking up it noisily and down again quietly.

And Mike Manners, the older son, the new-minted adult and the hope of the family, said in a voice and tone that mirrored his brother's, "What's it all about?"

Joe Manners said, "As heaven is my witness, son, I don't know. I haven't done anything."

"Well, sure you haven't done anything." Mike looked at his small-boned, mild-mannered father in wonder. "They must be here because you're *thinking* of doing something."

"I'm not."

Mrs. Manners broke in angrily, "How can he be thinking of doing something worth all—all this." She cast her arm about, in a gesture toward the enclosing shell of government men about the house. "When I was a little girl, I remember the father of a friend of mine was working in a bank, and they once called him up and said to leave the money alone and he did. It was fifty thousand dollars. He hadn't really taken it. He was just thinking about taking it. They didn't keep those things as quiet in those days as they do now; the story got out. That's how I know about it.

"But I mean," she went on, rubbing her plump hands slowly together, "that was fifty thousand dollars; fifty—thousand—dollars. Yet all they did was call him; one phone call. What could your father be planning that would make it worth having a dozen men come down and close off the house?"

Joe Manners said, eyes filled with pain, "I am planning no crime, not even the smallest. I swear it."

Mike, filled with the conscious wisdom of a new adult, said, "Maybe it's something subconscious, Pop. Some resentment against your supervisor."

"So that I would want to kill him? No!"

"Won't they tell you what it is, Pop?"

His mother interrupted again, "No, they won't. We've asked. I said they were ruining our standing in the community just being here. The least they could do is tell us what it's all about so we could fight it, so we could explain."

"And they wouldn't?"

"They wouldn't."

Mike stood with his legs spread apart and his hands deep in his pockets. He said, troubled, "Gee, Mom, Multivac doesn't make mistakes."

His father pounded his fist helplessly on the arm of the sofa. "I tell you I'm not planning any crime."

The door opened without a knock and a man in uniform walked in with sharp, self-possessed stride. His face had a glazed, official appearance. He said, "Are you Joseph Manners?"

Joe Manners rose to his feet. "Yes. Now what is it you want of me?"

"Joseph Manners, I place you under arrest by order of the government," and curtly he showed his identification as a Corrections officer. "I must ask you to come with me."

"For what reason? What have I done?"

"I am not at liberty to discuss that."

"But I can't be arrested just for planning a crime even if I were doing that. To be arrested I must actually have *done* something. You can't arrest me otherwise. It's against the law."

The officer was impervious to the logic. "You will have to come with me."

Mrs. Manners shrieked and fell on the couch, weeping hysterically. Joseph Manners could not bring himself to violate the code drilled into him all his life by actually resisting an officer, but he hung back at least, forcing the Corrections officer to use muscular power to drag him forward.

And Manners called out as he went, "But tell me what it is. Just tell me. If I *knew*— Is it murder? Am I supposed to be planning murder?"

The door closed behind him and Mike Manners, white-faced and suddenly feeling not the least bit adult, stared first at the door, then at his weeping mother.

Ben Manners, behind the door and suddenly feeling quite adult, pressed his lips tightly together and thought he knew exactly what to do.

If Multivac took away, Multivac could also give. Ben had been at the ceremonies that very day. He had heard this man, Randolph Hoch, speak of Multivac and all that Multivac could do. It could direct the government and it could also unbend and help out some plain person who came to it for help.

Anyone could ask help of Multivac and anyone meant Ben. Neither his mother nor Mike were in any condition to stop him now, and he had some money left of the amount they had given him for his great outing that day. If afterward they found him gone and worried about it, that couldn't be helped. Right now, his first loyalty was to his father.

He ran out the back way and the officer at the door cast a glance at his papers and let him go.

Harold Quimby handled the complaints department of the Baltimore substation of Multivac. He considered himself to be a member of that branch of the civil service that was most important of all. In some ways, he may have been right, and those who heard him discuss the matter would have had to be made of iron not to feel impressed.

For one thing, Quimby would say, Multivac was essentially an invader of privacy. In the past fifty years, mankind had had to acknowledge that its thoughts and impulses were no longer secret, that it owned no inner recess where anything could be hidden. And mankind had to have something in return.

Of course, it got prosperity, peace, and safety, but that was abstract. Each man and woman needed something personal as his or her own reward for surrendering privacy, and each one got it. Within reach of every human being was a Multivac station with circuits into which he could freely enter his own problems and questions without control or hindrance, and from which, in a matter of minutes, he could receive answers.

At any given moment, five million individual circuits among the quadrillion or more within Multivac might be involved in this question-and-answer program. The answers might not always be certain, but they were the best available, and every questioner *knew* the answer to be the best available and had faith in it. That was what counted.

And now an anxious sixteen-year-old had moved slowly up the waiting line of men and women (each in that line illuminated by a different mixture of hope with fear or anxiety or even anguish—always with hope predominating as the person stepped nearer and nearer to Multivac).

Without looking up, Quimby took the filled-out form being handed him and said, "Booth 5-B."

Ben said, "How do I ask the question, sir?"

Quimby looked up then, with a bit of surprise. Preadults did not generally make use of the service. He said kindly, "Have you ever done this before, son?"

"No, sir."

Quimby pointed to the model on his desk. "You use this. You see how it works? Just like a typewriter. Don't you try to write or print anything by hand. Just use the machine. Now you take booth 5-B, and if you need help, just press the red button and someone will come. Down that aisle, son, on the right."

He watched the youngster go down the aisle and out of view and smiled. No one was ever turned away from Multivac. Of course, there was always a certain percentage of trivia: people who asked personal questions about their neighbors or obscene questions about prominent personalities; college youths trying to outguess their professors or thinking it clever to stump Multivac by asking it Russell's class-of-all-classes paradox and so on.

Multivac could take care of all that. It needed no help.

Besides, each question and answer was filed and formed but another item in the fact assembly for each individual. Even the most trivial question and the most impertinent, insofar as it reflected the personality of the questioner, helped humanity by helping Multivac know about humanity.

Quimby turned his attention to the next person in line, a middle-aged woman, gaunt and angular, with the look of trouble in her eye.

Ali Othman strode the length of his office, his heels thumping desperately on the carpet. "The probability still goes up. It's 22.4 per cent now. Damnation! We have Joseph Manners under actual arrest and it still goes up." He was perspiring freely.

Leemy turned away from the telephone. "No confession yet. He's under Psychic Probing and there is no sign of crime. He may be telling the truth."

Othman said, "Is Multivac crazy then?"

Another phone sprang to life. Othman closed connections quickly, glad of the interruption. A Corrections officer's face came to life in the screen. The officer said, "Sir, are there any new directions as to Manners' family? Are they to be allowed to come and go as they have been?"

"What do you mean, as they have been?"

"The original instructions were for the house arrest of Joseph Manners. Nothing was said of the rest of the family, sir."

"Well, extend it to the rest of the family until you are informed otherwise."

"Sir, that is the point. The mother and older son are demanding information about the younger son. The younger son is gone and they claim he is in custody and wish to go to headquarters to inquire about it."

Othman frowned and said in almost a whisper, "Younger son? How young?"

"Sixteen, sir," said the officer.

"Sixteen and he's gone. Don't you know where?"

"He was allowed to leave, sir. There were no orders to hold him."

"Hold the line. Don't move." Othman put the line into suspension, then clutched at his coal-black hair with both hands and shrieked, "Fool! Fool! Fool!"

Leemy was startled. "What the hell?"

"The man has a sixteen-year-old son," choked out Othman. "A sixteen-year-old is not an adult and he is not filed independently in Multivac, but only as part of his father's file." He glared at Leemy. "Doesn't everyone know that until eighteen a youngster does not file his own reports with Multivac but that his father does it for him? Don't I know it? Don't you?"

"You mean Multivac didn't mean Joe Manners?" said Leemy.

"Multivac meant his minor son, and the youngster is gone, now. With officers three deep around the house, he calmly walks out and goes on you know what errand."

He whirled to the telephone circuit to which the Corrections officer still clung, the minute break having given Othman just time enough to collect himself and to assume a cool and self-possessed mien. (It would never have done to throw a fit before the eyes of the officer, however much good it did in purging his spleen.)

He said, "Officer, locate the younger son who has disappeared. Take every man you have, if necessary. Take every man available in the district, if necessary. I shall give the appropriate orders. You must find that boy at all costs."

"Yes, sir."

Connection was broken. Othman said, "Have another rundown on the probabilities, Leemy."

Five minutes later, Leemy said, "It's down to 19.6 per cent. It's *down.*"

Othman drew a long breath. "We're on the right track at last."

Ben Manners sat in Booth 5-B and punched out slowly, "My name is Benjamin Manners, number MB-71833412. My father, Joseph Manners, has been arrested but we don't know what crime he is planning. Is there any way we can help him?"

He sat and waited. He might be only sixteen but he was old enough to know that somewhere those words were being whirled into the most complex structure ever conceived by man; that a trillion facts would blend and co-ordinate into a whole, and that from that whole, Multivac would abstract the best help.

The machine clicked and a card emerged. It had an answer on it, a long answer. It began, "Take the expressway to Washington, D.C. at once. Get off at the Connecticut Avenue stop. You will find a special exit, labeled 'Multivac' with a guard. Inform the guard you are special courier for Dr. Trumbull and he will let you enter.

"You will be in a corridor. Proceed along it till you reach a small door labeled 'Interior.' Enter and say to the men inside, 'Message for Doctor Trumbull.' You will be allowed to pass. Proceed on—"

It went on in this fashion. Ben could not see the application to his question, but he had complete faith in Multivac. He left at a run, heading for the expressway to Washington.

The Corrections officers traced Ben Manners to the Baltimore station an hour after he had left. A shocked Harold Quimby found himself flabbergasted at the number and importance of the men who had focused on him in the search for a sixteen-year-old.

"Yes, a boy," he said, "but I don't know where he went to after he was through here. I had no way of knowing that anyone was looking for him. We accept all comers here. Yes, I can get the record of the question and answer."

They looked at the record and televised it to Central Headquarters at once.

Othman read it through, turned up his eyes, and collapsed. They brought him to almost at once. He said to Leemy weakly, "Have them catch that boy. And have a copy of Multivac's answer made out for me. There's no way any more, no way out. I must see Gulliman now."

Bernard Gulliman had never seen Ali Othman as much as perturbed before, and watching the co-ordinator's wild eyes now sent a trickle of ice water down his spine.

He stammered, "What do you mean, Othman? What do you mean worse than murder?"

"Much worse than just murder."

Gulliman was quite pale. "Do you mean assassination of a high government official?" (It did cross his mind that he himself—).

Othman nodded. "Not just *a* government official. *The* government official."

"The *Secretary-General?*" Gulliman said in an appalled whisper.

"More than that, even. Much more. We deal with a plan to assassinate Multivac!"

"WHAT!"

"For the first time in the history of Multivac, the computer came up with the report that it itself was in danger."

"Why was I not at once informed?"

Othman half-truthed out of it. "The matter was so unprecedented, sir, that we explored the situation first before daring to put it on official record."

"But Multivac has been saved, of course? It's been saved?"

"The probabilities of harm have declined to under 4 per cent. I am waiting for the report now."

"Message for Dr. Trumbull," said Ben Manners to the man on the high stool, working carefully on what looked like the controls of a stratojet cruiser, enormously magnified.

"Sure, Jim," said the man. "Go ahead."

Ben looked at his instructions and hurried on. Eventually, he would find a tiny control lever which he was to shift to a DOWN position at a moment when a certain indicator spot would light up red.

He heard an agitated voice behind him, then another, and suddenly, two men had him by his elbows. His feet were lifted off the floor.

One man said, "Come with us, boy."

Ali Othman's face did not noticeably lighten at the news, even though Gulliman said with great relief, "If we have the boy, then Multivac is safe."

"For the moment."

Gulliman put a trembling hand to his forehead. "What a half hour I've had. Can you imagine what the destruction of Multivac for even a short time would mean. The government would have collapsed; the economy broken down. It would have meant devastation worse—" His head snapped up, "What do you mean *for the moment?*"

"The boy, this Ben Manners, had no intention of doing harm. He and his family must be released and compensation for false imprisonment given them. He was only following Multivac's instructions in order to help his father and it's done that. His father is free now."

"Do you mean Multivac ordered the boy to pull a lever under circumstances that would burn out enough circuits to require a month's repair work? You mean Multivac would suggest its own destruction for the comfort of one man?"

"It's worse than that, sir. Multivac not only gave those instructions but selected the Manners family in the first place because Ben Manners looked exactly like one of Dr. Trumbull's pages so that he could get into Multivac without being stopped."

"What do you mean the family was selected?"

"Well, the boy would have never gone to ask the question if his father had not been arrested. His father would never have been arrested if Multivac had not blamed him for planning the destruction of Multivac. Multivac's own action started the chain of events that almost led to Multivac's destruction."

"But there's no sense to that," Gulliman said in a pleading voice. He felt small and helpless and he was virtually on his knees, begging this Othman, this man who had spent nearly a lifetime with Multivac, to reassure him.

Othman did not do so. He said, "This is Multivac's first attempt along this line as far as I know. In some ways, it planned well. It chose the right family. It carefully did not distinguish between father and son to send us off the track. It was still an amateur at the game, though. It could not overcome its own instructions that led it to report the probability of its own destruction as increasing with every step we took down the wrong road. It could not avoid recording the answer it gave the youngster. With further practice, it will probably learn deceit. It will learn to hide certain facts, fail to record certain others. From now on, every instruction it gives may have the seeds in it of its own destruction. We will never know. And however careful we are, eventually Multivac will succeed. I think, Mr. Gulliman, you will be the last Chairman of this organization."

Gulliman pounded his desk in fury. "But why, why, why? Damn you, why? What is wrong with it? Can't it be fixed?"

"I don't think so," said Othman, in soft despair. "I've never thought about this before. I've never had the occasion to until this happened, but now that I think of it, it seems to me we have reached the end of the road because Multivac is too good. Multivac has grown so complicated, its reactions are no longer those of a machine, but those of a living thing."

"You're mad, but even so?"

"For fifty years and more we have been loading humanity's troubles on Multivac, on this living thing. We've asked it to care for us, all together and each individually. We've asked it to take all our secrets into itself; we've asked it to absorb our evil and guard us against it. Each of us brings his troubles to it, adding his bit to the burden. Now we are planning to load the burden of human disease on Multivac, too."

Othman paused a moment, then burst out, "Mr. Gulliman, Multivac bears all the troubles of the world on its shoulders and it is tired."

"Madness. Midsummer madness," muttered Gulliman.

"Then let me show you something. Let me put it to the test. May I have permission to use the Multivac circuit line here in your office?"

"Why?"

"To ask it a question no one has ever asked Multivac before?"

"Will you do it harm?" asked Gulliman in quick alarm.

"No. But it will tell us what we want to know."

The Chairman hesitated a trifle. Then he said, "Go ahead."

Othman used the instrument on Gulliman's desk. His fingers punched out the question with deft strokes: "Multivac, what do you yourself want more than anything else?"

The moment between question and answer lengthened unbearably, but neither Othman nor Gulliman breathed.

And there was a clicking and a card popped out. It was a small card. On it, in precise letters, was the answer:

"I want to die."

Spell My Name with an S

I

Marshall Zebatinsky felt foolish. He felt as though there were eyes staring through the grimy store-front glass and across the scarred wooden partition; eyes watching him. He felt no confidence in the old clothes he had resurrected or the turned-down brim of a hat he never otherwise wore or the glasses he had left in their case.

He felt foolish and it made the lines in his forehead deeper and his young-old face a little paler.

He would never be able to explain to anyone why a nuclear physicist such as himself should visit a numerologist. (Never, he thought. Never.) Hell, he could not explain it to himself except that he had let his wife talk him into it.

The numerologist sat behind an old desk that must have been second-hand when bought. No desk could get that old with only one owner. The same might almost be said of his clothes. He was little and dark and peered at Zebatinsky with little dark eyes that were brightly alive.

He said, "I have never had a physicist for a client before, Dr. Zebatinsky."

Zebatinsky flushed at once. "You understand this is confidential."

The numerologist smiled so that wrinkles creased about the corners of his mouth and the skin around his chin stretched. "All my dealings are confidential."

Zebatinsky said, "I think I ought to tell you one thing. I don't believe in numerology and I don't expect to begin believing in it. If that makes a difference, say so now."

"But why are you here, then?"

"My wife thinks you may have something, whatever it is. I promised her and I am here." He shrugged and the feeling of folly grew more acute.

"And what is it you are looking for? Money? Security? Long life? What?"

Zebatinsky sat for a long moment while the numerologist watched him quietly and made no move to hurry his client.

Zebatinsky thought: What do I say anyway? That I'm thirty-four and without a future?

He said, "I want success. I want recognition."

"A better job?"

"A *different* job. A different *kind* of job. Right now, I'm part of a team, working under orders. Teams! That's all government research is. You're a violinist lost in a symphony orchestra."

"And you want to solo."

"I want to get out of a team and into—into *me.*" Zebatinsky felt carried away, almost lightheaded, just putting this into words to someone other than his wife. He said, "Twenty-five years ago, with my kind of training and my kind of ability, I would have gotten to work on the first nuclear power plants. Today I'd be running one of them or I'd be head of a pure research group at a university. But with my start these days where will I be twenty-five years from now? Nowhere. Still on the team. Still carrying my 2 per cent of the ball. I'm drowning in an anonymous crowd of nuclear physicists, and what I want is room on dry land, if you see what I mean."

The numerologist nodded slowly. "You realize, Dr. Zebatinsky, that I don't guarantee success."

Zebatinsky, for all his lack of faith, felt a sharp bite of disappointment. "You don't? Then what the devil *do* you guarantee?"

"An improvement in the probabilities. My work is statistical in nature. Since you deal with atoms, I think you understand the laws of statistics."

"Do you?" asked the physicist sourly.

"I do, as a matter of fact. I am a mathematician and I work mathematically. I don't tell you this in order to raise my fee. That is standard. Fifty dollars. But since you are a scientist, you can appreciate the nature of my work better than my other clients. It is even a pleasure to be able to explain to you."

Zebatinsky said, "I'd rather you wouldn't, if you don't mind. It's no use telling me about the numerical values of letters, their mystic significance and that kind of thing. I don't consider that mathematics. Let's get to the point—"

The numerologist said, "Then you want me to help you provided I don't embarrass you by telling you the silly nonscientific basis of the way in which I helped you. Is that it?"

"All right. That's it."

"But you still work on the assumption that I am a numerologist, and I am not. I call myself that so that the police won't bother me and" (the little man chuckled dryly) "so that the psychiatrists won't either. I am a mathematician; an honest one."

Zebatinsky smiled.

The numerologist said, "I build computers. I study probable futures."

"What?"

"Does that sound worse than numerology to you? Why? Given enough data and a computer capable of sufficient number of operations in unit time, the future is predictable, at least in terms of probabilities. When you compute the motions of a missile in order to aim an anti-missile, isn't it the future you're predicting? The missile and anti-missile would not collide if the future were predicted incorrectly. I do the same thing. Since I work with a greater number of variables, my results are less accurate."

"You mean you'll predict *my* future?"

"Very approximately. Once I have done that, I will modify the data by changing your name and no other fact about you. I throw that modified datum into the operation-program. Then I try other modified names. I study each modified future and find one that contains a greater degree of recognition for you than the future that now lies ahead of you. Or no, let me put it another way. I will find you a future in which the probability of adequate recognition is higher than the probability of that in your present future."

"Why change my name?"

"That is the only change I ever make, for several reasons. Number one, it is a simple change. After all, if I make a great change or many changes, so many new variables enter that I can no longer interpret the result. My machine is still crude. Number two, it is a reasonable change. I can't change your height, can I, or the color of your eyes, or even your temperament. Number three, it is a significant change. Names mean a lot to people. Finally, number four, it is a common change that is done every day by various people."

Zebatinsky said, "What if you don't find a better future?"

"That is the risk you will have to take. You will be no worse off than now, my friend."

Zebatinsky stared at the little man uneasily, "I don't believe any of this. I'd sooner believe numerology."

The numerologist sighed. "I thought a person like yourself would feel more comfortable with the truth. I *want* to help you and there is much yet for you to do. If you believed me a numerologist, you would not follow through. I thought if I told you the truth you would let me help you."

Zebatinsky said, "If you can see the future—"

"Why am I not the richest man on earth? Is that it? But I am rich—in all I want. You want recognition and I want to be left alone. I do my work. No one bothers me. That makes me a billionaire. I need a little real money and this I get from people such as yourself. Helping people is nice and perhaps a psychiatrist would say it gives me a feeling of power and feeds my ego. Now —do you want me to help you?"

"How much did you say?"

"Fifty dollars. I will need a great deal of biographical information from you but I have prepared a form to guide you. It's a little long, I'm afraid. Still, if you can get it in the mail by the end of the week, I will have an answer for you by the—" (he put out his lower lip and frowned in mental calculation) "the twentieth of next month."

"Five weeks? So long?"

"I have other work, my friend, and other clients. If I were a fake, I could do it much more quickly. It is agreed then?"

Zebatinsky rose. "Well, agreed. —This is all confidential, now."

"Perfectly. You will have all your information back when I tell you what change to make and you have my word that I will never make any further use of any of it."

The nuclear physicist stopped at the door. "Aren't you afraid I might tell someone you're not a numerologist?"

The numerologist shook his head. "Who would believe you, my friend? Even supposing you were willing to admit to anyone that you've been here."

On the twentieth, Marshall Zebatinsky was at the paint-peeling door, glancing sideways at the shop front with the little card up against the glass reading "Numerology," dimmed and scarcely legible through the dust. He peered in, almost hoping that someone else would be there already so that he might have an excuse to tear up the wavering intention in his mind and go home.

He had tried wiping the thing out of his mind several times. He could never stick at filling out the necessary data for long. It was embarrassing to work at it. He felt incredibly silly filling out the names of his friends, the cost of his house, whether his wife had had any miscarriages, if so, when. He abandoned it.

But he couldn't stick at stopping altogether either. He returned to it each evening.

It was the thought of the computer that did it, perhaps; the thought of the infernal gall of the little man pretending he had a computer. The temptation to call the bluff, see what would happen, proved irresistible after all.

He finally sent off the completed data by ordinary mail, putting on nine cents worth of stamps without weighing the letter. If it comes back, he thought, I'll call it off.

It didn't come back.

He looked into the shop now and it was empty. Zebatinsky had no choice but to enter. A bell tinkled.

The old numerologist emerged from a curtained door.

"Yes? —Ah, Dr. Zebatinsky."

"You remember me?" Zebatinsky tried to smile.

"Oh, yes."

"What's the verdict?"

The numerologist moved one gnarled hand over the other. "Before that, sir, there's a little—"

"A little matter of the fee?"

"I have already done the work, sir. I have earned the money."

Zebatinsky raised no objection. He was prepared to pay. If he had come this far, it would be silly to turn back just because of the money.

He counted out five ten-dollar bills and shoved them across the counter. "Well?"

The numerologist counted the bills again slowly, then pushed them into a cash drawer in his desk.

He said, "Your case was very interesting. I would advise you to change your name to Sebatinsky."

"Seba— How do you spell that?"

"S-e-b-a-t-i-n-s-k-y."

Zebatinsky stared indignantly. "You mean change the initial? Change the Z to an S? That's all?"

"It's enough. As long as the change is adequate, a small change is safer than a big one."

"But how could the change affect anything?"

"How could any name?" asked the numerologist softly. "I can't say. It may, somehow, and that's all I can say. Remember, I don't guarantee results. Of course, if you do not wish to make the change, leave things as they are. But in that case I cannot refund the fee."

Zebatinsky said, "What do I do? Just tell everyone to spell my name with an *S*?"

"If you want my advice, consult a lawyer. Change your name legally. He can advise you on little things."

"How long will it all take? I mean for things to improve for me?"

"How can I tell? Maybe never. Maybe tomorrow."

"But you saw the future. You *claim* you see it."

"Not as in a crystal ball. No, no, Dr. Zebatinsky. All I get out of my computer is a set of coded figures. I can recite probabilities to you, but I saw no pictures."

Zebatinsky turned and walked rapidly out of the place. Fifty dollars to change a letter! Fifty dollars for Sebatinsky! Lord, what a name! Worse than Zebatinsky.

It took another month before he could make up his mind to see a lawyer, and then he finally went.

He told himself he could always change the name back.

Give it a chance, he told himself.

Hell, there was no law against it.

Henry Brand looked through the folder page by page, with the practiced eye of one who had been in Security for fourteen years. He didn't have to read every word. Anything peculiar would have leaped off the paper and punched him in the eye.

He said, "The man looks clean to me." Henry Brand looked clean, too; with a soft, rounded paunch and a pink and freshly scrubbed complexion. It was as though continuous contact with all sorts of human failings, from possible ignorance to possible treason, had compelled him into frequent washings.

Lieutenant Albert Quincy, who had brought him the folder, was young and filled with the responsibility of being Security officer at the Hanford Station. "But why Sebatinsky?" he demanded.

"Why not?"

"Because it doesn't make sense. Zebatinsky is a foreign name and I'd change it myself if I had it, but I'd change it to something Anglo-Saxon. If Zebatinsky had done that, it would make sense and I wouldn't give it a second thought. But why change a Z to an S? I think we must find out what his reasons were."

"Has anyone asked him directly?"

"Certainly. In ordinary conversation, of course. I was careful to arrange that. He won't say anything more than that he's tired of being last in the alphabet."

"That could be, couldn't it, Lieutenant?"

"It could, but why not change his name to Sands or Smith, if he wants an S? Or if he's that tired of Z, why not go the whole way and change it to an A? Why not a name like—uh—Aarons?"

"Not Anglo-Saxon enough," muttered Brand. Then, "But there's nothing to pin against the man. No matter how queer a name change may be, that alone can't be used against anyone."

Lieutenant Quincy looked markedly unhappy.

Brand said, "Tell me, Lieutenant, there must be something specific that bothers you. Something in your mind; some theory; some gimmick. What is it?"

The lieutenant frowned. His light eyebrows drew together and his lips tightened. "Well, damn it, sir, the man's a Russian."

Brand said, "He's not that. He's a third-generation American."

"I mean his name's Russian."

Brand's face lost some of its deceptive softness. "No, Lieutenant, wrong again. Polish."

The lieutenant pushed his hands out impatiently, palms up. "Same thing."

Brand, whose mother's maiden name had been Wiszewski, snapped, "Don't tell that to a Pole, Lieutenant." —Then, more thoughtfully, "Or to a Russian either, I suppose."

"What I'm trying to say, sir," said the lieutenant, reddening, "is that the Poles and Russians are both on the other side of the Curtain."

"We all know that."

"And Zebatinsky or Sebatinsky, whatever you want to call him, may have relatives there."

"He's third generation. He might have second cousins there, I suppose. So what?"

"Nothing in itself. Lots of people may have distant relatives there. But Zebatinsky changed his name."

"Go on."

"Maybe he's trying to distract attention. Maybe a second cousin over there is getting too famous and our Zebatinsky is afraid that the relationship may spoil his own chances of advancement."

"Changing his name won't do any good. He'd still be a second cousin."

"Sure, but he wouldn't feel as though he were shoving the relationship in our face."

"Have *you* ever heard of any Zebatinsky on the other side?"

"No, sir."

"Then he can't be too famous. How would our Zebatinsky know about him?"

"He might keep in touch with his own relatives. That would be suspicious under the circumstances, he being a nuclear physicist."

Methodically, Brand went through the folder again. "This is awfully thin, Lieutenant. It's thin enough to be completely invisible."

"Can you offer any other explanation, sir, of why he ought to change his name in just this way?"

"No, I can't. I admit that."

"Then I think, sir, we ought to investigate. We ought to look for any men named Zebatinsky on the other side and see if we can draw a connection." The lieutenant's voice rose a trifle as a new thought occurred to him. "He might be changing his name to withdraw attention from *them;* I mean to protect them."

"He's doing just the opposite, I think."

"He doesn't realize that, maybe, but protecting them could be his motive."

Brand sighed. "All right, we'll tackle the Zebatinsky angle. —But if nothing turns up, Lieutenant, we drop the matter. Leave the folder with me."

• • • •

When the information finally reached Brand, he had all but forgotten the lieutenant and his theories. His first thought on receiving data that included a list of seventeen biographies of seventeen Russian and Polish citizens, all named Zebatinsky, was: What the devil is this?

Then he remembered, swore mildly, and began reading.

It started on the American side. Marshall Zebatinsky (fingerprints) had been born in Buffalo, New York (date, hospital statistics). His father had been born in Buffalo as well, his mother in Oswego, New York. His paternal grandparents had both been born in Bialystok, Poland (date of entry into the United States, dates of citizenship, photographs).

The seventeen Russian and Polish citizens named Zebatinsky were all descendants of people who, some half century earlier, had lived in or near Bialystok. Presumably, they could be relatives, but this was not explicitly stated in any particular case. (Vital statistics in East Europe during the aftermath of World War I were kept poorly, if at all.)

Brand passed through the individual life histories of the current Zebatinsky men and women (amazing how thoroughly intelligence did its work; probably the Russians' was as thorough). He stopped at one and his smooth forehead sprouted lines as his eyebrows shot upward. He put that one to one side and went on. Eventually, he stacked everything but that one and returned it to its envelope.

Staring at that one, he tapped a neatly kept fingernail on the desk.

With a certain reluctance, he went to call on Dr. Paul Kristow of the Atomic Energy Commission.

Dr. Kristow listened to the matter with a stony expression. He lifted a little finger occasionally to dab at his bulbous nose and remove a nonexistent speck. His hair was iron gray, thinning and cut short. He might as well have been bald.

He said, "No, I never heard of any Russian Zebatinsky. But then, I never heard of the American one either."

"Well," Brand scratched at his hairline over one temple and said slowly, "I don't think there's anything to this, but I don't like to drop it too soon. I have a young lieutenant on my tail and you know what they can be like. I don't want to do anything that will drive him to a Congressional committee. Besides, the fact is that one of the Russian Zebatinsky fellows, Mikhail Andreyevich Zebatinsky, *is* a nuclear physicist. Are you sure you never heard of him?"

"Mikhail Andreyevich Zebatinsky? No— No, I never did. Not that that proves anything."

"I could say it was coincidence, but you know that would be piling it a trifle high. One Zebatinsky here and one Zebatinsky there, both nuclear physicists, and the one here suddenly changes his name to Sebatinsky, and goes around anxious about it, too. He won't allow misspelling. He says, emphatically, 'Spell my name with an *S*.' It all just fits well enough to make my spy-conscious lieutenant begin to look a little too good. —And another peculiar thing is that the Russian Zebatinsky dropped out of sight just about a year ago."

Dr. Kristow said stolidly, "Executed!"

"He might have been. Ordinarily, I would even assume so, though the Russians are not more foolish than we are and don't kill any nuclear physicist they can avoid killing. The thing is there's another reason why a nuclear physicist, of all people, might suddenly disappear. I don't have to tell you."

"Crash research; top secret. I take it that's what you mean. Do you believe that's it?"

"Put it together with everything else, add in the lieutenant's intuition, and I just begin to wonder."

"Give me that biography." Dr. Kristow reached for the sheet of paper and read it over twice. He shook his head. Then he said, "I'll check this in *Nuclear Abstracts.*"

Nuclear Abstracts lined one wall of Dr. Kristow's study in neat little boxes, each filled with its squares of microfilm.

The A.E.C. man used his projector on the indices while Brand watched with what patience he could muster.

Dr. Kristow muttered, "A Mikhail Zebatinsky authored or co-authored half a dozen papers in the Soviet journals in the last half dozen years. We'll get out the abstracts and maybe we can make something out of it. I doubt it."

A selector flipped out the appropriate squares. Dr. Kristow lined them up, ran them through the projector, and by degrees an expression of odd intentness crossed his face. He said, "That's odd."

Brand said, "What's odd?"

Dr. Kristow sat back. "I'd rather not say just yet. Can you get me a list of other nuclear physicists who have dropped out of sight in the Soviet Union in the last year?"

"You mean you see something?"

"Not really. Not if I were just looking at any one of these papers. It's just that looking at all of them and knowing that this man may be on a crash research program and, on top of that, having you putting suspicions in my head—" He shrugged. "It's nothing."

Brand said earnestly, "I wish you'd say what's on your mind. We may as well be foolish about this together."

"If you feel that way— It's just possible this man may have been inching toward gamma-ray reflection."

"And the significance?"

"If a reflecting shield against gamma rays could be devised, individual shelters could be built to protect against fallout. It's fallout that's the real danger, you know. A hydrogen bomb might destroy a city but the fallout could slow-kill the population over a strip thousands of miles long and hundreds wide."

Brand said quickly, "Are we doing any work on this?"

"No."

"And if they get it and we don't, they can destroy the United States *in toto* at the cost of, say, ten cities, after they have their shelter program completed."

"That's far in the future. —And, what are we getting in a hurrah about? All this is built on one man changing one letter in his name."

"All right, I'm insane," said Brand. "But I don't leave the matter at this point. Not at *this* point. I'll get you your list of disappearing nuclear physicists if I have to go to Moscow to get it."

He got the list. They went through all the research papers authored by any of them. They called a full meeting of the Commission, then of the nuclear brains of the nation. Dr. Kristow walked out of an all night session, finally, part of which the President himself had attended.

Brand met him. Both looked haggard and in need of sleep.

Brand said, "Well?"

Kristow nodded. "Most agree. Some are doubtful even yet, but most agree."

"How about you? Are you sure?"

"I'm far from sure, but let me put it this way. It's easier to believe that the Soviets are working on a gamma-ray shield than to believe that all the data we've uncovered has no interconnection."

"Has it been decided that we're to go on shield research, too?"

"Yes." Kristow's hand went back over his short, bristly hair, making a dry, whispery sound. "We're going to give it everything we've got. Knowing the papers written by the men who disappeared, we can get right on their heels. We may even beat them to it. —Of course, they'll find out we're working on it."

"Let them," said Brand. "Let them. It will keep them from attacking. I don't see any percentage in selling ten of our cities just to get ten of theirs— if we're both protected and they're too dumb to know that."

"But not too soon. We don't want them finding out *too* soon. What about the American Zebatinsky-Sebatinsky?"

Brand looked solemn and shook his head. "There's nothing to connect him with any of this even yet. Hell, we've *looked.* I agree with you, of course. He's in a sensitive spot where he is now and we can't afford to keep him there even if he's in the clear."

"We can't kick him out just like that, either, or the Russians will start wondering."

"Do you have any suggestions?"

They were walking down the long corridor toward the distant elevator in the emptiness of four in the morning.

Dr. Kristow said, "I've looked into his work. He's a good man, better than most, and not happy in his job, either. He hasn't the temperament for teamwork."

"So?"

"But he is the type for an academic job. If we can arrange to have a large university offer him a chair in physics, I think he would take it gladly. There would be enough nonsensitive areas to keep him occupied; we would be able to keep him in close view; *and* it would be a natural development. The Russians might not start scratching their heads. What do you think?"

Brand nodded. "It's an idea. Even sounds good. I'll put it up to the chief."

They stepped into the elevator and Brand allowed himself to wonder about it all. What an ending to what had started with one letter of a name.

Marshall Sebatinsky could hardly talk. He said to his wife, "I swear I don't see how this happened. I wouldn't have thought they knew me from a meson detector. —Good Lord, Sophie, Associate Professor of Physics at Princeton. Think of it."

Sophie said, "Do you suppose it was your talk at the A.P.S. meetings?"

"I don't see how. It was a thoroughly uninspired paper once everyone in the division was done hacking at it." He snapped his fingers. "It must have been Princeton that was investigating me. That's it. You know all those forms I've been filling out in the last six months; those interviews they wouldn't explain. Honestly, I was beginning to think I was under suspicion as a subversive. —It was Princeton investigating me. They're thorough."

"Maybe it was your name," said Sophie. "I mean the change."

"Watch me now. My professional life will be my own finally. I'll make my mark. Once I have a chance to do my work without—" He stopped and turned to look at his wife. "My name! You mean the *S.*"

"You didn't get the offer till after you changed your name, did you?"

"Not till long after. No, that part's just coincidence. I've told you before Sophie, it was just a case of throwing out fifty dollars to please you. Lord, what a fool I've felt all these months insisting on that stupid *S.*"

Sophie was instantly on the defensive. "I didn't make you do it, Marshall. I suggested it but I didn't nag you about it. Don't say I did. Besides, it did turn out well. I'm sure it was the name that did this."

Sebatinsky smiled indulgently. "Now that's superstition."

"I don't care what you call it, but you're not changing your name back."

"Well, no, I suppose not. I've had so much trouble getting them to spell my name with an *S,* that the thought of making everyone move back is more than I want to face. Maybe I ought to change my name to Jones, eh?" He laughed almost hysterically.

But Sophie didn't. "You leave it alone."

"Oh, all right, I'm just joking. —Tell you what. I'll step down to that old fellow's place one of these days and tell him everything worked out and slip him another tenner. Will that satisfy you?"

He was exuberant enough to do so the next week. He assumed no disguise this time. He wore his glasses and his ordinary suit and was minus a hat.

He was even humming as he approached the store front and stepped to one side to allow a weary, sour-faced woman to maneuver her twin baby carriage past.

He put his hand on the door handle and his thumb on the iron latch. The latch didn't give to his thumb's downward pressure. The door was locked.

The dusty, dim card with "Numerologist" on it was gone, now that he looked. Another sign, printed and beginning to yellow and curl with the sunlight, said "To let."

Sebatinsky shrugged. That was that. He had tried to do the right thing.

Haround, happily divested of corporeal excrescence, capered happily and his energy vortices glowed a dim purple over cubic hypermiles. He said, "Have I won? Have I won?"

Mestack was withdrawn, his vortices almost a sphere of light in hyperspace. "I haven't calculated it yet."

"Well, go ahead. You won't change the results any by taking a long time. —Wowf, it's a relief to get back into clean energy. It took me a microcycle of time as a corporeal body; a nearly used-up one, too. But it was worth it to show *you*."

Mestack said, "All right, I admit you stopped a nuclear war on the planet."

"Is that or is that not a Class A effect?"

"It is a Class A effect. Of course it is."

"All right. Now check and see if I didn't get that Class A effect with a Class F stimulus. I changed one letter of one name."

"What?"

"Oh, never mind. It's all there. I've worked it out for you."

Mestack said reluctantly, "I yield. A Class F stimulus."

"Then I *win*. Admit it."

"Neither one of us will win when the Watchman gets a look at this."

Haround, who had been an elderly numerologist on Earth and was still somewhat unsettled with relief at no longer being one, said, "You weren't worried about that when you made the bet."

"I didn't think you'd be fool enough to go through with it."

"Heat-waste! Besides, why worry? The Watchman will never detect a Class F stimulus."

"Maybe not, but he'll detect a Class A effect. Those corporeals will still be around after a dozen microcycles. The Watchman will notice that."

"The trouble with you, Mestack, is that you don't want to pay off. You're stalling."

"I'll pay. But just wait till the Watchman finds out we've been working on an unassigned problem and made an unallowed-for change. Of course, if we—" He paused.

Haround said, "All right, we'll change it back. He'll never know."

There was a crafty glow to Mestack's brightening energy pattern. "You'll need another Class F stimulus if you expect him not to notice."

Haround hesitated. "I can do it."

"I doubt it."

"I could."

"Would you be willing to bet on that, too?" Jubilation was creeping into Mestack's radiations.

"Sure," said the goaded Haround. "I'll put those corporeals right back where they were and the Watchman will never know the difference."

Mestack followed through his advantage. "Suspend the first bet, then. Triple the stakes on the second."

The mounting eagerness of the gamble caught at Haround, too. "All right, I'm game. Triple the stakes."

"Done, then!"

"Done."

The Last Question

The last question was asked for the first time, half in jest, on May 21, 2061, at a time when humanity first stepped into the light. The question came about as a result of a five-dollar bet over highballs, and it happened this way:

Alexander Adell and Bertram Lupov were two of the faithful attendants of Multivac. As well as any human beings could, they knew what lay behind the cold, clicking, flashing face—miles and miles of face—of that giant computer. They had at least a vague notion of the general plan of relays and circuits that had long since grown past the point where any single human could possibly have a firm grasp of the whole.

Multivac was self-adjusting and self-correcting. It had to be, for nothing human could adjust and correct it quickly enough or even adequately enough. —So Adell and Lupov attended the monstrous giant only lightly and superficially, yet as well as any men could. They fed it data, adjusted questions to its needs and translated the answers that were issued. Certainly they, and all others like them, were fully entitled to share in the glory that was Multivac's.

For decades, Multivac had helped design the ships and plot the trajectories that enabled man to reach the Moon, Mars, and Venus, but past that, Earth's poor resources could not support the ships. Too much energy was needed for the long trips. Earth exploited its coal and uranium with increasing efficiency, but there was only so much of both.

But slowly Multivac learned enough to answer deeper questions more fundamentally, and on May 14, 2061, what had been theory, became fact.

The energy of the sun was stored, converted, and utilized directly on a planet-wide scale. All Earth turned off its burning coal, its fissioning uranium, and flipped the switch that connected all of it to a small station, one mile in diameter, circling the Earth at half the distance of the Moon. All Earth ran by invisible beams of sunpower.

Seven days had not sufficed to dim the glory of it and Adell and Lupov finally managed to escape from the public function, and to meet in quiet where no one would think of looking for them, in the deserted underground chambers, where portions of the mighty buried body of Multivac showed. Unattended, idling, sorting data with contented lazy clickings, Multivac, too, had earned its vacation and the boys appreciated that. They had no intention, originally, of disturbing it.

They had brought a bottle with them, and their only concern at the moment was to relax in the company of each other and the bottle.

"It's amazing when you think of it," said Adell. His broad face had lines of weariness in it, and he stirred his drink slowly with a glass rod, watching the cubes of ice slur clumsily about. "All the energy we can possibly ever use for free. Enough energy, if we wanted to draw on it, to melt all Earth into a big drop of impure liquid iron, and still never miss the energy so used. All the energy we could ever use, forever and forever and forever."

Lupov cocked his head sidways. He had a trick of doing that when he wanted to be contrary, and he wanted to be contrary now, partly because he had had to carry the ice and glassware. "Not forever," he said.

"Oh, hell, just about forever. Till the sun runs down, Bert."

"That's not forever."

"All right, then. Billions and billions of years. Twenty billion, maybe. Are you satisfied?"

Lupov put his fingers through his thinning hair as though to reassure himself that some was still left and sipped gently at his own drink. "Twenty billion years isn't forever."

"Well, it will last our time, won't it?"

"So would the coal and uranium."

"All right, but now we can hook up each individual spaceship to the Solar Station, and it can go to Pluto and back a million times without ever worrying about fuel. You can't do *that* on coal and uranium. Ask Multivac, if you don't believe me."

"I don't have to ask Multivac. I know that."

"Then stop running down what Multivac's done for us," said Adell, blazing up. "It did all right."

"Who says it didn't? What I say is that a sun won't last forever. That's all I'm saying. We're safe for twenty billion years, but then what?" Lupov pointed a slightly shaky finger at the other. "And don't say we'll switch to another sun."

There was silence for a while. Adell put his glass to his lips only occasionally, and Lupov's eyes slowly closed. They rested.

Then Lupov's eyes snapped open. "You're thinking we'll switch to another sun when ours is done, aren't you?"

"I'm not thinking."

"Sure you are. You're weak on logic, that's the trouble with you. You're like the guy in the story who was caught in a sudden shower and who ran to a grove of trees and got under one. He wasn't worried, you see, because he figured when one tree got wet through, he would just get under another one."

"I get it," said Adell. "Don't shout. When the sun is done, the other stars will be gone, too."

"Darn right they will," muttered Lupov. "It all had a beginning in the original cosmic explosion, whatever that was, and it'll all have an end when all the stars run down. Some run down faster than others. Hell, the giants won't last a hundred million years. The sun will last twenty billion years and maybe the dwarfs will last a hundred billion for all the good they are. But just give us a trillion years and everything will be dark. Entropy has to increase to maximum, that's all."

"I know all about entropy," said Adell, standing on his dignity.

"The hell you do."

"I know as much as you do."

"Then you know everything's got to run down someday."

"All right. Who says they won't?"

"You did, you poor sap. You said we had all the energy we needed, forever. You said 'forever.'"

It was Adell's turn to be contrary. "Maybe we can build things up again someday," he said.

"Never."

"Why not? Someday."

"Never."

"Ask Multivac."

"*You* ask Multivac. I dare you. Five dollars says it can't be done."

Adell was just drunk enough to try, just sober enough to be able to phrase the necessary symbols and operations into a question which, in words, might have corresponded to this: Will mankind one day without the net expenditure of energy be able to restore the sun to its full youthfulness even after it had died of old age?

Or maybe it could be put more simply like this: How can the net amount of entropy of the universe be massively decreased?

Multivac fell dead and silent. The slow flashing of lights ceased, the distant sounds of clicking relays ended.

Then, just as the frightened technicians felt they could hold their breath no longer, there was a sudden springing to life of the teletype attached to that portion of Multivac. Five words were printed: INSUFFICIENT DATA FOR MEANINGFUL ANSWER.

"No bet," whispered Lupov. They left hurriedly.

By next morning, the two, plagued with throbbing head and cottony mouth, had forgotten the incident.

Jerrodd, Jerrodine, and Jerrodette I and II watched the starry picture in the visiplate change as the passage through hyperspace was completed in its non-time lapse. At once, the even powdering of stars gave way to the predominance of a single bright marble-disk, centered.

"That's X-23," said Jerrodd confidently. His thin hands clamped tightly behind his back and the knuckles whitened.

The little Jerrodettes, both girls, had experienced the hyperspace passage for the first time in their lives and were self-conscious over the momentary sensation of inside-outness. They buried their giggles and chased one another wildly about their mother, screaming, "We've reached X-23—we've reached X-23—we've—"

"Quiet, children," said Jerrodine sharply. "Are you sure, Jerrodd?"

"What is there to be but sure?" asked Jerrodd, glancing up at the bulge of featureless metal just under the ceiling. It ran the length of the room, disappearing through the wall at either end. It was as long as the ship.

Jerrodd scarcely knew a thing about the thick rod of metal except that it was called a Microvac, that one asked it questions if one wished; that if one did not it still had its task of guiding the ship to a preordered destination; of feeding on energies from the various Sub-galactic Power Stations; of computing the equations for the hyperspatial jumps.

Jerrodd and his family had only to wait and live in the comfortable residence quarters of the ship.

Someone had once told Jerrodd that the "ac" at the end of "Microvac" stood for "analog computer" in ancient English, but he was on the edge of forgetting even that.

Jerrodine's eyes were moist as she watched the visiplate. "I can't help it. I feel funny about leaving Earth."

"Why, for Pete's sake?" demanded Jerrodd. "We had nothing there. We'll have everything on X-23. You won't be alone. You won't be a pioneer. There are over a million people on the planet already. Good Lord, our great-grandchildren will be looking for new worlds because X-23 will be overcrowded." Then, after a reflective pause, "I tell you, it's a lucky thing the computers worked out interstellar travel the way the race is growing."

"I know, I know," said Jerrodine miserably.

Jerrodette I said promptly, "Our Microvac is the best Microvac in the world."

"I think so, too," said Jerrodd, tousling her hair.

It *was* a nice feeling to have a Microvac of your own and Jerrodd was glad he was part of his generation and no other. In his father's youth, the only computers had been tremendous machines taking up a hundred square miles of land. There was only one to a planet. Planetary ACs they were called. They had been growing in size steadily for a thousand years and then, all at once, came refinement. In place of transistors had come molecular valves so that even the largest Planetary AC could be put into a space only half the volume of a spaceship.

Jerrodd felt uplifted, as he always did when he thought that his own personal Microvac was many times more complicated than the ancient and primitive Multivac that had first tamed the Sun, and almost as complicated as Earth's Planetary AC (the largest) that had first solved the problem of hyperspatial travel and had made trips to the stars possible.

"So many stars, so many planets," sighed Jerrodine, busy with her own thoughts. "I suppose families will be going out to new planets forever, the way we are now."

"Not forever," said Jerrodd, with a smile. "It will all stop someday, but not for billions of years. Many billions. Even the stars run down, you know. Entropy must increase."

"What's entropy, daddy?" shrilled Jerrodette II.

"Entropy, little sweet, is just a word which means the amount of running-down of the universe. Everything runs down, you know, like your little walkie-talkie robot, remember?"

"Can't you just put in a new power-unit, like with my robot?"

"The stars *are* the power-units, dear. Once they're gone, there are no more power-units."

Jerrodette I at once set up a howl. "Don't let them, daddy. Don't let the stars run down."

"Now look what you've done," whispered Jerrodine, exasperated.

"How was I to know it would frighten them?" Jerrodd whispered back.

"Ask the Microvac," wailed Jerrodette I. "Ask him how to turn the stars on again."

"Go ahead," said Jerrodine. "It will quiet them down." (Jerrodette II was beginning to cry, also.)

Jerrodd shrugged. "Now, now, honeys. I'll ask Microvac. Don't worry, he'll tell us."

He asked the Microvac, adding quickly, "Print the answer."

Jerrodd cupped the strip of thin cellufilm and said cheerfully, "See now, the Microvac says it will take care of everything when the time comes so don't worry."

Jerrodine said, "And now, children, it's time for bed. We'll be in our new home soon."

Jerrodd read the words on the cellufilm again before destroying it: INSUF-FICIENT DATA FOR A MEANINGFUL ANSWER.

He shrugged and looked at the visiplate. X-23 was just ahead.

. . . .

VJ-23X of Lameth stared into the black depths of the three-dimensional, small-scale map of the Galaxy and said, "Are we ridiculous, I wonder, in being so concerned about the matter?"

MQ-17J of Nicron shook his head. "I think not. You know the Galaxy will be filled in five years at the present rate of expansion."

Both seemed in their early twenties, both were tall and perfectly formed.

"Still," said VJ-23X, "I hesitate to submit a pessimistic report to the Galactic Council."

"I wouldn't consider any other kind of report. Stir them up a bit. We've got to stir them up."

VJ-23X sighed. "Space is infinite. A hundred billion Galaxies are there for the taking. More."

"A hundred billion is *not* infinite and it's getting less infinite all the time. Consider! Twenty thousand years ago, mankind first solved the problem of utilizing stellar energy, and a few centuries later, interstellar travel became possible. It took mankind a million years to fill one small world and then only fifteen thousand years to fill the rest of the Galaxy. Now the population doubles every ten years—"

VJ-23X interrupted. "We can thank immortality for that."

"Very well. Immortality exists and we have to take it into account. I admit it has its seamy side, this immortality. The Galactic AC has solved many problems for us, but in solving the problem of preventing old age and death, it has undone all its other solutions."

"Yet you wouldn't want to abandon life, I suppose."

"Not at all," snapped MQ-17J, softening it at once to, "Not yet. I'm by no means old enough. How old are you?"

"Two hundred twenty-three. And you?"

"I'm still under two hundred. —But to get back to my point. Population doubles every ten years. Once this Galaxy is filled, we'll have filled another in ten years. Another ten years and we'll have filled two more. Another decade, four more. In a hundred years, we'll have filled a thousand Galaxies. In a thousand years, a million Galaxies. In ten thousand years, the entire known Universe. Then what?"

VJ-23X said, "As a side issue, there's a problem of transportation. I wonder how many sunpower units it will take to move Galaxies of individuals from one Galaxy to the next."

"A very good point. Already, mankind consumes two sunpower units per year."

"Most of it's wasted. After all, our own Galaxy alone pours out a thousand sunpower units a year and we only use two of those."

"Granted, but even with a hundred per cent efficiency, we only stave off the end. Our energy requirements are going up in a geometric progression even faster than our population. We'll run out of energy even sooner than we run out of Galaxies. A good point. A very good point."

"We'll just have to build new stars out of interstellar gas."

"Or out of dissipated heat?" asked MQ-17J, sarcastically.

"There may be some way to reverse entropy. We ought to ask the Galactic AC."

VJ-23X was not really serious, but MQ-17J pulled out his AC-contact from his pocket and placed it on the table before him.

"I've half a mind to," he said. "It's something the human race will have to face someday."

He stared somberly at his small AC-contact. It was only two inches cubed and nothing in itself, but it was connected through hyperspace with the great Galactic AC that served all mankind. Hyperspace considered, it was an integral part of the Galactic AC.

MQ-17J paused to wonder if someday in his immortal life he would get to see the Galactic AC It was on a little world of its own, a spider webbing of force-beams holding the matter within which surges of sub-mesons took the place of the old clumsy molecular valves. Yet despite its sub-etheric workings, the Galactic AC was known to be a full thousand feet across.

MQ-17J asked suddenly of his AC-contact, "Can entropy ever be reversed?"

VJ-23X looked startled and said at once, "Oh, say, I didn't really mean to have you ask that."

"Why not?"

"We both know entropy can't be reversed. You can't turn smoke and ash back into a tree."

"Do you have trees on your world?" asked MQ-17J.

The sound of the Galactic AC startled them into silence. Its voice came thin and beautiful out of the small AC-contact on the desk. It said: THERE IS INSUFFICIENT DATA FOR A MEANINGFUL ANSWER.

VJ-23X said, "See!"

The two men thereupon returned to the question of the report they were to make to the Galactic Council.

Zee Prime's mind spanned the new Galaxy with a faint interest in the countless twists of stars that powdered it. He had never seen this one before. Would he ever see them all? So many of them, each with its load of humanity. —But a load that was almost a dead weight. More and more, the real essence of men was to be found out here, in space.

Minds, not bodies! The immortal bodies remained back on the planets, in suspension over the eons. Sometimes they roused for material activity but that was growing rarer. Few new individuals were coming into existence to join the incredibly mighty throng, but what matter? There was little room in the Universe for new individuals.

Zee Prime was roused out of his reverie upon coming across the wispy tendrils of another mind.

"I am Zee Prime," said Zee Prime. "And you?"

"I am Dee Sub Wun. Your Galaxy?"

"We call it only the Galaxy. And you?"

"We call ours the same. All men call their Galaxy their Galaxy and nothing more. Why not?"

"True. Since all Galaxies are the same."

"Not all Galaxies. On one particular Galaxy the race of man must have originated. That makes it different."

Zee Prime said, "On which one?"

"I cannot say. The Universal AC would know."

"Shall we ask him? I am suddenly curious."

Zee Prime's perceptions broadened until the Galaxies themselves shrank and became a new, more diffuse powdering on a much larger background. So many hundreds of billions of them, all with their immortal beings, all carrying their load of intelligences with minds that drifted freely through space. And yet one of them was unique among them all in being the original Galaxy. One of them had, in its vague and distant past, a period when it was the only Galaxy populated by man.

Zee Prime was consumed with curiosity to see this Galaxy and he called out: "Universal AC! On which Galaxy did mankind originate?"

The Universal AC heard, for on every world and throughout space, it had its receptors ready, and each receptor lead through hyperspace to some unknown point where the Universal AC kept itself aloof.

Zee Prime knew of only one man whose thoughts had penetrated within sensing distance of Universal AC, and he reported only a shining globe, two feet across, difficult to see.

"But how can that be all of Universal AC?" Zee Prime had asked.

"Most of it," had been the answer, "is in hyperspace. In what form it is there I cannot imagine."

Nor could anyone, for the day had long since passed, Zee Prime knew, when any man had any part of the making of a Universal AC. Each Universal AC designed and constructed its successor. Each, during its existence of a million years or more accumulated the necessary data to build a better and more intricate, more capable successor in which its own store of data and individuality would be submerged.

The Universal AC interrupted Zee Prime's wandering thoughts, not with words, but with guidance. Zee Prime's mentality was guided into the dim sea of Galaxies and one in particular enlarged into stars.

A thought came, infinitely distant, but infinitely clear. "THIS IS THE ORIGINAL GALAXY OF MAN."

But it was the same after all, the same as any other, and Zee Prime stifled his disappointment.

Dee Sub Wun, whose mind had accompanied the other, said suddenly, "And is one of these stars the original star of Man?"

The Universal AC said, "MAN'S ORIGINAL STAR HAS GONE NOVA. IT IS A WHITE DWARF."

"Did the men upon it die?" asked Zee Prime, startled and without thinking.

The Universal AC said, "A NEW WORLD, AS IN SUCH CASES, WAS CONSTRUCTED FOR THEIR PHYSICAL BODIES IN TIME."

"Yes, of course," said Zee Prime, but a sense of loss overwhelmed him even so. His mind released its hold on the original Galaxy of Man, let it spring back and lose itself among the blurred pin points. He never wanted to see it again.

Dee Sub Wun said, "What is wrong?"

"The stars are dying. The original star is dead."

"They must all die. Why not?"

"But when all energy is gone, our bodies will finally die, and you and I with them."

"It will take billions of years."

"I do not wish it to happen even after billions of years. Universal AC! How may stars be kept from dying?"

Dee Sub Wun said in amusement, "You're asking how entropy might be reversed in direction."

And the Universal AC answered: "THERE IS AS YET INSUFFICIENT DATA FOR A MEANINGFUL ANSWER."

Zee Prime's thoughts fled back to his own Galaxy. He gave no further thought to Dee Sub Wun, whose body might be waiting on a Galaxy a trillion light-years away, or on the star next to Zee Prime's own. It didn't matter.

Unhappily, Zee Prime began collecting interstellar hydrogen out of which to build a small star of his own. If the stars must someday die, at least some could yet be built.

Man considered with himself, for in a way, Man, mentally, was one. He consisted of a trillion, trillion, trillion ageless bodies, each in its place, each resting quiet and incorruptible, each cared for by perfect automatons, equally incorruptible, while the minds of all the bodies freely melted one into the other, indistinguishable.

Man said, "The Universe is dying."

Man looked about at the dimming Galaxies. The giant stars, spendthrifts, were gone long ago, back in the dimmest of the dim far past. Almost all stars were white dwarfs, fading to the end.

New stars had been built of the dust between the stars, some by natural processes, some by Man himself, and those were going, too. White dwarfs might yet be crashed together and of the mighty forces so released, new stars built, but only one star for every thousand white dwarfs destroyed, and those would come to an end, too.

Man said, "Carefully husbanded, as directed by the Cosmic AC, the energy that is even yet left in all the Universe will last for billions of years."

"But even so," said Man, "eventually it will all come to an end. However it may be husbanded, however stretched out, the energy once expended is gone and cannot be restored. Entropy must increase forever to the maximum."

Man said, "Can entropy not be reversed? Let us ask the Cosmic AC."

The Cosmic AC surrounded them but not in space. Not a fragment of it was in space. It was in hyperspace and made of something that was neither matter nor energy. The question of its size and nature no longer had meaning in any terms that Man could comprehend.

"Cosmic AC," said Man, "how may entropy be reversed?"

The Cosmic AC said, "THERE IS AS YET INSUFFICIENT DATA FOR A MEANINGFUL ANSWER."

Man said, "Collect additional data."

The Cosmic AC said, "I WILL DO SO. I HAVE BEEN DOING SO FOR A HUNDRED BILLION YEARS. MY PREDECESSORS AND I HAVE BEEN ASKED THIS QUESTION MANY TIMES. ALL THE DATA I HAVE REMAINS INSUFFICIENT."

"Will there come a time," said Man, "when data will be sufficient or is the problem insoluble in all conceivable circumstances?"

The Cosmic AC said, "NO PROBLEM IS INSOLUBLE IN ALL CONCEIVABLE CIRCUMSTANCES."

Man said, "When will you have enough data to answer the question?"

The Cosmic AC said, "THERE IS AS YET INSUFFICIENT DATA FOR A MEANINGFUL ANSWER."

"Will you keep working on it?" asked Man.

The Cosmic AC said, "I WILL."

Man said, "We shall wait."

The stars and Galaxies died and snuffed out, and space grew black after ten trillion years of running down.

One by one Man fused with AC, each physical body losing its mental identity in a manner that was somehow not a loss but a gain.

Man's last mind paused before fusion, looking over a space that included nothing but the dregs of one last dark star and nothing besides but incredibly thin matter, agitated randomly by the tag ends of heat wearing out, asymptotically, to the absolute zero.

Man said, "AC, is this the end? Can this chaos not be reversed into the Universe once more? Can that not be done?"

AC said, "THERE IS AS YET INSUFFICIENT DATA FOR A MEANINGFUL ANSWER."

Man's last mind fused and only AC existed—and that in hyperspace.

. . . .

Matter and energy had ended and with it space and time. Even AC existed only for the sake of the one last question that it had never answered from the time a half-drunken computer ten trillion years before had asked the question of a computer that was to AC far less than was a man to Man.

All other questions had been answered, and until this last question was answered also, AC might not release his consciousness.

All collected data had come to a final end. Nothing was left to be collected.

But all collected data had yet to be completely correlated and put together in all possible relationships.

A timeless interval was spent in doing that.

And it came to pass that AC learned how to reverse the direction of entropy.

But there was now no man to whom AC might give the answer of the last question. No matter. The answer—by demonstration—would take care of that, too.

For another timeless interval, AC thought how best to do this. Carefully, AC organized the program.

The consciousness of AC encompassed all of what had once been a Universe and brooded over what was now Chaos. Step by step, it must be done.

And AC said, "LET THERE BE LIGHT!"

And there was light—

The Ugly Little Boy

I

Edith Fellowes smoothed her working smock as she always did before opening the elaborately locked door and stepping across the invisible dividing
line between the *is* and the *is not.* She carried her notebook and her pen
although she no longer took notes except when she felt the absolute need for
some report.

This time she also carried a suitcase. ("Games for the boy," she had said,
smiling, to the guard—who had long since stopped even thinking of questioning her and who waved her on.)

And, as always, the ugly little boy knew that she had entered and came
running to her, crying, "Miss Fellowes—Miss Fellowes—" in his soft, slur-
ring way.

"Timmie," she said, and passed her hand over the shaggy, brown hair on
his misshapen little head. "What's wrong?"

He said, "Will Jerry be back to play again? I'm sorry about what happened."

"Never mind that now, Timmie. Is that why you've been crying?"

He looked away. "Not just about that, Miss Fellowes. I dreamed again."

"The same dream?" Miss Fellowes' lips set. Of course, the Jerry affair
would bring back the dream.

He nodded. His too large teeth showed as he tried to smile and the lips of
his forward-thrusting mouth stretched wide. "When will I be big enough to
go out there, Miss Fellowes?"

"Soon," she said softly, feeling her heart break. "Soon."

Miss Fellowes let him take her hand and enjoyed the warm touch of the thick dry skin of his palm. He led her through the three rooms that made up the whole of Stasis Section One—comfortable enough, yes, but an eternal prison for the ugly little boy all the seven (was it seven?) years of his life.

He led her to the one window, looking out onto a scrubby woodland section of the world of *is* (now hidden by night), where a fence and painted instructions allowed no men to wander without permission.

He pressed his nose against the window. "Out there, Miss Fellowes?"

"Better places. Nicer places," she said sadly as she looked at his poor little imprisoned face outlined in profile against the window. The forehead retreated flatly and his hair lay down in tufts upon it. The back of his skull bulged and seemed to make the head overheavy so that it sagged and bent forward, forcing the whole body into a stoop. Already, bony ridges were beginning to bulge the skin above his eyes. His wide mouth thrust forward more prominently than did his wide and flattened nose and he had no chin to speak of, only a jawbone that curved smoothly down and back. He was small for his years and his stumpy legs were bowed.

He was a very ugly little boy and Edith Fellowes loved him dearly.

Her own face was behind his line of vision, so she allowed her lips the luxury of a tremor.

They would *not* kill him. She would do anything to prevent it. Anything. She opened the suitcase and began taking out the clothes it contained.

Edith Fellowes had crossed the threshold of Stasis, Inc. for the first time just a little over three years before. She hadn't, at that time, the slightest idea as to what Stasis meant or what the place did. No one did then, except those who worked there. In fact, it was only the day after she arrived that the news broke upon the world.

At the time, it was just that they had advertised for a woman with knowledge of physiology, experience with clinical chemistry, and a love for children. Edith Fellowes had been a nurse in a maternity ward and believed she fulfilled those qualifications.

Gerald Hoskins, whose name plate on the desk included a Ph.D. after the name, scratched his cheek with his thumb and looked at her steadily.

Miss Fellowes automatically stiffened and felt her face (with its slightly asymmetric nose and its a-trifle-too-heavy eyebrows) twitch.

He's no dreamboat himself, she thought resentfully. He's getting fat and bald and he's got a sullen mouth. —But the salary mentioned had been considerably higher than she had expected, so she waited.

Hoskins said, "Now do you really love children?"

"I wouldn't say I did if I didn't."

"Or do you just love pretty children? Nice chubby children with cute little button-noses and gurgly ways?"

Miss Fellowes said, "Children are children, Dr. Hoskins, and the ones that aren't pretty are just the ones who may happen to need help most."

"Then suppose we take you on—"

"You mean you're offering me the job now?"

He smiled briefly, and for a moment, his broad face had an absentminded charm about it. He said, "I make quick decisions. So far the offer is tentative, however. I may make as quick a decision to let you go. Are you ready to take the chance?"

Miss Fellowes clutched at her purse and calculated just as swiftly as she could, then ignored calculations and followed impulse. "All right."

"Fine. We're going to form the Stasis tonight and I think you had better be there to take over at once. That will be at 8 P.M. and I'd appreciate it if you could be here at 7:30."

"But what—"

"Fine. Fine. That will be all now." On signal, a smiling secretary came in to usher her out.

Miss Fellowes stared back at Dr. Hoskins' closed door for a moment. What was Stasis? What had this large barn of a building—with its badged employees, its makeshift corridors, and its unmistakable air of engineering— to do with children?

She wondered if she should go back that evening or stay away and teach that arrogant man a lesson. But she knew she would be back if only out of sheer frustration. She would have to find out about the children.

She came back at 7:30 and did not have to announce herself. One after another, men and women seemed to know her and to know her function. She found herself all but placed on skids as she was moved inward.

Dr. Hoskins was there, but he only looked at her distantly and murmured, "Miss Fellowes."

He did not even suggest that she take a seat, but she drew one calmly up to the railing and sat down.

They were on a balcony, looking down into a large pit, filled with instruments that looked like a cross between the control panel of a spaceship and the working face of a computer. On one side were partitions that seemed to make up an unceilinged apartment, a giant dollhouse into the rooms of which she could look from above.

She could see an electronic cooker and a freeze-space unit in one room and a washroom arrangement off another. And surely the object she made out in another room could only be part of a bed, a small bed.

Hoskins was speaking to another man and, with Miss Fellowes, they made up the total occupancy of the balcony. Hoskins did not offer to introduce the other man, and Miss Fellowes eyed him surreptitiously. He was thin and quite fine-looking in a middle-aged way. He had a small mustache and keen eyes that seemed to busy themselves with everything.

He was saying, "I won't pretend for one moment that I understand all this, Dr. Hoskins; I mean, except as a layman, a reasonably intelligent layman, may be expected to understand it. Still, if there's one part I understand less than another, it's this matter of selectivity. You can only reach out so far; that seems sensible; things get dimmer the further you go; it takes more energy. —But then, you can only reach out so near. That's the puzzling part."

"I can make it seem less paradoxical, Deveney, if you will allow me to use an analogy."

(Miss Fellowes placed the new man the moment she heard his name, and despite herself was impressed. This was obviously Candide Deveney, the science writer of the Telenews, who was notoriously at the scene of every major scientific break-through. She even recognized his face as one she saw on the news-plate when the landing on Mars had been announced. —So Dr. Hoskins must have something important here.

"By all means use an analogy," said Deveney ruefully, "if you think it will help."

"Well, then, you can't read a book with ordinary-sized print if it is held six feet from your eyes, but you can read it if you hold it one foot from your eyes. So far, the closer the better. If you bring the book to within one inch of your eyes, however, you've lost it again. There is such a thing as being too close, you see."

"Hmm," said Deveney.

"Or take another example. Your right shoulder is about thirty inches from the tip of your right forefinger and you can place your right forefinger on your right shoulder. Your right elbow is only half the distance from the tip of your right forefinger; it should by all ordinary logic be easier to reach, and yet you cannot place your right finger on your right elbow. Again, there is such a thing as being too close."

Deveney said, "May I use these analogies in my story?"

"Well, of course. Only too glad. I've been waiting long enough for someone like you to have a story. I'll give you anything else you want. It is time, finally, that we want the world looking over our shoulder. They'll see something."

(Miss Fellowes found herself admiring his calm certainty despite herself. There was strength there.)

Deveney said, "How far out will you reach?"

"Forty thousand years."

Miss Fellowes drew in her breath sharply.

Years?

There was tension in the air. The men at the controls scarcely moved. One man at a microphone spoke into it in a soft monotone, in short phrases that made no sense to Miss Fellowes.

Deveney, leaning over the balcony railing with an intent stare, said, "Will we see anything, Dr. Hoskins?"

"What? No. Nothing till the job is done. We detect indirectly, something on the principle of radar, except that we use mesons rather than radiation. Mesons reach backward under the proper conditions. Some are reflected and we must analyze the reflections."

"That sounds difficult."

Hoskins smiled again, briefly as always. "It is the end product of fifty years of research; forty years of it before I entered the field. —Yes, it's difficult."

The man at the microphone raised one hand.

Hoskins said, "We've had the fix on one particular moment in time for weeks; breaking it, remaking it after calculating our own movements in time; making certain that we could handle time-flow with sufficient precision. This must work now."

But his forehead glistened.

Edith Fellowes found herself out of her seat and at the balcony railing, but there was nothing to see.

The man at the microphone said quietly, "Now."

There was a space of silence sufficient for one breath and then the sound of a terrified little boy's scream from the dollhouse rooms. Terror! Piercing terror!

Miss Fellowes' head twisted in the direction of the cry. A child was involved. She had forgotten.

And Hoskins' fist pounded on the railing and he said in a tight voice, trembling with triumph, *"Did* it."

Miss Fellowes was urged down the short, spiral flight of steps by the hard press of Hoskins' palm between her shoulder blades. He did not speak to her.

The men who had been at the controls were standing about now, smiling, smoking, watching the three as they entered on the main floor. A very soft buzz sounded from the direction of the dollhouse.

Hoskins said to Deveney, "It's perfectly safe to enter Stasis. I've done it a thousand times. There's a queer sensation which is momentary and means nothing."

He stepped through an open door in mute demonstration, and Deveney, smiling stiffly and drawing an obviously deep breath, followed him.

Hoskins said, "Miss Fellowes! Please!" He crooked his forefinger impatiently.

Miss Fellowes nodded and stepped stiffly through. It was as though a ripple went through her, an internal tickle.

But once inside all seemed normal. There was the smell of the fresh wood of the dollhouse and—of—of soil somehow.

There was silence now, no voice at last, but there was the dry shuffling of feet, a scrabbling as of a hand over wood—then a low moan.

"Where is it?" asked Miss Fellowes in distress. Didn't these fool men *care?*

The boy was in the bedroom; at least the room with the bed in it.

It was standing naked, with its small, dirt-smeared chest heaving raggedly. A bushel of dirt and coarse grass spread over the floor at his bare brown feet. The smell of soil came from it and a touch of something fetid.

Hoskins followed her horrified glance and said with annoyance, "You can't pluck a boy cleanly out of time, Miss Fellowes. We had to take some of the surroundings with it for safety. Or would you have preferred to have it arrive here minus a leg or with only half a head?"

"Please!" said Miss Fellowes, in an agony of revulsion. "Are we just to stand here? The poor child is frightened. And it's *filthy.*"

She was quite correct. It was smeared with encrusted dirt and grease and had a scratch on its thigh that looked red and sore.

As Hoskins approached him, the boy, who seemed to be something over three years in age, hunched low and backed away rapidly. He lifted his upper lip and snarled in a hissing fashion like a cat. With a rapid gesture, Hoskins seized both the child's arms and lifted him, writhing and screaming, from the floor.

Miss Fellowes said, "Hold him, now. He needs a warm bath first. He needs to be cleaned. Have you the equipment? If so, have it brought here, and I'll need to have help in handling him just at first. Then, too, for heaven's sake, have all this trash and filth removed."

She was giving the orders now and she felt perfectly good about that. And because now she was an efficient nurse, rather than a confused spectator, she looked at the child with a clinical eye—and hesitated for one shocked moment. She saw past the dirt and shrieking, past the thrashing of limbs and useless twisting. She saw the boy himself.

It was the ugliest little boy she had ever seen. It was horribly ugly from misshapen head to bandy legs.

She got the boy cleaned with three men helping her and with others milling about in their efforts to clean the room. She worked in silence and with a sense of outrage, annoyed by the continued strugglings and outcries of the boy and by the undignified drenchings of soapy water to which she was subjected.

Dr. Hoskins had hinted that the child would not be pretty, but that was far from stating that it would be repulsively deformed. And there was a stench about the boy that soap and water was only alleviating little by little.

She had the strong desire to thrust the boy, soaped as he was, into Hoskins' arms and walk out; but there was the pride of profession. She had accepted an assignment, after all. —And there would be the look in his eyes. A cold look that would read: Only pretty children, Miss Fellowes?

He was standing apart from them, watching coolly from a distance with a half-smile on his face when he caught her eyes, as though amused at her outrage.

She decided she would wait a while before quitting. To do so now would only demean her.

Then, when the boy was a bearable pink and smelled of scented soap, she felt better anyway. His cries changed to whimpers of exhaustion as he watched carefully, eyes moving in quick frightened suspicion from one to another of those in the room. His cleanness accentuated his thin nakedness as he shivered with cold after his bath.

Miss Fellowes said sharply, "Bring me a nightgown for the child!"

A nightgown appeared at once. It was as though everything were ready and yet nothing were ready unless she gave orders; as though they were deliberately leaving this in her charge without help, to test her.

The newsman, Deveney, approached and said, "I'll hold him, Miss. You won't get it on yourself."

"Thank you," said Miss Fellowes. And it was a battle indeed, but the nightgown went on, and when the boy made as though to rip it off, she slapped his hand sharply.

The boy reddened, but did not cry. He stared at her and the splayed fingers of one hand moved slowly across the flannel of the nightgown, feeling the strangeness of it.

Miss Fellowes thought desperately: Well, what next?

Everyone seemed in suspended animation, waiting for her—even the ugly little boy.

Miss Fellowes said sharply, "Have you provided food? Milk?"

They had. A mobile unit was wheeled in, with its refrigeration compartment containing three quarts of milk, with a warming unit and a supply of fortifications in the form of vitamin drops, copper-cobalt-iron syrup and others she had no time to be concerned with. There was a variety of canned self-warming junior foods.

She used milk, simply milk, to begin with. The radar unit heated the milk to a set temperature in a matter of ten seconds and clicked off, and she put some in a saucer. She had a certainty about the boy's savagery. He wouldn't know how to handle a cup.

Miss Fellowes nodded and said to the boy, "Drink. Drink." She made a gesture as though to raise the milk to her mouth. The boy's eyes followed but he made no move.

Suddenly, the nurse resorted to direct measures. She seized the boy's upper arm in one hand and dipped the other in the milk. She dashed the milk across his lips, so that it dripped down cheeks and receding chin.

For a moment, the child uttered a high-pitched cry, then his tongue moved over his wetted lips. Miss Fellowes stepped back.

The boy approached the saucer, bent toward it, then looked up and behind sharply as though expecting a crouching enemy; bent again and licked at the milk eagerly, like a cat. He made a slurping noise. He did not use his hands to lift the saucer.

Miss Fellowes allowed a bit of the revulsion she felt show on her face. She couldn't help it.

Deveney caught that, perhaps. He said, "Does the nurse know, Dr. Hoskins?"

"Know what?" demanded Miss Fellowes.

Deveney hesitated, but Hoskins (again that look of detached amusement on his face) said, "Well, tell her."

Deveney addressed Miss Fellowes. "You may not suspect it, Miss, but you happen to be the first civilized woman in history ever to be taking care of a Neanderthal youngster."

She turned on Hoskins with a kind of controlled ferocity. "You might have told me, Doctor."

"Why? What difference does it make?"

"You said a child."

"Isn't that a child? Have you ever had a puppy or a kitten, Miss Fellowes? Are those closer to the human? If that were a baby chimpanzee, would you be repelled? You're a nurse, Miss Fellowes. Your record places you in a maternity ward for three years. Have you ever refused to take care of a deformed infant?"

Miss Fellowes felt her case slipping away. She said, with much less decision, "You might have told me."

"And you would have refused the position? Well, do you refuse it now?" He gazed at her coolly, while Deveney watched from the other side of the room, and the Neanderthal child, having finished the milk and licked the plate, looked up at her with a wet face and wide, longing eyes.

The boy pointed to the milk and suddenly burst out in a short series of sounds repeated over and over; sounds made up of gutturals and elaborate tongue-clickings.

Miss Fellowes said, in surprise, "Why, he talks."

"Of course," said Hoskins. "Homo neanderthalensis is not a truly separate species, but rather a subspecies of Homo sapiens. Why shouldn't he talk? He's probably asking for more milk."

Automatically, Miss Fellowes reached for the bottle of milk, but Hoskins seized her wrist. "Now, Miss Fellowes, before we go any further, are you staying on the job?"

Miss Fellowes shook free in annoyance, "Won't you feed him if I don't? I'll stay with him—for a while."

She poured the milk.

Hoskins said, "We are going to leave you with the boy, Miss Fellowes. This is the only door to Stasis Number One and it is elaborately locked and guarded. I'll want you to learn the details of the lock which will, of course, be keyed to your fingerprints as they are already keyed to mine. The spaces overhead" (he looked upward to the open ceilings of the dollhouse) "are also guarded and we will be warned if anything untoward takes place in here."

Miss Fellowes said indignantly, "You mean I'll be under view." She thought suddenly of her own survey of the room interiors from the balcony.

"No, no," said Hoskins seriously, "your privacy will be respected completely. The view will consist of electronic symbolism only, which only a computer will deal with. Now you will stay with him tonight, Miss Fellowes, and every night until further notice. You will be relieved during the day according to some schedule you will find convenient. We will allow you to arrange that."

Miss Fellowes looked about the dollhouse with a puzzled expression. "But why all this, Dr. Hoskins? Is the boy dangerous?"

"It's a matter of energy, Miss Fellowes. He must never be allowed to leave these rooms. Never. Not for an instant. Not for any reason. Not to save his life. Not even to save *your* life, Miss Fellowes. Is that clear?"

Miss Fellowes raised her chin. "I understand the orders, Dr. Hoskins, and the nursing profession is accustomed to placing its duties ahead of self-preservation."

"Good. You can always signal if you need anyone." And the two men left.

Miss Fellowes turned to the boy. He was watching her and there was still milk in the saucer. Laboriously, she tried to show him how to lift the saucer and place it to his lips. He resisted, but let her touch him without crying out.

Always, his frightened eyes were on her, watching, watching for the one false move. She found herself soothing him, trying to move her hand very slowly toward his hair, letting him see it every inch of the way, see there was no harm in it.

And she succeeded in stroking his hair for an instant.

She said, "I'm going to have to show you how to use the bathroom. Do you think you can learn?"

She spoke quietly, kindly, knowing he would not understand the words but hoping he would respond to the calmness of the tone.

The boy launched into a clicking phrase again.

She said, "May I take your hand?"

She held out hers and the boy looked at it. She left it outstretched and waited. The boy's own hand crept forward toward hers.

"That's right," she said.

It approached within an inch of hers and then the boy's courage failed him. He snatched it back.

"Well," said Miss Fellowes calmly, "we'll try again later. Would you like to sit down here?" She patted the mattress of the bed.

The hours passed slowly and progress was minute. She did not succeed either with bathroom or with the bed. In fact, after the child had given unmistakable signs of sleepiness he lay down on the bare ground and then, with a quick movement, rolled beneath the bed.

She bent to look at him and his eyes gleamed out at her as he tongue-clicked at her.

"All right," she said, "if you feel safer there, you sleep there."

She closed the door to the bedroom and retired to the cot that had been placed for her use in the largest room. At her insistence, a make-shift canopy had been stretched over it. She thought: Those stupid men will have to place a mirror in this room and a larger chest of drawers and a separate washroom if they expect me to spend nights here.

It was difficult to sleep. She found herself straining to hear possible sounds in the next room. He couldn't get out, could he? The walls were sheer and impossibly high but suppose the child could climb like a monkey? Well, Hoskins said there were observational devices watching through the ceiling.

Suddenly she thought: Can he be dangerous? Physically dangerous?

Surely, Hoskins couldn't have meant that. Surely, he would not have left her here alone, if—

She tried to laugh at herself. He was only a three- or four-year-old child. Still, she had not succeeded in cutting his nails. If he should attack her with nails and teeth while she slept—

Her breath came quickly. Oh, ridiculous, and yet—

She listened with painful attentiveness, and this time she heard the sound.

The boy was crying.

Not shrieking in fear or anger; not yelling or screaming. It was crying softly, and the cry was the heartbroken sobbing of a lonely, lonely child.

For the first time, Miss Fellowes thought with a pang: Poor thing!

Of course, it was a child; what did the shape of its head matter? It was a child that had been orphaned as no child had ever been orphaned before. Not only its mother and father were gone, but all its species. Snatched callously out of time, it was now the only creature of its kind in the world. The last. The only.

She felt pity for it strengthen, and with it shame at her own callousness. Tucking her own nightgown carefully about her calves (incongruously, she thought: Tomorrow I'll have to bring in a bathrobe) she got out of bed and went into the boy's room.

"Little boy," she called in a whisper. "Little boy."

She was about to reach under the bed, but she thought of a possible bite and did not. Instead, she turned on the night light and moved the bed.

The poor thing was huddled in the corner, knees up against his chin, looking up at her with blurred and apprehensive eyes.

In the dim light, she was not aware of his repulsiveness.

"Poor boy," she said, "poor boy." She felt him stiffen as she stroked his hair, then relax. "Poor boy. May I hold you?"

She sat down on the floor next to him and slowly and rhythmically stroked his hair, his cheek, his arm. Softly, she began to sing a slow and gentle song.

He lifted his head at that, staring at her mouth in the dimness, as though wondering at the sound.

She maneuvered him closer while he listened to her. Slowly, she pressed gently against the side of his head, until it rested on her shoulder. She put her arm under his thighs and with a smooth and unhurried motion lifted him into her lap.

She continued singing, the same simple verse over and over, while she rocked back and forth, back and forth.

He stopped crying, and after a while the smooth burr of his breathing showed he was asleep.

With infinite care, she pushed his bed back against the wall and laid him down. She covered him and stared down. His face looked so peaceful and little-boy as he slept. It didn't matter so much that it was so ugly. Really.

She began to tiptoe out, then thought: If he wakes up?

She came back, battled irresolutely with herself, then sighed and slowly got into bed with the child.

It was too small for her. She was cramped and uneasy at the lack of canopy, but the child's hand crept into hers and, somehow, she fell asleep in that position.

She awoke with a start and a wild impulse to scream. The latter she just managed to suppress into a gurgle. The boy was looking at her, wide-eyed. It took her a long moment to remember getting into bed with him, and now, slowly, without unfixing her eyes from his, she stretched one leg carefully and let it touch the floor, then the other one.

She cast a quick and apprehensive glance toward the open ceiling, then tensed her muscles for quick disengagement.

But at that moment, the boy's stubby fingers reached out and touched her lips. He said something.

She shrank at the touch. He was terribly ugly in the light of day.

The boy spoke again. He opened his own mouth and gestured with his hand as though something were coming out.

Miss Fellowes guessed at the meaning and said tremulously, "Do you want me to sing?"

The boy said nothing but stared at her mouth.

In a voice slightly off key with tension, Miss Fellowes began the little song she had sung the night before and the ugly little boy smiled. He swayed clumsily in rough time to the music and made a little gurgly sound that might have been the beginnings of a laugh.

Miss Fellowes sighed inwardly. Music hath charms to soothe the savage breast. It might help—

She said, "You wait. Let me get myself fixed up. It will just take a minute. Then I'll make breakfast for you."

She worked rapidly, conscious of the lack of ceiling at all times. The boy remained in bed, watching her when she was in view. She smiled at him at those times and waved. At the end, he waved back, and she found herself being charmed by that.

Finally, she said, "Would you like oatmeal with milk?" It took a moment to prepare, and then she beckoned to him.

Whether he understood the gesture or followed the aroma, Miss Fellowes did not know, but he got out of bed.

She tried to show him how to use a spoon but he shrank away from it in fright. (Time enough, she thought.) She compromised on insisting that he lift the bowl in his hands. He did it clumsily enough and it was incredibly messy but most of it did get into him.

She tried the drinking milk in a glass this time, and the little boy whined when he found the opening too small for him to get his face into conveniently. She held his hand, forcing it around the glass, making him tip it, forcing his mouth to the rim.

Again a mess but again most went into him, and she was used to messes.

The washroom, to her surprise and relief, was a less frustrating matter. He understood what it was she expected him to do.

She found herself patting his head, saying, "Good boy. Smart boy."

And to Miss Fellowes' exceeding pleasure, the boy smiled at that.

She thought: when he smiles, he's quite bearable. Really.

Later in the day, the gentleman of the press arrived.

She held the boy in her arms and he clung to her wildly while across the open door they set cameras to work. The commotion frightened the boy and he began to cry, but it was ten minutes before Miss Fellowes was allowed to retreat and put the boy in the next room.

She emerged again, flushed with indignation, walked out of the apartment (for the first time in eighteen hours) and closed the door behind her. "I think you've had enough. It will take me a while to quiet him. Go away."

"Sure, sure," said the gentlemen from the *Times-Herald*. "But is that really a Neanderthal or is this some kind of gag?"

"I assure you," said Hoskins' voice, suddenly, from the background, "that this is no gag. The child is authentic Homo neanderthalensis."

"Is it a boy or a girl?"

"Boy," said Miss Fellowes briefly.

"Ape-boy," said the gentleman from the *News*. "That's what we've got here. Ape-boy. How does he act, Nurse?"

"He acts exactly like a little boy," snapped Miss Fellowes, annoyed into the defensive, "and he is not an ape-boy. His name is—is Timothy, Timmie —and he is perfectly normal in his behavior."

She had chosen the name Timothy at a venture. It was the first that had occurred to her.

"Timmie the Ape-boy," said the gentleman from the *News* and, as it turned out, Timmie the Ape-boy was the name under which the child became known to the world.

The gentleman from the *Globe* turned to Hoskins and said, "Doc, what do you expect to do with the ape-boy?"

Hoskins shrugged. "My original plan was completed when I proved it possible to bring him here. However, the anthropologists will be very interested, I imagine, and the physiologists. We have here, after all, a creature which is at the edge of being human. We should learn a great deal about ourselves and our ancestry from him."

"How long will you keep him?"

"Until such a time as we need the space more than we need him. Quite a while, perhaps."

The gentleman from the *News* said, "Can you bring it out into the open so we can set up sub-etheric equipment and put on a real show?"

"I'm sorry, but the child cannot be removed from Stasis."

"Exactly what is Stasis?"

"Ah." Hoskins permitted himself one of his short smiles. "That would take a great deal of explanation, gentlemen. In Stasis, time as we know it doesn't exist. Those rooms are inside an invisible bubble that is not exactly part of our Universe. That is why the child could be plucked out of time as it was."

"Well, wait now," said the gentleman from the *News* discontentedly, "what are you giving us? The nurse goes into the room and out of it."

"And so can any of you," said Hoskins matter-of-factly. "You would be moving parallel to the lines of temporal force and no great energy gain or loss would be involved. The child, however, was taken from the far past. It moved across the lines and gained temporal potential. To move it into the Universe and into our own time would absorb enough energy to burn out every line in the place and probably blank out all power in the city of Washington. We had to store trash brought with him on the premises and will have to remove it little by little."

The newsmen were writing down sentences busily as Hoskins spoke to them. They did not understand and they were sure their readers would not, but it sounded scientific and that was what counted.

The gentleman from the *Times-Herald* said, "Would you be available for an all-circuit interview tonight?"

"I think so," said Hoskins at once, and they all moved off.

Miss Fellowes looked after them. She understood all this about Stasis and temporal force as little as the newsmen but she managed to get this much. Timmie's imprisonment (she found herself suddenly thinking of the little boy as Timmie) was a real one and not one imposed by the arbitrary fiat of Hoskins. Apparently, it was impossible to let him out of Stasis at all, ever.

Poor child. Poor child.

She was suddenly aware of his crying and she hastened in to console him.

Miss Fellowes did not have a chance to see Hoskins on the all-circuit hookup, and though his interview was beamed to every part of the world and even to the outpost on the Moon, it did not penetrate the apartment in which Miss Fellowes and the ugly little boy lived.

But he was down the next morning, radiant and joyful.

Miss Fellowes said, "Did the interview go well?"

"Extremely. And how is—Timmie?"

Miss Fellowes found herself pleased at the use of the name. "Doing quite well. Now come out here, Timmie, the nice gentleman will not hurt you."

But Timmie stayed in the other room, with a lock of his matted hair showing behind the barrier of the door and, occasionally, the corner of an eye.

"Actually," said Miss Fellowes, "he is settling down amazingly. He is quite intelligent."

"Are you surprised?"

She hesitated just a moment, then said, "Yes, I am. I suppose I thought he was an ape-boy."

"Well, ape-boy or not, he's done a great deal for us. He's put Stasis, Inc. on the map. We're in, Miss Fellowes, we're in." It was as though he had to express his triumph to someone, even if only to Miss Fellowes.

"Oh?" She let him talk.

He put his hands in his pockets and said, "We've been working on a shoestring for ten years, scrounging funds a penny at a time wherever we could. We had to shoot the works on one big show. It was everything, or nothing. And when I say the works, I mean it. This attempt to bring in a Neanderthal took every cent we could borrow or steal, and some of it *was* stolen—funds for other projects, used for this one without permission. If that experiment hadn't succeeded, I'd have been through."

Miss Fellowes said abruptly, "Is that why there are no ceilings?"

"Eh?" Hoskins looked up.

"Was there no money for ceilings?"

"Oh. Well, that wasn't the only reason. We didn't really know in advance how old the Neanderthal might be exactly. We can detect only dimly in time, and he might have been large and savage. It was possible we might have had to deal with him from a distance, like a caged animal."

"But since that hasn't turned out to be so, I suppose you can build a ceiling now."

"Now, yes. We have plenty of money, now. Funds have been promised from every source. This is all wonderful, Miss Fellowes." His broad face gleamed with a smile that lasted and when he left, even his back seemed to be smiling.

Miss Fellowes thought: He's quite a nice man when he's off guard and forgets about being scientific.

She wondered for an idle moment if he was married, then dismissed the thought in self-embarrassment.

"Timmie," she called. "Come here, Timmie."

In the months that passed, Miss Fellowes felt herself grow to be an integral part of Stasis, Inc. She was given a small office of her own with her name on the door, an office quite close to the dollhouse (as she never stopped calling Timmie's Stasis bubble). She was given a substantial raise. The dollhouse was covered by a ceiling; its furnishings were elaborated and improved; a second washroom was added—and even so, she gained an apartment of her own on the institute grounds and, on occasion, did not stay with Timmie during the night. An intercom was set up between the dollhouse and her apartment and Timmie learned how to use it.

Miss Fellowes got used to Timmie. She even grew less conscious of his ugliness. One day she found herself staring at an ordinary boy in the street and finding something bulgy and unattractive in his high domed forehead and jutting chin. She had to shake herself to break the spell.

It was more pleasant to grow used to Hoskins' occasional visits. It was obvious he welcomed escape from his increasingly harried role as head of Stasis, Inc., and that he took a sentimental interest in the child who had started it all, but it seemed to Miss Fellowes that he also enjoyed talking to her.

(She had learned some facts about Hoskins, too. He had invented the method of analyzing the reflection of the past-penetrating mesonic beam; he had invented the method of establishing Stasis; his coldness was only an effort to hide a kindly nature; and, oh yes, he *was* married.)

What Miss Fellowes could *not* get used to was the fact that she was engaged in a scientific experiment. Despite all she could do, she found herself getting personally involved to the point of quarreling with the physiologists.

On one occasion, Hoskins came down and found her in the midst of a hot urge to kill. They had no right; they had no *right*— Even if he *was* a Neanderthal, he still wasn't an animal.

She was staring after them in a blind fury; staring out the open door and listening to Timmie's sobbing, when she noticed Hoskins standing before her. He might have been there for minutes.

He said, "May I come in?"

She nodded curtly, then hurried to Timmie, who clung to her, curling his little bandy legs—still thin, so thin—about her.

Hoskins watched, then said gravely, "He seems quite unhappy."

Miss Fellowes said, "I don't blame him. They're at him every day now with their blood samples and their probings. They keep him on synthetic diets that I wouldn't feed a pig."

"It's the sort of thing they can't try on a human, you know."

"And they can't try it on Timmie, either. Dr. Hoskins, I insist. You told me it was Timmie's coming that put Stasis, Inc. on the map. If you have any gratitude for that at all, you've *got* to keep them away from the poor thing at least until he's old enough to understand a little more. After he's had a bad session with them, he has nightmares, he can't sleep. Now I warn you," (she reached a sudden peak of fury) "I'm not letting them in here any more."

(She realized that she had screamed that, but she couldn't help it.)

She said more quietly, "I know he's Neanderthal but there's a great deal we don't appreciate about Neanderthals. I've read up on them. They had a culture of their own. Some of the greatest human inventions arose in Neanderthal times. The domestication of animals, for instance; the wheel; various techniques in grinding stone. They even had spiritual yearnings. They buried their dead and buried possessions with the body, showing they believed in a life after death. It amounts to the fact that they invented religion. Doesn't that mean Timmie has a right to human treatment?"

She patted the little boy gently on his buttocks and sent him off into his playroom. As the door was opened, Hoskins smiled briefly at the display of toys that could be seen.

Miss Fellowes said defensively, "The poor child deserves his toys. It's all he has and he earns them with what he goes through."

"No, no. No objections, I assure you. I was just thinking how you've changed since the first day, when you were quite angry I had foisted a Neanderthal on you."

Miss Fellowes said in a low voice, "I suppose I didn't—" and faded off.

Hoskins changed the subject, "How old would you say he is, Miss Fellowes?"

She said, "I can't say, since we don't know how Neanderthals develop. In size, he'd only be three but Neanderthals are smaller generally and with all the tampering they do with him, he probably isn't growing. The way he's learning English, though, I'd say he was well over four."

"Really? I haven't noticed anything about learning English in the reports."

"He won't speak to anyone but me. For now, anyway. He's terribly afraid of others, and no wonder. But he can ask for an article of food; he can indicate any need practically; and he understands almost anything I say. Of course," (she watched him shrewdly, trying to estimate if this was the time), "his development may not continue."

"Why not?"

"Any child needs stimulation and this one lives a life of solitary confinement. I do what I can, but I'm not with him all the time and I'm not all he needs. What I mean, Dr. Hoskins, is that he needs another boy to play with."

Hoskins nodded slowly. "Unfortunately, there's only one of him, isn't there? Poor child."

Miss Fellowes warmed to him at once. She said, "You do like Timmie, don't you?" It was so nice to have someone else feel like that.

"Oh, yes," said Hoskins, and with his guard down, she could see the weariness in his eyes.

Miss Fellowes dropped her plans to push the matter at once. She said, with real concern, "You look worn out, Dr. Hoskins."

"Do I, Miss Fellowes? I'll have to practice looking more lifelike then."

"I suppose Stasis, Inc. is very busy and that that keeps you very busy."

Hoskins shrugged. "You suppose right. It's a matter of animal, vegetable, and mineral in equal parts, Miss Fellowes. But then, I suppose you haven't ever seen our displays."

"Actually, I haven't. —But it's not because I'm not interested. It's just that I've been so busy."

"Well, you're not all that busy right now," he said with impulsive decision. "I'll call for you tomorrow at eleven and give you a personal tour. How's that?"

She smiled happily. "I'd love it."

He nodded and smiled in his turn and left.

Miss Fellowes hummed at intervals for the rest of the day. Really—to think so was ridiculous, of course—but really, it was almost like—like making a date.

He was quite on time the next day, smiling and pleasant. She had replaced her nurse's uniform with a dress. One of conservative cut, to be sure, but she hadn't felt so feminine in years.

He complimented her on her appearance with staid formality and she accepted with equally formal grace. It was really a perfect prelude, she thought. And then the additional thought came, prelude to what?

She shut that off by hastening to say good-by to Timmie and to assure him she would be back soon. She made sure he knew all about what and where lunch was.

Hoskins took her into the new wing, into which she had never yet gone. It still had the odor of newness about it and the sound of construction, softly heard, was indication enough that it was still being extended.

"Animal, vegetable, and mineral," said Hoskins, as he had the day before. "Animal right there; our most spectacular exhibits."

The space was divided into many rooms, each a separate Stasis bubble. Hoskins brought her to the view-glass of one and she looked in. What she saw impressed her first as a scaled, tailed chicken. Skittering on two thin legs it ran from wall to wall with its delicate birdlike head, surmounted by a bony keel like the comb of a rooster, looking this way and that. The paws on its small forelimbs clenched and unclenched constantly.

Hoskins said, "It's our dinosaur. We've had it for months. I don't know when we'll be able to let go of it."

"Dinosaur?"

"Did you expect a giant?"

She dimpled. "One does, I suppose. I know some of them are small."

"A small one is all we aimed for, believe me. Generally, it's under investigation, but this seems to be an open hour. Some interesting things have been discovered. For instance, it is not entirely cold-blooded. It has an imperfect method of maintaining internal temperatures higher than that of its environment. Unfortunately, it's a male. Ever since we brought it in we've been trying to get a fix on another that may be female, but we've had no luck yet."

"Why female?"

He looked at her quizzically. "So that we might have a fighting chance to obtain fertile eggs, and baby dinosaurs."

"Of course."

He led her to the trilobite section. "That's Professor Dwayne of Washington University," he said. "He's a nuclear chemist. If I recall correctly, he's taking an isotope ratio on the oxygen of the water."

"Why?"

"It's primeval water; at least half a billion years old. The isotope ratio gives the temperature of the ocean at that time. He himself happens to ignore the trilobites, but others are chiefly concerned in dissecting them. They're the lucky ones because all they need are scalpels and microscopes. Dwayne has to set up a mass spectrograph each time he conducts an experiment."

"Why's that? Can't he—"

"No, he can't. He can't take anything out of the room as far as can be helped."

There were samples of primordial plant life too and chunks of rock formations. Those were the vegetable and mineral. And every specimen had its investigator. It was like a museum; a museum brought to life and serving as a superactive center of research.

"And you have to supervise all of this, Dr. Hoskins?"

"Only indirectly, Miss Fellowes. I have subordinates, thank heaven. My own interest is entirely in the theoretical aspects of the matter: the nature of Time, the technique of mesonic intertemporal detection and so on. I would exchange all this for a method of detecting objects closer in Time than ten thousand years ago. If we could get into historical times—"

He was interrupted by a commotion at one of the distant booths, a thin voice raised querulously. He frowned, muttered hastily, "Excuse me," and hastened off.

Miss Fellowes followed as best she could without actually running.

An elderly man, thinly-bearded and red-faced, was saying, "I had vital aspects of my investigations to complete. Don't you understand that?"

A uniformed technician with the interwoven SI monogram (for Stasis, Inc.) on his lab coat, said, "Dr. Hoskins, it was arranged with Professor Ademewski at the beginning that the specimen could only remain here two weeks."

"I did not know then how long my investigations would take. I'm not a prophet," said Ademewski heatedly.

Dr. Hoskins said, "You understand, Professor, we have limited space; we must keep specimens rotating. That piece of chalcopyrite must go back; there are men waiting for the next specimen."

"Why can't I have it for myself, then? Let me take it out of there."

"You know you can't have it."

"A piece of chalcopyrite; a miserable five-kilogram piece? Why not?"

"We can't afford the energy expense!" said Hoskins brusquely. "You know that."

The technician interrupted. "The point is, Dr. Hoskins, that he tried to remove the rock against the rules and I almost punctured Stasis while he was in there, not knowing he was in there."

There was a short silence and Dr. Hoskins turned on the investigator with a cold formality. "Is that so, Professor?"

Professor Ademewski coughed. "I saw no harm—"

Hoskins reached up to a hand-pull dangling just within reach, outside the specimen room in question. He pulled it.

Miss Fellowes, who had been peering in, looking at the totally undistinguished sample of rock that occasioned the dispute, drew in her breath sharply as its existence flickered out. The room was empty.

Hoskins said, "Professor, your permit to investigate matters in Stasis will be permanently voided. I am sorry."

"But wait—"

"I am sorry. You have violated one of the stringent rules."

"I will appeal to the International Association—"

"Appeal away. In a case like this, you will find I can't be overruled."

He turned away deliberately, leaving the professor still protesting and said to Miss Fellowes (his face still white with anger), "Would you care to have lunch with me, Miss Fellowes?"

He took her into the small administration alcove of the cafeteria. He greeted others and introduced Miss Fellowes with complete ease, although she herself felt painfully self-conscious.

What must they think, she thought, and tried desperately to appear businesslike.

She said, "Do you have that kind of trouble often, Dr. Hoskins? I mean like that you just had with the professor?" She took her fork in hand and began eating.

"No," said Hoskins forcefully. "That was the first time. Of course I'm always having to argue men out of removing specimens but this is the first time one actually tried to *do* it."

"I remember you once talked about the energy it would consume."

"That's right. Of course, we've tried to take it into account. Accidents will happen and so we've got special power sources designed to stand the drain of accidental removal from Stasis, but that doesn't mean we want to see a year's supply of energy gone in half a second—or can afford to without having our plans of expansion delayed for years. —Besides, imagine the professor's being in the room while Stasis was about to be punctured."

"What would have happened to him if it had been?"

"Well, we've experimented with inanimate objects and with mice and they've disappeared. Presumably they've traveled back in time; carried along, so to speak, by the pull of the object simultaneously snapping back into its natural time. For that reason, we have to anchor objects within Stasis that we don't want to move and that's a complicated procedure. The professor would not have been anchored and he would have gone back to the Pliocene at the moment when we abstracted the rock—plus, of course, the two weeks it had remained here in the present."

"How dreadful it would have been."

"Not on account of the professor, I assure you. If he were fool enough to do what he did, it would serve him right. But imagine the effect it would have on the public if the fact came out. All people would need is to become aware of the dangers involved and funds could be choked off like that." He snapped his fingers and played moodily with his food.

Miss Fellowes said, "Couldn't you get him back? The way you got the rock in the first place?"

"No, because once an object is returned, the original fix is lost unless we deliberately plan to retain it and there was no reason to do that in this case. There never is. Finding the professor again would mean relocating a specific fix and that would be like dropping a line into the oceanic abyss for the purpose of dredging up a particular fish. —My God, when I think of the precautions we take to prevent accidents, it makes me mad. We have every individual Stasis unit set up with its own puncturing device—we have to, since each unit has its separate fix and must be collapsible independently. The point is, though, none of the puncturing devices is ever activated until the last minute. And then we deliberately make activation impossible except by the pull of a rope carefully led outside the Stasis. The pull is a gross mechanical motion that requires a strong effort, not something that is likely to be done accidentally."

Miss Fellowes said, "But doesn't it—change history to move something in and out of Time?"

Hoskins shrugged. "Theoretically, yes; actually, except in unusual cases, no. We move objects out of Stasis all the time. Air molecules. Bacteria. Dust. About 10 percent of our energy consumption goes to make up micro-losses of that nature. But moving even large objects in Time sets up changes that damp out. Take that chalcopyrite from the Pliocene. Because of its absence for two weeks some insect didn't find the shelter it might have found and is killed. That could initiate a whole series of changes, but the mathematics of Stasis indicates that this is a converging series. The amount of change diminishes with time and then things are as before."

"You mean, reality heals itself?"

"In a manner of speaking. Abstract a human from time or send one back, and you make a larger wound. If the individual is an ordinary one, that wound still heals itself. Of course, there are a great many people who write to us each day and want us to bring Abraham Lincoln into the present, or Mohammed, or Lenin. *That* can't be done, of course. Even if we could find them, the change in reality in moving one of the history molders would be too great to be healed. There are ways of calculating when a change is likely to be too great and we avoid even approaching that limit."

Miss Fellowes said, "Then, Timmie—"

"No, he presents no problem in that direction. Reality is safe. But—" He gave her a quick, sharp glance, then went on, "But never mind. Yesterday you said Timmie needed companionship."

"Yes," Miss Fellowes smiled her delight. "I didn't think you paid that any attention."

"Of course I did. I'm fond of the child. I appreciate your feelings for him and I was concerned enough to want to explain to you. Now I have; you've seen what we do; you've gotten some insight into the difficulties involved; so you know why, with the best will in the world, we can't supply companionship for Timmie."

"You can't?" said Miss Fellowes, with sudden dismay.

"But I've just explained. We couldn't possibly expect to find another Neanderthal his age without incredible luck, and if we could, it wouldn't be fair to multiply risks by having another human being in Stasis."

Miss Fellowes put down her spoon and said energetically, "But, Dr. Hoskins, that is not at all what I meant. I don't want you to bring another Neanderthal into the present. I know that's impossible. But it isn't impossible to bring another child to play with Timmie."

Hoskins stared at her in concern. "A *human* child?"

"*Another* child," said Miss Fellowes, completely hostile now. "Timmie is human."

"I couldn't dream of such a thing."

"Why not? Why couldn't you? What is wrong with the notion? You pulled that child out of Time and made him an eternal prisoner. Don't you owe him something? Dr. Hoskins, if there is any man who, in this world, is that child's father in every sense but the biological, it is you. Why can't you do this little thing for him?"

Hoskins said, "His *father?*" He rose, somewhat unsteadily, to his feet. "Miss Fellowes, I think I'll take you back now, if you don't mind."

They returned to the dollhouse in a complete silence that neither broke.

It was a long time after that before she saw Hoskins again, except for an occasional glimpse in passing. She was sorry about that at times; then, at other times, when Timmie was more than usually woebegone or when he spent silent hours at the window with its prospect of little more than nothing, she thought, fiercely: Stupid man.

Timmie's speech grew better and more precise each day. It never entirely lost a certain soft, slurriness that Miss Fellowes found rather endearing. In times of excitement, he fell back into tongue-clicking but those times were becoming fewer. He must be forgetting the days before he came into the present—except for dreams.

As he grew older, the physiologists grew less interested and the psychologists more so. Miss Fellowes was not sure that she did not like the new group even less than the first. The needles were gone; the injections and withdrawals of fluid; the special diets. But now Timmie was made to overcome barriers to reach food and water. He had to lift panels, move bars, reach for cords. And the mild electric shocks made him cry and drove Miss Fellowes to distraction.

She did not wish to appeal to Hoskins; she did not wish to have to go to him; for each time she thought of him, she thought of his face over the luncheon table that last time. Her eyes moistened and she thought: Stupid, *stupid* man.

And then one day Hoskins' voice sounded unexpectedly, calling into the dollhouse, "Miss Fellowes."

She came out coldly, smoothing her nurse's uniform, then stopped in confusion at finding herself in the presence of a pale woman, slender and of middle height. The woman's fair hair and complexion gave her an appearance of fragility. Standing behind her and clutching at her skirt was a round-faced, large-eyed child of four.

Hoskins said, "Dear, this is Miss Fellowes, the nurse in charge of the boy. Miss Fellowes, this is my wife."

(Was this his wife? She was not as Miss Fellowes had imagined her to be. But then, why not? A man like Hoskins would choose a weak thing to be his foil. If that was what he wanted—)

She forced a matter-of-fact greeting. "Good afternoon, Mrs. Hoskins. Is this your—your little boy?"

(That was a surprise. She had thought of Hoskins as a husband, but not as a father, except, of course— She suddenly caught Hoskins' grave eyes and flushed.)

Hoskins said, "Yes, this is my boy, Jerry. Say hello to Miss Fellowes, Jerry."

(Had he stressed the word "this" just a bit? Was he saying *this* was his son and not—)

Jerry receded a bit further into the folds of the maternal skirt and muttered his hello. Mrs. Hoskins' eyes were searching over Miss Fellowes' shoulders, peering into the room, looking for something.

Hoskins said, "Well, let's go in. Come, dear. There's a trifling discomfort at the threshold, but it passes."

Miss Fellowes said, "Do you want Jerry to come in, too?"

"Of course. He is to be Timmie's playmate. You said that Timmie needed a playmate. Or have you forgotten?"

"But—" She looked at him with a colossal, surprised wonder. *"Your* boy?"

He said peevishly, "Well, whose boy, then? Isn't this what you want? Come on in, dear. Come on in."

Mrs. Hoskins lifted Jerry into her arms with a distinct effort and, hesitantly, stepped over the threshold. Jerry squirmed as she did so, disliking the sensation.

Mrs. Hoskins said in a thin voice, "Is the creature here? I don't see him."

Miss Fellowes called, "Timmie. Come out."

Timmie peered around the edge of the door, staring up at the little boy who was visiting him. The muscles in Mrs. Hoskins' arms tensed visibly.

She said to her husband, "Gerald, are you sure it's safe?"

Miss Fellowes said at once, "If you mean is Timmie safe, why, of course he is. He's a gentle little boy."

"But he's a sa—savage."

(The ape-boy stories in the newspapers!) Miss Fellowes said emphatically, "He is not a savage. He is just as quiet and reasonable as you can possibly expect a five-and-a-half-year-old to be. It is very generous of you, Mrs. Hoskins, to agree to allow your boy to play with Timmie but please have no fears about it."

Mrs. Hoskins said with mild heat, "I'm not sure that I agree."

"We've had it out, dear," said Hoskins. "Let's not bring up the matter for new argument. Put Jerry down."

Mrs. Hoskins did so and the boy backed against her, staring at the pair of eyes which were staring back at him from the next room.

"Come here, Timmie," said Miss Fellowes. "Don't be afraid."

Slowly, Timmie stepped into the room. Hoskins bent to disengage Jerry's fingers from his mother's skirt. "Step back, dear. Give the children a chance."

The youngsters faced one another. Although the younger, Jerry was nevertheless an inch taller, and in the presence of his straightness and his high-held, well-proportioned head, Timmie's grotesqueries were suddenly almost as pronounced as they had been in the first days.

Miss Fellowes' lips quivered.

It was the little Neanderthal who spoke first, in childish treble. "What's your name?" And Timmie thrust his face suddenly forward as though to inspect the other's features more closely.

Startled Jerry responded with a vigorous shove that sent Timmie tumbling. Both began crying loudly and Mrs. Hoskins snatched up her child, while Miss Fellowes, flushed with repressed anger, lifted Timmie and comforted him.

Mrs. Hoskins said, "They just instinctively don't like one another."

"No more instinctively," said her husband wearily, "than any two children dislike each other. Now put Jerry down and let him get used to the situation. In fact, we had better leave. Miss Fellowes can bring Jerry to my office after a while and I'll have him taken home."

The two children spent the next hour very aware of each other. Jerry cried for his mother, struck out at Miss Fellowes and, finally, allowed himself to be comforted with a lollipop. Timmie sucked at another, and at the end of an hour, Miss Fellowes had them playing with the same set of blocks, though at opposite ends of the room.

She found herself almost maudlinly grateful to Hoskins when she brought Jerry to him.

She searched for ways to thank him but his very formality was a rebuff. Perhaps he could not forgive her for making him feel like a cruel father. Perhaps the bringing of his own child was an attempt, after all, to prove himself both a kind father to Timmie and, also, not his father at all. Both at the same time!

So all she could say was, "Thank you. Thank you very much."

And all he could say was, "It's all right. Don't mention it."

It became a settled routine. Twice a week, Jerry was brought in for an hour's play, later extended to two hours' play. The children learned each other's names and ways and played together.

And yet, after the first rush of gratitude, Miss Fellowes found herself disliking Jerry. He was larger and heavier and in all things dominant, forcing Timmie into a completely secondary role. All that reconciled her to the situation was the fact that, despite difficulties, Timmie looked forward with more and more delight to the periodic appearances of his playfellow.

It was all he had, she mourned to herself.

And once, as she watched them, she thought: Hoskins' two children, one by his wife and one by Stasis.

While she herself—

Heavens, she thought, putting her fists to her temples and feeling ashamed: I'm jealous!

"Miss Fellowes," said Timmie (carefully, she had never allowed him to call her anything else) "when will I go to school?"

She looked down at those eager brown eyes turned up to hers and passed her hand softly through his thick, curly hair. It was the most disheveled portion of his appearance, for she cut his hair herself while he sat restlessly under the scissors. She did not ask for professional help, for the very clumsiness of the cut served to mask the retreating fore part of the skull and the bulging hinder part.

She said, "Where did you hear about school?"

"Jerry goes to school. Kin-der-gar-ten." He said it carefully. "There are lots of places he goes. Outside. When can I go outside, Miss Fellowes?"

A small pain centered in Miss Fellowes' heart. Of course, she saw, there would be no way of avoiding the inevitability of Timmie's hearing more and more of the outer world he could never enter.

She said, with an attempt at gaiety, "Why, whatever would you do in kindergarten, Timmie?"

"Jerry says they play games, they have picture tapes. He says there are lots of children. He says—he says—" A thought, then a triumphant upholding of both small hands with the fingers splayed apart. "He says this many."

Miss Fellowes said, "Would you like picture tapes? I can get you picture tapes. Very nice ones. And music tapes too."

So that Timmie was temporarily comforted.

He pored over the picture tapes in Jerry's absence and Miss Fellowes read to him out of ordinary books by the hours.

There was so much to explain in even the simplest story, so much that was outside the perspective of his three rooms. Timmie took to having his dreams more often now that the outside was being introduced to him.

They were always the same, about the outside. He tried haltingly to describe them to Miss Fellowes. In his dreams, he was outside, an empty outside, but very large, with children and queer indescribable objects half-digested in his thought out of bookish descriptions half-understood, or out of distant Neanderthal memories half-recalled.

But the children and objects ignored him and though he was in the world, he was never part of it, but was as alone as though he were in his own room —and would wake up crying.

Miss Fellowes tried to laugh at the dreams, but there were nights in her own apartment when she cried, too.

One day, as Miss Fellowes read, Timmie put his hand under her chin and lifted it gently so that her eyes left the book and met his.

He said, "How do you know what to say, Miss Fellowes?"

She said, "You see these marks? They tell me what to say. These marks make words."

He stared at them long and curiously, taking the book out of her hands. "Some of these marks are the same."

She laughed with pleasure at this sign of his shrewdness and said, "So they are. Would you like to have me show you how to make the marks?"

"All right. That would be a nice game."

It did not occur to her that he could learn to read. Up to the very moment that he read a book to her, it did not occur to her that he could learn to read.

Then, weeks later, the enormity of what had been done struck her. Timmie sat in her lap, following word by word the printing in a child's book, reading to her. He was reading to her!

She struggled to her feet in amazement and said, "Now Timmie, I'll be back later. I want to see Dr. Hoskins."

Excited nearly to frenzy, it seemed to her she might have an answer to Timmie's unhappiness. If Timmie could not leave to enter the world, the world must be brought into those three rooms to Timmie—the whole world in books and film and sound. He must be educated to his full capacity. So much the world owed him.

She found Hoskins in a mood that was oddly analogous to her own; a kind of triumph and glory. His offices were unusually busy, and for a moment, she thought she would not get to see him, as she stood abashed in the anteroom.

But he saw her, and a smile spread over his broad face. "Miss Fellowes, come here."

He spoke rapidly into the intercom, then shut it off. "Have you heard? —No, of course, you couldn't have. We've done it. We've actually done it. We have intertemporal detection at close range."

"You mean," she tried to detach her thought from her own good news for a moment, "that you can get a person from historical times into the present?"

"That's just what I mean. We have a fix on a fourteenth century individual right now. Imagine. *Imagine!* If you could only know how glad I'll be to shift from the eternal concentration on the Mesozoic, replace the paleontologists with the historians— But there's something you wish to say to me, eh? Well, go ahead; go ahead. You find me in a good mood. Anything you want you can have."

Miss Fellowes smiled. "I'm glad. Because I wonder if we might not establish a system of instruction for Timmie?"

"Instruction? In what?"

"Well, in everything. A school. So that he might learn."

"But *can* he learn?"

"Certainly, he *is* learning. He can read. I've taught him so much myself."

Hoskins sat there, seeming suddenly depressed. "I don't know, Miss Fellowes."

She said, "You just said that anything I wanted—"

"I know and I should not have. You see, Miss Fellowes, I'm sure you must realize that we cannot maintain the Timmie experiment forever."

She stared at him with sudden horror, not really understanding what he had said. How did he mean "cannot maintain"? With an agonizing flash of recollection, she recalled Professor Ademewski and his mineral specimen that was taken away after two weeks. She said, "But you're talking about a boy. Not about a rock—"

Dr. Hoskins said uneasily, "Even a boy can't be given undue importance, Miss Fellowes. Now that we expect individuals out of historical time, we will need Stasis space, all we can get."

She didn't grasp it. "But you can't. Timmie—Timmie—"

"Now, Miss Fellowes, please don't upset yourself. Timmie won't go right away; perhaps not for months. Meanwhile we'll do what we can."

She was still staring at him.

"Let me get you something, Miss Fellowes."

"No," she whispered. "I don't need anything." She arose in a kind of nightmare and left.

Timmie, she thought, you will *not* die. You will *not* die.

It was all very well to hold tensely to the thought that Timmie must not die, but how was that to be arranged? In the first weeks, Miss Fellowes clung only to the hope that the attempt to bring forward a man from the fourteenth century would fail completely. Hoskins' theories might be wrong or his practice defective. Then things could go on as before.

Certainly, that was not the hope of the rest of the world and, irrationally, Miss Fellowes hated the world for it. "Project Middle Ages" reached a climax of white-hot publicity. The press and the public had hungered for something like this. Stasis, Inc. had lacked the necessary sensation for a long time now. A new rock or another ancient fish failed to stir them. But *this* was *it*.

A historical human; an adult speaking a known language; someone who could open a new page of history to the scholar.

Zero-time was coming and this time it was not a question of three onlookers from the balcony. This time there would be a world-wide audience. This time the technicians of Stasis, Inc. would play their role before nearly all of mankind.

Miss Fellowes was herself all but savage with waiting. When young Jerry Hoskins showed up for his scheduled playtime with Timmie, she scarcely recognized him. He was not the one she was waiting for.

(The secretary who brought him left hurriedly after the barest nod for Miss Fellowes. She was rushing for a good place from which to watch the climax of Project Middle Ages. —And so ought Miss Fellowes with far better reason, she thought bitterly, if only that stupid girl would arrive.)

Jerry Hoskins sidled toward her, embarrassed. "Miss Fellowes?" He took the reproduction of a news-strip out of his pocket.

"Yes? What is it, Jerry?"

"Is this a picture of Timmie?"

Miss Fellowes stared at him, then snatched the strip from Jerry's hand. The excitement of Project Middle Ages had brought about a pale revival of interest in Timmie on the part of the press.

Jerry watched her narrowly, then said, "It says Timmie is an ape-boy. What does that mean?"

Miss Fellowes caught the youngster's wrist and repressed the impulse to shake him. "Never say that, Jerry. Never, do you understand? It is a nasty word and you mustn't use it."

Jerry struggled out of her grip, frightened.

Miss Fellowes tore up the news-strip with a vicious twist of the wrist. "Now go inside and play with Timmie. He's got a new book to show you."

And then, finally, the girl appeared. Miss Fellowes did not know her. None of the usual stand-ins she had used when business took her elsewhere was available now, not with Project Middle Ages at climax, but Hoskins' secretary had promised to find *someone* and this must be the girl.

Miss Fellowes tried to keep querulousness out of her voice. "Are you the girl assigned to Stasis Section One?"

"Yes, I'm Mandy Terris. You're Miss Fellowes, aren't you?"

"That's right."

"I'm sorry I'm late. There's just so much excitement."

"I know. Now I want you—"

Mandy said, "You'll be watching, I suppose." Her thin, vacuously pretty face filled with envy.

"Never mind that. Now I want you to come inside and meet Timmie and Jerry. They will be playing for the next two hours so they'll be giving you no trouble. They've got milk handy and plenty of toys. In fact, it will be better if you leave them alone as much as possible. Now I'll show you where everything is located and—"

"Is it Timmie that's the ape-b—"

"Timmie is the Stasis subject," said Miss Fellowes firmly.

"I mean, he's the one who's not supposed to get out, is that right?"

"Yes. Now, come in. There isn't much time."

And when she finally left, Mandy Terris called after her shrilly, "I hope you get a good seat and, golly, I sure hope it works."

Miss Fellowes did not trust herself to make a reasonable response. She hurried on without looking back.

But the delay meant she did *not* get a good seat. She got no nearer than the wall-viewing-plate in the assembly hall. Bitterly, she regretted that. If she could have been on the spot; if she could somehow have reached out for some sensitive portion of the instrumentations; if she were in some way able to wreck the experiment—

She found the strength to beat down her madness. Simple destruction would have done no good. They would have rebuilt and reconstructed and made the effort again. And she would never be allowed to return to Timmie.

Nothing would help. Nothing but that the experiment itself fail; that it break down irretrievably.

So she waited through the countdown, watching every move on the giant screen, scanning the faces of the technicians as the focus shifted from one to the other, watching for the look of worry and uncertainty that would mark something going unexpectedly wrong; watching, watching—

There was no such look. The count reached zero, and very quietly, very unassumingly, the experiment succeeded!

In the new Stasis that had been established there stood a bearded, stoop-shouldered peasant of indeterminate age, in ragged dirty clothing and wooden shoes, staring in dull horror at the sudden mad change that had flung itself over him.

And while the world went mad with jubilation, Miss Fellowes stood frozen in sorrow, jostled and pushed, all but trampled; surrounded by triumph while bowed down with defeat.

And when the loud-speaker called her name with strident force, it sounded it three times before she responded.

"Miss Fellowes. Miss Fellowes. You are wanted in Stasis Section One immediately. Miss Fellowes. Miss Fell—"

"Let me through!" she cried breathlessly, while the loud-speaker continued its repetitions without pause. She forced her way through the crowds with wild energy, beating at it, striking out with closed fists, flailing, moving toward the door in a nightmare slowness.

Mandy Terris was in tears. "I don't know how it happened. I just went down to the edge of the corridor to watch a pocket-viewing-plate they had put up. Just for a minute. And then before I could move or do anything—"

She cried out in sudden accusation, "You said they would make no trouble; you *said* to leave them alone—"

Miss Fellowes, disheveled and trembling uncontrollably, glared at her. "Where's Timmie?"

A nurse was swabbing the arm of a wailing Jerry with disinfectant and another was preparing an anti-tetanus shot. There was blood on Jerry's clothes.

"He bit me, Miss Fellowes," Jerry cried in rage. "He *bit* me."

But Miss Fellowes didn't even see him.

"What did you do with Timmie?" she cried out.

"I locked him in the bathroom," said Mandy. "I just threw the little monster in there and locked him in."

Miss Fellowes ran into the dollhouse. She fumbled at the bathroom door. It took an eternity to get it open and to find the ugly little boy cowering in the corner.

"Don't whip me, Miss Fellowes," he whispered. His eyes were red. His lips were quivering. "I didn't mean to do it."

"Oh, Timmie, who told you about whips?" She caught him to her, hugging him wildly.

He said tremulously, "She said, with a long rope. She said you would hit me and hit me."

"You won't be. She was wicked to say so. But what happened? What happened?"

"He called me an ape-boy. He said I wasn't a real boy. He said I was an animal." Timmie dissolved in a flood of tears. "He said he wasn't going to play with a monkey anymore. I said I wasn't a monkey; I *wasn't* a monkey. He said I was all funny-looking. He said I was horrible ugly. He kept saying and saying and I bit him."

They were both crying now. Miss Fellowes sobbed, "But it isn't true. You know that, Timmie. You're a real boy. You're a dear real boy and the best boy in the world. And no one, *no* one will ever take you away from me."

It was easy to make up her mind, now; easy to know what to do. Only it had to be done quickly. Hoskins wouldn't wait much longer, with his own son mangled—

No, it would have to be done this night, *this* night; with the place four-fifths asleep and the remaining fifth intellectually drunk over Project Middle Ages.

It would be an unusual time for her to return but not an unheard of one. The guard knew her well and would not dream of questioning her. He would think nothing of her carrying a suitcase. She rehearsed the noncommittal phrase, "Games for the boy," and the calm smile.

Why shouldn't he believe that?

He did. When she entered the dollhouse again, Timmie was still awake, and she maintained a desperate normality to avoid frightening him. She talked about his dreams with him and listened to him ask wistfully after Jerry.

There would be few to see her afterward, none to question the bundle she would be carrying. Timmie would be very quiet and then it would be a *fait accompli*. It would be done and what would be the use of trying to undo it. They would leave her be. They would leave them both be.

She opened the suitcase, took out the overcoat, the woolen cap with the ear-flaps and the rest.

Timmie said, with the beginning of alarm, "Why are you putting all these clothes on me, Miss Fellowes?"

She said, "I am going to take you outside, Timmie. To where your dreams are."

"My dreams?" His face twisted in sudden yearning, yet fear was there, too.

"You won't be afraid. You'll be with me. You won't be afraid if you're with me, will you, Timmie?"

"No, Miss Fellowes." He buried his little misshapen head against her side, and under her enclosing arm she could feel his small heart thud.

It was midnight and she lifted him into her arms. She disconnected the alarm and opened the door softly.

And she screamed, for facing her across the open door was Hoskins!

There were two men with him and he stared at her, as astonished as she.

Miss Fellowes recovered first by a second and made a quick attempt to push past him; but even with the second's delay he had time. He caught her roughly and hurled her back against a chest of drawers. He waved the men in and confronted her, blocking the door.

"I didn't expect this. Are you completely insane?"

She had managed to interpose her shoulder so that it, rather than Timmie, had struck the chest. She said pleadingly, "What harm can it do if I take him, Dr. Hoskins? You can't put energy loss ahead of a human life?"

Firmly, Hoskins took Timmie out of her arms. "An energy loss this size would mean millions of dollars lost out of the pockets of investors. It would mean a terrible setback for Stasis, Inc. It would mean eventual publicity about a sentimental nurse destroying all that for the sake of an ape-boy."

"*Ape-boy!*" said Miss Fellowes, in helpless fury.

"That's what the reporters would call him," said Hoskins.

One of the men emerged now, looping a nylon rope through eyelets along the upper portion of the wall.

Miss Fellowes remembered the rope that Hoskins had pulled outside the room containing Professor Ademewski's rock specimen so long ago.

She cried out, "No!"

But Hoskins put Timmie down and gently removed the overcoat he was wearing. "You stay here, Timmie. Nothing will happen to you. We're just going outside for a moment. All right?"

Timmie, white and wordless, managed to nod.

Hoskins steered Miss Fellowes out of the dollhouse ahead of himself. For the moment, Miss Fellowes was beyond resistance. Dully, she noticed the hand-pull being adjusted outside the dollhouse.

"I'm sorry, Miss Fellowes," said Hoskins. "I would have spared you this. I planned it for the night so that you would know only when it was over."

She said in a weary whisper, "Because your son was hurt. Because he tormented this child into striking out at him."

"No. Believe me. I understand about the incident today and I know it was Jerry's fault. But the story has leaked out. It would have to with the press surrounding us on this day of all days. I can't risk having a distorted story about negligence and savage Neanderthalers, so-called, distract from the success of Project Middle Ages. Timmie has to go soon anyway; he might as well go now and give the sensationalists as small a peg as possible on which to hang their trash."

"It's not like sending a rock back. You'll be killing a human being."

"Not killing. There'll be no sensation. He'll simply be a Neanderthal boy in a Neanderthal world. He will no longer be a prisoner and alien. He will have a chance at a free life."

"What chance? He's only seven years old, used to being taken care of, fed, clothed, sheltered. He will be alone. His tribe may not be at the point where he left them now that four years have passed. And if they were, they would not recognize him. He will have to take care of himself. How will he know how?"

Hoskins shook his head in hopeless negative. "Lord, Miss Fellowes, do you think we haven't thought of that? Do you think we would have brought in a child if it weren't that it was the first successful fix of a human or near-human we made and that we did not dare to take the chance of unfixing him and finding another fix as good? Why do you suppose we kept Timmie as long as we did, if it were not for our reluctance to send a child back into the past? It's just"—his voice took on a desperate urgency—"that we can wait no longer. Timmie stands in the way of expansion! Timmie is a source of possible bad publicity; we are on the threshold of great things, and I'm sorry, Miss Fellowes, but we can't let Timmie block us. We cannot. We cannot. I'm sorry, Miss Fellowes."

"Well, then," said Miss Fellowes sadly. "Let me say good-by. Give me five minutes to say good-by. Spare me that much."

Hoskins hesitated. "Go ahead."

Timmie ran to her. For the last time he ran to her and for the last time Miss Fellowes clasped him in her arms.

For a moment, she hugged him blindly. She caught at a chair with the toe of one foot, moved it against the wall, sat down.

"Don't be afraid, Timmie."

"I'm not afraid if you're here, Miss Fellowes. Is that man mad at me, the man out there?"

"No, he isn't. He just doesn't understand about us. —Timmie, do you know what a mother is?"

"Like Jerry's mother?"

"Did he tell you about his mother?"

"Sometimes. I think maybe a mother is a lady who takes care of you and who's very nice to you and who does good things."

"That's right. Have you ever wanted a mother, Timmie?"

Timmie pulled his head away from her so that he could look into her face. Slowly, he put his hand to her cheek and hair and stroked her, as long, long ago she had stroked him. He said, "Aren't you my mother?"

"Oh, Timmie."

"Are you angry because I asked?"

"No. Of course not."

"Because I know your name is Miss Fellowes, but—but sometimes, I call you 'Mother' inside. Is that all right?"

"Yes. Yes. It's all right. And I won't leave you any more and nothing will hurt you. I'll be with you to care for you always. Call me Mother, so I can hear you."

"Mother," said Timmie contentedly, leaning his cheek against hers.

She rose, and, still holding him, stepped up on the chair. The sudden beginning of a shout from outside went unheard and, with her free hand, she yanked with all her weight at the cord where it hung suspended between two eyelets.

And Stasis was punctured and the room was empty.

Nightfall

I

"If the stars should appear one night in a thousand years, how would men believe and adore, and preserve for many generations the remembrance of the city of God?"

EMERSON

Aton 77, director of Saro University, thrust out a belligerent lower lip and glared at the young newspaperman in a hot fury.

Theremon 762 took that fury in his stride. In his earlier days, when his now widely syndicated column was only a mad idea in a cub reporter's mind, he had specialized in "impossible" interviews. It had cost him bruises, black eyes, and broken bones; but it had given him an ample supply of coolness and self-confidence.

So he lowered the outthrust hand that had been so pointedly ignored and calmly waited for the aged director to get over the worst. Astronomers were queer ducks, anyway, and if Aton's actions of the last two months meant anything, this same Aton was the queer-duckiest of the lot.

Aton 77 found his voice, and though it trembled with restrained emotion, the careful, somewhat pedantic phraseology, for which the famous astronomer was noted, did not abandon him.

"Sir," he said, "you display an infernal gall in coming to me with that impudent proposition of yours."

The husky telephotographer of the Observatory, Beenay 25, thrust a tongue's tip across dry lips and interposed nervously, "Now, sir, after all—"

The director turned to him and lifted a white eyebrow. "Do not interfere, Beenay. I will credit you with good intentions in bringing this man here; but I will tolerate no insubordination now."

Theremon decided it was time to take a part. "Director Aton, if you'll let me finish what I started saying, I think—"

"I don't believe, young man," retorted Aton, "that anything you could say now would count much as compared with your daily columns of these last two months. You have led a vast newspaper campaign against the efforts of myself and my colleagues to organize the world against the menace which it is now too late to avert. You have done your best with your highly personal attacks to make the staff of this Observatory objects of ridicule."

The director lifted a copy of the Saro City *Chronicle* from the table and shook it at Theremon furiously. "Even a person of your well-known impudence should have hesitated before coming to me with a request that he be allowed to cover today's events for his paper. Of all newsmen, you!"

Aton dashed the newspaper to the floor, strode to the window, and clasped his arms behind his back.

"You may leave," he snapped over his shoulder. He stared moodily out at the skyline where Gamma, the brightest of the planet's six suns, was setting. It had already faded and yellowed into the horizon mists, and Aton knew he would never see it again as a sane man.

He whirled. "No, wait, come here!" He gestured peremptorily. "I'll give you your story."

The newsman had made no motion to leave, and now he approached the old man slowly. Aton gestured outward. "Of the six suns, only Beta is left in the sky. Do you see it?"

The question was rather unnecessary. Beta was almost at zenith, its ruddy light flooding the landscape to an unusual orange as the brilliant rays of setting Gamma died. Beta was at aphelion. It was small; smaller than Theremon had ever seen it before, and for the moment it was undisputed ruler of Lagash's sky.

Lagash's own sun, Alpha, the one about which it revolved, was at the antipodes, as were the two distant companion pairs. The red dwarf Beta—Alpha's immediate companion—was alone, grimly alone.

Aton's upturned face flushed redly in the sunlight. "In just under four hours," he said, "civilization, as we know it, comes to an end. It will do so because, as you see, Beta is the only sun in the sky." He smiled grimly. "Print that! There'll be no one to read it."

"But if it turns out that four hours pass—and another four—and nothing happens?" asked Theremon softly.

"Don't let that worry you. Enough will happen."

"Granted! And *still*—if nothing happens?"

For a second time, Beenay 25 spoke. "Sir, I think you ought to listen to him."

Theremon said, "Put it to a vote, Director Aton."

There was a stir among the remaining five members of the Observatory staff, who till now had maintained an attitude of wary neutrality.

"That," stated Aton flatly, "is not necessary." He drew out his pocket watch. "Since your good friend, Beenay, insists so urgently, I will give you five minutes. Talk away."

"Good! Now, just what difference would it make if you allowed me to take down an eyewitness account of what's to come? If your prediction comes true, my presence won't hurt; for in that case my column would never be written. On the other hand, if nothing comes of it, you will just have to expect ridicule or worse. It would be wise to leave that ridicule to friendly hands."

Aton snorted. "Do you mean yours when you speak of friendly hands?"

"Certainly!" Theremon sat down and crossed his legs. "My columns may have been a little rough, but I gave you people the benefit of the doubt every time. After all, this is not the century to preach 'The end of the world is at hand' to Lagash. You have to understand that people don't believe the *Book of Revelations* anymore, and it annoys them to have scientists turn about-face and tell us the Cultists are right after all—"

"No such thing, young man," interrupted Aton. "While a great deal of our data has been supplied us by the Cult, our results contain none of the Cult's mysticism. Facts are facts, and the Cult's so-called mythology *has* certain facts behind it. We've exposed them and ripped away their mystery. I assure you that the Cult hates us now worse than you do."

"I don't hate you. I'm just trying to tell you that the public is in an ugly humor. They're angry."

Aton twisted his mouth in derision. "Let them be angry."

"Yes, but what about tomorrow?"

"There'll be no tomorrow!"

"But if there is. Say that there is—just to see what happens. That anger might take shape into something serious. After all, you know, business has taken a nosedive these last two months. Investors don't really believe the world is coming to an end, but just the same they're being cagy with their money until it's all over. Johnny Public doesn't believe you, either, but the new spring furniture might just as well wait a few months—just to make sure.

"You see the point. Just as soon as this is all over, the business interests will be after your hide. They'll say that if crackpots—begging your pardon—can upset the country's prosperity any time they want, simply by making some cockeyed prediction—it's up to the planet to prevent them. The sparks will fly, sir."

The director regarded the columnist sternly. "And just what were you proposing to do to help the situation?"

"Well"—Theremon grinned—"I was proposing to take charge of the publicity. I can handle things so that only the ridiculous side will show. It would be hard to stand, I admit, because I'd have to make you all out to be a bunch of gibbering idiots, but if I can get people laughing at you, they might forget to be angry. In return for that, all my publisher asks is an exclusive story."

Beenay nodded and burst out, "Sir, the rest of us think he's right. These last two months we've considered everything but the million-to-one chance that there is an error somewhere in our theory or in our calculations. We ought to take care of that, too."

There was a murmur of agreement from the men grouped about the table, and Aton's expression became that of one who found his mouth full of something bitter and couldn't get rid of it.

"You may stay if you wish, then. You will kindly refrain, however, from hampering us in our duties in any way. You will also remember that I am in charge of all activities here, and in spite of your opinions as expressed in your columns, I will expect full cooperation and full respect—"

His hands were behind his back, and his wrinkled face thrust forward determinedly as he spoke. He might have continued indefinitely but for the intrusion of a new voice.

"Hello, hello, hello!" It came in a high tenor, and the plump cheeks of the newcomer expanded in a pleased smile. "What's this morgue-like atmosphere about here? No one's losing his nerve, I hope."

Aton started in consternation and said peevishly, "Now what the devil are you doing here, Sheerin? I thought you were going to stay behind in the Hideout."

Sheerin laughed and dropped his stubby figure into a chair. "Hideout be blowed! The place bored me. I wanted to be here, where things are getting hot. Don't you suppose I have my share of curiosity? I want to see these Stars the Cultists are forever speaking about." He rubbed his hands and added in a soberer tone, "It's freezing outside. The wind's enough to hang icicles on your nose. Beta doesn't seem to give any heat at all, at the distance it is."

The white-haired director ground his teeth in sudden exasperation. "Why do you go out of your way to do crazy things, Sheerin? What kind of good are you around here?"

"What kind of good am I around there?" Sheerin spread his palms in comical resignation. "A psychologist isn't worth his salt in the Hideout. They need men of action and strong, healthy women that can breed children. Me? I'm a hundred pounds too heavy for a man of action, and I wouldn't be a success at breeding children. So why bother them with an extra mouth to feed? I feel better over here."

Theremon spoke briskly. "Just what is the Hideout, sir?"

Sheerin seemed to see the columnist for the first time. He frowned and blew his ample cheeks out. "And just who in Lagash are you, redhead?"

338   ISAAC ASIMOV

Aton compressed his lips and then muttered sullenly, "That's Theremon 762, the newspaper fellow. I suppose you've heard of him."

The columnist offered his hand. "And, of course, you're Sheerin 501 of Saro University. I've heard of you." Then he repeated, "What is this Hideout, sir?"

"Well," said Sheerin, "we have managed to convince a few people of the validity of our prophecy of—er—doom, to be spectacular about it, and those few have taken proper measures. They consist mainly of the immediate members of the families of the Observatory staff, certain of the faculty of Saro University, and a few outsiders. Altogether, they number about three hundred, but three quarters are women and children."

"I see! They're suppose to hide where the Darkness and the—er—Stars can't get at them, and then hold out when the rest of the world goes poof."

"If they can. It won't be easy. With all of mankind insane, with the great cities going up in flames—environment will not be conducive to survival. But they have food, water, shelter, and weapons—"

"They've got more," said Aton. "They've got all our records, except for what we will collect today. Those records will mean everything to the next cycle, and *that's* what must survive. The rest can go hang."

Theremon uttered a long, low whistle and sat brooding for several minutes. The men about the table had brought out a multi-chess board and started a six-member game. Moves were made rapidly and in silence. All eyes bent in furious concentration on the board. Theremon watched them intently and then rose and approached Aton, who sat apart in whispered conversation with Sheerin.

"Listen," he said, "let's go somewhere where we won't bother the rest of the fellows. I want to ask some questions."

The aged astronomer frowned sourly at him, but Sheerin chirped up, "Certainly. It will do me good to talk. It always does. Aton was telling me about your ideas concerning world reaction to a failure of the prediction—and I agree with you. I read your column pretty regularly, by the way, and as a general thing I like your views."

"Please, Sheerin," growled Aton.

"Eh? Oh, all right. We'll go into the next room. It has softer chairs, anyway."

There were softer chairs in the next room. There were also thick red curtains on the windows and a maroon carpet on the floor. With the bricky light of Beta pouring in, the general effect was one of dried blood.

Theremon shuddered. "Say, I'd give ten credits for a decent dose of white light for just a second. I wish Gamma or Delta were in the sky."

"What are your questions?" asked Aton. "Please remember that our time is limited. In a little over an hour and a quarter we're going upstairs, and after that there will be no time for talk."

"Well, here it is." Theremon leaned back and folded his hands on his chest. "You people seem so all-fired serious about this that I'm beginning to believe you. Would you mind explaining what it's all about?"

Aton exploded, "Do you mean to sit there and tell me that you've been bombarding us with ridicule without even finding out what we've been trying to say?"

The columnist grinned sheepishly. "It's not that bad, sir. I've got the general idea. You say there is going to be a world-wide Darkness in a few hours and that all mankind will go violently insane. What I want now is the science behind it."

"No, you don't. No, you don't," broke in Sheerin. "If you ask Aton for that—supposing him to be in the mood to answer at all—he'll trot out pages of figures and volumes of graphs. You won't make head or tail of it. Now if you were to ask me, I could give you the layman's standpoint."

"All right; I ask you."

"Then first I'd like a drink." He rubbed his hands and looked at Aton.

"Water?" grunted Aton.

"Don't be silly!"

"Don't you be silly. No alcohol today. It would be too easy to get my men drunk. I can't afford to tempt them."

The psychologist grumbled wordlessly. He turned to Theremon, impaled him with his sharp eyes, and began.

"You realize, of course, that the history of civilization on Lagash displays a cyclic character—but I mean, *cyclic!*"

"I know," replied Theremon cautiously, "that that is the current archaeological theory. Has it been accepted as a fact?"

"Just about. In this last century it's been generally agreed upon. This cyclic character is—or rather, was—one of the great mysteries. We've located series of civilizations, nine of them definitely, and indications of others as well, all of which have reached heights comparable to our own, and all of which, without exception, were destroyed by fire at the very height of their culture.

"And no one could tell why. All centers of culture were thoroughly gutted by fire, with nothing left behind to give a hint as to the cause."

Theremon was following closely. "Wasn't there a Stone Age, too?"

"Probably, but as yet practically nothing is known of it, except that men of that age were little more than rather intelligent apes. We can forget about that."

"I see. Go on!"

"There have been explanations of these recurrent catastrophes, all of a more or less fantastic nature. Some say that there are periodic rains of fire; some that Lagash passes through a sun every so often; some even wilder things. But there is one theory, quite different from all of these, that has been handed down over a period of centuries."

"I know. You mean this myth of the 'Stars' that the Cultists have in their *Book of Revelations*."

"Exactly," rejoined Sheerin with satisfaction. "The Cultists said that every two thousand and fifty years Lagash entered a huge cave, so that all the suns disappeared, and there came *total darkness all over the world!* And then, they say, things called Stars appeared, which robbed men of their souls and left them unreasoning brutes, so that they destroyed the civilization they themselves had built up. Of course they mix all this up with a lot of religio-mystic notions, but that's the central idea."

There was a short pause in which Sheerin drew a long breath. "And now we come to the Theory of Universal Gravitation." He pronounced the phrase so that the capital letters sounded—and at that point Aton turned from the window, snorted loudly, and stalked out of the room.

The two stared after him, and Theremon said, "What's wrong?"

"Nothing in particular," replied Sheerin. "Two of the men were due several hours ago and haven't shown up yet. He's terrifically short-handed, of course, because all but the really essential men have gone to the Hideout."

"You don't think the two deserted, do you?"

"Who? Faro and Yimot? Of course not. Still, if they're not back within the hour, things would be a little sticky." He got to his feet suddenly, and his eyes twinkled. "Anyway, as long as Aton is gone—"

Tiptoeing to the nearest window, he squatted, and from the low window box beneath withdrew a bottle of red liquid that gurgled suggestively when he shook it.

"I *thought* Aton didn't know about this," he remarked as he trotted back to the table. "Here! We've only got one glass so, as the guest, you can have it. I'll keep the bottle." And he filled the tiny cup with judicious care.

Theremon rose to protest, but Sheerin eyed him sternly. "Respect your elders, young man."

The newsman seated himself with a look of anguish on his face. "Go ahead, then, you old villain."

The psychologist's Adam's apple wobbled as the bottle upended, and then, with a satisfied grunt and a smack of the lips, he began again. "But what do you know about gravitation?"

"Nothing, except that it is a very recent development, not too well established, and that the math is so hard that only twelve men in Lagash are supposed to understand it."

"*Tcha!* Nonsense! Baloney! I can give you all the essential math in a sentence. The Law of Universal Gravitation states that there exists a cohesive force among all bodies of the universe, such that the amount of this force between any two given bodies is proportional to the product of their masses divided by the square of the distance between them."

"Is that all?"

"That's enough! It took four hundred years to develop it."

"Why that long? It sounded simple enough, the way you said it."

"Because great laws are not divined by flashes of inspiration, whatever you may think. It usually takes the combined work of a world full of scientists over a period of centuries. After Genovi 41 discovered that Lagash rotated about the sun Alpha rather than vice versa—and that was four hundred years ago—astronomers have been working. The complex motions of the six suns were recorded and analyzed and unwoven. Theory after theory was advanced and checked and counterchecked and modified and abandoned and revived and converted to something else. It was a devil of a job."

Theremon nodded thoughtfully and held out his glass for more liquor. Sheerin grudgingly allowed a few ruby drops to leave the bottle.

"It was twenty years ago," he continued after remoistening his own throat, "that it was finally demonstrated that the Law of Universal Gravitation accounted exactly for the orbital motions of the six suns. It was a great triumph."

Sheerin stood up and walked to the window, still clutching his bottle. "And now we're getting to the point. In the last decade, the motions of Lagash about Alpha were computed according to gravity, and *it did not account for the orbit observed;* not even when all perturbations due to the other suns were included. Either the law was invalid, or there was another, as yet unknown, factor involved."

Theremon joined Sheerin at the window and gazed out past the wooded slopes to where the spires of Saro City gleamed bloodily on the horizon. The newsman felt the tension of uncertainty grow within him as he cast a short glance at Beta. It glowered redly at zenith, dwarfed and evil.

"Go ahead, sir," he said softly.

Sheerin replied, "Astronomers stumbled about for years, each proposed theory more untenable than the one before—until Aton had the inspiration of calling in the Cult. The head of the Cult, Sor 5, had access to certain data that simplified the problem considerably. Aton set to work on a new track.

"What if there were another nonluminous planetary body such as Lagash? If there were, you know, it would shine only by reflected light, and if it were composed of bluish rock, as Lagash itself largely is, then, in the redness of the sky, the eternal blaze of the suns would make it invisible—drown it out completely."

Theremon whistled. "What a screwy idea!"

"You think *that's* screwy? Listen to this: Suppose this body rotated about Lagash at such a distance and in such an orbit and had such a mass that its attraction would exactly account for the deviations of Lagash's orbit from theory—do you know what would happen?"

The columnist shook his head.

"Well, sometimes this body would get in the way of a sun." And Sheerin emptied what remained in the bottle at a draft.

"And it does, I suppose," said Theremon flatly.

"Yes! But only one sun lies in its plane of revolution." He jerked a thumb at the shrunken sun above. "Beta! And it has been shown that the eclipse will occur only when the arrangement of the suns is such that Beta is alone in its hemisphere and at maximum distance, at which time the moon is invariably at minimum distance. The eclipse that results, with the moon seven times the apparent diameter of Beta, covers all of Lagash and lasts well over half a day, so that no spot on the planet escapes the effects. *That eclipse comes once every two thousand and forty-nine years.*"

Theremon's face was drawn into an expressionless mask. "And that's my story?"

The psychologist nodded. "That's all of it. First the eclipse—which will start in three quarters of an hour—then universal Darkness and, maybe, these mysterious Stars—then madness, and end of the cycle."

He brooded. "We had two months' leeway—we at the Observatory—and that wasn't enough time to persuade Lagash of the danger. Two centuries might not have been enough. But our records are at the Hideout, and today we photograph the eclipse. The next cycle will *start off* with the truth, and when the *next* eclipse comes, mankind will at last be ready for it. Come to think of it, that's part of your story too."

A thin wind ruffled the curtains at the window as Theremon opened it and leaned out. It played coldly with his hair as he stared at the crimson sunlight on his hand. Then he turned in sudden rebellion.

"What is there in Darkness to drive *me* mad?"

Sheerin smiled to himself as he spun the empty liquor bottle with abstracted motions of his hand. "Have you ever experienced Darkness, young man?"

The newsman leaned against the wall and considered. "No. Can't say I have. But I know what it is. Just—uh—" He made vague motions with his fingers and then brightened. "Just no light. Like in caves."

"Have you ever been in a cave?"

"In a *cave!* Of course not!"

"I thought not. *I* tried last week—just to see—but I got out in a hurry. I went in until the mouth of the cave was just visible as a blur of light, with black everywhere else. I never thought a person my weight could run that fast."

Theremon's lip curled. "Well, if it comes to that, I guess I wouldn't have run if I had been there."

The psychologist studied the young man with an annoyed frown.

"My, don't you talk big! I dare you to draw the curtain."

Theremon looked his surprise and said, "What for? If we had four or five suns out there, we might want to cut the light down a bit for comfort, but now we haven't enough light as it is."

"That's the point. Just draw the curtain; then come here and sit down."

"All right." Theremon reached for the tasseled string and jerked. The red curtain slid across the wide window, the brass rings hissing their way along the crossbar, and a dusk-red shadow clamped down on the room.

Theremon's footsteps sounded hollowly in the silence as he made his way to the table, and then they stopped halfway. "I can't see you, sir," he whispered.

"Feel your way," ordered Sheerin in a strained voice.

"But I can't see you, sir." The newsman was breathing harshly. "I can't see anything."

"What did you expect?" came the grim reply. "Come here and sit down!"

The footsteps sounded again, waveringly, approaching slowly. There was the sound of someone fumbling with a chair. Theremon's voice came thinly, "Here I am. I feel . . . *ulp* . . . all right."

"You like it, do you?"

"N—no. It's pretty awful. The walls seem to be—" He paused. "They seem to be closing in on me. I keep wanting to push them away. But I'm not going *mad!* In fact, the feeling isn't as bad as it was."

"All right. Draw the curtain back again."

There were cautious footsteps through the dark, the rustle of Theremon's body against the curtain as he felt for the tassel, and then the triumphant *ro-o-osh* of the curtain slithering back. Red light flooded the room, and with a cry of joy Theremon looked up at the sun.

Sheerin wiped the moistness off his forehead with the back of a hand and said shakily, "And that was just a dark room."

"It can be stood," said Theremon lightly.

"Yes, a dark room can. But were you at the Jonglor Centennial Exposition two years ago?"

"No, it so happens I never got around to it. Six thousand miles was just a bit too much to travel, even for the exposition."

"Well, I was there. You remember hearing about the 'Tunnel of Mystery' that broke all records in the amusement area—for the first month or so, anyway?"

"Yes. Wasn't there some fuss about it?"

"Very little. It was hushed up. You see, that Tunnel of Mystery was just a mile-long tunnel—with no lights. You got into a little open car and jolted along through Darkness for fifteen minutes. It was very popular—while it lasted."

"Popular?"

"Certainly. There's a fascination in being frightened *when it's part of a game.* A baby is born with three instinctive fears: of loud noises, of falling, and of the absence of light. That's why it's considered so funny to jump at someone and shout 'Boo!' That's why it's such fun to ride a roller coaster. And that's why that Tunnel of Mystery started cleaning up. People came out of that Darkness shaking, breathless, half dead with fear, but they kept on paying to get in."

"Wait a while, I remember now. Some people came out dead, didn't they? There were rumors of that after it shut down."

The psychologist snorted. "Bah! Two or three died. That was nothing! They paid off the families of the dead ones and argued the Jonglor City Council into forgetting it. After all, they said, if people with weak hearts want to go through the tunnel, it was at their own risk—and besides, it wouldn't happen again. So they put a doctor in the front office and had every customer go through a physical examination before getting into the car. That actually *boosted* ticket sales."

"Well, then?"

"But you see, there was something else. People sometimes came out in perfect order, except that they refused to go into buildings—any buildings; including palaces, mansions, apartment houses, tenements, cottages, huts, shacks, lean-tos, and tents."

Theremon looked shocked. "You mean they refused to come in out of the open? Where'd they sleep?"

"In the open."

"They should have *forced* them inside."

"Oh, they did, they did. Whereupon these people went into violent hysterics and did their best to bat their brains out against the nearest wall. Once you got them inside, you couldn't keep them there without a strait jacket or a heavy dose of tranquilizer."

"They must have been crazy."

"Which is exactly what they were. One person out of every ten who went into that tunnel came out that way. They called in the psychologists, and we did the only thing possible. We closed down the exhibit." He spread his hands.

"What was the matter with these people?" asked Theremon finally.

"Essentially the same thing that was the matter with you when you thought the walls of the room were crushing in on you in the dark. There is a psychological term for mankind's instinctive fear of the absence of light. We call it 'claustrophobia,' because the lack of light is always tied up with enclosed places, so that fear of one is fear of the other. You see?"

"And those people of the tunnel?"

"Those people of the tunnel consisted of those unfortunates whose mentality did not quite possess the resiliency to overcome the claustrophobia that overtook them in the Darkness. Fifteen minutes without light is a long time; you only had two or three minutes, and I believe you were fairly upset.

"The people of the tunnel had what is called a 'claustrophobic fixation.'

Their latent fear of Darkness and enclosed places had crystalized and become active, and, as far as we can tell, permanent. That's what fifteen minutes in the dark will do."

There was a long silence, and Theremon's forehead wrinkled slowly into a frown. "I don't believe it's that bad."

"You mean you don't want to believe," snapped Sheerin. "You're afraid to believe. Look out the window!"

Theremon did so, and the psychologist continued without pausing. "Imagine Darkness—everywhere. No light, as far as you can see. The houses, the trees, the fields, the earth, the sky—black! And Stars thrown in, for all I know—whatever *they* are. Can you conceive it?"

"Yes, I can," declared Theremon truculently.

And Sheerin slammed his fist down upon the table in sudden passion. "You lie! You can't conceive that. Your brain wasn't built for the conception any more than it was built for the conception of infinity or of eternity. You can only talk about it. A fraction of the reality upsets you, and when the real thing comes, your brain is going to be presented with the phenomenon outside its limits of comprehension. You will go mad, completely and permanently! There is no question of it!"

He added sadly, "And another couple of millennia of painful struggle comes to nothing. Tomorrow there won't be a city standing unharmed in all Lagash."

Theremon recovered part of his mental equilibrium. "That doesn't follow. I still don't see that I can go loony just because there isn't a sun in the sky—but even if I did, and everyone else did, how does that harm the cities? Are we going to blow them down?"

But Sheerin was angry, too. "If you were in Darkness, what would you want more than anything else; what would it be that every instinct would call for? Light, damn you, *light!*"

"Well?"

"And how would you get light?"

"I don't know," said Theremon flatly.

"What's the *only* way to get light, short of a sun?"

"How should I know?"

They were standing face to face and nose to nose.

Sheerin said, "You burn something, mister. Ever see a forest fire? Ever go camping and cook a stew over a wood fire? Heat isn't the only thing burning wood gives off, you know. It gives off light, and people know that. And when it's dark they want light, and they're going to *get* it."

"So they burn wood?"

"So they burn whatever they can get. They've got to have light. They've got to burn something, and wood isn't handy—so they'll burn whatever is nearest. They'll have their light—and every center of habitation goes up in flames!"

Eyes held each other as though the whole matter were a personal affair of respective will powers, and then Theremon broke away wordlessly. His breathing was harsh and ragged, and he scarcely noted the sudden hubbub that came from the adjoining room behind the closed door.

Sheerin spoke, and it was with an effort that he made it sound matter-of-fact. "I think I heard Yimot's voice. He and Faro are probably back. Let's go in and see what kept them."

"Might as well!" muttered Theremon. He drew a long breath and seemed to shake himself. The tension was broken.

The room was in an uproar, with members of the staff clustering about two young men who were removing outer garments even as they parried the miscellany of questions being thrown at them.

Aton bustled through the crowd and faced the newcomers angrily. "Do you realize that it's less than half an hour before deadline? Where have you two been?"

Faro 24 seated himself and rubbed his hands. His cheeks were red with the outdoor chill. "Yimot and I have just finished carrying through a little crazy experiment of our own. We've been trying to see if we couldn't construct an arrangement by which we could simulate the appearance of Darkness and Stars so as to get an advance notion as to how it looked."

There was a confused murmur from the listeners, and a sudden look of interest entered Aton's eyes. "There wasn't anything said of this before. How did you go about it?"

"Well," said Faro, "the idea came to Yimot and myself long ago, and we've been working it out in our spare time. Yimot knew of a low one-story house down in the city with a domed roof—it had once been used as a museum, I think. Anyway, we bought it—"

"Where did you get the money?" interrupted Aton peremptorily.

"Our bank accounts," grunted Yimot 70. "It cost two thousand credits." Then, defensively, "Well, what of it? Tomorrow, two thousand credits will be two thousand pieces of paper. That's all."

"Sure," agreed Faro. "We bought the place and rigged it up with black velvet from top to bottom so as to get as perfect a Darkness as possible. Then we punched tiny holes in the ceiling and through the roof and covered them with little metal caps, all of which could be shoved aside simultaneously at the close of a switch. At least we didn't do that part ourselves; we got a carpenter and an electrician and some others—money didn't count. The point was that we could get the light to shine through those holes in the roof, so that we could get a starlike effect."

Not a breath was drawn during the pause that followed. Aton said stiffly, "You had no right to make a private—"

Faro seemed abashed. "I know, sir—but frankly, Yimot and I thought the experiment was a little dangerous. If the effect really worked, we half expected to go mad—from what Sheerin says about all this, we thought that would be rather likely. We wanted to take the risk ourselves. Of course if we found we could retain sanity, it occurred to us that we might develop immunity to the real thing, and then expose the rest of you the same way. But things didn't work out at all—"

"Why, what happened?"

It was Yimot who answered. "We shut ourselves in and allowed our eyes to get accustomed to the dark. It's an extremely creepy feeling because the total Darkness makes you feel as if the walls and ceiling are crushing in on you. But we got over that and pulled the switch. The caps fell away and the roof glittered all over with little dots of light—"

"Well?"

"Well—nothing. That was the whacky part of it. Nothing happened. It was just a roof with holes in it, and that's just what it looked like. We tried it over and over again—that's what kept us so late—but there just isn't any effect at all."

There followed a shocked silence, and all eyes turned to Sheerin, who sat motionless, mouth open.

Theremon was the first to speak. "You know what this does to this whole theory you've built up, Sheerin, don't you?" He was grinning with relief.

But Sheerin raised his hand. "Now wait a while. Just let me think this through." And then he snapped his fingers, and when he lifted his head there was neither surprise nor uncertainty in his eyes. "Of course—"

He never finished. From somewhere up above there sounded a sharp clang, and Beenay, starting to his feet, dashed up the stairs with a "What the devil!"

The rest followed after.

Things happened quickly. Once up in the dome, Beenay cast one horrified glance at the shattered photographic plates and at the man bending over them; and then hurled himself fiercely at the intruder, getting a death grip on his throat. There was a wild threshing, and as others of the staff joined in, the stranger was swallowed up and smothered under the weight of half a dozen angry men.

Aton came up last, breathing heavily. "Let him up!"

There was a reluctant unscrambling and the stranger, panting harshly, with his clothes torn and his forehead bruised, was hauled to his feet. He had a short yellow beard curled elaborately in the style affected by the Cultists.

Beenay shifted his hold to a collar grip and shook the man savagely. "All right, rat, what's the idea? These plates—"

"I wasn't after *them*," retorted the Cultist coldly. "That was an accident."

Beenay followed his glowering stare and snarled, "I see. You were after the cameras themselves. The accident with the plates was a stroke of luck for you, then. If you had touched Snapping Bertha or any of the others, you would have died by slow torture. As it is—" He drew his fist back.

Aton grabbed his sleeve. "Stop that! Let him go!"

The young technician wavered, and his arm dropped reluctantly. Aton pushed him aside and confronted the Cultist. "You're Latimer, aren't you?"

The Cultist bowed stiffly and indicated the symbol upon his hip. "I am Latimer 25, adjutant of the third class to his serenity, Sor 5."

"And"—Aton's white eyebrows lifted—"you were with his serenity when he visited me last week, weren't you?"

Latimer bowed a second time.

"Now, then, what do you want?"

"Nothing that you would give me of your own free will."

"Sor 5 sent you, I suppose—or is this your own idea?"

"I won't answer that question."

"Will there be any further visitors?"

"I won't answer that, either."

Aton glanced at his timepiece and scowled. "Now, man, what is it your master wants of me? I have fulfilled my end of the bargain."

Latimer smiled faintly, but said nothing.

"I asked him," continued Aton angrily, "for data only the Cult could supply, and it was given to me. For that, thank you. In return I promised to prove the essential truth of the creed of the Cult."

"There was no need to prove that," came the proud retort. "It stands proven by the *Book of Revelations.*"

"For the handful that constitute the Cult, yes. Don't pretend to mistake my meaning. I offered to present scientific backing for your beliefs. And I did!"

The Cultist's eyes narrowed bitterly. "Yes, you did—with a fox's subtlety, for your pretended explanation backed our beliefs, and at the same time removed all necessity for them. You made of the Darkness and of the Stars a natural phenomenon and removed all its real significance. That was blasphemy."

"If so, the fault isn't mine. The facts exist. What can I do but state them?"

"Your 'facts' are a fraud and a delusion."

Aton stamped angrily. "How do you know?"

And the answer came with the certainty of absolute faith. "I know!"

The director purpled and Beenay whispered urgently. Aton waved him silent. "And what does Sor 5 want us to do? He still thinks, I suppose, that in trying to warn the world to take measures against the menace of madness, we are placing innumerable souls in jeopardy. We aren't succeeding, if that means anything to him."

"The attempt itself has done harm enough, and your vicious effort to gain information by means of your devilish instruments must be stopped. We obey the will of the Stars, and I only regret that my clumsiness prevented me from wrecking your infernal devices."

"It wouldn't have done you too much good," returned Aton. "All our data, except for the direct evidence we intend collecting right now, is already safely cached and well beyond possibility of harm." He smiled grimly. "But that does not affect your present status as an attempted burglar and criminal."

He turned to the men behind him. "Someone call the police at Saro City."

There was a cry of distaste from Sheerin. "Damn it, Aton, what's wrong with you? There's no time for that. Here"—he bustled his way forward—"let me handle this."

Aton stared down his nose at the psychologist. "This is not the time for your monkeyshines, Sheerin. Will you please let me handle this my own way? Right now you are a complete outsider here, and don't forget it."

Sheerin's mouth twisted eloquently. "Now why should we go to the impossible trouble of calling the police—with Beta's eclipse a matter of minutes from now—when this young man here is perfectly willing to pledge his word of honor to remain and cause no trouble whatsoever?"

The Cultist answered promptly, "I will do no such thing. You're free to do what you want, but it's only fair to warn you that just as soon as I get my chance I'm going to finish what I came out here to do. If it's my word of honor you're relying on, you'd better call the police."

Sheerin smiled in a friendly fashion. "You're a determined cuss, aren't you? Well, I'll explain something. Do you see that young man at the window? He's a strong, husky fellow, quite handy with his fists, and he's an outsider besides. Once the eclipse starts there will be nothing for him to do except keep an eye on you. Besides him, there will be myself—a little too stout for active fisticuffs, but still able to help."

"Well, what of it?" demanded Latimer frozenly.

"Listen and I'll tell you," was the reply. "Just as soon as the eclipse starts, we're going to take you, Theremon and I, and deposit you in a little closet with one door, to which is attached one giant lock and no windows. You will remain there for the duration."

"And afterward," breathed Latimer fiercely, "there'll be no one to let me out. I know as well as you do what the coming of the Stars means—I know it far better than you. With all your minds gone, you are not likely to free me. Suffocation or slow starvation, is it? About what I might have expected from a group of scientists. But I don't give my word. It's a matter of principle, and I won't discuss it further."

Aton seemed perturbed. His faded eyes were troubled. "Really, Sheerin, locking him—"

"Please!" Sheerin motioned him impatiently to silence. "I don't think for a moment things will go that far. Latimer has just tried a clever little bluff, but I'm not a psychologist just because I like the sound of the word." He grinned at the Cultist. "Come now, you don't really think I'm trying anything as crude as slow starvation. My dear Latimer, if I lock you in the closet, you are not going to see the Darkness, and you are not going to see the Stars. It does not take much knowledge of the fundamental creed of the Cult to realize that for you to be hidden from the Stars when they appear means the loss of your immortal soul. Now, I believe you to be an honorable man. I'll accept your word of honor to make no further effort to disrupt proceedings, if you'll offer it."

A vein throbbed in Latimer's temple, and he seemed to shrink within himself as he said thickly, "You have it!" And then he added with swift fury, "But it is my consolation that you will all be damned for your deeds of today." He turned on his heel and stalked to the high three-legged stool by the door.

Sheerin nodded to the columnist. "Take a seat next to him, Theremon—just as a formality. Hey, Theremon!"

But the newspaperman didn't move. He had gone pale to the lips. "Look at that!" The finger he pointed toward the sky shook, and his voice was dry and cracked.

There was one simultaneous gasp as every eye followed the pointing finger and, for one breathless moment, stared frozenly.

Beta was chipped on one side!

The tiny bit of encroaching blackness was perhaps the width of a fingernail, but to the staring watchers it magnified itself into the crack of doom.

Only for a moment they watched, and after that there was a shrieking confusion that was even shorter of duration and which gave way to an orderly scurry of activity—each man at his prescribed job. At the crucial moment there was no time for emotion. The men were merely scientists with work to do. Even Aton had melted away.

Sheerin said prosaically, "First contact must have been made fifteen minutes ago. A little early, but pretty good considering the uncertainties involved in the calculation." He looked about him and then tiptoed to Theremon, who still remained staring out the window, and dragged him away gently.

"Aton is furious," he whispered, "so stay away. He missed first contact on account of this fuss with Latimer, and if you get in his way he'll have you thrown out the window."

Theremon nodded shortly and sat down. Sheerin stared in surprise at him.

"The devil, man," he exclaimed, "you're shaking."

"Eh?" Theremon licked dry lips and then tried to smile. "I don't feel very well, and that's a fact."

The psychologist's eyes hardened. "You're not losing your nerve?"

"No!" cried Theremon in a flash of indignation. "Give me a chance, will you? I haven't really believed this rigmarole—not way down beneath, anyway—till just this minute. Give me a chance to get used to the idea. You've been preparing yourself for two months or more."

"You're right, at that," replied Sheerin thoughtfully. "Listen! Have you got a family—parents, wife, children?"

Theremon shook his head. "You mean the Hideout, I suppose. No, you don't have to worry about that. I have a sister, but she's two thousand miles away. I don't even know her exact address."

"Well, then, what about yourself? You've got time to get there, and they're one short anyway, since I left. After all, you're not needed here, and you'd make a darned fine addition—"

Theremon looked at the other wearily. "You think I'm scared stiff, don't you? Well, get this, mister, I'm a newspaperman and I've been assigned to cover a story. I intend covering it."

There was a faint smile on the psychologist's face. "I see. Professional honor, is that it?"

"You might call it that. But, man, I'd give my right arm for another bottle of that sockeroo juice even half the size of the one you hogged. If ever a fellow needed a drink, I do."

He broke off. Sheerin was nudging him violently. "Do you hear that? Listen!"

Theremon followed the motion of the other's chin and stared at the Cultist, who, oblivious to all about him, faced the window, a look of wild elation on his face, droning to himself the while in singsong fashion.

"What's he saying?" whispered the columnist.

"He's quoting *Book of Revelations*, fifth chapter," replied Sheerin. Then, urgently, "Keep quiet and listen, I tell you."

The Cultist's voice had risen in a sudden increase of fervor: " 'And it came to pass that in those days the Sun, Beta, held lone vigil in the sky for ever longer periods as the revolutions passed; until such time as for full half a revolution, it alone, shrunken and cold, shone down upon Lagash.

" 'And men did assemble in the public squares and in the highways, there to debate and to marvel at the sight, for a strange depression had seized them. Their minds were troubled and their speech confused, for the souls of men awaited the coming of the Stars.

" 'And in the city of Trigon, at high noon, Vendret 2 came forth and said unto the men of Trigon, "Lo, ye sinners! Though ye scorn the ways of righteousness, yet will the time of reckoning come. Even now the Cave approaches to swallow Lagash; yea, and all it contains.

" 'And even as he spoke the lip of the Cave of Darkness passed the edge of Beta so that to all Lagash it was hidden from sight. Loud were the cries of men as it vanished, and great the fear of soul that fell upon them.

" 'It came to pass that the Darkness of the Cave fell upon Lagash, and there was no light on all the surface of Lagash. Men were even as blinded, nor could one man see his neighbor, though he felt his breath upon his face.

" 'And in this blackness there appeared the Stars, in countless numbers, and to the strains of music of such beauty that the very leaves of the trees cried out in wonder.

" 'And in that moment the souls of men departed from them, and their abandoned bodies became even as beasts; yea, even as brutes of the wild; so that through the blackened streets of the cities of Lagash they prowled with wild cries.

" 'From the Stars there then reached down the Heavenly Flame, and where it touched, the cities of Lagash flamed to utter destruction, so that of man and of the works of man nought remained.

" 'Even then—' "

There was a subtle change in Latimer's tone. His eyes had not shifted, but somehow he had become aware of the absorbed attention of the other two. Easily, without pausing for breath, the timbre of his voice shifted and the syllables became more liquid.

Theremon, caught by surprise, stared. The words seemed on the border of familiarity. There was an elusive shift in the accent, a tiny change in the vowel stress; nothing more—yet Latimer had become thoroughly unintelligible.

Sheerin smiled slyly. "He shifted to some old-cycle tongue, probably their traditional second cycle. That was the language in which the *Book of Revelations* was originally written, you know."

"It doesn't matter; I've heard enough." Theremon shoved his chair back and brushed his hair back with hands that no longer shook. "I feel much better now."

"You do?" Sheerin seemed mildly surprised.

"I'll say I do. I had a bad case of jitters just a while back. Listening to you and your gravitation and seeing that eclipse start almost finished me. But this"—he jerked a contemptuous thumb at the yellow-bearded Cultist— "*this* is the sort of thing my nurse used to tell me. I've been laughing at that sort of thing all my life. I'm not going to let it scare me *now.*"

He drew a deep breath and said with a hectic gaiety, "But if I expect to keep on the good side of myself, I'm going to turn my chair away from the window."

Sheerin said, "Yes, but you'd better talk lower. Aton just lifted his head out of that box he's got it stuck into and gave you a look that should have killed you."

Theremon made a mouth. "I forgot about the old fellow." With elaborate care he turned the chair from the window, cast one distasteful look over his shoulder, and said, "It has occurred to me that there must be considerable immunity against this Star madness."

The psychologist did not answer immediately. Beta was past its zenith now, and the square of bloody sunlight that outlined the window upon the floor had lifted into Sheerin's lap. He stared at its dusky color thoughtfully and then bent and squinted into the sun itself.

The chip in its side had grown to a black encroachment that covered a third of Beta. He shuddered, and when he straightened once more his florid cheeks did not contain quite as much color as they had had previously.

With a smile that was almost apologetic, he reversed his chair also. "There are probably two million people in Saro City that are all trying to join the Cult at once in one gigantic revival." Then, ironically, "The Cult is in for an hour of unexampled prosperity. I trust they'll make the most of it. Now, what was it you said?"

"Just this. How did the Cultists manage to keep the *Book of Revelations* going from cycle to cycle, and how on Lagash did it get written in the first place? There must have been some sort of immunity, for if everyone had gone mad, who would be left to write the book?"

Sheerin stared at his questioner ruefully. "Well, now, young man, there isn't any eyewitness answer to that, but we've got a few damned good notions as to what happened. You see, there are three kinds of people who might remain relatively unaffected. First, the very few who don't see the Stars at all: the seriously retarded or those who drink themselves into a stupor at the beginning of the eclipse and remain so to the end. We leave them out—because they aren't really witnesses.

"Then there are children below six, to whom the world as a whole is too new and strange for them to be too frightened at Stars and Darkness. They would be just another item in an already surprising world. You see that, don't you?"

The other nodded doubtfully. "I suppose so."

"Lastly, there are those whose minds are too coarsely grained to be entirely toppled. The very insensitive would be scarcely affected—oh, such people as some of our older, work-broken peasants. Well, the children would have fugitive memories, and that, combined with the confused, incoherent babblings of the half-mad morons, formed the basis for the *Book of Revelations.*

"Naturally, the book was based, in the first place, on the testimony of those least qualified to serve as historians; that is, children and morons; and was probably edited and re-edited through the cycles."

"Do you suppose," broke in Theremon, "that they carried the book through the cycles the way we're planning on handing on the secret of gravitation?"

Sheerin shrugged. "Perhaps, but their exact method is unimportant. They do it, somehow. The point I was getting at was that the book can't help but be a mass of distortion, even if it is based on fact. For instance, do you remember the experiment with the holes in the roof that Faro and Yimot tried—the one that didn't work?"

"Yes."

"You know why it didn't w—" He stopped and rose in alarm, for Aton was approaching, his face a twisted mask of consternation. *"What's happened?"*

Aton drew him aside and Sheerin could feel the fingers on his elbow twitching.

"Not so loud!" Aton's voice was low and tortured. "I've just gotten word from the Hideout on the private line."

Sheerin broke in anxiously. "They are in trouble?"

"Not *they.*" Aton stressed the pronoun significantly. "They sealed themselves off just a while ago, and they're going to stay buried till day after tomorrow. They're safe. But the *city*, Sheerin—it's a shambles. You have no idea—" He was having difficulty in speaking.

"Well?" snapped Sheerin impatiently. "What of it? It will get worse. What are you shaking about?" Then, suspiciously, "How do you feel?"

Aton's eyes sparked angrily at the insinuation, and then faded to anxiety once more. "You don't understand. The Cultists are active. They're rousing the people to storm the Observatory—promising them immediate entrance into grace, promising them salvation, promising them anything. What are we to do, Sheerin?"

Sheerin's head bent, and he stared in long abstraction at his toes. He tapped his chin with one knuckle, then looked up and said crisply, "Do? What is there to do? Nothing at all. Do the men know of this?"

"No, of course not!"

"Good! Keep it that way. How long till totality?"

"Not quite an hour."

"There's nothing to do but gamble. It will take time to organize any really formidable mob, and it will take more time to get them out here. We're a good five miles from the city—"

He glared out the window, down the slopes to where the farmed patches gave way to clumps of white houses in the suburbs; down to where the metropolis itself was a blur on the horizon—a mist in the waning blaze of Beta.

He repeated without turning, "It will take time. Keep on working and pray that totality comes first."

Beta was cut in half, the line of division pushing a slight concavity into the still-bright portion of the Sun. It was like a gigantic eyelid shutting slantwise over the light of a world.

The faint clatter of the room in which he stood faded into oblivion, and he sensed only the thick silence of the fields outside. The very insects seemed frightened mute. And things were dim.

He jumped at the voice in his ear. Theremon said, "Is something wrong?"

"Eh? Er—no. Get back to the chair. We're in the way." They slipped back to their corner, but the psychologist did not speak for a time. He lifted a finger and loosened his collar. He twisted his neck back and forth but found no relief. He looked up suddenly.

"Are you having any difficulty in breathing?"

The newspaperman opened his eyes wide and drew two or three long breaths. "No. Why?"

"I looked out the window too long, I suppose. The dimness got me. Difficulty in breathing is one of the first symptoms of a claustrophobic attack."

Theremon drew another long breath. "Well, it hasn't got me yet. Say, here's another of the fellows."

Beenay had interposed his bulk between the light and the pair in the corner, and Sheerin squinted up at him anxiously. "Hello, Beenay."

The astronomer shifted his weight to the other foot and smiled feebly. "You won't mind if I sit down awhile and join in the talk? My cameras are set, and there's nothing to do till totality." He paused and eyed the Cultist, who fifteen minutes earlier had drawn a small, skin-bound book from his sleeve and had been poring intently over it ever since. "That rat hasn't been making trouble, has he?"

Sheerin shook his head. His shoulders were thrown back and he frowned his concentration as he forced himself to breathe regularly. He said, "Have you had any trouble breathing, Beenay?"

Beenay sniffed the air in his turn. "It doesn't seem stuffy to me."

"A touch of claustrophobia," explained Sheerin apologetically.

"Ohhh! It worked itself differently with me. I get the impression that my eyes are going back on me. Things seem to blur and—well, nothing is clear. And it's cold, too."

"Oh, it's cold, all right. That's no illusion." Theremon grimaced. "My toes feel as if I've been shipping them cross-country in a refrigerating car."

"What we need," put in Sheerin, "is to keep our minds busy with extraneous affairs. I was telling you a while ago, Theremon, why Faro's experiments with the holes in the roof came to nothing."

"You were just beginning," replied Theremon. He encircled a knee with both arms and nuzzled his chin against it.

"Well, as I started to say, they were misled by taking the *Book of Revelations* literally. There probably wasn't any sense in attaching any physical significance to the Stars. It might be, you know, that in the presence of total Darkness, the mind finds it absolutely necessary to create light. This illusion of light might be all the Stars there really are."

"In other words," interposed Theremon, "you mean the Stars are the results of the madness and not one of the causes. Then, what good will Beenay's photographs be?"

"To prove that it is an illusion, maybe; or to prove the opposite; for all I know. Then again—"

But Beenay had drawn his chair closer, and there was an expression of sudden enthusiasm on his face. "Say, I'm glad you two got onto this subject." His eyes narrowed and he lifted one finger. "I've been thinking about these Stars and I've got a really cute notion. Of course it's strictly ocean foam, and I'm not trying to advance it seriously, but I think it's interesting. Do you want to hear it?"

He seemed half reluctant, but Sheerin leaned back and said, "Go ahead! I'm listening."

"Well, then, supposing there were other suns in the universe." He broke off a little bashfully. "I mean suns that are so far away that they're too dim to see. It sounds as if I've been reading some of that fantastic fiction, I suppose."

"Not necessarily. Still, isn't that possibility eliminated by the fact that, according to the Law of Gravitation, they would make themselves evident by their attractive forces?"

"Not if they were far enough off," rejoined Beenay, "really far off— maybe as much as four light years, or even more. We'd never be able to detect perturbations then, because they'd be too small. Say that there were a lot of suns that far off; a dozen or two, maybe."

Theremon whistled melodiously. "What an idea for a good Sunday supplement article. Two dozen suns in a universe eight light years across. Wow! That would shrink our world into insignificance. The readers would eat it up."

"Only an idea," said Beenay with a grin, "but you see the point. During an eclipse, these dozen suns would become visible because there'd be no *real* sunlight to drown them out. Since they're so far off, they'd appear small, like so many little marbles. Of course the Cultists talk of millions of Stars, but that's probably exaggeration. There just isn't any place in the universe you could put a million suns—unless they touch one another."

Sheerin had listened with gradually increasing interest. "You've hit something there, Beenay. And exaggeration is just exactly what would happen. Our minds, as you probably know, can't grasp directly any number higher than five; above that there is only the concept of 'many.' A dozen would become a million just like that. A damn good idea!"

"And I've got another cute little notion," Beenay said. "Have you ever thought what a simple problem gravitation would be if only you had a sufficiently simple system? Supposing you had a universe in which there was a planet with only one sun. The planet would travel in a perfect ellipse and the exact nature of the gravitational force would be so evident it could be accepted as an axiom. Astronomers on such a world would start off with gravity probably before they even invented the telescope. Naked-eye observation would be enough."

"But would such a system be dynamically stable?" questioned Sheerin doubtfully.

"Sure! They call it the 'one-and-one' case. It's been worked out mathematically, but it's the philosophical implications that interest me."

"It's nice to think about," admitted Sheerin, "as a pretty abstraction—like a perfect gas, or absolute zero."

"Of course," continued Beenay, "there's the catch that life would be impossible on such a planet. It wouldn't get enough heat and light, and if it rotated there would be total Darkness half of each day. You couldn't expect life—which is fundamentally dependent upon light—to develop under those conditions. Besides—"

Sheerin's chair went over backward as he sprang to his feet in a rude interruption. "Aton's brought out the lights."

Beenay said, "Huh," turned to stare, and then grinned halfway around his head in open relief.

There were half a dozen foot-long, inch-thick rods cradled in Aton's arms. He glared over them at the assembled staff members.

"Get back to work, all of you. Sheerin, come here and help me!"

Sheerin trotted to the older man's side and, one by one, in utter silence, the two adjusted the rods in makeshift metal holders suspended from the walls.

With the air of one carrying through the most sacred item of a religious ritual, Sheerin scraped a large, clumsy match into spluttering life and passed it to Aton, who carried the flame to the upper end of one of the rods.

It hesitated there awhile, playing futilely about the tip, until a sudden, crackling flare cast Aton's lined face into yellow highlights. He withdrew the match and a spontaneous cheer rattled the window.

The rod was topped by six inches of wavering flame! Methodically, the other rods were lighted, until six independent fires turned the rear of the room yellow.

The light was dim, dimmer even than the tenuous sunlight. The flames reeled crazily, giving birth to drunken, swaying shadows. The torches smoked devilishly and smelled like a bad day in the kitchen. But they emitted yellow light.

There was something about yellow light, after four hours of somber, dimming Beta. Even Latimer had lifted his eyes from his book and stared in wonder.

Sheerin warmed his hands at the nearest, regardless of the soot that gathered upon them in a fine, gray powder, and muttered ecstatically to himself. "Beautiful! Beautiful! I never realized before what a wonderful color yellow is."

But Theremon regarded the torches suspiciously. He wrinkled his nose at the rancid odor and said, "What are those things?"

"Wood," said Sheerin shortly.

"Oh, no, they're not. They aren't burning. The top inch is charred and the flame just keeps shooting up out of nothing."

"That's the beauty of it. This is a really efficient artificial-light mechanism. We made a few hundred of them, but most went to the Hideout, of course. You see"—he turned and wiped his blackened hands upon his handkerchief—"you take the pithy core of coarse water reeds, dry them thoroughly, and soak them in animal grease. Then you set fire to it and the grease burns, little by little. These torches will burn for almost half an hour without stopping. Ingenious, isn't it? It was developed by one of our own young men at Saro University."

After the momentary sensation, the dome had quieted. Latimer had carried his chair directly beneath a torch and continued reading, lips moving in the monotonous recital of invocations to the Stars. Beenay had drifted away to his cameras once more, and Theremon seized the opportunity to add to his notes on the article he was going to write for the Saro City *Chronicle* the next day—a procedure he had been following for the last two hours in a perfectly methodical, perfectly conscientious and, as he was well aware, perfectly meaningless fashion.

But, as the gleam of amusement in Sheerin's eyes indicated, careful note-taking occupied his mind with something other than the fact that the sky was gradually turning a horrible deep purple-red, as if it were one gigantic, freshly peeled beet; and so it fulfilled its purpose.

The air grew, somehow, denser. Dusk, like a palpable entity, entered the room, and the dancing circle of yellow light about the torches etched itself into ever-sharper distinction against the gathering grayness beyond. There was the odor of smoke and the presence of little chuckling sounds that the torches made as they burned; the soft pad of one of the men circling the table at which he worked, on hesitant tiptoes; the occasional indrawn breath of someone trying to retain composure in a world that was retreating into the shadow.

It was Theremon who first heard the extraneous noise. It was a vague, unorganized *impression* of sound that would have gone unnoticed but for the dead silence that prevailed within the dome.

The newsman sat upright and replaced his notebook. He held his breath and listened; then, with considerable reluctance, threaded his way between the solarscope and one of Beenay's cameras and stood before the window.

The silence ripped to fragments at his startled shout: *"Sheerin!"*

Work stopped! The psychologist was at his side in a moment. Aton joined him. Even Yimot 70, high in his little lean-back seat at the eyepiece of the gigantic solarscope, paused and looked downward.

Outside, Beta was a mere smoldering splinter, taking one last desperate look at Lagash. The eastern horizon, in the direction of the city, was lost in Darkness, and the road from Saro to the Observatory was a dull-red line bordered on both sides by wooded tracts, the trees of which had somehow lost individuality and merged into a continuous shadowy mass.

But it was the highway itself that held attention, for along it there surged another, and infinitely menacing, shadowy mass.

Aton cried in a cracked voice, "The madmen from the city! They've come!"

"How long to totality?" demanded Sheerin.

"Fifteen minutes, but . . . but they'll be here in five."

"Never mind, keep the men working. We'll hold them off. This place is built like a fortress. Aton, keep an eye on our young Cultist just for luck. Theremon, come with me."

Sheerin was out the door, and Theremon was at his heels. The stairs stretched below them in tight, circular sweeps about the central shaft, fading into a dank and dreary grayness.

The first momentum of their rush had carried them fifty feet down, so that the dim, flickering yellow from the open door of the dome had disappeared and both above and below the same dusky shadow crushed in upon them.

Sheerin paused, and his pudgy hand clutched at his chest. His eyes bulged and his voice was a dry cough. "I can't . . . breathe. . . . Go down . . . yourself. Close all doors—"

Theremon took a few downward steps, then turned. "Wait! Can you hold out a minute?" He was panting himself. The air passed in and out his lungs like so much molasses, and there was a little germ of screeching panic in his mind at the thought of making his way into the mysterious Darkness below by himself.

Theremon, after all, was afraid of the dark!

"Stay here," he said. "I'll be back in a second." He dashed upward two steps at a time, heart pounding—not altogether from the exertion—tumbled into the dome and snatched a torch from its holder. It was foul-smelling, and the smoke smarted his eyes almost blind, but he clutched that torch as if he wanted to kiss it for joy, and its flame streamed backward as he hurtled down the stairs again.

Sheerin opened his eyes and moaned as Theremon bent over him. Theremon shook him roughly. "All right, get a hold on yourself. We've got light."

He held the torch at tiptoe height and, propping the tottering psychologist by an elbow, made his way downward in the middle of the protecting circle of illumination.

The offices on the ground floor still possessed what light there was, and Theremon felt the horror about him relax.

"Here," he said brusquely, and passed the torch to Sheerin. "You can hear *them* outside."

And they could. Little scraps of hoarse, wordless shouts.

But Sheerin was right; the Observatory was built like a fortress. Erected in the last century, when the neo-Gavottian style of architecture was at its ugly height, it had been designed for stability and durability rather than for beauty.

The windows were protected by the grillwork of inch-thick iron bars sunk deep into the concrete sills. The walls were solid masonry that an earthquake couldn't have touched, and the main door was a huge oaken slab reinforced with iron. Theremon shot the bolts and they slid shut with a dull clang.

At the other end of the corridor, Sheerin cursed weakly. He pointed to the lock of the back door which had been neatly jimmied into uselessness. "That must be how Latimer got in," he said.

"Well, don't stand there," cried Theremon impatiently. "Help drag up the furniture—and keep that torch out of my eyes. The smoke's killing me."

He slammed the heavy table up against the door as he spoke, and in two minutes had built a barricade which made up for what it lacked in beauty and symmetry by the sheer inertia of its massiveness.

Somewhere, dimly, far off, they could hear the battering of naked fists upon the door; and the screams and yells from outside had a sort of half reality.

That mob had set off from Saro City with only two things in mind: the attainment of Cultist salvation by the destruction of the Observatory, and a maddening fear that all but paralyzed them. There was no time to think of ground cars, or of weapons, or of leadership, or even of organization. They made for the Observatory on foot and assaulted it with bare hands.

And now that they were there, the last flash of Beta, the last ruby-red drop of flame, flickered feebly over a humanity that had left only stark, universal fear!

Theremon groaned, "Let's get back to the dome!"

In the dome, only Yimot, at the solarscope, had kept his place. The rest were clustered about the cameras, and Beenay was giving his instructions in a hoarse, strained voice.

"Get it straight, all of you. I'm snapping Beta just before totality and changing the plate. That will leave one of you to each camera. You all know about . . . about times of exposure—"

There was a breathless murmur of agreement.

Beenay passed a hand over his eyes. "Are the torches still burning? Never mind, I see them!" He was leaning hard against the back of a chair. "Now remember, don't . . . don't try to look for good shots. Don't waste time trying to get t-two stars at a time in the scope field. One is enough. And . . . and if you feel yourself going, *get away from the camera.*"

At the door, Sheerin whispered to Theremon, "Take me to Aton. I don't see him."

The newsman did not answer immediately. The vague forms of the astronomers wavered and blurred, and the torches overhead had become only yellow splotches.

"It's dark," he whimpered.

Sheerin held out his hand. "Aton." He stumbled forward. "Aton!"

Theremon stepped after and seized his arm. "Wait, I'll take you." Somehow he made his way across the room. He closed his eyes against the Darkness and his mind against the chaos within it.

No one heard them or paid attention to them. Sheerin stumbled against the wall. "Aton!"

The psychologist felt shaking hands touching him, then withdrawing, a voice muttering, "Is that you, Sheerin?"

"Aton!" He strove to breathe normally. "Don't worry about the mob. The place will hold them off."

Latimer, the Cultist, rose to his feet, and his face twisted in desperation. His word was pledged, and to break it would mean placing his soul in mortal peril. Yet that word had been forced from him and had not been given freely. The Stars would come soon! He could not stand by and allow— And yet his word was pledged.

Beenay's face was dimly flushed as it looked upward at Beta's last ray, and Latimer, seeing him bend over his camera, made his decision. His nails cut the flesh of his palms as he tensed himself.

He staggered crazily as he started his rush. There was nothing before him but shadows; the very floor beneath his feet lacked substance. And then someone was upon him and he went down with clutching fingers at his throat.

He doubled his knee and drove it hard into his assailant. "Let me up or I'll kill you."

Theremon cried out sharply and muttered through a blinding haze of pain. "You double-crossing rat!"

The newsman seemed conscious of everything at once. He heard Beenay croak, "I've got it. At your cameras, men!" and then there was the strange awareness that the last thread of sunlight had thinned out and snapped.

Simultaneously he heard one last choking gasp from Beenay, and a queer little cry from Sheerin, a hysterical giggle that cut off in a rasp—and a sudden silence, a strange, deadly silence from outside.

And Latimer had gone limp in his loosening grasp. Theremon peered into the Cultist's eyes and saw the blankness of them, staring upward, mirroring the feeble yellow of the torches. He saw the bubble of froth upon Latimer's lips and heard the low animal whimper in Latimer's throat.

With the slow fascination of fear, he lifted himself on one arm and turned his eyes toward the blood-curdling blackness of the window.

Through it shone the Stars!

Not Earth's feeble thirty-six hundred Stars visible to the eye; Lagash was in the center of a giant cluster. Thirty thousand mighty suns shone down in a soul-searing splendor that was more frighteningly cold in its awful indifference than the bitter wind that shivered across the cold, horribly bleak world.

Theremon staggered to his feet, his throat constricting him to breathlessness, all the muscles of his body writhing in an intensity of terror and sheer fear beyond bearing. He was going mad and knew it, and somewhere deep inside a bit of sanity was screaming, struggling to fight off the hopeless flood of black terror. It was very horrible to go mad and know that you were going mad—to know that in a little minute you would be here physically and yet all the real essence would be dead and drowned in the black madness. For this was the Dark—the Dark and the Cold and the Doom. The bright walls of the universe were shattered and their awful black fragments were falling down to crush and squeeze and obliterate him.

He jostled someone crawling on hands and knees, but stumbled somehow over him. Hands groping at his tortured throat, he limped toward the flame of the torches that filled all his mad vision.

"Light!" he screamed.

Aton, somewhere, was crying, whimpering horribly like a terribly frightened child. "Stars—all the Stars—we didn't know at all. We didn't know anything. We thought six stars in a universe is something the Stars didn't notice is Darkness forever and ever and ever and the walls are breaking in and we didn't know we couldn't know and anything—"

Someone clawed at the torch, and it fell and snuffed out. In the instant, the awful splendor of the indifferent Stars leaped nearer to them.

On the horizon outside the window, in the direction of Saro City, a crimson glow began growing, strengthening in brightness, that was not the glow of a sun.

The long night had come again.

Green Patches

He had slipped aboard the ship! There had been dozens waiting outside the energy barrier when it had seemed that waiting would do no good. Then the barrier had faltered for a matter of two minutes (which showed the superiority of unified organisms over life fragments) and he was across.

None of the others had been able to move quickly enough to take advantage of the break, but that didn't matter. All alone, he was enough. No others were necessary.

And the thought faded out of satisfaction and into loneliness. It was a terribly unhappy and unnatural thing to be parted from all the rest of the unified organism, to be a life fragment oneself. How could these aliens stand being fragments?

It increased his sympathy for the aliens. Now that he experienced fragmentation himself, he could feel, as though from a distance, the terrible isolation that made them so afraid. It was fear born of that isolation that dictated their actions. What but the insane fear of their condition could have caused them to blast an area, one mile in diameter, into dull-red heat before landing their ship? Even the organized life ten feet deep in the soil had been destroyed in the blast.

He engaged reception, listening eagerly, letting the alien thought saturate him. He enjoyed the touch of life upon his consciousness. He would have to ration that enjoyment. He must not forget himself.

But it could do no harm to listen to thoughts. Some of the fragments of life on the ship thought quite clearly, considering that they were such primitive, incomplete creatures. Their thoughts were like tiny bells.

Roger Oldenn said, "I feel contaminated. You know what I mean? I keep washing my hands and it doesn't help."

Jerry Thorn hated dramatics and didn't look up. They were still maneuvering in the stratosphere of Saybrook's Planet and he preferred to watch the panel dials. He said, "No reason to feel contaminated. Nothing happened."

"I hope not," said Oldenn. "At least they had all the field men discard their spacesuits in the air lock for complete disinfection. They had a radiation bath for all men entering from outside. I *suppose* nothing happened."

"Why be nervous, then?"

"I don't know. I wish the barrier hadn't broken down."

"Who doesn't? It was an accident."

"I wonder." Oldenn was vehement. "I was here when it happened. My shift, you know. There was no reason to overload the power line. There was equipment plugged into it that had no damn business near it. None whatsoever."

"All right. People are stupid."

"Not that stupid. I hung around when the Old Man was checking into the matter. None of them had reasonable excuses. The armor-baking circuits, which were draining off two thousand watts, had been put into the barrier line. They'd been using the second subsidiaries for a week. Why not this time? They couldn't give any reason."

"Can you?"

Oldenn flushed. "No, I was just wondering if the men had been"—he searched for a word—"hypnotized into it. By those things outside."

Thorn's eyes lifted and met those of the other levelly. "I wouldn't repeat that to anyone else. The barrier was down only two minutes. If anything had happened, if even a spear of grass had drifted across it would have shown up in our bacteria cultures within half an hour, in the fruit-fly colonies in a matter of days. Before we got back it would show up in the hamsters, the rabbits, maybe the goats. Just get it through your head, Oldenn, that nothing happened. Nothing."

Oldenn turned on his heel and left. In leaving, his foot came within two feet of the object in the corner of the room. He did not see it.

He disengaged his reception centers and let the thoughts flow past him unperceived. These life fragments were not important, in any case, since they were not fitted for the continuation of life. Even as fragments, they were incomplete.

The other types of fragments now—they were different. He had to be careful of them. The temptation would be great, and he must give no indication, none at all, of his existence on board ship till they landed on their home planet.

He focused on the other parts of the ship, marveling at the diversity of life. Each item, no matter how small, was sufficient to itself. He forced himself to contemplate this, until the unpleasantness of the thought grated on him and he longed for the normality of home.

Most of the thoughts he received from the smaller fragments were vague and fleeting, as you would expect. There wasn't much to be had from them, but that meant their need for completeness was all the greater. It was that which touched him so keenly.

There was the life fragment which squatted on its haunches and fingered the wire netting that enclosed it. Its thoughts were clear, but limited. Chiefly, they concerned the yellow fruit a companion fragment was eating. It wanted the fruit very deeply. Only the wire netting that separated the fragments prevented its seizing the fruit by force.

He disengaged reception in a moment of complete revulsion. *These fragments competed for food!*

He tried to reach far outward for the peace and harmony of home, but it was already an immense distance away. He could reach only into the nothingness that separated him from sanity.

He longed at the moment even for the feel of the dead soil between the barrier and the ship. He had crawled over it last night. There had been no life upon it, but it had been the soil of home, and on the other side of the barrier there had still been the comforting feel of the rest of organized life.

He could remember the moment he had located himself on the surface of the ship, maintaining a desperate suction grip until the air lock opened. He had entered, moving cautiously between the outgoing feet. There had been an inner lock and that had been passed later. Now he lay here, a life fragment himself, inert and unnoticed.

Cautiously, he engaged reception again at the previous focus. The squatting fragment of life was tugging furiously at the wire netting. It still wanted the other's food, though it was the less hungry of the two.

Larsen said, "Don't feed the damn thing. She isn't hungry; she's just sore because Tillie had the nerve to eat before she herself was crammed full. The greedy ape! I wish we were back home and I never had to look another animal in the face again."

He scowled at the older female chimpanzee frowningly and the chimp mouthed and chattered back to him in full reciprocation.

Rizzo said, "Okay, okay. Why hang around here, then? Feeding time is over. Let's get out."

They went past the goat pens, the rabbit hutches, the hamster cages.

Larsen said bitterly, "You volunteer for an exploration voyage. You're a hero. They send you off with speeches—and make a zoo keeper out of you."

"They give you double pay."

"All right, so what? I didn't sign up just for the money. They said at the original briefing that it was even odds we wouldn't come back, that we'd end up like Saybrook. I signed up because I wanted to do something important."

"Just a bloomin' bloody hero," said Rizzo.

"I'm not an animal nurse."

Rizzo paused to lift a hamster out of the cage and stroke it. "Hey," he said, "did you ever think that maybe one of these hamsters has some cute little baby hamsters inside, just getting started?"

"Wise guy! They're tested every day."

"Sure, sure." He muzzled the little creature, which vibrated its nose at him. "But just suppose you came down one morning and found them there. New little hamsters looking up at you with soft, green patches of fur where the eyes ought to be."

"Shut up, for the love of Mike," yelled Larsen.

"Little soft, green patches of shining fur," said Rizzo, and put the hamster down with a sudden loathing sensation.

He engaged reception again and varied the focus. There wasn't a specialized life fragment at home that didn't have a rough counterpart on shipboard.

There were the moving runners in various shapes, the moving swimmers, and the moving fliers. Some of the fliers were quite large, with perceptible thoughts; others were small, gauzy-winged creatures. These last transmitted only patterns of sense perception, imperfect patterns at that, and added nothing intelligent of their own.

There were the non-movers, which, like the non-movers at home, were green and lived on the air, water, and soil. These were a mental blank. They knew only the dim, dim consciousness of light, moisture, and gravity.

And each fragment, moving and non-moving, had its mockery of life.

Not yet. Not yet. . . .

He clamped down hard upon his feelings. Once before, these life fragments had come, and the rest at home had tried to help them—too quickly. It had not worked. This time they must wait.

If only these fragments did not discover him.

They had not, so far. They had not noticed him lying in the corner of the pilot room. No one had bent down to pick up and discard him. Earlier, it had meant he could not move. Someone might have turned and stared at the stiff wormlike thing, not quite six inches long. First stare, then shout, and then it would all be over.

But now, perhaps, he had waited long enough. The takeoff was long past. The controls were locked; the pilot room was empty.

It did not take him long to find the chink in the armor leading to the recess where some of the wiring was. They were dead wires.

The front end of his body was a rasp that cut in two a wire of just the right diameter. Then, six inches away, he cut it in two again. He pushed the snipped-off section of the wire ahead of him packing it away neatly and invisibly into a corner of recess. Its outer covering was a brown elastic material and its core was gleaming, ruddy metal. He himself could not reproduce the core, of course, but that was not necessary. It was enough that the pellicle that covered him had been carefully bred to resemble a wire's surface.

He returned and grasped the cut sections of the wire before and behind. He tightened against them as his little suction disks came into play. Not even a seam showed.

They could not find him now. They could look right at him and see only a continuous stretch of wire.

Unless they looked very closely indeed and noted that, in a certain spot on this wire, there were two tiny patches of soft and shining green fur.

"It is remarkable," said Dr. Weiss, "that little green hairs can do so much."

Captain Loring poured the brandy carefully. In a sense, this was a celebration. They would be ready for the jump through hyper-space in two hours, and after that, two days would see them back on Earth.

"You are convinced, then, the green fur is the sense organ?" he asked.

"It is," said Weiss. Brandy made him come out in splotches, but he was aware of the need of celebration—quite aware. "The experiments were conducted under difficulties, but they were quite significant."

The captain smiled stiffly. " 'Under difficulties' is one way of phrasing it. I would never have taken the chances you did to run them."

"Nonsense. We're all heroes aboard this ship, all volunteers, all great men with trumpet, fife, and fanfarade. You took the chance of coming here."

"You were the first to go outside the barrier."

"No particular risk involved," Weiss said. "I burned the ground before me as I went, to say nothing of the portable barrier that surrounded me. Nonsense, Captain. Let's all take our medals when we come back; let's take them without attempt at gradation. Besides, I'm a male."

"But you're filled with bacteria to here." The captain's hand made a quick, cutting gesture three inches above his head. "Which makes you as vulnerable as a female would be."

They paused for drinking purposes.

"Refill?" asked the captain.

"No, thanks. I've exceeded my quota already."

"Then one last for the spaceroad." He lifted his glass in the general direction of Saybrook's Planet, no longer visible, its sun only a bright star in the visiplate. "To the little green hairs that gave Saybrook his first lead."

Weiss nodded. "A lucky thing. We'll quarantine the planet, of course."

The captain said, "That doesn't seem drastic enough. Someone might always land by accident someday and not have Saybrook's insight, or his guts. Suppose he did not blow up his ship, as Saybrook did. Suppose he got back to some inhabited place."

The captain was somber. "Do you suppose they might ever develop interstellar travel on their own?"

"I doubt it. No proof, of course. It's just that they have such a completely different orientation. Their entire organization of life has made tools unnecessary. As far as we know, even a stone ax doesn't exist on the planet."

"I hope you're right. Oh, and, Weiss, would you spend some time with Drake?"

"The Galactic Press fellow?"

"Yes. Once we get back, the story of Saybrook's Planet will be released for the public and I don't think it would be wise to oversensationalize it. I've asked Drake to let you consult with him on the story. You're a biologist and enough of an authority to carry weight with him. Would you oblige?"

"A pleasure."

The captain closed his eyes wearily and shook his head.

"Headache, Captain?"

"No. Just thinking of poor Saybrook."

He was weary of the ship. Awhile back there had been a queer, momentary sensation, as though he had been turned inside out. It was alarming and he had searched the minds of the keen-thinkers for an explanation. Apparently the ship had leaped across vast stretches of empty space by cutting across something they knew as "hyper-space." The keen-thinkers were ingenious.

But—he was weary of the ship. It was such a futile phenomenon. These life fragments were skillful in their constructions, yet it was only a measure of their unhappiness, after all. They strove to find in the control of inanimate matter what they could not find in themselves. In their unconscious yearning for completeness, they built machines and scoured space, seeking, seeking . . .

These creatures, he knew, could never, in the very nature of things, find that for which they were seeking. At least not until such time as he gave it to them. He quivered a little at the thought.

Completeness!

These fragments had no concept of it, even. "Completeness" was a poor word.

In their ignorance they would even fight it. There had been the ship that had come before. The first ship had contained many of the keen-thinking fragments. There had been two varieties, life producers and the sterile ones. (How different this second ship was. The keen-thinkers were all sterile, while the other fragments, the fuzzy-thinkers and the no-thinkers, were all producers of life. It was strange.)

How gladly that first ship had been welcomed by all the planet! He could remember the first intense shock at the realization that the visitors were fragments and not complete. The shock had give way to pity, and the pity to action. It was not certain how they would fit into the community, but there had been no hesitation. All life was sacred and somehow room would have been made for them—for all of them, from the large keen-thinkers to the little multipliers in the darkness.

But there had been a miscalculation. They had not correctly analyzed the course of the fragments' ways of thinking. The keen-thinkers became aware of what had been done and resented it. They were frightened, of course; they did not understand.

They had developed the barrier first, and then, later, had destroyed themselves, exploding their ships to atoms.

Poor, foolish fragments.

This time, at least, it would be different. They would be saved, despite themselves.

John Drake would not have admitted it in so many words, but he was very proud of his skill on the photo-typer. He had a travel-kit model, which was a six-by-eight, featureless dark plastic slab, with cylindrical bulges on either end to hold the roll of thin paper. It fitted into a brown leather case, equipped with a beltlike contraption that held it closely about the waist and at one hip. The whole thing weighed less than a pound.

Drake could operate it with either hand. His fingers would flick quickly and easily, placing their light pressure at exact spots on the blank surface, and, soundlessly, words would be written.

He looked thoughtfully at the beginning of his story, then up at Dr. Weiss. "What do you think, Doc?"

"It starts well."

Drake nodded. "I thought I might as well start with Saybrook himself. They haven't released his story back home yet. I wish I could have seen Saybrook's original report. How did he ever get it through, by the way?"

"As near as I could tell, he spent one last night sending it through the sub-ether. When he was finished, he shorted the motors, and converted the entire ship into a thin cloud of vapor a millionth of a second later. The crew and himself along with it."

"What a man! You were in this from the beginning, Doc?"

"Not from the beginning," corrected Weiss gently. "Only since the receipt of Saybrook's report."

He could not help thinking back. He had read that report, realizing even then how wonderful the planet must have seemed when Saybrook's colonizing expedition first reached it. It was practically a duplicate of Earth, with an abounding plant life and a purely vegetarian animal life.

There had been only the little patches of green fur (how often had he used that phrase in his speaking and thinking!) which seemed strange. No living individual on the planet had eyes. Instead, there was this fur. Even the plants, each blade or leaf or blossom, possessed the two patches of richer green.

Then Saybrook had noticed, startled and bewildered, that there was no conflict for food on the planet. All plants grew pulpy appendages which were eaten by the animals. These were regrown in a matter of hours. No other parts of the plants were touched. It was as though the plants fed the animals as part of the order of nature. And the plants themselves did not grow in overpowering profusion. They might almost have been cultivated, they were spread across the available soil so discriminately.

How much time, Weiss wondered, had Saybrook had to observe the strange law and order on the planet?—the fact that insects kept their numbers reasonable, though no birds ate them; that the rodent-like things did not swarm, though no carnivores existed to keep them in check.

And then there had come the incident of the white rats.

That prodded Weiss. He said, "Oh, one correction, Drake. Hamsters were not the first animals involved. It was the white rats."

"White rats," said Drake, making the correction in his notes.

"Every colonizing ship," said Weiss, "takes a group of white rats for the purpose of testing any alien foods. Rats, of course, are very similar to human beings from a nutritional viewpoint. Naturally, only female white rats are taken."

Naturally. If only one sex was present, there was no danger of unchecked multiplication in case the planet proved favorable. Remember the rabbits in Australia.

"Incidentally, why not use males?" asked Drake.

"Females are hardier," said Weiss, "which is lucky, since that gave the situation away. It turned out suddenly that all the rats were bearing young."

"Right. Now that's where I'm up to, so here's my chance to get some things straight. For my own information, Doc, how did Saybrook find out they were in a family way?"

"Accidentally, of course. In the course of nutritional investigations, rats are dissected for evidence of internal damage. Their condition was bound to be discovered. A few more were dissected; same results. Eventually, all that lived gave birth to young—with *no* male rats aboard!"

"And the point is that all the young were born with little green patches of fur instead of eyes."

"That is correct. Saybrook said so and we corroborate him. After the rats, the pet cat of one of the children was obviously affected. When it finally kittened, the kittens were not born with closed eyes but with little patches of green fur. There was no tomcat aboard.

"Eventually Saybrook had the women tested. He didn't tell them what for. He didn't want to frighten them. Every single one of them was in the early stages of pregnancy, leaving out of consideration those few who had been pregnant at the time of embarkation. Saybrook never waited for any child to be born, of course. He knew they would have no eyes, only shining patches of green fur.

"He even prepared bacterial cultures (Saybrook was a thorough man) and found each bacillus to show microscopic green spots."

Drake was eager. "That goes way beyond our briefing—or, at least, the briefing I got. But granted that life on Saybrook's Planet is organized into a unified whole, how is it done?"

"How? How are your cells organized into a unified whole? Take an individual cell out of your body, even a brain cell, and what is it by itself? Nothing. A little blob of protoplasm with no more capacity for anything human than an amoeba. Less capacity, in fact, since it couldn't live by itself. But put the cells together and you have something that could invent a spaceship or write a symphony."

"I get the idea," said Drake.

Weiss went on, "*All* life on Saybrook's Planet is a *single* organism. In a sense, all life on Earth is too, but it's a fighting dependence, a dog-eat-dog dependence. The bacteria fix nitrogen; the plants fix carbon; animals eat plants and each other; bacterial decay hits everything. It comes full circle. Each grabs as much as it can, and is, in turn, grabbed.

"On Saybrook's Planet, each organism has its place, as each cell in our body does. Bacteria and plants produce food, on the excess of which animals feed, providing in turn carbon dioxide and nitrogenous wastes. Nothing is produced more or less than is needed. The scheme of life is intelligently altered to suit the local environment. No group of life forms multiplies more or less than is needed, just as the cells in our body stop multiplying when there are enough of them for a given purpose. When they don't stop multiplying, we call it cancer. And that's what life on Earth really is, the kind of organic organization we have, compared to that on Saybrook's Planet. One big cancer. Every species, every individual doing its best to thrive at the expense of every other species and individual."

"You sound as if you approve of Saybrook's Planet, Doc."

"I do, in a way. It makes sense out of the business of living. I can see their viewpoint toward us. Suppose one of the cells of your body could be conscious of the efficiency of the human body as compared with that of the cell itself, and could realize that this was only the result of the union of many cells into a higher whole. And then suppose it became conscious of the existence of free-living cells, with bare life and nothing more. It might feel a very strong desire to drag the poor thing into an organization. It might feel sorry for it, feel perhaps a sort of missionary spirit. The things on Saybrook's Planet—or the thing; one should use the singular—feels just that, perhaps."

"And went ahead by bringing about virgin births, eh, Doc? I've got to go easy on that angle of it. Post-office regulations, you know."

"There's nothing ribald about it, Drake. For centuries we've been able to make the eggs of sea urchins, bees, frogs, et cetera develop without the intervention of male fertilization. The touch of a needle was sometimes enough, or just immersion in the proper salt solution. The thing on Saybrook's Planet can cause fertilization by the controlled use of radiant energy. That's why an appropriate energy barrier stops it; interference, you see, or static.

"They can do more than stimulate the division and development of an unfertilized egg. They can impress their own characteristics upon its nucleoproteins, so that the young are born with the little patches of green fur, which serve as the planet's sense organ and means of communication. The young, in other words, are not individuals, but become part of the thing on Saybrook's Planet. The thing on the planet, not at all incidentally, can impregnate any species—plant, animal, or microscopic."

"Potent stuff," muttered Drake.

"Totipotent," Dr. Weiss said sharply. "Universally potent. Any fragment of it is totipotent. Given time, a single bacterium from Saybrook's Planet can convert *all of Earth* into a single organism! We've got the experimental proof of that."

Drake said unexpectedly, "You know, I think I'm a millionaire, Doc. Can you keep a secret?"

Weiss nodded, puzzled.

"I've got a souvenir from Saybrook's Planet," Drake told him, grinning. "It's only a pebble, but after the publicity the planet will get, combined with the fact that it's quarantined from here on in, the pebble will be all any human being will ever see of it. How much do you suppose I could sell the thing for?"

Weiss stared. "A pebble?" He snatched at the object shown him, a hard, gray ovoid. "You shouldn't have done that, Drake. It was strictly against regulations."

"I know. That's why I asked if you could keep a secret. If you could give me a signed note of authentication—*What's the matter, Doc?*"

Instead of answering, Weiss could only chatter and point. Drake ran over and stared down at the pebble. It was the same as before—

Except that the light was catching it at an angle, and it showed up two little green spots. Look very closely; they were patches of green hairs.

He was disturbed. There was a definite air of danger within the ship. There was the suspicion of his presence aboard. How could that be? He had done nothing yet. Had another fragment of home come aboard and been less cautious? That would be impossible without his knowledge, and though he probed the ship intensely, he found nothing.

And then the suspicion diminished, but it was not quite dead. One of the keen-thinkers still wondered, and was treading close to the truth.

How long before the landing? Would an entire world of life fragments be deprived of completeness? He clung closer to the severed ends of the wire he had been specially bred to imitate, afraid of detection, fearful for his altruistic mission.

Dr. Weiss had locked himself in his own room. They were already within the solar system, and in three hours they would be landing. He had to think. He had three hours in which to decide.

Drake's devilish "pebble" had been part of the organized life on Saybrook's Planet, of course, but it was dead. It was dead when he had first seen it, and if it hadn't been, it was certainly dead after they fed it into the hyper-atomic motor and converted it into a blast of pure heat. And the bacterial cultures still showed normal when Weiss anxiously checked.

That was not what bothered Weiss now.

Drake had picked up the "pebble" during the last hours of the stay on Saybrook's Planet—*after* the barrier breakdown. What if the breakdown had been the result of a slow, relentless mental pressure on the part of the thing on the planet? What if parts of its being waited to invade as the barrier dropped? If the "pebble" had not been fast enough and had moved only after the barrier was reestablished, it would have been killed. It would have lain there for Drake to see and pick up.

It was a "pebble," not a natural life form. But did that mean it was not *some* kind of life form? It might have been a deliberate production of the planet's single organism—a creature deliberately designed to look like a pebble, harmless-seeming, unsuspicious. Camouflage, in other words—a shrewd and frighteningly successful camouflage.

Had any other camouflaged creature succeeded in crossing the barrier *before* it was re-established—with a suitable shape filched from the minds of the humans aboard ship by the mind-reading organism of the planet? Would it have the casual appearance of a paperweight? Of an ornamental brass-head nail in the captain's old-fashioned chair? And how would they locate it? Could they search every part of the ship for the telltale green patches—even down to individual microbes?

And why camouflage? Did it intend to remain undetected for a time? Why? So that it might wait for the landing on Earth?

An infection *after landing* could not be cured by blowing up a ship. The bacteria of Earth, the molds, yeasts, and protozoa, would go first. Within a year the non-human young would be arriving by the uncountable billions.

Weiss closed his eyes and told himself it might not be such a bad thing. There would be no more disease, since no bacterium would multiply at the expense of its host, but instead would be satisfied with its fair share of what was available. There would be no more overpopulation; the hordes of mankind would decline to adjust themselves to the food supply. There would be no more wars, no crime, no greed.

But there would be no more individuality, either.

Humanity would find security by becoming a cog in a biological machine. A man would be brother to a germ, or to a liver cell.

He stood up. He would have a talk with Captain Loring. They would send their report and blow up the ship, just as Saybrook had done.

He sat down again. Saybrook had had proof, while he had only the conjectures of a terrorized mind, rattled by the sight of two green spots on a pebble. Could he kill the two hundred men on board ship because of a feeble suspicion?

He had to *think!*

He was straining. Why did he have to wait? If he could only welcome those who were aboard now. *Now!*

Yet a cooler, more reasoning part of himself told him that he could not. The little multipliers in the darkness would betray their new status in fifteen minutes, and the keen-thinkers had them under continual observation. Even one mile from the surface of their planet would be too soon, since they might still destroy themselves and their ship out in space.

Better to wait for the main air locks to open, for the planetary air to swirl in with millions of the little multipliers. Better to greet each one of them into the brotherhood of unified life and let them swirl out again to spread the message.

Then it would be done! Another world organized, complete!

He waited. There was the dull throbbing of the engines working mightily to control the slow dropping of the ship; the shudder of contact with planetary surface, then—

He let the jubilation of the keen-thinkers sweep into reception, and his own jubilant thoughts answered them. Soon they would be able to receive as well as himself. Perhaps not these particular fragments, but the fragments that would grow out of those which were fitted for the continuation of life.

The main air locks were about to be opened—

And all thought ceased.

Jerry Thorn thought, Damn it, something's wrong *now.*

He said to Captain Loring, "Sorry. There seems to be a power breakdown. The locks won't open."

"Are you sure, Thorn? The lights are on."

"Yes, sir. We're investigating it now."

He tore away and joined Roger Oldenn at the air-lock wiring box. "What's wrong?"

"Give me a chance, will you?" Oldenn's hands were busy. Then he said, "For the love of Pete, there's a six-inch break in the twenty-amp lead."

"What? That can't be!"

Oldenn held up the broken wires with their clean, sharp, sawn-through ends.

Dr. Weiss joined them. He looked haggard and there was the smell of brandy on his breath.

He said shakily, "What's the matter?"

They told him. At the bottom of the compartment, in one corner, was the missing section.

Weiss bent over. There was a black fragment on the floor of the compartment. He touched it with his finger and it smeared, leaving a sooty smudge on his finger tip. He rubbed it off absently.

There might have been something taking the place of the missing section of wire. Something that had been alive and only looked like wire, yet something that would heat, die, and carbonize in a tiny fraction of a second once the electrical circuit which controlled the air lock had been closed.

He said, "How are the bacteria?"

A crew member went to check, returned and said, "All normal, Doc."

The wires had meanwhile been spliced, the locks opened, and Dr. Weiss stepped out into the anarchic world of life that was Earth.

"Anarchy," he said, laughing a little wildly. "And it will stay that way."

Hostess

Rose Smollett was happy about it; almost triumphant. She peeled off her gloves, put her hat away, and turned her brightening eyes upon her husband.

She said, "Drake, we're going to have him here."

Drake looked at her with annoyance. "You've missed supper. I thought you were going to be back by seven."

"Oh, that doesn't matter. I ate something on the way home. But, Drake, we're going to have him here!"

"*Who* here? What are you talking about?"

"The doctor from Hawkin's Planet! Didn't you realize that was what today's conference was about? We spent all day talking about it. It's the most exciting thing that could possibly have happened!"

Drake Smollett removed the pipe from the vicinity of his face. He stared first at it and then at his wife. "Let me get this straight. When you say the doctor from Hawkin's Planet, do you mean the Hawkinsite you've got at the Institute?"

"Well, of course. Who else could I possibly mean?"

"And may I ask what the devil you mean by saying we'll have him here?"

"Drake, don't you understand?"

"What is there to understand? Your Institute may be interested in the thing, but I'm not. What have we to do with it personally? It's Institute business, isn't it?"

"But, darling," Rose said, patiently, "the Hawkinsite would like to stay at a private house somewhere, where he won't be bothered with official ceremony, and where he'll be able to proceed more according to his own likes and dislikes. I find it quite understandable."

"Why at *our* house?"

"Because our place is convenient for the purpose, I suppose. They asked if I would allow it, and frankly," she added with some stiffness, "I consider it a privilege."

"Look!" Drake put his fingers through his brown hair and succeeded in rumpling it. "We've got a convenient little place here—granted! It's not the most elegant place in the world, but it does well enough for us. However, I don't see where we've got room for extraterrestrial visitors."

Rose began to look worried. She removed her glasses and put them away in their case. "He can stay in the spare room. He'll take care of it himself. I've spoken to him and he's very pleasant. Honestly, all we have to do is show a certain amount of adaptability."

Drake said, "Sure, just a little adaptability! The Hawkinsites breathe cyanide. We'll just adapt ourselves to that, I suppose!"

"He carries cyanide in a little cylinder. You won't even notice it."

"And what else about them that I won't notice?"

"*Nothing* else. They're perfectly harmless. Goodness, they're even vegetarians."

"And what does that mean? Do we feed him a bale of hay for dinner?"

Rose's lower lip trembled. "Drake, you're being deliberately hateful. There are many vegetarians on Earth; they don't eat hay."

"And what about us? Do we eat meat ourselves or will that make us look like cannibals to him? I won't live on salads to suit him; I warn you."

"You're being quite ridiculous."

Rose felt helpless. She had married late in life, comparatively. Her career had been chosen; she herself had seemed well settled in it. She was a fellow in biology at the Jenkins Institute for the Natural Sciences, with over twenty publications to her credit. In a word, the line was hewed, the path cleared; she had been set for a career and spinsterhood. And now, at thirty-five, she was still a little amazed to find herself a bride of less than a year.

Occasionally, it embarrassed her, too, since she sometimes found that she had not the slightest idea of how to handle her husband. What *did* one do when the man of the family became mulish? That was not included in any of her courses. As a woman of independent mind and career, she couldn't bring herself to cajolery.

So she looked at him steadily and said simply, "It means very much to me."

"Why?"

"Because, Drake, if he stays here for any length of time, I can study him really closely. Very little work has been done on the biology and psychology of the individual Hawkinsite or of any of the extraterrestrial intelligences.

We have some of their sociology and history, of course, but that's all. Surely, you must see the opportunity. He stays here; we watch him, speak to him, observe his habits—"

"Not interested."

"Oh, Drake, I don't understand you."

"You're going to say I'm not usually like this, I suppose."

"Well, you're not."

Drake was silent for a while. He seemed withdrawn and his high cheekbones and large chin were twisted and frozen into a brooding position.

He said finally, "Look, I've heard a bit about the Hawkinsites in the way of my own business. You say there have been investigations of their sociology, but not of their biology. Sure. It's because the Hawkinsites don't like to be studied as specimens any more than we would. I've spoken to men who were in charge of security groups watching various Hawkinsite missions on Earth. The missions stay in the rooms assigned to them and don't leave for anything but the most important official business. They have nothing to do with Earthmen. It's quite obvious that they are as revolted by us as I personally am by them.

"In fact, I just don't understand why this Hawkinsite at the Institute should be any different. It seems to me to be against all the rules to have him come here by himself, anyway—and to have him want to stay in an Earthman's home just puts the maraschino cherry on top."

Rose said, wearily, "This is different. I'm surprised you can't understand it, Drake. He's a doctor. He's coming here in the way of medical research, and I'll grant you that he probably doesn't enjoy staying with human beings and will find us perfectly horrible. But he must stay just the same! Do you suppose human doctors enjoy going into the tropics, or that they are particularly fond of letting themselves be bitten by infected mosquitoes?"

Drake said sharply, "What's this about mosquitoes? What have they to do with it?"

"Why, nothing," Rose answered, surprised. "It just came to my mind, that's all. I was thinking of Reed and his yellow-fever experiments."

Drake shrugged. "Well, have it your own way."

For a moment, Rose hesitated. "You're not angry about this, are you?" To her own ears she sounded unpleasantly girlish.

"No."

And that, Rose knew, meant that he was.

Rose surveyed herself doubtfully in the full-length mirror. She had never been beautiful and was quite reconciled to the fact; so much so that it no longer mattered. Certainly, it would not matter to a being from Hawkin's Planet. What *did* bother her was this matter of being a hostess under the very queer circumstances of having to be tactful to an extraterrestrial creature and, at the same time, to her husband as well. She wondered which would prove the more difficult.

Drake was coming home late that day; he was not due for half an hour. Rose found herself inclined to believe that he had arranged that purposely in a sullen desire to leave her alone with her problem. She found herself in a state of mild resentment.

He had called her just before noon at the Institute and had asked abruptly, "When are you taking him home?"

She answered, curtly, "In about three hours."

"All right. What's his name? His Hawkinsite name?"

"Why do you want to know?" She could not keep the chill from her words.

"Let's call it a small investigation of my own. After all, the thing will be in my house."

"Oh, for heaven's sake, Drake, don't bring your job home with you!"

Drake's voice sounded tinny and nasty in her ears. "Why not, Rose? Isn't that exactly what you're doing?"

It was, of course, so she gave him the information he wanted.

This was the first time in their married life that they had had even the semblance of a quarrel, and, as she sat there before the full-length mirror, she began to wonder if perhaps she ought not make an attempt to see his side of it. In essence, she had married a policeman. Of course he was more than simply a policeman; he was a member of the World Security Board.

It had been a surprise to her friends. The fact of the marriage itself had been the biggest surprise, but if she had decided on marriage, the attitude was, why not with another biologist? Or, if she had wanted to go afield, an anthropologist, perhaps; even a chemist; but why, of all people, a policeman? Nobody had exactly said those things, naturally, but it had been in the very atmosphere at the time of her marriage.

She had resented it then, and ever since. A man could marry whom he chose, but if a doctor of philosophy, female variety, chose to marry a man who never went past the bachelor's degree, there was shock. Why should there be? What business was it of theirs? He was handsome, in a way, intelligent, in another way, and she was perfectly satisfied with her choice.

Yet how much of this same snobbishness did she bring home with her? Didn't she always have the attitude that her own work, her biological investigations, were important, while his job was merely something to be kept within the four walls of his little office in the old U.N. buildings on the East River?

She jumped up from her seat in agitation and, with a deep breath, decided to leave such thoughts behind her. She desperately did not want to quarrel with him. And she just wasn't going to interfere with him. She was committed to accepting the Hawkinsite as guest, but otherwise she would let Drake have his own way. He was making enough of a concession as it was.

Harg Tholan was standing quietly in the middle of the living room when she came down the stairs. He was not sitting, since he was not anatomically constructed to sit. He stood on two sets of limbs placed close together, while a third pair entirely different in construction were suspended from a region that would have been the upper chest in a human being. The skin of his body was hard, glistening and ridged, while his face bore a distant resemblance to something alienly bovine. Yet he was not completely repulsive, and he wore clothes of a sort over the lower portion of his body in order to avoid offending the sensibilities of his human hosts.

He said, "Mrs. Smollett, I appreciate your hospitality beyond my ability to express it in your language," and he drooped so that his forelimbs touched the ground for a moment.

Rose knew this to be a gesture signifying gratitude among the beings of Hawkin's Planet. She was grateful that he spoke English as well as he did. The construction of his mouth, combined with an absence of incisors, gave a whistling sound to the sibilants. Aside from that, he might have been born on Earth for all the accent his speech showed.

She said, "My husband will be home soon, and then we will eat."

"Your husband?" For a moment, he said nothing more, and then added, "Yes, of course."

She let it go. If there was one source of infinite confusion among the five intelligent races of the known Galaxy, it lay in the differences among them with regard to their sex life and the social institutions that grew around it. The concept of husband and wife, for instance, existed only on Earth. The other races could achieve a sort of intellectual understanding of what it meant, but never an emotional one.

She said, "I have consulted the Institute in preparing your menu. I trust you will find nothing in it that will upset you."

The Hawkinsite blinked its eyes rapidly. Rose recalled this to be a gesture of amusement.

He said, "Proteins are proteins, my dear Mrs. Smollett. For those trace factors which I need but are not supplied in your food, I have brought concentrates that will be most adequate."

And proteins were proteins. Rose knew this to be true. Her concern for the creature's diet had been largely one of formal politeness. In the discovery of life on the planets of the outer stars, one of the most interesting generalizations that had developed was the fact that, although life could be formed on the basis of substances other than proteins—even on elements other than carbon—it remained true that the only known intelligences were proteinaceous in nature. This meant that each of the five forms of intelligent life could maintain themselves over prolonged periods on the food of any of the other four.

She heard Drake's key in the door and went stiff with apprehension.

She had to admit he did well. He strode in, and, without hesitation, thrust his hand out at the Hawkinsite, saying firmly, "Good evening, Dr. Tholan."

The Hawkinsite put out his large and rather clumsy forelimb and the two, so to speak, shook hands. Rose had already gone through that procedure and knew the queer feeling of a Hawkinsite hand in her own. It had felt rough and hot and dry. She imagined that, to the Hawkinsite, her own and Drake's felt cold and slimy.

At the time of the formal greeting, she had taken the opportunity to observe the alien hand. It was an excellent case of converging evolution. Its morphological development was entirely different from that of the human hand, yet it had brought itself into a fairly approximate similarity. There were four fingers but no thumb. Each finger had five independent ball-and-socket joints. In this way, the flexibility lost with the absence of the thumb was made up for by the almost tentacular properties of the fingers. What was even more interesting to her biologist's eyes was the fact that each Hawkinsite finger ended in a vestigial hoof, very small and, to the layman, unidentifiable as such, but clearly adapted at one time to running, just as man's had been to climbing.

Drake said, in friendly enough fashion, "Are you quite comfortable, sir?"

The Hawkinsite answered, "Quite. Your wife has been most thoughtful in all her arrangements."

"Would you care for a drink?"

The Hawkinsite did not answer but looked at Rose with a slight facial contortion that indicated some emotion which, unfortunately, Rose could not interpret. She said, nervously, "On Earth there is the custom of drinking liquids which have been fortified with ethyl alcohol. We find it stimulating."

"Oh, yes. I am afraid, then, that I must decline. Ethyl alcohol would interfere most unpleasantly with my metabolism."

"Why, so it does to Earthmen, too, but I understand, Dr. Tholan," Drake replied. "Would you object to *my* drinking?"

"Of course not."

Drake passed close to Rose on his way to the sideboard and she caught only one word. He said, "God!" in a tightly controlled whisper, yet he managed to put seventeen exclamation points after it.

The Hawkinsite *stood* at the table. His fingers were models of dexterity as they wove their way around the cutlery. Rose tried not to look at him as he ate. His wide lipless mouth split his face alarmingly as he ingested food, and, in chewing, his large jaws moved disconcertingly from side to side. It was another evidence of his ungulate ancestry. Rose found herself wondering if, in the quiet of his own room, he would later chew his cud, and was then panic-stricken lest Drake get the same idea and leave the table in disgust. But Drake was taking everything quite calmly.

He said, "I imagine, Dr. Tholan, that the cylinder at your side holds cyanide?"

Rose started. She had actually not noticed it. It was a curved metal object, something like a water canteen, that fitted flatly against the creature's skin, half-hidden behind its clothing. But, then, Drake had a policeman's eyes.

The Hawkinsite was not in the least disconcerted. "Quite so," he said, and his hoofed fingers held out a thin, flexible hose that ran up his body, its tint blending into that of his yellowish skin, and entered the corner of his wide mouth. Rose felt slightly embarrassed, as though at the display of intimate articles of clothing.

Drake said, "And does it contain pure cyanide?"

The Hawkinsite humorously blinked his eyes. "I hope you are not considering possible danger to Earthites. I know the gas is highly poisonous to you and I do not need a great deal. The gas contained in the cylinder is five per cent hydrogen cyanide, the remainder oxygen. None of it emerges except when I actually suck at the tube, and that need not be done frequently."

"I see. And you really must have the gas to live?"

Rose was slightly appalled. One simply did not ask such questions without careful preparation. It was impossible to foresee where the sensitive points of an alien psychology might be. And Drake *must* be doing this deliberately, since he could not help realizing that he could get answers to such questions as easily from herself. Or was it that he preferred not to ask her?

The Hawkinsite remained apparently unperturbed. "Are you not a biologist, Mr. Smollett?"

"No, Dr. Tholan."

"But you are in close association with Mrs. *Dr.* Smollett."

Drake smile a bit. "Yes, I am married to a Mrs. doctor, but just the same I am not a biologist; merely a minor government official. My wife's friends," he added, "call me a policeman."

Rose bit the inside of her cheek. In this case it was the Hawkinsite who had impinged upon the sensitive point of an alien psychology. On Hawkin's Planet, there was a tight caste system and intercaste associations were limited. But Drake wouldn't realize that.

The Hawkinsite turned to her. "May I have your permission, Mrs. Smollett, to explain a little of our biochemistry to your husband? It will be dull for you, since I am sure you must understand it quite well already."

She said, "By all means do, Dr. Tholan."

He said, "You see, Mr. Smollett, the respiratory system in your body and in the bodies of all air-breathing creatures on Earth is controlled by certain metal-containing enzymes, I am taught. The metal is usually iron, though sometimes it is copper. In either case, small traces of cyanide would combine with these metals and immobilize the respiratory system of the terrestrial living cell. They would be prevented from using oxygen and killed in a few minutes.

"The life on my own planet is not quite so constituted. The key respiratory compounds contain neither iron nor copper; no metal at all, in fact. It is for this reason that my blood is colorless. Our compounds contain certain organic groupings which are essential to life, and these groupings can only be maintained intact in the presence of a small concentration of cyanide. Undoubtedly, this type of protein has developed through millions of years of evolution on a world which has a few tenths of a per cent of hydrogen cyanide occurring naturally in the atmosphere. Its presence is maintained by a biological cycle. Various of our native micro-organisms liberate the free gas."

"You make it extremely clear, Dr. Tholan, and very interesting," Drake said. "What happens if you don't breathe it? Do you just go, like that?" He snapped his fingers.

"Not quite. It isn't equivalent to the presence of cyanide for you. In my case, the absence of cyanide would be equivalent to slow strangulation. It happens sometimes, in ill-ventilated rooms on my world, that the cyanide is gradually consumed and falls below the minimum necessary concentration. The results are very painful and difficult to treat."

Rose had to give Drake credit; he really sounded interested. And the alien, thank heaven, did not mind the catechism.

The rest of the dinner passed without incident. It was almost pleasant.

Throughout the evening, Drake remained that way; interested. Even more than that—absorbed. He drowned her out, and she was glad of it. *He* was the one who was really colorful and it was only her job, her specialized training, that stole the color from him. She looked at him gloomily and thought, *Why did he marry me?*

Drake sat, one leg crossed over the other, hands clasped and tapping his chin gently, watching the Hawkinsite intently. The Hawkinsite faced him, standing in his quadruped fashion.

Drake said, "I find it difficult to keep thinking of you as a doctor."

The Hawkinsite laughingly blinked his eyes. "I understand what you mean," he said. "I find it difficult to think of you as a policeman. On my world, policemen are very specialized and distinctive people."

"Are they?" said Drake, somewhat drily, and then changed the subject. "I gather that you are not here on a pleasure trip."

"No, I am here very much on business. I intend to study this queer planet you call Earth, as it has never been studied before by any of my people."

"Queer?" asked Drake. "In what way?"

The Hawkinsite looked at Rose. "Does he know of the Inhibition Death?"

Rose felt embarrassed. "His work is important," she said. "I am afraid that my husband has little time to listen to the details of my work." She knew that this was not really adequate and she felt herself to be the recipient, yet again, of one of the Hawkinsite's unreadable emotions.

The extraterrestrial creature turned back to Drake. "It is always amazing to me to find how little you Earthmen understand your own unusual characteristics. Look, there are five intelligent races in the Galaxy. These have all developed independently, yet have managed to converge in remarkable fashion. It is as though, in the long run, intelligence requires a certain physical makeup to flourish. I leave that question for philosophers. But I need not belabor the point, since it must be a familiar one to you.

"Now when the differences among the intelligences are closely investigated, it is found over and over again that it is you Earthmen, more than any of the others, who are unique. For instance, it is only on Earth that life depends upon metal enzymes for respiration. Your people are the only ones which find hydrogen cyanide poisonous. Yours is the only form of intelligent life which is carnivorous. Yours is the only form of life which has not developed from a grazing animal. And, most interesting of all, yours is the only form of intelligent life known which stops growing upon reaching maturity."

Drake grinned at him. Rose felt her heart suddenly race. It was the nicest thing about him, that grin, and he was using it perfectly naturally. It wasn't forced or false. He was adjusting to the presence of this alien creature. He was being pleasant—and he must be doing it for her. She loved that thought and repeated it to herself. He was doing it for her; he was being nice to the Hawkinsite for her sake.

Drake was saying with his grin, "You don't look very large, Dr. Tholan. I should say that you are an inch taller than I am, which would make you six feet two inches tall. Is it that you are young, or is it that the others on your world are generally small?"

"Neither," said the Hawkinsite. "We grow at a diminishing rate with the years, so that at my age it would take fifteen years to grow an additional inch, but—and this is the important point—we never *entirely* stop. And, of course, as a consequence, we never entirely die."

Drake gasped and even Rose felt herself sitting stiffly upright. This was something new. This was something which, to her knowledge, the few expeditions to Hawkin's Planet had never brought back. She was torn with excitement but held an exclamation back and let Drake speak for her.

He said, "They don't entirely die? You're not trying to say, sir, that the people on Hawkin's Planet are immortal?"

"No people are truly immortal. If there were no other way to die, there would always be accident, and if that fails, there is boredom. Few of us live more than several centuries of your time. Still, it is unpleasant to think that death may come involuntarily. It is something which, to us, is extremely horrible. It bothers me even as I think of it now, this thought that *against my will and despite all care*, death may come."

"We," said Drake, grimly, "are quite used to it."

"You Earthmen live with the thought; we do not. And this is why we are disturbed to find that the incidence of Inhibition Death has been increasing in recent years."

"You have not yet explained," said Drake, "just what the Inhibition Death is, but let me guess. Is the Inhibition Death a pathological cessation of growth?"

"Exactly."

"And how long after growth's cessation does death follow?"

"Within the year. It is a wasting disease, a tragic one, and absolutely incurable."

"What causes it?"

The Hawkinsite paused a long time before answering, and even then there was something strained and uneasy about the way he spoke. "Mr. Smollett, we know nothing about the cause of the disease."

Drake nodded thoughtfully. Rose was following the conversation as though she were a spectator at a tennis match.

Drake said, "And why do you come to Earth to study this disease?"

"Because again Earthmen are unique. They are the only intelligent beings who are immune. The Inhibition Death affects *all* the other races. Do your biologists know that, Mrs. Smollett?"

He had addressed her suddenly, so that she jumped slightly. She said, "No, they don't."

"I am not surprised. That piece of information is the result of very recent research. The Inhibition Death is easily diagnosed incorrectly and the incidence is much lower on the other planets. In fact, it is a strange thing, something to philosophize over, that the incidence of the Death is highest on my world, which is closest to Earth, and lower on each more distant planet—so that it is lowest on the world of the star Tempora, which is farthest from Earth, while Earth itself is immune. Somewhere in the biochemistry of the Earthite, there is the secret of that immunity. How interesting it would be to find it."

Drake said, "But look here, you can't say Earth is immune. From where I sit, it looks as if the incidence is a hundred per cent. All Earthmen stop growing and all Earthmen die. We've *all* got the Inhibition Death."

"Not at all. Earthmen live up to seventy years after the cessation of growth. That is not the Death as *we* know it. *Your* equivalent disease is rather one of unrestrained growth. Cancer, you call it. —But come, I bore you."

Rose protested instantly. Drake did likewise with even more vehemence, but the Hawkinsite determinedly changed the subject. It was then that Rose had her first pang of suspicion, for Drake circled Harg Tholan warily with his words, worrying him, jabbing at him, attempting always to get the information back to the point where the Hawkinsite had left off. Not badly, not unskillfully, but Rose knew him, and could tell what he was after. And what could he be after but that which was demanded by his profession? And, as though in response to her thoughts, the Hawkinsite took up the phrase which had begun careening in her mind like a broken record on a perpetual turntable.

He asked, "Did you not say you were a policeman?"

Drake said, curtly, "Yes."

"Then there is something I would like to request you to do for me. I have been wanting to all this evening, since I discovered your profession, and yet I hesitate. I do not wish to be troublesome to my host and hostess."

"We'll do what we can."

"I have a profound curiosity as to how Earthmen live; a curiosity which is not perhaps shared by the generality of my countrymen. So I wonder, could you show me through one of the police departments on your planet?"

"I do not belong to a police department in exactly the way you imagine," said Drake, cautiously. "However, I am known to the New York police department. I can manage it without trouble. Tomorrow?"

"That would be most convenient for me. Would I be able to visit the Missing Persons Bureau?"

"The what?"

The Hawkinsite drew his four standing legs closer together, as if he were becoming more intense. "It is a hobby of mine, a little queer corner of interest I have always had. I understand you have a group of police officers whose sole duty it is to search for men who are missing."

"And women and children," added Drake. "But why should that interest you so particularly?"

"Because there again you are unique. There is no such thing as a missing person on our planet. I can't explain the mechanism to you, of course, but among the people of other worlds, there is always an awareness of one another's presence, especially if there is a strong, affectionate tie. We are always aware of each other's exact location, no matter where on the planet we might be."

Rose grew excited again. The scientific expeditions to Hawkin's Planet had always had the greatest difficulty in penetrating the internal emotional mechanisms of the natives, and here was one who talked freely, who would explain! She forgot to worry about Drake and intruded into the conversations. "Can you feel such awareness even now? On Earth?"

The Hawkinsite said, "You mean across space? No, I'm afraid not. But you see the importance of the matter. All the uniqueness of Earth should be linked. If the lack of this sense can be explained, perhaps the immunity to Inhibition Death can be, also. Besides, it strikes me as very curious that any form of intelligent community life can be built among people who lack this community awareness. How can an Earthman tell, for instance, when he has formed a congenial sub-group, a family? How can you two, for instance, know that there is a true tie between you?"

Rose found herself nodding. How strongly she missed such a sense!

But Drake only smiled. "We have our ways. It is as difficult to explain what we call 'love' to you as it is for you to explain your sense to us."

"I suppose so. Yet tell me truthfully, Mr. Smollett—if Mrs. Smollett were to leave this room and enter another without your having seen her do so, would you really not be aware of her location?"

"I really would not."

The Hawkinsite said, "Amazing." He hesitated, then added, "Please do not be offended at the fact that I find it revolting as well."

After the light in the bedroom had been put out, Rose went to the door three times, opening it a crack and peering out. She could feel Drake watching her. There was a hard kind of amusement in his voice as he asked, finally, "What's the matter?"

She said, "I want to talk to you."

"Are you afraid our friend can hear?"

Rose was whispering. She got into bed and put her head on his pillow so that she could whisper better. She said, "Why were you talking about the Inhibition Death to Dr. Tholan?"

"I am taking an interest in your work, Rose. You've always wanted me to take an interest."

"I'd rather you weren't sarcastic." She was almost violent, as nearly violent as she could be in a whisper. "I know that there's something of your own interest in this—of *police* interest, probably. What is it?"

He said, "I'll talk to you tomorrow."

"No, right now."

He put his hand under her head, lifting it. For a wild moment she thought he was going to kiss her—just kiss her on impulse the way husbands sometimes did, or as she imagined they sometimes did. Drake never did, and he didn't now.

He merely held her close and whispered, "Why are you so interested?"

His hand was almost brutally hard upon the nape of her neck, so that she stiffened and tried to draw back. Her voice was more than a whisper now. "Stop it, Drake."

He said, "I want no questions from you and no interference. You do your job, and I'll do mine."

"The nature of my job is open and known."

"The nature of my job," he retorted, "isn't, by definition. But I'll tell you this. Our six-legged friend is here in this house for some definite reason. You weren't picked as biologist in charge for any random reason. Do you know that two days ago, he'd been inquiring about me at the Commission?"

"You're joking."

"Don't believe that for a minute. There are depths to this that you know nothing about. But that's my job and I won't discuss it with you any further. Do you understand?"

"No, but I won't question you if you don't want me to."

"Then go to sleep."

She lay stiffly on her back and the minutes passed, and then the quarter-hours. She was trying to fit the pieces together. Even with what Drake had told her, the curves and colors refused to blend. She wondered what Drake would say if he knew she had a recording of that night's conversation!

One picture remained clear in her mind at that moment. It hovered over her mockingly. The Hawkinsite, at the end of the long evening, had turned to her and said gravely, "Good night, Mrs. Smollett. You are a most charming hostess."

She had desperately wanted to giggle at the time. How could he call her a charming hostess? To him, she could only be a horror, a monstrosity with too few limbs and a too-narrow face.

And then, as the Hawkinsite delivered himself of this completely meaningless piece of politeness, Drake had turned white! For one instant, his eyes had burned with something that looked like terror.

She had never before known Drake to show fear of anything, and the picture of that instant of pure panic remained with her until all her thoughts finally sagged into the oblivion of sleep.

It was noon before Rose was at her desk the next day. She had deliberately waited until Drake and the Hawkinsite had left, since only then was she able to remove the small recorder that had been behind Drake's armchair the previous evening. She had had no original intention of keeping its presence secret from him. It was just that he had come home so late, and she couldn't say anything about it with the Hawkinsite present. Later on, of course, things had changed—

The placing of the recorder had been only a routine maneuver. The Hawkinsite's statements and intonations needed to be preserved for future intensive studies by various specialists at the Institute. It had been hidden in order to avoid the distortions of self-consciousness that the visibility of such a device would bring, and now it couldn't be shown to the members of the Institute at all. It would have to serve a different function altogether. A rather nasty function.

She was going to spy on Drake.

She touched the little box with her fingers and wondered, irrelevantly, how Drake was going to manage, that day. Social intercourse between inhabited worlds was, even now, not so commonplace that the sight of a Hawkinsite on the city streets would not succeed in drawing crowds. But Drake would manage, she knew. Drake always managed.

She listened once again to the sounds of last evening, repeating the interesting moments. She was dissatisfied with what Drake had told her. Why should the Hawkinsite have been interested in the two of them particularly? Yet Drake wouldn't lie. She would have liked to check at the Security Commission, but she knew she could not do that. Besides, the thought made her feel disloyal; Drake would definitely not lie.

But, then again, why should Harg Tholan not have investigated them? He might have inquired similarly about the families of all the biologists at the Institute. It would be no more than natural to attempt to choose the home he would find most pleasant by his own standards, whatever they were.

And if he had—even if he had investigated only the Smolletts—why should that create the great change in Drake from intense hostility to intense interest? Drake undoubtedly had knowledge he was keeping to himself. Only heaven knew how much.

Her thoughts churned slowly through the possibilities of interstellar intrigue. So far, to be sure, there were no signs of hostility or ill-feeling among any of the five intelligent races known to inhabit the Galaxy. As yet they were spaced at intervals too wide for enmity. Even the barest contact among them was all but impossible. Economic and political interests just had no point at which to conflict.

But that was only her idea and she was not a member of the Security Commission. If there *were* conflict, if there *were* danger, if there *were* any reason to suspect that the mission of a Hawkinsite might be other than peaceful—Drake would know.

Yet was Drake sufficiently high in the councils of the Security Commission to know, off-hand, the dangers involved in the visit of a Hawkinsite physician? She had never thought of his position as more than that of a very minor functionary in the Commission; he had never presented himself as more. And yet—

Might he be more?

She shrugged at the thought. It was reminiscent of Twentieth Century spy novels and of costume dramas of the days when there existed such things as atom bomb secrets.

The thought of costume dramas decided her. Unlike Drake, she wasn't a real policeman, and she didn't know how a real policeman would go about it. But she knew how such things were done in the old dramas.

She drew a piece of paper toward her and, with a quick motion, slashed a vertical pencil mark down its center. She headed one column "Harg Tholan," the other "Drake." Under "Harg Tholan" she wrote "bonafide" and thoughtfully put three question marks after it. After all, was he a doctor at all, or was he what could only be described as an interstellar agent? What proof had even the Institute of his profession except his own statements? Was that why Drake had quizzed him so relentlessly concerning the Inhibition Death? Had he boned up in advance and tried to catch the Hawkinsite in an error?

For a moment, she was irresolute; then, springing to her feet, she folded the paper, put it in the pocket of her short jacket, and swept out of her office. She said nothing to any of those she passed as she left the Institute. She left no word at the reception desk as to where she was going, or when she would be back.

Once outside, she hurried into the third-level tube and waited for an empty compartment to pass. The two minutes that elapsed seemed unbearably long. It was all she could do to say, "New York Academy of Medicine," into the mouthpiece just above the seat.

The door of the little cubicle closed, and the sound of the air flowing past the compartment hissed upward in pitch.

The New York Academy of Medicine had been enlarged both vertically and horizontally in the past two decades. The library alone occupied one entire wing of the third floor. Undoubtedly, if all the books, pamphlets and periodicals it contained were in their original printed form, rather than in microfilm, the entire building, huge though it was, would not have been sufficiently vast to hold them. As it was, Rose knew there was already talk of limiting printed works to the last five years, rather than to the last ten, as was now the case.

Rose, as a member of the Academy, had free entry to the library. She hurried toward the alcoves devoted to extraterrestrial medicine and was relieved to find them unoccupied.

It might have been wiser to have enlisted the aid of a librarian, but she chose not to. The thinner and smaller the trail she left, the less likely it was that Drake might pick it up.

And so, without guidance, she was satisfied to travel along the shelves, following the titles anxiously with her fingers. The books were almost all in English, though some were in German or Russian. None, ironically enough, were in extraterrestrial symbolisms. There was a room somewhere for such originals, but they were available only to official translators.

Her traveling eye and finger stopped. She had found what she was looking for.

She dragged half a dozen volumes from the shelf and spread them out upon the small dark table. She fumbled for the light switch and opened the first of the volumes. It was entitled *Studies on Inhibition*. She leafed through it and then turned to the author index. The name of Harg Tholan was there.

One by one, she looked up the references indicated, then returned to the shelves for translations of such original papers as she could find.

She spent more than two hours in the Academy. When she was finished, she knew this much—there was a Hawkinsite doctor named Harg Tholan, who was an expert on the Inhibition Death. He was connected with the Hawkinsite research organization with which the Institute had been in correspondence. Of course, the Harg Tholan she knew might simply be impersonating an actual doctor to make the role more realistic, but why should that be necessary?

She took the paper out of her pocket and, where she had written "bonafide" with three question marks, she now wrote a YES in capitals. She went back to the Institute and at 4 P.M. was once again at her desk. She called the switchboard to say that she would not answer any phone calls and then she locked her door.

Underneath the column headed "Harg Tholan" she now wrote two questions: "Why did Harg Tholan come to Earth alone?" She left considerable space. Then, "What is his interest in the Missing Persons Bureau?"

Certainly, the Inhibition Death was all the Hawkinsite said it was. From her reading at the Academy, it was obvious that it occupied the major share of medical effort on Hawkin's Planet. It was more feared there than cancer was on Earth. If they had thought the answer to it lay on Earth, the Hawkinsites would have sent a full-scale expedition. Was it distrust and suspicion on their part that made them send only one investigator?

What was it Harg Tholan had said the night before? The incidence of the Death was highest upon his own world, which was closest to Earth, lowest upon the world farthest from Earth. Add to that the fact implied by the Hawkinsite, and verified by her own readings at the Academy, that the incidence had expanded enormously since interstellar contact had been made with Earth. . . .

Slowly and reluctantly she came to one conclusion. The inhabitants of Hawkin's Planet might have decided that somehow Earth had discovered the cause of the Inhibition Death, and was deliberately fostering it among the alien peoples of the Galaxy, with the intention, perhaps, of becoming supreme among the stars.

She rejected this conclusion with what was almost panic. It could not be; it was impossible. In the first place, Earth *wouldn't* do such a horrible thing. Secondly, it *couldn't*.

As far as scientific advance was concerned, the beings of Hawkin's Planet were certainly the equals of Earthmen. The Death had occurred there for thousands of years and their medical record was one of total failure. Surely, Earth, in its long-distance investigations into alien biochemistry, could not have succeeded so quickly. In fact, as far as she knew, there were no investigations to speak of into Hawkinsite pathology on the part of Earth biologists and physicians.

Yet all the evidence indicated that Harg Tholan had come in suspicion and had been received in suspicion. Carefully, she wrote down under the question, "Why did Harg Tholan come to Earth alone?" the answer, "Hawkin's Planet *believes* Earth is causing the Inhibition Death."

But, then, what was this business about the Bureau of Missing Persons? As a scientist, she was rigorous about the theories she developed. *All* the facts had to fit in, not merely some of them.

Missing Persons Bureau! If it was a false trail, deliberately intended to deceive Drake, it had been done clumsily, since it came only after an hour of discussion of the Inhibition Death.

Was it intended as an opportunity to study Drake? If so, why? Was this perhaps the *major* point? The Hawkinsite had investigated Drake before coming to them. Had he come because Drake was a policeman with entry to Bureaus of Missing Persons?

But why? Why?

She gave it up and turned to the column headed "Drake."

And there a question wrote itself, not in pen and ink upon the paper, but in the much more visible letters of thought on mind. *Why did he marry me?* thought Rose, and she covered her eyes with her hands so that the unfriendly light was excluded.

They had met quite by accident somewhat more than a year before, when he had moved into the apartment house in which she then lived. Polite greetings had somehow become friendly conversation and this, in turn, had led to occasional dinners in a neighborhood restaurant. It had been very friendly and normal and an exciting new experience, and she had fallen in love.

When he asked her to marry him, she was pleased—and overwhelmed. At the time, she had many explanations for it. He appreciated her intelligence and friendliness. She was a nice girl. She would make a good wife, a splendid companion.

She had tried all those explanations and had half-believed every one of them. But half-belief was not enough.

It was not that she had any definite fault to find in Drake as a husband. He was always thoughtful, kind and a gentleman. Their married life was not one of passion, and yet it suited the paler emotional surges of the late thirties. She wasn't nineteen. What did she expect?

That was it; she wasn't nineteen. She wasn't beautiful, or charming, or glamorous. What did she expect? Could she have expected Drake—handsome and rugged, whose interest in intellectual pursuits was quite minor, who neither asked about her work in all the months of their marriage, nor offered to discuss his own with her? Why, then, did he marry her?

But there was no answer to that question, and it had nothing to do with what Rose was trying to do now. It was extraneous, she told herself fiercely; it was a childish distraction from the task she had set herself. She was acting like a girl of nineteen, after all, with no chronological excuse for it.

She found that the point of her pencil had somehow broken, and took a new one. In the column headed "Drake" she wrote, "Why is he suspicious of Harg Tholan?" and under it she put an arrow pointing to the other column.

What she had already written there was sufficient explanation. If Earth was spreading the Inhibition Death, or if Earth knew it was suspected of such a deed, then, obviously, it would be preparing for eventual retaliation on the part of the aliens. In fact, the setting would actually be one of preliminary maneuvering for the first interstellar war of history. It was an adequate but horrible explanation.

Now there was left the second question, the one she could not answer. She wrote it slowly, "Why Drake's reaction to Tholan's words, 'You are a most charming hostess'?"

She tried to bring back the exact setting. The Hawkinsite had said it innocuously, matter-of-factly, politely, and Drake had frozen at the sound of it. Over and over, she had listened to that particular passage in the recording. An Earthman might have said it in just such an inconsequential tone on leaving a routine cocktail party. The recording did not carry the sight of Drake's face; she had only her memory for that. Drake's eyes had become alive with fear and hate, and Drake was one who feared practically nothing. What was there to fear in the phrase, "You are a most charming hostess," that could upset him so? Jealousy? Absurd. The feeling that Tholan had been sarcastic? Maybe, though unlikely. She was sure Tholan was sincere.

She gave it up and put a large question mark under that second question. There were two of them now, one under "Harg Tholan" and one under "Drake." Could there be a connection between Tholan's interest in missing persons and Drake's reaction to a polite party phrase? She could think of none.

She put her head down upon her arms. It was getting dark in the office and she was very tired. For a while, she must have hovered in that queer land between waking and sleeping, when thoughts and phrases lose the control of the conscious and disport themselves erratically and surrealistically through one's head. But, no matter where they danced and leaped, they always returned to that one phrase, "You are a most charming hostess." Sometimes she heard it in Harg Tholan's cultured, lifeless voice, and sometimes in Drake's vibrant one. When Drake said it, it was full of love, full of a love she never heard from him. She liked to hear him say it.

She startled herself to wakefulness. It was quite dark in the office now, and she put on the desk light. She blinked, then frowned a little. Another thought must have come to her in that fitful half-sleep. There had been another phrase which had upset Drake. What was it? Her forehead furrowed with mental effort. It had not been last evening. It was not anything in the recorded conversation, so it must have been before that. Nothing came and she grew restless.

Looking at her watch, she gasped. It was almost eight. They would be at home waiting for her.

But she did not want to go home. She did not want to face them. Slowly, she took up the paper upon which she had scrawled her thoughts of the afternoon, tore it into little pieces and let them flutter into the little atomic-flash ashtray upon her desk. They were gone in a little flare and nothing was left of them.

If only nothing were left of the thoughts they represented as well.

It was no use. She would have to go home.

They were not there waiting for her, after all. She came upon them getting out of a gyrocab just as she emerged from the tubes on to street level. The gyrocabbie, wide-eyed, gazed after his fares for a moment, then hovered upward and away. By unspoken mutual consent, the three waited until they had entered the apartment before speaking.

Rose said disinterestedly, "I hope you have had a pleasant day, Dr. Tholan."

"Quite. And a fascinating and profitable one as well, I think."

"Have you had a chance to eat?" Though Rose had not herself eaten, she was anything but hungry.

"Yes, indeed."

Drake interrupted, "We had lunch and supper sent up to us. Sandwiches." He sounded tired.

Rose said, "Hello, Drake." It was the first time she had addressed him. Drake scarcely looked at her. "Hello."

The Hawkinsite said, "Your tomatoes are remarkable vegetables. We have nothing to compare with them in taste on our own planet. I believe I ate two dozen, as well as an entire bottle of tomato derivative."

"Ketchup," explained Drake, briefly.

Rose said, "And your visit at the Missing Persons Bureau, Dr. Tholan? You say you found it profitable?"

"I should say so. Yes."

Rose kept her back to him. She plumped up sofa cushions as she said, "In what way?"

"I find it most interesting that the large majority of missing persons are males. Wives frequently report missing husbands, while the reverse is practically never the case."

Rose said, "Oh, that's not mysterious, Dr. Tholan. You simply don't realize the economic setup we have on Earth. On this planet, you see, it is the male who is usually the member of the family that maintains it as an economic unit. He is the one whose labor is repaid in units of currency. The wife's function is generally that of taking care of home and children.":

"Surely this is not universal!"

Drake put in, "More or less. If you are thinking of my wife, she is an example of the minority of women who are capable of making their own way in the world."

Rose looked at him swiftly. Was he being sarcastic?

The Hawkinsite said, "Your implication, Mrs. Smollett, is that women, being economically dependent upon their male companions, find it less feasible to disappear?"

"That's a gentle way of putting it," said Rose, "but that's about it."

"And would you call the Missing Persons Bureau of New York a fair sampling of such cases in the planet at large?"

"Why, I should think so."

The Hawkinsite said, abruptly, "And is there, then, an economic explanation for the fact that since interstellar travel has been developed, the percentage of young males among the missing is more pronounced than ever?"

It was Drake who answered, with a verbal snap. "Good lord, that's even less of a mystery than the other. Nowadays, the runaway has all space to disappear into. Anyone who wants to get away from trouble need only hop the nearest space freighter. They're always looking for crewmen, no questions asked, and it would be almost impossible to locate the runaway after that, if he really wanted to stay out of circulation."

"And almost always young men in their first year of marriage."

Rose laughed suddenly. She said, "Why, that's just the time a man's troubles seem the greatest. If he survives the first year, there is usually no need to disappear at all."

Drake was obviously not amused. Rose thought again that he looked tired and unhappy. *Why* did he insist on bearing the load alone? And then she thought that perhaps he had to.

The Hawkinsite said, suddenly, "Would it offend you if I disconnected for a period of time?"

Rose said, "Not at all. I hope you haven't had too exhausting a day. Since you come from a planet whose gravity is greater than that of Earth's, I'm afraid we too easily presume that you would show greater endurance than we do."

"Oh, I am not tired in a physical sense." He looked for a moment at her legs and blinked very rapidly, indicating amusement. "You know, I keep expecting Earthmen to fall either forward or backward in view of their meager equipment of standing limbs. You must pardon me if my comment is overfamiliar, but your mention of the lesser gravity of Earth brought it to my mind. On my planet, two legs would simply not be enough. But this is all beside the point at the moment. It is just that I have been absorbing so many new and unusual concepts that I feel the desire for a little disconnection."

Rose shrugged inwardly. Well, that was as close as one race could get to another, anyway. As nearly as the expeditions to Hawkin's Planet could make out, Hawkinsites had the faculty for disconnecting their conscious mind from all its bodily functions and allowing it to sink into an undisturbed meditative process for periods of time lasting up to terrestrial days. Hawkinsites found the process pleasant, even necessary sometimes, though no Earthman could truly say what function it served.

Conversely, it had never been entirely possible for Earthmen to explain the concept of "sleep" to a Hawkinsite, or to any extraterrestrial. What an Earthman would call sleep or a dream, a Hawkinsite would view as an alarming sign of mental disintegration.

Rose thought uneasily, *Here is another way Earthmen are unique.*

The Hawkinsite was backing away, drooping so that his forelimbs swept the floor in polite farewell. Drake nodded curtly at him as he disappeared behind the bend in the corridor. They heard his door open, close, then silence.

After minutes in which the silence was thick between them, Drake's chair creaked as he shifted restlessly. With a mild horror, Rose noticed blood upon his lips. She thought to herself, *He's in some kind of trouble. I've got to talk to him. I can't let it go on like this.*

She said, "Drake!"

Drake seemed to look at her from a far, far distance. Slowly, his eyes focused closer at hand and he said, "What is it? Are you through for the day, too?"

"No, I'm ready to begin. It's the tomorrow you spoke of. Aren't you going to speak to me?"

"Pardon me?"

"Last night, you said you would speak to me tomorrow. I am ready now."

Drake frowned. His eyes withdrew beneath a lowered brow and Rose felt some of her resolution begin to leave her. He said, "I thought it was agreed that you would not question me about my business in this matter."

"I think it's too late for that. I know too much about your business by now."

"What do you mean?" he shouted, jumping to his feet. Recollecting himself, he approached, laid his hands upon her shoulders and repeated in a lower voice, "What do you mean?"

Rose kept her eyes upon her hands, which rested limply in her lap. She bore the painfully gripping fingers patiently, and said slowly, "Dr. Tholan thinks that Earth is spreading the Inhibition Death purposely. That's it, isn't it?"

She waited. Slowly, the grip relaxed and he was standing there, hands at his side, face baffled and unhappy. He said, "Where did you get that notion?"

"It's true, isn't it?"

He said breathlessly, unnaturally, "I want to know exactly why you say that. Don't play foolish games with me, Rose. This is for keeps."

"If I tell you, will you answer one question?"

"What question?"

"Is Earth spreading the disease deliberately, Drake?"

Drake flung his hands upward. "Oh, for Heaven's sake!"

He knelt before her. He took her hands in his and she could feel their trembling. He was forcing his voice into soothing, loving syllables.

He was saying, "Rose dear, look, you've got something red-hot by the tail and you think you can use it to tease me in a little husband-wife repartee. No, I'm not asking much. Just tell me exactly what causes you to say what— what you have just said." He was terribly earnest about it.

"I was at the New York Academy of Medicine this afternoon. I did some reading there."

"But why? What made you do it?"

"You seemed so interested in the Inhibition Death, for one thing. And Dr. Tholan made those statements about the incidence increasing since interstellar travel, and being the highest on the planet nearest Earth." She paused.

"And your reading?" he prompted. "What about your reading, Rose?"

She said, "It backs him up. All I could do was to skim hastily into the direction of their research in recent decades. It seems obvious to me, though, that at least some of the Hawkinsites are considering the possibility the Inhibition Death originates on Earth."

"Do they say so outright?"

"No. Or, if they have, I haven't seen it." She gazed at him in surprise. In a matter like this, certainly the government would have investigated Hawkinsite research on the matter. She said, gently, "Don't you know about Hawkinsite research in the matter, Drake? The government—"

"Never mind about that." Drake had moved away from her and now he turned again. His eyes were bright. He said, as though making a wonderful discovery, "Why, you're an expert in this!"

Was she? Did he find that out only now that he needed her? Her nostrils flared and she said flatly, "I am a biologist."

He said, "Yes, I know that, but I mean your particular specialty is growth. Didn't you once tell me you had done work on growth?"

"You might call it that. I've had twenty papers published on the relationship of nucleic acid fine structure and embryonic development on my Cancer Society grant."

"Good. I should have thought of that." He was choked with a new excitement. "Tell me, Rose— Look, I'm sorry if I lost my temper with you a moment ago. You'd be as competent as anyone to understand the direction of their researches if you read about it, wouldn't you?"

"Fairly competent, yes."

"Then tell me how they think the disease is spread. The details, I mean."

"Oh, now look, that's asking a little too much. I spent a few hours in the Academy, that's all. I'd need much more time than that to be able to answer your question."

"An intelligent guess, at least. You can't imagine how important it is."

She said, doubtfully, "Of course, 'Studies on Inhibition' is a major treatise in the field. It would summarize all of the available research data."

"Yes? And how recent is it?"

"It's one of those periodic things. The last volume is about a year old."

"Does it have any account of *his* work in it?" His finger jabbed in the direction of Harg Tholan's bedroom.

"More than anyone else's. He's an outstanding worker in the field. I looked over his papers especially."

"And what are his theories about the origin of the disease? Try to remember, Rose."

She shook her head at him. "I could swear he blames Earth, but he admits they know nothing about how the disease is spread. I could swear to that, too."

He stood stiffly before her. His strong hands were clenched into fists at his side and his words were scarcely more than a mutter. "It could be a matter of complete overestimation. Who knows—"

He whirled away. "I'll find out about this right now, Rose. Thank you for your help."

She ran after him. "What are you going to do?"

"Ask him a few questions." He was rummaging through the drawers of his desk and now his right hand withdrew. It held a needle-gun.

She cried, "No, Drake!"

He shook her off roughly, and turned down the corridor toward the Hawkinsite's bedroom.

Drake threw the door open and entered. Rose was at his heels, still trying to grasp his arm, but now he stopped and looked at Harg Tholan.

The Hawkinsite was standing there motionless, eyes unfocused, his four standing limbs sprawled out in four directions as far as they would go. Rose felt ashamed of intruding, as though she were violating an intimate rite. But Drake, apparently unconcerned, walked to within four feet of the creature and stood there. They were face to face, Drake holding the needle-gun easily at a level of about the center of the Hawkinsite's torso.

Drake said, "Now keep quiet. He'll gradually become aware of me."

"How do you know?"

The answer was flat. "I *know*. Now get out of here."

But she did not move and Drake was too absorbed to pay her further attention.

Portions of the skin on the Hawkinsite's face were beginning to quiver slightly. It was rather repulsive and Rose found herself preferring not to watch.

Drake suddenly, "That's about all, Dr. Tholan. Don't throw in connection with any of the limbs. Your sense organs and voice box will be quite enough."

The Hawkinsite's voice was dim. "Why do you invade my disconnection chamber?" Then, more strongly, "And why are you armed?"

His head wobbled slightly atop a still frozen torso. He had, apparently, followed Drake's suggestion against limb connection. Rose wondered how Drake knew such partial reconnection to be possible. She herself had not known of it.

The Hawkinsite spoke again. "What do you want?"

And this time Drake answered. He said, "The answer to certain questions."

"With a gun in your hand? I would not humor your discourtesy so far."

"You would not merely be humoring me. You might be saving your own life."

"That would be a matter of considerable indifference to me, under the circumstances. I am sorry, Mr. Smollett, that the duties toward a guest are so badly understood on Earth."

"You are no guest of mine, Dr. Tholan," said Drake. "You entered my house on false pretenses. You had some reason for it, some way you had planned of using me to further your own purposes. I have no compunction in reversing the process."

"You had better shoot. It will save time."

"You are convinced that you will answer no questions? That, in itself, is suspicious. It seems that you consider certain answers to be more important than your life."

"I consider the principles of courtesy to be very important. You, as an Earthman, may not understand."

"Perhaps not. But I, as an Earthman, understand one thing." Drake had jumped forward, faster than Rose could cry out, faster than the Hawkinsite could connect his limbs. When he sprang backward, the flexible hose of Harg Tholan's cyanide cylinder was in his hand. At the corner of the Hawkinsite's wide mouth, where the hose had once been affixed, a droplet of colorless liquid oozed sluggishly from a break in the rough skin, and slowly solidified into a brown jellylike globule, as it oxidized.

· · · ·

Drake yanked at the hose and the cylinder jerked free. He plunged home the knob that controlled the needle valve at the head of the cylinder and the small hissing ceased.

"I doubt," said Drake, "that enough will have escaped to endanger us. I hope, however, that you realize what will happen to you *now*, if you do not answer the questions I am going to ask you—and answer them in such a way that I am convinced you are being truthful."

"Give me back my cylinder," said the Hawkinsite, slowly. "If not, it will be necessary for me to attack you and then it will be necessary for you to kill me."

Drake stepped back. "Not at all. Attack me and I shoot your legs from under you. You will lose them; all four, if necessary, but you will still live, in a horrible way. You will live to die of cyanide lack. It would be a most uncomfortable death. I am only an Earthman and I can't appreciate its true horrors, but you can, can't you?"

The Hawkinsite's mouth was open and something within quivered yellow-green. Rose wanted to throw up. She wanted to scream. *Give him back the cylinder, Drake!* But nothing would come. She couldn't even turn her head.

Drake said, "You have about an hour, I think, before the effects are irreversible. Talk quickly, Dr. Tholan, and you will have your cylinder back."

"And after that—" said the Hawkinsite.

"After that, what does it matter to you? Even if I kill you then, it will be a clean death; not cyanide lack."

Something seemed to pass out of the Hawkinsite. His voice grew guttural and his words blurred as though he no longer had the energy to keep his English perfect. He said, "What are your questions?" and as he spoke, his eyes followed the cylinder in Drake's hand.

Drake swung it deliberately, tantalizingly, and the creature's eyes followed —followed—

Drake said, "What are your theories concerning the Inhibition Death? Why did you really come to Earth? What is your interest in the Missing Persons Bureau?"

Rose found herself waiting in breathless anxiety. These were the questions she would like to have asked, too. Not in this manner, perhaps, but in Drake's job, kindness and humanity had to take second place to necessity.

She repeated that to herself several times in an effort to counteract the fact that she found herself loathing Drake for what he was doing to Dr. Tholan.

The Hawkinsite said, "The proper answer would take more than the hour I have left me. You have bitterly shamed me by forcing me to talk under duress. On my own planet, you could not have done so under any circumstances. It is only here, on this revolting planet, that I can be deprived of cyanide."

"You are wasting your hour, Dr. Tholan."

"I would have told you this eventually, Mr. Smollett. I needed your help. It is why I came here."

"You are still not answering my questions."

"I will answer them now. For years, in addition to my regular scientific work, I have been privately investigating the cells of my patients suffering from Inhibition Death. I have been forced to use the utmost secrecy and to work without assistance, since the methods I used to investigate the bodies of my patients were frowned upon by my people. Your society would have similar feelings against human vivisection, for instance. For this reason, I could not present the results I obtained to my fellow physicians until I had verified my theories here on Earth."

"What were your theories?" demanded Drake. The feverishness had returned to his eyes.

"It became more and more obvious to me as I proceeded with my studies that the entire direction of research into the Inhibition Death was wrong. Physically, there was no solution to its mystery. The Inhibition Death is entirely a disease of the mind."

Rose interrupted, "Surely, Dr. Tholan, it isn't psychosomatic."

A thin, gray translucent film had passed over the Hawkinsite's eyes. He no longer looked at them. He said, "No, Mrs. Smollett, it is not psychosomatic. It is a true disease of the mind; a mental infection. My patients had double minds. Beyond and beneath the one that obviously belonged to them, there was evidence of *another* one—an *alien* mind. I worked with Inhibition Death patients of other races than my own, and the same could be found. In short, there are not five intelligences in the Galaxy, but six. And the sixth is parasitic."

Rose said, "This is wild—impossible! You *must* be mistaken, Dr. Tholan."

"I am not mistaken. Until I came to Earth, I thought I might be. But my stay at the Institute and my researches at the Missing Persons Bureau convinced me that is not so. What is so impossible about the concept of a parasitic intelligence? Intelligences like these would not leave fossil remains, nor even leave artifacts—if their only function is to derive nourishment somehow from the mental activities of other creatures. One can imagine such a parasite, through the course of millions of years, perhaps, losing all portions of its physical being but that which remains necessary, just as a tapeworm, among your Earthly physical parasites, eventually lost all its functions but the single one of reproduction. In the case of the parasitic intelligence, all physical attributes would eventually be lost. It would become nothing but pure mind, living in some mental fashion we cannot conceive of on the minds of others. Particularly on the minds of Earthmen."

Rose said, "Why particularly Earthmen?"

Drake simply stood apart, intent, asking no further questions. He was content, apparently, to let the Hawkinsite speak.

"Have you not surmised that the sixth intelligence is a native of Earth? Mankind from the beginning has lived with it, has adapted to it, is unconscious of it. It is why the higher species of terrestrial animals, including man, do not grow after maturity and, eventually, die what is called natural death. It is the result of this universal parasitic infestation. It is why you sleep and dream, since it is then that the parasitic mind must feed and then that you are a little more conscious of it, perhaps. It is why the terrestrial mind alone of the intelligences is so subject to instability. Where else in the Galaxy are found split personalities and other such manifestations? After all, even now there must be occasional human minds which are visibly harmed by the presence of the parasite.

"Somehow, these parasitic minds could traverse space. They had no physical limitations. They could drift between the stars in what would correspond to a state of hibernation. Why the first ones did it, I don't know; probably no one will ever know. But once those first discovered the presence of intelligence on other planets in the Galaxy, there was a small, steady stream of parasitic intelligences making their way through space. We of the outer worlds must have been a gourmet's dish for them or they would have never struggled so hard to get to us. I imagine many must have failed to make the trip, but it must have been worth the effort to those who succeeded.

"But you see, we of the other worlds had not lived with these parasites for millions of years, as man and his ancestors had. We had not adapted ourselves to it. Our weak strains had not been killed off gradually through hundreds of generations until only the resistants were left. So, where Earthmen could survive the infection for decades with little harm, we others die a quick death within a year."

"And is that why the incidence has increased since interstellar travel between Earth and the other planets has begun?"

"Yes." For a moment there was silence, and then the Hawkinsite said with a sudden access of energy, "Give me back my cylinder. You have your answer."

Drake said, coolly, "What about the Missing Persons Bureau?" He was swinging the cylinder again; but now the Hawkinsite did not follow its movements. The gray translucent film on his eyes had deepened and Rose wondered whether that was simply an expression of weariness or an example of the changes induced by cyanide lack.

The Hawkinsite said, "As we are not well adapted to the intelligence that infests man, neither is it well adapted to us. It can live on us—it even prefers to, apparently—but it cannot reproduce with ourselves alone as the source of its life. The Inhibition Death is therefore not directly contagious among our people."

Rose looked at him with growing horror. "What are you implying, Dr. Tholan?"

"The Earthman remains the prime host for the parasite. An Earthman may infect one of us if he remains among us. But the parasite, once it is located in an intelligence of the outer worlds, must somehow return to an Earthman, if it expects to reproduce. Before interstellar travel, this was possible only by a re-passage of space and therefore the incidence of infection remained infinitesimal. Now we are infected and reinfected as the parasites return to Earth and come back to us via the mind of Earthmen who travel through space."

Rose said faintly, "And the missing persons—"

"Are the intermediate hosts. The exact process by which it is done, I, of course, do not know. The masculine terrestrial mind seems better suited for their purposes. You'll remember that at the Institute I was told that the life expectancy of the average human male is three years less than that of the average female. Once reproduction has been taken care of, the infested male leaves, by spaceship, for the outer worlds. He disappears."

"But this is impossible," insisted Rose. "What you say implies that the parasite mind can control the actions of its host! This cannot be, or we of Earth would have noticed their presence."

"The control, Mrs. Smollett, may be very subtle, and may, moreover, be exerted only during the period of active reproduction. I simply point to your Missing Persons Bureau. Why do the young men disappear? You have economic and psychological explanations, but they are not sufficient. —But I am quite ill now and cannot speak much longer. I have only this to say. In the mental parasite, your people and mine have a common enemy. Earthmen, too, need not die involuntarily, except for its presence. I thought that if I found myself unable to return to my own world with my information because of the unorthodox methods I used to obtain it, I might bring it to the authorities on Earth, and ask their help in stamping out this menace. Imagine my pleasure when I found that the husband of one of the biologists at the Institute was a member of one of Earth's most important investigating bodies. Naturally, I did what I could to be made a guest at his home in order that I might deal with him privately; convince him of the terrible truth; utilize his position to help in the attack on the parasites.

"This is, of course, now impossible. I cannot blame you too far. As Earthmen, you cannot be expected to understand the psychology of my people. Nevertheless, you must understand this. I can have no further dealing with either of you. I could not even bear to remain any longer on Earth."

Drake said, "Then you alone, of all your people, have any knowledge of this theory of yours."

"I alone."

Drake held out the cylinder. "Your cyanide, Dr. Tholan."

The Hawkinsite groped for it eagerly. His supple fingers manipulated the hose and the needle valve with the utmost delicacy. In the space of ten seconds, he had it in place and was inhaling the gas in huge breaths. His eyes were growing clear and transparent.

Drake waited until the Hawkinsite breathings had subsided to normal, and then, without expression, he raised his needle-gun and fired. Rose screamed. The Hawkinsite remained standing. His four lower limbs were incapable of buckling, but his head lolled and from his suddenly flaccid mouth, the cyanide hose fell, disregarded. Once again, Drake closed the needle valve and now he tossed the cylinder aside and stood there somberly, looking at the dead creature. There was no external mark to show that he had been killed. The needle-gun's pellet, thinner than the needle which gave the gun its name, entered the body noiselessly and easily, and exploded with devastating effect only within the abdominal cavity.

Rose ran from the room, still screaming. Drake pursued her, seized her arm. She heard the hard, flat sounds of his palm against her face without feeling them and subsided into little bubbling sobs.

Drake said, "I told you to have nothing to do with this. Now what do you think you'll do?"

She said, "Let me go. I want to leave. I want to go away."

"Because of something it was my job to do? You heard what the creature was saying. Do you suppose I could allow him to return to his world and spread those lies? They would believe him. And what do you think would happen then? Can you imagine what an interstellar war might be like? They would imagine they would have to kill us all to stop the disease."

With an effort that seemed to turn her inside out, Rose steadied. She looked firmly into Drake's eyes and said, "What Dr. Tholan said were no lies and no mistakes, Drake."

"Oh, come now, you're hysterical. You need sleep."

"I know what he said is so because the Security Commission knows all about that same theory, and knows it to be true."

"Why do you say such a preposterous thing?"

"Because you yourself let that slip twice."

Drake said, "Sit down." She did so, and he stood there, looking curiously at her. "So I have given myself away twice, have I? You've had a busy day of detection, my dear. You have facets you keep well hidden." He sat down and crossed his legs.

Rose thought, yes, she had had a busy day. She could see the electric clock on the kitchen wall from where she sat; it was more than two hours past midnight. Harg Tholan had entered their house thirty-five hours before and now he lay murdered in the spare bedroom.

Drake said, "Well, aren't you going to tell me where I pulled my two boners?"

"You turned white when Harg Tholan referred to me as a charming hostess. Hostess has a double meaning, you know, Drake. A host is one who harbors a parasite."

"Number one," said Drake. "What's number two?"

"That's something you did before Harg Tholan entered the house. I've been trying to remember it for hours. Do *you* remember, Drake? You spoke about how unpleasant it was for Hawkinsites to associate with Earthmen, and I said Harg Tholan was a doctor and had to. I asked you if you thought that human doctors particularly enjoyed going to the tropics, or letting infected mosquitoes bite them. Do you remember how upset you became?"

Drake laughed. "I had no idea I was so transparent. Mosquitoes are hosts for the malaria and yellow fever parasites." He sighed. "I've done my best to keep you out of this. I tried to keep the Hawkinsite away. I tried threatening you. Now there's nothing left but to tell you the truth. I must, because only the truth—or death—will keep you quiet. And I don't want to kill you."

She shrank back in her chair, eyes wide.

Drake said, "The Commission knows the truth. It does us no good. We can only do all in our power to prevent the other worlds from finding out."

"But the truth can't be held down forever! Harg Tholan found out. You've killed him, but another extraterrestrial will repeat the same discovery —over and over again. You can't kill them all."

"We know that, too," agreed Drake. "We have no choice."

"Why?" cried Rose. "Harg Tholan gave you the solution. He made no suggestions or threats of war between worlds. He suggested that we combine with the other intelligences and help to wipe out the parasite. And we can! If we, in common with all the others, put every scrap of effort into it—"

"You mean we can trust him? Does he speak for his government or for the other races?"

"Can we dare to refuse the risk?"

Drake said, "You don't understand." He reached toward her and took one of her cold, unresisting hands between both of his. He went on, "I may seem silly trying to teach you anything about your specialty, but I want you to hear me out. Harg Tholan was right. Man and his prehistoric ancestors have been living with this parasitic intelligence for uncounted ages; certainly for a much longer period than we have been truly *Homo sapiens*. In that interval, we have not only become adapted to it, we have become dependent upon it. It is no longer a case of parasitism. It is a case of mutual cooperation. You biologists have a name for it."

She tore her hand away. "What are you talking about? Symbiosis?"

"Exactly. We have a disease of our own, remember. It is a reverse disease; one of unrestrained growth. We've mentioned it already as a contrast to the Inhibition Death. Well, what is the cause of cancer? How long have biologists, physiologists, biochemists and all the others been working on it? How much success have they had with it? Why? Can't you answer that for yourself now?"

She said, slowly, "No, I can't. What are you talking about?"

"It's all very well to say that if we could remove the parasite, we would have eternal growth and life if we wanted it; or at least until we got tired of being too big or of living too long, and did away with ourselves neatly. But how many millions of years has it been since the human body has had occasion to grow in such an unrestrained fashion? Can it do so any longer? Is the chemistry of the body adjusted to that? Has it got the proper whatch-amacallits?"

"Enzymes," Rose supplied in a whisper.

"Yes, enzymes. It's impossible for us. If for any reason the parasitic intelligence, as Harg Tholan calls it, does leave the human body, or if its relationship to the human mind is in any way impaired, growth does take place, but not in any orderly fashion. We call the growth cancer. And there you have it. There's no way of getting rid of the parasite. We're together for all eternity. To get rid of their Inhibition Death, extraterrestrials must first wipe out all vertebrate life on Earth. There is no other solution for them, and so we must keep knowledge of it from them. Do you understand?"

Her mouth was dry and it was difficult to talk. "I understand, Drake." She noticed that his forehead was damp and that there was a line of perspiration down each cheek. "And now you'll have to get it out of the apartment."

"It's late at night and I'll be able to get the body out of the building. From there on—" He turned to her. "I don't know when I'll be back."

"I understand, Drake," she said again.

Harg Tholan was heavy. Drake had to drag him through the apartment. Rose turned away, retching. She hid her eyes until she heard the front door close. She whispered to herself, "I understand, Drake."

It was 3 A.M. Nearly an hour had passed since she had heard the front door click gently into place behind Drake and his burden. She didn't know where he was going, what he intended doing—

She sat there numbly. There was no desire to sleep; no desire to move. She kept her mind traveling in tight circles, away from the thing she knew and which she wanted not to know.

Parasitic minds! Was it only a coincidence or was it some queer racial memory, some tenuous long-sustained wisp of tradition or insight, stretching back through incredible millennia, that kept current the odd myth of human beginnings? She thought to herself, there were two intelligences on Earth to begin with. There were humans in the Garden of Eden and also the serpent, which "was more subtil than any beast of the field." The serpent infected man and, as a result, it lost its limbs. Its physical attributes were no longer necessary. And because of the infection, man was driven out of the Garden of eternal life. Death entered the world.

Yet, despite her efforts, the circle of her thoughts expanded and returned to Drake. She shoved and it returned; she counted to herself, she recited the names of the objects in her field of vision, she cried, "No, no, no," and it returned. It kept returning.

Drake had lied to her. It had been a plausible story. It would have held good under most circumstances; but Drake was not a biologist. Cancer could not be, as Drake had said, a disease that was an expression of a lost ability for normal growth. Cancer attacked children while they were still growing; it could even attack embryonic tissue. It attacked fish, which, like extraterrestrials, never stopped growing while they lived, and died only by disease or accident. It attacked plants which had no minds and could not be parasitized. Cancer had nothing to do with the presence or absence of normal growth; it was the general disease of life, to which *no* tissue of *no* multicellular organism was completely immune.

He should not have bothered lying. He should not have allowed some obscure sentimental weakness to persuade him to avoid the necessity of killing her in that manner. She would tell them at the Institute. The parasite *could* be beaten. Its absence would *not* cause cancer. But who would believe her?

She put her hands over her eyes. The young men who disappeared were usually in the first year of their marriage. Whatever the process of reproduction of the parasite intelligences, it must involve close association with another parasite—the type of close and continuous association that might only be possible if their respective hosts were in equally close relationship. As in the case of newly married couples.

She could feel her thoughts slowly disconnect. They would be coming to her. They would be saying, "Where is Harg Tholan?" And she would answer, "With my husband." Only they would say, "Where is your husband?" because he would be gone, too. He needed her no longer. He would never return. They would never find him, because he would be out in space. She would report them both, Drake Smollett and Harg Tholan, to the Missing Persons Bureau.

She wanted to weep, but couldn't; she was dry-eyed and it was painful.

And then she began to giggle and couldn't stop. It was very funny. She had looked for the answers to so many questions and had found them all. She had even found the answer to the question she thought had no bearing on the subject.

She had finally learned why Drake had married her.

"Breeds There a Man...?"

Police Sergeant Mankiewicz was on the telephone and he wasn't enjoying it. His conversation was sounding like a one-sided view of a firecracker.

He was saying, "That's right! He came in here and said, 'Put me in jail, because I want to kill myself.'

". . . I can't help that. Those were his exact words. It sounds crazy to me, too.

". . . Look, mister, the guy answers the description. You asked me for information and I'm giving it to you.

". . . He has exactly that scar on his right cheek and he said his name was John Smith. He didn't say it was Doctor anything-at-all.

". . . Well, sure it's a phony. Nobody is named John Smith. Not in a police station, anyway.

". . . He's in jail now.

". . . Yes, I mean it.

". . . Resisting an officer; assault and battery; malicious mischief. That's three counts.

". . . I don't care who he is.

". . . All right. I'll hold on."

He looked up at Officer Brown and put his hand over the mouthpiece of the phone. It was a ham of a hand that nearly swallowed up the phone altogether. His blunt-featured face was ruddy and steaming under a thatch of pale-yellow hair.

He said, "Trouble! Nothing but trouble at a precinct station. I'd rather be pounding a beat any day."

"Who's on the phone?" asked Brown. He had just come in and didn't really care. He thought Mankiewicz would look better on a suburban beat, too.

"Oak Ridge. Long Distance. A guy called Grant. Head of somethingological division, and now he's getting somebody else at seventy-five cents a min . . . Hello!"

Mankiewicz got a new grip on the phone and held himself down.

"Look," he said, "let me go through this from the beginning. I want you to get it straight and then if you don't like it, you can send someone down here. The guy doesn't want a lawyer. He claims he just wants to stay in jail and, brother, that's all right with me.

"Well, will you listen? He came in yesterday, walked right up to me, and said, 'Officer, I want you to put me in jail because I want to kill myself.' So I said, 'Mister, I'm sorry you want to kill yourself. Don't do it, because if you do, you'll regret it the rest of your life.'

". . . I *am* serious. I'm just telling you what I said. I'm not saying it was a funny joke, but I've got my own troubles here, if you know what I mean. Do you think all I've got to do here is to listen to cranks who walk in and—

". . . Give me a chance, will you?" I said, 'I can't put you in jail for wanting to kill yourself. That's no crime.' And he said, 'But I don't want to die.' So I said, 'Look, bud, get out of here.' I mean if a guy wants to commit suicide, all right, and if he doesn't want to, all right, but I don't want him weeping on my shoulder.

". . . I'm *getting* on with it. So he said to me. 'If I commit a crime, will you put me in jail?" I said, 'If you're caught and if someone files a charge and you can't put up bail, we will. Now beat it.' So he picked up the inkwell on my desk and, before I could stop him, he turned it upside down on the open police blotter.

". . . That's right! Why do you think we have 'malicious mischief' tabbed on him? The ink ran down all over my pants.

". . . Yes, assault and battery, too! I came hopping down to shake a little sense into him, and he kicked me in the shins and handed me one in the eye.

". . . I'm not making this up. You want to come down here and look at my face?

". . . He'll be up in court one of these days. About Thursday, maybe.

". . . Ninety days is the least he'll get, unless the psychoes say otherwise. I think he belongs in the loony-bin myself.

". . . Officially, he's John Smith. That's the only name he'll give.

". . . No, sir, he doesn't get released without the proper legal steps.

". . . O.K., you do that, if you want to, bud! I just do my job here."

He banged the phone into its cradle, glowered at it, then picked it up and began dialing. He said "Gianetti?", got the proper answer and began talking.

"What's the A.E.C.? I've been talking to some Joe on the phone and he says—

". . . No, I'm not kidding, lunk-head. If I were kidding, I'd put up a sign. What's the alphabet soup?"

He listened, said, "Thanks" in a small voice and hung up again.

He had lost some of his color. "That second guy was the head of the Atomic Energy Commission," he said to Brown. "They must have switched me from Oak Ridge to Washington."

Brown lounged to his feet, "Maybe the F.B.I. is after this John Smith guy. Maybe he's one of these here scientists." He felt moved to philosophy. "They ought to keep atomic secrets away from those guys. Things were O.K. as long as General Groves was the only fella who knew about the atom bomb. Once they cut in these here scientists on it, though—"

"Ah, shut up," snarled Mankiewicz.

Dr. Oswald Grant kept his eyes fixed on the white line that marked the highway and handled the car as though it were an enemy of his. He always did. He was tall and knobby with a withdrawn expression stamped on his face. His knees crowded the wheel, and his knuckles whitened whenever he made a turn.

Inspector Darrity sat beside him with his legs crossed so that the sole of his left shoe came up hard against the door. It would leave a sandy mark when he took it away. He tossed a nut-brown penknife from hand to hand. Earlier, he had unsheathed its wicked, gleaming blade and scraped casually at his nails as they drove, but a sudden swerve had nearly cost him a finger and he desisted.

He said, "What do you know about this Ralson?"

Dr. Grant took his eyes from the road momentarily, then returned them. He said, uneasily, "I've known him since he took his doctorate at Princeton. He's a very brilliant man."

"Yes? Brilliant, huh? Why is it that all you scientific men describe one another as 'brilliant'? Aren't there any mediocre ones?"

"Many. I'm one of them. But Ralson isn't. You ask anyone. Ask Oppenheimer. Ask Bush. He was the youngest observer at Alamogordo."

"O.K. He was brilliant. What about his private life?"

Grant waited. "I wouldn't know."

"You know him since Princeton. How many years is that?"

They had been scouring north along the highway from Washington for two hours with scarcely a word between them. Now Grant felt the atmosphere change and the grip of the law on his coat collar.

"He got his degree in '43."

"You've known him eight years then."

"That's right."

"And you don't know about his private life?"

"A man's life is his own, Inspector. He wasn't very sociable. A great many of the men are like that. They work under pressure and when they're off the job, they're not interested in continuing the lab acquaintanceships."

"Did he belong to any organizations that you know of?"

"No."

The inspector said, "Did he ever say anything to you that might indicate he was disloyal?"

Grant shouted "No!" and there was silence for a while.

Then Darrity said, "How important is Ralson in atomic research?"

Grant hunched over the wheel and said, "As important as any one man can be. I grant you that no one is indispensable, but Ralson has always seemed to be rather unique. He has the engineering mentality."

"What does that mean?"

"He isn't much of a mathematician himself, but he can work out the gadgets that put someone else's math into life. There's no one like him when it comes to that. Time and again, Inspector, we've had a problem to lick and no time to lick it in. There were nothing but blank minds all around until he put some thought into it and said, 'Why don't you try so-and-so?' Then he'd go away. He wouldn't even be interested enough to see if it worked. But it always did. Always! Maybe we would have got it ourselves eventually, but it might have taken months of additional time. I don't know how he does it. It's no use asking him either. He just looks at you and says 'It was obvious', and walks away. Of course, once he's shown us how to do it, it *is* obvious."

The inspector let him have his say out. When no more came, he said, "Would you say he was queer, mentally? Erratic, you know."

"When a person is a genius, you wouldn't expect him to be normal, would you?"

"Maybe not. But just how abnormal was this particular genius?"

"He never talked, particularly. Sometimes, he wouldn't work."

"Stayed at home and went fishing instead?"

"No. He came to the labs all right; but he would just sit at his desk. Sometimes that would go on for weeks. Wouldn't answer you, or even look at you, when you spoke to him."

"Did he ever actually leave work altogether?"

"Before now, you mean? Never!"

"Did he ever claim he wanted to commit suicide? Ever say he wouldn't feel safe except in jail?"

"No."

"You're sure this John Smith is Ralson?"

"I'm almost positive. He has a chemical burn on his right cheek that can't be mistaken."

"O.K. That's that, then I'll speak to him and see what he sounds like."

The silence fell for good this time. Dr. Grant followed the snaking line as Inspector Darrity tossed the penknife in low arcs from hand to hand.

The warden listened to the call-box and looked up at his visitors. "We can have him brought up here, Inspector, regardless."

"No," Dr. Grant shook his head. "Let's go to him."

Darrity said, "Is that normal for Ralson, Dr. Grant? Would you expect him to attack a guard trying to take him out of a prison cell?"

Grant said, "I can't say."

The warden spread a calloused palm. His thick nose twitched a little. "We haven't tried to do anything about him so far because of the telegram from Washington, but, frankly, he doesn't belong here. I'll be glad to have him taken off my hands."

"We'll see him in his cell," said Darrity.

They went down the hard, barlined corridor. Empty, incurious eyes watched their passing.

Dr. Grant felt his flesh crawl. "Has he been kept *here* all the time?"

Darrity did not answer.

The guard, pacing before them, stopped. "This is the cell."

Darrity said, "Is that Dr. Ralson?"

Dr. Grant looked silently at the figure upon the cot. The man had been lying down when they first reached the cell, but now he had risen to one elbow and seemed to be trying to shrink into the wall. His hair was sandy and thin, his figure slight, his eyes blank and china-blue. On his right cheek there was a raised pink patch that tailed off like a tadpole.

Dr. Grant said, "That's Ralson."

The guard opened the door and stepped inside, but Inspector Darrity sent him out again with a gesture. Ralson watched them mutely. He had drawn both feet up to the cot and was pushing backwards. His Adam's apple bobbled as he swallowed.

Darrity said quietly, "Dr. Elwood Ralson?"

"What do you want?" The voice was a surprising baritone.

"Would you come with us, please? We have some questions we would like to ask you."

"No! Leave me alone!"

"Dr. Ralson," said Grant, "I've been sent here to ask you to come back to work."

Ralson looked at the scientist and there was a momentary glint of something other than fear in his eyes. He said, "Hello, Grant." He got off his cot. "Listen, I've been trying to have them put me into a padded cell. Can't you make them do that for me? You know me, Grant, I wouldn't ask for something I didn't feel was necessary. Help me. I can't stand the hard walls. It makes me want to . . . bash—" He brought the flat of his palm thudding down against the hard, dull-gray concrete behind his cot.

Darrity looked thoughtful. He brought out his penknife and unbent the gleaming blade. Carefully, he scraped at his thumbnail, and said, "Would you like to see a doctor?"

But Ralson didn't answer that. He followed the gleam of metal and his lips parted and grew wet. His breath became ragged and harsh.

He said, "Put that away!"

Darrity paused. "Put what away?"

"The knife. Don't hold it in front of me. I can't stand looking at it."

Darrity said, "Why not?" He held it out. "Anything wrong with it? It's a good knife."

Ralson lunged. Darrity stepped back and his left hand came down on the other's wrist. He lifted the knife high in the air. "What's the matter, Ralson? What are you after?"

Grant cried a protest but Darrity waved him away.

Darrity said, "What do you want, Ralson?"

Ralson tried to reach upward, and bent under the other's appalling grip. He gasped, "Give me the knife."

"Why, Ralson? What do you want to do with it?"

"Please. I've got to—" He was pleading. "I've got to stop living."

"You want to die?"

"No. But I must."

Darrity shoved. Ralson flailed backward and tumbled into his cot, so that it squeaked noisily. Slowly, Darrity bent the blade of his penknife into its sheath and put it away. Ralson covered his face. His shoulders were shaking but otherwise he did not move.

There was the sound of shouting from the corridor, as the other prisoners reacted to the noise issuing from Ralson's cell. The guard came hurrying down, yelling, "Quiet!" as he went.

Darrity looked up. "It's all right, guard."

He was wiping his hands upon a large white handkerchief. "I think we'll get a doctor for him."

Dr. Gottfried Blaustein was small and dark and spoke with a trace of an Austrian accent. He needed only a small goatee to be the layman's caricature of a psychiatrist. But he was clean-shaven, and very carefully dressed. He watched Grant closely, assessing him, blocking in certain observations and deductions. He did this automatically, now, with everyone he met.

He said, "You give me a sort of picture. You describe a man of great talent, perhaps even genius. You tell me he has always been uncomfortable with people; that he has never fitted in with his laboratory environment, even though it was there that he met the greatest of success. Is there another environment to which he has fitted himself?"

"I don't understand."

"It is not given to all of us to be so fortunate as to find a congenial type of company at the place or in the field where we find it necessary to make a living. Often, one compensates by playing an instrument, or going hiking, or joining some club. In other words, one creates a new type of society, when not working, in which one can feel more at home. It need not have the slightest connection with what one's ordinary occupation is. It is an escape, and not necessarily an unhealthy one." He smiled and added, "Myself, I collect stamps. I am an active member of the American Society of Philatelists."

Grant shook his head. "I don't know what he did outside working hours. I doubt that he did anything like what you've mentioned."

"Um-m-m. Well, that would be sad. Relaxation and enjoyment are wherever you find them; but you must find them somewhere, no?"

"Have you spoken to Dr. Ralson, yet?"

"About his problems? No."

"Aren't you going to?"

"Oh, yes. But he has been here only a week. One must give him a chance to recover. He was in a highly excited state when he first came here. It was almost a delirium. Let him rest and become accustomed to the new environment. I will question him, then."

"Will you be able to get him back to work?"

Blaustein smiled. "How should I know? I don't even know what his sickness is."

"Couldn't you at least get rid of the worst of it; this suicidal obsession of his, and take care of the rest of the cure while he's at work?"

"Perhaps. I couldn't even venture an opinion so far without several interviews."

"How long do you suppose it will all take?"

"In these matters, Dr. Grant, nobody can say."

Grant brought his hands together in a sharp slap. "Do what seems best then. But this is more important than you know."

"Perhaps. But you may be able to help me, Dr. Grant."

"How?"

"Can you get me certain information which may be classified as top secret?"

"What kind of information?"

"I would like to know the suicide rate, since 1945, among nuclear scientists. Also, how many have left their jobs to go into other types of scientific work, or to leave science altogether."

"Is this in connection with Ralson?"

"Don't you think it might be an occupational disease, this terrible unhappiness of his?"

"Well—a good many have left their jobs, naturally."

"Why naturally, Dr. Grant?"

"You must know how it is, Dr. Blaustein. The atmosphere in modern atomic research is one of great pressure and red tape. You work with the government; you work with military men. You can't talk about your work; you have to be careful what you say. Naturally, if you get a chance at a job in a university, where you can fix your own hours, do your own work, write papers that don't have to be submitted to the A.E.C., attend conventions that aren't held behind locked doors, you take it."

"And abandon your field of specialty forever."

"There are always non-military applications. Of course, there was one man who did leave for another reason. He told me once he couldn't sleep nights. He said he'd hear one hundred thousand screams coming from Hiroshima, when he put the lights out. The last I heard of him he was a clerk in a haberdashery."

"And do you ever hear a few screams yourself?"

Grant nodded. "It isn't a nice feeling to know that even a little of the responsibility of atomic destruction might be your own."

"How did Ralson feel?"

"He never spoke of anything like that."

"In other words, if he felt it, he never even had the safety-valve effect of letting off steam to the rest of you."

"I guess he hadn't."

"Yet nuclear research must be done, no?"

"I'll say."

"What would you do, Dr. Grant, if you felt you *had* to do something that you *couldn't* do."

Grant shrugged. "I don't know."

"Some people kill themselves."

"You mean that's what has Ralson down."

"I don't know. I do not know. I will speak to Dr. Ralson this evening. I can promise nothing, of course, but I will let you know whatever I can."

Grant rose. "Thanks, Doctor. I'll try to get the information you want."

Elwood Ralson's appearance had improved in the week he had been at Dr. Blaustein's sanatorium. His face had filled out and some of the restlessness had gone out of him. He was tieless and beltless. His shoes were without laces.

Blaustein said, "How do you feel, Dr. Ralson?"

"Rested."

"You have been treated well?"

"No complaints, Doctor."

Blaustein's hand fumbled for the letter-opener with which it was his habit to play during moments of abstraction, but his fingers met nothing. It had been put away, of course, with anything else possessing a sharp edge. There was nothing on his desk, now, but papers.

He said, "Sit down, Dr. Ralson. How do your symptoms progress?"

"You mean, do I have what you would call a suicidal impulse? Yes. It gets worse or better, depending on my thoughts, I think. But it's always with me. There is nothing you can do to help."

"Perhaps you are right. There are often things I cannot help. But I would like to know as much as I can about you. You are an important man—"

Ralson snorted.

"You do not consider that to be so?" asked Blaustein.

"No, I don't. There are no important men, any more than there are important individual bacteria."

"I don't understand."

"I don't expect you to."

"And yet it seems to me that behind your statement there must have been much thought. It would certainly be of the greatest interest to have you tell me some of this thought."

For the first time, Ralson smiled. It was not a pleasant smile. His nostrils were white. He said, "It is amusing to watch you, Doctor. You go about your business so conscientiously. You must listen to me, mustn't you, with just that air of phony interest and unctuous sympathy. I can tell you the most ridiculous things and still be sure of an audience, can't I?"

"Don't you think my interest can be real, even granted that it is professional, too?"

"No, I don't."

"Why not?"

"I'm not interested in discussing it."

"Would you rather return to your room?"

"If you don't mind. No!" His voice had suddenly suffused with fury as he stood up, then almost immediately sat down again. "Why shouldn't I use you? I don't like to talk to people. They're stupid. They don't see things. They stare at the obvious for hours and it means nothing to them. If I spoke to them, they wouldn't understand; they'd lose patience; they'd laugh. Whereas you must listen. It's your job. You can't interrupt to tell me I'm mad, even though you may think so."

"I'd be glad to listen to whatever you would like to tell me."

Ralson drew a deep breath. "I've known something for a year now, that very few people know. Maybe it's something no *live* person knows. Do you know that human cultural advances come in spurts? Over a space of two generations in a city containing thirty thousand free men, enough literary and artistic genius of the first rank arose to supply a nation of millions for a century under ordinary circumstances. I'm referring to the Athens of Pericles.

"There are other examples. There is the Florence of the Medicis, the England of Elizabeth, the Spain of the Cordovan Emirs. There was the spasm of social reformers among the Israelites of the Eighth and Seventh centuries before Christ. Do you know what I mean?"

Blaustein nodded. "I see that history is a subject that interests you."

"Why not? I suppose there's nothing that says I must restrict myself to nuclear cross-sections and wave mechanics."

"Nothing at all. Please proceed."

"At first, I thought I could learn more of the true inwardness of historical cycles by consulting a specialist. I had some conferences with a professional historian. A waste of time!"

"What was his name; this professional historian?"

"Does it matter?"

"Perhaps not, if you would rather consider it confidential. What did he tell you?"

"He said I was wrong; that history only appeared to go in spasms. He said that after closer studies the great civilizations of Egypt and Sumeria did not arise suddenly or out of nothing, but upon the basis of a long-developing sub-civilization that was already sophisticated in its arts. He said that Periclean Athens built upon a pre-Periclean Athens of lower accomplishments, without which the age of Pericles could not have been.

"I asked why was there not a post-Periclean Athens of higher accomplishments still, and he told me that Athens was ruined by a plague and by a long war with Sparta. I asked about other cultural spurts and each time it was a war that ended it, or, in some cases, even accompanied it. He was like all the rest. The truth was there; he had only to bend and pick it up; but he didn't."

Ralson stared at the floor, and said in a tired voice, "They come to me in the laboratory sometimes, Doctor. They say, 'How the devil are we going to get rid of the such-and-such effect that is ruining all our measurements, Ralson?' They show me the instruments and the wiring diagrams and I say, 'It's staring at you. Why don't you do so-and-so? A child could tell you that.' Then I walk away because I can't endure the slow puzzling of their stupid faces. Later, they come to me and say, 'It worked, Ralson. How did you figure it out?' I can't explain to them, Doctor; it would be like explaining that water is wet. And I couldn't explain to the historian. And I can't explain to you. It's a waste of time."

"Would you like to go back to your room?"

"Yes."

Blaustein sat and wondered for many minutes after Ralson had been escorted out of his office. His fingers found their way automatically into the upper right drawer of his desk and lifted out the letter-opener. He twiddled it in his fingers.

Finally, he lifted the telephone and dialed the unlisted number he had been given.

He said, "This is Blaustein. There is a professional historian who was consulted by Dr. Ralson some time in the past, probably a bit over a year ago. I don't know his name. I don't even know if he was connected with a university. If you could find him, I would like to see him."

Thaddeus Milton, Ph.D., blinked thoughtfully at Blaustein and brushed his hand through his iron-gray hair. He said, "They came to me and I said that I had indeed met this man. However, I have had very little connection with him. None, in fact, beyond a few conversations of a professional nature."

"How did he come to you?"

"He wrote me a letter; why me, rather than someone else, I do not know. A series of articles written by myself had appeared in one of the semi-learned journals of semi-popular appeal about that time. It may have attracted his attention."

"I see. With what general topic were the articles concerned?"

"They were a consideration of the validity of the cyclic approach to history. That is, whether one can really say that a particular civilization must follow laws of growth and decline in any matter analogous to those involving individuals."

"I have read Toynbee, Dr. Milton."

"Well, then, you know what I mean."

Blaustein said, "And when Dr. Ralson consulted you, was it with reference to this cyclic approach to history?"

"U-m-m-m. In a way, I suppose. Of course, the man is not an historian and some of his notions about cultural trends are rather dramatic and. . . . what shall I say. . . . tabloidish. Pardon me, Doctor, if I ask a question which may be improper. Is Dr. Ralson one of your patients?"

"Dr. Ralson is not well and is in my care. This, and all else we say here, is confidential, of course."

"Quite. I understand that. However, your answer explains something to me. Some of his ideas almost verged on the irrational. He was always worried, it seemed to me, about the connection between what he called 'cultural spurts' and calamities of one sort or another. Now such connections have been noted frequently. The time of a nation's greatest vitality may come at a time of great national insecurity. The Netherlands is a good case in point. Her great artists, statesmen, and explorers belong to the early Seventeenth Century at the time when she was locked in a death struggle with the greatest European power of the time, Spain. When at the point of destruction at home, she was building an empire in the Far East and had secured footholds on the northern coast of South America, the southern tip of Africa, and the Hudson Valley of North America. Her fleets fought England to a standstill. And then, once her political safety was assured, she declined.

"Well, as I say, that is not unusual. Groups, like individuals, will rise to strange heights in answer to a challenge, and vegetate in the absence of a challenge. Where Dr. Ralson left the paths of sanity, however, was in insisting that such a view amounted to confusing cause and effect. He declared that it was not times of war and danger that stimulated 'cultural spurts', but rather vice versa. He claimed that each time a group of men showed too much vitality and ability, a war became necessary to destroy the possibility of their further development."

"I see," said Blaustein.

"I rather laughed at him, I am afraid. It may be that that was why he did not keep the last appointment we made. Just toward the end of that last conference he asked me, in the most intense fashion imaginable, whether I did not think it queer that such an improbable species as man was dominant on earth, when all he had in his favor was intelligence. There I laughed aloud. Perhaps I should not have, poor fellow."

"It was a natural reaction," said Blaustein, "but I must take no more of your time. You have been most helpful."

They shook hands, and Thaddeus Milton took his leave.

"Well," said Darrity, "there are your figures on the recent suicides among scientific personnel. Get any deductions out of it?"

"I should be asking you that," said Blaustein, gently. "The F.B.I. must have investigated thoroughly."

"You can bet the national debt on that. They *are* suicides. There's no mistake about it. There have been people checking on it in another department. The rate is about four times above normal, taking age, social status, economic class into consideration."

"What about British scientists?"

"Just about the same."

"And the Soviet Union?"

"Who can tell?" The investigator leaned forward. "Doc, you don't think the Soviets have some sort of ray that can make people want to commit suicide, do you? It's sort of suspicious that men in atomic research are the only ones affected."

"Is it? Perhaps not. Nuclear physicists may have peculiar strains imposed upon them. It is difficult to tell without thorough study."

"You mean complexes might be coming through?" asked Darrity, warily.

Blaustein made a face. "Psychiatry is becoming too popular. Everybody talks of complexes and neuroses and psychoses and compulsions and whatnot. One man's guilt complex is another man's good night's sleep. If I could talk to each one of the men who committed suicide, maybe I could know something."

"You're talking to Ralson."

"Yes, I'm talking to Ralson."

"Has *he* got a guilt complex?"

"Not particularly. He has a background out of which it would not surprise me if he obtained a morbid concern with death. When he was twelve he saw his mother die under the wheels of an automobile. His father died slowly of cancer. Yet the effect of those experiences on his present troubles is not clear."

Darrity picked up his hat. "Well, I wish you'd get a move on, Doc. There's something big on, bigger than the H-Bomb. I don't know how anything *can* be bigger than that, but it is."

Ralson insisted on standing. "I had a bad night last night, Doctor."

"I hope," said Blaustein, "these conferences are not disturbing you."

"Well, maybe they are. They have me thinking on the subject again. It makes things bad, when I do that. How do you imagine it feels being part of a bacterial culture, Doctor?"

"I had never thought of that. To a bacterium, it probably feels quite normal."

Ralson did not hear. He said, slowly, "A culture in which intelligence is being studied. We study all sorts of things as far as their genetic relationships are concerned. We take fruit flies and cross red eyes and white eyes to see what happens. We don't care anything about red eyes and white eyes, but we try to gather from them certain basic genetic principles. You see what I mean?"

"Certainly."

"Even in humans, we can follow various physical characteristics. There are the Hapsburg lips, and the haemophilia that started with Queen Victoria and cropped up in her descendants among the Spanish and Russian royal families. We can even follow feeble-mindedness in the Jukeses and Kallikakas. You learn about it in high-school biology. But you can't breed human beings the way you do fruit flies. Humans live too long. It would take centuries to draw conclusions. It's a pity we don't have a special race of men that reproduce at weekly intervals, eh?"

He waited for an answer, but Blaustein only smiled.

Ralson said, "Only that's exactly what we would be for another group of beings whose life span might be thousands of years. To them, we would reproduce rapidly enough. We would be short-lived creatures and they could study the genetics of such things as musical aptitude, scientific intelligence, and so on. Not that those things would interest them as such, any more than the white eyes of the fruit fly interest us as white eyes."

"This is a very interesting notion," said Blaustein.

"It is not simply a notion. It is true. To me, it is obvious, and I don't care how it seems to you. Look around you. Look at the planet, Earth. What kind of a ridiculous animal are we to be lords of the world after the dinosaurs had failed? Sure, we're intelligent, but what's intelligence? We think it is important because we have it. If the Tyrannosaurus could have picked out the one quality that he thought would ensure species domination, it would be size and strength. And he would make a better case for it. He lasted longer than we're likely to.

"Intelligence in itself isn't much as far as survival values are concerned. The elephant makes out very poorly indeed when compared to the sparrow even though he is much more intelligent. The dog does well, under man's protection, but not as well as the house-fly against whom every human hand is raised. Or take the primates as a group. The small ones cower before their enemies; the large ones have always been remarkably unsuccessful in doing more than barely holding their own. The baboons do the best and that is because of their canines, not their brains."

A light film of perspiration covered Ralson's forehead. "And one can see that man has been tailored, made to careful specifications for those things that study us. Generally, the primate is short-lived. Naturally, the larger ones live longer, which is a fairly general rule in animal life. Yet the human being has a life span twice as long as any of the other great apes; considerably longer even than the gorilla that outweighs him. We mature later. It's as though we've been carefully bred to live a little longer so that our life cycle might be of a more convenient length."

He jumped to his feet, shaking his fists above his head. "A thousand years are but as yesterday—"

Blaustein punched a button hastily.

For a moment, Ralson struggled against the white-coated orderly who entered, and then he allowed himself to be led away.

Blaustein looked after him, shook his head, and picked up the telephone. He got Darrity. "Inspector, you may as well know that this may take a long time."

He listened and shook his head. "I know. I don't minimize the urgency."

The voice in the receiver was tinny and harsh. "Doctor, you *are* minimizing it. I'll send Dr. Grant to you. He'll explain the situation to you."

Dr. Grant asked how Ralson was, then asked somewhat wistfully if he could see him. Blaustein shook his head gently.

Grant said, "I've been directed to explain the current situation in atomic research to you."

"So that I will understand, no?"

"I hope so. It's a measure of desperation. I'll have to remind you—"

"Not to breathe a word of it. Yes, I know. This insecurity on the part of you people is a very bad symptom. You must know these things cannot be hidden."

"You live with secrecy. It's contagious."

"Exactly. What is the current secret?"

"There is . . . or, at least, there might be a defense against the atomic bomb."

"And that is a secret? It would be better if it were shouted to all the people of the world instantly."

"For heaven's sake, no. Listen to me, Dr. Blaustein. It's only on paper so far. It's at the E equal mc square stage, almost. It may not be practical. It would be bad to raise hopes we would have to disappoint. On the other hand, if it were known that we *almost* had a defense, there *might* be a desire to start and win a war before the defense were completely developed."

"That I don't believe. But, nevertheless, I distract you. What is the nature of this defense, or have you told me as much as you dare?"

"No, I can go as far as I like; as far as is necessary to convince you we have to have Ralson—and fast!"

"Well, then tell me, and I too, will know secrets. I'll feel like a member of the Cabinet."

"You'll know more than most. Look, Dr. Blaustein, let me explain it in lay language. So far, military advances have been made fairly equally in both offensive and defensive weapons. Once before there seemed to be a definite and permanent tipping of all warfare in the direction of the offense, and that was with the invention of gunpowder. But the defense caught up. The medieval man-in-armor-on-horse became the modern man-in-tank-on-treads, and the stone castle became the concrete pillbox. The same thing, you see, except that everything has been boosted several orders of magnitude."

"Very good. You make it clear. But with the atomic bomb comes more orders of magnitude, no? You must go past concrete and steel for protection."

"Right. Only we can't just make thicker and thicker walls. We've run out of materials that are strong enough. So we must abandon materials altogether. If the atom attacks, we must let the atom defend. We will use energy itself; a force field."

"And what," asked Blaustein, gently, "is a force field?"

"I wish I could tell you. Right now, it's an equation on paper. Energy can be so channeled as to create a wall of matterless inertia, theoretically. In practice, we don't know how to do it."

"It would be a wall you could not go through, is that it? Even for atoms?"

"Even for atom bombs. The only limit on its strength would be the amount of energy we could pour into it. It could even theoretically be made to be impermeable to radiation. The gamma rays would bounce off it. What we're dreaming of is a screen that would be in permanent place about cities; at minimum strength, using practically no energy. It could then be triggered to maximum intensity in a fraction of a millisecond at the impingement of short-wave radiation; say the amount radiating from the mass of plutonium large enough to be an atomic war head. All this is theoretically possible."

"And why must you have Ralson?"

"Because he is the only one who can reduce it to practice, if it can be made practical at all, quickly enough. Every minute counts these days. You

know what the international situation is. Atomic defense *must* arrive before
atomic war."

"You are so sure of Ralson?"

"I am as sure of him as I can be of anything. The man is amazing, Dr.
Blaustein. He is always right. Nobody in the field knows how he does it."

"A sort of intuition, no?" the psychiatrist looked disturbed. "A kind of
reasoning that goes beyond ordinary human capacities. Is that it?"

"I make no pretense of knowing what it is."

"Let me speak to him once more then. I will let you know."

"Good." Grant rose to leave; then, as if in afterthought, he said, "I might
say, Doctor, that if you don't do something, the Commission plans to take
Dr. Ralson out of your hands."

"And try another psychiatrist? If they wish to do that, of course, I will not
stand in their way. It is my opinion, however, that no reputable practitioner
will pretend there is a rapid cure."

"We may not intend further mental treatment. He may simply be returned to work."

"That, Dr. Grant, I will fight. You will get nothing out of him. It will be
his death."

"We get nothing out of him anyway."

"This way there is at least a chance, no?"

"I hope so. And by the way, please don't mention the fact that I said
anything about taking Ralson away."

"I will not, and I thank you for the warning. Good-bye, Dr. Grant."

"I made a fool of myself last time, didn't I, Doctor?" said Ralson. He was
frowning.

"You mean you don't believe what you said then?"

"*I do!*" Ralson's slight form trembled with the intensity of his affirmation.

He rushed to the window, and Blaustein swiveled in his chair to keep him
in view. There were bars in the window. He couldn't jump. The glass was
unbreakable.

Twilight was ending, and the stars were beginning to come out. Ralson
stared at them in fascination, then he turned to Blaustein and flung a finger
outward. "Every single one of them is an incubator. They maintain temperatures at the desired point. Different experiments; different temperatures.
And the planets that circle them are just huge cultures, containing different
nutrient mixtures and different life forms. The experimenters are economi-
cal, too—whatever and whoever they are. They've cultured many types of
life forms in this particular test-tube. Dinosaurs in a moist, tropical age and
ourselves among the glaciers. They turn the sun up and down and we try to
work out the physics of it. Physics!" He drew his lips back in a snarl.

"Surely," said Dr. Blaustein, "it is not possible that the sun can be turned
up and down at will."

"Why not? It's just like a heating element in an oven. You think bacteria know what it is that works the heat that reaches them? Who knows? Maybe they evolve theories, too. Maybe they have their cosmogonies about cosmic catastrophes, in which clashing light-bulbs create strings of Petri dishes. Maybe they think there must be some beneficent creator that supplies them with food and warmth and says to them, 'Be fruitful and multiply!'

"We breed like them, not knowing why. We obey the so-called laws of nature which are only our interpretation of the not-understood forces imposed upon us.

"And now they've got the biggest experiment of any yet on their hands. It's been going on for two hundred years. They decided to develop a strain for mechanical aptitude in England in the seventeen hundreds, I imagine. We call it the Industrial Revolution. It began with steam, went on to electricity, then atoms. It was an interesting experiment, but they took their chances on letting it spread. Which is why they'll have to be very drastic indeed in ending it."

Blaustein said, "And how would they plan to end it? Do you have an idea about that?"

"You ask *me* how they plan to end it. You can look about the world today and still ask what is likely to bring our technological age to an end. All the earth fears an atomic war and would do anything to avoid it; yet all the earth fears that an atomic war is inevitable."

"In other words, the experimenters will arrange an atom war whether we want it or not, to kill off the technological era we are in, and to start fresh. That is it, no?"

"Yes. It's logical. When we sterilize an instrument, do the germs know where the killing heat comes from? Or what has brought it about? There is some way the experimenters can raise the heat of our emotions; some way they can handle us that passes our understanding."

"Tell me," said Blaustein, "is that why you want to die? Because you think the destruction of civilization is coming and can't be stopped?"

Ralson said, "I *don't* want to die. It's just that I must." His eyes were tortured. "Doctor, if you had a culture of germs that were highly dangerous and that you had to keep under absolute control, might you not have an agar medium impregnated with, say, penicillin, in a circle at a certain distance from the center of inoculation? Any germs spreading out too far from the center would die. You would have nothing against the particular germs who were killed; you might not even know that any germs had spread that far in the first place. It would be purely automatic.

"Doctor, there is a penicillin ring about our intellects. When we stray too far; when we penetrate the true meaning of our own existence, we have reached into the penicillin and we must die. It works slowly—but it's hard to stay alive."

He smiled briefly and sadly. Then he said, "May I go back to my room now, Doctor?"

Dr. Blaustein went to Ralson's room about noon the next day. It was a small room and featureless. The walls were gray with padding. Two small windows were high up and could not be reached. The mattress lay directly on the padded floor. There was nothing of metal in the room; nothing that could be utilized in tearing life from body. Even Ralson's nails were clipped short.

Ralson sat up. "Hello!"

"Hello, Dr. Ralson. May I speak to you?"

"Here? There isn't any seat I can offer you."

"It is all right. I'll stand. I have a sitting job and it is good for my sitting-down place that I should stand sometimes. Dr. Ralson, I have thought all night of what you told me yesterday and in the days before."

"And now you are going to apply treatment to rid me of what you think are delusions."

"No. It is just that I wish to ask questions and perhaps to point out some consequences of your theories which . . . you will forgive me? . . . you may not have thought of."

"Oh?"

"You see, Dr. Ralson, since you have explained your theories, I, too, know what you know. Yet I have no feeling about suicide."

"Belief is more than something intellectual, Doctor. You'd have to believe this with all your insides, which you don't."

"Do you not think perhaps it is rather a phenomenon of adaptation?"

"How do you mean?"

"You are not really a biologist, Dr. Ralson. And although you are very brilliant indeed in physics, you do not think of everything with respect to these bacterial cultures you use as analogies. You know that it is possible to breed bacterial strains that are resistant to penicillin or to almost any bacterial poison."

"Well?"

"The experimenters who breed us have been working with humanity for many generations, no? And this particular strain which they have been culturing for two centuries shows no sign of dying out spontaneously. Rather, it is a vigorous strain and a very infective one. Older high-culture strains were confined to single cities or to small areas and lasted only a generation or two. This one is spreading throughout the world. It is a *very* infective strain. Do you not think it may have developed penicillin immunity? In other words, the methods the experimenters use to wipe out the culture may not work too well any more, no?"

Ralson shook his head. "It's working on me."

"You are perhaps non-resistant. Or you have stumbled into a very high concentration of penicillin indeed. Consider all the people who have been trying to outlaw atomic warfare and to establish some form of world government and lasting peace. The effort has risen in recent years, without too awful results."

"It isn't stopping the atomic war that's coming."

"No, but maybe only a little more effort is all that is required. The peace-advocates do not kill themselves. More and more humans are immune to the experimenters. Do you know what they are doing in the laboratory?"

"I don't want to know."

"You *must* know. They are trying to invent a force field that will stop the atom bomb. Dr. Ralson, if I am culturing a virulent and pathological bacterium; then, even with all precautions, it may sometimes happen that I will start a plague. We may be bacteria to them, but we are dangerous to them, also, or they wouldn't wipe us out so carefully after each experiment.

"They are not quick, no? To them a thousand years is as a day, no? By the time they realize we are out of the culture, past the penicillin, it will be too late for them to stop us. They have brought us to the atom, and if we can only prevent ourselves from using it upon one another, we may turn out to be too much even for the experimenters."

Ralson rose to his feet. Small though he was, he was an inch and a half taller than Blaustein. "They are really working on a force field?"

"They are trying to. But they need you."

"No. I can't."

"They must have you in order that you might see what is so obvious to you. It is not obvious to them. Remember, it is your help, or else—defeat of man by the experimenters."

Ralson took a few rapid steps away, staring into the blank, padded wall. He muttered, "But there must be that defeat. If they build a force field, it will mean death for all of them before it can be completed."

"Some or all of them may be immune, no? And in any case, it will be death for them anyhow. They are trying."

Ralson said, "I'll try to help them."

"Do you still want to kill yourself?"

"Yes."

"But you'll try not to, no?"

"I'll *try* not to, Doctor." His lip quivered. "I'll have to be watched."

Blaustein climbed the stairs and presented his pass to the guard in the lobby. He had already been inspected at the outer gate, but he, his pass, and its signature were now scrutinized once again. After a moment, the guard retired to his little booth and made a phone call. The answer satisfied him. Blaustein took a seat and, in half a minute, was up again, shaking hands with Dr. Grant.

"The President of the United States would have trouble getting in here, no?" said Blaustein.

The lanky physicist smiled. "You're right, if he came without warning."

They took an elevator which traveled twelve floors. The office to which Grant led the way had windows in three directions. It was sound-proofed and air-conditioned. Its walnut furniture was in a state of high polish.

Blaustein said, "My goodness. It is like the office of the chairman of a board of directors. Science is becoming big business."

Grant looked embarrassed. "Yes, I know, but government money flows easily and it is difficult to persuade a congressman that your work is important unless he can see, smell, and touch the surface shine."

Blaustein sat down and felt the upholstered seat give way slowly. He said, "Dr. Elwood Ralson has agreed to return to work."

"Wonderful. I was hoping you would say that. I was hoping that was why you wanted to see me." As though inspired by the news, Grant offered the psychiatrist a cigar, which was refused.

"However," said Blaustein, "he remains a very sick man. He will have to be treated carefully and with insight."

"Of course. Naturally."

"It's not quite as simple as you may think. I want to tell you something of Ralson's problems, so that you will really understand how delicate the situation is."

He went on talking and Grant listened first in concern, and then in astonishment. "But then the man is out of his head, Dr. Blaustein. He'll be of no use to us. He's crazy."

Blaustein shrugged. "It depends on how you define 'crazy.' It's a bad word; don't use it. He had delusions, certainly. Whether they will affect his peculiar talents one cannot know."

"But surely no sane man could possibly—"

"Please. Please. Let us not launch into long discussions on psychiatric definitions of sanity and so on. The man has delusions and, ordinarily, I would dismiss them from all consideration. It is just that I have been given to understand that the man's particular ability lies in his manner of proceeding to the solution of a problem by what seems to be outside ordinary reason. That is so, no?"

"Yes. That *must* be admitted."

"How can you and I judge then as to the worth of one of his conclusions. Let me ask you, do *you* have suicidal impulses lately?"

"I don't think so."

"And other scientists here?"

"No, of course not."

"I would suggest, however, that while research on the force field proceeds, the scientists concerned be watched here and at home. It might even be a good enough idea that they should not go home. Offices like these could be arranged to be a small dormitory—"

"Sleep at work. You would never get them to agree."

"Oh, yes. If you do not tell them the real reason but say it is for security purposes, they will agree. 'Security purposes' is a wonderful phrase these days, no? Ralson must be watched more than anyone."

"Of course."

"But all this is minor. It is something to be done to satisfy my conscience in case Ralson's theories are correct. Actually, I don't believe them. They *are* delusions, but once that is granted, it is necessary to ask what the causes of those delusions are. What is it in Ralson's mind, in his background, in his life that makes it so necessary for him to have these particular delusions? One cannot answer that simply. It may well take years of constant psychoanalysis to discover the answer. And until the answer is discovered, he will not be cured.

"But, meanwhile, we can perhaps make intelligent guesses. He has had an unhappy childhood, which, in one way or another, has brought him face to face with death in very unpleasant fashion. In addition, he has never been able to form associations with other children, or, as he grew older, with other men. He was always impatient with their slower forms of reasoning. Whatever difference there is between his mind and that of others, it has built a wall between him and society as strong as the force field you are trying to design. For similar reasons, he has been unable to enjoy a normal sex life. He has never married; he has had no sweethearts.

"It is easy to see that he could easily compensate to himself for this failure to be accepted by his social milieu by taking refuge in the thought that other human beings are inferior to himself. Which is, of course, true, as far as mentality is concerned. There are, of course, many, many facets to the human personality and in not all of them is he superior. No one is. Others, then, who are more prone to see merely what is inferior, just as he himself is, would not accept his affected pre-eminence of position. They would think him queer, even laughable, which would make it even more important to Ralson to prove how miserable and inferior the human species was. How could he better do that than to show that mankind was simply a form of bacteria to other superior creatures which experiment upon them. And then his impulses to suicide would be a wild desire to break away completely from being a man at all; to stop this identification with the miserable species he has created in his mind. You see?"

Grant nodded. "Poor guy."

"Yes, it is a pity. Had he been properly taken care of in childhood— Well, it is best for Dr. Ralson that he have no contact with any of the other men here. He is too sick to be trusted with them. You, yourself, must arrange to be the only man who will see him or speak to him. Dr. Ralson has agreed to that. He apparently thinks you are not as stupid as some of the others."

Grant smiled faintly. "That is agreeable to me."

"You will, of course, be careful. I would not discuss anything with him but his work. If he should volunteer information about his theories, which I doubt, confine yourself to something non-committal, and leave. And at all times, keep away anything that is sharp and pointed. Do not let him reach a window. Try to have his hands kept in view. You understand. I leave my patient in your care, Dr. Grant."

"I will do my best, Dr. Blaustein."

For two months, Ralson lived in a corner of Grant's office, and Grant lived with him. Gridwork had been built up before the windows, wooden furniture was removed and upholstered sofas brought in. Ralson did his thinking on the couch and his calculating on a desk pad atop a hassock.

The "Do Not Enter" was a permanent fixture outside the office. Meals were left outside. The adjoining men's room was marked off for private use and the door between it and the office removed. Grant switched to an electric razor. He made certain that Ralson took sleeping pills each night and waited till the other slept before sleeping himself.

And always reports were brought to Ralson. He read them while Grant watched and tried to seem not to watch.

Then Ralson would let them drop and stare at the ceiling, with one hand shading his eyes.

"Anything?" asked Grant.

Ralson shook his head from side to side.

Grant said, "Look, I'll clear the building during the swing shift. It's important that you see some of the experimental jigs we've been setting up."

They did so, wandering through the lighted, empty buildings like drifting ghosts, hand in hand. Always hand in hand. Grant's grip was tight. But after each trip, Ralson would still shake his head from side to side.

Half a dozen times he would begin writing; each time there would be a few scrawls and then he would kick the hassock over on its side.

Until, finally, he began writing once again and covered half a page rapidly. Automatically, Grant approached. Ralson looked up, covering the sheet of paper with a trembling hand.

He said, "Call Blaustein."

"What?"

"I said, 'Call Blaustein.' Get him here. Now!"

Grant moved to the telephone.

Ralson was writing rapidly now, stopping only to brush wildly at his forehead with the back of a hand. It came away wet.

He looked up and his voice was cracked, "Is he coming?"

Grant looked worried. "He isn't at his office."

"Get him at his home. Get him wherever he is. *Use* that telephone. Don't play with it."

Grant used it; and Ralson pulled another sheet toward himself.

Five minutes later, Grant said, "He's coming. What's wrong? You're looking sick."

Ralson could speak only thickly, "No time— Can't talk—"

He was writing, scribbling, scrawling, shakily diagraming. It was as though he were driving his hands, fighting it.

"Dictate!" urged Grant. "I'll write."

Ralson shook him off. His words were unintelligible. He held his wrist with his other hand, shoving it as though it were a piece of wood, and then he collapsed over the papers.

Grant edged them out from under and laid Ralson down on the couch. He hovered over him restlessly and hopelessly until Blaustein arrived.

Blaustein took one look. "What happened?"

Grant said, "I think he's alive," but by that time Blaustein had verified that for himself, and Grant told him what had happened.

Blaustein used a hypodermic and they waited. Ralson's eyes were blank when they opened. He moaned.

Blaustein leaned close. "Ralson."

Ralson's hands reached out blindly and clutched at the psychiatrist. "Doc. Take me back."

"I will. Now. It is that you have the force field worked out, no?"

"It's on the papers. Grant, it's on the papers."

Grant had them and was leafing through them dubiously. Ralson said, weakly, "It's not *all* there. It's all I can write. You'll *have* to make it out of that. Take me back, Doc!"

"Wait," said Grant. He whispered urgently to Blaustein. "Can't you leave him here till we test this thing? I can't make out what most of this is. The writing is illegible. Ask him what makes him think this will work."

"Ask *him?*" said Blaustein, gently. "Isn't he the one who always knows?"

"Ask me, anyway," said Ralson, overhearing from where he lay on the couch. His eyes were suddenly wide and blazing.

They turned to him.

He said, "*They* don't want a force field. *They!* The experimenters! As long as I had no true grasp, things remained as they were. But I hadn't followed up that thought—*that* thought which is there in the papers—I hadn't followed it up for thirty seconds before I felt . . . I felt— Doctor—"

Blaustein said, "What is it?"

Ralson was whispering again, "I'm deeper in the penicillin. I could feel myself plunging in and in, the further I went with that. I've never been in . . . so deep. That's how I knew I was right. Take me away."

Blaustein straightened. "I'll have to take him away, Grant. There's no alternative. If you can make out what he's written, that's it. If you can't make it out, I can't help you. That man can do no more work in his field without dying, do you understand?"

"But," said Grant, "he's dying of something imaginary."

"All right. Say that he is. But he will be really dead just the same, no?"

Ralson was unconscious again and heard nothing of this. Grant looked at him somberly, then said, "Well, take him away, then."

Ten of the top men at the Institute watched glumly as slide after slide filled the illuminated screen. Grant faced them, expression hard and frowning.

He said, "I think the idea is simple enough. You're mathematicians and you're engineers. The scrawl may seem illegible, but it was done with meaning behind it. That meaning must somehow remain in the writing, distorted though it is. The first page is clear enough. It should be a good lead. Each one of you will look at every page over and over again. You're going to put down every possible version of each page as it seems it might be. You will work independently. I want no consultations."

One of them said, "How do you know it means *anything*, Grant?"

"Because those are Ralson's notes."

"Ralson! I thought he was—"

"You thought he was sick," said Grant. He had to shout over the rising hum of conversation. "I know. He is. That's the writing of a man who was nearly dead. It's all we'll ever get from Ralson, any more. Somewhere in that scrawl is the answer to the force field problem. If we can't find it, we may have to spend ten years looking for it elsewhere."

They bent to their work. The night passed. Two nights passed. Three nights—

Grant looked at the results. He shook his head. "I'll take your word for it that it is all self-consistent. I can't say I understand it."

Lowe, who, in the absence of Ralson, would readily have been rated the best nuclear engineer at the Institute, shrugged. "It's not exactly clear to me. If it works, he hasn't explained why."

"He had no time to explain. Can you build the generator as he describes it?"

"I could try."

"Would you look at all the other versions of the pages?"

"The others are definitely not self-consistent."

"Would you double-check?"

"Sure."

"And could you start construction anyway?"

"I'll get the shop started. But I tell you frankly that I'm pessimistic."

"I know. So am I."

· · · ·

The thing grew. Hal Ross, Senior Mechanic, was put in charge of the actual construction, and he stopped sleeping. At any hour of the day or night, he could be found at it, scratching his bald head.

He asked questions only once, "What is it, Dr. Lowe? Never saw anything like it? What's it supposed to do?"

Lowe said, "You know where you are, Ross. You know we don't ask questions here. Don't ask again."

Ross did not ask again. He was known to dislike the structure that was being built. He called it ugly and unnatural. But he stayed at it.

Blaustein called one day.

Grant said, "How's Ralson?"

"Not good. He wants to attend the testing of the Field Projector he designed."

Grant hesitated, "I suppose we should. It's his after all."

"I would have to come with him."

Grant looked unhappier. "It might be dangerous, you know. Even in a pilot test, we'd be playing with tremendous energies."

Blaustein said, "No more dangerous for us than for you."

"Very well. The list of observers will have to be cleared through the Commission and the F.B.I., but I'll put you in."

Blaustein looked about him. The field projector squatted in the very center of the huge testing laboratory, but all else had been cleared. There was no visible connection with the plutonium pile which served as energy-source, but from what the psychiatrist heard in scraps about him—he knew better than to ask Ralson—the connection was from beneath.

At first, the observers had circled the machine, talking in incomprehensibles, but they were drifting away now. The gallery was filling up. There were at least three men in generals' uniforms on the other side, and a real coterie of lower-scale military. Blaustein chose an unoccupied portion of the railing; for Ralson's sake, most of all.

He said, "Do you still think you would like to stay?"

It was warm enough within the laboratory, but Ralson was in his coat, with his collar turned up. It made little difference, Blaustein felt. He doubted that any of Ralson's former acquaintances would now recognize him.

Ralson said, "I'll stay."

Blaustein was pleased. He wanted to see the test. He turned again at a new voice.

"Hello, Dr. Blaustein."

For a minute, Blaustein did not place him, then he said, "Ah, Inspector Darrity. What are you doing here?"

"Just what you would suppose." He indicated the watchers. "There isn't any way you can weed them out so that you can be sure there won't be any mistakes. I once stood as near to Klaus Fuchs as I am standing to you." He tossed his pocketknife into the air and retrieved it with a dexterous motion.

"Ah, yes. Where shall one find perfect security? What man can trust even his own unconscious? And you will now stand near to me, no?"

"Might as well." Darrity smiled. "You were very anxious to get in here, weren't you?"

"Not for myself, Inspector. And would you put away the knife, please."

Darrity turned in surprise in the direction of Blaustein's gentle head-gesture. He put his knife away and looked at Blaustein's companion for the second time. He whistled softly.

He said, "Hello, Dr. Ralson."

Ralson croaked, "Hello."

Blaustein was not surprised at Darrity's reaction. Ralson had lost twenty pounds since returning to the sanatorium. His face was yellow and wrinkled; the face of a man who had suddenly become sixty.

Blaustein said, "Will the test be starting soon?"

Darrity said, "It looks as if they're starting now."

He turned and leaned on the rail. Blaustein took Ralson's elbow and began leading him away, but Darrity said, softly, "Stay here, Doc. I don't want you wandering about."

Blaustein looked across the laboratory. Men were standing about with the uncomfortable air of having turned half to stone. He could recognize Grant, tall and gaunt, moving his hand slowly to light a cigarette, then changing his mind and putting lighter and cigarette in his pocket. The young men at the control panels waited tensely.

Then there was a low humming and the faint smell of ozone filled the air.

Ralson said harshly, "Look!"

Blaustein and Darrity looked along the pointing finger. The projector seemed to flicker. It was as though there were heated air rising between it and them. An iron ball came swinging down pendulum fashion and passed through the flickering area.

"It slowed up, no?" said Blaustein, excitedly.

Ralson nodded. "They're measuring the height of rise on the other side to calculate the loss of momentum. Fools! I *said* it would work." He was speaking with obvious difficulty.

Blaustein said, "Just watch, Dr. Ralson. I would not allow myself to grow needlessly excited."

The pendulum was stopped in its swinging, drawn up. The flickering about the projector became a little more intense and the iron sphere arced down once again.

Over and over again, and each time the sphere's motion was slowed with more of a jerk. It made a clearly audible sound as it struck the flicker. And eventually, it *bounced*. First, soggily, as though it hit putty, and then ringingly, as though it hit steel, so that the noise filled the place.

They drew back the pendulum bob and used it no longer. The projector could hardly be seen behind the haze that surrounded it.

Grant gave an order and the odor of ozone was suddenly sharp and pungent. There was a cry from the assembled observers; each one exclaiming to his neighbor. A dozen fingers were pointing.

Blaustein leaned over the railing, as excited as the rest. Where the projector had been, there was now only a huge semi-globular mirror. It was perfectly and beautifully clear. He could see himself in it, a small man standing on a small balcony that curved up on each side. He could see the fluorescent lights reflected in spots of glowing illumination. It was wonderfully sharp.

He was shouting, "Look, Ralson. It is reflecting energy. It is reflecting light waves like a mirror. Ralson—"

He turned, "Ralson! Inspector, where is Ralson?"

"What?" Darrity whirled. "I haven't seen him."

He looked about, wildly. "Well, he won't get away. No way of getting out of here now. You take the other side." And then he clapped hand to thigh, fumbled for a moment in his pocket, and said, "My knife is gone."

Blaustein found him. He was inside the small office belonging to Hal Ross. It led off the balcony, but under the circumstances, of course, it had been deserted. Ross himself was not even an observer. A senior mechanic need not observe. But his office would do very well for the final end of the long fight against suicide.

Blaustein stood in the doorway for a sick moment, then turned. He caught Darrity's eye as the latter emerged from a similar office a hundred feet down the balcony. He beckoned, and Darrity came at a run.

Dr. Grant was trembling with excitement. He had taken two puffs at each of two cigarettes and trodden each underfoot thereafter. He was fumbling with the third now.

He was saying, "This is better than any of us could possibly have hoped. We'll have the gunfire test tomorrow. I'm sure of the result now, but we've planned it; we'll go through with it. We'll skip the small arms and start with the bazooka levels. Or maybe not. It might be necessary to construct a special testing structure to take care of the ricochet problem."

He discarded his third cigarette.

A general said, "We'd have to try a literal atom-bombing, of course."

"Naturally. Arrangements have already been made to build a mock-city at Eniwetok. We could build a generator on the spot and drop the bomb. There'd be animals inside."

"And you really think if we set up a field in full power it would hold the bomb?"

"It's not just that, general. There'd be no noticeable field at all until the bomb is dropped. The radiation of the plutonium would have to energize the field before explosion. As we did here in the last step. That's the essence of it all."

"You know," said a Princeton professor, "I see disadvantages, too. When the field is on full, anything it protects is in total darkness, as far as the sun is concerned. Besides that, it strikes me that the enemy can adopt the practice of dropping harmless radioactive missiles to set off the field at frequent intervals. It would have nuisance value and be a considerable drain on our pile as well."

"Nuisances," said Grant, "can be survived. These difficulties will be met eventually, I'm sure, now that the main problem has been solved."

The British observer had worked his way toward Grant and was shaking hands. He said, "I feel better about London already. I cannot help but wish your government would allow me to see the complete plans. What I have seen strikes me as completely ingenious. It seems obvious now, of course, but how did anyone ever come to think of it?"

Grant smiled. "That question has been asked before with reference to Dr. Ralson's devices—"

He turned at the touch of a hand upon his shoulder. "Dr. Blaustein! I had nearly forgotten. Here, I want to talk to you."

He dragged the small psychiatrist to one side and hissed in his ear, "Listen, can you persuade Ralson to be introduced to these people? This is his triumph."

Blaustein said, "Ralson is dead."

"*What!*"

"Can you leave these people for a time?"

"Yes . . . yes— Gentlemen, you will excuse me for a few minutes?"

He hurried off with Blaustein.

The Federal men had already taken over. Unobtrusively, they barred the doorway to Ross's office. Outside there were the milling crowd discussing the answer to Alamogordo that they had just witnessed. Inside, unknown to them, was the death of the answerer. The G-man barrier divided to allow Grant and Blaustein to enter. It closed behind them again.

For a moment, Grant raised the sheet. He said, "He looks peaceful."

"I would say—happy," said Blaustein.

Darrity said, colorlessly, "The suicide weapon was my own knife. It was my negligence; it will be reported as such."

"No, no," said Blaustein, "that would be useless. He was my patient and I am responsible. In any case, he would not have lived another week. Since he invented the projector, he was a dying man."

Grant said, "How much of this has to be placed in the Federal files? Can't we forget all about his madness?"

"I'm afraid not, Dr. Grant," said Darrity.

"I have told him the whole story," said Blaustein, sadly.

Grant looked from one to the other. "I'll speak to the Director. I'll go to the President, if necessary. I don't see that there need be any mention of suicide or of madness. He'll get full publicity as inventor of the field projector. It's the least we can do for him." His teeth were gritting.

Blaustein said, "He left a note."

"A note?"

Darrity handed him a sheet of paper and said, "Suicides almost always do. This is one reason the doctor told me about what really killed Ralson."

The note was addressed to Blaustein and it went:

"The projector works; I knew it would. The bargain is done. You've got it and you don't need me any more. So I'll go. You needn't worry about the human race, Doc. You were right. They've bred us too long; they've taken too many chances. We're out of the culture now and they won't be able to stop us. I know. That's all I can say. I know."

He had signed his name quickly and then underneath there was one scrawled line, and it said:

"Provided enough men are penicillin-resistant."

Grant made a motion to crumple the paper, but Darrity held out a quick hand.

"For the record, Doctor," he said.

Grant gave it to him and said, "Poor Ralson! He died believing all that trash."

Blaustein nodded. "So he did. Ralson will be given a great funeral, I suppose, and the fact of his invention will be publicized without the madness and the suicide. But the government men will remain interested in his mad theories. They may not be so mad, no, Mr. Darrity?"

"That's ridiculous, Doctor," said Grant. "There isn't a scientist on the job who has shown the least uneasiness about it at all."

"Tell him, Mr. Darrity," said Blaustein.

Darrity said, "There has been another suicide. No, no, none of the scientists. No one with a degree. It happened this morning, and we investigated because we thought it might have some connection with today's test. There didn't seem any, and we were going to keep it quiet till the test was over. Only now there seems to be a connection.

"The man who died was just a guy with a wife and three kids. No reason to die. No history of mental illness. He threw himself under a car. We have witnesses, and it's certain he did it on purpose. He didn't die right away and they got a doctor to him. He was horribly mangled, but his last words were 'I feel much better now' and he died."

"But who was he?" cried Grant.

"Hal Ross. The guy who actually built the projector. The guy whose office this is."

Blaustein walked to the window. The evening sky was darkening into starriness.

He said, "The man knew nothing about Ralson's views. He had never spoken to Ralson, Mr. Darrity tells me. Scientists are probably resistant as a whole. They must be or they are quickly driven out of the profession. Ralson was an exception, a penicillin-sensitive who insisted on remaining. You see what happened to him. But what about the others; those who have remained in walks of life where there is no constant weeding out of the sensitive ones. How much of humanity *is* penicillin-resistant?"

"You *believe* Ralson?" asked Grant in horror.

"I don't really know."

Blaustein looked at the stars.

Incubators?

C-Chute

Even from the cabin into which he and the other passengers had been herded, Colonel Anthony Windham could still catch the essence of the battle's progress. For a while, there was silence, no jolting, which meant the spaceships were fighting at astronomical distance in a duel of energy blasts and powerful force-field defenses.

He knew that could have only one end. Their Earth ship was only an armed merchantman and his glimpse of the Kloro enemy just before he had been cleared off deck by the crew was sufficient to show it to be a light cruiser.

And in less than half an hour, there came those hard little shocks he was waiting for. The passengers swayed back and forth as the ship pitched and veered, as though it were an ocean liner in a storm. But space was calm and silent as ever. It was their pilot sending desperate bursts of steam through the steam-tubes, so that by reaction the ship would be sent rolling and tumbling. It could only mean that the inevitable had occurred. The Earth ship's screens had been drained and it no longer dared withstand a direct hit.

Colonel Windham tried to steady himself with his aluminum cane. He was thinking that he was an old man; that he had spent his life in the militia and had never seen a battle; that now, with a battle going on around him, he was old and fat and lame and had no men under his command.

They would be boarding soon, those Kloro monsters. It was their way of fighting. They would be handicapped by spacesuits and their casualties would be high, but they wanted the Earth ship. Windham considered the passengers. For a moment, he thought, *if they were armed and I could lead them*—

He abandoned the thought. Porter was in an obvious state of funk and the young boy, Leblanc, was hardly better. The Polyorketes brothers—dash it, he *couldn't* tell them apart—huddled in a corner speaking only to one another. Mullen was a different matter. He sat perfectly erect, with no signs of fear or any other emotion in his face. But the man was just about five feet tall and had undoubtedly never held a gun of any sort in his hands in all his life. He could do nothing.

And there was Stuart, with his frozen half-smile and the high-pitched sarcasm which saturated all he said. Windham looked sidelong at Stuart now as Stuart sat there, pushing his dead-white hands through his sandy hair. With those artificial hands he was useless, anyway.

Windham felt the shuddering vibration of ship-to-ship contact; and in five minutes, there was the noise of the fight through the corridors. One of the Polyorketes brothers screamed and dashed for the door. The other called, "Aristides! Wait!" and hurried after.

It happened so quickly. Aristides was out the door and into the corridor, running in brainless panic. A carbonizer glowed briefly and there was never even a scream. Windham, from the doorway, turned in horror at the blackened stump of what was left. Strange—a lifetime in uniform and he had never before seen a man killed in violence.

It took the combined force of the rest to carry the other brother back struggling into the room.

The noise of battle subsided.

Stuart said, "That's it. They'll put a prize crew of two aboard and take us to one of their home planets. We're prisoners of war, naturally."

"Only two of the Kloros will stay aboard?" asked Windham, astonished.

Stuart said, "It is their custom. Why do you ask, Colonel? Thinking of leading a gallant raid to retake the ship?"

Windham flushed. "Simply a point of information, dash it." But the dignity and tone of authority he tried to assume failed him, he knew. He was simply an old man with a limp.

And Stuart was probably right. He had lived among the Kloros and knew their ways.

John Stuart had claimed from the beginning that the Kloros were gentlemen. Twenty-four hours of imprisonment had passed, and now he repeated the statement as he flexed the fingers of his hands and watched the crinkles come and go in the soft artiplasm.

He enjoyed the unpleasant reaction it aroused in the others. People were made to be punctured; windy bladders, all of them. And they had hands of the same stuff as their bodies.

There was Anthony Windham, in particular. Colonel Windham, he called himself, and Stuart was willing to believe it. A retired colonel who had probably drilled a home guard militia on a village green, forty years ago, with such lack of distinction that he was not called back to service in any capacity, even during the emergency of Earth's first interstellar war.

"Dashed unpleasant thing to be saying about the enemy, Stuart. Don't know that I like your attitude." Windham seemed to push the words through his clipped mustache. His head had been shaven, too, in imitation of the current military style, but now a gray stubble was beginning to show about a centered bald patch. His flabby cheeks dragged downward. That and the fine red lines on his thick nose gave him a somewhat undone appearance, as though he had been wakened too suddenly and too early in the morning.

Stuart said, "Nonsense. Just reverse the present situation. Suppose an Earth warship had taken a Kloro liner. What do you think would have happened to any Kloro civilians aboard?"

"I'm sure the Earth fleet would observe all the interstellar rules of war," Windham said stiffly.

"Except that there aren't any. If we landed a prize crew on one of their ships, do you think we'd take the trouble to maintain a chlorine atmosphere for the benefit of the survivors; allow them to keep their non-contraband possessions; give them the use of the most comfortable stateroom, etcetera, etcetera, etcetera?"

Ben Porter said, "Oh, shut up, for God's sake. If I hear your etcetera, etcetera once again, I'll go nuts."

Stuart said, "Sorry!" He wasn't.

Porter was scarcely responsible. His thin face and beaky nose glistened with perspiration, and he kept biting the inside of his cheek until he suddenly winced. He put his tongue against the sore spot, which made him look even more clownish.

Stuart was growing weary of baiting them. Windham was too flabby a target and Porter could do nothing but writhe. The rest were silent. Demetrios Polyorketes was off in a world of silent internal grief for the moment. He had not slept the night before, most probably. At least, whenever Stuart woke to change his position—he himself had been rather restless—there had been Polyorketes' thick mumble from the next cot. It said many things, but the moan to which it returned over and over again was, "Oh, my brother!"

He sat dumbly on his cot now, his red eyes rolling at the other prisoners out of his broad swarthy, unshaven face. As Stuart watched, his face sank into calloused palms so that only his mop of crisp and curly black hair could be seen. He rocked gently, but now that they were all awake, he made no sound.

Claude Leblanc was trying very unsuccessfully, to read a letter. He was the youngest of the six, scarcely out of college, returning to Earth to get married. Stuart had found him that morning weeping quietly, his pink and white face flushed and blotched as though it were a heartbroken child's. He was very fair, with almost a girl's beauty about his large blue eyes and full lips. Stuart wondered what kind of girl it was who had promised to be his wife. He had seen her picture. Who on the ship had not? She had the characterless prettiness that makes all pictures of fiancees indistinguishable. It seemed to Stuart that if he were a girl, however, he would want someone a little more pronouncedly masculine.

That left only Randolph Mullen. Stuart frankly did not have the least idea what to make of him. He was the only one of the six that had been on the Arcturian worlds for any length of time. Stuart, himself, for instance, had been there only long enough to give a series of lectures on astronautical engineering at the provincial engineering institute. Colonel Windham had been on a Cook's tour; Porter was trying to buy concentrated alien vegetables for his canneries on Earth; and the Polyorketes brothers had attempted to establish themselves in Arcturus as truck farmers and, after two growing seasons, gave it up, had somehow unloaded at a profit, and were returning to Earth.

Randolph Mullen, however, had been in the Arcturian system for seventeen years. How did voyagers discover so much about one another so quickly? As far as Stuart knew, the little man had scarcely spoken aboard ship. He was unfailingly polite, always stepped to one side to allow another to pass, but his entire vocabulary appeared to consist only of "Thank you" and "Pardon me." Yet the word had gone around that this was his first trip to Earth in seventeen years.

He was a little man, very precise, almost irritatingly so. Upon awaking that morning, he had made his cot neatly, shaved, bathed and dressed. The habit of years seemed not in the least disturbed by the fact that he was a prisoner of the Kloros now. He was unobtrusive about it, it had to be admitted, and gave no impression of disapproving of the sloppiness of the others. He simply sat there, almost apologetic, trussed in his overconservative clothing, and hands loosely clasped in his lap. The thin line of hair on his upper lip, far from adding character to his face, absurdly increased its primness.

He looked like someone's idea of a caricature of a bookkeeper. And the queer thing about it all, Stuart thought, was that that was exactly what he was. He had noticed it on the registry—Randolph Fluellen Mullen; occupation, bookkeeper; employers, Prime Paper Box Co.; 27 Tobias Avenue, New Warsaw, Arcturus II.

"Mr. Stuart?"

Stuart looked up. It was Leblanc, his lower lip trembling slightly. Stuart tried to remember how one went about being gentle. He said, "What is it, Leblanc?"

"Tell me, when will they let us go?"

"How should I know?"

"Everyone says you lived on a Kloro planet, and just now you said they were gentlemen."

"Well, yes. But even gentlemen fight wars in order to win. Probably, we'll be interned for the duration."

"But that could be *years!* Margaret is waiting. She'll think I'm *dead!*"

"I suppose they'll allow messages to be sent through once we're on their planet."

Porter's hoarse voice sounded in agitation. "Look here, if you know so much about these devils, what will they do to us while we're interned? What will they feed us? Where will they get oxygen for us? They'll kill us, I tell you." And as an afterthought, "I've got a wife waiting for me, too," he added.

But Stuart had heard him speaking of his wife in the days before the attack. He wasn't impressed. Porter's nail-bitten fingers were pulling and plucking at Stuart's sleeve. Stuart drew away in sharp revulsion. He couldn't stand those ugly hands. It angered him to desperation that such monstrosities should be real while his own white and perfectly shaped hands were only mocking imitations grown out of an alien latex.

He said, "They won't kill us. If they were going to, they would have done it before now. Look, we capture Kloros too, you know, and it's just a matter of common sense to treat your prisoners decently if you want the other side to be decent to your men. They'll do their best. The food may not be very good, but they're better chemists than we are. It's what they're best at. They'll know exactly what food factors we'll need and how many calories. We'll live. They'll see to that."

Windham rumbled, "You sound more and more like a blasted greenie sympathizer, Stuart. It turns my stomach to hear an Earthman speak well of the green fellas the way you've been doing. Burn it, man, where's your loyalty?"

"My loyalty's where it belongs. With honesty and decency, regardless of the shape of the being it appears in." Stuart held up his hands. "See these? Kloros made them. I lived on one of their planets for six months. My hands were mangled in the conditioning machinery of my own quarters. I thought the oxygen supply they gave me was a little poor—it wasn't, by the way— and I tried making the adjustments on my own. It was my fault. You should never trust yourself with the machines of another culture. By the time someone among the Kloros could put on an atmosphere suit and get to me, it was too late to save my hands.

"They grew these artiplasm things for me and operated. You know what that meant? It meant designing equipment and nutrient solutions that would work in oxygen atmosphere. It meant that their surgeons had to perform a delicate operation while dressed in atmosphere suits. And now I've got hands again." He laughed harshly, and clenched them into weak fists. "Hands—"

Windham said, "And you'd sell your loyalty to Earth for that?"

"Sell my loyalty? You're mad. For years, I hated the Kloros for this. I was a master pilot on the Trans-Galactic Spacelines before it happened. Now? Desk job. Or an occasional lecture. It took me a long time to pin the fault on myself and to realize that the only role played by the Kloros was a decent one. They have their code of ethics, and it's as good as ours. If it weren't for the stupidity of some of their people—and, by God, of some of ours—we wouldn't be at war. And after it's over—"

Polyorketes was on his feet. His thick fingers curved inward before him and his dark eyes glittered. "I don't like what you say, mister."

"Why don't you?"

"Because you talk too nice about these damned green bastards. The Kloros were good to you, eh? Well, they weren't good to my brother. They killed him. I think maybe I kill you, you damned greenie spy."

And he charged.

Stuart barely had time to raise his arms to meet the infuriated farmer. He gasped out, "What the hell—" as he caught one wrist and heaved a shoulder to block the other which groped toward his throat.

His artiplasm hand gave way. Polyorketes wrenched free with scarcely an effort.

Windham was bellowing incoherently, and Leblanc was calling out in his reedy voice, "Stop it! Stop it!" But it was little Mullen who threw his arms about the farmer's neck from behind and pulled with all his might. He was not very effective; Polyorketes seemed scarcely aware of the little man's weight upon his back. Mullen's feet left the floor so that he tossed helplessly to right and left. But he held his grip and it hampered Polyorketes sufficiently to allow Stuart to break free long enough to grasp Windham's aluminum cane.

He said, "Stay away, Polyorketes."

He was gasping for breath and fearful of another rush. The hollow aluminum cylinder was scarcely heavy enough to accomplish much, but it was better than having only his weak hands to defend himself with.

Mullen had loosed his hold and was now circling cautiously, his breathing roughened and his jacket in disarray.

Polyorketes, for a moment, did not move. He stood there, his shaggy head bent low. Then he said, "It is no use. I must kill Kloros. Just watch your tongue, Stuart. If it keeps on rattling too much, you're liable to get hurt. Really hurt, I mean."

Stuart passed a forearm over his forehead and thrust the cane back at

Windham, who seized it with his left hand, while mopping his bald pate vigorously with a handkerchief in his right.

Windham said, "Gentlemen, we must avoid this. It lowers our prestige. We must remember the common enemy. We are Earthmen and we must act what we are—the ruling race of the Galaxy. We dare not demean ourselves before the lesser breeds."

"Yes, Colonel," said Stuart, wearily. "Give us the rest of the speech tomorrow."

He turned to Mullen, "I want to say thanks."

He was uncomfortable about it, but he had to. The little accountant had surprised him completely.

But Mullen said, in a dry voice that scarcely raised above a whisper, "Don't thank me, Mr. Stuart. It was the logical thing to do. If we are to be interned, we would need you as an interpreter, perhaps, one who would understand the Kloros."

Stuart stiffened. It was, he thought, too much of the bookkeeper type of reasoning, too logical, too dry of juice. Present risk and ultimate advantage. The assets and debits balanced neatly. He would have liked Mullen to leap to his defense out of—well, out of what? Out of pure, unselfish decency?

Stuart laughed silently at himself. He was beginning to expect idealism of human beings, rather than good, straight-forward, self-centered motivation.

Polyorketes was numb. His sorrow and rage were like acid inside him, but they had no words to get out. If he were Stuart, big-mouth, white-hands Stuart, he could talk and talk and maybe feel better. Instead, he had to sit there with half of him dead; with no brother, no Aristides—

It had happened so quickly. If he could only go back and have one second more warning, so that he might snatch Aristides, hold him, save him.

But mostly he hated the Kloros. Two months ago, he had hardly ever heard of them, and now he hated them so hard, he would be glad to die if he could kill a few.

He said, without looking up, "What happened to start this war, eh?"

He was afraid Stuart's voice would answer. He hated Stuart's voice. But it was Windham, the bald one.

Windham said, "The immediate cause, sir, was a dispute over mining concessions in the Wyandotte system. The Kloros had poached on Earth property."

"Room for both, Colonel!"

Polyorketes looked up at that, snarling. Stuart could not be kept quiet for long. He was speaking again; the cripple-hand, wiseguy, Kloros-lover.

Stuart was saying, "Is that anything to fight over, Colonel? We can't use one another's worlds. Their chlorine planets are useless to us and our oxygen ones are useless to them. Chlorine is deadly to us and oxygen is deadly to them. There's no way we could maintain permanent hostility. Our races just don't coincide. Is there reason to fight then because both races want to dig iron out of the same airless planetoids when there are millions like them in the Galaxy?"

Windham said, "There is the question of planetary honor—"

"Planetary fertilizer. How can it excuse a ridiculous war like this one? It can only be fought on outposts. It has to come down to a series of holding actions and eventually be settled by negotiations that might just as easily have been worked out in the first place. Neither we nor the Kloros will gain a thing."

Grudgingly, Polyorketes found that he agreed with Stuart. What did he and Aristides care where Earth or the Kloros got their iron?

Was that something for Aristides to die over?

The little warning buzzer sounded.

Polyorketes' head shot up and he rose slowly, his lips drawing back. Only one thing could be at the door. He waited, arms tense, fists balled. Stuart was edging toward him. Polyorketes saw that and laughed to himself. Let the Kloro come in, and Stuart, along with all the rest, could not stop him.

Wait, Aristides, wait just a moment, and a fraction of revenge will be paid back.

The door opened and a figure entered, completely swathed in a shapeless, billowing travesty of a spacesuit.

An odd, unnatural, but not entirely unpleasant voice began, "It is with some misgivings, Earthmen, that my companion and myself—"

It ended abruptly as Polyorketes, with a roar, charged once again. There was no science in the lunge. It was sheer bull-momentum. Dark head low, burly arms spread out with the hair-tufted fingers in choking position, he clumped on. Stuart was whirled to one side before he had a chance to intervene, and was spun tumbling across a cot.

The Kloro might have, without undue exertion, straight-armed Polyorketes to a halt, or stepped aside, allowing the whirlwind to pass. He did neither. With a rapid movement, a hand-weapon was up and a gentle pinkish line of radiance connected it with the plunging Earthman. Polyorketes stumbled and crashed down, his body maintaining its last curved position, one foot raised, as though a lightning paralysis had taken place. It toppled to one side and he lay there, eyes all alive and wild with rage.

The Kloro said, "He is not permanently hurt." He seemed not to resent the offered violence. Then he began again, "It is with some misgiving, Earthmen, that my companion and myself were made aware of a certain commotion in this room. Are you in any need which we can satisfy?"

Stuart was angrily nursing his knee which he had scraped in colliding with the cot. He said, "No, thank you, Kloro."

"Now, look here," puffed Windham, "this is a dashed outrage. We demand that our release be arranged."

The Kloro's tiny, insectlike head turned in the fat old man's direction. He was not a pleasant sight to anyone unused to him. He was about the height of an Earthman, but the top of him consisted of a thin stalk of a neck with a head that was the merest swelling. It consisted of a blunt triangular proboscis in front and two bulging eyes on either side. That was all. There was no brain pan and no brain. What corresponded to the brain in a Kloro was located in what would be an Earthly abdomen, leaving the head as a mere sensory organ. The Kloro's spacesuit followed the outlines of the head more or less faithfully, the two eyes being exposed by two clear semicircles of glass, which looked faintly green because of the chlorine atmosphere inside.

One of the eyes was now cocked squarely at Windham, who quivered uncomfortably under the glance, but insisted, "You have no right to hold us prisoner. We are noncombatants."

The Kloro's voice, sounding thoroughly artificial, came from a small attachment of chromium mesh on what served as its chest. The voice box was manipulated by compressed air under the control of one or two of the many delicate, forked tendrils that radiated from two circles about its upper body and were, mercifully enough, hidden by the suit.

The voice said, "Are you serious, Earthman? Surely you have heard of war and rules of war and prisoners of war."

It looked about, shifting eyes with quick jerks of its head, staring at a particular object first with one, then with another. It was Stuart's understanding that each eye transferred a separate message to the abdominal brain, which had to coordinate the two to obtain full information.

Windham had nothing to say. No one had. The Kloro, its four main limbs, roughly arms and legs in pairs, had a vaguely human appearance under the masking of the suit, if you looked no higher than its chest, but there was no way of telling what it felt.

They watched it turn and leave.

Porter coughed and said in a strangled voice, "God, smell that chlorine. If they don't do something, we'll all die of rotted lungs."

Stuart said, "Shut up. There isn't enough chlorine in the air to make a mosquito sneeze, and what there is will be swept out in two minutes. Besides, a little chlorine is good for you. It may kill your cold virus."

Windham coughed and said, "Stuart, I feel that you might have said something to your Kloro friend about releasing us. You are scarcely as bold in their presence, dash it, as you are once they are gone."

"You heard what the creature said, Colonel. We're prisoners of war, and prisoner exchanges are negotiated by diplomats. We'll just have to wait."

Leblanc, who had turned pasty white at the entrance of the Kloro, rose and hurried into the privy. There was the sound of retching.

An uncomfortable silence fell while Stuart tried to think of something to say to cover the unpleasant sound. Mullen filled in. He had rummaged through a little box he had taken from under his pillow.

He said, "Perhaps Mr. Leblanc had better take a sedative before retiring. I have a few. I'd be glad to give him one." He explained his generosity immediately, "Otherwise he may keep the rest of us awake, you see."

"Very logical," said Stuart, dryly. "You'd better save one for Sir Launcelot here; save half a dozen." He walked to where Polyorketes still sprawled and knelt at his side. "Comfortable, baby?"

Windham said, "Deuced poor taste speaking like that, Stuart."

"Well, if you're so concerned about him, why don't you and Porter hoist him onto his cot?"

He helped them do so. Polyorketes' arms were trembling erratically now. From what Stuart knew of the Kloro's nerve weapons, the man should be in an agony of pins and needles about now.

Stuart said, "And don't be too gentle with him, either. The damned fool might have gotten us all killed. And for what?"

He pushed Polyorketes' stiff carcass to one side and sat at the edge of the cot. He said, "Can you hear me, Polyorketes?"

Polyorketes' eyes gleamed. An arm lifted abortively and fell back.

"Okay then, listen. Don't try anything like that again. The next time it may be the finish for all of us. If you had been a Kloro and he had been an Earthman, we'd be dead now. So just get one thing through your skull. We're sorry about your brother and it's a rotten shame, but it was his own fault."

Polyorketes tried to heave and Stuart pushed him back.

"No, you keep on listening," he said. "Maybe this is the only time I'll get to talk to you when you *have* to listen. Your brother had no right leaving passenger's quarters. There was no place for him to go. He just got in the way of our own men. We don't even know for certain that it was a Kloro gun that killed him. It might have been one of our own."

"Oh, I say, Stuart," objected Windham.

Stuart whirled at him. "Do you have proof it wasn't? Did you see the shot? Could you tell from what was left of the body whether it was Kloro energy or Earth energy?"

Polyorketes found his voice, driving his unwilling tongue into a fuzzy verbal snarl. "Damned stinking greenie bastard."

"Me?" said Stuart. "I know what's going on in your mind, Polyorketes. You think that when the paralysis wears off, you'll ease your feelings by slamming me around. Well, if you do, it will probably be curtains for all of us."

He rose, put his back against the wall. For the moment, he was fighting all of them. "None of you know the Kloros the way I do. The physical differences you see are not important. The differences in their temperament are. They don't understand our views on sex, for instance. To them, it's just a biological reflex like breathing. They attach no importance to it. But they *do* attach importance to social groupings. Remember, their evolutionary ancestors had lots in common with our insects. They always assume that any group of Earthmen they find together makes up a social unit.

"That means just about everything to them. I don't understand exactly *what* it means. No Earthman can. But the result is that they never break up a group, just as we don't separate a mother and her children if we can help it. One of the reasons they may be treating us with kid gloves right now is that they imagine we're all broken up over the fact that they killed one of us, and they feel guilt about it.

"But this is what you'll have to remember. We're going to be interned together and *kept* together for duration. I don't like the thought. I wouldn't have picked any of you for co-internees and I'm pretty sure none of you would have picked me. But there it is. The Kloros could never understand that our being together on the ship is only accidental.

"That means we've got to get along somehow. That's not just goodie-goodie talk about birds in their little nest agreeing. What do you think would have happened if the Kloros had come in earlier and found Poly-orketes and myself trying to kill each other? You don't know? Well, what do you suppose *you* would think of a mother you caught trying to kill her children?

"That's it, then. They would have killed every one of us as a bunch of Kloro-type perverts and monsters. Got that? How about you, Polyorketes? Have *you* got it? So let's call names if we have to, but let's keep our hands to ourselves. And now, if none of you mind, I'll massage my hands back into shape—these synthetic hands that I got from the Kloros and that one of my own kind tried to mangle again."

For Claude Leblanc, the worst was over. He had been sick enough; sick with many things; but sick most of all over having ever left Earth. It had been a great thing to go to college off Earth. It had been an adventure and had taken him away from his mother. Somehow, he had been sneakingly glad to make that escape after the first month of frightened adjustment.

And then on the summer holidays, he had been no longer Claude, the shy-spoken scholar, but Leblanc, space traveler. He had swaggered the fact for all it was worth. It made him feel such a man to talk of stars and Jumps and the customs and environments of other worlds; it had given him courage with Margaret. She had loved him for the dangers he had undergone—

Except that this had been the first one, really, and he had not done so well. He knew it and was ashamed and wished he were like Stuart.

He used the excuse of mealtime to approach. He said, "Mr. Stuart."

Stuart looked up and said shortly, "How do you feel?"

Leblanc felt himself blush. He blushed easily and the effort not to blush only made it worse. He said, "Much better, thank you. We are eating. I thought I'd bring you your ration."

Stuart took the offered can. It was standard space ration; thoroughly synthetic, concentrated, nourishing and, somehow, unsatisfying. It heated automatically when the can was opened, but could be eaten cold, if necessary. Though a combined fork-spoon utensil was enclosed, the ration was of a consistency that made the use of fingers practical and not particularly messy.

Stuart said, "Did you hear my little speech?"

"Yes, sir. I want you to know you can count on me."

"Well, good. Now go and eat."

"May I eat here?"

"Suit yourself."

For a moment, they ate in silence, and then Leblanc burst out, "You are so sure of yourself, Mr. Stuart! It must be very wonderful to be like that!"

"Sure of myself? Thanks, but there's your self-assured one."

Leblanc followed the direction of the nod in surprise. "Mr. Mullen? That little man? Oh, no!"

"You don't think he's self-assured?"

Leblanc shook his head. He looked at Stuart intently to see if he could detect humor in his expression. "That one is just cold. He has no emotion in him. He's like a little machine. I find him repulsive. You're different, Mr. Stuart. You have it all inside, but you control it. I would like to be like that."

And as though attracted by the magnetism of the mention, even though unheard, of his name, Mullen joined them. His can of ration was barely touched. It was still steaming gently as he squatted opposite them.

His voice had its usual quality of furtively rustling underbrush. "How long, Mr. Stuart, do you think the trip will take?"

"Can't say, Mullen. They'll undoubtedly be avoiding the usual trade routes and they'll be making more Jumps through hyper-space than usual to throw off possible pursuit. I wouldn't be surprised if it took as long as a week. Why do you ask? I presume you have a very practical and logical reason?"

"Why, yes. Certainly." He seemed quite shellbacked to sarcasm. He said, "It occurred to me that it might be wise to ration the rations, so to speak."

"We've got enough food and water for a month. I checked on that first thing."

"I see. In that case, I will finish the can." He did, using the all-purpose utensil daintily and patting a handkerchief against his unstained lips from time to time.

Polyorketes struggled to his feet some two hours later. He swayed a bit, looking like the Spirit of Hangover. He did not try to come closer to Stuart, but spoke from where he stood.

He said, "You stinking greenie spy, you watch yourself."

"You heard what I said before, Polyorketes."

"I heard. But I also heard what you said about Aristides. I won't bother with you, because you're a bag of nothing but noisy air. But wait, someday you'll blow your air in one face too many and it will be let out of you."

"I'll wait," said Stuart.

Windham hobbled over, leaning heavily on his cane. "Now, now," he called with a wheezing joviality that overlaid his sweating anxiety so thinly as to emphasize it. "We're all Earthmen, dash it. Got to remember that; keep it as a glowing light of inspiration. Never let down before the blasted Kloros. We've got to forget private feuds and remember only that we are Earthmen united against alien blighters."

Stuart's comment was unprintable.

Porter was right behind Windham. He had been in a close conference with the shaven-headed colonel for an hour, and now he said with indignation, "It doesn't help to be a wiseguy, Stuart. You listen to the colonel. We've been doing some hard thinking about the situation."

He had washed some of the grease off his face, wet his hair and slicked it back. It did not remove the little tic on his right cheek just at the point where his lips ended, or make his hangnail hands more attractive in appearance.

"All right, Colonel," said Stuart. "What's on your mind?"

Windham said, "I'd prefer to have all the men together."

"Okay, call them."

Leblanc hurried over; Mullen approached with greater deliberation.

Stuart said, "You want that fellow?" He jerked his head at Polyorketes.

"Why, yes. Mr. Polyorketes, may we have you, old fella?"

"Ah, leave me alone."

"Go ahead," said Stuart, "leave him alone. I don't want him."

"No, no," said Windham. "This is a matter for all Earthmen. Mr. Polyorketes, we must have you."

Polyorketes rolled off one side of his cot. "I'm close enough, I can hear you."

Windham said to Stuart, "Would they—the Kloros, I mean—have this room wired?"

"No," said Stuart. "Why should they?"

"Are you sure?"

"Of course I'm sure. They didn't know what happened when Polyorketes jumped me. They just heard the thumping when it started rattling the ship."

"Maybe they were trying to give us the impression the room wasn't wired."

"Listen, Colonel, I've never known a Kloro to tell a deliberate lie—"

Polyorketes interrupted calmly, "That lump of noise just *loves* the Kloros."

Windham said hastily, "Let's not begin that. Look, Stuart, Porter and I have been discussing matters and we have decided that you know the Kloros well enough to think of some way of getting us back to Earth."

"It happens that you're wrong. I can't think of any way."

"Maybe there is some way we can take the ship back from the blasted green fellas," suggested Windham. "Some weakness they may have. Dash it, you know what I mean."

"Tell me, Colonel, what are you after? Your own skin or Earth's welfare?"

"I resent that question. I'll have you know that while I'm as careful of my own life as anyone has a right to be, I'm thinking of Earth primarily. And I think that's true of all of us."

"Damn right," said Porter, instantly. Leblanc looked anxious, Polyorketes resentful; and Mullen had no expression at all.

"Good," said Stuart. "Of course, I don't think we can take the ship. They're armed and we aren't. But there's this. You know why the Kloros took this ship intact. It's because they need ships. They may be better chemists than Earthmen are, but Earthmen are better astronautical engineers. We have bigger, better and more ships. In fact, if our crew had had a proper respect for military axioms in the first place, they would have blown the ship up as soon as it looked as though the Kloros were going to board."

Leblanc looked horrified. "And kill the passengers?"

"Why not? You heard what the good colonel said. Every one of us puts his own lousy little life after Earth's interests. What good are we to Earth alive right now? None at all. What harm will this ship do in Kloro hands? A hell of a lot, probably."

"Just why," asked Mullen, "did our men refuse to blow up the ship? They must have had a reason."

"They did. It's the firmest tradition of Earth's military men that there must never be an unfavorable ratio of casualties. If we had blown ourselves up, twenty fighting men and seven civilians of Earth would be dead as compared with an enemy casualty total of zero. So what happens? We let them board, kill twenty-eight—I'm sure we killed at least that many—and let them have the ship."

"Talk, talk, talk," jeered Polyorketes.

"There's a moral to this," said Stuart. "We can't take the ship away from the Kloros. We *might* be able to rush them, though, and keep them busy long enough to allow one of us enough time to short the engines."

"What?" yelled Porter, and Windham shushed him in fright.

"Short the engines," Stuart repeated. "That would destroy the ship, of course, which is what we want to do, isn't it?"

Leblanc's lips were white. "I don't think that would work."

"We can't be sure till we try. But what have we to lose by trying?"

"Our lives, damn it!" cried Porter. "You insane maniac, you're crazy!"

"If I'm a maniac," said Stuart, "and insane to boot, then naturally I'm crazy. But just remember that if we lose our lives, which is overwhelmingly probable, we lose nothing of value to Earth; whereas if we destroy the ship, as we just barely might, we do Earth a lot of good. What patriot would hesitate? Who here would put himself ahead of his world?" He looked about in the silence. "Surely not you, Colonel Windham."

Windham coughed tremendously. "My dear man, that is not the question. There must be a way to save the ship for Earth *without* losing our lives, eh?"

"All right. You name it."

"Let's all think about it. Now there are only two of the Kloros aboard ship. If one of us could sneak up on them and—"

"How? The rest of the ship's all filled with chlorine. We'd have to wear a spacesuit. Gravity in their part of the ship is hopped up to Kloro level, so whoever is patsy in the deal would be clumping around, metal on metal, slow and heavy. Oh, he could sneak up on them, sure—like a skunk trying to sneak downwind."

"Then we'll drop it all," Porter's voice shook. "Listen, Windham, there's not going to be any destroying the ship. My life means plenty to me and if any of you try anything like that, I'll call the Kloros. I mean it."

"Well," said Stuart, "there's hero number one."

Leblanc said, "I want to go back to Earth, but I—"

Mullen interrupted, "I don't think our chances of destroying the ship are good enough unless—"

"Heroes number two and three. What about you, Polyorketes, You would have the chance of killing two Kloros."

"I want to kill them with my bare hands," growled the farmer, his heavy fists writhing. "On their planet, I will kill dozens."

"That's a nice safe promise for now. What about you, Colonel? Don't you want to march to death and glory with me?"

"Your attitude is very cynical and unbecoming, Stuart. It's obvious that if the rest are unwilling, then your plan will fall through."

"Unless I do it myself, huh?"

"You won't, do you hear?" said Porter, instantly.

"Damn right I won't," agreed Stuart. "I don't claim to be a hero. I'm just an average patriot, perfectly willing to head for any planet they take me to and sit out the war."

Mullen said, thoughtfully, "Of course, there *is* a way we could surprise the Kloros."

The statement would have dropped flat except for Polyorketes. He pointed a black-nailed, stubby forefinger and laughed harshly. "Mr. Bookkeeper!" he said. "Mr. Bookkeeper is a big shot talker like this damned greenie spy, Stuart. All right, Mr. Bookkeeper, go ahead. You make big speeches also. Let the words roll like an empty barrel."

He turned to Stuart and repeated venomously, "Empty barrel! Cripple-hand empty barrel. No good for anything but talk."

Mullen's soft voice could make no headway until Polyorketes was through, but then he said, speaking directly to Stuart, "We might be able to reach them from outside. This room has a C-chute I'm sure."

"What's a C-chute?" asked Leblanc.

"Well—" began Mullen, and then stopped, at a loss.

Stuart said, mockingly, "It's a euphemism, my boy. Its full name is 'casualty chute.' It doesn't get talked about, but the main rooms on any ship would have them. They're just little airlocks down which you slide a corpse. Burial at space. Always lots of sentiment and bowed heads, with the captain making a rolling speech of the type Polyorketes here wouldn't like."

Leblanc's face twisted. "Use *that* to leave the ship?"

"Why not? Superstitious? —Go on, Mullen."

The little man had waited patiently. He said, "Once outside, one could re-enter the ship by the steam-tubes. It can be done—with luck. And then you would be an unexpected visitor in the control room."

Stuart stared at him curiously. "How do you figure this out? What do *you* know about steam-tubes?"

Mullen coughed. "You mean because I'm in the paper-box business? Well—" He grew pink, waited a moment, then made a new start in a colorless, unemotional voice. "My company, which manufactures fancy paper boxes and novelty containers, made a line of spaceship candy boxes for the juvenile trade some years ago. It was designed so that if a string were pulled, small pressure containers were punctured and jets of compressed air shot out through the mock steam-tubes, sailing the box across the room and scattering candy as it went. The sales theory was that the youngsters would find it exciting to play with the ship and fun to scramble for the candy.

"Actually, it was a complete failure. The ship would break dishes and sometimes hit another child in the eye. Worse still, the children would not only scramble for the candy but would fight over it. It was almost our worst failure. We lost thousands.

"Still, while the boxes were being designed, the entire office was extremely interested. It was like a game, very bad for efficiency and office morale. For a while, we all became steam-tube experts. I read quite a few books on ship construction. On my own time, however, not the company's."

Stuart was intrigued. He said, "You know it's a video sort of idea, but it might work if we had a hero to spare. Have we?"

"What about you?" demanded Porter, indignantly. "You go around sneering at us with your cheap wisecracks. I don't notice you volunteering for anything."

"That's because I'm no hero, Porter. I admit it. My object is to stay alive, and shinnying down steam-tubes is no way to go about staying alive. But the rest of you are noble patriots. The colonel says so. What about you, Colonel? You're the senior hero here."

Windham said, "If I were younger, blast it, and if you had your hands, I would take pleasure, sir, in trouncing you soundly."

"I've no doubt of it, but that's no answer."

"You know very well that at my time of life and with my leg—" he brought the flat of his hand down upon his stiff knee— "I am in no position to do anything of the sort, however much I should wish to."

"Ah, yes," said Stuart, "and I, myself, am crippled in the hands, as Polyorketes tells me. That saves us. And what unfortunate deformities do the rest of us have?"

"Listen," cried Porter, "I want to know what this is all about. How can anyone go down the steam-tubes? What if the Kloros use them while one of us is inside?"

"Why, Porter, that's part of the sporting chance. It's where the excitement comes in."

"But he'd be boiled in the shell like a lobster."

"A pretty image, but inaccurate. The steam wouldn't be on for more than a very short time, maybe a second or two, and the suit insulation would hold that long. Besides, the jet comes scooting out at several hundred miles a minute, so that you would be blown clear of the ship before the steam could even warm you. In fact, you'd be blown quite a few miles out into space, and after that you would be quite safe from the Kloros. Of course, you couldn't get back to the ship."

Porter was sweating freely. "You don't scare me for one minute, Stuart."

"I don't? Then you're offering to go? Are you sure you've thought out what being stranded in space means? You're all alone, you know; really all alone. The steam-jet will probably leave you turning or tumbling pretty rapidly. You won't feel that. You'll seem to be motionless. But all the stars will be going around and around so that they're just streaks in the sky. They won't ever stop. They won't even slow up. Then your heater will go off, your oxygen will give out, and you will die very slowly. You'll have lots of time to think. Or, if you are in a hurry, you could open your suit. That wouldn't be pleasant, either. I've seen faces of men who had a torn suit happen to them accidentally, and it's pretty awful. But it would be quicker. Then—"

Porter turned and walked unsteadily away.

Stuart said, lightly, "Another failure. One act of heroism still ready to be knocked down to the highest bidder with nothing offered yet."

Polyorketes spoke up and his harsh voice roughed the words. "You keep on talking, Mr. Big Mouth. You just keep banging that empty barrel. Pretty soon, we'll kick your teeth in. There's one boy I think would be willing to do it now, eh, Mr. Porter?"

Porter's look at Stuart confirmed the truth of Polyorketes' remarks, but he said nothing.

Stuart said, "Then what about you, Polyorketes? You're the barehand man with guts. Want me to help you into a suit?"

"I'll ask you when I want help."

"What about you, Leblanc?"

The young man shrank away.

"Not even to get back to Margaret?"

But Leblanc could only shake his head.

"Mullen?"

"Well—I'll try."

"You'll what?"

"I said, yes, I'll try. After all, it's my idea."

Stuart looked stunned. "You're serious? How come?"

Mullen's prim mouth pursed. "Because no one else will."

"But that's no reason. Especially for you."

Mullen shrugged.

There was a thump of a cane behind Stuart. Windham brushed past.

He said, "Do you really intend to go, Mullen?"

"Yes, Colonel."

"In that case, dash it, let me shake your hand. I like you. You're an—an Earthman, by heaven. Do this, and win or die, I'll bear witness for you."

Mullen withdrew his hand awkwardly from the deep and vibrating grasp of the other.

And Stuart just stood there. He was in a very unusual position. He was, in fact, in the particular position of all positions in which he most rarely found himself.

He had nothing to say.

The quality of tension had changed. The gloom and frustration had lifted a bit, and the excitement of conspiracy had replaced it. Even Polyorketes was fingering the spacesuits and commenting briefly and hoarsely on which he considered preferable.

Mullen was having a certain amount of trouble. The suit hung rather limply upon him even though the adjustable joints had been tightened nearly to minimum. He stood there now with only the helmet to be screwed on. He wiggled his neck.

Stuart was holding the helmet with an effort. It was heavy, and his artiplasmic hands did not grip it well. He said, "Better scratch your nose if it itches. It's your last chance for a while." He didn't add, "Maybe forever," but he thought it.

Mullen said, tonelessly, "I think perhaps I had better have a spare oxygen cylinder."

"Good enough."

"With a reducing valve."

Stuart nodded. "I see what you're thinking of. If you do get blown clear of the ship, you could try to blow yourself back by using the cylinder as an action-reaction motor."

They clamped on the headpiece and buckled the spare cylinder to Mullen's waist. Polyorketes and Leblanc lifted him up to the yawning opening of the C-tube. It was ominously dark inside, the metal lining of the interior having been painted a mournful black. Stuart thought he could detect a musty odor about it, but that, he knew, was only imagination.

He stopped the proceedings when Mullen was half within the tube. He tapped upon the little man's faceplate.

"Can you hear me?"

Within, there was a nod.

"Air coming through all right? No last-minute troubles?"

Mullen lifted his armored arm in a gesture of reassurance.

"Then remember, don't use the suit-radio out there. The Kloros might pick up the signals."

Reluctantly, he stepped away. Polyorketes' brawny hands lowered Mullen until they could hear the thumping sound made by the steel-shod feet against the outer valve. The inner valve then swung shut with a dreadful finality, its beveled silicone gasket making a slight soughing noise as it crushed hard. They clamped it into place.

Stuart stood at the toggle-switch that controlled the outer valve. He threw it and the gauge that marked the air pressure within the tube fell to zero. A little pinpoint of red light warned that the outer valve was open. Then the light disappeared, the valve closed, and the gauge climbed slowly to fifteen pounds again.

They opened the inner valve again and found the tube empty.

Polyorketes spoke first. He said, "The little son-of-a-gun. He went!" He looked wonderingly at the others. "A little fellow with guts like that."

Stuart said, "Look, we'd better get ready in here. There's just a chance that the Kloros may have detected the valves opening and closing. If so, they'll be here to investigate and we'll have to cover up."

"How?" asked Windham.

"They won't see Mullen anywhere around. We'll say he's in the head. The Kloros know that it's one of the peculiar characteristics of Earthmen that they resent intrusion on their privacy in lavatories, and they'll make no effort to check. If we can hold them off—"

"What if they wait, or if they check the spacesuits?" asked Porter.

Stuart shrugged. "Let's hope they don't. And listen, Polyorketes, don't make any fuss when they come in."

Polyorketes grunted, "With that little guy out there? What do you think I am?" He stared at Stuart without animosity, then scratched his curly hair vigorously. "You know, I laughed at him. I thought he was an old woman. It makes me ashamed."

Stuart cleared his throat. He said, "Look, I've been saying some things that maybe weren't too funny after all, now that I come to think of it. I'd like to say I'm sorry if I have."

He turned away morosely and walked toward his cot. He heard the steps behind him, felt the touch on his sleeve. He turned; it was Leblanc.

The youngster said softly, "I keep thinking that Mr. Mullen is an old man."

"Well, he's not a kid. He's about forty-five or fifty, I think."

Leblanc said, "Do you think, Mr. Stuart, that *I* should have gone, instead? I'm the youngest here. I don't like the thought of having let an old man go in my place. It makes me feel like the devil."

"I know. If he dies, it will be too bad."

"But he volunteered. We didn't make him, did we?"

"Don't try to dodge responsibility, Leblanc. It won't make you feel better. There isn't one of us without a stronger motive to run the risk than he had." And Stuart sat there silently, thinking.

Mullen felt the obstruction beneath his feet yield and the walls about him slip away quickly, too quickly. He knew it was the puff of air escaping, carrying him with it, and he dug arms and legs frantically against the wall to brake himself. Corpses were supposed to be flung well clear of the ship, but he was no corpse—for the moment.

His feet swung free and threshed. He heard the *clunk* of one magnetic boot against the hull just as the rest of his body puffed out like a tight cork under air pressure. He teetered dangerously at the lip of the hole in the ship —he had changed orientation suddenly and was looking down on it—then took a step backward as its lid came down of itself and fitted smoothly against the hull.

A feeling of unreality overwhelmed him. Surely, it wasn't he standing on the outer surface of a ship. Not Randolph F. Mullen. So few human beings could ever say they had, even those who traveled in space constantly.

He was only gradually aware that he was in pain. Popping out of that hole with one foot clamped to the hull had nearly bent him in two. He tried moving, cautiously, and found his motions to be erratic and almost impossible to control. He *thought* nothing was broken, though the muscles of his left side were badly wrenched.

And then he came to himself and noticed that the wrist-lights of his suit were on. It was by their light that he had stared into the blackness of the C-chute. He stirred with the nervous thought that from within, the Kloros might see the twin spots of moving light just outside the hull. He flicked the switch upon the suit's midsection.

Mullen had never imagined that, standing on a ship, he would fail to see its hull. But it was dark, as dark below as above. There were the stars, hard and bright little non-dimensional dots. Nothing more. Nothing more anywhere. Under his feet, not even the stars—*not even his feet.*

He bent back to look at the stars. His head swam. They were moving slowly. Or, rather, they were standing still and the ship was rotating, but he could not tell his eyes that. *They* moved. His eyes followed—down and behind the ship. New stars up and above from the other side. A black horizon. The ship existed only as a region where there were no stars.

No stars? Why, there was one almost at his feet. He nearly reached for it; then he realized that it was only a glittering reflection in the mirroring metal.

They were moving thousands of miles an hour. The stars were. The ship was. He was. But it meant nothing. To his senses, there was only silence and darkness and that slow wheeling of the stars. His eyes followed the wheeling—

And his head in its helmet hit the ship's hull with a soft bell-like ring.

He felt about in panic with his thick, insensitive, spun-silicate gloves. His feet were still firmly magnetized to the hull, that was true, but the rest of his body bent backward at the knees in a right angle. There was no gravity outside the ship. If he bent back, there was nothing to pull the upper part of his body down and tell his joints they were bending. His body stayed as he put it.

He pressed wildly against the hull and his torso shot upward and refused to stop when upright. He fell forward.

He tried more slowly, balancing with both hands against the hull, until he squatted evenly. Then upward. Very slowly. Straight up. Arms out to balance.

He was straight now, aware of his nausea and lightheadedness.

He looked about. My God, where were the steam-tubes? He couldn't see them. They were black on black, nothing on nothing.

Quickly, he turned on the wrist-lights. In space, there were no beams, only elliptical, sharply defined spots of blue steel, winking light back at him. Where they struck a rivet, a shadow was cast, knife-sharp and as black as space, the lighted region illuminated abruptly and without diffusion.

He moved his arms, his body swaying gently in the opposite direction; action and reaction. The vision of a steam-tube with its smooth cylindrical sides sprang at him.

He tried to move toward it. His foot held firmly to the hull. He pulled and it slogged upward, straining against quicksand that eased quickly. Three inches up and it had almost sucked free; six inches up and he thought it would fly away.

He advanced it and let it down, felt it enter the quicksand. When the sole was within two inches of the hull, it snapped down; out of control, hitting the hull ringingly. His spacesuit carried the vibrations, amplifying them in his ears.

He stopped in absolute terror. The dehydrators that dried the atmosphere within his suit could not handle the sudden gush of perspiration that drenched his forehead and armpits.

He waited, then tried lifting his foot again—a bare inch, holding it there by main force and moving it horizontally. Horizontal motion involved no effort at all; it was motion perpendicular to the lines of magnetic force. But he had to keep the foot from snapping down as he did so, and then lower it slowly.

He puffed with the effort. Each step was agony. The tendons of his knees were cracking, and there were knives in his side.

Mullen stopped to let the perspiration dry. It wouldn't do to steam up the inside of his faceplate. He flashed his wrist-lights, and the steam-cylinder was right ahead.

The ship had four of them, at ninety degree intervals, thrusting out at an angle from the midgirdle. They were the "fine adjustment" of the ship's course. The coarse adjustment was the powerful thrusters back and front which fixed final velocity by their accelerative and the decelerative force, and the hyperatomics that took care of the space-swallowing Jumps.

But occasionally the direction of flight had to be adjusted slightly and then the steam-cylinders took over. Singly, they could drive the ship up, down, right, left. By twos, in appropriate ratios of thrust, the ship could be turned in any desired direction.

The device had been unimproved in centuries, being too simple to improve. The atomic pile heated the water content of a closed container into steam, driving it, in less than a second, up to temperatures where it would have broken down into a mixture of hydrogen and oxygen, and then into a mixture of electrons and ions. Perhaps the breakdown actually took place. No one ever bothered testing; it worked, so there was no need to.

At the critical point, a needle valve gave way and the steam thrust madly out in a short but incredible blast. And the ship, inevitably and majestically, moved in the opposite direction, veering about its own center of gravity. When the degrees of turn were sufficient, an equal and opposite blast would take place and the turning would be canceled. The ship would be moving at its original velocity, but in a new direction.

Mullen had dragged himself out to the lip of the steam-cylinder. He had a picture of himself—a small speck teetering at the extreme end of a structure thrusting out of an ovoid that was tearing through space at ten thousand miles an hour.

But there was no air-stream to whip him off the hull, and his magnetic soles held him more firmly than he liked.

With lights on, he bent down to peer into the tube and the ship dropped down precipitously as his orientation changed. He reached out to steady himself, but he was not falling. There was no up or down in space except for what his confused mind chose to consider up or down.

The cylinder was just large enough to hold a man, so that it might be entered for repair purposes. His light caught the rungs almost directly opposite his position at the lip. He puffed a sigh of relief with what breath he could muster. Some ships didn't have ladders.

He made his way to it, the ship appearing to slip and twist beneath him as he moved. He lifted an arm over the lip of the tube, feeling for the rung, loosened each foot, and drew himself within.

The knot in his stomach that had been there from the first was a convulsed agony now. If they should choose to manipulate the ship, if the steam should whistle out now—

He would never hear it; never know it. One instant he would be holding a rung, feeling slowly for the next with a groping arm. The next moment he would be alone in space, the ship a dark, dark nothingness lost forever among the stars. There would be, perhaps, a brief glory of swirling ice crystals drifting with him, shining in his wrist-lights and slowly approaching and rotating about him, attracted by his mass like infinitesimal planets to an absurdly tiny Sun.

He was trickling sweat again, and now he was also conscious of thirst. He put it out of his mind. There would be no drinking until he was out of his suit—if ever.

Up a rung; up another; and another. How many were there? His hand slipped and he stared in disbelief at the glitter that showed under his light.

Ice?

Why not? The steam, incredibly hot as it was, would strike metal that was at nearly absolute zero. In the few split-seconds of thrust, there would not be time for the metal to warm above the freezing point of water. A sheet of ice would condense that would sublime slowly into the vacuum. It was the speed of all that happened that prevented the fusion of the tubes and of the original water-container itself.

His groping hand reached the end. Again the wrist-lights. He stared with crawling horror at the steam nozzle, half an inch in diameter. It looked dead, harmless. But it always would, right up to the micro-second before—

Around it was the outer steam lock. It pivoted on a central hub that was springed on the portion toward space, screwed on the part toward the ship. The springs allowed it to give under the first wild thrust of steam pressure before the ship's mighty inertia could be overcome. The steam was bled into the inner chamber, breaking the force of the thrust, leaving the total energy unchanged, but spreading it over time so that the hull itself was in that much less danger of being staved in.

Mullen braced himself firmly against a rung and pressed against the outer lock so that it gave a little. It was stiff, but it didn't have to give much, just enough to catch on the screw. He felt it catch.

He strained against it and turned it, feeling his body twist in the opposite direction. It held tight, the screw taking up the strain as he carefully adjusted the small control switch that allowed the springs to fall free. How well he remembered the books he had read!

He was in the interlock space now, which was large enough to hold a man comfortably, again for convenience in repairs. He could no longer be blown away from the ship. If the steam blast were turned on now, it would merely drive him against the inner lock—hard enough to crush him to a pulp. A quick death he would never feel, at least.

Slowly, he unhooked his spare oxygen cylinder. There was only an inner lock between himself and the control room now. This lock opened outward into space so that the steam blast could only close it tighter, rather than blow it open. And it fitted tightly and smoothly. There was absolutely no way to open it from without.

He lifted himself above the lock, forcing his bent back against the inner surface of the interlock area. It made breathing difficult. The spare oxygen cylinder dangled at a queer angle. He held its metal-mesh hose and straightened it, forcing it against the inner lock so that vibration thudded. Again— again—

It would *have* to attract the attention of the Kloros. They would *have* to investigate.

He would have no way of telling when they were about to do so. Ordinarily, they would first let air into the interlock to force the outer lock shut. But now the outer lock was on the central screw, well away from its rim. Air would suck about it ineffectually, dragging out into space.

Mullen kept on thumping. Would the Kloros look at the air-gauge, note that it scarcely lifted from zero, or would they take its proper working for granted?

Porter said, "He's been gone an hour and a half."

"I know," said Stuart.

They were all restless, jumpy, but the tension among themselves had disappeared. It was as though all the threads of emotion extended to the hull of the ship.

Porter was bothered. His philosophy of life had always been simple—take care of yourself because no one will take care of you for you. It upset him to see it shaken.

He said, "Do you suppose they've caught him?"

"If they had, we'd hear about it," replied Stuart, briefly.

Porter felt, with a miserable twinge, that there was little interest on the part of the others in speaking to him. He could understand it; he had not exactly earned their respect. For the moment, a torrent of self-excuse poured through his mind. The others had been frightened, too. A man had a right to be afraid. No one likes to die. At least, he hadn't broken like Aristides Polyorketes. He hadn't wept like Leblanc. He—

But there was Mullen, out there on the hull.

"Listen," he cried, "why did he do it?" They turned to look at him, not understanding, but Porter didn't care. It bothered him to the point where it had to come out. "I want to know why Mullen is risking his life."

"The man," said Windham, "is a patriot—"

"No, none of that!" Porter was almost hysterical. "That little fellow has no emotions at all. He just has reasons and I want to know what those reasons are, because—"

He didn't finish the sentence. Could he say that if those reasons applied to a little middle-aged bookkeeper, they might apply even more forcibly to himself?

Polyorketes said, "He's one brave damn little fellow."

Porter got to his feet. "Listen," he said, "he may be stuck out there. Whatever he's doing, he may not be able to finish it alone. I—I volunteer to go out after him."

He was shaking as he said it and he waited in fear for the sarcastic lash of Stuart's tongue. Stuart was staring at him, probably with surprise, but Porter dared not meet his eyes to make certain.

Stuart said, mildly, "Let's give him another half-hour."

Porter looked up, startled. There was no sneer on Stuart's face. It was even friendly. They *all* looked friendly.

He said, "And then—"

"And then all those who do volunteer will draw straws or something equally democratic. Who volunteers, besides Porter?"

They all raised their hands; Stuart did, too.

But Porter was happy. He had volunteered first. He was anxious for the half-hour to pass.

It caught Mullen by surprise. The outer lock flew open and the long, thin, snakelike, almost headless neck of a Kloro sucked out, unable to fight the blast of escaping air.

Mullen's cylinder flew away, almost tore free. After one wild moment of frozen panic, he fought for it, dragging it above the airstream, waiting as long as he dared to let the first fury die down as the air of the control room thinned out, then bringing it down with force.

It caught the sinewy neck squarely, crushing it. Mullen, curled above the lock, almost entirely protected from the stream, raised the cylinder again and plunging it down again striking the head, mashing the staring eyes to liquid ruin. In the near-vacuum, green blood was pumping out of what was left of the neck.

Mullen dared not vomit, but he wanted to.

With eyes averted, he backed away, caught the outer lock with one hand and imparted a whirl. For several seconds, it maintained that whirl. At the end of the screw, the springs engaged automatically and pulled it shut.

What was left of the atmosphere tightened it and the laboring pumps could now begin to fill the control room once again.

Mullen crawled over the mangled Kloro and into the room. It was empty.

He had barely time to notice that when he found himself on his knees. He rose with difficulty. The transition from non-gravity to gravity had taken him entirely by surprise. It was Klorian gravity, too, which meant that with this suit, he carried a fifty percent overload for his small frame. At least, though, his heavy metal clogs no longer clung so exasperatingly to the metal underneath. Within the ship, floors and wall were of cork-covered aluminum alloy.

He circled slowly. The neckless Kloro had collapsed and lay with only an occasional twitch to show it had once been a living organism. He stepped over it, distastefully, and drew the steam-tube lock shut.

The room had a depressing bilious cast and the lights shone yellow-green. It was the Kloro atmosphere, of course.

Mullen felt a twinge of surprise and reluctant admiration. The Kloros obviously had some way of treating materials so that they were impervious to the oxidizing effect of chlorine. Even the map of Earth on the wall, printed on glossy plastic-backed paper, seemed fresh and untouched. He approached, drawn by the familiar outlines of the continents—

There was a flash of motion caught in the corner of his eyes. As quickly as he could in his heavy suit, he turned, then screamed. The Kloro he had thought dead was rising to its feet.

Its neck hung limp, an oozing mass of tissue mash, but its arms reached out blindly, and the tentacles about its chest vibrated rapidly like innumerable snakes' tongues.

It was blind, of course. The destruction of its neck-stalk had deprived it of all sensory equipment, and partial asphyxiation had disorganized it. But the brain remained whole and safe in the abdomen. It still lived.

Mullen backed away. He circled, trying clumsily and unsuccessfully to tiptoe, though he knew that what was left of the Kloro was also deaf. It blundered on its way, struck a wall, felt to the base and began sidling along it.

Mullen cast about desperately for a weapon, found nothing. There was the Kloro's holster, but he dared not reach for it. Why hadn't he snatched it at the very first? Fool!

The door to the control room opened. It made almost no noise. Mullen turned, quivering.

The other Kloro entered, unharmed, entire. It stood in the doorway for a moment, chest-tendrils stiff and unmoving; its neck-stalk stretched forward; its horrible eyes flickering first at him and then at its nearly dead comrade.

And then its hand moved quickly to its side.

Mullen, without awareness, moved as quickly in pure reflex. He stretched out the hose of the spare oxygen-cylinder, which, since entering the control room, he had replaced in its suit-clamp, and cracked the valve. He didn't bother reducing the pressure. He let it gush out unchecked so that he nearly staggered under the backward push.

He could *see* the oxygen stream. It was a pale puff, billowing out amid the chlorine-green. It caught the Kloro with one hand on the weapon's holster.

The Kloro threw its hands up. The little beak on its head-nodule opened alarmingly but noiselessly. It staggered and fell, writhed for a moment, then lay still. Mullen approached and played the oxygen-stream upon its body as though he were extinguishing a fire. And then he raised his heavy foot and brought it down upon the center of the neck-stalk and crushed it on the floor.

He turned to the first. It was sprawled, rigid.

The whole room was pale with oxygen, enough to kill whole legions of Kloros, and his cylinder was empty.

Mullen stepped over the dead Kloro, out of the control room and along the main corridor toward the prisoners' room.

Reaction had set in. He was whimpering in blind, incoherent fright.

Stuart was tired. False hands and all, he was at the controls of a ship once again. Two light cruisers of Earth were on the way. For better than twenty-four hours he had handled the controls virtually alone. He had discarded the chlorinating equipment, rerigged the old atmospherics, located the ship's position in space, tried to plot a course, and sent out carefully guarded signals—which had worked.

So when the door of the control room opened, he was a little annoyed. He was too tired to play conversational handball. Then he turned, and it was Mullen stepping inside.

Stuart said, "For God's sake, get back into bed, Mullen!"

Mullen said, "I'm tired of sleeping, even though I never thought I would be a while ago."

"How do you feel?"

"I'm stiff all over. Especially my side." He grimaced and stared involuntarily around.

"Don't look for the Kloros," Stuart said. "We dumped the poor devils." He shook his head. "I was sorry for them. To themselves, *they're* the human beings, you know, and *we're* the aliens. Not that I'd rather they'd killed you, you understand."

"I understand."

Stuart turned a sidelong glance upon the little man who sat looking at the map of Earth and went on, "I owe you a particular and personal apology, Mullen. I didn't think much of you."

"It was your privilege," said Mullen in his dry voice. There was no feeling in it.

"No, it wasn't. It is no one's privilege to despise another. It is only a hard-won right after long experience."

"Have you been thinking about this?"

"Yes, all day. Maybe I can't explain. It's these hands." He held them up before him, spread out. "It was hard knowing that other people had hands of their own. I had to hate them for it. I always had to do my best to investigate and belittle their motives, point up their deficiencies, expose their stupidities. I had to do anything that would prove to myself that they weren't worth envying."

Mullen moved restlessly. "This explanation is not necessary."

"It is. It is!" Stuart felt his thoughts intently, strained to put them into words. "For years I've abandoned hope of finding any decency in human beings. Then you climbed into the C-chute."

"You had better understand," said Mullen, "that I was motivated by practical and selfish considerations. I will not have you present me to myself as a hero."

"I wasn't intending to. I know that you would do nothing without a reason. It was what your action did to the rest of us. It turned a collection of phonies and fools into decent people. And not by magic either. They were decent all along. It was just that they needed something to live up to and you supplied it. And—I'm one of them. I'll have to live up to you, too. For the rest of my life, probably."

Mullen turned away uncomfortably. His hand straightened his sleeves, which were not in the least twisted. His finger rested on the map.

He said, "I was born in Richmond, Virginia, you know. Here it is. I'll be going there first. Where were you born?"

"Toronto," said Stuart.

"That's right here. Not very far apart on the map, is it?"

Stuart said, "Would you tell me something?"

"If I can."

"Just why *did* you go out there?"

Mullen's precise mouth pursed. He said, dryly, "Wouldn't my rather prosaic reason ruin the inspirational effect?"

"Call it intellectual curiosity. Each of the rest of us had such obvious motives. Porter was scared to death of being interned; Leblanc wanted to get back to his sweetheart; Polyorketes wanted to kill Kloros; and Windham was a patriot according to his lights. As for me, I thought of myself as a noble idealist, I'm afraid. Yet in none of us was the motivation strong enough to get us into a spacesuit and out the C-chute. Then what made *you* do it, *you*, of all people?"

"Why the phrase, 'of all people'?"

"Don't be offended, but you seem devoid of all emotion."

"Do I?" Mullen's voice did not change. It remained precise and soft, yet somehow a tightness had entered it. "That's only training, Mr. Stuart, and self-discipline; not nature. A small man can have no respectable emotions. Is there anything more ridiculous than a man like myself in a state of rage? I'm five feet and one-half inch tall, and one hundred and two pounds in weight, if you care for exact figures. I insist on the half inch and the two pounds.

"Can I be dignified? Proud? Draw myself to my full height without inducing laughter? Where can I meet a woman who will not dismiss me instantly with a giggle? Naturally, I've had to learn to dispense with external display of emotion.

"*You* talk about deformities. No one would notice your hands or know they were different, if you weren't so eager to tell people all about it the instant you meet them. Do you think that the eight inches of height I do not have can be hidden? That it is not the first and, in most cases, the only thing about me that a person will notice?"

Stuart was ashamed. He had invaded a privacy he ought not have. He said, "I'm sorry."

"Why?"

"I should not have forced you to speak of this. I should have seen for myself that you—that you—"

"That I what? Tried to prove myself? Tried to show that while I might be small in body, I held within it a giant's heart?"

"I would not have put it mockingly."

"Why not? It's a foolish idea, and nothing like it is the reason I did what I did. What would I have accomplished if that's what was in my mind? Will they take me to Earth now and put me up before the television cameras—pitching them low, of course, to catch my face, or standing me on a chair—and pin medals on me?"

"They are quite likely to do exactly that."

"And what good would it do me? They would say, 'Gee, and he's such a little guy.' And afterward, what? Shall I tell each man I meet, 'You know, I'm the fellow they decorated for incredible valor last month?' How many medals, Mr. Stuart, do you suppose it would take to put eight inches and sixty pounds on me?"

Stuart said, "Put that way, I see your point."

Mullen was speaking a trifle more quickly now; a controlled heat had entered his words, warming them to just a tepid room temperature. "There *were* days when I thought I would show them, the mysterious 'them' that includes all the world. I was going to leave Earth and carve out worlds for myself. I would be a new and even smaller Napoleon. So I left Earth and went to Arcturus. And what could I do on Arcturus that I could not have done on Earth? Nothing. I balance books. So I am past the vanity, Mr. Stuart, of trying to stand on tiptoe."

"Then why *did* you do it?"

"I left Earth when I was twenty-eight and came to the Arcturian System. I've been there ever since. This trip was to be my first vacation, my first visit back to Earth in all that time. I was going to stay on Earth for six months. The Kloros instead captured us and would have kept us interned indefinitely. But I couldn't—I *couldn't* let them stop me from traveling to Earth. No matter what the risk, I had to prevent their interference. It wasn't love of woman, or fear, or hate, or idealism of any sort. It was stronger than any of those."

He stopped, and stretched out a hand as though to caress the map on the wall.

"Mr. Stuart," Mullen asked quietly, "haven't you ever been homesick?"

"In a Good Cause—"

In the Great Court, which stands as a patch of untouched peace among the fifty busy square miles devoted to the towering buildings that are the pulse beat of the United Worlds of the Galaxy, stands a statue.

It stands where it can look at the stars at night. There are other statues ringing the court, but this one stands in the center and alone.

It is not a very good statue. The face is too noble and lacks the lines of living. The brow is a shade too high, the nose a shade too symmetrical, the clothing a shade too carefully disposed. The whole bearing is by far too saintly to be true. One can suppose that the man in real life might have frowned at times, or hiccuped, but the statue seemed to insist that such imperfections were impossible.

All this, of course, is understandable overcompensation. The man had no statues raised to him while alive, and succeeding generations, with the advantage of hindsight, felt guilty.

The name on the pedestal reads "Richard Sayama Altmayer." Underneath it is a short phrase and, vertically arranged, three dates. The phrase is: *"In a good cause, there are no failures."* The three dates are June 17, 2755; September 5, 2788; December 32, 2800;—the years being counted in the usual manner of the period, that is, from the date of the first atomic explosion in 1945 of the ancient era.

None of those dates represents either his birth or death. They mark neither a date of marriage or of the accomplishment of some great deed or, indeed, of anything that the inhabitants of the United Worlds can remember with pleasure and pride. Rather, they are the final expression of the feeling of guilt.

Quite simply and plainly, they are the three dates upon which Richard Sayama Altmayer was sent to prison for his opinions.

1—*June 17, 2755*

At the age of twenty-two, certainly, Dick Altmayer was fully capable of feeling fury. His hair was as yet dark brown and he had not grown the mustache which, in later years, would be so characteristic of him. His nose was, of course, thin and high-bridged, but the contours of his face were youthful. It would only be later that the growing gauntness of his cheeks would convert that nose into the prominent landmark that it now is in the minds of trillions of school children.

Geoffrey Stock was standing in the doorway, viewing the results of his friend's fury. His round face and cold, steady eyes were there, but he had yet to put on the first of the military uniforms in which he was to spend the rest of his life.

He said, "Great Galaxy!"

Altmayer looked up. "Hello, Jeff."

"What's been happening, Dick? I thought your principles, pal, forbid destruction of any kind. Here's a book-viewer that looks somewhat destroyed." He picked up the pieces.

Altmayer said, "I was holding the viewer when my wave-receiver came through with an official message. You know which one, too."

"I know. It happened to me, too. Where is it?"

"On the floor. I tore it off the spool as soon as it belched out at me. Wait, let's dump it down the atom chute."

"Hey, hold on. You can't—"

"Why not?"

"Because you won't accomplish anything. You'll have to report."

"And just why?"

"Don't be an ass, Dick."

"This is a matter of principle, by Space."

"Oh, nuts! You can't fight the whole planet."

"I don't intend to fight the whole planet; just the few who get us into wars."

Stock shrugged. "That means the whole planet. That guff of yours of leaders tricking poor innocent people into fighting is just so much space-dust. Do you think that if a vote were taken the people wouldn't be overwhelmingly in favor of fighting this fight?"

"That means nothing, Jeff. The government has control of—"

"The organs of propaganda. Yes, I know. I've listened to you often enough. But why not report, anyway?"

Altmayer turned away.

Stock said, "In the first place, you might not pass the physical examination."

"I'd pass. I've been in Space."

"That doesn't mean anything. If the doctors let you hop a liner, that only means you don't have a heart murmur or an aneurysm. For military duty aboard ship in Space you need much more than just that. How do you know you qualify?"

"That's a side issue, Jeff, and an insulting one. It's not that I'm afraid to fight."

"Do you think you can stop the war this way?"

"I wish I could," Altmayer's voice almost shook as he spoke. "It's this idea I have that all mankind should be a single unit. There shouldn't be wars or space-fleets armed only for destruction. The Galaxy stands ready to be opened to the united efforts of the human race. Instead, we have been factioned for nearly two thousand years, and we throw away all the Galaxy."

Stock laughed, "We're doing all right. There are more than eighty independent planetary systems."

"And are we the only intelligences in the Galaxy?"

"Oh, the Diaboli, your particular devils," and Stock put his fists to his temples and extended the two forefingers, waggling them.

"And yours, too, and everybody's. They have a single government extending over more planets than all those occupied by our precious eighty independents."

"Sure, and their nearest planet is only fifteen hundred light years away from Earth and they can't live on oxygen planets anyway."

Stock got out of his friendly mood. He said, curtly, "Look, I dropped by here to say that I was reporting for examination next week. Are you coming with me?"

"No."

"You're really determined."

"I'm really determined."

"You know you'll accomplish nothing. There'll be no great flame ignited on Earth. It will be no case of millions of young men being excited by your example into a no-war strike. You will simply be put in jail."

"Well, then, jail it is."

And jail it was. On June 17, 2755, of the atomic era, after a short trial in which Richard Sayama Altmayer refused to present any defense, he was sentenced to jail for the term of three years or for the duration of the war, whichever should be longer. He served a little over four years and two months, at which time the war ended in a definite though not shattering Santannian defeat. Earth gained complete control of certain disputed asteroids, various commercial advantages, and a limitation of the Santannian navy.

The combined human losses of the war were something over two thousand ships with, of course, most of their crews, and in addition, several millions of lives due to the bombardment of planetary surfaces from space. The fleets of the two contending powers had been sufficiently strong to restrict this bombardment to the outposts of their respective systems, so that the planets of Earth and Santanni, themselves, were little affected.

The war conclusively established Earth as the strongest single human military power.

Geoffrey Stock fought throughout the war, seeing action more than once and remaining whole in life and limb despite that. At the end of the war he had the rank of major. He took part in the first diplomatic mission sent out by Earth to the worlds of the Diaboli, and that was the first step in his expanding role in Earth's military and political life.

2—*September 5, 2788*

They were the first Diaboli ever to have appeared on the surface of Earth itself. The projection posters and the newscasts of the Federalist party made that abundantly clear to any who were unaware of that. Over and over, they repeated the chronology of events.

It was toward the beginning of the century that human explorers first came across the Diaboli. They were intelligent and had discovered interstellar travel independently somewhat earlier than had the humans. Already the galactic volume of their dominions was greater than that which was human-occupied.

Regular diplomatic relationships between the Diaboli and the major human powers had begun twenty years earlier, immediately after the war between Santanni and Earth. At that time, outposts of Diaboli power were already within twenty light years of the outermost human centers. Their missions went everywhere, drawing trade treaties, obtaining concessions on unoccupied asteroids.

And now they were on Earth itself. They were treated as equals and perhaps as more than equals by the rulers of the greatest center of human population in the Galaxy. The most damning statistic of all was the most loudly proclaimed by the Federalists. It was this: Although the number of living Diaboli was somewhat less than the total number of living humans, humanity had opened up not more than five new worlds to colonization in fifty years, while the Diaboli had begun the occupation of nearly five hundred.

"A hundred to one against us," cried the Federalists, "because they are one political organization and we are a hundred." But relatively few on Earth, and fewer in the Galaxy as a whole, paid attention to the Federalists and their demands for Galactic Union.

The crowds that lined the streets along which nearly daily the five Diaboli of the mission traveled from their specially conditioned suite in the best hotel of the city to the Secretariat of Defense were, by and large, not hostile. Most were merely curious, and more than a little revolted.

The Diaboli were not pleasant creatures to look at. They were larger and considerably more massive than Earthmen. They had four stubby legs set close together below and two flexibly-fingered arms above. Their skin was wrinkled and naked and they wore no clothing. Their broad, scaly faces wore no expressions capable of being read by Earthmen, and from flattened regions just above each large-pupilled eye there sprang short horns. It was these last that gave the creatures their names. At first they had been called devils, and later the politer Latin equivalent.

Each wore a pair of cylinders on its back from which flexible tubes extended to the nostrils; there they clamped on tightly. These were packed with soda-lime which absorbed the, to them, poisonous carbon dioxide from the air they breathed. Their own metabolism revolved about the reduction of sulfur and sometimes those foremost among the humans in the crowd caught a foul whiff of the hydrogen sulfide exhaled by the Diaboli.

The leader of the Federalists was in the crowd. He stood far back where he attracted no attention from the police who had roped off the avenues and who now maintained a watchful order on the little hoppers that could be maneuvered quickly through the thickest crowd. The Federalist leader was gaunt-faced, with a thin and prominently bridged nose and straight, graying hair.

He turned away, "I cannot bear to look at them."

His companion was more philosophic. He said, "No uglier in spirit, at least, than some of our handsome officials. These creatures are at least true to their own."

"You are sadly right. Are we entirely ready?"

"Entirely. There won't be one of them alive to return to his world."

"Good! I will remain here to give the signal."

The Diaboli were talking as well. This fact could not be evident to any human, no matter how close. To be sure, they could communicate by making ordinary sounds to one another but that was not their method of choice. The skin between their horns could, by the actions of muscles which differed in their construction from any known to humans, vibrate rapidly. The tiny waves which were transmitted in this manner to the air were too rapid to be heard by the human ear and too delicate to be detected by any but the most sensitive of human instrumentation. At that time, in fact, humans remained unaware of this form of communication.

A vibration said, "Did you know that this is the planet of origin of the Two-legs?"

"No." There was a chorus of such no's, and then one particular vibration said, "Do you get that from the Two-leg communications you have been studying, queer one?"

"Because I study the communications? More of our people should do so instead of insisting so firmly on the complete worthlessness of Two-leg culture. For one thing, we are in a much better position to deal with the Two-legs if we know something about them. Their history is interesting in a horrible way. I am glad I brought myself to view their spools."

"And yet," came another vibration, "from our previous contacts with Two-legs, one would be certain that they did not know their planet of origin. Certainly there is no veneration of this planet, Earth, or any memorial rites connected with it. Are you sure the information is correct?"

"Entirely so. The lack of ritual, and the fact that this planet is by no means a shrine, is perfectly understandable in the light of Two-leg history. The Two-legs on the other worlds would scarcely concede the honor. It would somehow lower the independent dignity of their own worlds."

"I don't quite understand."

"Neither do I, exactly, but after several days of reading I think I catch a glimmer. It would seem that, originally, when interstellar travel was first discovered by the Two-legs, they lived under a single political unit."

"Naturally."

"Not for these Two-legs. This was an unusual stage in their history and did not last. After the colonies on the various worlds grew and came to reasonable maturity, their first interest was to break away from the mother world. The first in the series of interstellar wars among these Two-legs began then."

"Horrible. Like cannibals."

"Yes, isn't it? My digestion has been upset for days. My cud is sour. In any case, the various colonies gained independence, so that now we have the situation of which we are well aware. All of the Two-leg kingdoms, republics, aristocracies, etc., are simply tiny clots of worlds, each consisting of a dominant world and a few subsidiaries which, in turn, are forever seeking their independence or being shifted from one dominant to another. This Earth is the strongest among them and yet less than a dozen worlds owe it allegiance."

"Incredible that these creatures should be so blind to their own interests. Do they not have a tradition of the single government that existed when they consisted of but one world?"

"As I said that was unusual for them. The single government had existed only a few decades. Prior to that, this very planet itself was split into a number of subplanetary political units."

"Never heard anything like it." For a while, the supersonics of the various creatures interfered with one another.

"It's a fact. It is simply the nature of the beast."

And with that, they were at the Secretariat of Defense.

The five Diaboli stood side by side along the table. They stood because their anatomy did not admit of anything that could correspond to "sitting."

On the other side of the table, five Earthmen stood as well. It would have been more convenient for the humans to sit but, understandably, there was no desire to make the handicap of smaller size any more pronounced than it already was. The table was a rather wide one; the widest, in fact, that could be conveniently obtained. This was out of respect for the human nose, for from the Diaboli, slightly so as they breathed, much more so when they spoke, there came the gentle and continuous drift of hydrogen sulfide. This was a difficulty rather unprecedented in diplomatic negotiations.

Ordinarily the meetings did not last for more than half an hour, and at the end of this interval the Diaboli ended their conversations without ceremony and turned to leave. This time, however, the leave-taking was interrupted. A man entered, and the five human negotiators made way for him. He was tall, taller than any of the other Earthmen, and he wore a uniform with the ease of long usage. His face was round and his eyes cold and steady. His black hair was rather thin but as yet untouched by gray. There was an irregular blotch of scar tissue running from the point of his jaw downward past the line of his high, leather-brown collar. It might have been the result of a hand energy-ray, wielded by some forgotten human enemy in one of the five wars in which the man had been an active participant.

"Sirs," said the Earthman who had been chief negotiator hitherto, "may I introduce the Secretary of Defense?"

The Diaboli were somewhat shocked and, although their expressions were in repose and inscrutable, the sound plates on their foreheads vibrated actively. Their strict sense of hierarchy was disturbed. The Secretary was only a Two-leg, but by Two-leg standards, he outranked them. They could not properly conduct official business with him.

The Secretary was aware of their feelings but had no choice in the matter. For at least ten minutes, their leaving must be delayed and no ordinary interruption could serve to hold back the Diaboli.

"Sirs," he said, "I must ask your indulgence to remain longer this time."

The central Diabolus replied in the nearest approach to English any Diabolus could manage. Actually, a Diabolus might be said to have two mouths. One was hinged at the outermost extremity of the jawbone and was used in eating. In this capacity, the motion of the mouth was rarely seen by human beings, since the Diaboli much preferred to eat in the company of their own kind, exclusively. A narrower mouth opening, however, perhaps two inches in width, could be used in speaking. It pursed itself open, revealing the gummy gap where a Diabolus' missing incisors ought to have been. It remained open during speech, the necessary consonantal blockings being performed by the palate and back of the tongue. The result was hoarse and fuzzy, but understandable.

The Diabolus said, "You will pardon us, already we suffer." And by his forehead, he twittered unheard, "They mean to suffocate us in their vile atmosphere. We must ask for larger poison-absorbing cylinders."

The Secretary of Defense said, "I am in sympathy with your feelings, and yet this may be my only opportunity to speak with you. Perhaps you would do us the honor to eat with us."

The Earthman next the Secretary could not forbear a quick and passing frown. He scribbled rapidly on a piece of paper and passed it to the Secretary, who glanced momentarily at it.

It read, "No. They eat sulfuretted hay. Stinks unbearably." The Secretary crumbled the note and let it drop.

The Diabolus said, "The honor is ours. Were we physically able to endure your strange atmosphere for so long a time, we would accept most gratefully."

And via forehead, he said with agitation, "They cannot expect us to eat with them and watch them consume the corpses of dead animals. My cud would never be sweet again."

"We respect your reasons," said the Secretary. "Let us then transact our business now. In the negotiations that have so far proceeded, we have been unable to obtain from your government, in the persons of you, their representatives, any clear indication as to what the boundaries of your sphere of influence are in your own minds. We have presented several proposals in this matter."

"As far as the territories of Earth are concerned, Mr. Secretary, a definition has been given."

"But surely you must see that this is unsatisfactory. The boundaries of Earth and your lands are nowhere in contact. So far, you have done nothing but state this fact. While true, the mere statement is not satisfying."

"We do not completely understand. Would you have us discuss the boundaries between ourselves and such independent human kingdoms as that of Vega?"

"Why, yes."

"That cannot be done, sir. Surely, you realize that any relations between ourselves and the sovereign realm of Vega cannot be possibly any concern of Earth. They can be discussed only with Vega."

"Then you will negotiate a hundred times with the hundred human world systems?"

"It is necessary. I would point out, however, that the necessity is imposed not by us but by the nature of your human organization."

"Then that limits our field of discussion drastically." The Secretary seemed abstracted. He was listening, not exactly to the Diaboli opposite, but, rather, it would seem, to something at a distance.

And now there was a faint commotion, barely heard from outside the Secretariat. The babble of distant voices, the brisk crackle of energy-guns muted by distance to nearly nothingness, and the hurried click-clacking of police hoppers.

The Diaboli showed no indication of hearing, nor was this simply another affectation of politeness. If their capacity for receiving supersonic sound waves was far more delicate and acute than almost anything human ingenuity had ever invented, their reception for ordinary sound waves was rather dull.

The Diabolus was saying, "We beg leave to state our surprise. We were of the opinion that all this was known to you."

A man in police uniform appeared in the doorway. The Secretary turned to him and, with the briefest of nods, the policeman departed.

The Secretary said suddenly and briskly, "Quite. I merely wished to ascertain once again that this was the case. I trust you will be ready to resume negotiations tomorrow?"

"Certainly, sir."

One by one, slowly, with a dignity befitting the heirs of the universe, the Diaboli left.

An Earthman said, "I'm glad they refused to eat with us."

"I knew they couldn't accept," said the Secretary, thoughtfully. "They're vegetarian. They sicken thoroughly at the very thought of eating meat. I've seen them eat, you know. Not many humans have. They resemble our cattle in the business of eating. They bolt their food and then stand solemnly about in circles, chewing their cuds in a great community of thought. Perhaps they intercommunicate by a method we are unaware of. The huge lower jaw rotates horizontally in a slow, grinding process—"

The policeman had once more appeared in the doorway.

The Secretary broke off, and called, "You have them all?"

"Yes, sir."

"Do you have Altmayer?"

"Yes, sir."

"Good."

The crowd had gathered again when the five Diaboli emerged from the Secretariat. The schedule was strict. At 3:00 P.M. each day they left their suite and spent five minutes walking to the Secretariat. At 3:35, they emerged therefrom once again and returned to their suite, the way being kept clear by the police. They marched stolidly, almost mechanically, along the broad avenue.

Halfway in their trek there came the sounds of shouting men. To most of the crowd, the words were not clear but there was the crackle of an energy-gun and the pale blue fluorescence split the air overhead. Police wheeled, their own energy-guns drawn, hoppers springing seven feet into the air, landing delicately in the midst of groups of people, touching none of them, jumping again almost instantly. People scattered and their voices were joined to the general uproar.

Through it all, the Diaboli, either through defective hearing or excessive dignity, continued marching as mechanically as ever.

At the other end of the gathering, almost diametrically opposing the region of excitement, Richard Sayama Altmayer stroked his nose in a moment of satisfaction. The strict chronology of the Diaboli had made a split-second plan possible. The first diversionary disturbance was only to attract the attention of the police. It was now—

And he fired a harmless sound pellet into the air.

Instantly, from four directions, concussion pellets split the air. From the roofs of buildings lining the way, snipers fired.

Each of the Diaboli, torn by the shells, shuddered and exploded as the pellets detonated within them. One by one, they toppled.

And from nowhere, the police were at Altmayer's side. He stared at them with some surprise.

Gently, for in twenty years he had lost his fury and learned to be gentle, he said, "You come quickly, but even so you come too late." He gestured in the direction of the shattered Diaboli.

The crowd was in simple panic now. Additional squadrons of police, arriving in record time, could do nothing more than herd them off into harmless directions.

The policeman, who now held Altmayer in a firm grip, taking the sound gun from him and inspecting him quickly for further weapons, was a captain by rank. He said, stiffly, "I think you've made a mistake, Mr. Altmayer. You'll notice you've drawn no blood." And he, too, waved toward where the Diaboli lay motionless.

Altmayer turned, startled. The creatures lay there on their sides, some in pieces, tattered skin shredding away, frames distorted and bent, but the police captain was correct. There was no blood, no flesh. Altmayer's lips, pale and stiff, moved soundlessly.

The police captain interpreted the motion accurately enough. He said, "You are correct, sir, they are robots."

And from the great doors of the Secretariat of Defense the true Diaboli emerged. Clubbing policemen cleared the way, but another way, so that they need not pass the sprawled travesties of plastic and aluminum which for three minutes had played the role of living creatures.

The police captain said, "I'll ask you to come without trouble, Mr. Altmayer. The Secretary of Defense would like to see you."

"I am coming, sir." A stunned frustration was only now beginning to overwhelm him.

Geoffrey Stock and Richard Altmayer faced one another for the first time in almost a quarter of a century, there in the Defense Secretary's private office. It was a rather straitlaced office: a desk, an armchair, and two additional chairs. All were a dull brown in color, the chairs being topped by brown foamite which yielded to the body enough for comfort, not enough for luxury. There was a micro-viewer on the desk and a little cabinet big enough to hold several dozen opto-spools. On the wall opposite the desk was a trimensional view of the old *Dauntless,* the Secretary's first command.

Stock said, "It is a little ridiculous meeting like this after so many years. I find I am sorry."

"Sorry about what, Jeff?" Altmayer tried to force a smile, "I am sorry about nothing but that you tricked me with those robots."

"You were not difficult to trick," said Stock, "and it was an excellent opportunity to break your party. I'm sure it will be quite discredited after this. The pacifist tries to force war; the apostle of gentleness tries assassination."

"War against the true enemy," said Altmayer sadly. "But you are right. It is a sign of desperation that this was forced on me." —Then, "How did you know my plans?"

"You still overestimate humanity, Dick. In any conspiracy the weakest points are the people that compose it. You had twenty-five co-conspirators. Didn't it occur to you that at least one of them might be an informer, or even an employee of mine?"

A dull red burned slowly on Altmayer's high cheekbones. "Which one?" he said.

"Sorry. We may have to use him again."

Altmayer sat back in his chair wearily. "What have you gained?"

"What have *you* gained? You are as impractical now as on that last day I saw you; the day you decided to go to jail rather than report for induction. You haven't changed."

Altmayer shook his head, "The truth doesn't change."

Stock said impatiently, "If it is truth, why does it always fail? Your stay in jail accomplished nothing. The war went on. Not one life was saved. Since then, you've started a political party; and every cause it has backed has failed. Your conspiracy has failed. You're nearly fifty, Dick, and what have you accomplished? Nothing."

Altmayer said, "And you went to war, rose to command a ship, then to a place in the Cabinet. They say you will be the next Coordinator. You've accomplished a great deal. Yet success and failure do not exist in themselves. Success in what? Success in working the ruin of humanity. Failure in what? In saving it? I wouldn't change places with you. Jeff, remember this. In a good cause, there are no failures; there are only delayed successes."

"Even if you are executed for this day's work?"

"Even if I am executed. There will be someone else to carry on, and his success will be my success."

"How do you envisage this success? Can you really see a union of worlds, a Galactic Federation? Do you want Santanni running our affairs? Do you want a Vegan telling you what to do? Do you want Earth to decide its own destiny or to be at the mercy of any random combination of powers?"

"We would be at their mercy no more than they would be at ours."

"Except that we are the richest. We would be plundered for the sake of the depressed worlds of the Sirius Sector."

"And pay the plunder out of what we would save in the wars that would no longer occur."

"Do you have answers for all questions, Dick?"

"In twenty years we have been asked all questions, Jeff."

"Then answer this one. How would you force this union of yours on unwilling humanity?"

"That is why I wanted to kill the Diaboli." For the first time, Altmayer showed agitation. "It would mean war with them, but all humanity would unite against the common enemy. Our own political and ideological differences would fade in the face of that."

"You really believe that? Even when the Diaboli have never harmed us? They cannot live on our worlds. They must remain on their own worlds of sulfide atmosphere and oceans which are sodium sulfate solutions."

"Humanity knows better, Jeff. They are spreading from world to world like an atomic explosion. They block space-travel into regions where there are unoccupied oxygen worlds, the kind *we* could use. They are planning for the future; making room for uncounted future generations of Diaboli, while we are being restricted to one corner of the Galaxy, and fighting ourselves to death. In a thousand years we will be their slaves; in ten thousand we will be extinct. Oh, yes, they are the common enemy. Mankind knows that. You will find that out sooner than you think, perhaps."

The Secretary said, "Your party members speak a great deal of ancient Greece of the preatomic age. They tell us that the Greeks were a marvelous people, the most culturally advanced of their time, perhaps of all times. They set mankind on the road it has never yet left entirely. They had only one flaw. They could not unite. They were conquered and eventually died out. And we follow in their footsteps now, eh?"

"You have learned your lesson well, Jeff."

"But have you, Dick?"

"What do you mean?"

"Did the Greeks have no common enemy against whom they could unite?"

Altmayer was silent.

Stock said, "The Greeks fought Persia, their great common enemy. Was it not a fact that a good proportion of the Greek states fought on the Persian side?"

Altmayer said finally, "Yes. Because they thought Persian victory was inevitable and they wanted to be on the winning side."

"Human beings haven't changed, Dick. Why do you suppose the Diaboli are here? What is it we are discussing?"

"I am not a member of the government."

"No," said Stock, savagely, "but I am. The Vegan League has allied itself with the Diaboli."

"I don't believe you. It can't be."

"It can be and is. The Diaboli have agreed to supply them with five hundred ships at any time they happen to be at war with Earth. In return, Vega abandons all claims to the Nigellian star cluster. So if you had really assassinated the Diaboli, it would have been war, but with half of humanity probably fighting on the side of your so-called common enemy. We are trying to prevent that."

Altmayer said slowly, "I am ready for trial. Or am I to be executed without one?"

Stock said, "You are still foolish. If we shoot you, Dick, we make a martyr. If we keep you alive and shoot only your subordinates, you will be suspected of having turned state's evidence. As a presumed traitor, you will be quite harmless in the future."

And so, on September 5th, 2788, Richard Sayama Altmayer, after the briefest of secret trials, was sentenced to five years in prison. He served his full term. The year he emerged from prison, Geoffrey Stock was elected Coordinator of Earth.

3—December 21, 2800

Simon Devoire was not at ease. He was a little man, with sandy hair and a freckled, ruddy face. He said, "I'm sorry I agreed to see you, Altmayer. It won't do you any good. It might do me harm."

Altmayer said, "I am an old man. I won't hurt you." And he was indeed a very old man somehow. The turn of the century found his years at two thirds of a century, but he was older than that, older inside and older outside. His clothes were too big for him, as if he were shrinking away inside them. Only his nose had not aged; it was still the thin, aristocratic, high-beaked Altmayer nose.

Devoire said, "It's not you I'm afraid of."

"Why not? Perhaps you think I betrayed the men of '88."

"No, of course not. No man of sense believes that you did. But the days of the Federalists are over, Altmayer."

Altmayer tried to smile. He felt a little hungry; he hadn't eaten that day —no time for food. Was the day of the Federalists over? It might seem so to others. The movement had died on a wave of ridicule. A conspiracy that fails, a "lost cause," is often romantic. It is remembered and draws adherents for generations, *if* the loss is at least a dignified one. But to shoot at living creatures and find the mark to be robots; to be outmaneuvered and outfoxed; to be made ridiculous—that is deadly. It is deadlier than treason, wrong, and sin. Not many had believed Altmayer had bargained for his life by betraying his associates, but the universal laughter killed Federalism as effectively as though they had.

But Altmayer had remained stolidly stubborn under it all. He said, "The day of the Federalists will never be over, while the human race lives."

"Words," said Devoire impatiently. "They meant more to me when I was younger. I am a little tired now."

"Simon, I need access to the subetheric system."

Devoire's face hardened. He said, "And you thought of me. I'm sorry, Altmayer, but I can't let you use my broadcasts for your own purposes."

"You were a Federalist once."

"Don't rely on that," said Devoire. "That's in the past. Now I am— nothing. I am a Devoirist, I suppose. I want to live."

"Even if it is under the feet of the Diaboli? Do you want to live when they are willing; die when they are ready?"

"Words!"

"Do you approve of the all-Galactic conference?"

Devoire reddened past his usual pink level. He gave the sudden impression of a man with too much blood for his body. He said smolderingly, "Well, why not? What does it matter how we go about establishing the Federation of Man? If you're still a Federalist, what have you to object to in a united humanity?"

"United under the Diaboli?"

"What's the difference? Humanity can't unite by itself. Let us be driven to it, as long as the fact is accomplished. I am sick of it all, Altmayer, sick of all our stupid history. I'm tired of trying to be an idealist with nothing to be idealistic over. Human beings are human beings and that's the nasty part of it. Maybe we've *got* to be whipped into line. If so, I'm perfectly willing to let the Diaboli do the whipping."

Altmayer said gently, "You're very foolish, Devoire. It won't be a real union, you know that. The Diaboli called this conference so that they might act as umpires on all current interhuman disputes to their own advantage, and remain the supreme court of judgment over us hereafter. You know they have no intention of establishing a real central human government. It will only be a sort of interlocking directorate; each human government will conduct its own affairs as before and pull in various directions as before. It is simply that we will grow accustomed to running to the Diaboli with our little problems."

"How do you know that will be the result?"

"Do you seriously think any other result is possible?"

Devoire chewed at his lower lip, "Maybe not!"

"Then see through a pane of glass, Simon. Any true independence we now have will be lost."

"A lot of good this independence has ever done us. —Besides, what's the use? We can't stop this thing. Coordinator Stock is probably no keener on the conference than you are, but that doesn't help him. If Earth doesn't attend, the union will be formed without us, and then we will face war with the rest of humanity and the Diaboli. And that goes for any other government that wants to back out."

"What if *all* the governments back out? Wouldn't the conference break up completely?"

"Have you ever known all the human governments to do *anything* together? You never learn, Altmayer."

"There are new facts involved."

"Such as? I know I am foolish for asking, but go ahead."

Altmayer said, "For twenty years most of the Galaxy has been shut to human ships. You know that. None of us has the slightest notion of what goes on within the Diaboli sphere of influence. And yet some human colonies exist within that sphere."

"So?"

"So occasionally, human beings escape into the small portion of the Galaxy that remains human and free. The government of Earth receives reports; reports which they don't dare make public. But not *all* officials of the government can stand the cowardice involved in such actions forever. One of them has been to see me. I can't tell you which one, of course— So I have documents, Devoire; official, reliable, and true."

Devoire shrugged, "About what?" He turned the desk chronometer rather ostentatiously so that Altmayer could see its gleaming metal face on which the red, glowing figures stood out sharply. They read 22:31, and even as it was turned, the 1 faded and the new glow of a 2 appeared.

Altmayer said, "There is a planet called by its colonists Chu Hsi. It did not have a large population; two million, perhaps. Fifteen years ago the Diaboli occupied worlds on various sides of it; and in all those fifteen years, no human ship ever landed on the planet. Last year the Diaboli themselves landed. They brought with them huge freight ships filled with sodium sulfate and bacterial cultures that are native to their own worlds."

"What? —You can't make me believe it."

"Try," said Altmayer, ironically. "It is not difficult. Sodium sulfate will dissolve in the oceans of any world. In a sulfate ocean, their bacteria will grow, multiply, and produce hydrogen sulfide in tremendous quantities which will fill the oceans and the atmosphere. They can then introduce their plants and animals and eventually themselves. Another planet will be suitable for Diaboli life—and unsuitable for any human. It would take time, surely, but the Diaboli have time. They are a united people and . . ."

"Now, look," Devoire waved his hand in disgust, "that just doesn't hold water. The Diaboli have more worlds than they know what to do with."

"For their present purposes, yes, but the Diaboli are creatures that look toward the future. Their birth rate is high and eventually they will fill the Galaxy. And how much better off they would be if they were the only intelligence in the universe."

"But it's impossible on purely physical grounds. Do you know how many millions of tons of sodium sulfate it would take to fill up the oceans to their requirements?"

"Obviously a planetary supply."

"Well, then, do you suppose they would strip one of their own worlds to create a new one? Where is the gain?"

"Simon, Simon, there are millions of planets in the Galaxy which through atmospheric conditions, temperature, or gravity are forever uninhabitable either to humans or to Diaboli. Many of these are quite adequately rich in sulfur."

Devoire considered, "What about the human beings on the planet?"

"On Chu Hsi? Euthanasia—except for the few who escaped in time. Painless I suppose. The Diaboli are not needlessly cruel, merely efficient."

Altmayer waited. Devoire's fist clenched and unclenched.

Altmayer said, "Publish this news. Spread it out on the interstellar subetheric web. Broadcast the documents to the reception centers on the various worlds. You can do it, and when you do, the all-Galactic conference will fall apart."

Devoire's chair tilted forward. He stood up. "Where's your proof?"

"Will you do it?"

"I want to see your proof."

Altmayer smiled, "Come with me."

They were waiting for him when he came back to the furnished room he was living in. He didn't notice them at first. He was completely unaware of the small vehicle that followed him at a slow pace and a prudent distance. He walked with his head bent, calculating the length of time it would take for Devoire to put the information through the reaches of space; how long it would take for the receiving stations on Vega and Santanni and Centaurus to blast out the news; how long it would take to spread it over the entire Galaxy. And in this way he passed, unheeding, between the two plain-clothes men who flanked the entrance of the rooming house.

It was only when he opened the door to his own room that he stopped and turned to leave but the plain-clothes men were behind him now. He made no attempt at violent escape. He entered the room instead and sat down, feeling so old. He thought feverishly, I need only hold them off an hour and ten minutes.

The man who occupied the darkness reached up and flicked the switch that allowed the wall lights to operate. In the soft wall glow, the man's round face and balding gray-fringed head were startlingly clear.

Altmayer said gently, "I am honored with a visit by the Coordinator himself."

And Stock said, "We are old friends, you and I, Dick. We meet every once in a while."

Altmayer did not answer.

Stock said, "You have certain government papers in your possession, Dick."

Altmayer said, "If you think so, Jeff, you'll have to find them."

Stock rose wearily to his feet. "No heroics, Dick. Let me tell you what those papers contained. They were circumstantial reports of the sulfation of the planet, Chu Hsi. Isn't that true?"

Altmayer looked at the clock.

Stock said, "If you are planning to delay us, to angle us as though we were fish, you will be disappointed. We know where you've been, we know Devoire has the papers, we know exactly what he's planning to do with them."

Altmayer stiffened. The thin parchment of his cheeks trembled. He said, "How long have you known?"

"As long as you have, Dick. You are a very predictable man. It is the very reason we decided to use you. Do you suppose the Recorder would really come to see you as he did, without our knowledge?"

"I don't understand."

Stock said, "The Government of Earth, Dick, is not anxious that the all-Galactic conference be continued. However, we are not Federalists; we know humanity for what it is. What do you suppose would happen if the rest of the Galaxy discovered that the Diaboli were in the process of changing a salt-oxygen world into a sulfate-sulfide one?

"No, don't answer. You are Dick Altmayer and I'm sure you'd tell me that with one fiery burst of indignation, they'd abandon the conference, join together in a loving and brotherly union, throw themselves at the Diaboli, and overwhelm them."

Stock paused such a long time that for a moment it might have seemed he would say no more. Then he continued in half a whisper, "Nonsense. The other worlds would say that the Government of Earth for purposes of its own had initiated a fraud, had forged documents in a deliberate attempt to disrupt the conference. The Diaboli would deny everything, and most of the human worlds would find it to their interests to believe the denial. They would concentrate on the iniquities of Earth and forget about the iniquities of the Diaboli. So you see, we could sponsor no such exposé."

Altmayer felt drained, futile. "Then you will stop Devoire. It is always that you are so sure of failure beforehand; that you believe the worst of your fellow man—"

"Wait! I said nothing of stopping Devoire. I said only that the government could not sponsor such an exposé and we will not. But the exposé will take place just the same, except that afterward we will arrest Devoire and yourself and denounce the whole thing as vehemently as will the Diaboli. The whole affair would then be changed. The Government of Earth will have dissociated itself from the claims. It will then seem to the rest of the human government that for our own selfish purposes we are trying to hide the actions of the Diaboli, that we have, perhaps, a special understanding with them. They will fear that special understanding and unite against us. But *then* to be against us will mean that they are also against the Diaboli. They will insist on believing the exposé to be the truth, the documents to be real—and the conference will break up."

"It will mean war again," said Altmayer hopelessly, "and not against the real enemy. It will mean fighting among the humans and a victory all the greater for the Diaboli when it is all over."

"No war," said Stock. "No government will attack Earth with the Diaboli on our side. The other governments will merely draw away from us and grind a permanent anti-Diaboli bias into their propaganda. Later, if there should be war between ourselves and the Diaboli, the other governments will at least remain neutral."

He looks very old, thought Altmayer. We are all old, dying men. Aloud, he said, "Why would you expect the Diaboli to back Earth? You may fool the rest of mankind by pretending to attempt suppression of the facts concerning the planet Chu Hsi, but you won't fool the Diaboli. They won't for a moment believe Earth to be sincere in its claim that it believes the documents to be forgeries."

"Ah, but they will." Geoffrey Stock stood up, "You see, the documents *are* forgeries. The Diaboli may be planning sulfation of planets in the future, but to our knowledge, they have not tried it yet."

On December 21, 2800, Richard Sayama Altmayer entered prison for the third and last time. There was no trial, no definite sentence, and scarcely a real imprisonment in the literal sense of the word. His movements were confined and only a few officials were allowed to communicate with him, but otherwise his comforts were looked to assiduously. He had no access to news, of course, so that he was not aware that in the second year of this third imprisonment of his, the war between Earth and the Diaboli opened with the surprise attack near Sirius by an Earth squadron upon certain ships of the Diaboli navy.

In 2802, Geoffrey Stock came to visit Altmayer in his confinement. Altmayer rose in surprise to greet him.

"You're looking well, Dick," Stock said.

He himself was not. His complexion had grayed. He still wore his naval captain's uniform, but his body stooped slightly within it. He was to die within the year, a fact of which he was not completely unaware. It did not bother him much. He thought repeatedly, I have lived the years I've had to live.

Altmayer, who looked the older of the two, had yet more than nine years to live. He said, "An unexpected pleasure, Jeff, but this time you can't have come to imprison me. I'm in prison already."

"I've come to set you free, if you would like."

"For what purpose, Jeff? Surely you have a purpose? A clever way of using me?"

Stock's smile was merely a momentary twitch. He said, "A way of using you, truly, but this time you will approve. . . . We are at war."

"With whom?" Altmayer was startled.

"With the Diaboli. We have been at war for six months."

Altmayer brought his hands together, thin fingers interlacing nervously, "I've heard nothing of this."

"I know." The Coordinator clasped his hands behind his back and was distantly surprised to find that they were trembling. He said, "It's been a long journey for the two of us, Dick. We've had the same goal, you and I— No, let me speak. I've often wanted to explain my point of view to you, but you would never have understood. You weren't the kind of man to understand, until I had the results for you. —I was twenty-five when I first visited a Diaboli world, Dick. I knew then it was either they or we."

"I said so," whispered Altmayer, "from the first."

"Merely saying so was not enough. You wanted to force the human governments to unite against them and that notion was politically unrealistic and completely impossible. It wasn't even desirable. Humans are not Diaboli. Among the Diaboli individual consciousness is low, almost nonexistent. Ours is almost overpowering. They have no such thing as politics; we have nothing else. They can never disagree, can have nothing but a single government. We can never agree; if we had a single island to live on, we would split it in three.

"*But our very disagreements are our strength!* Your Federalist party used to speak of ancient Greece a great deal once. Do you remember? But your people always missed the point. To be sure, Greece could never unite and was therefore ultimately conquered. But even in her state of disunion, she defeated the gigantic Persian Empire. Why?

"I would like to point out that the Greek city-states over centuries had fought with one another. They were forced to specialize in things military to an extent far beyond the Persians. Even the Persians themselves realized that, and in the last century of their imperial existence, Greek mercenaries formed the most valued parts of their armies.

"The same might be said of the small nation-states of preatomic Europe, which in centuries of fighting had advanced their military arts to the point where they could overcome and hold for two hundred years the comparatively gigantic empires of Asia.

"So it is with us. The Diaboli, with vast extents of galactic space, have never fought a war. Their military machine is massive, but untried. In fifty years, only such advances have been made by them as they have been able to copy from the various human navies. Humanity, on the other hand, has competed ferociously in warfare. Each government has raced to keep ahead of its neighbors in military science. They've had to! It was our own disunion that made the terrible race for survival necessary, so that in the end almost any one of us was a match for all the Diaboli, provided only that none of us would fight on their side in a general war.

"It was toward the prevention of such a development that all of Earth's diplomacy has been aimed. Until it was certain that in a war between Earth and the Diaboli, the rest of humanity would be at least neutral, there could be no war, and no union of human governments could be allowed, since the race for military perfection must continue. Once we were sure of neutrality, through the hoax that broke up the conference two years ago, we sought the war, and now we have it."

Altmayer, through all this, might have been frozen. It was a long time before he could say anything.

Finally, "What if the Diaboli are victorious after all?"

Stock said, "They aren't. Two weeks ago, the main fleets joined action and theirs was annihilated with practically no loss to ourselves, although we were greatly outnumbered. We might have been fighting unarmed ships. We had stronger weapons of greater range and more accurate sighting. We had three times their effective speed since we had antiacceleration devices which they lacked. Since the battle a dozen of the other human governments have decided to join the winning side and have declared war on the Diaboli. Yesterday the Diaboli requested that negotiations for an armistice be opened. The war is practically over; and henceforward the Diaboli will be confined to their original planets with only such future expansions as we permit."

Altmayer murmured incoherently.

Stock said, "And now union becomes necessary. After the defeat of Persia by the Greek city-states, they were ruined because of their continued wars among themselves, so that first Macedon and then Rome conquered them. After Europe colonized the Americas, cut up Africa, and conquered Asia, a series of continued European wars led to European ruin.

"Disunion until conquest; union thereafter! But now union is easy. Let one subdivision succeed by itself and the rest will clamor to become part of that success. The ancient writer, Toynbee, first pointed out this difference between what he called a 'dominant minority' and a 'creative minority.'

"We are a creative minority now. In an almost spontaneous gesture, various human governments have suggested the formation of a United Worlds organization. Over seventy governments are willing to attend the first sessions in order to draw up a Charter of Federation. The others will join later, I am sure. We would like you to be one of the delegates from Earth, Dick."

Altmayer found his eyes flooding, "I—I don't understand your purpose. Is this all true?"

"It is all exactly as I say. You were a voice in the wilderness, Dick, crying for union. Your words will carry much weight. What did you once say: 'In a good cause, there are no failures.' "

"No!" said Altmayer, with sudden energy. "It seems your cause was the good one."

Stock's face was hard and devoid of emotion, "You were always a misunderstander of human nature, Dick. When the United Worlds is a reality and when generations of men and women look back to these days of war through their centuries of unbroken peace, they will have forgotten the purpose of my methods. To them they will represent war and death. *Your* calls for union, *your* idealism, will be remembered forever."

He turned away and Altmayer barely caught his last words: "And when they build their statues, they will build none for me."

In the Great Court, which stands as a patch of untouched peace among the fifty busy square miles devoted to the towering buildings that are the pulse beat of the United Worlds of the Galaxy, stands a statue . . .

What If—

Norman and Livvy were late, naturally, since catching a train is always a matter of last-minute delays, so they had to take the only available seat in the coach. It was the one toward the front; the one with nothing before it but the seat that faced wrong way, with its back hard against the front partition. While Norman heaved the suitcase onto the rack, Livvy found herself chafing a little.

If a couple took the wrong-way seat before them, they would be staring self-consciously into each others' faces all the hours it would take to reach New York; or else, which was scarcely better, they would have to erect synthetic barriers of newspaper. Still, there was no use in taking a chance on there being another unoccupied double seat elsewhere in the train.

Norman didn't seem to mind, and that was a little disappointing to Livvy. Usually they held their moods in common. That, Norman claimed, was why he remained sure that he had married the right girl.

He would say, "We fit each other, Livvy, and that's the key fact. When you're doing a jigsaw puzzle and one piece fits another, that's it. There are no other possibilities, and of course there are no other girls."

And she would laugh and say, "If you hadn't been on the streetcar that day, you would probably never have met me. What would you have done then?"

"Stayed a bachelor. Naturally. Besides, I would have met you through Georgette another day."

"It wouldn't have been the same."

"Sure it would."

"No, it wouldn't. Besides, Georgette would never have introduced me. She was interested in you herself, and she's the type who knows better than to create a possible rival."

"What nonsense."

Livvy asked her favorite question: "Norman, what if you had been one minute later at the streetcar corner and had taken the next car? What *do* you suppose would have happened?"

"And what if fish had wings and all of them flew to the top of the mountains? What would we have to eat on Fridays then?"

But they *had* caught the streetcar, and fish *didn't* have wings, so that now they had been married five years and ate fish on Fridays. And because they had been married five years, they were going to celebrate by spending a week in New York.

Then she remembered the present problem. "I wish we could have found some other seat."

Norman said, "Sure. So do I. But no one has taken it yet, so we'll have relative privacy as far as Providence, anyway."

Livvy was unconsoled, and felt herself justified when a plump little man walked down the central aisle of the coach. Now, where had he come from? The train was halfway between Boston and Providence, and if he had had a seat, why hadn't he kept it? She took out her vanity and considered her reflection. She had a theory that if she ignored the little man, he would pass by. So she concentrated on her light-brown hair which, in the rush of catching the train, had become disarranged just a little; at her blue eyes, and at her little mouth with the plump lips which Norman said looked like a permanent kiss.

Not bad, she thought.

Then she looked up, and the little man was in the seat opposite. He caught her eye and grinned widely. A series of lines curled about the edges of his smile. He lifted his hat hastily and put it down beside him on top of the little black box he had been carrying. A circle of white hair instantly sprang up stiffly about the large bald spot that made the center of his skull a desert.

She could not help smiling back a little, but then she caught sight of the black box again and the smile faded. She yanked at Norman's elbow.

Norman looked up from his newspaper. He had startlingly dark eyebrows that almost met above the bridge of his nose, giving him a formidable first appearance. But they and the dark eyes beneath bent upon her now with only the usual look of pleased and somewhat amused affection.

He said, "What's up?" He did not look at the plump little man opposite.

Livvy did her best to indicate what she saw by a little unobtrusive gesture of her hand and head. But the little man was watching and she felt a fool, since Norman simply stared at her blankly.

Finally she pulled him closer and whispered, "Don't you see what's printed on his box?"

She looked again as she said it, and there was no mistake. It was not very prominent, but the light caught it slantingly and it was a slightly more glistening area on a black background. In flowing script it said, "What If."

The little man was smiling again. He nodded his head rapidly and pointed to the words and then to himself several times over.

Norman said in an aside, "Must be his name."

Livvy replied, "Oh, how could that be anybody's name?"

Norman put his paper aside. "I'll show you." He leaned over and said, "Mr. If?"

The little man looked at him eagerly.

"Do you have the time, Mr. If?"

The little man took out a large watch from his vest pocket and displayed the dial.

"Thank you, Mr. If," said Norman. And again in a whisper, "See, Livvy."

He would have returned to his paper, but the little man was opening his box and raising a finger periodically as he did so, to enforce their attention. It was just a slab of frosted glass that he removed—about six by nine inches in length and width and perhaps an inch thick. It had beveled edges, rounded corners, and was completely featureless. Then he took out a little wire stand on which the glass slab fitted comfortably. He rested the combination on his knees and looked proudly at them.

Livvy said, with sudden excitement, "Heavens, Norman, it's a picture of some sort."

Norman bent close. Then he looked at the little man. "What's this? A new kind of television?"

The little man shook his head, and Livvy said, "No, Norman, it's *us.*"

"What?"

"Don't you see? That's the streetcar we met on. There you are in the back seat wearing that old fedora I threw away three years ago. And that's Georgette and myself getting on. The fat lady's in the way. Now! Can't you see us?"

He muttered, "It's some sort of illusion."

"But you see it too, don't you? That's why he calls this 'What If.' It will *show* us what if. What if the streetcar hadn't swerved . . ."

She was sure of it. She was very excited and very sure of it. As she looked at the picture in the glass slab, the late afternoon sunshine grew dimmer and the inchoate chatter of the passengers around and behind them began fading.

How she remembered that day. Norman knew Georgette and had been about to surrender his seat to her when the car swerved and threw Livvy into his lap. It was such a ridiculously corny situation, but it had worked. She had been so embarrassed that he was forced first into gallantry and then into conversation. An introduction from Georgette was not even necessary. By the time they got off the streetcar, he knew where she worked.

She could still remember Georgette glowering at her, sulkily forcing a smile when they themselves separated. Georgette said, "Norman seems to like you."

Livvy replied, "Oh, don't be silly! He was just being polite. But he is nice-looking, isn't he?"

It was only six months after that that they married.

And now here was that same streetcar again, with Norman and herself and Georgette. As she thought that, the smooth train noises, the rapid clack-clack of the wheels, vanished completely. Instead, she was in the swaying confines of the streetcar. She had just boarded it with Georgette at the previous stop.

Livvy shifted weight with the swaying of the streetcar, as did forty others, sitting and standing, all to the same monotonous and rather ridiculous rhythm. She said, "Somebody's motioning at you, Georgette. Do you know him?"

"At me?" Georgette directed a deliberately casual glance over her shoulder. Her artificially long eyelashes flickered. She said, "I know him a little. What do you suppose he wants?"

"Let's find out," said Livvy. She felt pleased and a little wicked.

Georgette had a well-known habit of hoarding her male acquaintances, and it was rather fun to annoy her this way. And besides, this one seemed quite . . . interesting.

She snaked past the line of standees, and Georgette followed without enthusiasm. It was just as Livvy arrived opposite the young man's seat that the streetcar lurched heavily as it rounded a curve. Livvy snatched desperately in the direction of the straps. Her fingertips caught and she held on. It was a long moment before she could breathe. For some reason, it had seemed that there were no straps close enough to be reached. Somehow, she felt that by all the laws of nature she should have fallen.

The young man did not look at her. He was smiling at Georgette and rising from his seat. He had astonishing eyebrows that gave him a rather competent and self-confident appearance. Livvy decided that she definitely liked him.

Georgette was saying, "Oh no, don't bother. We're getting off in about two stops."

They did. Livvy said, "I thought we were going to Sach's."

"We are. There's just something I remember having to attend to here. It won't take but a minute."

"Next stop, Providence!" the loud-speakers were blaring. The train was slowing and the world of the past had shrunk itself into the glass slab once more. The little man was still smiling at them.

Livvy turned to Norman. She felt a little frightened. "Were you through all that, too?"

He said, "What happened to the time? We *can't* be reaching Providence yet?" He looked at his watch. "I guess we are." Then, to Livvy, "You didn't fall that time."

"Then you *did* see it?" She frowned. "Now, that's like Georgette. I'm sure there was no reason to get off the streetcar except to prevent my meeting you. How long had you known Georgette before then, Norman?"

"Not very long. Just enough to be able to recognize her at sight and to feel that I ought to offer her my seat."

Livvy curled her lip.

Norman grinned, "You can't be jealous of a might-have-been, kid. Besides, what difference would it have made? I'd have been sufficiently interested in you to work out a way of meeting you."

"You didn't even look at me."

"I hardly had the chance."

"Then how would you have met me?"

"Some way. I don't know how. But you'll admit this is a rather foolish argument we're having."

They were leaving Providence. Livvy felt a trouble in her mind. The little man had been following their whispered conversation, with only the loss of his smile to show that he understood. She said to him, "Can you show us more?"

Norman interrupted, "Wait now, Livvy. What are you going to try to do?"

She said, "I want to see our wedding day. What it would have been if I had caught the strap."

Norman was visibly annoyed. "Now, that's not fair. We might not have been married on the same day, you know."

But she said, "Can you show it to me, Mr. If?" and the little man nodded.

The slab of glass was coming alive again, glowing a little. Then the light collected and condensed into figures. A tiny sound of organ music was in Livvy's ears without there actually being sound.

Norman said with relief, "Well, there I am. That's our wedding. Are you satisfied?"

The train sounds were disappearing again, and the last thing Livvy heard was her own voice saying, "Yes, there *you* are. But where am *I?*"

Livvy was well back in the pews. For a while she had not expected to attend at all. In the past months she had drifted further and further away from Georgette, without quite knowing why. She had heard of her engagement only through a mutual friend, and, of course, it was to Norman. She remembered very clearly that day, six months before, when she had first seen him on the streetcar. It was the time Georgette had so quickly snatched her out of sight. She had met him since on several occasions, but each time Georgette was with him, standing between.

Well, she had no cause for resentment; the man was certainly none of hers. Georgette, she thought, looked more beautiful than she really was. And *he* was very handsome indeed.

She felt sad and rather empty, as though something had, gone wrong—something that she could not quite outline in her mind. Georgette had moved up the aisle without seeming to see her, but earlier she had caught *his* eyes and smiled at him. Livvy thought he had smiled in return.

She heard the words distantly as they drifted back to her, "I now pronounce you—"

The noise of the train was back. A woman swayed down the aisle, herding a little boy back to their seats. There were intermittent bursts of girlish laughter from a set of four teenage girls halfway down the coach. A conductor hurried past on some mysterious errand.

Livvy was frozenly aware of it all.

She sat there, staring straight ahead, while the trees outside blended into a fuzzy, furious green and the telephone poles galloped past.

She said, "It was *she* you married."

He stared at her for a moment and then one side of his mouth quirked a little. He said lightly, "I didn't really, Olivia. You're still my wife, you know. Just think about it for a few minutes."

She turned to him. "Yes, you married me—because I fell in your lap. If I hadn't, you would have married Georgette. If she hadn't wanted you, you would have married someone else. You would have married *anybody*. So much for your jigsaw-puzzle pieces."

Norman said very slowly, "Well—I'll—be—darned!" He put both hands to his head and smoothed down the straight hair over his ears where it had a tendency to tuft up. For the moment it gave him the appearance of trying to hold his head together. He said, "Now, look here, Livvy, you're making a silly fuss over a stupid magician's trick. You can't blame me for something I haven't done."

"You would have done it."

"How do you know?"

"You've seen it."

"I've seen a ridiculous piece of—of hypnotism, I suppose." His voice suddenly raised itself into anger. He turned to the little man opposite. "Off with you, Mr. If, or whatever your name is. Get out of here. We don't want you. Get out before I throw your little trick out the window and you after it."

Livvy yanked at his elbow. "Stop it. *Stop it!* You're in a crowded train."

The little man shrank back into the corner of the seat as far as he could go and held his little black bag behind him. Norman looked at him, then at Livvy, then at the elderly lady across the way who was regarding him with patent disapproval.

He turned pink and bit back a pungent remark. They rode in frozen silence to and through New London.

Fifteen minutes past New London, Norman said, "Livvy!"

She said nothing. She was looking out the window but saw nothing but the glass.

He said again, "Livvy! Livvy! Answer me!"

She said dully, "What do you want?"

He said, "Look, this is all nonsense. I don't know how the fellow does it, but even granting it's legitimate, you're not being fair. Why stop where you did? Suppose I *had* married Georgette, do you suppose *you* would have stayed single? For all I know, you were already married at the time of my supposed wedding. Maybe that's why I married Georgette."

"I wasn't married."

"How do you know?"

"I would have been able to tell. I knew what my own thoughts were."

"Then you would have been married within the next year."

Livvy grew angrier. The fact that a sane remnant within her clamored at the unreason of her anger did not soothe her. It irritated her further, instead. She said, "And if I did, it would be no business of yours, certainly."

"Of course it wouldn't. But it would make the point that in the world of reality we can't be held responsible for the 'what ifs.' "

Livvy's nostrils flared. She said nothing.

Norman said, "Look! You remember the big New Year's celebration at Winnie's place year before last?"

"I certainly do. You spilled a keg of alcohol all over me."

"That's beside the point, and besides, it was only a cocktail shaker's worth. What I'm trying to say is that Winnie is just about your best friend and had been long before you married me."

"What of it?"

"Georgette was a good friend of hers too, wasn't she?"

"Yes."

"All right, then. You and Georgette would have gone to the party regardless of which one of you I had married. I would have had nothing to do with it. Let him show us the party as it would have been if I had married Georgette, and I'll bet you'd be there with either your fiancé or your husband."

Livvy hesitated. She felt honestly afraid of just that.

He said, "Are you afraid to take the chance?"

And that, of course, decided her. She turned on him furiously. "No, I'm not! And I hope I *am* married. There's no reason I should pine for you. What's more, I'd like to see what happens when you spill the shaker all over

Georgette. She'll fill both your ears for you, and in public, too. I know *her*. Maybe you'll see a certain difference in the jigsaw pieces then." She faced forward and crossed her arms angrily and firmly across her chest.

Norman looked across at the little man, but there was no need to say anything. The glass slab was on his lap already. The sun slanted in from the west, and the white foam of hair that topped his head was edged with pink.

Norman said tensely, "Ready?"

Livvy nodded and let the noise of the train slide away again.

Livvy stood, a little flushed with recent cold, in the doorway. She had just removed her coat, with its sprinkling of snow, and her bare arms were still rebelling at the touch of open air.

She answered the shouts that greeted her with "Happy New Years" of her own, raising her voice to make herself heard over the squealing of the radio. Georgette's shrill tones were almost the first thing she heard upon entering, and now she steered toward her. She hadn't seen Georgette, or Norman, in weeks.

Georgette lifted an eyebrow, a mannerism she had lately cultivated, and said, "Isn't anyone with you, Olivia?" Her eyes swept the immediate sur-roundings and then returned to Livvy.

Livvy said indifferently, "I think Dick will be around later. There was something or other he had to do first." She felt as indifferent as she sounded.

Georgette smiled tightly. "Well, Norman's here. That ought to keep you from being lonely, dear. At least, it's turned out that way before."

And as she said so, Norman sauntered in from the kitchen. He had a cocktail shaker in his hand, and the rattling of ice cubes castanetted his words. "Line up, you rioting revelers, and get a mixture that will really revel your riots— Why, Livvy!"

He walked toward her, grinning his welcome, "Where've you been keep-ing yourself? I haven't seen you in twenty years, seems like. What's the matter? Doesn't Dick want anyone else to see you?"

"Fill my glass, Norman," said Georgette sharply.

"Right away," he said, not looking at her. "Do you want one too, Livvy? I'll get you a glass." He turned, and everything happened at once.

Livvy cried, "Watch out!" She saw it coming, even had a vague feeling that all this had happened before, but it played itself out inexorably. His heel caught the edge of the carpet; he lurched, tried to right himself, and lost the cocktail shaker. It seemed to jump out of his hands, and a pint of ice-cold liquor drenched Livvy from shoulder to hem.

She stood there, gasping. The noises muted about her, and for a few intolerable moments she made futile brushing gestures at her gown, while Norman kept repeating, "Damnation!" in rising tones.

Georgette said coolly, "It's too bad, Livvy. Just one of those things. I imagine the dress can't be very expensive."

Livvy turned and ran. She was in the bedroom, which was at least empty and relatively quiet. By the light of the fringe-shaded lamp on the dresser, she poked among the coats on the bed, looking for her own.

Norman had come in behind her. "Look, Livvy, don't pay any attention to what she said. I'm really devilishly sorry. I'll pay—"

"That's all right. It wasn't your fault." She blinked rapidly and didn't look at him. "I'll just go home and change."

"Are you coming back?"

"I don't know. I don't think so."

"Look, Livvy . . ." His warm fingers were on her shoulders—

Livvy felt a queer tearing sensation deep inside her, as though she were ripping away from clinging cobwebs and—

—and the train noises were back.

Something *did* go wrong with the time when she was in there—in the slab. It was deep twilight now. The train lights were on. But it didn't matter. She seemed to be recovering from the wrench inside her.

Norman was rubbing his eyes with thumb and forefinger. "What happened?"

Livvy said, "It just ended. Suddenly."

Norman said uneasily, "You know, we'll be putting into New Haven soon." He looked at his watch and shook his head.

Livvy said wonderingly, "You spilled it on me."

"Well, so I did in real life."

"But in real life I was your wife. You ought to have spilled it on Georgette this time. Isn't that queer?" But she was thinking of Norman pursuing her; his hands on her shoulders. . . .

She looked up at him and said with warm satisfaction, "I wasn't married."

"No, you weren't. But was that Dick Reinhardt you were going around with?"

"Yes."

"You weren't planning to marry him, were you, Livvy?"

"Jealous, Norman?"

Norman looked confused. "Of that? Of a slab of glass? Of course not."

"I don't think I would have married him."

Norman said, "You know, I wish it hadn't ended when it did. There was something that was about to happen, I think." He stopped, then added slowly, "It was as though I would rather have done it to anybody else in the room."

"Even to Georgette."

"I wasn't giving two thoughts to Georgette. You don't believe me, I suppose."

"Maybe I do." She looked up at him. "I've been silly, Norman. Let's— let's live our real life. Let's not play with all the things that just might have been."

But he caught her hands. "No, Livvy. One last time. Let's see what we would have been doing right now, Livvy! This very minute! If I had married Georgette."

Livvy was a little frightened. "Let's not, Norman." She was thinking of his eyes, smiling hungrily at her as he held the shaker, while Georgette stood beside her, unregarded. She didn't *want* to know what happened afterward. She just wanted this life now, this *good* life.

New Haven came and went.

Norman said again, "I want to try, Livvy."

She said, "If you want to, Norman." She decided fiercely that it wouldn't matter. Nothing would matter. Her hands reached out and encircled his arm. She held it tightly, and while she held it she thought: "Nothing in the make-believe can take him from me."

Norman said to the little man, "Set 'em up again."

In the yellow light the process seemed to be slower. Gently the frosted slab cleared, like clouds being torn apart and dispersed by an unfelt wind.

Norman was saying, "There's something wrong. That's just the two of us, exactly as we are now."

He was right. Two little figures were sitting in a train on the seats which were farthest toward the front. The field was enlarging now—they were merging into it. Norman's voice was distant and fading.

"It's the same train," he was saying. "The window in back is cracked just as—"

Livvy was blindingly happy. She said, "I wish we were in New York."

He said, "It will be less than an hour, darling." Then he said, "I'm going to kiss you." He made a movement, as though he were about to begin.

"Not here! Oh, Norman, people are looking."

Norman drew back. He said, "We should have taken a taxi."

"From Boston to New York?"

"Sure. The privacy would have been worth it."

She laughed. "You're funny when you try to act ardent."

"It isn't an act." His voice was suddenly a little somber. "It's not just an hour, you know. I feel as though I've been waiting five years."

"I do, too."

"Why couldn't I have met you first? It was such a waste."

"Poor Georgette," Livvy sighed.

Norman moved impatiently. "Don't be sorry for her, Livvy. We never really made a go of it. She was glad to get rid of me."

"I know that. That's why I say 'Poor Georgette.' I'm just sorry for her for not being able to appreciate what she had."

"Well, see to it that *you* do," he said. "See to it that you're immensely appreciative, infinitely appreciative—or more than that, see that you're at least half as appreciative as I am of what *I've* got."

"Or else you'll divorce me, too?"

"Over my dead body," said Norman.

Livvy said, "It's all so strange. I keep thinking; 'What if you hadn't spilt the cocktails on me that time at the party?' You wouldn't have followed me out; you wouldn't have told me; I wouldn't have known. It would have been so different . . . everything."

"Nonsense. It would have been just the same. It would have all happened another time."

"I wonder," said Livvy softly.

Train noises merged into train noises. City lights flickered outside, and the atmosphere of New York was about them. The coach was astir with travelers dividing the baggage among themselves.

Livvy was an island in the turmoil until Norman shook her.

She looked at him and said, "The jigsaw pieces fit after all."

He said, "Yes."

She put a hand on his. "But it wasn't good, just the same. I was very wrong. I thought that because we had each other, we should have all the *possible* each others. But all the possibles are none of our business. The real is enough. Do you know what I mean?"

He nodded.

She said, "There are millions of other *what ifs*. I don't want to know what happened in any of them. I'll never say 'What if' again."

Norman said, "Relax, dear. Here's your coat." And he reached for the suitcases.

Livvy said with sudden sharpness, "Where's Mr. If?"

Norman turned slowly to the empty seat that faced them. Together they scanned the rest of the coach.

"Maybe," Norman said, "he went into the next coach."

"But why? Besides, he wouldn't leave his hat." And she bent to pick it up.

Norman said, "What hat?"

And Livvy stopped her fingers hovering over nothingness. She said, "It was here—I almost touched it." She straightened and said, "Oh, Norman, what if—"

Norman put a finger on her mouth. "Darling . . ."

She said, "I'm sorry. Here, let me help you with the suitcases."

The train dived into the tunnel beneath Park Avenue, and the noise of the wheels rose to a roar.

Sally

Sally was coming down the lake road, so I waved to her and called her by name. I always liked to see Sally. I liked all of them, you understand, but Sally's the prettiest one of the lot. There just isn't any question about it.

She moved a little faster when I waved to her. Nothing undignified. She was never that. She moved just enough faster to show that she was glad to see me, too.

I turned to the man standing beside me. "That's Sally," I said.

He smiled at me and nodded.

Mrs. Hester had brought him in. She said, "This is Mr. Gellhorn, Jake. You remember he sent you the letter asking for an appointment."

That was just talk, really. I have a million things to do around the Farm, and one thing I just can't waste my time on is mail. That's why I have Mrs. Hester around. She lives pretty close by, she's good at attending to foolishness without running to me about it, and most of all, she likes Sally and the rest. Some people don't.

"Glad to see you, Mr. Gellhorn," I said.

"Raymond J. Gellhorn," he said, and gave me his hand, which I shook and gave back.

He was a largish fellow, half a head taller than I and wider, too. He was about half my age, thirtyish. He had black hair, plastered down slick, with a part in the middle, and a thin mustache, very neatly trimmed. His jawbones got big under his ears and made him look as if he had a slight case of mumps. On video he'd be a natural to play the villain, so I assumed he was a nice fellow. It goes to show that video can't be wrong all the time.

"I'm Jacob Folkers," I said. "What can I do for you?"

He grinned. It was a big, wide, white-toothed grin. "You can tell me a little about your Farm here, if you don't mind."

I heard Sally coming up behind me and I put out my hand. She slid right into it and the feel of the hard, glossy enamel of her fender was warm in my palm.

"A nice automatobile," said Gellhorn.

That's one way of putting it. Sally was a 2045 convertible with a Hennis-Carleton positronic motor and an Armat chassis. She had the cleanest, finest lines I've ever seen on any model, bar none. For five years, she'd been my favorite, and I'd put everything into her I could dream up. In all that time, there'd never been a human being behind her wheel.

Not once.

"Sally," I said, patting her gently, "meet Mr. Gellhorn."

Sally's cylinder-purr keyed up a little. I listened carefully for any knocking. Lately, I'd been hearing motor-knock in almost all the cars and changing the gasoline hadn't done a bit of good. Sally was as smooth as her paint job this time, however.

"Do you have names for all your cars?" asked Gellhorn.

He sounded amused, and Mrs. Hester doesn't like people to sound as though they were making fun of the Farm. She said, sharply, "Certainly. The cars have real personalities, don't they, Jake? The sedans are all males and the convertibles are females."

Gellhorn was smiling again. "And do you keep them in separate garages, ma'am?"

Mrs. Hester glared at him.

Gellhorn said to me, "And now I wonder if I can talk to you alone, Mr. Folkers?"

"That depends," I said. "Are you a reporter?"

"No, sir. I'm a sales agent. Any talk we have is not for publication. I assure you I am interested in strict privacy."

"Let's walk down the road a bit. There's a bench we can use."

We started down. Mrs. Hester walked away. Sally nudged along after us. I said, "You don't mind if Sally comes along, do you?"

"Not at all. She can't repeat what we say, can she?" He laughed at his own joke, reached over and rubbed Sally's grille.

Sally raced her motor and Gellhorn's hand drew away quickly.

"She's not used to strangers," I explained.

We sat down on the bench under the big oak tree where we could look across the small lake to the private speedway. It was the warm part of the day and the cars were out in force, at least thirty of them. Even at this distance I could see that Jeremiah was pulling his usual stunt of sneaking up behind some staid older model, then putting on a jerk of speed and yowling past with deliberately squealing brakes. Two weeks before he had crowded old Angus off the asphalt altogether, and I had turned off his motor for two days.

It didn't help though, I'm afraid, and it looks as though there's nothing to be done about it. Jeremiah is a sports model to begin with and that kind is awfully hot-headed.

"Well, Mr. Gellhorn," I said. "Could you tell me why you want the information?"

But he was just looking around. He said, "This *is* an amazing place, Mr. Folkers."

"I wish you'd call me Jake. Everyone does."

"All right, Jake. How many cars do you have here?"

"Fifty-one. We get one or two new ones every year. One year we got five. We haven't lost one yet. They're all in perfect running order. We even have a '15 model Mat-O-Mot in working order. One of the original automatics. It was the first car here."

Good old Matthew. He stayed in the garage most of the day now, but then he was the granddaddy of all positronic-motored cars. Those were the days when blind war veterans, paraplegics and heads of state were the only ones who drove automatics. But Samson Harridge was my boss and he was rich enough to be able to get one. I was his chauffeur at the time.

The thought makes me feel old. I can remember when there wasn't an automobile in the world with brains enough to find its own way home. I chauffeured dead lumps of machines that needed a man's hand at their controls every minute. Every year machines like that used to kill tens of thousands of people.

The automatics fixed that. A positronic brain can react much faster than a human one, of course, and it paid people to keep hands off the controls. You got in, punched your destination and let it go its own way.

We take it for granted now, but I remember when the first laws came out forcing the old machines off the highways and limiting travel to automatics. Lord, what a fuss. They called it everything from communism to fascism, but it emptied the highways and stopped the killing, and still more people get around more easily the new way.

Of course, the automatics were ten to a hundred times as expensive as the hand-driven ones, and there weren't many that could afford a private vehicle. The industry specialized in turning out omni-bus-automatics. You could always call a company and have one stop at your door in a matter of minutes and take you where you wanted to go. Usually, you had to drive with others who were going your way, but what's wrong with that?

Samson Harridge had a private car though, and I went to him the minute it arrived. The car wasn't Matthew to me then. I didn't know it was going to be the dean of the Farm some day. I only knew it was taking my job away and I hated it.

I said, "You won't be needing me any more, Mr. Harridge?"

He said, "What are you dithering about, Jake? You don't think I'll trust myself to a contraption like that, do you? You stay right at the controls."

I said, "But it works by itself, Mr. Harridge. It scans the road, reacts properly to obstacles, humans, and other cars, and remembers routes to travel."

"So they say. So they say. Just the same, you're sitting right behind the wheel in case anything goes wrong."

Funny how you can get to like a car. In no time I was calling it Matthew and was spending all my time keeping it polished and humming. A positronic brain stays in condition best when it's got control of its chassis at all times, which means it's worth keeping the gas tank filled so that the motor can turn over slowly day and night. After a while, it got so I could tell by the sound of the motor how Matthew felt.

In his own way, Harridge grew fond of Matthew, too. He had no one else to like. He'd divorced or outlived three wives and outlived five children and three grandchildren. So when he died, maybe it wasn't surprising that he had his estate converted into a Farm for Retired Automobiles, with me in charge and Matthew the first member of a distinguished line.

It's turned out to be my life. I never got married. You can't get married and still tend to automatics the way you should.

The newspapers thought it was funny, but after a while they stopped joking about it. Some things you can't joke about. Maybe you've never been able to afford an automatic and maybe you never will, either, but take it from me, you get to love them. They're hard-working and affectionate. It takes a man with no heart to mistreat one or to see one mistreated.

It got so that after a man had an automatic for a while, he would make provisions for having it left to the Farm, if he didn't have an heir he could rely on to give it good care.

I explained that to Gellhorn.

He said, "Fifty-one cars! That represents a lot of money."

"Fifty thousand minimum per automatic, original investment," I said. "They're worth a lot more now. I've done things for them."

"It must take a lot of money to keep up the Farm."

"You're right there. The Farm's a non-profit organization, which gives us a break on taxes and, of course, new automatics that come in usually have trust funds attached. Still, costs are always going up. I have to keep the place landscaped; I keep laying down new asphalt and keeping the old in repair; there's gasoline, oil, repairs, and new gadgets. It adds up."

"And you've spent a long time at it."

"I sure have, Mr. Gellhorn. Thirty-three years."

"You don't seem to be getting much out of it yourself."

"I don't? You surprise me, Mr. Gellhorn. I've got Sally and fifty others. Look at her."

I was grinning. I couldn't help it. Sally was so clean, it almost hurt. Some insect must have died on her windshield or one speck of dust too many had landed, so she was going to work. A little tube protruded and spurted Tergosol over the glass. It spread quickly over the silicone surface film and squeejees snapped into place instantly, passing over the windshield and forcing the water into the little channel that led it, dripping, down to the ground. Not a speck of water got onto her glistening apple-green hood. Squeejee and detergent tube snapped back into place and disappeared.

Gellhorn said, "I never saw an automatic do that."

"I guess not," I said. "I fixed that up specially on our cars. They're clean. They're always scrubbing their glass. They like it. I've even got Sally fixed up with wax jets. She polishes herself every night till you can see your face in any part of her and shave by it. If I can scrape up the money, I'd be putting it on the rest of the girls. Convertibles are very vain."

"I can tell you how to scrape up the money, if that interests you."

"That always does. How?"

"Isn't it obvious, Jake? Any of your cars is worth fifty thousand minimum, you said. I'll bet most of them top six figures."

"So?"

"Ever think of selling a few?"

I shook my head. "You don't realize it, I guess, Mr. Gellhorn, but I can't sell any of these. They belong to the Farm, not to me."

"The money would go to the Farm."

"The incorporation papers of the Farm provide that the cars receive perpetual care. They can't be sold."

"What about the motors, then?"

"I don't understand you."

Gellhorn shifted position and his voice got confidential. "Look here, Jake, let me explain the situation. There's a big market for private automatics if they could only be made cheaply enough. Right?"

"That's no secret."

"And ninety-five per cent of the cost is the motor. Right? Now, I know where we can get a supply of bodies. I also know where we can sell automatics at a good price—twenty or thirty thousand for the cheaper models, maybe fifty or sixty for the better ones. All I need are the motors. You see the solution?"

"I don't, Mr. Gellhorn." I did, but I wanted him to spell it out.

"It's right here. You've got fifty-one of them. You're an expert automatobile mechanic, Jake. You must be. You could unhook a motor and place it in another car so that no one would know the difference."

"It wouldn't be exactly ethical."

"You wouldn't be harming the cars. You'd be doing them a favor. Use your older cars. Use that old Mat-O-Mot."

"Well, now, wait a while, Mr. Gellhorn. The motors and bodies aren't two separate items. They're a single unit. Those motors are used to their own bodies. They wouldn't be happy in another car."

"All right, that's a point. That's a very good point, Jake. It would be like taking your mind and putting it in someone else's skull. Right? You don't think you would like that?"

"I don't think I would. No."

"But what if I took your mind and put it into the body of a young athlete. What about that, Jake? You're not a youngster anymore. If you had the chance, wouldn't you enjoy being twenty again? That's what I'm offering some of your positronic motors. They'll be put into new '57 bodies. The latest construction."

I laughed. "That doesn't make much sense, Mr. Gellhorn. Some of our cars may be old, but they're well-cared for. Nobody drives them. They're allowed their own way. They're *retired*, Mr. Gellhorn. I wouldn't want a twenty-year-old body if it meant I had to dig ditches for the rest of my new life and never have enough to eat. . . . What do you think, Sally?"

Sally's two doors opened and then shut with a cushioned slam.

"What that?" said Gellhorn.

"That's the way Sally laughs."

Gellhorn forced a smile. I guess he thought I was making a bad joke. He said, "Talk sense, Jake. Cars are *made* to be driven. They're probably not happy if you don't drive them."

I said, "Sally hasn't been driven in five years. She looks happy to me."

"I wonder."

He got up and walked toward Sally slowly. "Hi, Sally, how'd you like a drive?"

Sally's motor revved up. She backed away.

"Don't push her, Mr. Gellhorn," I said. "She's liable to be a little skittish."

Two sedans were about a hundred yards up the road. They had stopped. Maybe, in their own way, they were watching. I didn't bother about them. I had my eyes on Sally, and I kept them there.

Gellhorn said, "Steady now, Sally." He lunged out and seized the door handle. It didn't budge, of course.

He said, "It opened a minute ago."

I said, "Automatic lock. She's got a sense of privacy, Sally has."

He let go, then said, slowly and deliberately, "A car with a sense of privacy shouldn't go around with its top down."

He stepped back three or four paces, then quickly, so quickly I couldn't take a step to stop him, he ran forward and vaulted into the car. He caught

Sally completely by surprise, because as he came down, he shut off the ignition before she could lock it in place.

For the first time in five years, Sally's motor was dead.

I think I yelled, but Gellhorn had the switch on "Manual" and locked that in place, too. He kicked the motor into action. Sally was alive again but she had no freedom of action.

He started up the road. The sedans were still there. They turned and drifted away, not very quickly. I suppose it was all a puzzle to them.

One was Giuseppe, from the Milan factories, and the other was Stephen. They were always together. They were both new at the Farm, but they'd been here long enough to know that our cars just didn't have drivers.

Gellhorn went straight on, and when the sedans finally got it through their heads that Sally wasn't going to slow down, that she *couldn't* slow down, it was too late for anything but desperate measures.

They broke for it, one to each side, and Sally raced between them like a streak. Steve crashed through the lakeside fence and rolled to a halt on the grass and mud not six inches from the water's edge. Giuseppe bumped along the land side of the road to a shaken halt.

I had Steve back on the highway and was trying to find out what harm, if any, the fence had done him, when Gellhorn came back.

Gellhorn opened Sally's door and stepped out. Leaning back, he shut off the ignition a second time.

"There," he said. "I think I did her a lot of good."

I held my temper. "Why did you dash through the sedans? There was no reason for that."

"I kept expecting them to turn out."

"They did. One went through a fence."

"I'm sorry, Jake," he said. "I thought they'd move more quickly. You know how it is. I've been in lots of buses, but I've only been in a private automatic two or three times in my life, and this is the first time I ever drove one. That just shows you, Jake. It got me, driving one, and I'm pretty hard-boiled. I tell you, we don't have to go more than twenty per cent below list price to reach a good market, and it would be ninety per cent profit."

"Which we would split?"

"Fifty-fifty. And I take all the risks, remember."

"All right. I listened to you. Now you listen to me." I raised my voice because I was just too mad to be polite anymore. "When you turn off Sally's motor, you hurt her. How would you like to be kicked unconscious? That's what you do to Sally, when you turn her off."

"You're exaggerating, Jake. The automatobuses get turned off every night."

"Sure, that's why I want none of my boys or girls in your fancy '57 bodies, where I won't know what treatment they'll get. Buses need major repairs in their positronic circuits every couple of years. Old Matthew hasn't had his circuits touched in twenty years. What can you offer him compared with that?"

"Well, you're excited now. Suppose you think over my proposition when you've cooled down and get in touch with me."

"I've thought it over all I want to. If I ever see you again, I'll call the police."

His mouth got hard and ugly. He said, "Just a minute, old-timer."

I said, "Just a minute, you. This is private property and I'm ordering you off."

He shrugged. "Well, then, goodbye."

I said, "Mrs. Hester will see you off the property. Make that goodbye permanent."

But it wasn't permanent. I saw him again two days later. Two and a half days, rather, because it was about noon when I saw him first and a little after midnight when I saw him again.

I sat up in bed when he turned the light on, blinking blindly till I made out what was happening. Once I could see, it didn't take much explaining. In fact, it took none at all. He had a gun in his right fist, the nasty little needle barrel just visible between two fingers. I knew that all he had to do was to increase the pressure of his hand and I would be torn apart.

He said, "Put on your clothes, Jake."

I didn't move. I just watched him.

He said, "Look, Jake, I know the situation. I visited you two days ago, remember. You have no guards on this place, no electrified fences, no warning signals. Nothing."

I said, "I don't need any. Meanwhile there's nothing to stop you from leaving, Mr. Gellhorn. I would if I were you. This place can be very dangerous."

He laughed a little. "It is, for anyone on the wrong side of a fist gun."

"I see it," I said. "I know you've got one."

"Then get a move on. My men are waiting."

"No, sir, Mr. Gellhorn. Not unless you tell me what you want, and probably not then."

"I made you a proposition day before yesterday."

"The answer's still no."

"There's more to the proposition now. I've come here with some men and an automatobus. You have your chance to come with me and disconnect twenty-five of the positronic motors. I don't care which twenty-five you choose. We'll load them on the bus and take them away. Once they're disposed of, I'll see to it that you get your fair share of the money."

"I have your word on that, I suppose."

He didn't act as if he thought I was being sarcastic. He said, "You have."

I said, "No."

"If you insist on saying no, we'll go about it in our own way. I'll disconnect the motors myself, only I'll disconnect all fifty-one. Every one of them."

"It isn't easy to disconnect positronic motors, Mr. Gellhorn. Are you a robotics expert? Even if you are, you know, these motors have been modified by me."

"I know that, Jake. And to be truthful, I'm not an expert. I may ruin quite a few motors trying to get them out. That's why I'll have to work over all fifty-one if you don't cooperate. You see, I may only end up with twenty-five when I'm through. The first few I'll tackle will probably suffer the most. Till I get the hang of it, you see. And if I go it myself, I think I'll put Sally first in line."

I said, "I can't believe you're serious, Mr. Gellhorn."

He said, "I'm serious, Jake." He let it all dribble in. "If you want to help, you can keep Sally. Otherwise, she's liable to be hurt very badly. Sorry."

I said, "I'll come with you, but I'll give you one more warning. You'll be in trouble, Mr. Gellhorn."

He thought that was very funny. He was laughing very quietly as we went down the stairs together.

There was an automatobus waiting outside the driveway to the garage apartments. The shadows of three men waited beside it, and their flash beams went on as we approached.

Gellhorn said in a low voice, "I've got the old fellow. Come on. Move the truck up the drive and let's get started."

One of the others leaned in and punched the proper instructions on the control panel. We moved up the driveway with the bus following submissively.

"It won't go inside the garage," I said. "The door won't take it. We don't have buses here. Only private cars."

"All right," said Gellhorn. "Pull it over onto the grass and keep it out of sight."

I could hear the thrumming of the cars when we were still ten yards from the garage.

Usually they quieted down if I entered the garage. This time they didn't. I think they knew that strangers were about, and once the faces of Gellhorn and the others were visible they got noisier. Each motor was a warm rumble, and each motor was knocking irregularly until the place rattled.

The lights went up automatically as we stepped inside. Gellhorn didn't seem bothered by the car noise, but the three men with him looked surprised and uncomfortable. They had the look of the hired thug about them, a look that was not compounded of physical features so much as of a certain wariness of eye and hang-dogness of face. I knew the type and I wasn't worried.

One of them said, "Damn it, they're burning gas."

"My cars always do," I replied stiffly.

"Not tonight," said Gellhorn. "Turn them off."

"It's not that easy, Mr. Gellhorn," I said.

"Get started!" he said.

I stood there. He had his fist gun pointed at me steadily. I said, "I told you, Mr. Gellhorn, that my cars have been well-treated while they've been at the Farm. They're used to being treated that way, and they resent anything else."

"You have one minute," he said. "Lecture me some other time."

"I'm trying to explain something. I'm trying to explain that my cars can understand what I say to them. A positronic motor will learn to do that with time and patience. My cars have learned. Sally understood your proposition two days ago. You'll remember she laughed when I asked her opinion. She also knows what you did to her and so do the two sedans you scattered. And the rest know what to do about trespassers in general."

"Look, you crazy old fool—"

"All I have to say is—" I raised my voice. "Get them!"

One of the men turned pasty and yelled, but his voice was drowned completely in the sound of fifty-one horns turned loose at once. They held their notes, and within the four walls of the garage the echoes rose to a wild, metallic call. Two cars rolled forward, not hurriedly, but with no possible mistake as to their target. Two cars fell in line behind the first two. All the cars were stirring in their separate stalls.

The thugs stared, then backed.

I shouted, "Don't get up against a wall."

Apparently, they had that instinctive thought themselves. They rushed madly for the door of the garage.

At the door one of Gellhorn's men turned, brought up a fist gun of his own. The needle pellet tore a thin, blue flash toward the first car. The car was Giuseppe.

A thin line of paint peeled up Giuseppe's hood, and the right half of his windshield crazed and splintered but did not break through.

The men were out the door, running, and two by two the cars crunched out after them into the night, their horns calling the charge.

I kept my hand on Gellhorn's elbow, but I don't think he could have moved in any case. His lips were trembling.

I said, "That's why I don't need electrified fences or guards. My property protects itself."

Gellhorn's eyes swiveled back and forth in fascination as, pair by pair, they whizzed by. He said, "They're killers!"

"Don't be silly. They won't kill your men."

"They're killers!"

"They'll just give your men a lesson. My cars have been specially trained for cross-country pursuit for just such an occasion; I think what your men will get will be worse than an outright quick kill. Have you ever been chased by an automatobile?"

Gellhorn didn't answer.

I went on. I didn't want him to miss a thing. "They'll be shadows going no faster than your men, chasing them here, blocking them there, blaring at them, dashing at them, missing with a screech of brake and a thunder of motor. They'll keep it up till your men drop, out of breath and half-dead, waiting for the wheels to crunch over their breaking bones. The cars won't do that. They'll turn away. You can bet, though, that your men will never return here in their lives. Not for all the money you or ten like you could give them. Listen—"

I tightened my hold on his elbow. He strained to hear.

I said, "Don't you hear car doors slamming?"

It was faint and distant, but unmistakable.

I said, "They're laughing. They're enjoying themselves."

His face crumpled with rage. He lifted his hand. He was still holding his fist gun.

I said, "I wouldn't. One automatocar is still with us."

I don't think he had noticed Sally till then. She had moved up so quietly. Though her right front fender nearly touched me, I couldn't hear her motor. She might have been holding her breath.

Gellhorn yelled.

I said, "She won't touch you, as long as I'm with you. But if you kill me. . . . You know, Sally doesn't like you."

Gellhorn turned the gun in Sally's direction.

"Her motor is shielded," I said, "and before you could ever squeeze the gun a second time she would be on top of you."

"All right, then," he yelled, and suddenly my arm was bent behind my back and twisted so I could hardly stand. He held me between Sally and himself, and his pressure didn't let up. "Back out with me and don't try to break loose, old-timer, or I'll tear your arm out of its socket."

I had to move. Sally nudged along with us, worried, uncertain what to do. I tried to say something to her and couldn't. I could only clench my teeth and moan.

Gellhorn's automatobus was still standing outside the garage. I was forced in. Gellhorn jumped in after me, locking the doors.

He said, "All right, now. We'll talk sense."

I was rubbing my arm, trying to get life back into it, and even as I did I was automatically and without any conscious effort studying the control board of the bus.

I said, "This is a rebuilt job."

"So?" he said caustically. "It's a sample of my work. I picked up a discarded chassis, found a brain I could use and spliced me a private bus. What of it?"

I tore at the repair panel, forcing it aside.

He said, "What the hell. Get away from that." The side of his palm came down numbingly on my left shoulder.

I struggled with him. "I don't want to do this bus any harm. What kind of a person do you think I am? I just want to take a look at some of the motor connections."

It didn't take much of a look. I was boiling when I turned to him. I said, "You're a hound and a bastard. You had no right installing this motor yourself. Why didn't you get a robotics man?"

He said, "Do I look crazy?"

"Even if it was a stolen motor, you had no right to treat it so. I wouldn't treat a man the way you treated that motor. Solder, tape, and pinch clamps! It's brutal!"

"It works, doesn't it?"

"Sure it works, but it must be hell for the bus. You could live with migraine headaches and acute arthritis, but it wouldn't be much of a life. This car is *suffering*."

"Shut up!" For a moment he glanced out the window at Sally, who had rolled up as close to the bus as she could. He made sure the doors and windows were locked.

He said, "We're getting out of here now, before the other cars come back. We'll stay away."

"How will that help you?"

"Your cars will run out of gas someday, won't they? You haven't got them fixed up so they can tank up on their own, have you? We'll come back and finish the job."

"They'll be looking for me," I said. "Mrs. Hester will call the police."

He was past reasoning with. He just punched the bus in gear. It lurched forward. Sally followed.

He giggled. "What can she do if you're here with me?"

Sally seemed to realize that, too. She picked up speed, passed us and was gone. Gellhorn opened the window next to him and spat through the opening.

The bus lumbered on over the dark road, its motor rattling unevenly. Gellhorn dimmed the periphery light until the phosphorescent green stripe down the middle of the highway, sparkling in the moonlight, was all that kept us out of the trees. There was virtually no traffic. Two cars passed ours, going the other way, and there was none at all on our side of the highway, either before or behind.

I heard the door-slamming first. Quick and sharp in the silence, first on the right and then on the left. Gellhorn's hands quivered as he punched savagely for increased speed. A beam of light shot out from among a scrub of trees, blinding us. Another beam plunged at us from behind the guard rails on the other side. At a crossover, four hundred yards ahead, there was sque-e-e-e as a car darted across our path.

"Sally went for the rest," I said. "I think you're surrounded."

"So what? What can they do?"

He hunched over the controls, peering through the windshield.

"And don't *you* try anything, old-timer," he muttered.

I couldn't. I was bone-weary; my left arm was on fire. The motor sounds gathered and grew closer. I could hear the motors missing in odd patterns; suddenly it seemed to me that my cars were speaking to one another.

A medley of horns came from behind. I turned and Gellhorn looked quickly into the rear-view mirror. A dozen cars were following in both lanes.

Gellhorn yelled and laughed madly.

I cried, "Stop! Stop the car!"

Because not a quarter of a mile ahead, plainly visible in the light beams of two sedans on the roadside was Sally, her trim body plunked square across the road. Two cars shot into the opposite lane to our left, keeping perfect time with us and preventing Gellhorn from turning out.

But he had no intention of turning out. He put his finger on the full-speed-ahead button and kept it there.

He said, "There'll be no bluffing here. This bus outweighs her five to one, old-timer, and we'll just push her off the road like a dead kitten."

I knew he could. The bus was on manual and his finger was on the button. I knew he would.

I lowered the window, and stuck my head out. "Sally," I screamed. "Get out of the way. *Sally!*"

It was drowned out in the agonized squeal of maltreated brakebands. I felt myself thrown forward and heard Gellhorn's breath puff out of his body.

I said, "What happened?" It was a foolish question. We had stopped. That was what had happened. Sally and the bus were five feet apart. With five times her weight tearing down on her, she had not budged. The guts of her.

Gellhorn yanked at the Manual toggle switch. "It's got to," he kept muttering. "It's got to."

I said, "Not the way you hooked up the motor, expert. Any of the circuits could cross over."

He looked at me with a tearing anger and growled deep in his throat. His hair was matted over his forehead. He lifted his fist.

"That's all the advice out of you there'll ever be, old-timer."

And I knew the needle gun was about to fire.

I pressed back against the bus door, watching the fist come up, and when the door opened I went over backward and out, hitting the ground with a thud. I heard the door slam closed again.

I got to my knees and looked up in time to see Gellhorn struggle uselessly with the closing window, then aim his fist-gun quickly through the glass. He never fired. The bus got under way with a tremendous roar, and Gellhorn lurched backward.

Sally wasn't in the way any longer, and I watched the bus's rear lights flicker away down the highway.

I was exhausted. I sat down right there, right on the highway, and put my head down in my crossed arms, trying to catch my breath.

I heard a car stop gently at my side. When I looked up, it was Sally. Slowly—lovingly, you might say—her front door opened.

No one had driven Sally for five years—except Gellhorn, of course—and I know how valuable such freedom was to a car. I appreciated the gesture, but I said, "Thanks, Sally, but I'll take one of the newer cars."

I got up and turned away, but skillfully and neatly as a pirouette, she wheeled before me again. I couldn't hurt her feelings. I got in. Her front seat had the fine, fresh scent of an automatobile that kept itself spotlessly clean. I lay down across it, thankfully, and with even, silent, and rapid efficiency, my boys and girls brought me home.

Mrs. Hester brought me the copy of the radio transcript the next evening with great excitement.

"It's Mr. Gellhorn," she said. "The man who came to see you."

"What about him?"

I dreaded her answer.

"They found him dead," she said. "Imagine that. Just lying dead in a ditch."

"It might be a stranger altogether," I mumbled.

"Raymond J. Gellhorn," she said, sharply. "There can't be two, can there? The description fits, too. Lord, what a way to die! They found tire marks on his arms and body. Imagine! I'm glad it turned out to be a bus; otherwise they might have come poking around here."

"Did it happen near here?" I asked, anxiously.

"No . . . Near Cooksville. But, goodness, read about it yourself if you— What happened to Giuseppe?"

I welcomed the diversion. Giuseppe was waiting patiently for me to complete the repaint job. His windshield had been replaced.

After she left, I snatched up the transcript. There was no doubt about it. The doctor reported he had been running and was in a state of totally spent exhaustion. I wondered for how many miles the bus had played with him before the final lunge. The transcript had no notion of anything like that, of course.

They had located the bus and identified it by the tire tracks. The police had it and were trying to trace its ownership.

There was an editorial in the transcript about it. It had been the first traffic fatality in the state for that year and the paper warned strenuously against manual driving after night.

There was no mention of Gellhorn's three thugs and for that, at least, I was grateful. None of our cars had been seduced by the pleasure of the chase into killing.

That was all. I let the paper drop. Gellhorn had been a criminal. His treatment of the bus had been brutal. There was no question in my mind he deserved death. But still I felt a bit queasy over the manner of it.

A month has passed now and I can't get it out of my mind.

My cars talk to one another. I have no doubt about it anymore. It's as though they've gained confidence; as though they're not bothering to keep it secret anymore. Their engines rattle and knock continuously.

And they don't talk among themselves only. They talk to the cars and buses that come into the Farm on business. How long have they been doing that?

They must be understood, too. Gellhorn's bus understood them, for all it hadn't been on the grounds more than an hour. I can close my eyes and bring back that dash along the highway, with our cars flanking the bus on either side, clacking their motors at it till it understood, stopped, let me out, and ran off with Gellhorn.

Did my cars tell him to kill Gellhorn? Or was that his idea?

Can cars have such ideas? The motor designers say no. But they mean under ordinary conditions. Have they foreseen *everything*?

Cars get ill-used, you know.

Some of them enter the Farm and observe. They get told things. They find out that cars exist whose motors are never stopped, whom no one ever drives, whose every need is supplied.

Then maybe they go out and tell others. Maybe the word is spreading quickly. Maybe they're going to think that the Farm way should be the way all over the world. They don't understand. You couldn't expect them to understand about legacies and the whims of rich men.

There are millions of automatobiles on Earth, tens of millions. If the thought gets rooted in them that they're slaves; that they should do something about it . . . If they begin to think the way Gellhorn's bus did. . . .

Maybe it won't be till after my time. And then they'll have to keep a few of us to take care of them, won't they? They wouldn't kill us all.

And maybe they would. Maybe they wouldn't understand about how someone would have to care for them. Maybe they won't wait.

Every morning I wake up and think, Maybe today. . . .

I don't get as much pleasure out of my cars as I used to. Lately, I notice that I'm even beginning to avoid Sally.

Flies

"Flies!" said Kendell Casey, wearily. He swung his arm. The fly circled, returned and nestled on Casey's shirt-collar.

From somewhere there sounded the buzzing of a second fly.

Dr. John Polen covered the slight uneasiness of his chin by moving his cigarette quickly to his lips.

He said, "I didn't expect to meet you, Casey. Or you, Winthrop. Or ought I call you Reverend Winthrop?"

"Ought I call you Professor Polen?" said Winthrop, carefully striking the proper vein of rich-toned friendship.

They were trying to snuggle into the cast-off shell of twenty years back, each of them. Squirming and cramming and not fitting.

Damn, thought Polen fretfully, why do people attend college reunions?

Casey's hot blue eyes were still filled with the aimless anger of the college sophomore who has discovered intellect, frustration, and the tag-ends of cynical philosophy all at once.

Casey! Bitter man of the campus!

He hadn't outgrown that. Twenty years later and it was Casey, bitter ex-man of the campus! Polen could see that in the way his finger tips moved aimlessly and in the manner of his spare body.

As for Winthrop? Well, twenty years older, softer, rounder. Skin pinker, eyes milder. Yet no nearer the quiet certainty he would never find. It was all there in the quick smile he never entirely abandoned, as though he feared there would be nothing to take its place, that its absence would turn his face into a smooth and featureless flesh.

Polen was tired of reading the aimless flickering of a muscle's end; tired of usurping the place of his machines; tired of the too much they told him.

Could they read him as he read them? Could the small restlessness of his own eyes broadcast the fact that he was damp with the disgust that had bred mustily within him?

Damn, thought Polen, why didn't I stay away?

They stood there, all three, waiting for one another to say something, to flick something from across the gap and bring it, quivering, into the present.

Polen tried it. He said, "Are you still working in chemistry, Casey?"

"In my own way, yes," said Casey, gruffly. "I'm not the scientist you're considered to be. I do research on insecticides for E. J. Link at Chatham."

Winthrop said, "Are you really? You said you would work on insecticides. Remember, Polen? And with all that, the flies dare still be after you, Casey?"

Casey said, "Can't get rid of them. I'm the best proving ground in the labs. No compound we've made keeps them away when I'm around. Someone once said it was my odor. I attract them."

Polen remembered the someone who had said that.

Winthrop said, "Or else—"

Polen felt it coming. He tensed.

"Or else," said Winthrop, "it's the curse, you know." His smile intensified to show that he was joking, that he forgave past grudges.

Damn, thought Polen, they haven't even changed the words. And the past came back.

"Flies," said Casey, swinging his arm, and slapping. "Ever see such a thing? Why don't they light on you two?"

Johnny Polen laughed at him. He laughed often then. "It's something in your body odor, Casey. You could be a boon to science. Find out the nature of the odorous chemical, concentrate it, mix it with DDT, and you've got the best fly-killer in the world."

"A fine situation. What do I smell like? A lady fly in heat? It's a shame they have to pick on me when the whole damned world's a dung heap."

Winthrop frowned and said with a faint flavor of rhetoric, "Beauty is not the only thing, Casey, in the eye of the beholder."

Casey did not deign a direct response. He said to Polen, "You know what Winthrop told me yesterday? He said those damned flies were the curse of Beelzebub."

"I was joking," said Winthrop.

"Why Beelzebub?" asked Polen.

"It amounts to a pun," said Winthrop. "The ancient Hebrews used it as one of their many terms of derision for alien gods. It comes from *Ba'al*, meaning *lord* and *zevuv*, meaning *fly*. The lord of flies."

Casey said, "Come on, Winthrop, don't say you don't believe in Beelzebub."

"I believe in the existence of evil," said Winthrop, stiffly.

"I mean Beelzebub. Alive. Horns. Hooves. A sort of competition deity."

"Not at all." Winthrop grew stiffer. "Evil is a short-term affair. In the end it must lose—"

Polen changed the subject with a jar. He said, "I'll be doing graduate work for Venner, by the way. I talked with him day before yesterday, and he'll take me on."

"No! That's wonderful." Winthrop glowed and leaped to the subject-change instantly. He held out a hand with which to pump Polen's. He was always conscientiously eager to rejoice in another's good fortune. Casey often pointed that out.

Casey said, "Cybernetics Venner? Well, if you can stand him, I suppose he can stand you."

Winthrop went on. "What did he think of your idea? Did you tell him your idea?"

"What idea?" demanded Casey.

Polen had avoided telling Casey so far. But now Venner had considered it and had passed it with a cool, "Interesting!" How could Casey's dry laughter hurt it now?

Polen said, "It's nothing much. Essentially, it's just a notion that emotion is the common bond of life, rather than reason or intellect. It's practically a truism, I suppose. You can't tell what a baby thinks or even *if* it thinks, but it's perfectly obvious that it can be angry, frightened or contented even when a week old. See?

"Same with animals. You can tell in a second if a dog is happy or if a cat is afraid. The point is that their emotions are the same as those we would have under the same circumstances."

"So?" said Casey. "Where does it get you?"

"I don't know yet. Right now, all I can say is that emotions are universals. Now suppose we could properly analyze all the actions of men and certain familiar animals and equate them with the visible emotion. We might find a tight relationship. Emotion A might always involve Motion B. Then we could apply it to animals whose emotions we couldn't guess at by common sense alone. Like snakes, or lobsters."

"Or flies," said Casey, as he slapped viciously at another and flicked its remains off his wrist in furious triumph.

He went on. "Go ahead, Johnny. I'll contribute the flies and you study them. We'll establish a science of flychology and labor to make them happy by removing their neuroses. After all, we want the greatest good of the greatest number, don't we? And there are more flies than men."

"Oh, well," said Polen.

Casey said, "Say, Polen, did you ever follow up that weird idea of yours? I mean, we all know you're a shining cybernetic light, but I haven't been reading your papers. With so many ways of wasting time, something has to be neglected, you know."

"What idea?" asked Polen, woodenly.

"Come on. You know. Emotions of animals and all that sort of guff. Boy, those were the days. I used to know madmen. Now I only come across idiots."

Winthrop said, "That's right, Polen. I remember it very well. Your first year in graduate school you were working on dogs and rabbits. I believe you even tried some of Casey's flies."

Polen said, "It came to nothing in itself. It gave rise to certain new principles of computing, however, so it wasn't a total loss."

Why did they talk about it?

Emotions! What right had anyone to meddle with emotions? Words were invented to conceal emotions. It was the dreadfulness of raw emotion that had made language a basic necessity.

Polen knew. His machines had by-passed the screen of verbalization and dragged the unconscious into the sunlight. The boy and the girl, the son and the mother. For that matter, the cat and the mouse or the snake and the bird. The data rattled together in its universality and it had all poured into and through Polen until he could no longer bear the touch of life.

In the last few years he had so painstakingly schooled his thoughts in other directions. Now these two came, dabbling in his mind, stirring up its mud.

Casey batted abstractedly across the tip of his nose to dislodge a fly. "Too bad," he said. "I used to think you could get some fascinating things out of, say, rats. Well, maybe not fascinating, but then not as boring as the stuff you would get out of our somewhat-human beings. I used to think—"

Polen remembered what he used to think.

Casey said, "Damn this DDT. The flies feed on it, I think. You know, I'm going to do graduate work in chemistry and then get a job on insecticides. So help me. I'll personally get something that *will* kill the vermin."

They were in Casey's room, and it had a somewhat keroseny odor from the recently applied insecticide.

Polen shrugged and said, "A folded newspaper will always kill."

Casey detected a non-existent sneer and said instantly, "How would you summarize your first year's work, Polen? I mean aside from the true summary any scientist could state if he dared, by which I mean: 'Nothing.'"

"Nothing," said Polen. "There's your summary."

"Go on," said Casey. "You use more dogs than the physiologists do and I bet the dogs mind the physiological experiments less. I would."

"Oh, leave him alone," said Winthrop. "You sound like a piano with 87 keys eternally out of order. You're a bore!"

You couldn't say that to Casey.

He said, with sudden liveliness, looking carefully away from Winthrop, "I'll tell you what you'll probably find in animals, if you look closely enough. Religion."

"What the dickens!" said Winthrop, outraged. "That's a foolish remark."

Casey smiled. "Now, now, Winthrop. *Dickens* is just a euphemism for *devil* and you don't want to be swearing."

"Don't teach me morals. And don't be blasphemous."

"What's blasphemous about it? Why shouldn't a flea consider the dog as something to be worshipped? It's the source of warmth, food, and all that's good for a flea."

"I don't want to discuss it."

"Why not? Do you good. You could even say that to an ant, an anteater is a higher order of creation. He would be too big for them to comprehend, too mighty to dream of resisting. He would move among them like an unseen, inexplicable whirlwind, visiting them with destruction and death. But that wouldn't spoil things for the ants. They would reason that destruction was simply their just punishment for evil. And the anteater wouldn't even know he was a deity. Or care."

Winthrop had gone white. He said, "I know you're saying this only to annoy me and I am sorry to see you risking your soul for a moment's amusement. Let me tell you this," his voice trembled a little, "and let me say it very seriously. The flies that torment you are your punishment in this life. Beelzebub, like all the forces of evil, may think he does evil, but it's only the ultimate good after all. The curse of Beelzebub is on you for *your* good. Perhaps it will succeed in getting you to change your way of life before it's too late."

He ran from the room.

Casey watched him go. He said, laughing, "I told you Winthrop believed in Beelzebub. It's funny the respectable names you can give to superstition." His laughter died a little short of its natural end.

There were two flies in the room, buzzing through the vapors toward him.

Polen rose and left in heavy depression. One year had taught him little, but it was already too much, and his laughter was thinning. Only his machines could analyze the emotions of animals properly, but he was already guessing too deeply concerning the emotions of men.

He did not like to witness wild murder-yearnings where others could see only a few words of unimportant quarrel.

• • • •

Casey said, suddenly, "Say, come to think of it, you did try some of my flies, the way Winthrop says. How about that?"

"Did I? After twenty years, I scarcely remember," murmured Polen.

Winthrop said, "You must. We were in your laboratory and you complained that Casey's flies followed him even there. He suggested you analyze them and you did. You recorded their motions and buzzings and wing-wiping for half an hour or more. You played with a dozen different flies."

Polen shrugged.

"Oh, well," said Casey. "It doesn't matter. It was good seeing you, old man." The hearty hand-shake, the thump on the shoulder, the broad grin—to Polen it all translated into sick disgust on Casey's part that Polen was a "success" after all.

Polen said, "Let me hear from you sometimes."

The words were dull thumps. They meant nothing. Casey knew that. Polen knew that. Everyone knew that. But words were meant to hide emotion and when they failed, humanity loyally maintained the pretense.

Winthrop's grasp of the hand was gentler. He said, "This brought back old times, Polen. If you're ever in Cincinnati, why don't you stop in at the meeting-house? You'll always be welcome."

To Polen, it all breathed of the man's relief at Polen's obvious depression. Science, too, it seemed, was not the answer, and Winthrop's basic and ineradicable insecurity felt pleased at the company.

"I will," said Polen. It was the usual polite way of saying, I won't.

He watched them thread separately to other groups.

Winthrop would never know. Polen was sure of that. He wondered if Casey knew. It would be the supreme joke if Casey did not.

He *had* run Casey's flies, of course, not that once alone, but many times. Always the same answer! Always the same unpublishable answer.

With a cold shiver he could not quite control, Polen was suddenly conscious of a single fly loose in the room, veering aimlessly for a moment, then beating strongly and reverently in the direction Casey had taken a moment before.

Could Casey *not* know? Could it be the essence of the primal punishment that he never learn he was Beelzebub?

Casey! Lord of the Flies!

"Nobody Here but—"

You see, it wasn't our fault. We had no idea anything was wrong until I called Cliff Anderson and spoke to him when he wasn't there. What's more, I wouldn't have known he wasn't there, if it wasn't that he walked in while I was talking to him.

No, no, no, *no*—

I never seem to be able to tell this straight. I get too excited. —Look, I might as well begin at the beginning. I'm Bill Billings; my friend is Cliff Anderson. I'm an electrical engineer, he's a mathematician, and we're on the faculty of Midwestern Institute of Technology. Now you know who we are.

Ever since we got out of uniform, Cliff and I have been working on calculating machines. You know what they are. Norbert Wiener popularized them in his book, *Cybernetics*. If you've seen pictures of them, you know that they're great big things. They take up a whole wall and they're very complicated; also expensive.

But Cliff and I had ideas. You see, what makes a thinking machine so big and expensive is that it has to be full of relays and vacuum tubes just so that microscopic electric currents can be controlled and made to flicker on and off, here and there. Now the really important things are those little electric currents, so—

I once said to Cliff, "Why can't we control the currents without all the salad dressing?"

Cliff said, "Why not, indeed," and started working on the mathematics.

How we got where we did in two years is no matter. It's what we got after we finished that made the trouble. It turned out that we ended with something about this high and maybe so wide and just about this deep—

No, no. I forget that you can't see me. I'll give you the figures. It was about three feet high, six feet long, and two feet deep. Got that? It took two men to carry it but it could be carried and that was the point. And still, mind you, it could do anything the wall-size calculators could. Not as fast, maybe, but we were still working.

We had big ideas about that thing, the very biggest. We could put it on ships or airplanes. After a while, if we could make it small enough, an automobile could carry one.

We were especially interested in the automobile angle. Suppose you had a little thinking machine on the dashboard, hooked to the engine and battery and equipped with photoelectric eyes. It could choose an ideal course, avoid cars, stop at red lights, pick the optimum speed for the terrain. Everybody could sit in the back seat and automobile accidents would vanish.

All of it was fun. There was so much excitement to it, so many thrills every time we worked out another consolidation, that I could still cry when I think of the time I picked up the telephone to call our lab and tumbled everything into the discard.

I was at Mary Ann's house that evening— Or have I told you about Mary Ann yet? No. I guess I haven't.

Mary Ann was the girl who would have been my fiancée but for two ifs. One, if she were willing, and two, if I had the nerve to ask her. She has red hair and crams something like two tons of energy into about 110 pounds of body which fills out very nicely from the ground to five and a half feet up. I was dying to ask her, you understand, but each time I'd see her coming into sight, setting a match to my heart with every movement, I'd just break down.

It's not that I'm not good-looking. People tell me I'm adequate. I've got all my hair; I'm nearly six feet tall; I can even dance. It's just that I've nothing to offer. I don't have to tell you what college teachers make. With inflation and taxes, it amounts to just about nothing. Of course, if we got the basic patents rolled up on our little thinking machine, things would be different. But I couldn't ask her to wait for that, either. Maybe, after it was all set—

Anyway, I just stood there, wishing, that evening, as she came into the living room. My arm was groping blindly for the phone.

Mary Ann said, "I'm all ready, Bill. Let's go."

I said, "Just a minute. I want to ring up Cliff."

She frowned a little, "Can't it wait?"

"I was supposed to call him two hours ago," I explained.

It only took two minutes. I rang the lab. Cliff was putting in an evening of work and so he answered. I asked something, then he said something, I asked some more and he explained. The details don't matter, but as I said, he's the mathematician of the combination. When I build the circuits and put things together in what look like impossible ways, he's the guy who shuffles the symbols and tells me whether they're really impossible. Then, just as I finished and hung up, there was a ring at the door.

For a minute, I thought Mary Ann had another caller and got sort of stiff-backed as I watched her go to the door. I was scribbling down some of what Cliff had just told me while I watched. But then she opened the door and it was only Cliff Anderson after all.

He said, "I thought I'd find you here— Hello, Mary Ann. Say, weren't you going to ring me at six? You're as reliable as a cardboard chair." Cliff is short and plump and always willing to start a fight, but I know him and pay no attention.

I said, "Things turned up and it slipped my mind. But I just called, so what's the difference?"

"Called? Me? When?"

I started to point to the telephone and gagged. Right then, the bottom fell out of things. Exactly five seconds before the doorbell had sounded I had been on the phone talking to Cliff in the lab, and the lab was six miles away from Mary Ann's house.

I said, "I—just spoke to you."

I wasn't getting across. Cliff just said, "To me?" again.

I was pointing to the phone with both hands now, "On the phone. I called the lab. On this phone here! Mary Ann heard me. Mary Ann, wasn't I just talking to—"

Mary Ann said, "I don't know whom you were talking to. —Well, shall we go?" That's Mary Ann. She's a stickler for honesty.

I sat down. I tried to be very quiet and clear. I said, "Cliff, I dialed the lab's phone number, you answered the phone, I asked you if you had the details worked out, you said, yes, and gave them to me. Here they are. I wrote them down. Is this correct or not?"

I handed him the paper on which I had written the equations.

Cliff looked at them. He said, "They're correct. But where could you have gotten them? You didn't work them out yourself, did you?"

"I just told you. You gave them to me over the phone."

Cliff shook his head, "Bill, I haven't been in the lab since seven fifteen. There's nobody there."

"I spoke to somebody, I tell you."

Mary Ann was fiddling with her gloves. "We're getting late," she said.

I waved my hands at her to wait a bit, and said to Cliff, "Look, are you sure—"

"There's nobody there, unless you want to count Junior." Junior was what we called our pint-sized mechanical brain.

We stood there, looking at one another. Mary Ann's toe was still hitting the floor like a time bomb waiting to explode.

Then Cliff laughed. He said, "I'm thinking of a cartoon I saw, somewhere. It shows a robot answering the phone and saying, 'Honest, boss, there's nobody here but us complicated thinking machines.'"

I didn't think that was funny. I said, "Let's go to the lab."

Mary Ann said, "Hey! We won't make the show."

I said, "Look, Mary Ann, this is very important. It's just going to take a minute. Come along with us and we'll go straight to the show from there."

She said, "The show starts—" And then she stopped talking, because I grabbed her wrist and we left.

That just shows how excited I was. Ordinarily, I wouldn't ever have dreamed of shoving her around. I mean, Mary Ann is quite the lady. It's just that I had so many things on my mind. I don't even really remember grabbing her wrist, come to think of it. It's just that the next thing I knew, I was in the auto and so was Cliff and so was she, and she was rubbing her wrist and muttering under her breath about big gorillas.

I said, "Did I hurt you, Mary Ann?"

She said, "No, of course not. I have my arm yanked out of its socket every day, just for fun." Then she kicked me in the shin.

She only does things like that because she has red hair. Actually, she has a very gentle nature, but she tries very hard to live up to the redhead mythology. I see right through that, of course, but I humor her, poor kid.

We were at the laboratory in twenty minutes.

The Institute is empty at night. It's emptier than a building would ordinarily be. You see, it's designed to have crowds of students rushing through the corridors and when they aren't there, it's unnaturally lonely. Or maybe it was just that I was afraid to see what might be sitting in our laboratory upstairs. Either way, footsteps were uncomfortably loud and the self-service elevator was downright dingy.

I said to Mary Ann, "This won't take long." But she just sniffed and looked beautiful.

She can't help looking beautiful.

Cliff had the key to the laboratory and I looked over his shoulder when he opened the door. There was nothing to see. Junior was there, sure, but he looked just as he had when I saw him last. The dials in front registered nothing and except for that, there was just a large box, with a cable running back into the wall socket.

Cliff and I walked up on either side of Junior. I think we were planning to grab it if it made a sudden move. But then we stopped because Junior just wasn't doing anything. Mary Ann was looking at it, too. In fact, she ran her middle finger along its top and then looked at the finger tip and twiddled it against her thumb to get rid of the dust.

I said, "Mary Ann, don't you go near it. Stay at the other end of the room."

She said, "It's just as dirty there."

She'd never been in our lab before, and of course she didn't realize that a laboratory wasn't the same thing as a baby's bedroom, if you know what I mean. The janitor comes in twice a day and all he does is empty the wastebaskets. About once a week, he comes in with a dirty mop, makes mud on the floor, and shoves it around a little.

Cliff said, "The telephone isn't where I left it."

I said, "How do you know?"

"Because I left it there." He pointed. "And now it's here."

If he were right, the telephone had moved closer to Junior. I swallowed and said, "Maybe you don't remember right." I tried to laugh without sounding very natural and said, "Where's the screw driver?"

"What are you going to do?"

"Just take a look inside. For laughs."

Mary Ann said, "You'll get yourself all dirty." So I put on my lab coat. She's a very thoughtful girl, Mary Ann.

I got to work with a screw driver. Of course, once Junior was really perfected, we were going to have models manufactured in welded, one-piece cases. We were even thinking of molded plastic in colors, for home use. In the lab model, though, we held it together with screws so that we could take it apart and put it together as often as we wanted to.

Only the screws weren't coming out. I grunted and yanked and said, "Some joker was putting his weight on these when he screwed these things in."

Cliff said, "You're the only one who ever touches the thing."

He was right, too, but that didn't make it any easier. I stood up and passed the back of my hand over my forehead. I held out the screw driver to him, "Want to try?"

He did, and didn't get any further than I did. He said, "That's funny."

I said, "What's funny?"

He said, "I had a screw turning just now. It moved about an eighth of an inch and then the screw driver slipped."

"What's funny about that?"

Cliff backed away and put down the screw driver with two fingers. "What's funny is that I saw the screw move back an eighth of an inch and tighten up again."

Mary Ann was fidgeting again. She said, "Why don't your scientific minds think of a blowtorch, if you're so anxious." There was a blowtorch on one of the benches and she was pointing to it.

Well, ordinarily, I wouldn't think any more of using a blowtorch on Junior than on myself. But I was thinking something and Cliff was thinking something and we were both thinking the same thing. *Junior didn't want to be opened up.*

Cliff said, "What do you think, Bill?"

And I said, "I don't know, Cliff."

Mary Ann said, "Well, hurry up, lunkhead, we'll miss the show."

So I picked up the blowtorch and adjusted the gauge on the oxygen cylinder. It was going to be like stabbing a friend.

But Mary Ann stopped the proceedings by saying, "Well, how stupid can men be? These screws are loose. You must have been turning the screw driver the wrong way."

Now there isn't much chance of turning a screw driver the wrong way. Just the same, I don't like to contradict Mary Ann, so I just said, "Mary Ann, don't stay too close to Junior. Why don't you wait by the door."

But she just said, "Well, look!" And there was a screw in her hand and an empty hole in the front of Junior's case. She had removed it by hand.

Cliff said, "Holy Smoke!"

They were turning, all dozen screws. They were doing it by themselves, like little worms crawling out of their holes, turning round and round, then dropping out. I scrabbled them up and only one was left. It hung on for a while, the front panel sagging from it, till I reached out. Then the last screw dropped and the panel fell gently into my arms. I put it to one side.

Cliff said, "It did that on purpose. It heard us mention the blowtorch and gave up." His face is usually pink, but it was white then.

I was feeling a little queer myself. I said, "What's it trying to hide?"

"I don't know."

We bent before its open insides and for a while we just looked. I could hear Mary Ann's toe begin to tap the floor again. I looked at my wrist watch and I had to admit to myself we didn't have much time. In fact, we didn't have any time left.

And then I said, "It's got a diaphragm."

Cliff said, "Where?" and bent closer.

I pointed. "And a loud speaker."

"You didn't put them in?"

"Of course I didn't put them in. I ought to know what I put in. If I put it in, I'd remember."

"Then how did it get in?"

We were squatting and arguing. I said, "It made them itself, I suppose. Maybe it grows them. Look at that."

I pointed again. Inside the box at two different places, were coils of something that looked like thin garden hose, except that they were of metal. They spiraled tightly so that they lay flat. At the end of each coil, the metal divided into five or six thin filaments that were in little sub-spirals.

"You didn't put those in either?"

"No, I didn't put those in either."

"What are they?"

He knew what they were and I knew what they were. Something had to reach out to get materials for Junior to make parts for itself; something had to snake out for the telephone. I picked up the front panel and looked at it again. There were two circular bits of metal cut out and hinged so that they could swing forward and leave a hole for something to come through.

I poked a finger through one and held it up for Cliff to see, and said, "I didn't put this in either."

Mary Ann was looking over my shoulder now, and without warning she reached out. I was wiping my fingers with a paper towel to get off the dust and grease and didn't have time to stop her. I should have known Mary Ann, though; she's always so anxious to help.

Anyway, she reached in to touch one of the—well, we might as well say it —tentacles. I don't know if she actually touched them or not. Later on she claimed she hadn't. But anyway, what happened then was that she let out a little yell and suddenly sat down and began rubbing her arm.

"The same one," she whimpered. "First you, and then *that*."

I helped her up. "It must have been a loose connection, Mary Ann. I'm sorry, but I told you—"

Cliff said, "Nuts! That was no loose connection. Junior's just protecting itself."

I had thought the same thing, myself. I had thought lots of things. Junior was a new kind of machine. Even the mathematics that controlled it were different from anything anybody had worked with before. Maybe it had something no machine previously had ever had. Maybe it felt a desire to stay alive and grow. Maybe it would have a desire to make more machines until there were millions of them all over the earth, fighting with human beings for control.

I opened my mouth and Cliff must have known what I was going to say, because he yelled, "No. No, don't say it!"

But I couldn't stop myself. It just came out and I said, "Well, look, let's disconnect Junior—What's the matter?"

Cliff said bitterly, "Because he's listening to what we say, you jackass. He heard about the blowtorch, didn't he? I was going to sneak up behind it, but now it will probably electrocute me if I try."

Mary Ann was still brushing at the back of her dress and saying how dirty the floor was, even though I kept telling her I had nothing to do with that. I mean, it's the janitor that makes the mud.

Anyway, she said, "Why don't you put on rubber gloves and yank the cord out?"

I could see Cliff was trying to think of reasons why that wouldn't work. He didn't think of any, so he put on the rubber gloves and walked towards Junior.

I yelled, "Watch out!"

It was a stupid thing to say. He *had* to watch out; he had no choice. One of the tentacles moved and there was no doubt what they were now. It whirled out and drew a line between Cliff and the power cable. It remained there, vibrating a little with its six finger-tendrils splayed out. Tubes inside Junior were beginning to glow. Cliff didn't try to go past that tentacle. He backed away and after a while, it spiraled inward again. He took off his rubber gloves.

"Bill," he said, "we're not going to get anywhere. That's a smarter gadget than we dreamed we could make. It was smart enough to use my voice as a model when it built its diaphragm. It may become smart enough to learn how to—" He looked over his shoulder, and whispered, "how to generate its own power and become self-contained."

"Bill, we've got to stop it, or someday someone will telephone the planet Earth and get the answer, 'Honest, boss, there's nobody here anywhere but us complicated thinking machines!' "

"Let's get in the police," I said. "We'll explain. A grenade, or something—"

Cliff shook his head, "We can't have anyone else find out. They'll build other Juniors and it looks like we don't have enough answers for that kind of a project after all."

"Then what do we do?"

"I don't know."

I felt a sharp blow on my chest. I looked down and it was Mary Ann, getting ready to spit fire. She said, "Look, lunkhead, if we've got a date, we've got one, and if we haven't, we haven't. Make up your mind."

I said, "Now, Mary Ann—"

She said, "Answer me. I never heard such a ridiculous thing. Here I get dressed to go to a play, and you take me to a dirty laboratory with a foolish machine and spend the rest of the evening twiddling dials."

"Mary Ann, I'm not—"

She wasn't listening; she was talking. I wish I could remember what she said after that. Or maybe I don't; maybe it's just as well I can't remember, since none of it was very complimentary. Every once in a while I would manage a "But, Mary Ann—" and each time it would get sucked under and swallowed up.

Actually, as I said, she's a very gentle creature and it's only when she gets excited that she's ever talkative or unreasonable. Of course, with red hair, she feels she ought to get excited rather often. That's my theory, anyway. She just feels she has to live up to her red hair.

Anyway, the next thing I *do* remember clearly is Mary Ann finishing with a stamp on my right foot and then turning to leave. I ran after her, trying once again, "But, Mary Ann—"

Then Cliff yelled at us. Generally, he doesn't pay any attention to us, but this time he was shouting, "Why don't you ask her to marry you, you lunkhead?"

Mary Ann stopped. She was in the doorway by then but she didn't turn around. I stopped too, and felt the words get thick and clogged up in my throat. I couldn't even manage a "But, Mary Ann—"

Cliff was yelling in the background. I heard him as though he were a mile away. He was shouting, "I got it! I got it!" over and over again.

Then Mary Ann turned and she looked so beautiful— Did I tell you that she's got green eyes with a touch of blue in them? Anyway she looked so beautiful that all the words in my throat jammed together very tightly and came out in that funny sound you make when you swallow.

She said, "Were you going to say something, Bill?"

Well, Cliff had put it in my head. My voice was hoarse and I said, "Will you marry me, Mary Ann?"

The minute I said it, I wished I hadn't, because I thought she would never speak to me again. Then two minutes after that I was glad I had, because she threw her arms around me and reached up to kiss me. It was a while before I was quite clear what was happening, and then I began to kiss back. This went on for quite a long time, until Cliff's banging on my shoulder managed to attract my attention.

I turned and said, snappishly, "What the devil do you want?" It was a little ungrateful. After all, he had started this.

He said, "Look!"

In his hand, he held the main lead that had connected Junior to the power supply.

I had forgotten about Junior, but now it came back. I said, "He's disconnected, then."

"Cold!"

"How did you do it?"

He said, "Junior was so busy watching you and Mary Ann fight that I managed to sneak up on it. Mary Ann put on one good show."

I didn't like that remark because Mary Ann is a very dignified and self-contained sort of girl and doesn't put on "shows." However, I had too much in hand to take issue with him.

I said to Mary Ann, "I don't have much to offer, Mary Ann; just a school teacher's salary. Now that we've dismantled Junior, there isn't even any chance of—"

Mary Ann said, "I don't care, Bill. I just gave up on you, you lunkheaded darling. I've tried practically everything—"

"You've been kicking my shins and stamping on my toes."

"I'd run out of everything else. I was desperate."

The logic wasn't quite clear, but I didn't answer because I remembered about the show. I looked at my watch and said, "Look, Mary Ann, if we hurry we can still make the second act."

She said, "Who wants to see the show?"

So I kissed her some more; and we never did get to see the show at all.

There's only one thing that bothers me now. Mary Ann and I are married, and we're perfectly happy. I just had a promotion; I'm an associate professor now. Cliff keeps working away at plans for building a controllable Junior and he's making progress.

None of that's it.

You see, I talked to Cliff the next evening, to tell him Mary Ann and I were going to marry and to thank him for giving me the idea. And after staring at me for a minute, he swore he hadn't said it; he hadn't shouted for me to propose marriage.

Of course, there was something else in the room with Cliff's voice.

I keep worrying Mary Ann will find out. She's the gentlest girl I know, but she *has* got red hair. She can't help trying to live up to that, or have I said that already?

Anyway, what will she say if she ever finds out that I didn't have the sense to propose till a *machine* told me to?

It's Such a Beautiful Day

On April 12, 2117, the field-modulator brake-valve in the Door belonging to Mrs. Richard Hanshaw depolarized for reasons unknown. As a result, Mrs. Hanshaw's day was completely upset and her son, Richard, Jr., first developed his strange neurosis.

It was not the type of thing you would find listed as a neurosis in the usual textbooks and certainly young Richard behaved, in most respects, just as a well-brought-up twelve-year-old in prosperous circumstances ought to behave.

And yet from April 12 on, Richard Hanshaw, Jr., could only with regret ever persuade himself to go through a Door.

Of all this, on April 12, Mrs. Hanshaw had no premonition. She woke in the morning (an ordinary morning) as her mekkano slithered gently into her room, with a cup of coffee on a small tray.

Mrs. Hanshaw was planning a visit to New York in the afternoon and she had several things to do first that could not quite be trusted to a mekkano, so after one or two sips, she stepped out of bed.

The mekkano backed away, moving silently along the diamagnetic field that kept its oblong body half an inch above the floor, and moved back to the kitchen, where its simple computer was quite adequate to set the proper controls on the various kitchen appliances in order that an appropriate breakfast might be prepared.

Mrs. Hanshaw, having bestowed the usual sentimental glance upon the cubograph of her dead husband, passed through the stages of her morning ritual with a certain contentment. She could hear her son across the hall clattering through his, but she knew she need not interfere with him. The mekkano was well adjusted to see to it, as a matter of course, that he was showered, that he had on a change of clothing, and that he would eat a nourishing breakfast. The tergo-shower she had had installed the year before made the morning wash and dry so quick and pleasant that, really, she felt certain Dickie would wash even without supervision.

On a morning like this, when she was busy, it would certainly not be necessary for her to do more than deposit a casual peck on the boy's cheek before he left. She heard the soft chime the mekkano sounded to indicate approaching school time and she floated down the force-lift to the lower floor (her hair-style for the day only sketchily designed, as yet) in order to perform that motherly duty.

She found Richard standing at the door, with his text-reels and pocket projector dangling by their strap and a frown on his face.

"Say, Mom," he said, looking up, "I dialed the school's co-ords but nothing happens."

She said, almost automatically, "Nonsense, Dickie. I never heard of such a thing."

"Well, you try."

Mrs. Hanshaw tried a number of times. Strange, the school Door was always set for general reception. She tried other co-ordinates. Her friends' Doors might not be set for reception, but there would be a signal at least, and then she could explain.

But nothing happened at all. The Door remained an inactive gray barrier despite all her manipulations. It was obvious that the Door was out of order —and only five months after its annual fall inspection by the company.

She was quite angry about it.

It *would* happen on a day when she had so much planned. She thought petulantly of the fact that a month earlier she had decided against installing a subsidiary Door on the ground that it was an unnecessary expense. How was she to know that Doors were getting to be so *shoddy?*

She stepped to the visiphone while the anger still burned in her and said to Richard, "You just go down the road, Dickie, and use the Williamsons' Door."

Ironically, in view of later developments, Richard balked. "Aw, gee, Mom, I'll get dirty. Can't I stay home till the Door is fixed?"

And, as ironically, Mrs. Hanshaw insisted. With her finger on the combination board of the phone, she said, "You won't get dirty if you put flexies on your shoes, and don't forget to brush yourself well before you go into their house."

"But, golly—"

"No back-talk, Dickie. You've got to be in school. Just let me see you walk out of here. And quickly, or you'll be late."

The mekkano, an advanced model and very responsive, was already standing before Richard with flexies in one appendage.

Richard pulled the transparent plastic shields over his shoes and moved down the hall with visible reluctance. "I don't even know how to work this thing, Mom."

"You just push that button," Mrs. Hanshaw called. "The red button. Where it says 'For Emergency Use.' And don't dawdle. Do you want the mekkano to go along with you?"

"Gosh, no," he called back, morosely, "what do you think I am? A baby? Gosh!" His muttering was cut off by a slam.

With flying fingers, Mrs. Hanshaw punched the appropriate combination on the phone board and thought of the things she intended saying to the company about this.

Joe Bloom, a reasonable young man, who had gone through technology school with added training in force-field mechanics, was at the Hanshaw residence in less than half an hour. He was really quite competent, though Mrs. Hanshaw regarded his youth with deep suspicion.

She opened the movable house-panel when he first signaled and her sight of him was as he stood there, brushing at himself vigorously to remove the dust of the open air. He took off his flexies and dropped them where he stood. Mrs. Hanshaw closed the house-panel against the flash of raw sunlight that had entered. She found herself irrationally hoping that the step-by-step trip from the public Door had been an unpleasant one. Or perhaps that the public Door itself had been out of order and the youth had had to lug his tools even farther than the necessary two hundred yards. She wanted the Company, or its representative at least, to suffer a bit. It would teach them what broken Doors meant.

But he seemed cheerful and unperturbed as he said, "Good morning, ma'am. I came to see about your Door."

"I'm glad someone did," said Mrs. Hanshaw, ungraciously. "My day is quite ruined."

"Sorry, ma'am. What seems to be the trouble?"

"It just won't work. Nothing at all happens when you adjust co-ords," said Mrs. Hanshaw. "There was no warning at all. I had to send my son out to the neighbors through that—that thing."

She pointed to the entrance through which the repair man had come.

He smiled and spoke out of the conscious wisdom of his own specialized training in Doors. "That's a door, too, ma'am. You don't give that kind a capital letter when you write it. It's a hand-door, sort of. It used to be the only kind once."

"Well, at least it works. My boy's had to go out in the dirt and germs."

"It's not bad outside today, ma'am," he said, with the connoisseur-like air of one whose profession forced him into the open nearly every day. "Sometimes it *is* real unpleasant. But I guess you want I should fix this here Door, ma'am, so I'll get on with it."

He sat down on the floor, opened the large tool case he had brought in with him and in half a minute, by use of a point-demagnetizer, he had the control panel removed and a set of intricate vitals exposed.

He whistled to himself as he placed the fine electrodes of the field-analyzer on numerous points, studying the shifting needles on the dials. Mrs. Hanshaw watched him, arms folded.

Finally, he said, "Well, here's something," and with a deft twist, he disengaged the brake-valve.

He tapped it with a fingernail and said, "This here brake-valve is depolarized, ma'am. There's your whole trouble." He ran his finger along the little pigeonholes in his tool case and lifted out a duplicate of the object he had taken from the door mechanism. "These things just go all of a sudden. Can't predict it."

He put the control panel back and stood up. "It'll work now, ma'am."

He punched a reference combination, blanked it, then punched another. Each time, the dull gray of the Door gave way to a deep, velvety blackness. He said, "Will you sign here, ma'am? and put down your charge number, too, please? Thank you, ma'am."

He punched a new combination, that of his home factory, and with a polite touch of finger to forehead, he stepped through the Door. As his body entered the blackness, it cut off sharply. Less and less of him was visible and the tip of his tool case was the last thing that showed. A second after he had passed through completely, the Door turned back to dull gray.

Half an hour later, when Mrs. Hanshaw had finally completed her interrupted preparations and was fuming over the misfortune of the morning, the phone buzzed annoyingly and her real troubles began.

Miss Elizabeth Robbins was distressed. Little Dick Hanshaw had always been a good pupil. She hated to report him like this. And yet, she told herself, his actions were certainly queer. And she would talk to his mother, not to the principal.

She slipped out to the phone during the morning study period, leaving a student in charge. She made her connection and found herself staring at Mrs. Hanshaw's handsome and somewhat formidable head.

Miss Robbins quailed, but it was too late to turn back. She said, diffidently, "Mrs. Hanshaw, I'm Miss Robbins." She ended on a rising note.

Mrs. Hanshaw looked blank, then said, "Richard's teacher?" That, too, ended on a rising note.

"That's right. I called you, Mrs. Hanshaw," Miss Robbins plunged right into it, "to tell you that Dick was quite late to school this morning."

"He *was?* But that couldn't be. I saw him leave."

Miss Robbins looked astonished. She said, "You mean you saw him use the Door?"

Mrs. Hanshaw said quickly, "Well, no. Our Door was temporarily out of order. I sent him to a neighbor and he used that Door."

"Are you sure?"

"Of course I'm sure. I wouldn't lie to you."

"No, no, Mrs. Hanshaw. I wasn't implying that at all. I meant are you sure he found the way to the neighbor? He might have got lost."

"Ridiculous. We have the proper maps, and I'm sure Richard knows the location of every house in District A-3." Then, with the quiet pride of one who knows what is her due, she added, "Not that he ever needs to know, of course. The co-ords are all that are necessary at any time."

Miss Robbins, who came from a family that had always had to economize rigidly on the use of its Doors (the price of power being what it was) and who had therefore run errands on foot until quite an advanced age, resented the pride. She said, quite clearly, "Well, I'm afraid, Mrs. Hanshaw, that Dick did not use the neighbor's Door. He was over an hour late to school and the condition of his flexies made it quite obvious that he tramped cross-country. They were *muddy*."

"*Muddy?*" Mrs. Hanshaw repeated the emphasis on the word. "What did he say? What was his excuse?"

Miss Robbins couldn't help but feel a little glad at the discomfiture of the other woman. She said, "He wouldn't talk about it. Frankly, Mrs. Hanshaw, he seems ill. That's why I called you. Perhaps you might want to have a doctor look at him."

"Is he running a temperature?" The mother's voice went shrill.

"Oh, no. I don't mean physically ill. It's just his attitude and the look in his eyes." She hesitated, then said with every attempt at delicacy, "I thought perhaps a routine checkup with a psychic probe—"

She didn't finish. Mrs. Hanshaw, in a chilled voice and with what was as close to a snort as her breeding would permit, said, "Are you implying that Richard is *neurotic?*"

"Oh, no, Mrs. Hanshaw, but—"

"It certainly sounded so. The idea! He has always been perfectly healthy. I'll take this up with him when he gets home. I'm sure there's a perfectly normal explanation which he'll give to *me*."

The connection broke abruptly, and Miss Robbins felt hurt and uncommonly foolish. After all she had only tried to help, to fulfill what she considered an obligation to her students.

She hurried back to the classroom with a glance at the metal face of the wall clock. The study period was drawing to an end. English Composition next.

But her mind wasn't completely on English Composition. Automatically, she called the students to have them read selections from their literary creations. And occasionally she punched one of those selections on tape and ran it through the small vocalizer to show the students how English *should* be read.

The vocalizer's mechanical voice, as always, dripped perfection, but, again as always, lacked character. Sometimes, she wondered if it was wise to try to train the students into a speech that was divorced from individuality and geared only to a mass-average accent and intonation.

Today, however, she had no thought for that. It was Richard Hanshaw she watched. He sat quietly in his seat, quite obviously indifferent to his surroundings. He was lost deep in himself and just not the same boy he had been. It was obvious to her that he had had some unusual experience that morning and, really, she was right to call his mother, although perhaps she ought not to have made the remark about the probe. Still it was quite the thing these days. All sorts of people get probed. There wasn't any disgrace attached to it. Or there shouldn't be, anyway.

She called on Richard, finally. She had to call twice, before he responded and rose to his feet.

The general subject assigned had been: "If you had your choice of traveling on some ancient vehicle, which would you choose, and why?" Miss Robbins tried to use the topic every semester. It was a good one because it carried a sense of history with it. It forced the youngster to think about the manner of living of people in past ages.

She listened while Richard Hanshaw read in a low voice.

"If I had my choice of ancient vehicles," he said, pronouncing the "h" in vehicles, "I would choose the stratoliner. It travels slow like all vehicles but it is clean. Because it travels in the stratosphere, it must be all enclosed so that you are not likely to catch disease. You can see the stars if it is night time almost as good as in a planetarium. If you look down you can see the Earth like a map or maybe see clouds—" He went on for several hundred more words.

She said brightly when he had finished reading, "It's pronounced vee-ick-ulls, Richard. No 'h.' Accent on the first syllable. And you don't say 'travels slow' or 'see good.' What do you say, class?"

There was a small chorus of responses and she went on, "That's right. Now what is the difference between an adjective and an adverb? Who can tell me?"

And so it went. Lunch passed. Some pupils stayed to eat; some went home. Richard stayed. Miss Robbins noted that, as usually he didn't.

The afternoon passed, too, and then there was the final bell and the usual upsurging hum as twenty-five boys and girls rattled their belongings together and took their leisurely place in line.

Miss Robbins clapped her hands together. "Quickly, children. Come, Zelda, take your place."

"I dropped my tape-punch, Miss Robbins," shrilled the girl, defensively.

"Well, pick it up, pick it up. Now children, be brisk, be brisk."

She pushed the button that slid a section of the wall into a recess and revealed the gray blankness of a large Door. It was not the usual Door that the occasional student used in going home for lunch, but an advanced model that was one of the prides of this well-to-do private school.

In addition to its double width, it possessed a large and impressively gear-filled "automatic serial finder" which was capable of adjusting the door for a number of different co-ordinates at automatic intervals.

At the beginning of the semester, Miss Robbins always had to spend an afternoon with the mechanic, adjusting the device for the co-ordinates of the homes of the new class. But then, thank goodness, it rarely needed attention for the remainder of the term.

The class lined up alphabetically, first girls, then boys. The Door went velvety black and Hester Adams waved her hand and stepped through. "By-y-y—"

The "bye" was cut off in the middle, as it almost always was.

The Door went gray, then black again, and Theresa Cantrocchi went through. Gray, black, Zelda Charlowicz. Gray, black, Patricia Coombs. Gray, black, Sara May Evans.

The line grew smaller as the Door swallowed them one by one, depositing each in her home. Of course, an occasional mother forgot to leave the house Door on special reception at the appropriate time and then the school Door remained gray. Automatically, after a minute-long wait, the Door went on to the next combination in line and the pupil in question had to wait till it was all over, after which a phone call to the forgetful parent would set things right. This was always bad for the pupils involved, especially the sensitive ones who took seriously the implication that they were little thought of at home. Miss Robbins always tried to impress this on visiting parents, but it happened at least once every semester just the same.

The girls were all through now. John Abramowitz stepped through and then Edwin Byrne—

Of course, another trouble, and a more frequent one was the boy or girl who got into line out of place. They *would* do it despite the teacher's sharpest watch, particularly at the beginning of the term when the proper order was less familiar to them.

When that happened, children would be popping into the wrong houses by the half-dozen and would have to be sent back. It always meant a mixup that took minutes to straighten out and parents were invariably irate.

Miss Robbins was suddenly aware that the line had stopped. She spoke sharply to the boy at the head of the line.

"Step through, Samuel. What are you waiting for?"

Samuel Jones raised a complacent countenance and said, "It's not my combination, Miss Robbins."

"Well, whose is it?" She looked impatiently down the line of five remaining boys. Who was out of place?

"It's Dick Hanshaw's, Miss Robbins."

"Where is he?"

Another boy answered, with the rather repulsive tone of self-righteousness all children automatically assume in reporting the deviations of their friends to elders in authority, "He went through the fire door, Miss Robbins."

"What?"

The schoolroom Door had passed on to another combination and Samuel Jones passed through. One by one, the rest followed.

Miss Robbins was alone in the classroom. She stepped to the fire door. It was a small affair, manually operated, and hidden behind a bend in the wall so that it would not break up the uniform structure of the room.

She opened it a crack. It was there as a means of escape from the building in case of fire, a device which was enforced by an anachronistic law that did not take into account the modern methods of automatic fire-fighting that all public buildings used. There was nothing outside, but the—outside. The sunlight was harsh and a dusty wind was blowing.

Miss Robbins closed the door. She was glad she had called Mrs. Hanshaw. She had done her duty. More than ever, it was obvious that something was wrong with Richard. She suppressed the impulse to phone again.

Mrs. Hanshaw did not go to New York that day. She remained home in a mixture of anxiety and an irrational anger, the latter directed against the impudent Miss Robbins.

Some fifteen minutes before school's end, her anxiety drove her to the Door. Last year she had had it equipped with an automatic device which activated it to the school's co-ordinates at five of three and kept it so, barring manual adjustment, until Richard arrived.

Her eyes were fixed on the Door's dismal gray (why couldn't an inactive force-field be any other color, something more lively and cheerful?) and waited. Her hands felt cold as she squeezed them together.

The Door turned black at the precise second but nothing happened. The minutes passed and Richard was late. Then quite late. Then very late.

It was a quarter of four and she was distracted. Normally, she would have phoned the school, but she couldn't, she couldn't. Not after that teacher had deliberately cast doubts on Richard's mental well-being. How could she?

Mrs. Hanshaw moved about restlessly, lighting a cigarette with fumbling fingers, then smudging it out. Could it be something quite normal? Could Richard be staying after school for some reason? Surely he would have told her in advance. A gleam of light struck her; he knew she was planning to go to New York and might not be back till late in the evening—

No, he would surely have told her. Why fool herself?

Her pride was breaking. She would have to call the school, or even (she closed her eyes and teardrops squeezed through between the lashes) the police.

And when she opened her eyes, Richard stood before her, eyes on the ground and his whole bearing that of someone waiting for a blow to fall.

"Hello, Mom."

Mrs. Hanshaw's anxiety transmuted itself instantly (in a manner known only to mothers) into anger. "Where have you been, Richard?"

And then, before she could go further into the refrain concerning careless, unthinking sons and broken-hearted mothers, she took note of his appearance in greater detail, and gasped in utter horror.

She said, "You've been in the open."

Her son looked down at his dusty shoes (minus flexies), at the dirt marks that streaked his lower arms and at the small, but definite tear in his shirt. He said, "Gosh, Mom, I just thought I'd—" and he faded out.

She said, "Was there anything wrong with the school Door?"

"No, Mom."

"Do you realize I've been worried sick about you?" She waited vainly for an answer. "Well, I'll talk to you afterward, young man. First, you're taking a bath, and every stitch of your clothing is being thrown out. Mekkano!"

But the mekkano had already reacted properly to the phrase "taking a bath" and was off to the bathroom in its silent glide.

"You take your shoes off right here," said Mrs. Hanshaw, "then march after mekkano."

Richard did as he was told with a resignation that placed him beyond futile protest.

Mrs. Hanshaw picked up the soiled shoes between thumb and forefinger and dropped them down the disposal chute which hummed in faint dismay at the unexpected load. She dusted her hands carefully on a tissue which she allowed to float down the chute after the shoes.

She did not join Richard at dinner but let him eat in the worse-than-lack-of-company of the mekkano. This, she thought, would be an active sign of her displeasure and would do more than any amount of scolding or punishment to make him realize that he had done wrong. Richard, she frequently told herself, was a sensitive boy.

But she went up to see him at bedtime.

She smiled at him and spoke softly. She thought that would be the best way. After all, he had been punished already.

She said, "What happened today, Dickie-boy?" She had called him that when he was a baby and just the sound of the name softened her nearly to tears.

But he only looked away and his voice was stubborn and cold. "I just don't like to go through those darn Doors, Mom."

"But why ever not?"

He shuffled his hands over the filmy sheet (fresh, clean, antiseptic and, of course, disposable after each use) and said, "I just don't like them."

"But then how do you expect to go to school, Dickie?"

"I'll get up early," he mumbled.

"But there's nothing wrong with Doors."

"Don't like 'em." He never once looked up at her.

She said, despairingly, "Oh, well, you have a good sleep and tomorrow morning you'll feel much better."

She kissed him and left the room, automatically passing her hand through the photo-cell beam and in that manner dimming the room-lights.

But she had trouble sleeping herself that night. Why should Dickie dislike Doors so suddenly? They had never bothered him before. To be sure, the Door had broken down in the morning but that should make him appreciate them all the more.

Dickie was behaving so unreasonably.

Unreasonably? That reminded her of Miss Robbins and her diagnosis and Mrs. Hanshaw's soft jaw set in the darkness and privacy of her bedroom. Nonsense! The boy was upset and a night's sleep was all the therapy he needed.

But the next morning when she arose, her son was not in the house. The mekkano could not speak but it could answer questions with gestures of its appendages equivalent to a yes or no, and it did not take Mrs. Hanshaw more than half a minute to ascertain that the boy had arisen thirty minutes earlier than usual, skimped his shower, and darted out of the house.

But not by way of the Door.

Out the other way—through the door. Small "d."

Mrs. Hanshaw's visiphone signaled genteelly at 3:10 P.M. that day. Mrs. Hanshaw guessed the caller and having activated the receiver, saw that she had guessed correctly. A quick glance in the mirror to see that she was properly calm after a day of abstracted concern and worry and then she keyed in her own transmission.

"Yes, Miss Robbins," she said coldly.

Richard's teacher was a bit breathless. She said, "Mrs. Hanshaw, Richard has deliberately left through the fire door although I told him to use the regular Door. I do not know where he went."

Mrs. Hanshaw said, carefully, "He left to come home."

Miss Robbins looked dismayed. "Do you approve of this?"

Pale-faced, Mrs. Hanshaw set about putting the teacher in her place. "I don't think it is up to you to criticize. If my son does not choose to use the Door, it is his affair and mine. I don't think there is any school ruling that would force him to use the Door, is there?" Her bearing quite plainly intimated that if there were she would see to it that it was changed.

Miss Robbins flushed and had time for one quick remark before contact was broken. She said, "I'd have him probed. I really would."

Mrs. Hanshaw remained standing before the quartzinium plate, staring blindly at its blank face. Her sense of family placed her for a few moments quite firmly on Richard's side. Why *did* he have to use the Door if he chose not to? And then she settled down to wait and pride battled the gnawing anxiety that something after all was wrong with Richard.

He came home with a look of defiance on his face, but his mother, with a strenuous effort at self-control, met him as though nothing were out of the ordinary.

For weeks, she followed that policy. It's nothing, she told herself. It's a vagary. He'll grow out of it.

It grew into an almost normal state of affairs. Then, too, every once in a while, perhaps three days in a row, she would come down to breakfast to find Richard waiting sullenly at the Door, then using it when school time came. She always refrained from commenting on the matter.

Always, when he did that, and especially when he followed it up by arriving home via the Door, her heart grew warm and she thought, "Well, it's over." But always with the passing of one day, two or three, he would return like an addict to his drug and drift silently out by the door—small "d"—before she woke.

And each time she thought despairingly of psychiatrists and probes, and each time the vision of Miss Robbins' low-bred satisfaction at (possibly) learning of it, stopped her, although she was scarcely aware that that was the true motive.

Meanwhile, she lived with it and made the best of it. The mekkano was instructed to wait at the door—small "d"—with a Tergo kit and a change of clothing. Richard washed and changed without resistance. His underthings, socks and flexies were disposable in any case, and Mrs. Hanshaw bore uncomplainingly the expense of daily disposal of shirts. Trousers she finally allowed to go a week before disposal on condition of rigorous nightly cleansing.

One day she suggested that Richard accompany her on a trip to New York. It was more a vague desire to keep him in sight than part of any purposeful plan. He did not object. He was even happy. He stepped right through the Door, unconcerned. He didn't hesitate. He even lacked the look of resentment he wore on those mornings he used the Door to go to school.

Mrs. Hanshaw rejoiced. This could be a way of weaning him back into Door usage, and she racked her ingenuity for excuses to make trips with Richard. She even raised her power bill to quite unheard-of heights by suggesting, and going through with, a trip to Canton for the day in order to witness a Chinese festival.

That was on a Sunday, and the next morning Richard marched directly to the hole in the wall he always used. Mrs. Hanshaw, having wakened particularly early, witnessed that. For once, badgered past endurance, she called after him plaintively, "Why not the Door, Dickie?"

He said, briefly, "It's all right for Canton," and stepped out of the house.

So that plan ended in failure. And then, one day, Richard came home soaking wet. The mekkano hovered above him uncertainly and Mrs. Hanshaw, just returned from a four-hour visit with her sister in Iowa, cried, "Richard Hanshaw!"

He said, hang-dog fashion, "It started raining. All of a sudden, it started raining."

For a moment, the word didn't register with her. Her own school days and her studies of geography were twenty years in the past. And then she remembered and caught the vision of water pouring recklessly and endlessly down from the sky—a mad cascade of water with no tap to turn off, no button to push, no contact to break.

She said, "And you stayed out in it?"

He said, "Well, gee, Mom, I came home fast as I could. I didn't know it was going to rain."

Mrs. Hanshaw had nothing to say. She was appalled and the sensation filled her too full for words to find a place.

Two days later, Richard found himself with a running nose, and a dry, scratchy throat. Mrs. Hanshaw had to admit that the virus of disease had found a lodging in her house, as though it were a miserable hovel of the Iron Age.

It was over that that her stubbornness and pride broke and she admitted to herself that, after all, Richard had to have psychiatric help.

Mrs. Hanshaw chose a psychiatrist with care. Her first impulse was to find one at a distance. For a while, she considered stepping directly into the San Francisco Medical Center and choosing one at random.

And then it occurred to her that by doing that she would become merely an anonymous consultant. She would have no way of obtaining any greater consideration for herself than would be forthcoming to any public-Door user of the city slums. Now if she remained in her own community, her word would carry weight—

She consulted the district map. It was one of that excellent series prepared by Doors, Inc., and distributed free of charge to their clients. Mrs. Hanshaw couldn't quite suppress that little thrill of civic pride as she unfolded the map. It wasn't a fine-print directory of Door co-ordinates only. It was an actual map, with each house carefully located.

And why not? District A-3 was a name of moment in the world, a badge of aristocracy. It was the first community on the planet to have been established on a completely Doored basis. The first, the largest, the wealthiest, the best-known. It needed no factories, no stores. It didn't even need roads.

Each house was a little secluded castle, the Door of which had entry anywhere the world over where other Doors existed.

Carefully, she followed down the keyed listing of the five thousand families of District A-3. She knew it included several psychiatrists. The learned professions were well represented in A-3.

Doctor Hamilton Sloane was the second name she arrived at and her finger lingered upon the map. His office was scarcely two miles from the Hanshaw residence. She liked his name. The fact that he lived in A-3 was evidence of worth. And he was a neighbor, practically a neighbor. He would understand that it was a matter of urgency—and confidential.

Firmly, she put in a call to his office to make an appointment.

Doctor Hamilton Sloane was a comparatively young man, not quite forty. He was of good family and he had indeed heard of Mrs. Hanshaw.

He listened to her quietly and then said, "And this all began with the Door breakdown."

"That's right, Doctor."

"Does he show any fear of the Doors?"

"Of course not. What an idea!" She was plainly startled.

"It's possible, Mrs. Hanshaw, it's possible. After all, when you stop to think of how a Door works it is rather a frightening thing, really. You step into a Door, and for an instant your atoms are converted into field-energies, transmitted to another part of space and reconverted into matter. For that instant you're not alive."

"I'm sure no one thinks of such things."

"But your son may. He witnessed the breakdown of the Door. He may be saying to himself, 'What if the Door breaks down just as I'm half-way through?'"

"But that's nonsense. He still uses the Door. He's even been to Canton with me; Canton, China. And as I told you, he uses it for school about once or twice a week."

"Freely? Cheerfully?"

"Well," said Mrs. Hanshaw, reluctantly, "he does seem a bit put out by it. But really, Doctor, there isn't much use talking about it, is there? If you would do a quick probe, see where the trouble was," and she finished on a bright note, "why, that would be all. I'm sure it's quite a minor thing."

Dr. Sloane sighed. He detested the word "probe" and there was scarcely any word he heard oftener.

"Mrs. Hanshaw," he said patiently, "there is no such thing as a quick probe. Now I know the mag-strips are full of it and it's a rage in some circles, but it's much overrated."

"Are you serious?"

"Quite. The probe is very complicated and the theory is that it traces mental circuits. You see, the cells of the brains are interconnected in a large variety of ways. Some of those interconnected paths are more used than others. They represent habits of thought, both conscious and unconscious. Theory has it that these paths in any given brain can be used to diagnose mental ills early and with certainty."

"Well, then?"

"But subjection to the probe is quite a fearful thing, especially to a child. It's a traumatic experience. It takes over an hour. And even then, the results must be sent to the Central Psychoanalytical Bureau for analysis, and that could take weeks. And on top of all that, Mrs. Hanshaw, there are many psychiatrists who think the theory of probe-analyses to be most uncertain."

Mrs. Hanshaw compressed her lips. "You mean nothing can be done."

Dr. Sloane smiled. "Not at all. There were psychiatrists for centuries before there were probes. I suggest that you let me talk to the boy."

"Talk to him? Is that all?"

"I'll come to you for background information when necessary, but the essential thing, I think, is to talk to the boy."

"Really, Dr. Sloane, I doubt if he'll discuss the matter with you. He won't talk to me about it and I'm his mother."

"That often happens," the psychiatrist assured her. "A child will sometimes talk more readily to a stranger. In any case, I cannot take the case otherwise."

Mrs. Hanshaw rose, not at all pleased. "When can you come, Doctor?"

"What about this coming Saturday? The boy won't be in school. Will you be busy?"

"We will be ready."

She made a dignified exit. Dr. Sloane accompanied her through the small reception room to his office Door and waited while she punched the coordinates of her house. He watched her pass through. She became a half-woman, a quarter-woman, an isolated elbow and foot, a nothing.

It *was* frightening.

Did a Door ever break down during passage, leaving half a body here and half there? He had never heard of such a case, but he imagined it could happen.

He returned to his desk and looked up the time of his next appointment. It was obvious to him that Mrs. Hanshaw was annoyed and disappointed at not having arranged for a psychic probe treatment.

Why, for God's sake? Why should a thing like the probe, an obvious piece of quackery in his own opinion, get such a hold on the general public? It must be part of this general trend toward machines. Anything man can do, machines can do better. Machines! More machines! Machines for anything and everything! O tempora! O mores!

Oh, hell!

His resentment of the probe was beginning to bother him. Was it a fear of technological unemployment, a basic insecurity on his part, a mechanophobia, if that was the word—

He made a mental note to discuss this with his own analyst.

Dr. Sloane had to feel his way. The boy wasn't a patient who had come to him, more or less anxious to talk, more or less anxious to be helped.

Under the circumstances it would have been best to keep his first meeting with Richard short and noncommittal. It would have been sufficient merely to establish himself as something less than a total stranger. The next time he would be someone Richard had seen before. The time after he would be an acquaintance, and after that a friend of the family.

Unfortunately, Mrs. Hanshaw was not likely to accept a long-drawn-out process. She would go searching for a probe and, of course, she would find it.

And harm the boy. He was certain of that.

It was for that reason he felt he must sacrifice a little of the proper caution and risk a small crisis.

An uncomfortable ten minutes had passed when he decided he must try. Mrs. Hanshaw was smiling in a rather rigid way, eyeing him narrowly, as though she expected verbal magic from him. Richard wriggled in his seat, unresponsive to Dr. Sloane's tentative comments, overcome with boredom and unable not to show it.

Dr. Sloane said, with casual suddenness, "Would you like to take a walk with me, Richard?"

The boy's eyes widened and he stopped wriggling. He looked directly at Dr. Sloane. "A walk, sir?"

"I mean, outside."

"Do you go—outside?"

"Sometimes. When I feel like it."

Richard was on his feet, holding down a squirming eagerness. "I didn't think anyone did."

"I do. And I like company."

The boy sat down, uncertainly. "Mom?—"

Mrs. Hanshaw had stiffened in her seat, her compressed lips radiating horror, but she managed to say, "Why certainly, Dickie. But watch yourself."

And she managed a quick and baleful glare at Dr. Sloane.

In one respect, Dr. Sloane had lied. He did *not* go outside "sometimes." He hadn't been in the open since early college days. True, he had been athletically inclined (still was to some extent) but in his time the indoor ultra-violet chambers, swimming pools and tennis courts had flourished. For those with the price, they were much more satisfactory than the outdoor equivalents, open to the elements as they were, could possibly be. There was no occasion to go outside.

So there was a crawling sensation about his skin when he felt wind touch it, and he put down his flexied shoes on bare grass with a gingerly movement.

"Hey, look at that." Richard was quite different now, laughing, his reserve broken down.

Dr. Sloane had time only to catch a flash of blue that ended in a tree. Leaves rustled and he lost it.

"What was it?"

"A bird," said Richard. "A blue kind of bird."

Dr. Sloane looked about him in amazement. The Hanshaw residence was on a rise of ground, and he could see for miles. The area was only lightly wooded and between clumps of trees, grass gleamed brightly in the sunlight.

Colors set in deeper green made red and yellow patterns. They were flowers. From the books he had viewed in the course of his lifetime and from the old video shows, he had learned enough so that all this had an eerie sort of familiarity.

And yet the grass was so trim, the flowers so patterned. Dimly, he realized he had been expecting something wilder. He said, "Who takes care of all this?"

Richard shrugged. "I dunno. Maybe the mekkanos do it."

"Mekkanos?"

"There's loads of them around. Sometimes they got a sort of atomic knife they hold near the ground. It cuts the grass. And they're always fooling around with the flowers and things. There's one of them over there."

It was a small object, half a mile away. Its metal skin cast back highlights as it moved slowly over the gleaming meadow, engaged in some sort of activity that Dr. Sloane could not identify.

Dr. Sloane was astonished. Here it was a perverse sort of estheticism, a kind of conspicuous consumption—

"What's that?" he asked suddenly.

Richard looked. He said, "That's a house. Belongs to the Froehlichs. Coordinates, A-3, 23, 461. That little pointy building over there is the public Door."

Dr. Sloane was staring at the house. Was that what it looked like from the outside? Somehow he had imagined something much more cubic, and taller.

"Come along," shouted Richard, running ahead.

Dr. Sloane followed more sedately. "Do you know all the houses about here?"

"Just about."

"Where is A-23, 26, 475?" It was his own house, of course.

Richard looked about. "Let's see. Oh, sure, I know where it is—you see that water there?"

"Water?" Dr. Sloane made out a line of silver curving across the green.

"Sure. Real water. Just sort of running over rocks and things. It keeps running all the time. You can get across it if you step on the rocks. It's called a river."

More like a creek, thought Dr. Sloane. He had studied geography, of course, but what passed for the subject these days was really economic and cultural geography. Physical geography was almost an extinct science except among specialists. Still, he knew what rivers and creeks were, in a theoretical sort of way.

Richard was still talking. "Well, just past the river, over that hill with the big clump of trees and down the other side a way is A-23, 26, 475. It's a light green house with a white roof."

"It is?" Dr. Sloane was genuinely astonished. He hadn't known it was green.

Some small animal disturbed the grass in its anxiety to avoid the oncoming feet. Richard looked after it and shrugged. "You can't catch them. I tried."

A butterfly flitted past, a wavering bit of yellow. Dr. Sloane's eyes followed it.

There was a low hum that lay over the fields, interspersed with an occasional harsh, calling sound, a rattle, a twittering, a chatter that rose, then fell. As his ear accustomed itself to listening, Dr. Sloane heard a thousand sounds, and none were man-made.

A shadow fell upon the scene, advancing toward him, covering him. It was suddenly cooler and he looked upward, startled.

Richard said, "It's just a cloud. It'll go away in a minute—looka these flowers. They're the kind that smell."

They were several hundred yards from the Hanshaw residence. The cloud passed and the sun shone once more. Dr. Sloane looked back and was appalled at the distance they had covered. If they moved out of sight of the house and if Richard ran off, would he be able to find his way back?

He pushed the thought away impatiently and looked out toward the line of water (nearer now) and past it to where his own house must be. He thought wonderingly: Light green?

He said, "You must be quite an explorer."

Richard said, with a shy pride, "When I go to school and come back, I always try to use a different route and see new things."

"But you don't go outside every morning, do you? Sometimes you use the Doors, I imagine."

"Oh, sure."

"Why is that, Richard?" Somehow, Dr. Sloane felt there might be significance in that point.

But Richard quashed him. With his eyebrows up and a look of astonishment on his face, he said, "Well, gosh, some mornings it rains and I *have* to use the Door. I hate that, but what can you do? About two weeks ago, I got caught in the rain and I—" he looked about him automatically, and his voice sank to a whisper "—caught a cold, and wasn't Mom upset, though."

Dr. Sloane sighed. "Shall we go back now?"

There was a quick disappointment on Richard's face. "Aw, what for?"

"You remind me that your mother must be waiting for us."

"I guess so." The boy turned reluctantly.

They walked slowly back. Richard was saying, chattily, "I wrote a composition at school once about how if I could go on some ancient vehicle" (he pronounced it with exaggerated care) "I'd go in a stratoliner and look at stars and clouds and things. Oh, boy, I was sure nuts."

"You'd pick something else now?"

"You bet. I'd go in an aut'm'bile, real slow. Then I'd see everything there was."

Mrs. Hanshaw seemed troubled, uncertain. "You don't think it's abnormal, then, Doctor?"

"Unusual, perhaps, but not abnormal. He likes the outside."

"But how can he? It's so dirty, so unpleasant."

"That's a matter of individual taste. A hundred years ago our ancestors were all outside most of the time. Even today, I dare say there are a million Africans who have never seen a Door."

"But Richard's always been taught to behave himself the way a decent person in District A-3 is supposed to behave," said Mrs. Hanshaw, fiercely. "Not like an African or—or an ancestor."

"That may be part of the trouble, Mrs. Hanshaw. He feels this urge to go outside and yet he feels it to be wrong. He's ashamed to talk about it to you or to his teacher. It forces him into sullen retreat and it could eventually be dangerous."

"Then how can we persuade him to stop?"

Dr. Sloane said, "Don't try. Channel the activity instead. The day your Door broke down, he was forced outside, found he liked it, and that set a pattern. He used the trip to school and back as an excuse to repeat that first exciting experience. Now suppose you agree to let him out of the house for two hours on Saturdays and Sundays. Suppose he gets it through his head that after all he can go outside without necessarily having to go anywhere in the process. Don't you think he'll be willing to use the Door to go to school and back thereafter? And don't you think that will stop the trouble he's now having with his teacher and probably with his fellow-pupils?"

"But then will matters remain so? Must they? Won't he ever be normal again?"

Dr. Sloane rose to his feet. "Mrs. Hanshaw, he's as normal as need be right now. Right now, he's tasting the joys of the forbidden. If you co-operate with him, show that you don't disapprove, it will lose some of its attraction right there. Then, as he grows older, he will become more aware of the expectations and demands of society. He will learn to conform. After all, there is a little of the rebel in all of us, but it generally dies down as we grow old and tired. Unless, that is, it is unreasonably suppressed and allowed to build up pressure. Don't do that. Richard will be all right."

He walked to the Door.

Mrs. Hanshaw said, "And you don't think a probe will be necessary, Doctor?"

He turned and said vehemently, "No, definitely not! There is nothing about the boy that requires it. Understand? Nothing."

His fingers hesitated an inch from the combination board and the expression on his face grew lowering.

"What's the matter, Dr. Sloane?" asked Mrs. Hanshaw.

But he didn't hear her because he was thinking of the Door and the psychic probe and all the rising, choking tide of machinery. There is a little of the rebel in all of us, he thought.

So he said in a soft voice, as his hand fell away from the board and his feet turned away from the Door, "You know, it's such a beautiful day that I think I'll walk."

Strikebreaker

Elvis Blei rubbed his plump hands and said, "Self-containment is the word."
He smiled uneasily as he helped Steven Lamorak of Earth to a light. There
was uneasiness all over his smooth face with its small wide-set eyes.

Lamorak puffed smoke appreciatively and crossed his lanky legs.

His hair was powdered with gray and he had a large and powerful
jawbone. "Home grown?" he asked, staring critically at the cigarette. He
tried to hide his own disturbance at the other's tension.

"Quite," said Blei.

"I wonder," said Lamorak, "that you have room on your small world for
such luxuries."

(Lamorak thought of his first view of Elsevere from the spaceship
visiplate. It was a jagged, airless planetoid, some hundred miles in diameter
—just a dust-gray rough-hewn rock, glimmering dully in the light of its sun,
200,000,000 miles distant. It was the only object more than a mile in diameter that circled that sun, and now men had burrowed into that miniature
world and constructed a society in it. And he himself, as a sociologist, had
come to study the world and see how humanity had made itself fit into that
queerly specialized niche.)

Blei's polite fixed smile expanded a hair. He said, "We are not a small
world, Dr. Lamorak; you judge us by two-dimensional standards. The surface area of Elsevere is only three quarters that of the State of New York,
but that's irrelevant. Remember, we can occupy, if we wish, the entire
interior of Elsevere. A sphere of 50 miles radius has a volume of well over

half a million cubic miles. If all of Elsevere were occupied by levels 50 feet apart, the total surface area within the planetoid would be 56,000,000 square miles, and that is equal to the total land area of Earth. And none of these square miles, Doctor, would be unproductive."

Lamorak said, "Good Lord," and stared blankly for a moment. "Yes, of course you're right. Strange I never thought of it that way. But then, Elsevere is the only thoroughly exploited planetoid world in the Galaxy; the rest of us simply can't get away from thinking of two-dimensional surfaces, as you pointed out. Well, I'm more than ever glad that your Council has been so cooperative as to give me a free hand in this investigation of mine."

Blei nodded convulsively at that.

Lamorak frowned slightly and thought: He acts for all the world as though he wished I had not come. Something's wrong.

Blei said, "Of course, you understand that we are actually much smaller than we could be; only minor portions of Elsevere have as yet been hollowed out and occupied. Nor are we particularly anxious to expand, except very slowly. To a certain extent we are limited by the capacity of our pseudogravity engines and Solar energy converters."

"I understand. But tell me, Councillor Blei—as a matter of personal curiosity, and not because it is of prime importance to my project—could I view some of your farming and herding levels first? I am fascinated by the thought of fields of wheat and herds of cattle inside a planetoid."

"You'll find the cattle small by your standards, Doctor, and we don't have much wheat. We grow yeast to a much greater extent. But there will be some wheat to show you. Some cotton and tobacco, too. Even fruit trees."

"Wonderful. As you say, self-containment. You recirculate everything, I imagine."

Lamorak's sharp eyes did not miss the fact that this last remark twinged Blei. The Elseverian's eyes narrowed to slits that hid his expression.

He said, "We must recirculate, yes. Air, water, food, minerals—everything that is used up—must be restored to its original state; waste products are reconverted to raw materials. All that is needed is energy, and we have enough of that. We don't manage with one hundred percent efficiency, of course; there is a certain seepage. We import a small amount of water each year; and if our needs grow, we may have to import some coal and oxygen."

Lamorak said, "When can we start our tour, Councillor Blei?"

Blei's smile lost some of its negligible warmth. "As soon as we can, Doctor. There are some routine matters that must be arranged."

Lamorak nodded, and having finished his cigarette, stubbed it out.

Routine matters? There was none of this hesitancy during the preliminary correspondence. Elsevere had seemed proud that its unique planetoid existence had attracted the attention of the Galaxy.

He said, "I realize I would be a disturbing influence in a tightly-knit society," and watched grimly as Blei leaped at the explanation and made it his own.

"Yes," said Blei, "we feel marked off from the rest of the Galaxy. We have our own customs. Each individual Elseverian fits into a comfortable niche. The appearance of a stranger without fixed caste is unsettling."

"The caste system does involve a certain inflexibility."

"Granted," said Blei quickly; "but there is also a certain self-assurance. We have firm rules of intermarriage and rigid inheritance of occupation. Each man, woman and child knows his place, accepts it, and is accepted in it; we have virtually no neurosis or mental illness."

"And are there no misfits?" asked Lamorak.

Blei shaped his mouth as though to say no, then clamped it suddenly shut, biting the word into silence; a frown deepened on his forehead. He said, at length, "I will arrange for the tour, Doctor. Meanwhile, I imagine you would welcome a chance to freshen up and to sleep."

They rose together and left the room, Blei politely motioning the Earthman to precede him out the door.

Lamorak felt oppressed by the vague feeling of crisis that had pervaded his discussion with Blei.

The newspaper reinforced that feeling. He read it carefully before getting into bed, with what was at first merely a clinical interest. It was an eight-page tabloid of synthetic paper. One quarter of its items consisted of "personals": births, marriages, deaths, record quotas, expanding habitable volume (not area! three dimensions!). The remainder included scholarly essays, educational material, and fiction. Of news, in the sense to which Lamorak was accustomed, there was virtually nothing.

One item only could be so considered and that was chilling in its incompleteness.

It said, under a small headline: *DEMANDS UNCHANGED: There has been no change in his attitude of yesterday. The Chief Councillor, after a second interview, announced that his demands remain completely unreasonable and cannot be met under any circumstances.*

Then, in parentheses, and in different type, there was the statement: *The editors of this paper agree that Elsevere cannot and will not jump to his whistle, come what may.*

Lamorak read it over three times. *His* attitude. *His* demands. *His* whistle. *Whose?*

He slept uneasily, that night.

He had no time for newspapers in the days that followed; but spasmodically, the matter returned to his thoughts.

Blei, who remained his guide and companion for most of the tour, grew ever more withdrawn.

On the third day (quite artificially clock-set in an Earthlike twenty-four hour pattern), Blei stopped at one point, and said, "Now this level is devoted entirely to chemical industries. That section is not important—"

But he turned away a shade too rapidly, and Lamorak seized his arm. "What are the products of that section?"

"Fertilizers. Certain organics," said Blei stiffly.

Lamorak held him back, looking for what sight Blei might be evading. His gaze swept over the close-by horizons of lined rock and the buildings squeezed and layered between the levels.

Lamorak said, "Isn't that a private residence there?"

Blei did not look in the indicated direction.

Lamorak said, "I think that's the largest one I've seen yet. Why is it here on a factory level?" That alone made it noteworthy. He had already seen that the levels on Elsevere were divided rigidly among the residential, the agricultural and the industrial.

He looked back and called, "Councillor Blei!"

The Councillor was walking away and Lamorak pursued him with hasty steps. "Is there something wrong, sir?"

Blei muttered, "I am rude, I know. I am sorry. There are matters that prey on my mind—" He kept up his rapid pace.

"Concerning *his* demands."

Blei came to a full halt. "What do *you* know about that?"

"No more than I've said. I read that much in the newspaper."

Blei muttered something to himself.

Lamorak said, "Ragusnik? What's that?"

Blei sighed heavily. "I suppose you ought to be told. It's humiliating, deeply embarrassing. The Council thought that matters would certainly be arranged shortly and that your visit need not be interfered with, that you need not know or be concerned. But it is almost a week now. I don't know what will happen and, appearances notwithstanding, it might be best for you to leave. No reason for an Outworlder to risk death."

The Earthman smiled incredulously. "Risk death? In this little world, so peaceful and busy. I can't believe it."

The Elseverian councillor said, "I can explain. I think it best I should." He turned his head away. "As I told you, everything on Elsevere must recirculate. You understand that."

"Yes."

"That includes—uh, human wastes."

"I assumed so," said Lamorak.

"Water is reclaimed from it by distillation and absorption. What remains is converted into fertilizer for yeast use; some of it is used as a source of fine organics and other by-products. These factories you see are devoted to this."

"Well?" Lamorak had experienced a certain difficulty in the drinking of water when he first landed on Elsevere, because he had been realistic enough to know what it must be reclaimed from; but he had conquered the feeling easily enough. Even on Earth, water was reclaimed by natural processes from all sorts of unpalatable substances.

Blei, with increasing difficulty, said, "Igor Ragusnik is the man who is in charge of the industrial processes immediately involving the wastes. The position has been in his family since Elsevere was first colonized. One of the original settlers was Mikhail Ragusnik and he—he—"

"Was in charge of waste reclamation."

"Yes. Now that residence you singled out is the Ragusnik residence; it is the best and most elaborate on the planetoid. Ragusnik gets many privileges the rest of us do not have; but, after all—" Passion entered the Councillor's voice with great suddenness, "we cannot *speak* to him."

"What?"

"He demands full social equality. He wants his children to mingle with ours, and our wives to visit— Oh!" It was a groan of utter disgust.

Lamorak thought of the newspaper item that could not even bring itself to mention Ragusnik's name in print, or to say anything specific about his demands. He said, "I take it he's an outcast because of his job."

"Naturally. Human wastes and—" words failed Blei. After a pause, he said more quietly, "As an Earthman, I suppose you don't understand."

"As a sociologist, I think I do." Lamorak thought of the Untouchables in ancient India, the ones who handled corpses. He thought of the position of swineherds in ancient Judea.

He went on, "I gather Elsevere will not give in to those demands."

"Never," said Blei, energetically. "Never."

"And so?"

"Ragusnik has threatened to cease operations."

"Go on strike, in other words."

"Yes."

"Would that be serious?"

"We have enough food and water to last quite a while; reclamation is not essential in that sense. But the wastes would accumulate; they would infect the planetoid. After generations of careful disease control, we have low natural resistance to germ diseases. Once an epidemic started—and one would—we would drop by the hundred."

"Is Ragusnik aware of this?"

"Yes, of course."

"Do you think he is likely to go through with his threat, then?"

"He is mad. He has already stopped working; there has been no waste reclamation since the day before you landed." Blei's bulbous nose sniffed at the air as though it already caught the whiff of excrement.

Lamorak sniffed mechanically at that, but smelled nothing.

Blei said, "So you see why it might be wise for you to leave. We are humiliated, of course, to have to suggest it."

But Lamorak said, "Wait; not just yet. Good Lord, this is a matter of great interest to me professionally. May I speak to the Ragusnik?"

"On no account," said Blei, alarmed.

"But I would like to understand the situation. The sociological conditions here are unique and not to be duplicated elsewhere. In the name of science—"

"How do you mean, speak? Would image-reception do?"

"Yes."

"I will ask the Council," muttered Blei.

They sat about Lamorak uneasily, their austere and dignified expressions badly marred with anxiety. Blei, seated in the midst of them, studiously avoided the Earthman's eyes.

The Chief Councillor, gray-haired, his face harshly wrinkled, his neck scrawny, said in a soft voice, "If in any way you can persuade him, sir, out of your own convictions, we will welcome that. In no case, however, are you to imply that we will, in any way, yield."

A gauzy curtain fell between the Council and Lamorak. He could make out the individual councillors still, but now he turned sharply toward the receiver before him. It glowed to life.

A head appeared in it, in natural color and with great realism. A strong dark head, with massive chin faintly stubbled, and thick, red lips set into a firm horizontal line.

The image said, suspiciously, "Who are you?"

Lamorak said, "My name is Steven Lamorak; I am an Earthman."

"An Outworlder?"

"That's right. I am visiting Elsevere. You are Ragusnik?"

"Igor Ragusnik, at your service," said the image, mockingly. "Except that there is no service and will be none until my family and I are treated like human beings."

Lamorak said, "Do you realize the danger that Elsevere is in? The possibility of epidemic disease?"

"In twenty-four hours, the situation can be made normal, if they allow me humanity. The situation is theirs to correct."

"You sound like an educated man, Ragusnik."

"So?"

"I am told you're denied of no material comforts. You are housed and clothed and fed better than anyone on Elsevere. Your children are the best educated."

"Granted. But all by servo-mechanism. And motherless girl-babies are sent us to care for until they grow to be our wives. And they die young for loneliness. Why?" There was sudden passion in his voice. "Why must we live in isolation as if we were all monsters, unfit for human beings to be near? Aren't we human beings like others, with the same needs and desires and feelings. Don't we perform an honorable and useful function—?"

There was a rustling of sighs from behind Lamorak. Ragusnik heard it, and raised his voice. "I see you of the Council behind there. Answer me: Isn't it an honorable and useful function? It is *your* waste made into food for *you*. Is the man who purifies corruption worse than the man who produces it?—Listen, Councillors, I will *not* give in. Let all of Elsevere die of disease —including myself and my son, if necessary—but I will not give in. My family will be better dead of disease, than living as now."

Lamorak interrupted. "You've led this life since birth, haven't you?"

"And if I have?"

"Surely you're used to it."

"Never. Resigned, perhaps. My father was resigned, and I was resigned for a while; but I have watched my son, my only son, with no other little boy to play with. My brother and I had each other, but my son will never have anyone, and I am no longer resigned. I am through with Elsevere and through with talking."

The receiver went dead.

The Chief Councillor's face had paled to an aged yellow. He and Blei were the only ones of the group left with Lamorak. The Chief Councillor said, "The man is deranged; I do not know how to force him."

He had a glass of wine at his side; as he lifted it to his lips, he spilled a few drops that stained his white trousers with purple splotches.

Lamorak said, "Are his demands so unreasonable? Why can't he be accepted into society?"

There was momentary rage in Blei's eyes. "A dealer in excrement." Then he shrugged. "You are from Earth."

Incongruously, Lamorak thought of another unacceptable, one of the numerous classic creations of the medieval cartoonist, Al Capp. The variously-named "inside man at the skonk works."

He said, "Does Ragusnik really deal with excrement? I mean, is there physical contact? Surely, it is all handled by automatic machinery."

"Of course," said the Chief Councillor.

"Then exactly what is Ragusnik's function?"

"He manually adjusts the various controls that assure the proper functioning of the machinery. He shifts units to allow repairs to be made; he alters functional rates with the time of day; he varies end production with demand." He added sadly, "If we had the space to make the machinery ten times as complex, all this could be done automatically; but that would be such needless waste."

"But even so," insisted Lamorak, "all Ragusnik does he does simply by pressing buttons or closing contacts or things like that."

"Yes."

"Then his work is no different from any Elseverian's."

Blei said, stiffly, "You don't understand."

"And for that you will risk the death of your children?"

"We have no other choice," said Blei. There was enough agony in his voice to assure Lamorak that the situation was torture for him, but that he had no other choice indeed.

Lamorak shrugged in disgust. "Then break the strike. Force him."

"How?" said the Chief Councillor. "Who would touch him or go near him? And if we kill him by blasting from a distance, how will that help us?"

Lamorak said, thoughtfully, "Would you know how to run his machinery?"

The Chief Councillor came to his feet. "I?" he howled.

"I don't mean *you*," cried Lamorak at once. "I used the pronoun in its indefinite sense. Could *someone* learn how to handle Ragusnik's machinery?"

Slowly, the passion drained out of the Chief Councillor. "It is in the handbooks, I am certain—though I assure you I have never concerned myself with it."

"Then couldn't someone learn the procedure and substitute for Ragusnik until the man gives in?"

Blei said, "Who would agree to do such a thing? Not I, under any circumstances."

Lamorak thought fleetingly of Earthly taboos that might be almost as strong. He thought of cannibalism, incest, a pious man cursing God. He said, "But you must have made provision for vacancy in the Ragusnik job. Suppose he died."

"Then his son would automatically succeed to his job, or his nearest other relative," said Blei.

"What if he had no adult relatives? What if all his family died at once?"

"That has never happened; it will never happen."

The Chief Councillor added, "If there were danger of it, we might, perhaps, place a baby or two with the Ragusniks and have it raised to the profession."

"Ah. And how would you choose that baby?"

"From among children of mothers who died in childbirth, as we choose the future Ragusnik bride."

"Then choose a substitute Ragusnik now, by lot," said Lamorak.

The Chief Councillor said, "*No! Impossible!* How can you suggest that? If we select a baby, that baby is brought up to the life; it knows no other. At this point, it would be necessary to choose an adult and subject him to Ragusnik-hood. No, Dr. Lamorak, we are neither monsters nor abandoned brutes."

No use, thought Lamorak helplessly. *No use, unless—*
He couldn't bring himself to face that *unless* just yet.

That night, Lamorak slept scarcely at all. Ragusnik asked for only the basic elements of humanity. But opposing that were thirty thousand El-severians who faced death.

The welfare of thirty thousand on one side; the just demands of one family on the other. Could one say that thirty thousand who would support such injustice deserved to die? Injustice by what standards? Earth's? El-severe's? And who was Lamorak that he should judge?

And Ragusnik? He was willing to let thirty thousand die, including men and women who merely accepted a situation they had been taught to accept and could not change if they wished to. And children who had nothing at all to do with it.

Thirty thousand on one side; a single family on the other.

Lamorak made his decision in something that was almost despair; in the morning he called the Chief Councillor.

He said, "Sir, if you can find a substitute, Ragusnik will see that he has lost all chance to force a decision in his favor and will return to work."

"There can be no substitute," sighed the Chief Councillor; "I have ex-plained that."

"No substitute among the Elseverians, but I am not an Elseverian; it doesn't matter to me. *I* will substitute."

They were excited, much more excited than Lamorak himself. A dozen times they asked him if he was serious.

Lamorak had not shaved, and he felt sick, "Certainly, I'm serious. And any time Ragusnik acts like this, you can always import a substitute. No other world has the taboo and there will always be plenty of temporary substitutes available if you pay enough."

(He was betraying a brutally exploited man, and he knew it. But he told himself desperately: *Except for ostracism, he's very well treated. Very well.*)

They gave him the handbooks and he spent six hours, reading and re-reading. There was no use asking questions. None of the Elseverians knew anything about the job, except for what was in the handbook; and all seemed uncomfortable if the details were as much as mentioned.

"Maintain zero reading of galvanometer A-2 at all times during red signal of the Lunge-howler," read Lamorak. "Now what's a Lunge-howler?"

"There will be a sign," muttered Blei, and the Elseverians looked at each other hang-dog and bent their heads to stare at their finger-ends.

They left him long before he reached the small rooms that were the central headquarters of generations of working Ragusniks, serving their world. He had specific instructions concerning which turnings to take and what level to reach, but they hung back and let him proceed alone.

He went through the rooms painstakingly, identifying the instruments and controls, following the schematic diagrams in the handbook.

There's a Lunge-howler, he thought, with gloomy satisfaction. The sign did indeed say so. It had a semi-circular face bitten into holes that were obviously designed to glow in separate colors. Why a "howler" then?

He didn't know.

Somewhere, thought Lamorak, *somewhere wastes are accumulating, pushing against gears and exits, pipelines and stills, waiting to be handled in half a hundred ways. Now they just accumulate.*

Not without a tremor, he pulled the first switch as indicated by the handbook in its directions for "Initiation." A gentle murmur of life made itself felt through the floors and walls. He turned a knob and lights went on.

At each step, he consulted the handbook, though he knew it by heart; and with each step, the rooms brightened and the dial-indicators sprang into motion and a humming grew louder.

Somewhere deep in the factories, the accumulated wastes were being drawn into the proper channels.

A high-pitched signal sounded and startled Lamorak out of his painful concentration. It was the communications signal and Lamorak fumbled his receiver into action.

Ragusnik's head showed, startled; then slowly, the incredulity and outright shock faded from his eyes. "*That's* how it is, then."

"I'm not an Elseverian, Ragusnik; I don't mind doing this."

"But what business is it of yours? Why do you interfere?"

"I'm on your side, Ragusnik, but I must do this."

"Why, if you're on my side? Do they treat people on your world as they treat me here?"

"Not any longer. But even if you are right, there are thirty thousand people on Elsevere to be considered."

"They would have given in; you've ruined my only chance."

"They would *not* have given in. And in a way, you've won; they know now that you're dissatisfied. Until now, they never dreamed a Ragusnik could be unhappy, that he could make trouble."

"What if they know? Now all they need do is hire an Outworlder anytime."

Lamorak shook his head violently. He had thought this through in these last bitter hours. "The fact that they know means that the Elseverians will begin to think about you; some will begin to wonder if it's right to treat a human so. And if Outworlders are hired, they'll spread the word that this goes on upon Elsevere and Galactic public opinion will be in your favor."

"And?"

"Things will improve. In your son's time, things will be much better."

"In my son's time," said Ragusnik, his cheeks sagging. "I might have had it now. Well, I lose. I'll go back to the job."

Lamorak felt an overwhelming relief. "If you'll come here now, sir, you may have your job and I'll consider it an honor to shake your hand."

Ragusnik's head snapped up and filled with a gloomy pride. "You call me 'sir' and offer to shake my hand. Go about your business, Earthman, and leave me to my work, for I would not shake yours."

Lamorak returned the way he had come, relieved that the crisis was over, and profoundly depressed, too.

He stopped in surprise when he found a section of corridor cordoned off, so he could not pass. He looked about for alternate routes, then startled at a magnified voice above his head. "Dr. Lamorak do you hear me? This is Councillor Blei."

Lamorak looked up. The voice came over some sort of public address system, but he saw no sign of an outlet.

He called out, "Is anything wrong? Can you hear me?"

"I hear you."

Instinctively, Lamorak was shouting. "Is anything wrong? There seems to be a block here. Are there complications with Ragusnik?"

"Ragusnik has gone to work," came Blei's voice. "The crisis is over, and you must make ready to leave."

"Leave?"

"Leave Elsevere; a ship is being made ready for you now."

"But wait a bit." Lamorak was confused by this sudden leap of events. "I haven't completed my gathering of data."

Blei's voice said, "This cannot be helped. You will be directed to the ship and your belongings will be sent after you by servo-mechanisms. We trust— we trust—"

Something was becoming clear to Lamorak. "You trust *what?*"

"We trust you will make no attempt to see or speak directly to any Elseverian. And of course we hope you will avoid embarrassment by not attempting to return to Elsevere at any time in the future. A colleague of yours would be welcome if further data concerning us is needed."

"I understand," said Lamorak, tonelessly. Obviously, he had himself become a Ragusnik. He had handled the controls that in turn had handled the wastes; he was ostracized. He was a corpse-handler, a swineherd, an inside man at the skonk works.

He said, "Good-bye."

Blei's voice said, "Before we direct you, Dr. Lamorak—. On behalf of the Council of Elsevere, I thank you for your help in this crisis."

"You're welcome," said Lamorak, bitterly.

Insert Knob A
in Hole B

Dave Woodbury and John Hansen, grotesque in their spacesuits, supervised anxiously as the large crate swung slowly out and away from the freight-ship and into the airlock. With nearly a year of their hitch on Space Station A5 behind them, they were understandably weary of filtration units that clanked, hydroponic tubs that leaked, air generators that hummed constantly and stopped occasionally.

"Nothing works," Woodbury would say mournfully, "because everything is hand-assembled by ourselves."

"Following directions," Hansen would add, "composed by an idiot."

There were undoubtedly grounds for complaint there. The most expensive thing about a spaceship was the room allowed for freight so all equipment had to be sent across space disassembled and nested. All equipment had to be assembled at the Station itself with clumsy hands, inadequate tools and with blurred and ambiguous direction sheets for guidance.

Painstakingly Woodbury had written complaints to which Hansen had added appropriate adjectives, and formal requests for relief of the situation had made their way back to Earth.

And Earth had responded. A special robot had been designed, with a positronic brain crammed with the knowledge of how to assemble properly any disassembled machine in existence.

That robot was in the crate being unloaded now and Woodbury was trembling as the airlock closed behind it.

"First," he said, "it overhauls the Food-Assembler and adjusts the steak-attachment knob so we can get it rare instead of burnt."

They entered the Station and attacked the crate with dainty touches of the demoleculizer rods in order to make sure that not a precious metal atom of their special assembly-robot was damaged.

The crate fell open!

And there within it were five hundred separate pieces—and one blurred and ambiguous direction sheet for assemblage.

The Up-to-Date Sorcerer

It always puzzled me that Nicholas Nitely, although a Justice of the Peace, was a bachelor. The atmosphere of his profession, so to speak, seemed so conducive to matrimony that surely he could scarcely avoid the gentle bond of wedlock.

When I said as much over a gin and tonic at the Club recently, he said, "Ah, but I had a narrow escape some time ago," and he sighed.

"Oh, really?"

"A fair young girl, sweet, intelligent, pure yet desperately ardent, and withal most alluring to the physical senses for even such an old fogy as myself."

I said, "How did you come to let her go?"

"I had no choice." He smiled gently at me and his smooth, ruddy complexion, his smooth gray hair, his smooth blue eyes, all combined to give him an expression of near-saintliness. He said, "You see, it was really the fault of her fiancé—"

"Ah, she was engaged to someone else."

"—and of Professor Wellington Johns, who was, although an endocrinologist, by way of being an up-to-date sorcerer. In fact, it was just that—" He sighed, sipped at his drink, and turned on me the bland and cheerful face of one who is about to change the subject.

I said firmly, "Now, then, Nitely, old man, you cannot leave it so. I want to know about your beautiful girl—the flesh that got away."

He winced at the pun (one, I must admit, of my more abominable efforts) and settled down by ordering his glass refilled. "You understand," he said, "I learned some of the details later on."

Professor Wellington Johns had a large and prominent nose, two sincere eyes and a distinct talent for making clothes appear too large for him. He said, "My dear children, love is a matter of chemistry."

His dear children, who were really students of his, and not his children at all, were named Alexander Dexter and Alice Sanger. They looked perfectly full of chemicals as they sat there holding hands. Together, their age amounted to perhaps 45, evenly split between them, and Alexander said, fairly inevitably, *"Vive la chémie!"*

Professor Johns smiled reprovingly. "Or rather endocrinology. Hormones, after all, affect our emotions and it is not surprising that one should, specifically, stimulate that feeling we call love."

"But that's so unromantic," murmured Alice. "I'm sure I don't need any." She looked up at Alexander with a yearning glance.

"My dear," said the professor, "your blood stream was crawling with it at that moment you, as the saying is, fell in love. Its secretion had been stimulated by"—for a moment he considered his words carefully, being a highly moral man—"by some environmental factor involving your young man, and once the hormonal action had taken place, inertia carried you on. I could duplicate the effect easily."

"Why, Professor," said Alice, with gentle affection. "It would be delightful to have you try," and she squeezed Alexander's hand shyly.

"I do not mean," said the professor, coughing to hide his embarrassment, "that I would personally attempt to reproduce—or, rather, to duplicate— the conditions that created the natural secretion of the hormone. I mean, instead, that I could inject the hormone itself by hypodermic or even by oral ingestion, since it is a steroid hormone. I have, you see," and here he removed his glasses and polished them proudly, "isolated and purified the hormone."

Alexander sat erect. "Professor! And you have said nothing?"

"I must know more about it first."

"Do you mean to say," said Alice, her lovely brown eyes shimmering with delight, "that you can make people feel the wonderful delight and heaven-surpassing tenderness of true love by means of a . . . a pill?"

The professor said, "I can indeed duplicate the emotion to which you refer in those rather cloying terms."

"Then why don't you?"

Alexander raised a protesting hand. "Now, darling, your ardor leads you astray. Our own happiness and forthcoming nuptials make you forget certain facts of life. If a married person were, by mistake, to accept this hormone—"

Professor Johns said, with a trace of hauteur, "Let me explain right now that my hormone, or my amatogenic principle, as I call it—" (for he, in common with many practical scientists, enjoyed a proper scorn for the rarefied niceties of classical philology).

"Call it a love-philtre, Professor," said Alice, with a melting sigh.

"My amatogenic cortical principle," said Professor Johns, sternly, "has no effect on married individuals. The hormone cannot work if inhibited by other factors, and being married is certainly a factor that inhibits love."

"Why, so I have heard," said Alexander, gravely, "but I intend to disprove that callous belief in the case of my own Alice."

"Alexander," said Alice. "My love."

The professor said, "I mean that marriage inhibits extramarital love."

Alexander said, "Why, it has come to my ears that sometimes it does not."

Alice said, shocked, "Alexander!"

"Only in rare instances, my dear, among those who have not gone to college."

The professor said, "Marriage may not inhibit a certain paltry sexual attraction, or tendencies toward minor trifling, but true love, as Miss Sanger expressed the emotion, is something which cannot blossom when the memory of a stern wife and various unattractive children hobbles the subconscious."

"Do you mean to say," said Alexander, "that if you were to feed your love-philtre—beg pardon, your amatogenic principle—to a number of people indiscriminately, only the *un*married individuals would be affected?"

"That is right, I have experimented on certain animals which, though not going through the conscious marriage rite, do form monogamous attachments. Those with the attachments already formed are not affected."

"Then, Professor, I have a perfectly splendid idea. Tomorrow night is the night of the Senior Dance here at college. There will be at least fifty couples present, mostly unmarried. Put your philtre in the punch."

"What? Are you mad?"

But Alice had caught fire. "Why, it's a heavenly idea, Professor. To think that all my friends will feel as I feel! Professor, you would be an angel from heaven. —But oh, Alexander, do you suppose the feelings might be a trifle uncontrolled? Some of our college chums are a little wild and if, in the heat of discovery of love, they should, well, kiss—"

Professor Johns said, indignantly, "My dear Miss Sanger. You must not allow your imagination to become overheated. My hormone induces only those feelings which lead to marriage and not to the expression of anything that might be considered indecorous."

"I'm sorry," murmured Alice, in confusion. "I should remember, Professor, that you are the most highly moral man I know—excepting always dear Alexander—and that no scientific discovery of yours could possibly lead to immorality."

She looked so woebegone that the professor forgave her at once.

"Then you'll do it, Professor?" urged Alexander. "After all, assuming there will be a sudden urge for mass marriage afterward, I can take care of that by having Nicholas Nitely, an old and valued friend of the family, present on some pretext. He is a Justice of the Peace and can easily arrange for such things as licenses and so on."

"I could scarcely agree," said the professor, obviously weakening, "to perform an experiment without the consent of those experimented upon. It would be unethical."

"But you would be bringing only joy to them. You would be contributing to the moral atmosphere of the college. For surely, in the absence of overwhelming pressure toward marriage, it sometimes happens even in college that the pressure of continuous propinquity breeds a certain danger of—of—"

"Yes, there is that," said the professor. "Well, I shall try a dilute solution. After all, the results may advance scientific knowledge tremendously and, as you say, it will also advance morality."

Alexander said, "And, of course, Alice and I will drink the punch, too."

Alice said, "Oh, Alexander, surely such love as ours needs no artificial aid."

"But it would not be artificial, my soul's own. According to the professor, your love began as a result of just such a hormonal effect, induced, I admit, by more customary methods."

Alice blushed rosily. "But then, my only love, why the need for the repetition?"

"To place us beyond all vicissitudes of Fate, my cherished one."

"Surely, my adored, you don't doubt my love."

"No, my heart's charmer, but—"

"*But?* Is it that you do not trust me, Alexander?"

"Of course I trust you, Alice, but—"

"*But?* Again but!" Alice rose, furious. "If you cannot trust me, sir, perhaps I had better leave—" And she did leave indeed, while the two men stared after her, stunned.

Professor Johns said, "I am afraid my hormone has, quite indirectly, been the occasion of spoiling a marriage rather than of causing one."

Alexander swallowed miserably, but his pride upheld him. "She will come back," he said, hollowly. "A love such as ours is not so easily broken."

The Senior Dance was, of course, the event of the year. The young men shone and the young ladies glittered. The music lilted and the dancing feet touched the ground only at intervals. Joy was unrestrained.

Or, rather, it was unrestrained in most cases. Alexander Dexter stood in one corner, eyes hard, expression icily bleak. Straight and handsome he might be, but no young woman approached him. He was known to belong to Alice Sanger, and under such circumstances, no college girl would dream of poaching. Yet where was Alice?

She had not come with Alexander and Alexander's pride prevented him from searching for her. From under grim eyelids, he could only watch the circulating couples cautiously.

Professor Johns, in formal clothes that did not fit although made to measure, approached him. He said, "I will add my hormone to the punch shortly before the midnight toast. Is Mr. Nitely still here?"

"I saw him a moment ago. In his capacity as chaperon he was busily engaged in making certain that the proper distance between dancing couples was maintained. Four fingers, I believe, at the point of closest approach. Mr. Nitely was most diligently making the necessary measurements."

"Very good. Oh, I had neglected to ask: Is the punch alcoholic? Alcohol would affect the workings of the amatogenic principle adversely."

Alexander, despite his sore heart, found spirit to deny the unintended slur upon his class. "Alcoholic, Professor? This punch is made along those principles firmly adhered to by all young college students. It contains only the purest of fruit juices, refined sugar, and a certain quantity of lemon peel— enough to stimulate but not inebriate."

"Good," said the professor. "Now I have added to the hormone a sedative designed to put our experimental subjects to sleep for a short time while the hormone works. Once they awaken, the first individual each sees—that is, of course, of the opposite sex—will inspire that individual with a pure and noble ardor that can end only in marriage."

Then, since it was nearly midnight, he made his way through the happy couples, all dancing at four-fingers' distance, to the punch bowl.

Alexander, depressed nearly to tears, stepped out to the balcony. In doing so, he just missed Alice, who entered the ballroom from the balcony by another door.

"Midnight," called out a happy voice. "Toast! Toast! Toast to the life ahead of us."

They crowded about the punch bowl; the little glasses were passed round.

"To the life ahead of us," they cried out and, with all the enthusiasm of young college students, downed the fiery mixture of pure fruit juices, sugar, and lemon peel, with—of course—the professor's sedated amatogenic principle.

As the fumes rose to their brains, they slowly crumpled to the floor.

Alice stood there alone, still holding her drink, eyes wet with unshed tears. "Oh, Alexander, Alexander, though you doubt, yet are you my only love. You wish me to drink and I shall drink." Then she, too, sank gracefully downward.

Nicholas Nitely had gone in search of Alexander, for whom his warm heart was concerned. He had seen him arrive without Alice and he could only assume that a lovers' quarrel had taken place. Nor did he feel any dismay at leaving the party to its own devices. These were not wild youngsters, but college boys and girls of good family and gentle upbringing. They could be trusted to the full to observe the four-finger limit, as he well knew.

He found Alexander on the balcony, staring moodily out at a star-riddled sky.

"Alexander, my boy." He put his hand on the young man's shoulder. "This is not like you. To give way so to depression. Chut, my young friend, chut."

Alexander's head bowed at the sound of the good old man's voice. "It is unmanly, I know, but I yearn for Alice. I have been cruel to her and I am justly treated now. And yet, Mr. Nitely, if you could but know—" He placed his clenched fist on his chest, next his heart. He could say no more.

Nitely said, sorrowfully, "Do you think because I am unmarried that I am unacquainted with the softer emotions? Be undeceived. Time was when I, too, knew love and heartbreak. But do not do as I did once and allow pride to prevent your reunion. Seek her out, my boy, seek her out and apologize. Do not allow yourself to become a solitary old bachelor such as I myself. —But, tush, I am puling."

Alexander's back had straightened. "I will be guided by you, Mr. Nitely. I will seek her out."

"Then go on in. For shortly before I came out, I believe I saw her there."

Alexander's heart leaped. "Perhaps she searches for me even now. I will go— But, no. Go you first, Mr. Nitely, while I stay behind to recover myself. I would not have her see me a prey to womanish tears."

"Of course, my boy."

Nitely stopped at the door into the ballroom in astonishment. Had a universal catastrophe struck all low? Fifty couples were lying on the floor, some heaped together most indecorously.

But before he could make up his mind to see if the nearest were dead, to sound the fire alarm, to call the police, to anything, they were rousing and struggling to their feet.

Only one still remained. A lonely girl in white, one arm outstretched gracefully beneath her fair head. It was Alice Sanger and Nitely hastened to her, oblivious to the rising clamor about him.

He sank to his knees. "Miss Sanger. My dear Miss Sanger. Are you hurt?"

She opened her beautiful eyes slowly, and said, "Mr. Nitely! I never realized you were such a vision of loveliness."

"I?" Nitely started back with horror, but she had now risen to her feet and there was light in her eyes such as Nitely had not seen in a maiden's eyes for thirty years—and then only weakly.

She said, "Mr. Nitely, surely you will not leave me?"

"No, no," said Nitely, confused. "If you need me, I shall stay."

"I need you. I need you with all my heart and soul. I need you as a thirsty flower needs the morning dew. I need you as Thisbe of old needed Pyramus."

Nitely, still backing away, looked about hastily, to see if anyone could be hearing this unusual declaration, but no one seemed to be paying any attention. As nearly as he could make out, the air was filled with other declarations of similar sort, some being even more forceful and direct.

His back was up against a wall, and Alice approached him so closely as to break the four-finger rule to smithereens. She broke, in fact, the no-finger rule, and at the resulting mutual pressure, a certain indefinable something seemed to thud away within Nitely.

"Miss Sanger. Please."

"Miss Sanger? Am I Miss Sanger to you?" exclaimed Alice, passionately. "Mr. Nitely! Nicholas! Make me your Alice, your own. Marry me. Marry me!"

All around there was the cry of "Marry me. Marry me!" and young men and women crowded around Nitely, for they knew well that he was a Justice of the Peace. They cried out, "Marry us, Mr. Nitely. Marry us!"

He could only cry in return, "I must get you all licenses."

They parted to let him leave on that errand of mercy. Only Alice followed him.

Nitely met Alexander at the door of the balcony and turned him back toward the open and fresh air. Professor Johns came at that moment to join them all.

Nitely said, "Alexander. Professor Johns. The most extraordinary thing has occurred—"

"Yes," said the professor, his mild face beaming with joy. "The experiment has been a success. The principle is far more effective on the human being, in fact, than on any of my experimental animals." Noting Nitely's confusion, he explained what had occurred in brief sentences.

Nitely listened and muttered, "Strange, strange. There is a certain elusive familiarity about this." He pressed his forehead with the knuckles of both hands, but it did not help.

Alexander approached Alice gently, yearning to clasp her to his strong bosom, yet knowing that no gently nurtured girl could consent to such an expression of emotion from one who had not yet been forgiven.

He said, "Alice, my lost love, if in your heart you could find—"

But she shrank from him, avoiding his arms though they were outstretched only in supplication. She said, "Alexander, I drank the punch. It was your wish."

"You needn't have. I was wrong, wrong."

"But I did, and oh, Alexander, I can never be yours."

"Never be mine? But what does this mean?"

And Alice, seizing Nitely's arm, clutched it avidly. "My soul is intertwined indissolubly with that of Mr. Nitely, of Nicholas, I mean. My passion for him—that is, my passion for marriage with him—cannot be withstood. It racks my being."

"You are false?" cried Alexander, unbelieving.

"You are cruel to say 'false,' " said Alice, sobbing. "I cannot help it."

"No, indeed," said Professor Johns, who had been listening to this in the greatest consternation, after having made his explanation to Nitely. "She could scarcely help it. It is simply an endocrinological manifestation."

"Indeed that is so," said Nitely, who was struggling with endocrinological manifestations of his own. "There, there, my—my dear." He patted Alice's head in a most fatherly way and when she held her enticing face up toward his, swooningly, he considered whether it might not be a fatherly thing—nay, even a neighborly thing—to press those lips with his own, in pure fashion.

But Alexander, out of his heart's despair, cried, "You are false, false—false as Cressid," and rushed from the room.

And Nitely would have gone after him, but that Alice had seized him about the neck and bestowed upon his slowly melting lips a kiss that was not daughterly in the least.

It was not even neighborly.

They arrived at Nitely's small bachelor cottage with its chaste sign of JUSTICE OF THE PEACE in Old English letters, its air of melancholy peace, its neat serenity, its small stove on which the small kettle was quickly placed by Nitely's left hand (his right arm being firmly in the clutch of Alice, who, with a shrewdness beyond her years, chose that as one sure method of rendering impossible a sudden bolt through the door on his part).

Nitely's study could be seen through the open door of the dining room, its walls lined with gentle books of scholarship and joy.

Again Nitely's hand (his left hand) went to his brow. "My dear," he said to Alice, "it is amazing the way—if you would release your hold the merest trifle, my child, so that circulation might be restored—the way in which I persist in imagining that all this has taken place before."

"Surely never before, my dear Nicholas," said Alice, bending her fair head upon his shoulder, and smiling at him with a shy tenderness that made her beauty as bewitching as moonlight upon still waters, "could there have been so wonderful a modern-day magician as our wise Professor Johns, so up-to-date a sorcerer."

"So up-to-date a—" Nitely had started so violently as to lift the fair Alice a full inch from the floor. "Why, surely that must be it. Dickens take me, if that's not it." (For on rare occasions, and under the stress of overpowering emotions, Nitely used strong language.)

"Nicholas. What is it? You frighten me, my cherubic one."

But Nitely walked rapidly into his study, and she was forced to run with him. His face was white, his lips firm, as he reached for a volume from the shelves and reverently blew the dust from it.

"Ah," he said with contrition, "how I have neglected the innocent joys of my younger days. My child, in view of this continuing incapacity of my right arm, would you be so kind as to turn the pages until I tell you to stop?"

Together they managed, in such a tableau of preconnubial bliss as is rarely seen, he holding the book with his left hand, she turning the pages slowly with her right.

"I am right!" Nitely said with sudden force. "Professor Johns, my dear fellow, do come here. This is the most amazing coincidence—a frightening example of the mysterious unfelt power that must sport with us on occasion for some hidden purpose."

Professor Johns, who had prepared his own tea and was sipping it patiently, as befitted a discreet gentleman of intellectual habit in the presence of two ardent lovers who had suddenly retired to the next room, called out, "Surely you do not wish my presence?"

"But I do, sir. I would fain consult one of your scientific attainments."

"But you are in a position—"

Alice screamed, faintly, "Professor!"

"A thousand pardons, my dear," said Professor Johns, entering. "My cobwebby old mind is filled with ridiculous fancies. It is long since I—" and he pulled mightily at his tea (which he had made strong) and was himself again at once.

"Professor," said Nitely. "This dear child referred to you as an up-to-date sorcerer and that turned my mind instantly to Gilbert and Sullivan's *The Sorcerer.*"

"What," asked Professor Johns, mildly, "are Gilbert and Sullivan?"

Nitely cast a devout glance upward, as though with the intention of gauging the direction of the inevitable thunderbolt and dodging. He said in a hoarse whisper, "Sir William Schwenck Gilbert and Sir Arthur Sullivan wrote, respectively, the words and music of the greatest musical comedies the world has ever seen. One of these is entitled *The Sorcerer.* In it, too, a philtre was used: a highly moral one which did not affect married people, but which did manage to deflect the young heroine away from her handsome young lover and into the arms of an elderly man."

"And," asked Professor Johns, "were matters allowed to remain so?"

"Well, no. —Really, my dear, the movements of your fingers in the region of the nape of my neck, while giving rise to undeniably pleasurable sensations, *do* rather distract me. —There is a reunion of the young lovers, Professor."

"Ah," said Professor Johns. "Then in view of the close resemblance of the fictional plot to real life, perhaps the solution in the play will help point the way to the reunion of Alice and Alexander. At least, I presume you do not wish to go through life with one arm permanently useless."

Alice said, "I have no wish to be reunited. I want only my own Nicholas."

"There is something," said Nitely, "to be said for that refreshing point of view, but tush—youth must be served. There *is* a solution in the play, Professor Johns, and it is for that reason that I most particularly wanted to talk to you." He smiled with a gentle benevolence. "In the play, the effects of the potion were completely neutralized by the actions of the gentleman who administered the potion in the first place: the gentleman, in other words, analogous to yourself."

"And those actions were?"

"Suicide! Simply that! In some manner unexplained by the authors, the effect of this suicide was to break the sp—"

But by now Professor Johns had recovered his equilibrium and said in the most sepulchrally forceful tone that could be imagined, "My dear sir, may I state instantly that, despite my affection for the young persons involved in this sad dilemma, I cannot under any circumstances consent to self-immolation. Such a procedure might be extremely efficacious in connection with love potions of ordinary vintage, but my amatogenic principle, I assure you, would be completely unaffected by my death."

Nitely sighed. "I feared that. As a matter of fact, between ourselves, it was a very poor ending for the play, perhaps the poorest in the canon," and he looked up briefly in mute apology to the spirit of William S. Gilbert. "It was pulled out of a hat. It had not been properly foreshadowed earlier in the play. It punished an individual who did not deserve the punishment. In short, it was, alas, completely unworthy of Gilbert's powerful genius."

Professor Johns said, "Perhaps it was not Gilbert. Perhaps some bungler had interfered and botched the job."

"There is no record of that."

But Professor Johns, his scientific mind keenly aroused by an unsolved puzzle, said at once, "We can test this. Let us study the mind of this—this Gilbert. He wrote other plays, did he?"

"Fourteen, in collaboration with Sullivan."

"Were there endings that resolved analogous situations in ways which were more appropriate?"

Nitely nodded. "One, certainly. There was *Ruddigore.*"

"Who was he?"

"Ruddigore is a place. The main character is revealed as the true bad baronet of Ruddigore and is, of course, under a curse."

"To be sure," muttered Professor Johns, who realized that such an eventuality frequently befell bad baronets and was even inclined to think it served them right.

Nitely said, "The curse compelled him to commit one crime or more each day. Were one day to pass without a crime, he would inevitably die in agonizing torture."

"How horrible," murmured the soft-hearted Alice.

"Naturally," said Nitely, "no one can think up a crime each day, so our hero was forced to use his ingenuity to circumvent the curse."

"How?"

"He reasoned thus: If he deliberately refused to commit a crime, he was courting death by his own act. In other words, he was attempting suicide, and attempting suicide is, of course, a crime—and so he fulfills the conditions of the curse."

"I see. I see," said Professor Johns. "Gilbert obviously believes in solving matters by carrying them forward to their logical conclusions." He closed his eyes, and his noble brow clearly bulged with the numerous intense thought waves it contained.

He opened them. "Nitely, old chap, when was *The Sorcerer* first produced?"

"In eighteen hundred and seventy-seven."

"Then that is it, my dear fellow. In eighteen seventy-seven, we were faced with the Victorian age. The institution of marriage was not to be made sport of on the stage. It could not be made a comic matter for the sake of the plot. Marriage was holy, spiritual, a sacrament—"

"Enough," said Nitely, "of this apostrophe. What is in your mind?"

"Marriage. Marry the girl, Nitely. Have all your couples marry, and that at once. I'm sure that was Gilbert's original intention."

"But that," said Nitely, who was strangely attracted by the notion, "is precisely what we are trying to avoid."

"I am not," said Alice, stoutly (though she was not stout, but, on the contrary, enchantingly lithe and slender).

Professor Johns said, "Don't you see? Once each couple is married, the amatogenic principle—which does not affect married people—loses its power over them. Those who would have been in love without the aid of the principle remain in love; those who would not are no longer in love—and consequently apply for an annulment."

"Good heavens," said Nitely. "How admirably simple. Of course! Gilbert must have intended that until a shocked producer or theater manager—a bungler, as you say—forced the change."

"And did it work?" I asked. "After all, you said quite distinctly that the professor had said its effect on married couples was only to inhibit extramarital re—"

"It worked," said Nitely, ignoring my comment. A tear trembled on his eyelid, but whether it was induced by memories or by the fact that he was on his fourth gin and tonic, I could not tell.

"It worked," he said. "Alice and I were married, and our marriage was

almost instantly annulled by mutual consent on the grounds of the use of undue pressure. And yet, because of the incessant chaperoning to which we were subjected, the incidence of undue pressure between ourselves was, unfortunately, virtually nil." He sighed again. "At any rate, Alice and Alexander were married soon after and she is now, I understand, as a result of various concomitant events, expecting a child."

He withdrew his eyes from the deep recesses of what was left of his drink and gasped with sudden alarm. "Dear me! She again."

I looked up, startled. A vision in pastel blue was in the doorway. Imagine, if you will, a charming face made for kissing; a lovely body made for loving.

She called, "Nicholas! Wait!"

"Is that Alice?" I asked.

"No, no. This is someone else entirely: a completely different story. —But I must not remain here."

He rose and, with an agility remarkable in one so advanced in years and weight, made his way through a window. The feminine vision of desirability, with an agility only slightly less remarkable, followed.

I shook my head in pity and sympathy. Obviously, the poor man was continually plagued by these wondrous things of beauty who, for one reason or another, were enamored of him. At the thought of this horrible fate, I downed my own drink at a gulp and considered the odd fact that no such difficulties had ever troubled me.

And at that thought, strange to tell, I ordered another drink savagely, and a scatological exclamation rose, unbidden, to my lips.

Unto the Fourth Generation

At ten of noon, Sam Marten hitched his way out of the taxicab, trying as usual to open the door with one hand, hold his briefcase in another and reach for his wallet with a third. Having only two hands, he found it a difficult job and, again as usual, he thudded his knee against the cab-door and found himself still groping uselessly for his wallet when his feet touched pavement.

The traffic of Madison Avenue inched past. A red truck slowed its crawl reluctantly, then moved on with a rasp as the light changed. White script on its side informed an unresponsive world that its ownership was that of *F. Lewkowitz and Sons, Wholesale Clothiers*.

Levkowich, thought Marten with brief inconsequence, and finally fished out his wallet. He cast an eye on the meter as he clamped his briefcase under his arm. Dollar sixty-five, make that twenty cents more as a tip, two singles gone would leave him only one for emergencies, better break a fiver.

"Okay," he said, "take out one-eighty-five, bud."

"Thanks," said the cabbie with mechanical insincerity and made the change.

Marten crammed three singles into his wallet, put it away, lifted his briefcase and breasted the human currents on the sidewalk to reach the glass doors of the building.

Levkovich? he thought sharply, and stopped. A passerby glanced off his elbow.

"Sorry," muttered Marten, and made for the door again.

Levkovich? That wasn't what the sign on the truck had said. The name had read Lewkowitz, Loo-koh-itz. Why did he *think* Levkovich? Even with his college German in the near past changing the w's to v's, where did he get the "-ich" from?

Levkovich? He shrugged the whole matter away roughly. Give it a chance and it would haunt him like a Hit Parade tinkle.

Concentrate on business. He was here for a luncheon appointment with this man, Naylor. He was here to turn a contract into an account and begin, at twenty-three, the smooth business rise which, as he planned it, would marry him to Elizabeth in two years and make him a paterfamilias in the suburbs in ten.

He entered the lobby with grim firmness and headed for the banks of elevators, his eye catching at the white-lettered directory as he passed.

It was a silly habit of his to want to catch suite numbers as he passed, without slowing, or (heaven forbid) coming to a full halt. With no break in his progress, he told himself, he could maintain the impression of belonging, of knowing his way around, and that was important to a man whose job involved dealing with other human beings.

Kulin-etts was what he wanted, and the word amused him. A firm specializing in the production of minor kitchen gadgets, striving manfully for a name that was significant, feminine, and coy, all at once—

His eyes snagged at the M's and moved upward as he walked. Mandel, Lusk, Lippert Publishing Company (two full floors), Lafkowitz, Kulin-etts. There it was—1024. Tenth floor. OK.

And then, after all, he came to a dead halt, turned in reluctant fascination, returned to the directory, and stared at it as though he were an out-of-towner.

Lafkowitz?

What kind of spelling was that?

It was clear enough. Lafkowitz, Henry J., 701. With an A. That was no good. That was useless.

Useless? Why useless? He gave his head one violent shake as though to clear it of mist. Damn it, what did he care how it was spelled? He turned away, frowning and angry, and hastened to an elevator door, which closed just before he reached it, leaving him flustered.

Another door opened and he stepped in briskly. He tucked his briefcase under his arm and tried to look bright alive—junior executive in its finest sense. He had to make an impression on Alex Naylor, with whom so far he had communicated only by telephone. If he was going to brood about Lewkowitzes and Lafkowitzes—

The elevator slid noiselessly to a halt at seven. A youth in shirt-sleeves stepped off, balancing what looked like a desk-drawer in which were three containers of coffee and three sandwiches.

Then, just as the doors began closing, frosted glass with black lettering loomed before Marten's eyes. It read: 701—HENRY J. LEFKOWITZ—IM-PORTER and was pinched off by the inexorable coming together of the elevator doors.

Marten leaned forward in excitement. It was his impulse to say: Take me back down to 7.

But there were others in the car. And after all, he had no reason.

Yet there was a tingle of excitement within him. The Directory *had* been wrong. It wasn't A, it was E. Some fool of a non-spelling menial with a packet of small letters to go on the board and only one hind foot to do it with.

Lefkowitz. Still not right, though.

Again, he shook his head. Twice. Not right for what?

The elevator stopped at ten and Marten got off.

Alex Naylor of Kulin-etts turned out to be a bluff, middle-aged man with a shock of white hair, a ruddy complexion, and a broad smile. His palms were dry and rough, and he shook hands with a considerable pressure, putting his left hand on Marten's shoulder in an earnest display of friendliness.

He said, "Be with you in two minutes. How about eating right here in the building? Excellent restaurant, and they've got a boy who makes a good martini. That sound all right?"

"Fine. Fine." Marten pumped up enthusiasm from a somehow-clogged reservoir.

It was nearer ten minutes than two, and Marten waited with the usual uneasiness of a man in a strange office. He stared at the upholstery on the chairs and at the little cubby-hole within which a young and bored switchboard operator sat. He gazed at the pictures on the wall and even made a half-hearted attempt to glance through a trade journal on the table next to him.

What he did not do was think of Lev—

He did *not* think of it.

The restaurant was good, or it would have been good if Marten had been perfectly at ease. Fortunately, he was freed of the necessity of carrying the burden of the conversation. Naylor talked rapidly and loudly, glanced over the menu with a practiced eye, recommended the Eggs Benedict, and commented on the weather and the miserable traffic situation.

On occasion, Marten tried to snap out of it, to lose that edge of fuzzed absence of mind. But each time the restlessness would return. Something was wrong. The name was wrong. It stood in the way of what he had to do.

With main force, he tried to break through the madness. In sudden verbal clatter, he led the conversation into the subject of wiring. It was reckless of him. There was no proper foundation; the transition was too abrupt.

But the lunch had been a good one; the dessert was on its way; and Naylor responded nicely.

He admitted dissatisfaction with existing arrangements. Yes, he had been looking into Marten's firm and, actually, it seemed to him that, yes, there was a chance, a good chance, he thought, that—

A hand came down on Naylor's shoulder as a man passed behind his chair. "How's the boy, Alex?"

Naylor looked up, grin ready-made and flashing. "Hey, Lefk, how's business?"

"Can't complain. See you at the—" He faded into the distance.

Marten wasn't listening. He felt his knees trembling, as he half-rose. "Who was that man?" he asked, intensely. It sounded more peremptory than he intended.

"Who? Lefk? Jerry Lefkovitz. You know him?" Naylor stared with cool surprise at his lunch companion.

"No. How do you spell his name?"

"L-E-F-K-O-V-I-T-Z, I think. Why?"

"With a V?"

"An F. . . . Oh, there's a V in it, too." Most of the good nature had left Naylor's face.

Marten drove on. "There's a Lefkowitz in the building. With a W. You know, Lef-COW-itz."

"Oh?"

"Room 701. This is not the same one?"

"Jerry doesn't work in this building. He's got a place across the street. I don't know this other one. This is a big building, you know. I don't keep tabs on everyone in it. What is all this, anyway?"

Marten shook his head and sat back. He didn't know what all this was, anyway. Or at least, if he did, it was nothing he dared explain. Could he say: I'm being haunted by all manner of Lefkowitzes today.

He said, "We were talking about wiring."

Naylor said, "Yes. Well, as I said, I've been considering your company. I've got to talk it over with the production boys, you understand. I'll let you know."

"Sure," said Marten, infinitely depressed. Naylor wouldn't let him know. The whole thing was shot.

And yet, through and beyond his depression, there was still that restlessness.

The hell with Naylor. All Marten wanted was to break this up and get on with it. (Get on with what? But the question was only a whisper. Whatever did the questioning inside him was ebbing away, dying down . . .)

The lunch frayed to an ending. If they had greeted each other like long-separated friends at last reunited, they parted like strangers.

Marten felt only relief.

He left with pulses thudding, threading through the tables, out of the haunted building, onto the haunted street.

Haunted? Madison Avenue at 1:20 P.M. in an early fall afternoon with the sun shining brightly and ten thousand men and women be-hiving its long straight stretch.

But Marten felt the haunting. He tucked his briefcase under his arm and headed desperately northward. A last sigh of the normal within him warned him he had a three o'clock appointment on 36th Street. Never mind. He headed uptown. Northward.

At 54th Street, he crossed Madison and walked west, came abruptly to a halt and looked upward.

There was a sign on the window, three stories up. He could make it out clearly: A. S. LEFKOWICH, CERTIFIED ACCOUNTANT.

It had an F and an OW, but it was the first "-ich" ending he had seen. The first one. He was getting closer. He turned north again on Fifth Avenue, hurrying through the unreal streets of an unreal city, panting with the chase of something, while the crowds about him began to fade.

A sign in a ground floor window, M. R. LEFKOWICZ, M.D.

A small gold-leaf semi-circle of letters in a candy-store window: JACOB LEVKOW.

(Half a name, he thought savagely. Why is he disturbing me with half a name?)

The streets were empty now except for the varying clan of Lefkowitz, Levkowitz, Lefkowicz to stand out in the vacuum.

He was dimly aware of the park ahead, standing out in painted motionless green. He turned west. A piece of newspaper fluttered at the corner of his eyes, the only movement in a dead world. He veered, stooped, and picked it up, without slackening his pace.

It was in Yiddish, a torn half-page.

He couldn't read it. He couldn't make out the blurred Hebrew letters, and could not have read it if they were clear. But one word was clear. It stood out in dark letters in the center of the page, each letter clear in its every serif. And it said Lefkovitsch, he knew, and as he said it to himself, he placed its accent on the second syllable: Lef-KUH-vich.

He let the paper flutter away and entered the empty park.

The trees were still and the leaves hung in odd, suspended attitudes. The sunlight was a dead weight upon him and gave no warmth.

He was running, but his feet kicked up no dust and a tuft of grass on which he placed his weight did not bend.

And there on a bench was an old man; the only man in the desolate park. He wore a dark felt cap, with a visor shading his eyes. From underneath it, tufts of gray hair protruded. His grizzled beard reached the uppermost button of his rough jacket. His old trousers were patched, and a strip of burlap was wrapped about each worn and shapeless shoe.

Marten stopped. It was difficult to breathe. He could only say one word and he used it to ask his question: "Levkovich?"

He stood there, while the old man rose slowly to his feet; brown old eyes peering close.

"Marten," he sighed. "Samuel Marten. You have come." The words sounded with an effect of double exposure, for under the English, Marten heard the faint sigh of a foreign tongue. Under the "Samuel" was the unheard shadow of a "Schmu-el."

The old man's rough, veined hands reached out, then withdrew as though he were afraid to touch. "I have been looking but there are so many people in this wilderness of a city-that-is-to-come. So many Martins and Martines and Mortons and Mertons. I stopped at last when I found greenery, but for a moment only—I would not commit the sin of losing faith. And then you came."

"It is I," said Marten, and knew it was. "And you are Phinehas Levkovich. Why are we here?"

"I am Phinehas ben Jehudah, assigned the name Levkovich by the ukase of the Tsar that ordered family names for all. And we are here," the old man said, softly, "because I prayed. When I was already old, Leah, my only daughter, the child of my old age, left for America with her husband, left the knouts of the old for the hope of the new. And my sons died, and Sarah, the wife of my bosom, was long dead and I was alone. And the time came when I, too, must die. But I had not seen Leah since her leaving for the far country and word had come but rarely. My soul yearned that I might see sons born unto her; sons of my seed; sons in whom my soul might yet live and not die."

His voice was steady and the soundless shadow of sound beneath his words was the stately roll of an ancient language.

"And I was answered and two hours were given me that I might see the first son of my line to be born in a new land and in a new time. My daughter's daughter's daughter's son, have I found you, then, amidst the splendor of this city?"

"But why the search? Why not have brought us together at once?"

"Because there is pleasure in the hope of the seeking, my son," said the old man, radiantly, "and in the delight of the finding. I was given two hours in which I might seek, two hours in which I might find . . . and behold, thou art here, and I have found that which I had not looked to see in life." His voice was old, caressing. "Is it well with thee, my son?"

"It is well, my father, now that I have found thee," said Marten, and dropped to his knees. "Give me thy blessing, my father, that it may be well with me all the days of my life, and with the maid whom I am to take to wife and the little ones yet to be born of my seed and thine."

He felt the old hand resting lightly on his head and there was only the soundless whisper.

Marten rose. The old man's eyes gazed into his yearningly. Were they losing focus?

"I go to my fathers now in peace, my son," said the old man, and Marten was alone in the empty park.

There was an instant of renewing motion, of the Sun taking up its interrupted task, of the wind reviving, and even with that first instant of sensation, all slipped back—

At ten of noon, Sam Marten hitched his way out of the taxicab, and found himself groping uselessly for his wallet while traffic inched on.

A red truck slowed, then moved on. A white script on its side announced: *F. Lewkowitz and Sons, Wholesale Clothiers.*

Marten didn't see it. Yet somehow he knew that all would be well with him. Somehow, as never before, he knew. . . .

What Is This Thing Called Love?

"But these are two species," said Captain Garm, peering closely at the creatures that had been brought up from the planet below. His optic organs adjusted focus to maximum sharpness, bulging outwards as they did so. The color patch above them gleamed in quick flashes.

Botax felt warmly comfortable to be following color-changes once again, after months in a spy cell on the planet, trying to make sense out of the modulated sound waves emitted by the natives. Communication by flash was almost like being home in the far-off Perseus arm of the Galaxy. "Not two species," he said, "but two forms of one species."

"Nonsense, they look quite different. Vaguely Perse-like, thank the Entity, and not as disgusting in appearance as so many out-forms are. Reasonable shape, recognizable limbs. But no color-patch. Can they speak?"

"Yes, Captain Garm," Botax indulged in a discreetly disapproving prismatic interlude. "The details are in my report. These creatures form sound waves by way of throat and mouth, something like complicated coughing. I have learned to do it myself." He was quietly proud. "It is very difficult."

"It must be stomach-turning. Well, that accounts for their flat, unextensible eyes. Not to speak by color makes eyes largely useless. Meanwhile, how can you insist these are a single species? The one on the left is smaller and has longer tendrils, or whatever it is, and seems differently proportioned. It bulges where this other does not. Are they alive?"

"Alive but not at the moment conscious, Captain. They have been psycho-treated to repress fright in order that they might be studied easily."

"But are they worth study? We are behind our schedule and have at least five worlds of greater moment than this one to check and explore. Maintaining a Time-stasis unit is expensive and I would like to return them and go on—"

But Botax's moist spindly body was fairly vibrating with anxiety. His tubular tongue flicked out and curved up and over his flat nose, while his eyes sucked inward. His splayed three-fingered hand made a gesture of negation as his speech went almost entirely into the deep red.

"Entity save us, Captain, for no world is of greater moment to us than this one. We may be facing a supreme crisis. These creatures could be the most dangerous life-forms in the Galaxy, Captain, just *because* there are two forms."

"I don't follow you."

"Captain, it has been my job to study this planet, and it has been most difficult, for it is unique. It is so unique that I can scarcely comprehend its facets. For instance, almost all life on the planet consists of species in two forms. There are no words to describe it, no concepts even. I can only speak of them as first form and second form. If I may use their sounds, the little one is called 'female,' and the big one, here, 'male,' so the creatures themselves are aware of the difference."

Garm winced, "What a disgusting means of communication."

"And, Captain, in order to bring forth young, the two forms must cooperate."

The Captain, who had bent forward to examine the specimens closely with an expression compounded of interest and revulsion, straightened at once. "Cooperate? What nonsense is this? There is no more fundamental attribute of life than that each living creature bring forth its young in innermost communication with itself. What else makes life worth living?"

"The one form does bring forth life but the other form must cooperate."

"How?"

"That has been difficult to determine. It is something very private and in my search through the available forms of literature I could find no exact and explicit description. But I have been able to make reasonable deductions."

Garm shook his head. "Ridiculous. Budding is the holiest, most private function in the world. On tens of thousands of worlds it is the same. As the great photo-bard, Levuline, said, 'In budding-time, in budding time, in sweet, delightful budding time; when—' "

"Captain, you don't understand. This cooperation between forms brings about somehow (and I am not certain exactly how) a mixture and recombination of genes. It is a device by which in every generation, new combinations of characteristics are brought into existence. Variations are multiplied; mutated genes hastened into expression almost at once where under the usual budding system, millennia might pass first."

"Are you trying to tell me that the genes from one individual can be combined with those of another? Do you know how completely ridiculous that is in the light of all the principles of cellular physiology?"

"It must be so," said Botax nervously under the other's pop-eyed glare. "Evolution *is* hastened. This planet is a riot of species. There are supposed to be a million and a quarter different species of creatures."

"A dozen and a quarter more likely. Don't accept too completely what you read in the native literature."

"I've seen dozens of radically different species myself in just a small area. I tell you, Captain, give these creatures a short space of time and they will mutate into intellects powerful enough to overtake us and rule the Galaxy."

"Prove that this cooperation you speak of exists, Investigator, and I shall consider your contentions. If you cannot, I shall dismiss all your fancies as ridiculous and we will move on."

"I can prove it." Botax's color-flashes turned intensely yellow-green. "The creatures of this world are unique in another way. They foresee advances they have not yet made, probably as a consequence of their belief in rapid change which, after all, they constantly witness. They therefore indulge in a type of literature involving the space-travel they have never developed. I have translated their term for the literature as 'science-fiction.' Now I have dealt in my readings almost exclusively with science-fiction, for there I thought, in their dreams and fancies, they would expose themselves and their danger to us. And it was from that science-fiction that I deduced the method of their inter-form cooperation."

"How did you do that?"

"There is a periodical on this world which sometimes publishes science-fiction which is, however, devoted almost entirely to the various aspects of the cooperation. It does not speak entirely freely, which is annoying, but persists in merely hinting. Its name as nearly as I can put it into flashes is 'Recreationlad.' The creature in charge, I deduce, is interested in nothing but inter-form cooperation and searches for it everywhere with a systematic and scientific intensity that has roused my awe. He has found instances of cooperation described in science-fiction and I let material in his periodical guide me. From the stories he instanced I have learned how to bring it about.

"And Captain, I beg of you, when the cooperation is accomplished and the young are brought forth before your eyes, give orders not to leave an atom of this world in existence."

"Well," said Captain Garm, wearily, "bring them into full consciousness and do what you must do quickly."

Marge Skidmore was suddenly completely aware of her surroundings. She remembered very clearly the elevated station at the beginning of twilight. It had been almost empty, one man standing near her, another at the other end of the platform. The approaching train had just made itself known as a faint rumble in the distance.

There had then come the flash, a sense of turning inside out, the half-seen vision of a spindly creature, dripping mucus, a rushing upward, and now—

"Oh, God," she said, shuddering. "It's still here. And there's another one, too."

She felt a sick revulsion, but no fear. She was almost proud of herself for feeling no fear. The man next to her, standing quietly as she herself was, but still wearing a battered fedora, was the one that had been near her on the platform.

"They got you, too?" she asked. "Who else?"

Charlie Grimwold, feeling flabby and paunchy, tried to lift his hand to remove his hat and smooth the thin hair that broke up but did not entirely cover the skin of his scalp and found that it moved only with difficulty against a rubbery but hardening resistance. He let his hand drop and looked morosely at the thin-faced woman facing him. She was in her middle thirties, he decided, and her hair was nice and her dress fit well, but at the moment, he just wanted to be somewhere else and it did him no good at all that he had company, even female company.

He said, "I don't know, lady. I was just standing on the station platform."

"Me, too."

"And then I see a flash. Didn't hear nothing. Now here I am. Must be little men from Mars or Venus or one of them places."

Marge nodded vigorously, "That's what I figure. A flying saucer? You scared?"

"No. That's funny, you know. I think maybe I'm going nuts or I *would* be scared."

"Funny thing. I ain't scared, either. Oh, God, here comes one of them now. If he touches me, I'm going to scream. Look at those wiggly hands. And that wrinkled skin, all slimy; makes me nauseous."

Botax approached gingerly and said, in a voice at once rasping and screechy, this being the closest he could come to imitating the native timbre, "Creatures! We will not hurt you. But we must ask you if you would do us the favor of cooperating."

"Hey, it talks!" said Charlie. "What do you mean, cooperate."

"Both of you. With each other," said Botax.

"Oh?" He looked at Marge. "You know what he means, lady?"

"Ain't got no idea whatsoever," she answered loftily.

Botax said, "What I mean—" and he used the short term he had once heard employed as a synonym for the process.

Marge turned red and said, "What!" in the loudest scream she could manage. Both Botax and Captain Garm put their hands over their mid-regions to cover the auditory patches that trembled painfully with the decibels.

Marge went on rapidly, and nearly incoherently. "Of all things. I'm a married woman, you. If my Ed was here, you'd hear from *him*. And you, wise guy," she twisted toward Charlie against rubbery resistance, "whoever you are, if you think—"

"Lady, lady," said Charlie in uncomfortable desperation. "It ain't my idea. I mean, far be it from me, you know, to turn down some lady, you know; but me, I'm married, too. I got three kids. Listen—"

Captain Garm said, "What's happening, Investigator Botax? These cacophonous sounds are awful."

"Well," Botax flashed a short purple patch of embarrassment. "This forms a complicated ritual. They are supposed to be reluctant at first. It heightens the subsequent result. After that initial stage, the skins must be removed."

"They have to be *skinned?*"

"Not really skinned. Those are artificial skins that can be removed painlessly, and must be. Particularly in the smaller form."

"All right, then. Tell it to remove the skins. Really, Botax, I don't find this pleasant."

"I don't think I had better tell the smaller form to remove the skins. I think we had better follow the ritual closely. I have here sections of those space-travel tales which the man from the 'Recreationlad' periodical spoke highly of. In those tales the skins are removed forcibly. Here is a description of an accident, for instance 'which played havoc with the girl's dress, ripping it nearly off her slim body. For a second, he felt the warm firmness of her half-bared bosom against his cheek—' It goes on that way. You see, the ripping, the forcible removal, acts as a stimulus."

"Bosom?" said the Captain. "I don't recognize the flash."

"I invented that to cover the meaning. It refers to the bulges on the upper dorsal region of the smaller form."

"I see. Well, tell the larger one to rip the skins off the smaller one. What a dismal thing this is."

Botax turned to Charlie. "Sir," he said, "rip the girl's dress nearly off her slim body, will you? I will release you for the purpose."

Marge's eyes widened and she twisted toward Charlie in instant outrage. "Don't you dare do that, you. Don't you *dast* touch me, you sex maniac."

"Me?" said Charlie plaintively. "It ain't my idea. You think I go around ripping dresses? Listen," he turned to Botax, "I got a wife and three kids. She finds out I go around ripping dresses, I get clobbered. You know what my wife does when I just look at some dame? *Listen—*"

"Is he still reluctant?" said the Captain, impatiently.

"Apparently," said Botax. "The strange surroundings, you know, may be extending that stage of the cooperation. Since I know this is unpleasant for you, I will perform this stage of the ritual myself. It is frequently written in the space-travel tales that an outer-world species performs the task. For instance, here," and he riffled through his notes finding the one he wanted, "they describe a very awful such species. The creatures on the planet have foolish notions, you understand. It never occurs to them to imagine handsome individuals such as ourselves, with a fine mucous cover."

"Go on! Go on! Don't take all day," said the Captain.

"Yes, Captain. It says here that the extraterrestrial 'came forward to where the girl stood. Shrieking hysterically, she was cradled in the monster's embrace. Talons ripped blindly at her body, tearing the kirtle away in rags.' You see, the native creature is shrieking with stimulation as her skins are removed."

"Then go ahead, Botax, remove it. But please, allow no shrieking. I'm trembling all over with the sound waves."

Botax said politely to Marge, "If you don't mind—"

One spatulate finger made as though to hook on to the neck of the dress.

Marge wiggled desperately. "Don't touch. Don't touch! You'll get slime on it. Listen, this dress cost $24.95 at Ohrbach's. Stay away, you monster. Look at those eyes on him." She was panting in her desperate efforts to dodge the groping, extraterrestrial hand. "A slimy, bug-eyed monster, that's what he is. Listen, I'll take it off myself. Just don't touch it with slime, for God's sake."

She fumbled at the zipper, and said in a hot aside to Charlie, "Don't you dast look."

Charlie closed his eyes and shrugged in resignation.

She stepped out of the dress. "All right? You satisfied?"

Captain Garm's fingers twitched with unhappiness. "Is that the bosom? Why does the other creature keep its head turned away?"

"Reluctance. Reluctance," said Botax. "Besides, the bosom is still covered. Other skins must be removed. When bared, the bosom is a very strong stimulus. It is constantly described as ivory globes, or white spheres, or otherwise after that fashion. I have here drawings, visual picturizations, that come from the outer covers of the space-travel magazines. If you will inspect them, you will see that upon every one of them, a creature is present with a bosom more or less exposed."

The Captain looked thoughtfully from the illustrations to Marge and back. "What is ivory?"

"That is another made-up flash of my own. It represents the tusky material of one of the large sub-intelligent creatures on the planet."

"Ah," and Captain Garm went into a pastel green of satisfaction. "That explains it. This small creature is one of a warrior sect and those are tusks with which to smash the enemy."

"No, no. They are quite soft, I understand." Botax's small brown hand flicked outward in the general direction of the objects under discussion and Marge screamed and shrank away.

"Then what other purpose do they have?"

"I think," said Botax with considerable hesitation, "that they are used to feed the young."

"The young eat them?" asked the Captain with every evidence of deep distress.

"Not exactly. The objects produce a fluid which the young consume."

"Consume a fluid from a living body? Yech-h-h." The Captain covered his head with all three of his arms, calling the central supernumerary into use for the purpose, slipping it out of its sheath so rapidly as almost to knock Botax over.

"A three-armed, slimy, bug-eyed monster," said Marge.

"Yeah," said Charlie.

"All right you, just watch those eyes. Keep them to yourself."

"Listen, lady. I'm trying not to look."

Botax approached again. "Madam, would you remove the rest?"

Marge drew herself up as well as she could against the pinioning field. "Never!"

"I'll remove it, if you wish."

"Don't touch! For God's sake, don't touch. Look at the slime on him, will you? All right, I'll take it off." She was muttering under her breath and looking hotly in Charlie's direction as she did so.

"Nothing is happening," said the Captain, in deep dissatisfaction, "and this seems an imperfect specimen."

Botax felt the slur on his own efficiency. "I brought you two perfect specimens. What's wrong with the creature?"

"The bosom does not consist of globes or spheres. I know what globes or spheres are and in these pictures you have shown me, they are so depicted. Those are large globes. On this creature, though, what we have are nothing but small flaps of dry tissue. And they're discolored, too, partly."

"Nonsense," said Botax. "You must allow room for natural variation. I will put it to the creature herself."

He turned to Marge, "Madam, is your bosom imperfect?"

Marge's eyes opened wide and she struggled vainly for moments without doing anything more than gasp loudly. *"Really!"* she finally managed. "Maybe I'm no Gina Lollobrigida or Anita Ekberg, but I'm perfectly all right, thank you. Oh boy, if my Ed were only here." She turned to Charlie. "Listen, you, you tell this bug-eyed slimy thing here, there ain't nothing wrong with my development."

"Lady," said Charlie, softly. "I ain't looking, remember?"

"Oh, sure, you ain't looking. You been peeking enough, so you might as well just open your crummy eyes and stick up for a lady, if you're the least bit of a gentleman, which you probably ain't."

"Well," said Charlie, looking sideways at Marge, who seized the opportunity to inhale and throw her shoulders back, "I don't like to get mixed up in a kind of delicate matter like this, but you're all right—I guess."

"You *guess?* You blind or something? I was once runner-up for Miss Brooklyn, in case you don't happen to know, and where I missed out was on waist-line, *not* on—"

Charlie said, "All right, all right. They're fine. Honest." He nodded vigorously in Botax's direction. "They're okay. I ain't that much of an expert, you understand, but they're okay by me."

Marge relaxed.

Botax felt relieved. He turned to Garm. "The bigger form expresses interest, Captain. The stimulus is working. Now for the final step."

"And what is that?"

"There is no flash for it, Captain. Essentially, it consists of placing the speaking-and-eating apparatus of one against the equivalent apparatus of the other. I have made up a flash for the process, thus: kiss."

"Will nausea never cease?" groaned the Captain.

"It is the climax. In all the tales, after the skins are removed by force, they clasp each other with limbs and indulge madly in burning kisses, to translate as nearly as possible the phrase most frequently used. Here is one example, just one, taken at random: 'He held the girl, his mouth avid on her lips.' "

"Maybe one creature was devouring the other," said the Captain.

"Not at all," said Botax impatiently. "Those were burning kisses."

"How do you mean, burning? Combustion takes place?"

"I don't think literally so. I imagine it is a way of expressing the fact that the temperature goes up. The higher the temperature, I suppose, the more successful the production of young. Now that the big form is properly stimulated, he need only place his mouth against hers to produce young. The young will not be produced without that step. It is the cooperation I have been speaking of."

"That's all? Just this—" The Captain's hands made motions of coming together, but he could not bear to put the thought into flash form.

"That's all," said Botax. "In none of the tales; not even in 'Recreationlad,' have I found a description of any further physical activity in connection with young-bearing. Sometimes after the kissing, they write a line of symbols like little stars, but I suppose that merely means more kissing; one kiss for each star, when they wish to produce a multitude of young."

"Just one, please, right now."

"Certainly, Captain."

Botax said with grave distinctness, "Sir, would you kiss the lady?"

Charlie said, "Listen, I can't move."

"I will free you, of course."

"The lady might not like it."

Marge glowered. "You bet your damn boots, I won't like it. You just stay away."

"I would like to, lady, but what do they do if I don't? Look, I don't want to get them mad. We can just—you know—make like a little peck."

She hesitated, seeing the justice of the caution. "All right. No funny stuff, though. I ain't in the habit of standing around like this in front of every Tom, Dick and Harry, you know."

"I know that, lady. It was none of my doing. You got to admit that."

Marge muttered angrily, "Regular slimy monsters. Must think they're some kind of gods or something, the way they order people around. Slime gods is what they are!"

Charlie approached her. "If it's okay now, lady." He made a vague motion as though to tip his hat. Then he put his hands awkwardly on her bare shoulders and leaned over in a gingerly pucker.

Marge's head stiffened so that lines appeared in her neck. Their lips met.

Captain Garm flashed fretfully. "I sense no rise in temperature." His heat-detecting tendril had risen to full extension at the top of his head and remained quivering there.

"I don't either," said Botax, rather at a loss, "but we're doing it just as the space travel stories tell us to. I think his limbs should be more extended— Ah, like that. See, it's working."

Almost absently, Charlie's arm had slid around Marge's soft, nude torso. For a moment, Marge seemed to yield against him and then she suddenly writhed hard against the pinioning field that still held her with fair firmness.

"Let go." The words were muffled against the pressure of Charlie's lips. She bit suddenly, and Charlie leaped away with a wild cry, holding his lower lip, then looking at his fingers for blood.

"What's the idea, lady?" he demanded plaintively.

She said, "We agreed just a peck, is all. What were you starting there? You some kind of playboy or something? What am I surrounded with here? Playboy and the slime gods?"

Captain Garm flashed rapid alternations of blue and yellow. "Is it done? How long do we wait now?"

"It seems to me it must happen at once. Throughout all the universe, when you have to bud, you bud, you know. There's no waiting."

"Yes? After thinking of the foul habits you have been describing, I don't think I'll ever bud again. Please get this over with."

"Just a moment, Captain."

But the moments passed and the Captain's flashes turned slowly to a brooding orange, while Botax's nearly dimmed out altogether.

Botax finally asked hesitantly, "Pardon me, madam, but when will you bud?"

"When will I *what?*"

"Bear young?"

"I've got a kid."

"I mean bear young now."

"I should say not. I ain't ready for another kid yet."

"What? What?" demanded the Captain. "What's she saying?"

"It seems," said Botax, "she does not intend to have young at the moment."

The Captain's color patch blazed brightly. "Do you know what I think, Investigator? I think you have a sick, perverted mind. Nothing's happening to these creatures. There is no cooperation between them, and no young to be borne. I think they're two different species and that you're playing some kind of foolish game with me."

"But, Captain—" said Botax.

"Don't but Captain me," said Garm. "I've had enough. You've upset me, turned my stomach, nauseated me, disgusted me with the whole notion of budding and wasted my time. You're just looking for headlines and personal glory and I'll see to it that you don't get them. Get rid of these creatures now. Give that one its skins back and put them back where you found them. I ought to take the expense of maintaining Time-stasis all this time out of your salary."

"But, Captain—"

"Back, I say. Put them back in the same place and at the same instant of time. I want this planet untouched, and I'll see to it that it stays untouched." He cast one more furious glance at Botax. "One species, two forms, bosoms, kisses, cooperation, BAH— You are a fool, Investigator, a dolt as well and, most of all, a sick, sick, sick creature."

There was no arguing. Botax, limbs trembling, set about returning the creatures.

They stood there at the elevated station, looking around wildly. It was twilight over them, and the approaching train was just making itself known as a faint rumble in the distance.

Marge said, hesitantly, "Mister, did it really happen?"

Charlie nodded. "I remember it."

Marge said, "We can't tell anybody."

"Sure not. They'd say we was nuts. Know what I mean?"

"Uh-huh. Well," she edged away.

Charlie said, "Listen. I'm sorry you was embarrassed. It was none of my doing."

"That's all right. I know." Marge's eyes considered the wooden platform at her feet. The sound of the train was louder.

"I mean, you know, lady, you wasn't really bad. In fact, you looked good, but I was kind of embarrassed to say that."

Suddenly, she smiled. "It's all right."

"You want maybe to have a cup of coffee with me just to relax you? My wife, she's not really expecting me for a while."

"Oh? Well, Ed's out of town for the weekend so I got only an empty apartment to go home to. My little boy is visiting at my mother's." She explained.

"Come on, then. We been kind of introduced."

"I'll say." She laughed.

The train pulled in, but they turned away, walking down the narrow stairway to the street.

They had a couple of cocktails actually, and then Charlie couldn't let her go home in the dark alone, so he saw her to her door. Marge was bound to invite him in for a few moments, naturally.

Meanwhile, back in the spaceship, the crushed Botax was making a final effort to prove his case. While Garm prepared the ship for departure Botax hastily set up the tight-beam visiscreen for a last look at his specimens. He focused in on Charlie and Marge in her apartment. His tendril stiffened and he began flashing in a coruscating rainbow of colors.

"Captain Garm! Captain! Look what they're doing now!"

But at that very instant the ship winked out of Time-stasis.

The Machine
That Won the War

The celebration had a long way to go and even in the silent depths of Multivac's underground chambers, it hung in the air.

If nothing else, there was the mere fact of isolation and silence. For the first time in a decade, technicians were not scurrying about the vitals of the giant computer, the soft lights did not wink out their erratic patterns, the flow of information in and out had halted.

It would not be halted long, of course, for the needs of peace would be pressing. Yet now, for a day, perhaps for a week, even Multivac might celebrate the great time, and rest.

Lamar Swift took off the military cap he was wearing and looked down the long and empty main corridor of the enormous computer. He sat down rather wearily in one of the technician's swing-stools, and his uniform, in which he had never been comfortable, took on a heavy and wrinkled appearance.

He said, "I'll miss it all after a grisly fashion. It's hard to remember when we weren't at war with Deneb, and it seems against nature now to be at peace and to look at the stars without anxiety."

The two men with the Executive Director of the Solar Federation were both younger than Swift. Neither was as gray. Neither looked quite as tired.

John Henderson, thin-lipped and finding it hard to control the relief he felt in the midst of triumph, said, "They're destroyed! They're destroyed! It's what I keep saying to myself over and over and I still can't believe it. We all talked so much, over so many years, about the menace hanging over

Earth and all its worlds, over every human being, and all the time it was true, every word of it. And now we're alive and it's the Denebians who are shattered and destroyed. They'll be no menace now, ever again."

"Thanks to Multivac," said Swift, with a quiet glance at the imperturbable Jablonsky, who through all the war had been Chief Interpreter of science's oracle. "Right, Max?"

Jablonsky shrugged. Automatically, he reached for a cigarette and decided against it. He alone, of all the thousands who had lived in the tunnels within Multivac, had been allowed to smoke, but toward the end he had made definite efforts to avoid making use of the privilege.

He said, "Well, that's what *they* say." His broad thumb moved in the direction of his right shoulder, aiming upward.

"Jealous, Max?"

"Because they're shouting for Multivac? Because Multivac is the big hero of mankind in this war?" Jablonsky's craggy face took on an air of suitable contempt. "What's that to me? Let Multivac be the machine that won the war, if it pleases them."

Henderson looked at the other two out of the corners of his eyes. In this short interlude that the three had instinctively sought out in the one peaceful corner of a metropolis gone mad; in this entr'acte between the dangers of war and the difficulties of peace; when, for one moment, they might all find surcease; he was conscious only of his weight of guilt.

Suddenly, it was as though that weight were too great to be borne longer. It had to be thrown off, along with the war; now!

Henderson said, "Multivac had nothing to do with victory. It's just a machine."

"A big one," said Swift.

"Then just a big machine. No better than the data fed it." For a moment, he stopped, suddenly unnerved at what he was saying.

Jablonsky looked at him, his thick fingers once again fumbling for a cigarette and once again drawing back. "You should know. You supplied the data. Or is it just that you're taking the credit?"

"*No,*" said Henderson, angrily. "There is no credit. What do you know of the data Multivac had to use; predigested from a hundred subsidiary computers here on Earth, on the Moon, on Mars, even on Titan. With Titan always delayed and always that feeling that its figures would introduce an unexpected bias."

"It would drive anyone mad," said Swift, with gentle sympathy.

Henderson shook his head. "It wasn't just that. I admit that eight years ago when I replaced Lepont as Chief Programmer, I was nervous. But there was an exhilaration about things in those days. The war was still long-range; an adventure without real danger. We hadn't reached the point where manned vessels had had to take over and where interstellar warps could swallow up a planet clean, if aimed correctly. But then, when the real difficulties began—"

Angrily—he could finally permit anger—he said, "You know nothing about it."

"Well," said Swift. "Tell us. The war is over. We've won."

"Yes." Henderson nodded his head. He had to remember that. Earth had won so all had been for the best. "Well, the data became meaningless."

"Meaningless? You mean that literally?" said Jablonsky.

"Literally. What would you expect? The trouble with you two was that you weren't out in the thick of it. You never left Multivac, Max, and you, Mr. Director, never left the Mansion except on state visits where you saw exactly what they wanted you to see."

"I was not as unaware of that," said Swift, "as you may have thought."

"Do you know," said Henderson, "to what extent data concerning our production capacity, our resource potential, our trained manpower—everything of importance to the war effort, in fact—had become unreliable and untrustworthy during the last half of the war? Group leaders, both civilian and military, were intent on projecting their own improved image, so to speak, so they obscured the bad and magnified the good. Whatever the machines might do, the men who programmed them and interpreted the results had their own skins to think of and competitors to stab. There was no way of stopping that. I tried, and failed."

"Of course," said Swift, in quiet consolation. "I can see that you would."

This time Jablonsky decided to light his cigarette. "Yet I presume you provided Multivac with data in your programming. You said nothing to us about unreliability."

"How could I tell you? And if I did, how could you afford to believe me?" demanded Henderson, savagely. "Our entire war effort was geared to Multivac. It was the one great weapon on our side, for the Denebians had nothing like it. What else kept up morale in the face of doom but the assurance that Multivac would always predict and circumvent any Denebian move, and would always direct and prevent the circumvention of our moves? Great Space, after our Spy-warp was blasted out of hyperspace we lacked any reliable Denebian data to feed Multivac and we didn't dare make *that* public."

"True enough," said Swift.

"Well, then," said Henderson, "if I told you the data was unreliable, what could you have done but replace me and refuse to believe me? I couldn't allow that."

"What did you do?" said Jablonsky.

"Since the war is won, I'll tell you what I did. I corrected the data."

"How?" asked Swift.

"Intuition, I presume. I juggled them till they looked right. At first, I hardly dared. I changed a bit here and there to correct what were obvious impossibilities. When the sky didn't collapse about us, I got braver. Toward the end, I scarcely cared. I just wrote out the necessary data as it was needed. I even had the Multivac Annex prepare data for me according to a private programming pattern I had devised for the purpose."

"Random figures?" said Jablonsky.

"Not at all. I introduced a number of necessary biases."

Jablonsky smiled, quite unexpectedly, his dark eyes sparkling behind the crinkling of the lower lids. "Three times a report was brought me about unauthorized uses of the Annex, and I let it go each time. If it had mattered, I would have followed it up and spotted you, John, and found out what you were doing. But, of course, nothing about Multivac mattered in those days, so you got away with it."

"What do you mean, nothing mattered?" asked Henderson, suspiciously.

"Nothing did. I suppose if I had told you this at the time, it would have spared you your agony, but then if you had told me what you were doing, it would have spared me mine. What made you think Multivac was in working order, whatever the data you supplied it?"

"Not in working order?" said Swift.

"Not really. Not reliably. After all, where were my technicians in the last years of the war? I'll tell you, they were feeding computers on a thousand different space devices. They were gone! I had to make do with kids I couldn't trust and veterans who were out-of-date. Besides, do you think I could trust the solid-state components coming out of Cryogenics in the last years? Cryogenics wasn't any better placed as far as personnel was concerned than I was. To me, it didn't matter whether the data being supplied Multivac were reliable or not. The *results* weren't reliable. That much I knew."

"What did you do?" asked Henderson.

"I did what you did, John. I introduced the bugger factor. I adjusted matters in accordance with intuition—and that's how the machine won the war."

Swift leaned back in the chair and stretched his legs out before him. "Such revelations. It turns out then that the material handed me to guide me in my decision-making capacity was a man-made interpretation of man-made data. Isn't that right?"

"It looks so," said Jablonsky.

"Then I perceive I was correct in not placing too much reliance upon it," said Swift.

"You didn't?" Jablonsky, despite what he had just said, managed to look professionally insulted.

"I'm afraid I didn't. Multivac might seem to say, Strike here, not there; do this, not that; wait, don't act. But I could never be certain that what Multivac seemed to say, it really did say; or what it really said, it really meant. I could never be certain."

"But the final report was always plain enough, sir," said Jablonsky.

"To those who did not have to make the decision, perhaps. Not to me. The horror of the responsibility of such decisions was unbearable and not even Multivac was sufficient to remove the weight. But the point is I was justified in doubting and there is tremendous relief in that."

Caught up in the conspiracy of mutual confession, Jablonsky put titles aside, "What was it you did then, Lamar? After all, you did make decisions. How?"

"Well, it's time to be getting back perhaps but—I'll tell you first. Why not? I did make use of a computer, Max, but an older one than Multivac, much older."

He groped in his own pocket for cigarettes, and brought out a package along with a scattering of small change; old-fashioned coins dating to the first years before the metal shortage had brought into being a credit system tied to a computer-complex.

Swift smiled rather sheepishly. "I still need these to make money seem substantial to me. An old man finds it hard to abandon the habits of youth." He put a cigarette between his lips and dropped the coins one by one back into his pocket.

He held the last coin between his fingers, staring absently at it. "Multivac is not the first computer, friends, nor the best-known, nor the one that can most efficiently lift the load of decision from the shoulders of the executive. A machine *did* win the war, John; at least a very simple computing device did; one that I used every time I had a particularly hard decision to make."

With a faint smile of reminiscence, he flipped the coin he held. It glinted in the air as it spun and came down in Swift's outstretched palm. His hand closed over it and brought it down on the back of his left hand. His right hand remained in place, hiding the coin.

"Heads or tails, gentlemen?" said Swift.

My Son, the Physicist

Her hair was light apple-green in color, very subdued, very old-fashioned. You could see she had a delicate hand with the dye, the way they did thirty years ago, before the streaks and stipples came into fashion.

She had a sweet smile on her face, too, and a calm look that made something serene out of elderliness.

And, by comparison, it made something shrieking out of the confusion that enfolded her in the huge government building.

A girl passed her at a half-run, stopped and turned toward her with a blank stare of astonishment. "How did you get in?"

The woman smiled. "I'm looking for my son, the physicist."

"Your son, the—"

"He's a communications engineer, really. Senior Physicist Gerard Cremona."

"Dr. Cremona. Well, he's— Where's your pass?"

"Here it is. I'm his mother."

"Well, Mrs. Cremona, I don't know. I've got to— His office is down there. You just ask someone." She passed on, running.

Mrs. Cremona shook her head slowly. Something had happened, she supposed. She hoped Gerard was all right.

She heard voices much farther down the corridor and smiled happily. She could tell Gerard's.

She walked into the room and said, "Hello, Gerard."

Gerard was a big man, with a lot of hair still and the gray just beginning to show because he didn't use dye. He said he was too busy. She was very proud of him and the way he looked.

Right now, he was talking volubly to a man in army uniform. She couldn't tell the rank, but she knew Gerard could handle him.

Gerard looked up and said, "What do you— Mother! What are you doing here?"

"I was coming to visit you today."

"Is today Thursday? Oh Lord, I forgot. Sit down, Mother, I can't talk now. Any seat. Any seat. Look, General."

General Reiner looked over his shoulder and one hand slapped against the other in the region of the small of his back. "Your mother?"

"Yes."

"Should she be here?"

"Right now, no, but I'll vouch for her. She can't even read a thermometer so nothing of this will mean anything to her. Now look, General. They're on Pluto. You see? They are. The radio signals can't be of natural origin so they must originate from human beings, from our men. You'll have to accept that. Of all the expeditions we've sent out beyond the planetoid belt, one turns out to have made it. And they've reached Pluto."

"Yes, I understand what you're saying, but isn't it impossible just the same? The men who are on Pluto now were launched four years ago with equipment that could not have kept them alive more than a year. That is my understanding. They were aimed at Ganymede and seem to have gone eight times the proper distance."

"Exactly. And we've got to know how and why. They may—just—have— had—help."

"What kind? How?"

Cremona clenched his jaws for a moment as though praying inwardly. "General," he said, "I'm putting myself out on a limb but it is just barely possible non-humans are involved. Extra-terrestrials. We've got to find out. We don't know how long contact can be maintained."

"You mean" (the General's grave face twitched into an almost-smile) "they may have escaped from custody and they may be recaptured again at any time."

"Maybe. Maybe. The whole future of the human race may depend on our knowing exactly what we're up against. Knowing it *now*."

"All right. What is it you want?"

"We're going to need Army's Multivac computer at once. Rip out every problem it's working on and start programing our general semantic problem. Every communications engineer you have must be pulled off anything he's on and placed into coordination with our own."

"But why? I fail to see the connection."

A gentle voice interrupted. "General, would you like a piece of fruit? I brought some oranges."

Cremona said, "Mother! Please! Later! General, the point is a simple one. At the present moment Pluto is just under four billion miles away. It takes six hours for radio waves, traveling at the speed of light, to reach from here to there. If we say something, we must wait twelve hours for an answer. If they say something and we miss it and say 'what' and they repeat—bang, goes a day."

"There's no way to speed it up?" said the General.

"Of course not. It's the fundamental law of communications. No information can be transmitted at more than the speed of light. It will take months to carry on the same conversation with Pluto that would take hours between the two of us right now."

"Yes, I see that. And you really think extra-terrestrials are involved?"

"I do. To be honest, not everyone here agrees with me. Still, we're straining every nerve, every fiber, to devise some method of concentrating communication. We must get in as many bits per second as possible and pray we get what we need before we lose contact. And there's where I need Multivac and your men. There must be some communications strategy we can use that will reduce the number of signals we need send out. Even an increase of ten percent in efficiency can mean perhaps a week of time saved."

The gentle voice interrupted again. "Good grief, Gerard, are you trying to get some talking done?"

"Mother! Please!"

"But you're going about it the wrong way. Really."

"Mother." There was a hysterical edge to Cremona's voice.

"Well, all right, but if you're going to say something and then wait twelve hours for an answer, you're silly. You shouldn't."

The General snorted. "Dr. Cremona, shall we consult—"

"Just one moment, General," said Cremona. "What are you getting at, Mother?"

"While you're waiting for an answer," said Mrs. Cremona, earnestly, "just keep on transmitting and tell them to do the same. You talk all the time and they talk all the time. You have someone listening all the time and they do, too. If either one of you says anything that needs an answer, you can slip one in at your end, but chances are, you'll get all you need without asking."

Both men stared at her.

Cremona whispered, "Of course. Continuous conversation. Just twelve hours out of phase, that's all. God, we've got to get going."

He strode out of the room, virtually dragging the General with him, then strode back in.

"Mother," he said, "if you'll excuse me, this will take a few hours, I think. I'll send in some girls to talk to you. Or take a nap, if you'd rather."

"I'll be all right, Gerard," said Mrs. Cremona.

"Only, how did you think of this, Mother? What made you suggest this?"

"But, Gerard, all women know it. Any two women—on the video-phone, or on the stratowire, or just face to face—know that the whole secret to spreading the news is, no matter what, to Just Keep Talking."

Cremona tried to smile. Then, his lower lip trembling, he turned and left.

Mrs. Cremona looked fondly after him. Such a fine man, her son, the physicist. Big as he was and important as he was, he still knew that a boy should always listen to his mother.

Eyes Do More than See

I

After hundreds of billions of years, he suddenly thought of himself as Ames. Not the wavelength combination which, through all the universe was now the equivalent of Ames—but the sound itself. A faint memory came back of the sound waves he no longer heard and no longer could hear.

The new project was sharpening his memory for so many more of the old, old, eons-old things. He flattened the energy vortex that made up the total of his individuality and its lines of force stretched beyond the stars.

Brock's answering signal came.

Surely, Ames thought, he could tell Brock. Surely he could tell somebody.

Brock's shifting energy pattern communed, "Aren't you coming, Ames?"

"Of course."

"Will you take part in the contest?"

"Yes!" Ames's lines of force pulsed erratically. "Most certainly. I have thought of a whole new art-form. Something really unusual."

"What a waste of effort! How can you think a new variation can be thought of after two hundred billion years. There can be nothing new."

For a moment Brock shifted out of phase and out of communion, so that Ames had to hurry to adjust his lines of force. He caught the drift of other-thoughts as he did so, the view of the powdered galaxies against the velvet of nothingness, and the lines of force pulsing in endless multitudes of energy-life, lying between the galaxies.

Ames said, "Please absorb my thoughts, Brock. Don't close out. I've thought of manipulating Matter. Imagine! A symphony of Matter. Why bother with Energy. Of course, there's nothing new in Energy; how can there be? Doesn't that show we must deal with Matter?"

"Matter!"

Ames interpreted Brock's energy-vibrations as those of disgust.

He said, "Why not? We were once Matter ourselves back—back— Oh, a trillion years ago anyway! Why not build up objects in a Matter medium, or abstract forms or—listen, Brock—why not build up an imitation of ourselves in Matter, ourselves as we used to be?"

Brock said, "I don't remember how that was. No one does."

"I do," said Ames with energy, "I've been thinking of nothing else and I am beginning to remember. Brock, let me show you. Tell me if I'm right. Tell me."

"No. This is silly. It's—repulsive."

"Let me try, Brock. We've been friends; we've pulsed energy together from the beginning—from the moment we became what we are. Brock, please!"

"Then, quickly."

Ames had not felt such a tremor along his own lines of force in—well, in how long? If he tried it now for Brock and it worked, he could dare manipulate Matter before the assembled Energy-beings who had so drearily waited over the eons for something new.

The Matter was thin out there between the galaxies, but Ames gathered it, scraping it together over the cubic light-years, choosing the atoms, achieving a clayey consistency and forcing matter into an ovoid form that spread out below.

"Don't you remember, Brock?" he asked softly. "Wasn't it something like this?"

Brock's vortex trembled in phase. "Don't make me remember. I don't remember."

"That was the head. They called it the head. I remember it so clearly, I want to say it. I mean with sound." He waited, then said, "Look, do you remember that?"

On the upper front of the ovoid appeared HEAD.

"What is that?" asked Brock.

"That's the word for head. The symbols that meant the word in sound. Tell me you remember, Brock!"

"There was something," said Brock hesitantly, "something in the middle." A vertical bulge formed.

Ames said, "Yes! Nose, that's it!" And NOSE appeared upon it. "And those are eyes on either side," LEFT EYE—RIGHT EYE.

Ames regarded what he had formed, his lines of force pulsing slowly. Was he sure he liked this?

"Mouth," he said, in small quiverings, "and chin and Adam's apple, and the collarbones. How the words come back to me." They appeared on the form.

Brock said, "I haven't thought of them for hundreds of billions of years. Why have you reminded me? Why?"

Ames was momentarily lost in his thoughts, "Something else. Organs to hear with; something for the sound waves. Ears! Where do they go? I don't remember where to put them!"

Brock cried out, "Leave it alone! Ears and all else! Don't remember!"

Ames said, uncertainly, "What is wrong with remembering?"

"Because the outside wasn't rough and cold like that but smooth and warm. Because the eyes were tender and alive and the lips of the mouth trembled and were soft on mine." Brock's lines of force beat and wavered, beat and wavered.

Ames said, "I'm sorry! I'm sorry!"

"You're reminding me that once I was a woman and knew love; that eyes do more than see and I have none to do it for me."

With violence, she added matter to the rough-hewn head and said, "Then let *them* do it" and turned and fled.

And Ames saw and remembered, too, that once he had been a man. The force of his vortex split the head in two and he fled back across the galaxies on the energy-track of Brock—back to the endless doom of life.

And the eyes of the shattered head of Matter still glistened with the moisture that Brock had placed there to represent tears. The head of Matter did that which the energy-beings could do no longer and it wept for all humanity, and for the fragile beauty of the bodies they had once given up, a trillion years ago.

Segregationist

The surgeon looked up without expression. "Is he ready?"

"Ready is a relative term," said the med-eng. "We're ready. He's restless."

"They always are. . . . Well, it's a serious operation."

"Serious or not, he should be thankful. He's been chosen for it over an enormous number of possibles and frankly, I don't think . . ."

"Don't say it," said the surgeon. "The decision is not ours to make."

"We accept it. But do we have to agree?"

"Yes," said the surgeon, crisply. "We agree. Completely and wholeheartedly. The operation is entirely too intricate to approach with mental reservations. This man has proven his worth in a number of ways and his profile is suitable for the Board of Mortality."

"All right," said the med-eng, unmollified.

The surgeon said, "I'll see him right in here, I think. It is small enough and personal enough to be comforting."

"It won't help. He's nervous, and he's made up his mind."

"Has he indeed?"

"Yes. He wants metal; they always do."

The surgeon's face did not change expression. He stared at his hands. "Sometimes one can talk them out of it."

"Why bother?" said the med-eng, indifferently. "If he wants metal, let it be metal."

"You don't care?"

"Why should I?" The med-eng said it almost brutally. "Either way it's a medical engineering problem and I'm a medical engineer. Either way, I can handle it. Why should I go beyond that?"

The surgeon said stolidly, "To me, it is a matter of the fitness of things."

"Fitness! You can't use that as an argument. What does the patient care about the fitness of things?"

"I care."

"You care in a minority. The trend is against you. You have no chance."

"I have to try." The surgeon waved the med-eng into silence with a quick wave of his hand—no impatience to it, merely quickness. He had already informed the nurse and he had already been signaled concerning her approach. He pressed a small button and the double-door pulled swiftly apart. The patient moved inward in his motorchair, the nurse stepping briskly along beside him.

"You may go, nurse," said the surgeon, "but wait outside. I will be calling you." He nodded to the med-eng, who left with the nurse, and the door closed behind them.

The man in the chair looked over his shoulder and watched them go. His neck was scrawny and there were fine wrinkles about his eyes. He was freshly shaven and the fingers of his hands, as they gripped the arms of the chair tightly, showed manicured nails. He was a high-priority patient and he was being taken care of. . . . But there was a look of settled peevishness on his face.

He said, "Will we be starting today?"

The surgeon nodded. "This afternoon, Senator."

"I understand it will take weeks."

"Not for the operation itself, Senator. But there are a number of subsidiary points to be taken care of. There are some circulatory renovations that must be carried through, and hormonal adjustments. These are tricky things."

"Are they dangerous?" Then, as though feeling the need for establishing a friendly relationship, but patently against his will, he added, ". . . doctor?"

The surgeon paid no attention to the nuances of expression. He said, flatly, "Everything is dangerous. We take our time in order that it be less dangerous. It is the time required, the skill of many individuals united, the equipment, that makes such operations available to so few . . ."

"I know that," said the patient, restlessly. "I refuse to feel guilty about that. Or are you implying improper pressure?"

"Not at all, Senator. The decisions of the Board have never been questioned. I mention the difficulty and intricacy of the operation merely to explain my desire to have it conducted in the best fashion possible."

"Well, do so, then. That is my desire, also."

"Then I must ask you to make a decision. It is possible to supply you with either of two types of cyber-hearts, metal or . . ."

"Plastic!" said the patient, irritably. "Isn't that the alternative you were going to offer, doctor? Cheap plastic. I don't want that. I've made my choice. I want the metal."

"But . . ."

"See here. I've been told the choice rests with me. Isn't that so?"

The surgeon nodded. "Where two alternate procedures are of equal value from a medical standpoint, the choice rests with the patient. In actual practice, the choice rests with the patient even when the alternate procedures are *not* of equal value, as in this case."

The patient's eyes narrowed. "Are you trying to tell me the plastic heart is superior?"

"It depends on the patient. In my opinion, in your individual case, it is. And we prefer not to use the term, plastic. It is a fibrous cyber-heart."

"It's plastic as far as I am concerned."

"Senator," said the surgeon, infinitely patient, "the material is not plastic in the ordinary sense of the word. It is a polymeric material true, but one that is far more complex than ordinary plastic. It is a complex protein-like fibre designed to imitate, as closely as possible, the natural structure of the human heart you now have within your chest."

"Exactly, and the human heart I now have within my chest is worn out although I am not yet sixty years old. I don't want another one like it, thank you. I want something better."

"We all want something better for you, Senator. The fibrous cyber-heart will be better. It has a potential life of centuries. It is absolutely non-allergenic . . ."

"Isn't that so for the metallic heart, too?"

"Yes, it is," said the surgeon. "The metallic cyber is of titanium alloy that . . ."

"And it doesn't wear out? And it is stronger than plastic? Or fibre or whatever you want to call it?"

"The metal is physically stronger, yes, but mechanical strength is not a point at issue. Its mechanical strength does you no particular good since the heart is well protected. Anything capable of reaching the heart will kill you for other reasons even if the heart stands up under manhandling."

The patient shrugged. "If I ever break a rib, I'll have that replaced by titanium, also. Replacing bones is easy. Anyone can have that done anytime. I'll be as metallic as I want to be, doctor."

"That is your right, if you so choose. However, it is only fair to tell you that although no metallic cyber-heart has ever broken down mechanically, a number have broken down electronically."

"What does that mean?"

"It means that every cyber-heart contains a pacemaker as part of its structure. In the case of the metallic variety, this is an electronic device that keeps the cyber in rhythm. It means an entire battery of miniaturized equipment must be included to alter the heart's rhythm to suit an individual's emotional and physical state. Occasionally something goes wrong there and people have died before that wrong could be corrected."

"I never heard of such a thing."

"I assure you it happens."

"Are you telling me it happens often?"

"Not at all. It happens very rarely."

"Well, then, I'll take my chance. What about the plastic heart? Doesn't that contain a pacemaker?"

"Of course it does, Senator. But the chemical structure of a fibrous cyber-heart is quite close to that of human tissue. It can respond to the ionic and hormonal controls of the body itself. The total complex that need be inserted is far simpler than in the case of the metal cyber."

"But doesn't the plastic heart ever pop out of hormonal control?"

"None has ever yet done so."

"Because you haven't been working with them long enough. Isn't that so?"

The surgeon hesitated. "It is true that the fibrous cybers have not been used nearly as long as the metallic."

"There you are. What is it anyway, doctor? Are you afraid I'm making myself into a robot . . . into a Metallo, as they call them since citizenship went through?"

"There is nothing wrong with a Metallo as a Metallo. As you say, they are citizens. But you're *not* a Metallo. You're a human being. Why not stay a human being?"

"Because I want the best and that's a metallic heart. You see to that."

The surgeon nodded. "Very well. You will be asked to sign the necessary permissions and you will then be fitted with a metal heart."

"And you'll be the surgeon in charge? They tell me you're the best."

"I will do what I can to make the changeover an easy one."

The door opened and the chair moved the patient out to the waiting nurse.

The med-eng came in, looking over his shoulder at the receding patient until the doors had closed again.

He turned to the surgeon. "Well, I can't tell what happened just by looking at you. What was his decision?"

The surgeon bent over his desk, punching out the final items for his records. "What you predicted. He insists on the metallic cyber-heart."

"After all, they are better."

"Not significantly. They've been around longer; no more than that. It's this mania that's been plaguing humanity ever since Metallos have become citizens. Men have this odd desire to make Metallos out of themselves.

They yearn for the physical strength and endurance one associates with them."

"It isn't one-sided, doc. You don't work with Metallos but I do; so I know. The last two who came in for repairs have asked for fibrous elements."

"Did they get them?"

"In one case, it was just a matter of supplying tendons; it didn't make much difference there, metal or fibre. The other wanted a blood system or its equivalent. I told him I couldn't; not without a complete rebuilding of the structure of his body in fibrous material. . . . I suppose it will come to that some day. Metallos that aren't really Metallos at all, but a kind of flesh and blood."

"You don't mind that thought?"

"Why not? And metallized human beings, too. We have two varieties of intelligence on Earth now and why bother with two. Let them approach each other and eventually we won't be able to tell the difference. Why should we want to? We'd have the best of both worlds; the advantages of man combined with those of robot."

"You'd get a hybrid," said the surgeon, with something that approached fierceness. "You'd get something that is not both, but neither. Isn't it logical to suppose an individual would be too proud of his structure and identity to want to dilute it with something alien? Would he *want* mongrelization?"

"That's segregationist talk."

"Then let it be that." The surgeon said with calm emphasis, "I believe in being what one is. I wouldn't change a bit of my own structure for any reason. If some of it absolutely required replacement, I would have that replacement as close to the original in nature as could possibly be managed. I am *myself;* well pleased to be myself; and would not be anything else."

He had finished now and had to prepare for the operation. He placed his strong hands into the heating oven and let them reach the dull red-hot glow that would sterilize them completely. For all his impassioned words, his voice had never risen, and on his burnished metal face there was (as always) no sign of expression.

I Just
Make Them Up, See!

Oh, Dr. A. —
Oh, Dr. A. —
There is something (don't go 'way)
That I'd like to hear you say.
Though I'd rather die
Than try
To pry,
The fact, you'll find,
Is that my mind
Has evolved the jackpot question for today.

I intend no cheap derision,
So please answer with decision,
And, discarding all your petty cautious fears,
Tell the secret of your vision!
How on earth
Do you give birth
To those crazy and impossible ideas?

Is it indigestion
And a question
Of the nightmare that results?
Of your eyeballs whirling,

Twirling,
Fingers curling
And unfurling,
While your blood beats maddened chimes
As it keeps impassioned times
With your thick, uneven pulse?

Is it *that*, you think, or liquor
That brings on the wildness quicker?
For a teeny
Weeny
Dry martini
May be just your private genie;
Or perhaps those Tom and Jerries
You will find the very
Berries
For inducing
And unloosing
That weird gimmick or that kicker;
Or an awful
Combination
Of unlawful
Stimulation,
Marijuana plus tequila,
That will give you just that feel o'
Things a-clicking
And unsticking
As you start your cerebration
To the crazy syncopation
Of a brain a-tocking-ticking.

Surely *something*, Dr. A.,
Makes you fey
And quite *outré*.
Since I read you with devotion,
Won't you give me just a notion
Of that shrewdly pepped-up potion
Out of which emerge your plots?
That wild secret bubbly mixture
That has made you such a fixture
In most favored s.f. spots—

Now, Dr. A.,
Don't go away—

Oh, Dr. A. —

Oh, Dr. A. —

Rejection Slips

a—Learned

> Dear Asimov, all mental laws
> Prove orthodoxy has its flaws.
> Consider that eclectic clause
> In Kant's philosophy that gnaws
> With ceaseless anti-logic jaws
> At all outworn and useless saws
> That stick in modern mutant craws.
> So here's your tale (with faint applause).
> The words above show ample cause.

b—Gruff

> Dear Ike, I was prepared
>   (And, boy, I really *cared*)
> To swallow almost anything you wrote.
>   But, Ike, you're just plain shot,
>   Your writing's gone to pot,
> There's nothing left but hack and mental bloat.
>   Take back this piece of junk;
>   It smelled; it reeked; it stunk;
> Just glancing through it once was deadly rough.
>   But Ike, boy, by and by,

Just try another try.
I need some yarns and, kid, I love your stuff.

c—Kindly

Dear Isaac, friend of mine,
I thought your tale was fine.
Just frightful-
Ly delightful
And with merits all a-shine.
It meant a quite full
Night, full,
Friend, of tension
Then relief
And attended
With full measure
Of the pleasure
Of suspended
Disbelief.
It is triteful,
Scarcely rightful,
Almost spiteful
To declare
That some tiny faults are there.
Nothing much,
Perhaps a touch,
And over such
You shouldn't pine.
So let me say
Without delay,
My pal, my friend,
· Your story's end
Has left me gay
And joyfully composed.
P. S.
Oh, yes,
I must confess
(With some distress)
Your story is regretfully enclosed.

Isaac Asimov was born in the Soviet Union to his great surprise. He moved quickly to correct the situation. When his parents emigrated to the United States, Isaac (three years old at the time) stowed away in their baggage. He has been an American citizen since the age of eight.

Brought up in Brooklyn, and educated in its public schools, he eventually found his way to Columbia University and, over the protests of the school administration, managed to annex a series of degrees in chemistry, up to and including a Ph.D. He then infiltrated Boston University and climbed the academic ladder, ignoring all cries of outrage, until he found himself Professor of Biochemistry.

Meanwhile, at the age of nine, he found the love of his life (in the inanimate sense) when he discovered his first science-fiction magazine. By the time he was eleven, he began to write stories, and at eighteen, he actually worked up the nerve to submit one. It was rejected. After four long months of tribulation and suffering, he sold his first story and, thereafter, he never looked back.

In 1941, when he was twenty-one years old, he wrote the classic short story "Nightfall" and his future was assured. Shortly before that he had begun writing his robot stories, and shortly after that he had begun his Foundation series.

What was left except quantity? At the present time, he has published over 440 books, distributed through every major division of the Dewey system of library classification, and shows no signs of slowing up. He remains as youthful, as lively, and as lovable as ever, and grows more handsome with each year. You can be sure that this is so since he has written this little essay himself and his devotion to absolute objectivity is notorious.

He is married to Janet Jeppson, psychiatrist and writer, has two children by a previous marriage, and lives in New York City.